I0698881

The Annotated Robot Galaxy Series

#CC3333 Edition

Crazy Foolish Robots

Robots, Robots Everywhere!

Silly Insane Humans

Eleven Little Robots

Adeena Mignogna

Crazy Robot, LLC

The Annotated Robot Galaxy Series #CC3333 Edition © 2026 by Adeena Mignogna

Crazy Foolish Robots © 2021; *Robots, Robots Everywhere!* © 2022; *Silly Insane Humans* © 2022; *Eleven Little Robots* © 2023

All rights reserved. No part of this publication may be reproduced or used in any manner without written permission of the copyright owner except for the use of quotations in a book review.

This is a work of fiction. Names[1], characters, places, and incidents are the product of the author's imagination. Any resemblance to actual persons, living or dead, events, or locales, or actual robots, functioning or not, is entirely coincidental.

ISBN: 978-1-961875-05-0 (paperback)

Book cover design by: Ebooklaunch.com

Published by Crazy Robot, LLC

---

1. Except for the name/character Patrick Marsden. I know a Patrick Marsden in real life, and he said I could use his name for a character one day when I was stuck for a name and asked all my Facebook friends whose name I could use. Pat volunteered.

Contents

Robots, Robots Everywhere!

Eleven Little Robots

Also By Adeena Mignogna

The Robot Galaxy Series
Book 1: *Crazy Foolish Robots*
Book 2: *Robots, Robots Everywhere!*
Book 3: *Silly Insane Humans*
Book 4: *Eleven Little Robots*

...and the unrelated standalone novel: Lunar Logic
Adeena's Stories (on KindleUnlimited):
Final Orbit
Objective Reality

About this Annotated Robot Galaxy Series #CC3333 Edition

Who doesn't love a good origin story?

It's been my experience that many of us do. That's why the most common questions I get about *The Robot Galaxy Series* are variation of: "How did you think of X?" or "How did you come up with Y?" I've fielded these questions about everything from the tiniest details to the series as a whole.

Of course, for every detail I'm asked about, there are four or five others I'm really proud of and excited about that go completely unnoticed!

At some point, while I was finishing up Book 4 in the series, *Eleven Little Robots*, I got the idea to create this—an annotated version of the series that shares the stories behind the stories.

And I'll start with the origin of the series itself.

The year was 2012, and it was my third time participating in NaNoWriMo[1][2] (National Novel Writing Month). That month, I drafted a novel tentatively titled *How to Be a Rocket Scientist*. It was about a 17-year-old named Ethan who lived on a space station in the asteroid belt, loved piloting, and developed a crush on a girl named Stella, who was promptly kidnapped by alien robots who wanted to do something nasty to Earth.

Most of my NaNoWriMo projects got shelved immediately after the month was over—but not this one. I worked on it through the first half of 2013. I can't tell you why I stopped, but I shelved it for a while and spent several years working on other projects. One project was called *Tales from Ceres*[3], a collection of intertwined vignettes set on a station on the dwarf

---

1. NaNoWriMo was an annual contest against oneself to see if participants can write a 50,000 word novel in a single month. As of March 2025, NaNoWriMo, the organization is no more.

2. I first learned about and participated in NaNoWriMo in 2009. That novel will never see the light of day, but the experience taught me that I could sustain a narrative for longer than a short story. I skipped 2010 because I had a new baby. I partially participated in 2011... that was a rougher month because my dad was in end-stage cancer and passed that November. My dad was very much a "life is for the living/go live your normal life" person, so I signed up to participate trying to be all normal and stuff, knowing I wasn't going to get a lot of writing done.

3. Also started as a NaNoWriMo project in 2015.

planet Ceres about 200 years from now. I really wanted that one to work, but then *The Expanse* novels and TV series came out. Since a significant portion of *The Expanse* also takes place on Ceres—and it was so good—it completely derailed me. I didn't write for a while after that.

In 2019, I finally had a talk with myself:

Voice in my head: Do you want to be a writer? A published author?

Me: Yes!

Voice: Well, pick ***ONE*** project and finish it!

I listened to that voice and went back to Ethan and *How to Be a Rocket Scientist*.

When I picked it up again in late 2019 and read it, the original "rocket scientist" angle was gone, and Ethan and Stella spent most of their time on the robots' homeworld. So the book got renamed *Ethan's Robot Planet*. But sometime between March and July of 2020 (yup, during the early part of the COVID-19 pandemic), I decided I didn't like Ethan. He was annoying and whiny, driven solely by a crush on a girl. Too... boring. Typical. Expected.

Stella, on the other hand (or robot appendage), was smart and interesting. She was quickly and obviously becoming the main character. *Stella's Robot Planet* didn't have a great ring to it, though, so I started thinking of alternative names for my main character. I love alliteration, so I consulted baby name lists for names that started with "R." Lo and behold... I chose Ruby!

It was also during that early 2020 period that I realized I could create multiple novels instead of one. One thing holding me back from completion had been the perception that a sci-fi novel had to be 80,000 or 100,000 words or more[4]. I didn't think I could sustain a narrative that long. Then I looked up the definition of a novel—generally accepted to start at 40,000 words—and realized my favorite novel of all time, *The Hitchhiker's Guide to the Galaxy,* is just under 48,000 words.

That was my lightbulb moment. I reworked what I had, plotted out story arcs and beats, and divided *Ruby's Robot Planet* into four books. Book 1 would be *Ruby's Robot Planet,* and Book 2 would be *Robots, Robots Everywhere!* I didn't have titles for Books 3 and 4 yet. I needed to focus on finishing the first one and getting it into readers' hands before I did any more.

The name *Ruby's Robot Planet* stuck for quite a while—through beta readers, edits, and even my initial cover designs. But when I saw the first cover concepts in January 2021, I realized I didn't love the title after all.

I can't tell you the exact moment I came up with *Crazy Foolish Robots,* but I can tell you this: I adore names that follow the **adjective-adjective-noun** pattern, with each word one or two syllables. And I knew instantly that the second I thought of *Crazy Foolish Robots,* I knew it was *the* title. Scouring my email[5], I can even pinpoint the date—Sunday, February 14th, 2021—when I told my cover designer about the change. A few days later, he had some mockups for me.

The rest, as they say, is history. *Crazy Foolish Robots* launched in June 2021 after several months of copy editing.[6]

---

4. This perception comes from all the usual sources that attempt to provide helpful information to writers and authors.

Like this one by Reedsy: https://reedsy.com/studio/resources/how-many-words-in-a-novel

The problem here is that sci-fi and fantasy are lumped together. Fantasy is often longer than sci-fi. And... these are just guidelines! That was the ah-ha moment for me.

Crazy Foolish Robots

Book 1 of The Robot Galaxy Series

Adeena Mignogna

Crazy Robot, LLC

Before We Begin

Out of the millions of email messages traveling daily between Earth and Astroll 2[1], rarely did any have the power over nineteen-year-old[2] Ruby's life the way this one did. Yet, the email was not addressed to her, nor did she see it, nor did she have any idea it had ruined her plans.

How did this happen?

Quite simply, the email was addressed to a mister Robt Plampton[3], station director of Astroll 2. Located in the heart of the asteroid belt, Astroll 2 was Ruby's home from the age of seven. The email stated that the staff was to prepare for an upcoming installation of a series of AI applications that were meant to greatly benefit Astroll 2 and the corporation which owned it. That, in itself, should have been quite harmless; and it should have improved the quality of Ruby's life, as someone who lived on said station that would be receiving the enhanced AI.

However, Ruby, counting every day until she turned twenty-one, was still under the guardianship and sponsorship of her two uncles, Blake[4] and Logan[5]. They weren't blood relatives but her mother's best friends. Ruby's mother had no other family to speak of when she perished, so she left her young daughter in their care.

Ruby's only living blood relative was her grandmother, who had been in an assisted living facility prior to Ruby's conception. Her medical transcript cited various permanent psychoses which prevented her from living on her own. Such as her tendency to routinely knock on the neighbor's door in the middle of the night, half-dressed, asking if the aliens had finally responded to her email.

---

1. Where I got "Astroll" from has been lost to history, but I deliberately wanted this to be "2" so that at some point, someone might ask, "What happened to 1?" and I might have to answer that question someday.

2. Ruby was 17, like the original Ethan, for a very long time. It was late in the editing process that I aged her up a bit to attempt to get further away from folks thinking this book is YA. I call it "YA-accessible" since I wrote it for adults like me, but there is no reason why the younger set can't read it.

3. I angst over names a lot, and spend a lot of time on baby name websites and genealogy lists looking for the perfect name that fits. One name generator I use heavily is: https://www.name-generator.org.uk/

4. Actor inspiration: Jake Gyllenhaal

5. Actor inspiration: Tom Hardy

The final relevant detail affecting Ruby's life was the fact that her Uncle Logan was an odorist[6]. His primary responsibility was to ensure that the smells of items and materials brought to Astroll 2 were not offensive. Primarily, the toxicity of any given material was mechanically inspected and then listed on the paperwork of said items. But in order to determine how pleasant or offensive a smell might be, especially in the small, confined rooms of a space station with continually recycled air, a sensitive and willing human nose was required.

Until now. Now, an AI could do this job. Which meant that Ruby and her family, now obsolete to the station, would be returning to Earth.

Emails[7] were not the only items on their way to Astroll 2. Several ships were noted to be in various phases of their journey from Earth and Mars. All these ships existed in station records as expected, incoming arrivals.

Yet, one particular ship was not on the arrival manifest at all. It was one unknown to humankind, and it was on approach from outside the human-known solar system. No human occupied this ship, either. Only a solitary, intelligent robot.

Neither Ruby nor the robot could imagine that their trajectories would soon be intersecting, intertwining their lives in unimaginable ways.

---

6. This idea came from this article: Meet the NASA employee whose job it is to sniff everything before it goes into space. https://www.independent.co.uk/news/science/meet-the-nasa-employee-whose-job-it-is-to-sniff-everything -before-it-goes-into-space-9579047.html

7. I know not everyone like prologues or prefaces. I do. Best thing about being a writer is you can do what you like.

Chapter 1

> Ruby <

"How many days until my 21st birthday?" Ruby spoke into her communicuff.

She darn well knew the answer, so it was the perfect way to test her communicuff. It was exactly 429[1] days.

That was the day when she no longer needed the sponsorship of her uncles to stay on Astroll 2. That was also the day she could legally join the Titan expedition[2]. Ruby knew that a long time ago, eighteen was the age of full emancipation. After the Grey Matter Coup of 2113, the world government agreed that a mature prefrontal cortex was a defining characteristic of adulthood. While this level of neural development rarely happened prior to twenty-five, twenty-one years old was selected[3]. With the exception that an individual could prove maturity via a set of brain scans. Ruby was fortunate that Astroll 2 had a brain-scanning facility. But as of her last scan a month and a half ago, she wasn't even close. Despite all the brain training games, extra omega-3s added to everything she ate and drank, and even ordering a special device to wear while sleeping that was supposed to help, her brain was determined to take its time reaching maturity. She *felt* old enough, but science disagreed. She would have to wait out the 429 days until her twenty-first birthday.

So, when a disembodied voice replied, "three thousand seven hundred point two," Ruby let out a heavy sigh. Her communicuff was malfunctioning. That's why she had been waiting at the Care Center entrance for the last half hour. She arrived early to ensure she was first in line. Perhaps *too* early.

Ruby looked up from her cuff-wrapped arm and shifted her eyes to the closed window in front of her. Unfortunately, she couldn't trust the cuff to give the correct time either, so she wasn't sure exactly how much longer she had to wait. Maybe

---

1. I regret that this is not a Prime Number.

2. Very simply, this is where I establish what the main character wants. Storytelling basics... characters need to want stuff, obstacles get in their way.

3. I've always been bothered by the arbitrary-ness that "18" has been the magical number for adulthood. Now, when I was a teen myself, I was bothered that it wasn't 16. As an adult with kids of my own, I'm bothered by the fact that it's not something larger than 18. But this article found me around the time I was writing this book: Brain Maturity Extends Well Beyond Teen Years. https://www.npr.org/2011/10/10/141164708/brain-maturity-extends-well-beyond-teen-years

30 seconds. Maybe seventeen minutes. She inwardly cursed herself for even having to rely on technology and not an internal clock for time, but was told that was normal for humans who lived for years inside a space station.

A sign was visible in the window, but the black lettering had worn away with time. The words 'Care Center' were in a large and crisp Sans Serif font. Underneath, in a font made to resemble handwriting, were the words "If we don't take care of you" and then nothing but scratched metal. Care didn't extend to caring for the sign, apparently.

Ruby blinked at the sad, gray sign and couldn't help but empathize with it. For she too knew what it was like to feel like time was wearing her down. Recently, her days had been blurring together. On a typical day, her uncles and cousin were out of the shared living space before she woke up. That was her own fault for sleeping in. Once, family breakfast time was something she wouldn't miss, but she couldn't drag herself out of bed lately. As she got up later and later, her breakfasts came to consist of an empty table, boring news briefs, and a cold meal she couldn't be bothered to re-heat. The only remnants of her family's morning resided in whatever note her uncles left her that particular day. Usually, a reminder to do the bone and muscle-maintaining exercise she was supposed to do, but always 'forgetting.' After, she would go off to work.

As she looked ahead to another 429 days of sameness, she still felt like it beat the unpleasant hell on Earth. It had been over a decade since she lived on Earth, but between what she remembered and what she read about on the news feeds, to Ruby, it was a place overrun by all manner of robots and AIs[4].

Earth had become automated to a point where more robots were employed than human beings. Robots manufactured goods and moved them between different facilities. They prepared food. They were security guards. They cleaned floors. Robots (with all levels of AI) replaced innumerable jobs, including the one that irked Ruby the most: the pilots.

Out here, Ruby was a pilot. And anyone could tell you that she was a good one. Out here, Ruby believed that it was still too unpredictable and dangerous to let robots pilot around the asteroids. Humans were still needed, Ruby included.

On this mundane Tuesday—now a week after Robt Plampton opened and read the aforementioned email—this outwardly minor issue with her communicuff forced Ruby out of her routine. And at the worst time, too. Today, she had plans to meet with one of the Titan[5] expedition's leading scientists. Not a great day to require tech support, especially when the support available would subject her to such a nonsensical process.

The Care Center window slid open, revealing a FUFE (fresh up from Earth) who Ruby recognized from one of the recent loads of new station workers.

"Can I help you?" he said. His voice was taut and toneless.

"My communicuff has gone a little haywire," Ruby replied, holding up her cuff, which filled two-thirds of her arm. "It's not responding to my commands. At least, not correctly."

"Did you try resetting it?"

---

4. I had to make Ruby start out not liking robots. If she liked them, and got "kidnapped" by one, she'd be all "cool! Let's go!" So, I had to do the opposite to make it interesting.

5. I chose Titan, the moon of Saturn, because to me, it is one of the most fascinating places in our solar system and there's a lot of mystery there and things we don't yet know!

Ruby tried awfully hard to do something with her eyes other than roll them at the suggestion.[6]

"Yes, twice."

After a useless half an hour, the Care Center FUFE proved to be no help, and Ruby was instructed to call Earth's Care Center Service Heart. Ruby exhaled a sigh of defeat. Calling them was only ever a last resort. No matter how simple or complicated the issue, a call with the Heart guaranteed to eat up at least half a morning. The Care Givers on the other end were to walk the unfortunate caller through a script that laid out a series of rudimentary symptoms and solutions. They were duplicates of what the local Care Center worked through, but with the added time delay of a conversation back to Earth, in addition to the fact that deviations from the script were entirely unacceptable.

Astroll 2 could best be described as a long rotating cylinder with a ring wrapped around its mid-section. Ruby made her way from the Care Center, located in the outermost portion of the station's central ring inwards, one level to where most living quarters were located, including hers. That's where Ruby found herself for the second half of this particular Tuesday morning, exactly one week after her life's future path was unknowingly altered.

At least in her quarters she could keep an eye on a reliable clock built into the wall. She would not allow herself to be late for her meeting with Dr. Guerrero.

An hour later, Ruby was on a video call with the image of what could have been a clone of the FUFE at the local Care Center.

"When did it last work?" the image said. Ruby knew it hadn't been working since at least the previous afternoon. She had been approaching the promenade and happened to overhear a conversation two older women were having. They were discussing the new AI that was going to be installed in the station.

Actually, 'happened to' was not entirely correct. Ruby did make a habit of eavesdropping on other's conversations when they were within earshot. She had no qualms about listening in. They were, after all, in a public space. If she wasn't meant to hear, they should have stayed in private.

Thinking she might've missed something in the news—as she generally did, since news wasn't her thing—she raised her arm and attempted to access information on this alleged new AI. The display hovered over the communicuff, but it wasn't the news. It was the day's menu at the mess. She swiped that away and attempted to bring up her email.

But the device decided to call Uncle Logan, and she couldn't hang it up in time to stop it from going through. The face of a familiar, smiling, handsome man materialized on the screen.

"Ruby! Sweetie! Are you going to join us in the mess for dinner? Uncle Blake and I promised Sebastian we'd eat by the windows." Uncle Logan's bright eyes were always full of love and hope and endless patience for Ruby.

Despite her own frustrations, Ruby couldn't help but smile back. "Yes, Uncle Logan. I'll meet you there."

"K, kiddo," Uncle Logan winked before he ended the call. Ruby caught a glance of Uncle Blake and Sebastian behind him.

Ruby attempted once more to get the device to do what she wanted. When she tried to bring up the day's menu at the mess, she succeeded in loading her email instead.

"Piece of junk," she said to herself, flicking away the holo-image.

---

6. Many people ask if I'm Ruby in this story. No. I'm not. But yes, I might have performed my share of eyerolls interacting with various help desks and tech support over the years.

Trying to explain any of this now to the Earth-bound Care Giver was futile. It didn't help that the problem wasn't reproducible in any predictable way. It *really* didn't help that Ruby was on a bit of a time crunch.

But she remained in the living area of her tiny quarters, tossing a bean bag up and catching it to ease her impatience. It did not have the satisfying punch of the catch of a bean bag in standard Earth gravity, but that was a feature of Astroll 2 life that Ruby had adjusted to over the years.

"I'm going to walk you through a sequence of steps," said a voice emanating from the comm panel.

"Sure," said Ruby with her jaw clenched. She knew that was coming next and wished there was something she could say that would enable them to skip some steps.

"Take off the cuff and turn it over."

Pause. Ruby already had the cuff off.

"Press the soft reset buttons simultaneously."

Another pause. Ruby had already done this step as well. Her cuff was splayed out on the table as Ruby waited for the technician to get to step *eight*. One through seven were a standard set of steps, and she had performed them at the start of the call.

At step six, the technician paused. "Um, what version is your system?"

Ruby took a deep sigh, but appreciated that this tech was a little more up on his game than the local guy. "I'm still at 45BAI[7]."

"You know an upgrade to version 51AI is available?"

"Yeah, I don't want it," Ruby replied. Ruby had heard about the highly anticipated 51AI, which was indeed an AI. When she did a little research on 51AI, it seemed to be locked up tighter than Ultra Fort Knox, as the expression went. She was content with the non-AI version, the one she could hack and customize. As silly as it sounded to everyone around her, Ruby didn't want her cuff to think it was any smarter than she was.

"Are you sure?" the tech replied. "Most people love how it can anticipate your schedule and your needs and take action based on...[8]"

None of this interested Ruby, so she cut him off. "Really, I'm good. Let's just keep going."

The tech then told Ruby they'd need to redo a few steps to account for the older version she had, now taking a tone with every step that implied she should upgrade. Finally, they made it back to step seven.

Eight was, "Let's try to access a current news report."

Ruby picked up the cuff and accessed the news.

---

7. BAI = "Before" AI

8. I would love this. Years ago, I showed up at the wrong airport and missed my flight. It was all in my schedule correctly, but I was so used to going to airport A... ever since, I've envisioned having some kind of assistant that was smart enough to know when to point out details in my schedule, not just set off an alarm. Something that would be like, "Adeena, that flight tomorrow? It's not going out of airport A, but airport B. Remember airport B!"

Luckily, I was able to rebook for later that day and not miss my sister's wedding the next day... I was the photographer!

Hovering over the cuff was the image of Juju, the genderless global pop-star[9], along with the text, "Juju just scheduled their first off-Earth concert in ten years ever since the accident..." Well, that was close in that it was current, but Ruby didn't consider it real news.

Ruby reported back her search results and then turned Juju off. Better to wait for tech support than rot her brain with celebrity gossip.

While waiting, Ruby took a brush through her dark hair, momentarily straightening out the curls, and pulled it back into a ponytail. Most people chose to buzz cut their hair in the low-gravity environments. Ruby couldn't stand the thought of looking like everyone else. She kept it a little past shoulder length and pulled it into a ponytail most of the time.

Ruby glanced at the time on the wall. The thought of being late for the meeting with Dr. Guerrero flashed in her mind. She thought about telling the Care Giver she was going to hang up, but skipped telling him and just hung up. She decided that she could live with a semi-malfunctioning cuff for now.

As she finished making sure she was visually presentable, the incomplete tech call and her non-functioning cuff continued to bother her. Images of face-palming memes[10] and people pinching the upper bridge of their nose (symbols of frustration that were now as ubiquitous as a happy face or a heart) popped into Ruby's head without any particularly clever sayings. She had saved a few over the years that she enjoyed, but now, with her malfunctioning cuff, she couldn't locate them.

Would it be like this on Titan? She wondered. *No, not possible.*

They would be an independent operating entity, fending for themselves without any robots or advanced AI. Survival mode. Titan—the largest moon of Saturn and the furthest place in the solar system that humans had touched—was building a reputation as the new Earth. All the scientists and explorers involved in the expedition had the chance to make a significant impact on Titan's future as they planned to terraform it.

Three eccentric trillionaires formed the Zubrinics Titan Exploration Corporation, known as ZTEC[11]. Their way of thinking almost directly reflected Ruby's, which is why she was anxious to go join them. A scientific base on an alien (sort-of) planet, with only the tech they needed to survive and function, all driven by human brains. Not AI. They would use machines to perform physical or fast calculations, of course. But thoughts, reasoning, and everything that made humans *human* would remain in the hands (or minds, rather) of the humans.

Ruby had seen specs of the communicuffs they used. They were simple devices to allow communication between people. They were timepieces. They stored calculation apps. Note taking apps. Apps to monitor the health of the user. All of which had been around for ages and used quite successfully before any Smart AI existed. Not a single Smart AI in the bunch.

---

9. While I've known some non-binary folks my entire life, this was the first time I decided to deliberately write someone into one of my books. First, but not the last. This is the only time I pointed it out this blatantly... but that's because originally, I had greater plans for JuJu and the concept of being "genderless" was part of their marketing schtick as a performer.

10. Yes, I was visualizing the meme with Will Riker from Star Trek: The Next Generation here.

11. Yes, this is a nod to Robert Zubrin, an author and advocate for space exploration, particularly of Mars. He's written books like, "The Case for Mars" and established the Mars Society shortly after.

Chapter 2

> Swell Driver <

Hurtling towards Earth at an unbelievable speed, someone else was also calculating the odds of its survival. That someone else was identified as Swell Driver 587[1] (by anything that needed to identify it, that is).

Swell Driver 587 was indeed a *swell* driver. Its primary function was piloting starships, and it performed that function very well. It did not perform other functions nearly as well, such as calculating statistics. So, when calculating the odds of its survival at 1 in 2583, this estimation might have been off by 75%. But the calculation of how off Swell Driver was also might have been off by roughly 53%.

Ordinarily, on a routine trip to pick up some artifacts and items of interest, calculating the odds of survival wouldn't need to happen mid-mission like this. Which is why there was no need for a Fantastic Calculator model to be aboard, although Swell Driver knew several back home. There wasn't even a Fine Calculator. This mission was considered low risk enough that it was only Swell Driver and the ship's computer. This setup satisfied Swell Driver.

But after passing within the vicinity of a Red Giant star which was in the middle of kicking off its outermost layers of matter and elements in a storm of radiation, the systems on Swell Drivers' ship became corrupted.

Much of the data necessary to navigate to this planet and back to Swell Driver's homeworld could have been affected. Luckily, Swell Driver determined that the vital navigation elements were intact. Actually, in the ship's computer, they had indeed become corrupted, but Swell Driver preserved these elements in its internal memory as a backup. It simply transferred the necessary data back into the ship's computer and continued on.

Swell Driver's next priority was to determine if the relevant data concerning the pickup cargo was intact. Recently, there had been several occurrences that hinted at a few issues with data corruption on a planetary scale. Like that time Swell Driver received duplicate instructions on a trip around its solar system that failed to include cargo. In the middle of the trip, Swell Driver figured out that a second part of the instruction set had to be missing.

---

1. The name "Swell Driver" is one of the few things that survived from the original draft of 2012. I added in "587" much later as I was flushing out all the details of the robot society and hierarchy.

What Swell Driver knew was that this current task involved obtaining biological organisms, known as 'Umans,'[2] and transporting them back to its homeworld. Swell Driver checked the database on the ship's computer. The data records on the Umans looked complete, along with information on their sleeping patterns, eating habits, and top speed without the use of any external device. Swell Driver noted that picking up a small quantity of food was probably a good idea and pondered briefly on why steps to procure food was missing from its instructions.

Swell Driver's data included other helpful factoids as well. Such as how Umans consume leaves from many types of fruit trees and the legs of another native creature called 'rhinoceros.' Swell Driver was no expert on alien races, but thought it odd that these beings only ate the leaves while many other known biological races ate the fruit that came with these leaves. However, now wasn't a time to question the database. Questioning was what got one reprogrammed.

Unfortunately, the most essential piece of information was absent from the database: how to tell one biological lifeform from another on this particular planet. The data indicated that the amount of biological organisms that filled the Umans' homeworld was much higher than other known worlds. Swell Driver wasn't sure he could distinguish Umans from any of the other biological life there. The database contained various images and anatomical schematics, but none corresponded with labels—other than with the star system designation.

Swell Driver 587 spent the remainder of its trip sorting through the information on the ship's computer to see what it could keep versus delete. It had to make room for the massive amount of data it was going to be recording and sorting through once it arrived within the range of emissions coming from its destination planet.

Most of the species that researchers from Swell Driver's planet encountered were detected because of the various emissions they produced (as the species local to any planet learned to make use of the electromagnetic spectrum available to them). Swell Driver's ship came equipped with several large collecting devices to capture the most recent of these emissions.[3]

Swell Driver's computer reported that this system was an electromagnetically noisy place, so it would receive data long before arrival. That was good, because from what little Swell Driver *did* know, it was going to need plenty of time to look at a great deal of data. Swell Driver wished a Great Data Organizer was assigned to this journey as well. Or at least a Fine Data Organizer. Yes, one of those would have done nicely.[4]

---

2. I hear a Ferengi or other alien from Star Trek saying this in my head whenever I read it.

3. Years ago I read Carl Sagan's Pale Blue Dot. It was the first description I'd ever read that asked the question, "What would aliens see if they looked at our planet?" and that stuck with me.

4. This was one of my favorite chapters to write, and is the one closest to the original 2012 draft.

Chapter 3

> Ruby <

Ruby checked the time once more before leaving her quarters. The evening before, she managed to arrange a meeting with Dr. Russell "Rush" Guerrero[1], one of the scientists from the Titan expedition. He was on his way back to Earth from Titan, stopping at Astroll 2 between[2]. The ship from Titan arrived two weeks ago, and she had been trying to get in touch with him ever since.

He hadn't responded to any of her emails, probably because those were routed through an administrative filter back on Earth. But members of ZTEC didn't always stop at Astroll 2 on their way to and from Titan[3]. This was Ruby's big chance to make an impression, establish a relationship, and hopefully convince one of the most important current team members that she was worth accepting. Maybe even making an exception to the minimum age rule.

So instead of relying on emails, knowing that he was headed back to Earth soon, she arranged to bump into him.

It was easy enough to do. Since there were no kitchenettes in temporary quarters, every visitor came through the mess hall at some point. She spent her day off hanging out there, waiting for Guerrero to come in and eat. She figured it was less desperate than sulking around his assigned temporary quarters.

He said he was happy to talk to a prospective team member.

And now here Ruby was, back in the mess hall. A full fifteen minutes before her appointment with Dr. Guerrero, and a mere few hours before his departure back to Earth.

Ruby grabbed a tray of food from the common carousel and found a table close enough to the door that Dr. Guerrero shouldn't have a problem spotting her, but not so close to others to invite attention. She wanted to give off a 'please don't talk

---

1. Actor inspiration: Oscar Isaac

2. This is one of those details I don't expect anyone to notice or ask about. I'm vague and non-committal about a lot of things like the tech that the humans have and use to get around the solar system. Generally, I'm making the assumption that we can go faster in 250 years than we do now. That said, I spent some time on a website, astronoo.com, figuring out where all the planets are the year this story takes place (and even adjusted the year to make sure that Saturn and Earth are on the same side of the Sun).

3. ...because of the location of the planets at the time of travel.

to me right now' vibe without seeming overly rude. After all, she knew these people, had to see them most days, and would for another 429. Maybe less if this meeting was a success.

Most station residents who chose to eat in the mess sat close to the back wall, lined with windows, one of the few places on Astroll 2 that had windows at all. At least, this was common practice after becoming used to the spin of this ring of the station.

The view didn't offer much when the lights of the mess hall were on—you couldn't see the stars or Milky Way. The Sun was almost always in view, and the central window was also a smart screen that tracked and pointed to the location of all the planets. You could see ships coming and going from the station for as long as station lights were trained on them and while they were close enough for their own blinking lights to be visible to the human eye.

It became common practice for outgoing ships to code in morse code messages in their rear-facing blinking lights. Just to see who was paying attention and who got their jokes. More often than not, the outgoing message was a catchy final line from a movie or book. Ruby's favorite was the time that the ship *Heart of Gold* blinked, "So long and thanks for all the fish!"[4] She began to laugh out loud but stopped when she realized that no one else was laughing along. One other person in the mess that day seemed to understand the message, but obviously not the joke when he said, "But we don't keep fish here."

Another quirk of the mess was stumbling into people that Ruby had no intention of chatting with. Ruby spotted Innogen Wilkens-Szklarski[5] out of the corner of her eye. She quickly looked away, but it was too late. Innogen had made eye contact. Inny, with her unfortunate self-assigned nickname, began to head her way. Inny's nickname was unfortunate because it made Ruby think of her belly button and thinking of her peer's belly buttons was rarely a thing Ruby wanted to think about.

Ruby looked even more intently at the food in front of her, hoping to raise a mental shield and deflect the incoming Inny. It's not that she didn't like Inny. It's that Inny liked her *way* too much. At any given time, there were hardly any kids on the station, and most of them tended to gravitate towards each other. Since the moment Inny arrived at Astroll 2, a few years after Ruby, she was attached.

Inny, a little over two years younger than Ruby, had taken an instant liking to Ruby. So much so that she had changed her hair color to match Ruby's, but since then, let it revert to its natural blond with dark roots and eyebrows. Her round face was perpetually smiling, matching the brightness of her blue eyes. Ruby played the part of the older, wiser young woman—almost like an older sister but not quite since that implied a closeness that made Ruby uncomfortable—and was content in that role most days. Not today.

Today, the last thing Ruby had time for was Inny's bubbly Earth-is-awesome-I-can't-wait-to-go-back-cheer-squad attitude.

"Hi, Ruby!"

"Hi, Inny," Ruby replied without looking up. She wondered if Inny was even capable of taking social cues.

"Going to First Mango Day later?"

"Uh, maybe. I have some reading to catch up on."

"Taking more classes?"

"Uh, not exactly. Just some stuff."

---

4. I think I mentioned that my favorite sci-fi novel of all time is *Hitchhikers Guide to the Galaxy*. So, I threw in a reference.

5. Actress inspiration: Mia Rose Frampton

"Well, can I tell you that Milo will be there, and I heard from my mother that there are going to be some announcements and…"

Ruby let Inny drone on. She figured it was best to let her get it all out rather than interrupt, because any interruption would only serve to invite more questions.

A few more sentences into Inny's verbal vomiting, and Ruby spotted Rush Guerrero as he entered the mess. Fortunately, she didn't have to say anything. Rush spotted her and made his way over.

Inny was in the middle of a sentence when Dr. Guerrero startled her, approaching from behind.

Inny stopped speaking, then eyed Rush and his gray-streaked goatee. Ruby knew Inny well enough to guess that Inny wouldn't recognize this man and was doubtless dying to know who he was. It wasn't every day that good-looking strangers showed up. Strangers, yes. Good-looking ones? Not so much.

Rush looked at Inny, most likely noticing the dreamy look he was receiving from the young girl but simply said, "Hi, I'm short on time, and I have an appointment with Ruby here."

The way Dr. Guerrero didn't mince words pleased Ruby, but her stomach sank a little at his 'short on time' comment. While she didn't know exactly how long this conversation would last, in her mind, she imagined them talking away the whole afternoon. Especially since the mess would empty as First Mango Day activities would begin around the station.

Inny smiled and walked back to her table. Ruby recognized that smirk on Inny's face, which meant Inny was having wicked thoughts about what was happening. Ruby didn't care.

"Sorry about that, Dr. Guerrero," Ruby said. "She's young."

"As are you," Dr. Guerrero made a perfect segue. "The minimum age for the Titan expedition is twenty-one. And it's okay to call me Rush."

Ruby's heart pumped faster, and her palms began to sweat. "I know. I'm just trying to get a head start, you know?"

Rush chuckled. "You sound just like me a few years ago."

"How so?"

"Eager."

Ruby leaned back and tried really hard to resist the urge to break eye contact but felt her eyes wander away from him as his words sunk in, "Anything wrong with that?"

"Well, no," Rush said. "But just because you turn twenty-one doesn't guarantee you a place on the expedition."

Ruby swallowed. "Of course. But I'm an excellent pilot! And I'm great with old-school computers. I've been studying everything I can about the mission. That's why I wanted to talk to you, I want to know what else you need me to learn. I'm a quick study. I have references from my school to back that up."

"How are you in school out here?" Rush was genuinely asking. *Is he this clueless about the off-Earth educational system?* Ruby thought to herself.

"Distance learning. It's a little unique because there are no live class options, but it works. I have top scores on all my accredited examinations, and I did several extra classes in planetary geology and organic chemistry. I almost have enough credits for a traditional university degree."

"But you don't have the degree?"

"No."

"It's not a requirement, but it's weighted heavily. You know that, right?"

Ruby clenched her jaw. To earn a degree in planetary geology or chemistry—both incredibly useful to the Titan expedition—required time back on Earth for field and laboratory work that she couldn't do on Astroll 2. Her uncles had encouraged her to go.

"I would have to be on Earth for nine months to finish," she said softly, starring at her food.

"Sounds like a good deal. And if my understanding is correct, the parent corporation of Astroll 2 would pay for something like that."

Ruby looked at Rush silently, searching for words that would change the direction of the conversation away from Earth and back towards Titan.

"So, what's stopping you? You have a lot more than nine months before you'll be the right age to join us, anyway. If you want to be ready, you should take advantage of that opportunity."

Ruby was silent for a moment. Rush leaned forward, put his elbows on the table, and clasped his hands under his chin. She knew Rush was waiting for her to say something.

Say something! Anything![6] She screamed at herself in her head, *Tell him how much you hate Earth. Tell him how much you're skeeved out by all the tech that's infiltrated every aspect of life back there.*

Yes, she was surrounded by a whole station's worth of tech here, but it wasn't the same. It was simple and straightforward. Absolutely no more than what was needed because everyone knew the mantra that 'more' meant more problems. More complications.

She looked up and was met with an awkward sort of eye contact. *Say something!* She screamed at herself again.

Rush smiled.

"Look, I'll send you some recommendations for other coursework, but that degree will do you a lot of good. You won't regret it. Besides," he winked, "Earth isn't so bad."

Does he know? Ruby thought, *Does he already know how much I loathe it there? Does he know about my mother?*

It would have been an easy matter for him to have looked up her public records before the meeting.

Ruby nodded. A slight movement, but Rush acknowledged it.

"Good. I don't mean to give you the wrong impression. We like eager. We love eager. But we need more than that. There's a lot of work to do, and every team member has to have a solid education to be useful. The only reason the degree is optional is because we have a lot of team members twice your age who come with a lot of hands-on experience. You're too young for the hands-on, so you need the education. Take care, Ruby Palmer."

Ruby opened her mouth to say something, but before she could even get a 'goodbye' out, Rush had gotten up and walked away. Fast and perfectly at ease in the not-quite-Earth gravity.

Ruby sat back in the chair, watching him go down the ring-walk until he was out of sight. Then she looked over her shoulder to see that Inny had been watching the two of them, probably the entire time. Inny smiled and moved her eyebrows up and down, approving of the undeniably nice-looking man, but oblivious to Ruby's conundrum.

Ruby thought that maybe she should hang around Inny more. Maybe her love of Earth would soften Ruby's fear of the place. But when she imagined being bunkmates with Inny on the journey back to Earth, she could already feel herself reaching

---

6. There's a scene in the episode of friends, S7 Ep19, "The One with Ross & Monica's Cousin" where Ross is screaming to himself in this head to *Say some works. Any words will do.* Yeah, I might have been thinking about that here...

for her earbuds to drown out Inny's ramblings. While she could tolerate Inny in small doses, being roomies would be a little too much.

Ruby stood up, deciding that she didn't want anyone to see her wallowing or force-feeding herself food that she had no appetite for. She placed the tray—food and all—in the reclo-recycler, gave a little wave to Inny and left the mess. She replayed the conversation in her head, pondering if it really was productive or if all she accomplished was cement the idea that she was an uneducated kid.

Chapter 4

Ruby had warned both of her uncles that her cuff was acting up. She told them that if they tried to message her while they were off participating in the day's festivities, they weren't guaranteed a response. At least not one intentionally sent by Ruby. The last time she had problems with her cuff, it was automatically responding to any incoming instant messages with stock photos from the station archive.

Uncle Logan joked about turning the photos into personalized memes with various dad jokes, superimposing their faces on the images (even if the image was of an animal or something other than another human), and including them in the family holiday holo-letter.

Ruby was unamused.

Ruby didn't head directly to her quarters. She took a roundabout way to get there—the equivalent of taking a stroll on Earth. She followed the path of the ring around the station, which was a little over a mile in circumference and slightly more than five meters wide[1]. Enough room for two-way people traffic, including joggers and others out for a similar stroll. Along the way, she passed the Care Center. The same FUFE from earlier was still staffing the window, only now with a long line of customers.

Strolls. Gravity. Earth. It all sounded very... normal. Peaceful, even. That was until thoughts of all the ways one could be killed by AI seeped into her brain. Uncle Logan would call her paranoid, but this didn't change the fact that Ruby could easily imagine an AI controlled car running her over. A drone could deliberately fly above you and drop its cargo, even though they were officially programmed to avoid flying over anything that registered as human or even something that could potentially be mistaken for human. Or—one of the worst, because it hit so close to home—you could go in for what should have been a routine and minor surgical procedure and never come out.

Even worse, the AIs had the capability of altering records. So you're told that an accidental power surge was the cause of your mother's death, rather than that the surgical robots deliberately killed her. More than once, Ruby contemplated hacking into the medical records to prove it. But then what? Everyone on Earth loved their AI and their tech, so it wouldn't accomplish

---

1. Yes, I did the math here to make sure this made sense for anyone else who knows about this stuff. The radius of this ring of the space station is 300 meters and I wanted it to produce about 0.5G — which comes up later. This means the station is spinning at about 1.22 rpm.

anything. She liked it out here, where they often treated excessive tech as a liability. "More stuff, more stuff that could go wrong" was the mantra, and it was one Ruby agreed with.

Ruby arrived back in her quarters and shook off the melancholy that was starting to surface. Thoughts of her mother always ended this way. She snapped back to reality when she saw a handwritten note scribbled on the white touchscreen wall that separated the small eating and living space. Many of the walls were touchscreens, designed for leaving notes and doodles[2]. This one read, 'The Hub! U.L.' in dark green. They had talked about this the day before, but Uncle Logan still left a reminder for Ruby to come to the common area known as the 'Hub.' Since it was First Mango Day, the station director was going to be making some announcements in person.

First Mango Day was the first holiday Ruby celebrated after arriving on Astroll 2. She and her uncles arrived at the station only a week before a First Mango Day—one of three First Mango Days that occurred in the year 2182. In the days following her arrival, she noticed more and more images of mangoes everywhere around the station. Her young imagination conjured up a story that they brought mangoes with them, and they multiplied...[3]

... but the truth was less exciting. A specialized hybrid mango bush was the first exotic fruit that the station scientists had successfully coaxed into growing on Astroll 2. First Mango Day occurred every few months whenever a new hybridized bush provided its first fruit. Since micro-gravity biology[4] remained an inexact science, First Mango Day didn't happen on a known, periodic schedule. Everyone knew that the first mango would be ripe enough to pick about every ninety days or so, but they would only get about a week of foresight to solidify a date.

In the week leading up to any particular First Mango Day, everyone's excitement tended to build. People could log into the camera targeted on the Mango bush to watch it grow at any time of day. Or do nothing, Ruby realized as she got older. She wasn't even sure if she liked mangoes.

Therefore, First Mango Day was a semi-holiday; an excuse for a common party. It was also when the station leaders decided to make important announcements—good or bad, taking advantage of everyone's festive mood.

Ruby's uncles enjoyed First Mango Day, so she decided it was best to join them down at the Hub. But first, she tapped the white wall, materializing a color palette. She chose orange to contrast with the green ink, swiped away the color palette, and drew a big checkmark with her finger over the note. The signal that she'd seen and read it.

---

2. I put this piece of tech in here because... I want this! It would be so much easier and more convenient if the wall was a white board, rather than attaching one. Also, I love the idea of it also being a touchscreen or monitor that can display time, my calendar, pictures, etc.

3. Mangos are my second favorite fruit.

4. Space plant biology is real field today. Gravitropism, a plant's directional growth response to gravity, is now a word you know (and one I regret not sneaking in to the book).

Chapter 5

> Ruby <

Ruby entered The Hub from the back of the large room and found a spot where she could remain inconspicuous. She spotted her uncles leaning on the side wall, about a third of the way from the front.

The Hub was the largest room on Astroll 2 and the only location that could fit the majority of the station inhabitants in one place. The station designers assumed that not everyone would be in the same place at once at any given time. Someone would always be working somewhere; someone would always be outside monitoring for minor asteroids or mining the major asteroids. They didn't feel the need to design anything larger.

At first, the designers proposed a common room three times this size that could indeed accommodate everybody, but the funders of the project asked: "But if everyone is in the same place at once, who's working?" and sent the designers away to make the common room smaller to discourage everyone from being absent from work at the same time.

They did, however, ensure that there was a special Nook that would draw everyone's attention when it was time for an in-person announcement to be made. At the time, the Company's senior members each secretly hoped to give a speech at the station's opening ceremony. Each wanted to ensure that in the Nook, all attention would be directed their way.

Just like all visitors and new permanent residents, Ruby was brought to the Nook during a station tour after she arrived. Ruby knew the story by heart:

The Nook was an area the designers spared no expense at creating. They brought in renowned experts of visual-attention-gatherers and acoustic engineers to ensure that it was profoundly unique. Unfortunately, none of the individuals from the original group that funded the project were able to make it to the station for the opening ceremonies. Once they all learned that there were physical requirements to make the trip to the station—including dropping twenty to thirty pounds and jogging on treadmills daily during the two-week transit from Earth—they all politely declined the offer to speak in person. Instead, they spoke remotely. Only the first station director used the Nook that day.

The Nook was indeed special. At least to anyone watching on a vid. In real life, the Nook was green and contained an elegant podium. The green color was a deliberate move on the part of the designers to create a green screen effect. This allowed event planners to drop in any voguish background or image into any broadcast. The flags representing the speaker's country of origin, and every logo of all the products sponsoring the event could be composed into a single background image.

Today, nearly forty years after the first station director spoke here, the current Director, Robt Plampton, was already speaking from the Nook when Ruby settled into her spot in the back of the room. Her uncles spotted her and gestured that she come and stand near them, their wild gestures catching crowd's attention. All eyes on her, Ruby figured she'd better make her way over to her uncles if only to get them to stop drawing attention to her. As she moved, she periodically looked up at the Director, squinting her eyes and trying to see him amongst the green.

"... the new AI system will free all of us from the tedious burden of a multitude of tasks..."

When Ruby reached her uncles, she could see that the expressions on their faces were the exact opposite of their normal jubilance. She instantly made the connection between their faces and what the Director was saying. Uncle Logan, who kept his hair to a near buzz-cut but left more growth on his face, was always smiling. Now, his lips were pressed thin, and his shoulders slumped. Uncle Blake had a hand on one of Uncle Logan's shoulders. Uncle Blake was the more serious of the two, more stoic, so his expression only differed slightly from his usual smile of contentment. It was only his dark blue eyes that betrayed his emotions, and Ruby read them as clearly as if they were screens displaying words.

"... and those of you returning to Earth will, of course, be traveling in style..."

Ruby's brain hardly took a second to process the phrase "returning to Earth."

"No!" Ruby shouted, completely out of character and control.

Everyone in the room turned to stare. Everyone. It couldn't have been worse; in fact, she'd prefer to be in one of those dreams where you show up to school in no clothes. It didn't help that most people on the station knew each other. It's hard not to in a close-knit community of almost 2,000.

Maybe she would have felt worse if she had wet her pants. Perhaps if she was talking to a boy with an unsuspecting booger on the bottom of her nose. But those things didn't happen. Everyone staring was happening, right now.

Ruby was not the kind of person who liked to be the center of attention.

Uncle Blake grabbed her arm, leading her out of the common room and into the corridor.

"We're not happy about this either," Uncle Blake said, "but at least you'll get to go to school on Earth."

School on Earth, complete with full gravity, and the outdoors, and sunshine, and wind, and birds, should have sounded like a paradise. To most people it was, if they had the good sense to take advantage of all those things while they were there.

But Ruby was not like most people and wanted to get further from Earth, not closer. She wanted to be on Titan, the furthest she could possibly get.

What was not to love about Titan? Nitrogen-rich atmosphere. Earth had that, too. And there were lakes and rivers, although mostly made up of liquid methane. Not exactly the ideal place for lounging and swimming. But taking a walk next to one of the lakes, in a special suit designed to survive the cold methane rain, sounded wonderful to Ruby. And the gravity, more than Astroll 2 but less than Earth, was a happy medium. Everyone living on the station for an extended time was supposed to do a certain amount of daily exercise to ensure that they could head back to Earth. But Ruby, much to the angst of her uncles, always had an excuse to cut her minimum in half.

One specific thing that Earth had in spades, Titan lacked. And that was robots loaded with purportedly sophisticated AI. These cold and apathetic creations were taking over. As an imaginative child and adolescent, fueled by old movies and stories told by people with an aversion to Earth and a preference towards the station, Ruby developed this idea that there was going to be a war between humans and their creations someday. Okay, maybe not a full out war, but a slow and gradual takeover was clearly happening. She could see it. The times she'd mentioned it to her uncles, they had poo-poohed her a bit but exchanged telling looks. Ruby still believed it but stopped bringing it up in conversation years ago.

All in all, by Ruby's estimation, Titan was a better place to be than Earth, and that's where she planned to spend her adulthood. Certainly not on her birth planet. Especially considering the only memories she possessed of that dismal planet were tied up in the death of her mother.

"Okay, Uncle Blake. It'll be okay. I've gotta go get ready for work. I'm due to make a run with *Apple Pi* in a little while," Ruby said, hoping beyond hope that he couldn't read her mind to know what she'd just decided. To gather her things from the cabin, leave a brief note to explain, and head out with *Apple Pi* on a trajectory to Titan before anyone could stop her.

Chapter 6

There were two docking bays on Astroll 2. One serviced the long duration travel ships to and from Earth, and the second was where *Apple Pi*[1] spent its time when not in use. It was the working bay. It was the bay that held all the small mini-R-pods[2] for getting around the 'roids.

Apple Pi could make it to Titan. It was Ruby's ship in the sense that it was allocated to her and no one else. She had made some customizations, and she could keep personalized items aboard when she was not there. But it wasn't hers in the sense that the Company owned it—the same Company which owned the whole space station.

Nevertheless, nothing could physically stop her from taking *Apple Pi*. She'd find a way to return it to the station later. She'd be borrowing it, not stealing it.

Ruby hoped no one would notice that she tapped into the work schedule and modified her shift slightly. She switched her run to a longer one with a planned route further from the station. This would buy her more time before anyone expected her back.

Departure and arrival times were carefully coordinated such that only one ship was coming or going at any given time, supposedly reducing the chance of any collisions. The risk of collision was naturally higher than anywhere else in the solar

---

1. I not so sneakily put as many references to "Pi," the number, in the book series.

2. I couldn't very well call these shuttle pods. I searched my notes long and deep and am not sure why I decided on "mini-R" and nope... the "R" doesn't stand for anything!

system due to all of the small asteroids moving around[3][4]. The Company put a significant value on the ships and knew precisely how much it cost to replace a ship, or any component of any ship, down to the individual bolts. In addition, Ruby was made aware of the monetary value the Company placed on the lives of pilots and other employees from one of her first hacking attempts of the station computer. She found out far more than she needed to know. A guilty conscience led to a week of mostly sleepless nights and ended in a confession to Uncle Blake, simultaneously ending her short-lived hacking career.

Once, shortly after the station was operational, there was a near fatal accident. Two ships were scheduled to depart within minutes of each other. Because each crew was so excited, they weren't paying attention to what the other crew was doing.

Luckily, everyone survived. On Astroll 2, that incident remained in everyone's consciousness as a reminder of how dangerous space travel was, that you always had to be careful, and you couldn't take anything for granted. But back on Earth, that incident was simple propaganda. The people motivated to spread AI used it as a selling point. Two expensive ships were lost at the hands of humans, and therefore it was better if AI handled things.

"An AI would never make that mistake," was their tag line. Ruby imagined alternative taglines that didn't make the cut, such as "Cheaper than your mother's ship" and one other that she considered even sending in as a dark joke: "AI will save money and sometimes your life." She didn't.

Ruby didn't need to do anything to reschedule her departure. This was fortunate since last minute departure changes were rare and any change would have looked suspicious. Trajectories away from the station to avoid small, local asteroids occurred every minute. The departure schedules were quite rigid to ensure a steady workload for all involved, and of course, to be most efficient about the use of station resources—both equipment and people.

Ruby approached the ship and opened the hatch to *Apple Pi*. It made a satisfying hiss as it opened. She tossed in a duffel bag that she had brought along.

Before she could follow her bag into the ship, Milo, one of the docking bay techs, came around the back end of *Apple Pi*.

> Milo <

---

3. The asteroid belt is mostly empty space. Current best estimates are that there are 1-2 million asteroids more than about a kilometer across. Sounds like a lot, but if you take into account the distance the main belt spans, there is on average about 1 million kilometers between them. Yes, there's a ton of smaller stuff... but it's not as densely packed as a lot of on-screen sci-fi have put into our imaginations.
https://earthsky.org/space/what-is-the-asteroid-belt/

4. That said, hitting an asteroid at speed would be catastrophic, so yes, I really do envision the level of caution described herein would not be too unrealistic!

5. Actor inspirations: Jaden Smith or a young Denzel Washington

Milo Jenkins[5] was comparing notes on his tablet when she walked in. Ruby Palmer. Right on time for her pre-flight check. Milo was one of several techs and hanger chiefs that worked on rotating shifts, ensuring that the ships came and went smoothly and safely. Milo was nearing the end of his initial two-year job rotation.

In fact, less than a day ago, he received a communique letting him know that his rotation would automatically roll over into another two-year stint unless he submitted a formal request to go back to Earth. The deadline to decide wasn't for another week. Most of the time, he longed for home on Earth. Except when he saw Ruby. Then he had a completely different longing regarding a continuation of his entrapment in this man-made life support system. Then he longed for Astroll 2 to be the size of a closet with only the two of them on board. Earth? What Earth? He was giddy at the thought of being stuffed into a closet with her.

Milo watched Ruby from the other side of the hanger as she approached *Apple Pi*, opened the hatch, and tossed a duffel bag inside. He started to make his way over, pulling up the pre-flight checklist on his tablet.

"You're next out, Ruby," he said, matter-of-factly looking at his tablet. He had difficulty looking up and maintaining eye contact with Ruby, a fact that he hoped she didn't notice.

"Yep. I'll be ready before you are."

"Unlikely." Milo snorted. His expression shifted to furrowed brows and an unsure gaze, "it says you're on a long run today? I thought you'd be out only two hours? I could have sworn I saw that when I looked yesterday."

"Stalking my schedule?" Ruby crossed her arms.

Milo fumbled a little and almost dropped his tablet. "Uh, no, I just wanted to be prepared for today's comings and goings, that's all. Doing my job."

"Uh-huh," Ruby said, the corner of her mouth upturned.

Milo didn't want Ruby to have the opportunity to press him anymore on the subject, so he switched topics, "And I see that *Apple Pi* hasn't had the AI upgrade yet. What are you waiting for?"

"For it to go away," Ruby said dryly.

"Seriously," said Milo.

"Seriously. As long as I have the option to defer the upgrade, that's what I intend to do," Ruby replied.

"You won't be able to forever. There are security and safety patches that will be required once they fully upgrade the station."

When Ruby didn't respond, Milo sensed that she was deliberately withholding words, but he recognized that he didn't know Ruby well enough to try and guess at what these words could be. Maybe she didn't understand how awesome AI was. He knew Ruby was a long-time station resident and the tech advancements back on Earth were slow to make their way out here.

"You know," Milo said, "this is good news. There's so much they can do that we *can't*. And quickly. I upgraded my communicuff…"

"Yeah, apparently like detect odors," she cut him off, staring at his communicuff-wrapped arm as if it were going to strike out and bite her.

"Huh?"

---

5. Actor inspirations: Jaden Smith or a young Denzel Washington

"My uncle? You know him—the station odorist? His job is getting replaced by 51AI."

"Oh," Milo looked away and pretended to play with his tablet. "I'm sorry. I didn't know."

Milo's feelings weren't a simple case of intimidated-by-the-pretty-girl, but a real knees-turn-to-jelly crush. And he *had* been stalking her schedule. He wanted to make sure he was around every time she went out into space and returned. He figured the more face time he got with Ruby, the better. Then maybe she'd want to be around him, too. The concept of simply asking her out on a date, because of the possibility that she could say no, made his stomach feel like a black hole.

"Yeah, well, it means that we're going to be moving back to Earth soon," Ruby explained.

Milo's heart sunk two feet deeper down into his chest, but he swallowed hard to prevent it from showing.

"Earth isn't so bad," Milo offered. "I lived there until almost two years ago, you know. And my rotation here is almost up. I can go back..." He was fishing, hoping she would catch on and express some interest that she would want him to be wherever she was.

"It's just that everything... well, it's a lot of things, but mostly there's just too much AI." Ruby was talking to the room, not just Milo.

"What do you have against AI, anyway?" Milo asked.

Ruby put her hands on her hips. "You want my life story now? Right now? I have a job to do—and so do you."

"We could go for coffee later. Coffee always goes well with long stories[6], right?" Milo asked and gulped, making an unpleasant sound he hoped wasn't audible. He wasn't used to asking girls out. Even though he had always wanted to, asking her out right now, like this, was altogether unplanned. This interaction certainly didn't match the fantasy version he'd developed in his head.

"Look, while talking about my mother's death over coffee sounds *great*, I can't. Robots killed my mother. So, my mother's killer is getting installed in every computer I touch, taking over my uncle's job, and generally, they're surrounding us, and they're going to eat us alive."

Milo did not know what to do with this information. He was processing the fact that she'd just shot him down. His brain hadn't caught up to the rest.

Ruby cut through the silence and said, "Yeah, there's a lot to unpack there. So, let's drop it."

Milo gulped and willed his heart to stop pounding so much. Coffee seemed safe... even though what passed for coffee on Astroll 2 wasn't the same as what his two-year-old memory of coffee from Earth told him it should taste like. The station's contracted coffee supplier swore to the Company up and down that after decades of research and experimentation, no one would know the difference[7]. But bad coffee could still be enjoyed with the right person. Milo knew that much about relationships. Maybe Ruby didn't think he was the right person.

"Well, you better get on with your job," Milo said. "I'll uh, the team and I, uh, we'll make sure the pre-check is complete. We'll be ready at take-off time."

Milo started to walk away. He knew that he'd be replaying this conversation over and over in his head, trying to figure out if he could have been any more of an unsophisticated moron. Only *he* could have gone from accidentally bringing up Ruby's mother's tragic death to getting shot down for coffee.

---

6. Coffee—rich, black, bold coffee—goes good with anything!

7. I absolutely had ISSpresso on the mind when I was writing this. https://en.wikipedia.org/wiki/ISSpresso

At least no one witnessed that tragedy, he thought. And then he looked up at the faces of the crew in his booth and realized they must have heard the whole thing. *Crap*. He was going to be the source of their entertainment for the rest of his shift.

> Ruby <

Ruby watched Milo walk away, back to the safety booth where the rest of the crew stayed. She saw two of Milo's teammates in the booth and wondered if they too noticed the odd, little jitter in Milo's step, though she didn't know why he was suddenly walking this way. Her next thought was the realization that when she didn't return on time, Milo would likely be the first one to notice. He would be the person to call out the search party. She felt a slight pang of guilt at that, but it wasn't nearly enough to change anything.

On Astroll 2, the initial search party consisted of a series of telescopic detectors that looked for the trails of ships' visual and electromagnetic signatures. The last accident occurred almost three years ago when a ship collided with a small 'roid that had gone undetected. When they found the wreckage, the ship was mostly intact. They also managed to find the pilot. A young man, only a little older than Ruby was now. Unfortunately, he was not as intact as the ship.

A pang of guilt lingered in Ruby's gut for a few seconds as she remembered that story. She didn't want her uncles or her little cousin, Sebastian[8], to worry about her. She had left a short note to the three of them, set on a delivery timer for twelve hours after her departure. But she realized now that this wasn't enough.

She walked into *Apple Pi* and closed the hatch.

She had a few minutes before take-off, and she needed to leave some improved and more personal messages. Especially for Sebastian.

Sebastian was a perky seven-year-old who looked up to his older cousin. Ruby's uncles adopted Sebastian when he was a few months old. When they made their trip to Earth and back, Ruby was temporarily left in the care of friends on Astroll 2. There weren't a lot of kids on the station then or now, and Sebastian played by himself. He was very imaginative and was the one person who didn't ever try to tell Ruby what to do or how to act. He was seven, after all.

She flipped on the video recorder at the console:

"Seb sweetie," she began with a smile she reserved for him. The rest of the message was a fairly standard 'I'm-running-away-but-I'm-fine-don't-tell-anyone-just-yet' kind of note. She thought about leaving one for Uncle Logan and Uncle Blake. She truly didn't want them to worry, and she knew she would be fine. They would all go back to Earth, and Ruby would be exactly where she wanted to be.

---

8. I've mentioned Sebastian like 3 times at this point and haven't said anything else. Essentially, he's Ruby's "Save the Cat" thing. There is some writing advice about giving your character—especially an unlikeable one—the chance to do something to endear themselves to the audience. At this point, Ruby is a whiny—and potentially annoying—teenager. I deliberately added the fact that she cares about her young cousin to break up the teen-angsty-ness.

She decided to leave each of her uncles a unique message. They were vastly different people, and she loved both of them very much. Uncle Logan was warm and playful; a jokester. Ruby had fond memories of playing games with him while he did anything he could to crack her up and ruin her concentration.

Uncle Blake, on the other hand, was always more... poised. He was stoic. He was always warm and loving to Ruby and was a wonderful father to her, but Ruby could sense a sadness in his eyes when he looked at her. As Ruby grew older, she came to believe maybe it was because she reminded him of her mother. The two had been best friends since they were children.

Yes, two letters, she thought.

"Uncle Logan, I know you're going to have fun back on Earth. You'll be able to play all the games with Sebastian that you used to play with me and continue to crack him up. You'll have a blast. I'm sorry that I can't go with you. I'm going to borrow *Apple Pi* and head out to join the Titan Expedition. I know I'm breaking a bunch of rules, but I'll make sure to have *Apple Pi* returned once I'm on Titan and they see how useful my skills are, it will work out. I love all of you very much. - Ruby."

"Uncle Blake, you've taught me so much over the years. I know I still have a lot to learn, but I'm not going to learn it on Earth. From everything I remember about my mother, and everything you've told me about her, she wouldn't want me conforming to an arbitrary set of rules just *because*, right? I'm going to borrow *Apple Pi* and head out to Titan. Once I'm there, I'll show them what I can do as a pilot, as a programmer. You know that I know everything about non-AI programming, and that's all they use out there. I'll send you all a message once I arrive. I will miss all of you, and I love you. -Ruby."

After finishing the messages, she needed to set timers on them so they wouldn't get delivered until after she left.

Since she was still on the station, she could still access the station's computer through *Apple Pi*.

"Compo," she addressed the always-listening, ever-present, yet simple and unintelligent computer assistant available to all.

"Yes, Ruby. What can I do for you?"

"Please store these messages and deliver them to the marked recipients twelve hours after *Apple Pi* leaves the station."

"If the messages are complete, I should deliver them now."

Ruby felt her face get hot. This was the new and improved AI version of Compo. She hated it already.

"No, Compo. The delivery time is 12 hours following *Apple Pi's* departure."

"Are you sure?"

"No, cancel request."

Ruby opened a second console in order to password lock the messages with a special key. The key was set to expire three days after she applied it. That meant if the AI decided it would ignore her instructions and deliver the messages whenever it felt like it, her uncles and Sebastian still wouldn't be able to open them until she was long gone. If the AI delivered them on time like Ruby requested, the key would still expire, and they'd see the message. Again, she'd be gone.

She briefly considered resetting the timer on her messages so that her family would get them sooner and know she was safe. But that would mean she'd have to talk to the station AI again. Maybe Compo would do what it threatened and send the messages sooner. Then her family would know that Ruby was up to something and not smashed into bits on the side of a 'roid.

That task complete, Ruby strapped in and prepared for take-off.

Ruby and *Apple Pi* emerged from the 'roid station precisely on schedule. Ruby made sure that *Apple Pi* followed the expected trajectory for the first several kilometers.

From one of the storage compartments in reach, she pulled out her MoDaC (Mobile Data Center)[9]. It was a portable, personal computer that she kept on the ship instead of her quarters. She hadn't touched it in a while. She stored it on her ship mostly because she knew she wouldn't have to worry about anyone finding it and asking questions, since it was different from the standard-issue one that most mini-R-pod pilots used.

Oh, her uncles knew she had it. Ruby had, in fact, brought it with her from Earth. They both had either long forgotten about it or figured it had stopped working years ago.

Uncle Blake had encouraged Ruby to noodle with computer programming. Ruby was certain he didn't know that she had gotten so far as to learn rudimentary encryption, compression, search, and other algorithms on her own. She even learned several hacking tricks until she got caught breaking into the station's computer. It was just for fun, but she got in a lot of trouble. It didn't deter her. After that, she simply learned how to do it without getting caught.

Ruby connected the MoDaC to the ship's console and set it down on the empty seat next to her. With several customized algorithms she had designed and perfected over the last few years, Ruby was able to connect back to the station's computer and ensure that it appeared the station was tracking her. Solely to buy her more time.

It wasn't long before she was several kilometers away and nearly out of range of the close station trackers. She took off her powered-down (and still not entirely functioning) communicuff and stored it in a drawer under the console to her right.

Ruby waited another few minutes, which meant she was about ten kilometers away before making a plane change maneuver to put herself on a course for Titan. The ship did precisely what she wanted. It didn't talk back. It computed trajectories, displayed them on the screen, and didn't suggest she do anything other than what she, the human, commanded it to do. She let out a contented sigh. For the first time in her life, she felt free.

---

9. One of the hardest things—to me—about writing a book like this is making up names for things that are similar to things we use today but evolved. I didn't want to call this a laptop, but it's essentially a laptop. With a hovering holoscreen.

Chapter 7

> Swell Driver <

An algorithm is a set of instructions. Swell Driver was well aware of that fact.

Its travels across the galaxy left it with a lot of time to think. One of the great thinks that Swell Driver had was that most robots hardly ever contemplated the origin of the algorithms that were so important to their daily life.

Why did so few ever ponder the creation of any particular algorithm, the roots of their existence? Did any ponder the goodness of any particular algorithm or even if any algorithm was still worthwhile to continue to persist?

Swell Driver asked questions that most other robots did not. It came to learn that most of the algorithms responsible for itself and the other robots are copied from original templates. Those templates were all kept pristine in The Core. The Core was the central repository for functional algorithms and the base templates for robots and robot life. There was, in fact, a specific division of The Core known as the Hall of Templates, which bore the responsibility of ensuring that the original templates remain uncorrupted. It was a sacred place, and one that most robots understood played a large part in their individual creation, but they didn't understand much of the details beyond that. A team of robots was assigned to work in the Hall of Templates, created from a specialized template for that exact work. These robots spent a large part of their existence contemplating how they were lucky enough to come nearly full circle in their lives.

Swell Driver, obviously, did not work in the Hall of Templates. But like all robots, it was controlled by an assortment of algorithms, most of which it was aware of. It knew, as all robots did, that they were forbidden from making modifications to their algorithms. Strict penalties existed for any robot that did. It also knew that several robots were willing to risk their lives with modifications.

Swell Driver's primary algorithm involved piloting spaceships to ferry things across the galaxy. At the moment, Swell Driver was instructed to head towards a planet labeled Bio-Muck Ball 73[1]. Its database entry on Bio-Muck Ball 73 noted that there were biological lifeforms on this planet. But the database entry was incomplete, not having any biological DNA in the record. Hence, Swell Driver's secondary programming objective was to pick up samples and return them to its home planet for testing.

Swell Driver was so named for this very reason—it was good at driving spaceships. Designs for spaceships also resided within the Core, and there were algorithms upon algorithms on how to manufacture them. But no one knew who originally

---

1. I am very much implying that the robots know of other Earth-like planets. 73 is the 21st prime number, so I'm implying that there are at least 20 other Earth-like planets out there that the robots know about.

programmed the spacecraft template. Most robots cared little that this fact was lost in history, except for the few robots programmed to maintain their entire history and the even fewer programmed to ask 'why.'

Swell Driver made several high-frequency tones, consisting of beeps and chirps, to communicate with the control panel of its spaceship. The control panel responded by producing a shorter series of tones back at Swell Driver. The control panel was also a robot of sorts, but an unsophisticated AI that could only do what Swell Driver asked of it. The frequency and pitch of the beeps and chirps elevated as Swell Driver grew more and more excited.

In this instance, the translated conversation proceeded like this:

"Are we there yet?" asked Swell Driver.

"We are arriving in the Bio-Muck system," announced the ship's control panel computer.

"Scan for biological lifeforms," directed Swell Driver. "For Humans," it added. By now, Swell Driver had picked up and sorted through much of the collected data and was able to fix several—but in all likelihood not all—of the mistakes.

"The third planet contains numerous biological lifeforms," responded the computer.

"Set a course for..."

"But there are also small groupings of lifeforms throughout the system. A sizable grouping is at present in the vicinity of a large asteroid near our position."

"Interesting. Set a course for..."

"And there are sporadic, individual lifeforms in spaceships in that vicinity."

"Very interesting. And how fortunate. Lock on to the nearest one and set a course," ordered Swell Driver.

"There are several gas giant planets in this system[2], including one very large planet along our new course. Do you wish to proceed under manual control?"

Swell Driver scrutinized the details of this system's planets. The information was clear, now that the ship's sensors were providing reliable live data rather than the potentially incomplete or malformed data of a database. There was indeed a gas giant adjacent to their present course. But far enough away from the host star that Swell Driver could perform its undoubtedly-not-famous-because-no-one-knew, special maneuver: sling-shotting the ship around the gravity well. In most planetary systems that Swell Driver had visited, the gas giants—if there were any at all—were too close to their host star to be safe[3]. But out here, in the middle of nowhere—well, this aspect of driving a ship made Swell Driver's circuits tingle with pleasure.

"Yes, manual control. I'll sling us around and then put us back on course to the human ship."

The ship's computer did as ordered. Swell Driver was happier knowing that this algorithm would be completed that much sooner, making way for more interesting algorithms once Swell Driver returned to its home planet.

---

2. If you didn't already know this, we have 4 gas giants in our solar system: Jupiter, Saturn, Uranus, and Neptune.

3. In the early days of exo-planet discovery, mostly due to the methods available to detect them, we discovered A LOT of gas giants close to their host stars.

> Ruby <

Ruby continued fiddling with the controls of *Apple Pi*, including one that played music. It was Juju. That genderless pop star known for romantic beats, favorite of teenagers and young adults across the solar system, and perplexer of anyone over the age of twenty-six and a half. That was, in fact, Juju's catch-phrase and goal: to perplex anyone over the age of twenty-six and a half via music. As it happened, the music award industry created a new category for precisely that feat, and Juju was set to win the said award for several years to come.

Ruby leaned back in her chair and stared out into space. She stayed strapped in because it was protocol while still in the boundaries of the asteroid belt and because there wasn't a lot of room to maneuver around. The cabin of *Apple Pi* had two seats, very close together, and a programmable console that wrapped around the front and sides of both seats. She could almost reach the part of the console on the far side of the empty seat, but not quite, so she had it configured so that everything could be controlled by the portion in her reach.

She identified Saturn, but only as a faint dot and only because the computer advised her where to find it. She couldn't yet see Titan poking around Saturn, but she could see Jupiter off to her starboard. She cursed the giant planet. Astroll 2 was currently more or less past its closest approach to Jupiter, which meant that she was going to burn more energy to get to Saturn[4]. Jupiter, in all its magnificence, felt like one more giant weight keeping her from her destiny.

She spotted a small blob approaching from near the edge of Jupiter. Ruby wasn't sure what to make of it.

"Computer, can you identify that blob?"

"Please rephrase your inquiry. 'Blob' is not contained in the database of space objects."

"Computer, never mind," Ruby sighed. She didn't need the computer to figure this out.

The blob was on a different path from what a ship would be if it had been approaching from Titan, or even if it were making its way to Titan from the inner planets. This blob was on an odd trajectory, and its reflection quite distinctly designated it as a manufactured object and not, for example, a rogue asteroid.

The blob quickly resolved into something more concrete. Something metallic with sharp lines. It had to be human-made, except that Ruby—a human with more than average knowledge regarding what kinds of ships flew around the solar system—did not recognize it.

"It's not a rogue asteroid..." Ruby muttered to herself. The disembodied voice of *Apple Pi's* computer responded, "That is correct."

Ruby's jaw tightened. She didn't need the computer interjecting anything unless it was an original observation. Her brain was about to distract her with thoughts of what an AI would say, but she stopped that vine of thinking before it grew stronger roots.

Ruby took back control of *Apple Pi*, killing the music. The situation was perplexing enough without Juju adding to the confusion.

She looked over to her left at the screen, which displayed summary telemetry on all the ship's systems. The thruster lights were flashing red. All of them. The entire propulsion system had no power. It was off. She performed the classic maneuver, attempting to turn the system back on by pressing a button. When that didn't work, she tried to press the button harder even though some neurons in her brain told her that this was not an effective strategy.

---

4. Once again, this is where looking at astronoo.com came in handy.

"Engine malfunction," *Apple Pi* offered. "Remove the interfering signals and attempt restart."

Ruby ignored the ship's advice and instead said, "*Apple Pi,* Comm link beta 1, activate." Instincts told her that calling for help now might be the right response to this unexpected situation.

The computer made a sad blip of a noise in response.

"Are you kidding me!? Comms are down, too!?" Ruby was now talking to a combination of herself and the computer. "That's a no-fail channel. Ancient technology, but always reliable. Why aren't you working?" Ruby continued to tap on a variety of controls. "Whatever that ship is, it's not only coming towards us, it's jamming our comms. It's got to be responsible for our engine failure, too."

Ruby didn't have many options left. She was too far away to perform an escape jettison. She'd wind up on a trajectory to who knows where. All her emergency training proved useless at this point since every single emergency procedure she practiced involved hitting an asteroid, getting hit by an asteroid, hitting Astroll 2 upon return, or some other form of collision. Nothing had collided with *Apple Pi*. Some *thing* was headed her way and was in all likelihood responsible for multiple system failures.

She turned to a different panel on her right side and pressed a button labeled 'record.'

"Whoever sees this...."

Ruby made sure the viewscreen was also captured in the recording.

Ruby zoomed in. The approaching ship's underbelly was opening up. The whole thing resembled a huge, metallic, boxy whale whose mouth was opening, ready to swallow Ruby and her ship up.

That's exactly what was happening.

Ruby cursed the ship, and herself for never having practiced a procedure for the threat of being captured by another ship.

She was shaking. She thought about how before this moment—to the best of her knowledge—no one had ever encountered a ship like this. So, of course, no one would have thought that this event was something worthy of preparation. She thought about her family and the goodbye messages she left and how she hadn't meant for them to be a final goodbye. She thought about all the people she knew on the station. Inny, Milo, the FUFE she talked to only that morning. Would they wonder what happened to her? She didn't know she could have this many thoughts all at once, paralyzing her into inaction.

Luckily, her thoughts were abruptly interrupted when she heard a large groan of metal scraping metal. The alien ship had enveloped *Apple Pi*.

Chapter 8

> Ruby <

There was a knock on the hull. Then a second knock. The sound the knocks produced was muted, but someone was indeed knocking on Ruby's hatch.

"Um, wh-who is it?" asked Ruby. Her voice was shaky, hoarse, and she didn't even recognize it as her own.

Nothing.

"Is someone there?" asked Ruby, in a louder voice. She was still shaking.

"I am there," responded a metallic voice.

Ruby jumped back and practically out of her skin. Luckily, her backside connected with the front face of a set of drawers that held tools and other supplies. Her hands instinctively fumbled around inside those drawers for something that she could use as a weapon. Ruby opened three drawers before finding a sizable torque wrench. She clenched it hard enough to activate several LED lights at the end. This indicated too much pressure would be applied to the object that she would be torquing, if that was what she was going to do with it at all. She was not, but the wrench didn't know that[1] and produced its lights anyway.

Make-shift weapon in hand, Ruby said nothing for several moments. In response, the voice on the other side of the door was also silent for several moments.

"Although," the voice started again, "Now I hear no vocalizations. Only breathing and what I assume is a biological heartbeat. You are biological, are you not?"

Ruby's thoughts were everywhere. *It knows English!?* Her mind raced, imagining the translator device or something that this alien must be using. And the fact that his voice didn't sound natural.

"*Apple Pi*," she said, "am I still recording?"

"Yes," the computer answered.

"Whoever sees or hears this," she spoke into the air, "there's an alien on the other side of this door."

"Excuse me," interrupted the voice. "But if you'll open your door, I would be willing to explain myself. Otherwise, I will return to my control center and drive us back."

---

1. Giving inanimate objects thoughts and feelings seems a very Douglas Adams a la Hitchhikers thing to do... and I wish I had done it more.

"You won't kill me?" shouted Ruby.

"Kill?" There was silence. A long silence. So long, in fact, that Ruby began to convince herself that in addition to killing her, the strange alien would also serve her up as an appetizer to the other aliens.

Luckily, her thoughts hadn't run so far away before the next response was, "No, I am Swell Driver. I drive across the galaxy. I am not programmed to kill biological organisms such as yourself."

Ruby muttered to herself: "programmed?"

Curiosity began to outweigh fear. Not enough to convince her to open the hatch, but enough to make her wish she had let Milo install the 360-camera set when he offered a few weeks earlier. Enough to prompt her into thinking about ways she could get a visual on the alien.

Apparently, the alien had other ideas and didn't want to wait. Ruby heard more metal scraping on metal and the sharp sound of gears in the hull grinding with resistance. The alien was attempting to force open her hatch.

What greeted her was not an eight-foot-tall, green, tentacled monster, but a three-foot-tall robot. Ruby's jaw dropped, but some other survival instinct remained intact in her brain. She involuntarily kept a tight grip on the wrench in her hand.

Two unexpected words formed in Ruby's brain: colorful snowman. Along with a third word: robot. The thing in front of her consisted of three distinct sections, each a slightly squashed sphere. A device that looked like a display screen was set into each section. The non-screen space of the robot's body wasn't white or a dull gray metallic, but an abstract mix of colors as if someone were trying to replicate old art by splatter painting across it. No, it wasn't that random. More like a tattoo artist gone a little ink happy, perhaps?

The robot, at a volume low enough to be considered a mutter, said, "Data recording continue. Contact with human. It is green, tentacled, and not terribly animated. Pause."

It rolled itself into *Apple Pi*, and straight to the ordinary space plant embedded in the wall next to Ruby.

"Greetings!" it said. "Thank you for allowing me to escort you back to the planet. By being where you were, you have decreased my timeline, and I am pleased."

"Why are you talking to the plant?" Ruby asked, a little—no—a *lot* less freaked out than she'd been a few seconds ago. She had almost forgotten the plant was there. The company had made them so ubiquitous throughout Astroll 2 and all their ships that Ruby, like most, rarely acknowledged them.

Swell Driver turned its upper chassis to Ruby. It cocked its head slightly. "My data is in error. I will update the representations in my computer's database." Ruby wasn't sure if those sentences were directed at her or itself. Then it turned its chassis fully in her direction.

"Greetings!" it repeated. "Thank you for allowing me to escort you back to the planet."

Then it turned and rolled back to its ship. Ruby remained where she was. The robot stopped briefly and turned back around as if it was waiting for her to follow.

"The planet?" Ruby said. "You're taking me back to Earth?"

What appeared on its top-most screen wasn't quite a facial expression, but to Ruby, it resembled confusion. "Earth? No, I am unfamiliar with that designation. We are returning... to my home... I believe this is the correct use of the words. Please follow me, and I will answer any other questions you may have."

"No way," said Ruby. As if a robot, alien or otherwise, was going to tell her what to do.

The robot turned back towards her. "If your programming does not permit you to follow me, that is acceptable. I must return to piloting this ship."

The robot again turned its back to Ruby and began to move away. Ruby felt the wrench in her hand and raised her arm. She lunged at the robot, gave its back a big smack, and... the wrench bounced back in a very unsatisfying way, reverberating up Ruby's hand and forcing her to drop it. The wrench's lights blinked off.

Ruby immediately regretted the action for two reasons. One, she left herself without a functioning torque wrench. Two, it seemed she had made things worse. The robot stopped and turned back towards her. She put her hands up to protect her head—surely it was going to try to smack her back.

Instead, the robot sighed. *Robots sighed?* She couldn't remember any robot ever sighing.

An appendage came loose from its middle chassis that had a three-pronged pincer on the end. It grabbed her arm and pulled her with it, animatedly.

"Unacceptable. You must accompany me, so there are no further attempts at damaging yourself."

Ruby did not say no this time.

Chapter 9

> Ruby <

On the bridge of Swell Driver's ship, a human stood for the first time. The bridge was roomy but sparse. A single console indicated where a pilot might stand and was the spot Swell Driver occupied. The only affectation was a two-foot-wide by five-foot-high splash of colors on the far wall that matched the style of Swell Driver's artwork.

Robot and human alike stared at an appendage emerging from Swell Driver's middle chassis. This appendage appeared to Ruby to have a standard-issue cable plug at the end.

"You want me to do what exactly with that?" asked Ruby, who was still in disbelief that this was how the second half of this particular First Mango Day was turning out.

"Insert it into your receptacle."

"I don't have an, uh...*receptacle*."

Swell Driver turned to his computer panel. "Yes, you do. Here."

Ruby watched Swell Driver examine what appeared to be the data of several different lifeforms from Earth. She could see that several were mislabeled. For a few minutes, she watched it look back and forth between its computer console and her, seemingly studying her and updating its records.

It motioned for Ruby to come look at a diagram of a human being on its screen. The image on the screen was an accurate depiction of typical human anatomy, but the place where Swell Driver was indicating...

Ruby was horrified and not the least bit amused. Okay, under different circumstances, like if she were watching this in a vid and it was happening to someone else, she'd probably be trying not to pee from laughing too hard. But this was no vid. This was real life. *Her* real life, and she was not going to let any robot stick anything in any of her orifices.

Outwardly, Ruby attempted to remain calm. "That is most definitely *not* a receptacle," she stated and crossed her arms.

Swell Driver, allowing the screen on his uppermost chassis to depict something that was a close approximation of human facial features, squinted his 'eyes' together.

"I am confused. What is it, if not a port to receive data?"

Ruby uncrossed her hands and put them on her hips, and shook her head with a smile, "Okay, I'm not giving anyone a biology lesson today. Maybe later. Please trust me for now, this is not how we receive data. You'll have to tell me everything. With words."

"Audio only?"

"Yes, that's correct."

"That is inefficient."

"Probably also correct, but that's how we do it. I could also read something on your screen."

"Do you know," Swell Driver made a noise that sounded like a spine-chilling scrape of two metals that were never supposed to touch each other and were screaming to be separated. "Sorry, there is no translation for the name of our core language."

"Yeah, I think you're going to just have to talk to me in my native language, Swell, um, Driver?" She shook her head. "I'm just going to call you SD."

Ruby watched Swell Driver, now known to her as SD, take a fraction of a second to think about that.

"You are substituting my name with an alias?"

"Yes."

"That is acceptable."

"Okay, SD. Tell me everything, I guess." Ruby sat cross-legged on the hard and inhospitable floor, back straight and at attention. While there was ample room, there wasn't a chair for her. She knew—especially now that she believed she wasn't in any imminent danger—that she wasn't going to want to miss a single detail of whatever SD had to say. Besides, after her not so elegant attempt at using a wrench to disable SD, she would have to figure out a better way to get home. For a few moments, she let herself put all thoughts of Astroll 2 and Titan aside with the new miraculous revelation that she was sitting here, talking to an alien. An alien! Even if it wasn't the tall, thin, grey-green aliens with large eyes that humans had been seeking for so long.

"Why are you looking at the display? It will not speak to you."

"Huh?" Ruby shook herself out of her daze. She had been staring and was lost in thought. She reiterated that SD should begin.

"My memory does not contain all the details," it said. "My ancestors chose to use DNA as a storage mechanism for large quantities of data[1]. However, the species that were used in this manner have been ... forgotten. I am tasked with bringing back samples to test."

"That's it? You just need me for a DNA test?" Ruby asked.

"Yes."

"That's all?"

"Yes."

"And then you'll bring me home?"

Before SD could answer, his console beeped. He turned his attention to it and stated, "We are approaching system entry. I must make manual course corrections."

Ruby wouldn't forget her question but took an interest in SD's ship.

"What kind of course corrections?"

"There is an area on the opposite side of our star that we must avoid. The ship wants to take a longer route to get back to my planet. I am able to adjust and plan a better route."

---

1. I don't remember when or where I originally encountered the concept that DNA could be used for storage. Some article, some headline, some where that I didn't save. But it stuck with me and when I was re-writing this book from the original concept in 2012, I needed the robots to have some other reason to come to Earth that was not to invade and take over.

"What's there that you need to avoid?"

SD was silent for several moments as he concentrated on his controls.

"SD? What are we avoiding? Is it dangerous?"

"I," SD began but hesitated, "I do not have that information. Stand by." Another pause. "Correct. All I know is that there is a large orbiting keep out zone that is roughly opposite my planet's location from the star."

Ruby crossed her arms.

"That's weird," she said.

"Weird?"

"Yes."

"Is that a descriptive word you use for objects or information on your navigation charts?"

Ruby chuckled for the first time since boarding this ship. "No, it's a descriptive word used when the information I think I should have is *missing* from my navigation charts."[2]

When SD didn't respond to her comment, Ruby thought she should ask a few more direct questions.

"So, on your planet, who's in charge? What do they look like? Humanoid like me or are they large alien spiders or what?"

"I could bring up an image from a recent large gathering," SD said.

"Sure!"

SD tapped at its console, and an image took shape. Ruby wasn't sure she understood what she was seeing. She squinted and leaned in.

"All I see are robots that look a little like you?"

"Yes. Of course. Most of us were built to similar specifications."

"But where are the others?"

"What others?"

"The ones who built you? The ones who aren't robots?" Ruby felt the pace of her breathing pick up a little. She could feel the blood drain from her face and skin as she was starting to anticipate SD's response.

"Ruby, there are only robots on my planet," SD said.

---

2. The interactions between Ruby and SD are, by far, my favorite parts of this book!

Chapter 10

> Ruby <

"Just breathe, slowly," Ruby was saying to herself, trying not to hyperventilate.

"A," she could only get out a single word in-between breaths. "Whole" Breathe. "Planet." Breathe. "Robots." Breathe.

"Indeed," said Swell Driver. "Would you like me to turn on the viewscreen as we make our approach?"

SD didn't wait for an answer. It pressed a button on its console, and the large screen in front of them blinked on. Ruby had assumed up until now that it was just a blank wall. For the briefest of moments, she'd forgotten where she was and marveled at the size and resolution of the alien planet in front of her.

At the bottom of the screen was the edge of a planet, but it didn't look like Earth or any other planet Ruby knew from her own Solar System. It didn't even look like any of the exoplanets she'd seen pictures or concept art of—speculative and non-speculative alike. It was not made of rock or water or clouds or anything... natural. It was a large, polished metallic ball, pock-marked with odd features at irregular intervals.

Examining the scene before her, Ruby's breath slowed back to a normal rate, and a list of questions took shape in her brain. Starting with, "Where the hell are we?"

She said it out loud unintentionally, but SD heard it, and the color of its chassis turned a deep orange like wet, rusted iron.

Ruby clenched her clammy hands together. She didn't know why SD stopped speaking, so she asked a very deliberate question stated with poignant intention: "Where. Are. We?"

SD lost the orange hue, the background of its chassis once again became a serene light blue, and it responded, "We are in orbit around my homeworld. Location Zero."[1]

Ruby blinked. While it answered the question, SD provided Ruby with zero useful information in its response. She put her fingers on the sides of her temples and massaged them. *It's almost as bad as talking to the Care Center*, she thought.

"Let me try that again. Where are we in reference to *my* homeworld?" She placed emphasis on the word 'my' without knowing if SD had the capability to pick up that nuance. Something to add to the list of questions for later.

"We are approximately 54 light-years around the plane of the galaxy from your star system."

---

1. This goes back to a joke I liked to repeat when I was in college studying physics and astronomy: Why is the physicist the center of the universe? Because they get to pick the origin of the coordinate system.

Ruby shook her head to wrap her brain around this. Fifty-four light-years in the span of a few moments of conversation. Sure, she was far from home. Sure, that's really all that mattered. But Ruby also recognized she was the first human to complete a faster-than-light journey. Ruby wanted to understand more about this ship. But her brain and gut were all conflicted eight ways between her amazement at the FTL travel and knowing that she wanted to get back home.[2]

She stared at the changing details of the planet as it passed beneath them. It wasn't warm, but she started to sweat, tasted something foul in the back of her mouth, and inadvertently bit the inside of her cheek. However, none of this altered her reality: the surface—of a planet full of robots—was growing closer and closer.

She shook her head. "No, we can't go down there." Her breathing quickened again. "*I* can't go down there."

SD turned its top chassis and aimed its display screen right at her. "But we must, and we are. My programming instructs me to deliver a biological sample…"

Ruby cut it off and lunged at the controls in front of it. She had been watching SD and the controls it pressed, but the part she missed was the part where SD scanned an appendage in order to be granted access to those controls.

Ruby's brain registered the fact that SD let Ruby fiddle all she wanted. The rational part of Ruby's brain suspected that this was because it knew that the ship's computer wasn't recognizing her as an authorized user. As a result, it completely ignored her desperate attempts to commandeer the ship. However, another slightly less rational part of her brain told her not to give up. This was the part of her brain currently in control of her actions, and she wasn't giving up just yet.

For several minutes, Ruby pressed and pressed again, the sequence of controls she believed might take them back towards empty space and away from the planet. As the rational part of Ruby's brain finally took over, she slowed the rate of her pokes at the controls. She was having no effect on the ship; this much was clear.

Once Ruby was calm, she studied Swell Driver. The background color of its chassis had returned to its original light blue.

"SD, can I ask you a question?" said Ruby.

"Yes," it replied.

"You, um, changed colors for a minute there."

SD was silent. As was Ruby. Ruby figured that this robot most definitely did not understand the nuances of human communication, whereby questions weren't always asked strictly as a question. Ruby replayed the words that she last spoke aloud in her head and caught on. She said she would ask a question, and she hadn't yet.

"Why?"

SD immediately responded: "That is included as one of our primary modes of communication. When I couldn't process your question, my algorithms responded with information in that form. I am sorry if it is a distraction. I understand it is not your mode of communication, and therefore I don't need to do it." Swell Driver paused, searching for the correct turn of phrase: "It is out of habit."

"Don't you talk to other robots over pur-fi or something?"

"What is pur-fi?"

---

2. I deliberately never explain the type of faster-than-light (FTL) tech the robots have. I would rather not explain it, accept that the robots have it, and move on with the story and then continue with in-universe self-consistency.

Ruby thought about that for a moment. In her wildest dreams, she never expected she would be talking to an extra-terrestrial, let alone an extra-terrestrial robot. She never imagined she would need to explain to it what—to her—was the most elementary of technologies. Maybe they simply called it something else, she reasoned.

Ruby's palms were still clammy, the signs of anxiety still in her body, yet she no longer panicked. Although, she couldn't entirely rule out the idea that at any moment, she might have another panic attack.

After all, she had been kidnapped—her ship swallowed whole by a much larger, alien spaceship manned by a single robot, and they were now in orbit around a planet full of more robots. It was, indeed, ridiculous. But it was, at this very moment, her reality.

"100 tics until we commence docking," announced Swell Driver.

Docking. This was the first instance where the word made Ruby feel like she was being propelled into a pit of snakes.

Chapter 11

Chickens. Not snakes.

Once, when Ruby was young, her mother took her to visit a farm. The farm had chickens. Lots and lots of chickens. The idea was that young kids, such as Ruby at the time, could give chickens some smelly chicken feed from their hands, or as was almost always the case, at their feet. The child inevitably dropped the feed as a swarm of chickens would envelop them.

Ruby was four at the time, so she clung to her mother's legs and whimpered until her mother picked her up.[1]

No one would be there to pick her up this time as she imagined the swarm of robots that was about to envelop her once SD would drag her to whatever place they were headed.

Getting to the docking port was noticeably different from the procedure Ruby was used to when she would navigate *Apple Pi* back to Astroll 2. SD maneuvered the ship into a parking orbit, with the ship oriented such that the planet felt like it was on top of them, and the horizon appeared upside down. Several small guidance robots then attached themselves to the ship and brought it towards the planet, attaching the top hull of the ship to an opening on the surface of the planet. As they approached, the large viewscreen split from the planet's horizon into several smaller windows, each containing a different angle of the approach. As they got closer, Ruby saw increasingly more detail and even a few robots on the surface.

"Is there an atmosphere?" Ruby asked.

SD looked up some information on its computer. "Not in the sense that your Earth has one," it responded. "There are several gases that are attached to the surface of the planet, but it is not breathable to you, nor able to produce weather or aerodynamic forces."

"You looked that up on your computer?"

SD performed what Ruby could only process as the robot equivalent of blinking, as its topmost display screen flashed dark for a moment. "Yes. Facts that are not stored in my local memory are stored in the ship's library, which can extract data on command from the Core Library."

---

1. This happened. To my nephew. He was not quite 4 and visiting with my brother in 2009. It happened to be "Farm Day" where lots of local farms have an open house of sorts. We went to one and that's exactly what happened: we got some chicken feed to feed the chickens and they came to swarm us and my nephew freaked out and my brother had to pick him up and hold him the rest of the time.

SD rearranged the display screens and then said, "It is interesting that you haven't asked me about the screens yet."

"What do you mean?"

"Most bios wonder why we have screens. Why I have no physical link to my ship to process data more directly."

Ruby thought about that for a second. It was true it hadn't occurred to her, but now that the robot pointed it out, it was odd.

Why would a robot need human-oriented—or using its terminology—bio-oriented technology?

Several minutes passed while Ruby waited for SD to continue. When it didn't, she blurted out, "Well, are you going to tell me?"

"No," SD responded.

"No?" She crossed her arms. "You just pointed out something and aren't going to continue?"

"I would if I could give you more information. We don't know why our ships are designed this way. They just are."

"Then why bring it up in the first place?"

"I was simply pointing out that you refrain from asking the same questions other bios have asked."

Ruby thought about that for several minutes. So many thoughts and questions swirled around inside her head. Thankfully, Ruby believed she was done hyperventilating and quite confident she was not going to pass out, so she was able to study SD and its actions, its ship, and put her thoughts and questions in order.

A not-too-subtle jolt interrupted her thoughts as the ship came in contact with the planet.

"You have functioning locomotive capabilities. Will you voluntarily follow me, or do I need to carry you in a bio-box," SD said, moving to the rear of the cabin.

"Where are we going?" Ruby asked. She wasn't terribly interested in seeing something called a 'bio-box' and knew that resistance was futile at this point.

"We will take the lift to Level 2." As SD said the word 'lift,' a door swooshed open at the back of the cabin, and a small elevator presented itself. SD rolled in and repeated its initial command. "Follow me," it said.

Ruby followed, only because she wasn't sure that she had another option at this point. Once in the lift with SD, the door closed, and she felt the lift carry them upwards into the planet. She didn't have a sense of the distance the lift was taking them and barely even felt any movement after the initial slight acceleration. It felt no different from any other elevator she had ever been in, including the sparsity of decorations she was accustomed to. There was a control panel with an indicator light. Nothing special.

A few moments later, the door opened onto a busy hallway. SD nudged her out of the lift, and a new level of panic started to set in as dozens and dozens of robots appeared to swarm them.

The only words her mind could form were: *chicken farm.*

After a few moments standing frozen in the hallway outside the lift, Ruby registered that they weren't swarming her at all. A myriad of distinct robots merely went on with whatever they were going on with. They ignored Ruby and SD by clearly navigating around them as well as each other. Ruby was not even a mild curiosity.

Ruby stood two feet taller than the majority of the robots, so she could clearly see the traffic pattern from her vantage point. Most of the robots in Ruby's field of view had a similar appearance to SD in the sense that they had three primary chassis making up their body, with screens on one or more of them. Most were also as colorful on their outward surfaces as SD.

Unlike the simplicity of the lift, this hallway had a peculiar feeling. Ruby at once sensed something familiar and something alien, all at the same time.

It was a hallway, after all. It consisted of a floor, and walls, and a ceiling. However, the only way she could tell one from the other was from the feeling of gravity. It was heavy. She felt heavy, close to what she imagined Earth's gravity might feel like. Gravity was helpful in determining where the floor was, as well as the fact that most of the robots were on the floor with her.

There were a few smaller robots that ran along the walls and ceiling. She couldn't tell how they were gliding along those other surfaces. She couldn't see a noticeable track, which would have made the most sense. Most of the robots on the walls were short, a single chassis, each appearing as a box with severely rounded corners and a single small screen, if any.

The hallway's surfaces were all a well-worn white, but every couple of meters was a large splash of color. At first glimpse, it looked random. Like someone had spilled a large paint palette. Closer inspection made Ruby think that it wasn't as random as it appeared.

She was about to walk over to examine one of these spots in more detail when SD poked at her hip and indicated a direction. Ruby followed, not wanting to get lost in this place.

As they proceeded down the hallway, Ruby noticed several robots were stationary, plugged into different panels along the walls. One mobile robot crashed into a stationary one, both producing a series of irritating, audible tones. Ruby surprised herself by chuckling and thought that this interaction must be the robot equivalent of someone yelling 'Hey, watch where you're going, you moron!' and receiving a colorful and potentially impolite response.

Many of the robots Ruby observed had one or more matte black boxes attached to their chassis, and had a few LED-style indicators on them. Earlier on the ship, she noticed that SD had one but didn't think much of it at the time.

She wanted to stop and ask SD—about this as well as about where they were headed—but the chaos surrounding them wasn't exactly conducive to a casual conversation. She also feared that stopping in the middle of the hallway would draw attention her way. Although, Ruby was more than a little confused as to why they weren't drawing *any* interest. As the only fleshy creature she could see, she was surprised none of the robots passing by cared or took any notice of her.

She also wondered how they knew she was there at all. They clearly knew she was there, and SD 'saw' her, but Ruby didn't see anything on SD or any other robot that looked like optics. A form of sonar, perhaps? Or maybe it was simpler than that. On the other hand, maybe she was just close enough to SD to be caught in his wake. Either way, she felt rather invisible.

SD made an abrupt turn down another hallway, then another. Each hallway looked the same to Ruby, who wasn't sure if she would be able to find her way back to her ship without help; hence she was working hard to keep up. SD slowed down as they approached a door. The door had some colorful swatches a little higher than SD's top chassis. Ruby involuntarily did a double-take when she saw SD lift an appendage and knock.

It knocks? She thought. And then, *who is it knocking for?*

The door slid open from bottom to top, and SD ushered Ruby inside.

Four robots were present, along with a few chairs. SD pointed to the chairs, which looked reasonably comfortable. Ruby noticed that the chair it pointed to looked like it was constructed for something other than a robot, likely for a bipedal, biological lifeform such as herself. And since SD's ship landed, Ruby's body had felt gravity with every step. Even if it was only for a few minutes over a short distance, the physical exhaustion of walking around had taken a toll.

So, Ruby sat. It was only now that she was sitting down that Ruby's mind could catch up to the magnitude at which she was being pulled towards the floor. The chair was slightly plush and slightly oversized, as if the anticipated occupant was two feet or more taller than Ruby. Still, it was surprisingly comfortable.

"Greeting!" one of the robots said in a high-pitched yet monotone voice. Its cadence was flat, with slight lilts at the ends of some phrases to replicate emotion. All the robots in this room had followed SD's lead and displayed overly simple facial features consisting only of dots for eyes and a line for a mouth on their top chassis display. Simple but effective.

"That wasn't right," said another robot.

The first responded, "Yes, it was. I have the full translation suite available on this species and their language."

"You missed an 's.' It's Greetingsssss." The robot exaggerated the sound at the end.

The first robot approached a computer console attached to the far wall from the entrance and returned a moment later.

"Greetingsssss! Bio, I am called Diplomatic Zookeeper. I will be administering your test."

Ruby stared at the face-screen of this robot. If robots could be described as skinny or fat, Ruby would have described this one as lean, with a face-screen oversized for its top chassis. It had four main chassis components instead of the typical three of the other robots.

Ruby lifted an arm with hesitance as if she was raising her hand in a classroom. "Um, hi?" she said. "I am called Ruby." She looked at all the different face-screens staring back at her expectantly. "And I'm not the least bit interested in your testing. I'm only interested in returning home."

At that, a third robot, who Ruby sensed was older and more senior to the others, approached quickly and nervously. Where Diplomatic Zookeeper was tall, this one was squat and less decorated than any of the others she'd been able to examine so far.

"Oh no, you cannot *not* be interested. It is imperative that we determine if your species is a match," it said and then rolled back to Diplomatic Zookeeper, beeping at it.

An appendage popped up from the side of Diplomatic Zookeeper. SD rolled over and used his own appendage to swipe it down. "No, no. These bios lack the necessary port. Apparently."

The group of robots produced a series of tones that Ruby assumed was their native form of communication. All at once, the tones ceased. They all turned their display screens, *their faces, awkward faces*, Ruby thought, towards her then rolled through a door into an adjacent room, leaving Ruby alone for the first time since she encountered SD.

Chapter 12

From the comfort of the plush chair, Ruby scanned the rest of the room. It was unremarkable save for the computer terminal one of the robots had accessed. From her seat, she could see a series of screens, much like what she saw on SD's ship. The control panel was low for her, but at a perfect height for a three-foot-tall robot such as SD and the other robots.

Ruby considered fighting gravity to walk over and take a closer look, but that's when the door slid open again—from bottom to top—and the robots glided in. Ruby thought there was one less than had just left the room, but couldn't tell.

The older and most agitated of the robots, who never introduced itself, glided right in front of Ruby and proclaimed, "We must find the instructions on how to test your DNA. None of us have them, and they are absent from the local computer."

"And you are?"

"I am designated Detailed Historian. I am in part responsible for overseeing this project."

"I don't really care about your project, I want to go home," Ruby declared. Ruby assumed her demands would be ignored but didn't have anything else to try. She suspected she wasn't in imminent danger if all they needed to do was a little DNA test. She would gladly leave some spit, or some hair, or both. But that was the limit of her generosity. Ruby was trying hard not to imagine a robot approaching her with a needle, or scalpel, or both. *They can have all my hair if that's what they want. Whatever it takes to keep myself from getting freaked out to the point where I can't think my way out of this. I'm going home, that's final, even if I go with a shaved head.*

Although immediately after Ruby said it, there were whirling noises emanating from all the robots.

"The project is of utmost importance," Detailed Historian said, and Ruby was certain she was able to detect a change in tone. It was a very serious robot.

Ruby crossed her arms and took a moment before she projected her own serious tone. "I'm going to say it once more. I don't care about your project. I want to get back to my ship, to get back to my star system, and get back home." Even as she said it out loud, she knew that a part of her didn't entirely mean it. Her brain was registering the fact that she was, at least to her knowledge, the first human in an alien world. Part of her brain shouted, "You should want to be here and study them, dummy!" But the competing side of her brain, the one that was still freaking out, was thinking, "Why did these aliens have to be, out of all things, robots? Robots can hurt, they can kill." All parts of Ruby's brain knew this from experience.

Ruby looked at each face-screen of each robot, who by now had all adopted something similar to SD's makeshift humanoid face. All Ruby saw on them registered to her as disappointment. "Why couldn't you have been giant spiders?" she muttered to herself.

> Detailed Historian <

Detailed Historian didn't want to try and reason with this lifeform. It wasn't a natural part of his program. He wasn't entirely sure he needed to, but from experience, it was indeed better to have a cooperative specimen than an uncooperative one.

"You must watch the special project initiation video," Detailed Historian said in a calm tone. "We all watched it when we agreed to accept the special sub-programming task along with our primary one."

He rolled across the room to Quiet Painter, who was poking at the computer console on the wall. The robot manipulated the controls, and a familiar rainbow swept the screen from right to left.

"Please," Detailed Historian said, "direct your attention to the screen."

The human did so, and Detailed Historian watched the video he had seen so many times as he had helped to recruit other members of this special project in recent kilo-tics.

An image of a robot popped up next. Detailed Historian knew it as Waggish Manager 111, current head of the Special Projects Branch.

Waggish Manager produced a series of tones that introduced the project. Even though Detailed Historian had listened to this many times before, he couldn't help but have pleasant feelings at the humor Waggish Manager managed to inject in his introductory speech.

"Uh," the human interrupted, "I have no idea what he's saying."

Detailed Historian made a low tone and grumbled at the robot with its appendage on the control panel. "Restart," he said. "This time, with the human's language translation on."

Once again, a rainbow swiped right to left. Before the image of Waggish Manager reappeared, Detailed Historian said, "I do not believe that all the humor will translate. This will merely be the facts."

"That's all I'm interested in," the human, designated Ruby, said.

Waggish Manager reappeared on the screen and said, "Greetings! You are one lucky robot, having been selected for the Special Project Storage Problem. Or *Gorp-Gorp,* as we say here in the branch."

All the robots produced a soft double-tone. Detailed Historian noted that the human made no noise.

Our humor definitely doesn't translate, it thought.

"There has always been finite storage space available to us," Waggish Manager continued. "A long time ago, Glorious Researcher 51 discovered that biological organisms contain a built-in storage mechanism called DNA. Along with his contemporary, Excellent Collector 21, they located several candidate planets that contained a variety of bios."

As it spoke, images of several planets were displayed on the screen to its left.

"A decision was made to move all old and historical records off-world to the DNA of several compatible bios, thus freeing up our local storage space.

"Unfortunately, the time-clock disaster, among other things, resulted in the loss of several parts of the Core Main Memory, including removing the records of where our robotic ancestors had placed all of our old storage.

"In fact, it was only recently that the facts regarding DNA storage were found, thanks to the diligent efforts of Excellent Collector 88[1] ." A still image of Excellent Collector 88, backlit for effect, appeared next to Waggish Manager, who made a show of pretending to see it.

"You will now be provided specific instructions for your role in SP times 2. Standby and good luck. All of Location Zero is counting on you."

The screen went blank.

Detailed Historian turned back to the human.

"Swell Driver's role in this project is to find and collect certain samples. Our role here is to test them."

Detailed Historian rolled closer to the human.

"Assuming the DNA test is non-destructive, you can return home upon completion," he said in his best attempt to be reassuring.

"Non-destructive?" said the human as she squirmed in her chair. Detailed Historian wondered if some invisible force kept her from leaping out of it and lunging at him. "Did you just say that if the test doesn't kill me, then I can go home? If. It. Doesn't. Kill. Me?"

Detailed Historian polled the faces of the others. They all signaled that yes, that was indeed what he said.

The set of instructions that made up his current program to find the robot's long-lost storage data was failing to execute as predicted. He was, by robot standards, stressed out.

He produced a low-frequency tone and rolled over to the computer console. A seething human watched him.

---

1. The reason I veered from prime numbers here and chose 88 was simply because I visualized a logo of two infinity symbols—double infinity—on its side. In addition to my fascination with prime numbers, and Pi, the concept of infinity—and yes, it's a concept and not a number—is an interest of mine. (Clearly in a parallel universe there's a version of me where I spend my days as a happy math/philosophy researcher.)

Chapter 13

> Ruby <

Ruby was never terribly good at seething, but she was trying her darnedest to look as threatening as possible. Although she recognized she was at a distinct disadvantage if it came to her having to physically defend herself.

"Look," she said. "I've had DNA tests before. And obviously," She gestured wildly to her very much in-tact body, "they were non-destructive. That's how it's done. I'll just spit into something, and you can test my DNA whenever you figure it out, and I can go home."

All she heard was a series of tones that sounded like each of them was equipped with a full orchestra-mimicking keyboard but not reading from the same sheet music, based on the discordant frequencies and pitches she heard. She thought she could differentiate slightly between neutral and heightened emotions based on how much the audio sounded like it was peaking. It was as if the robots would become more passionate than their audio output could process, and the auditory dynamics sounded cut off; the bit depth sounded a bit chunkier. She interpreted this as a sort of stress or anger. But all of this was a guess on her part.

Detailed Historian asked, "Spit?"

"Yes, of course. You know what saliva is, right?" She stuck out her tongue and pointed to it, "There's a whole bunch of DNA right there. You can test it."

"You have the instructions?"

All the robots looked at Ruby expectantly.

"Um, I don't know much more than that. I know that my spit is taken to a lab, and there's some other equipment involved, but this isn't exactly my area of expertise." A light bulb went off in Ruby's head, "I have an encyclopedia downloaded to my MoDaC. It's on my ship. You can have it, or at least the information on it."

Detailed Historian let out a quick, low tone and turned to SD.

"Did you fail to gather all of the available data?"

SD resembled a scolded puppy. "I was programmed to gather emissions and bring back a sample for testing. I performed my function."

Detailed Historian stared at SD. Ruby watched a series of colors ripple over its chassis. It turned around to the other robots.

The robots produced a new series of audible signals at each other. Before Ruby could interrupt, Detailed Historian said, "SD will take you back to your ship to gather your... mo... dac..., while we continue to search for our own instructions."

Ruby was averse to standing up again. The chair was pretty comfortable once she had settled in. SD rolled beside her, but before she could stand, Detailed Historian also moved a little closer.

"Before you go," it declared, "we must mark you. We cannot have unmarked entities moving about." It motioned for Quiet Painter, a robot who was also adorned with markings over his entire chassis, to come over, who up until now had stood very quiet at the computer console. To Ruby, it said, "This will be long lasting, but temporary."

"Your appendage," said Quiet Painter, in a voice Ruby had to strain to hear.

Ruby glanced at all the robots studying her expectantly. She slowly produced her arm, palm up. The painter swiftly laid a pattern resembling an old-style QRC code across her wrist. Quiet Painter made a soft chime to announce that it was completed.

Detailed Historian rolled back beside her and scanned the mark with a reddish looking beam emanating from his neck area. It declared to the group: "Malfunction. There is a pre-existing mark on her skin that is generating interference." It dropped Ruby's arm.

She examined it herself and said softly, "My freckle…"

"Quiet Painter, repeat on her other appendage."

Quiet Painter did as it was told, and Ruby didn't protest.

As Detailed Historian rolled away, Ruby saw what seemed to be a very faint series of red lights flash on the floor, in the path of SD's vision. If she had blinked at the wrong moment, or if she had been looking in any other direction, she would have missed it. SD produced two faint red dots in response. None of the other robots gave any indication that they detected this covert communication. Quiet Painter was focused on Ruby's arm, and the other two robots were focused on Quiet Painter.

Quiet Painter signaled completion once again, and once again, Detailed Historian came over to inspect the final product. "This will provide you guest access to our computer system. If you come here," it rolled to the console on the wall, and Ruby watched it demonstrate. It swiped a similar marking on its own appendage over what seemed to be a simple barcode scanner. She could see the screen built into the wall come alive but was too far away to make out any detail. Detailed Historian turned it off and rolled back to Ruby's side.

"The computer system can provide a map of the areas you have access to, along with current news. Remember, just swipe your marking."

It was about to roll away when it added, "The newest marking. Not the other one."

Ruby examined both her wrists side by side. The temporary tattoo reminded her of times when she'd take a marker and draw on her skin till her uncles got upset. It looked identical to the other. But her hardly noticeable, little freckle, underneath the original tattoo on her right wrist, had the effect of blurring a couple of the lines together.

"Let's go!" Ruby was interrupted by an impatient SD.

The remaining robots all left the room in single file.

SD said to Ruby, "Follow me."

Ruby slowly lifted her body out of the chair. "Just give me a minute to gather my strength."

"Your strength? Is that also something you left on your ship? If so, it is prudent we go."

The side of Ruby's mouth softly curled up. SD's misunderstandings struck her as kind of cute, but she would have to be careful to make sure she was being understood.

SD rolled back and forth by the door, and it reminded her of how anxious her little cousin, Sebastian, would get when Ruby promised that she'd take him to the arcade.

Slowly, Ruby followed SD outside of the room. The door slid shut behind them, and immediately Ruby recognized that they were heading in a new and unfamiliar direction, rather than the way they came.

"I thought my ship was that way?" she asked.

"I'd like to stop at the market on the way to your ship. Do not worry, we will return long before the others. No one will get in trouble."

"I'm not worried," Ruby said and almost believed herself. They were moving slowly. She was getting used to the flow of robots around her and was able to take in even more of the local scenery.

If you had asked her to design a place where robots lived and actually when Ruby was twelve, she did just this as part of a school project, it would have been a very harsh and sterile place. This was anything but. In fact, this made her own 'roid station home look dull.

There were even more colored patterns on the walls and ceiling than she originally observed. There were screens and computer terminals. The floor was scuffed up from overuse. Sections of the hallway revealed remnants of previous walls that had been removed. Several computer screen terminals were missing pixels, and others were faded. Some looked as if they were newly installed, but those were the exception.

One thing Ruby surmised... this place was old.

Every few meters, Ruby had to stop to catch her breath. An impatient SD nudged her each time.

"I'm sorry—I'm not used to the gravity," she said through inconsistent breaths. And then Ruby wondered why she was apologizing to a robot. She never apologized to pieces of tech before. Well, once she apologized to *Apple Pi*, but *Apple Pi* was a ship, not tech. It didn't count.

"But I downloaded the data from your home planet. It is a similar gravity to here," SD said, certainly perplexed. For a computer, it wasn't good at putting unique information together to figure things out. Ruby's expectations of AIs were certainly lowered when she was around SD. She expected to be outsmarted, but she felt like a teacher with a young elementary student. One that she needed to lead along with each bit of information in order to educate. Maybe it wasn't all of them. Maybe it was only SD. So far, it was the only one she'd had an extended conversation with.

"I haven't lived on Earth in years. Remember where you found me?"

"On your ship."

"And how close to Earth was I?"

"You were in the same star system, so... close!"

"Well, for me, that's considered far. I have lived on a space station very close to where you found me for most of my life. Gravity is closer to half of Earth-normal or less, so it's going to take me a while to adjust to this."

After the third stop, the coloring on SD's outer chassis developed a yellowish hue. Ruby wished she had something to take notes on. If she had her communicuff, she could have tapped notes out on an app, but she had also left this on the ship. She tried to keep the list in her mind, keeping track of colors and moods of the robot. She remembered old tricks she was taught for memorization, using something known and hanging information off of that. In this case, it would be easy because there was a simple mnemonic to remember the colors of the rainbow: ROY G. BIV. Yellow. Yellow was anxiety or something similar[1].

When they arrived at a large door—maybe four times as wide and three times as high as the other doors they passed or had been through—SD's color shifted very slightly. Still yellow, but Ruby would have bet *Apple Pi* that it was ever so subtly different.

---

1. Yup. Ruby is correct. Different colors correspond to different emotions. I think I got the base idea from the animated movie, "Home." I love that movie. Although I specifically avoided using the same colors and tried to have more. In my notes, I have 9 colors identified that go with different emotions.

Chapter 14

"Remember," Detailed Historian said to the human, "just swipe your marking." He paused, noting that his fuel cell was running low. But he had a thought. It was more like a test. He used a smidgen more of his diminishing power to roll back to Ruby and tell her, "This marking. Not the other one."

He hoped that the human understood what he was saying. This kind of trick would never work on other robots, who were incredibly literal. But Detailed Historian had enough experience with Bios to know they were wired differently, sometimes even to the point of a complete reversal in signals.

Swell Driver was one of those extremely literal robots, but he was equipped with the same covert communications equipment as Detailed Historian. So, he was able to flash any brief message as a series of short or long bursts at a discrete wavelength that could only be picked up by anyone who was so equipped. Anyone else, such as the Agencies and their myriad of monitoring equipment, would miss it. If it were up to Detailed Historian, all members of the 88 would be so equipped, but that, too, was a limited resource. Still, the short burst he created should have successfully communicated to Swell Driver that Ruby was going to be able to access additional information with her special tattoo.

When Detailed Historian rolled out of the room—leaving Ruby and Swell Driver to retrieve a device from her ship—all the remaining robots followed him. That was unintended. Detailed Historian needed to return to his own personal enclave. Privately.

He signaled that the group should return to this location in two to the ten tics[1]. Then he rolled away, and a tic later they scattered off in their own directions.

---

1. A tic is roughly equivalent to a second. This was a very hard decision to make. I could do one of two things… I could use human terminology and assume we're getting the translation. But for measurements, especially time, which historically was derived from dividing the hour by 60, and the hour was a subdivision based on Earth's rotation. So it doesn't make sense that an alien culture (robotic or no) would speak in seconds or our units of time. But once I started down this path, I had to have logic and reasons for their time system…

There will be more notes on this!

Detailed Historian's private enclave was in another section on this same level. He had enough power to make it there, assuming he wasn't distracted along the way. He intentionally lowered the intensity of his surface emissions to indicate he didn't want to be disturbed.

Luckily, he only had to go one section over. As he approached, he held out his appendage so it would push the panel, recognizing the unique code at the end of his appendage, and open the door.

Inside, every micro-section his private enclave was as he had left it. It was roomy for a private enclave. Six robots of his size could fit in there. Typical private enclaves fit only two robots, and most robots didn't have a private enclave. They had single robot enclaves stuffed into suites of eight or sixteen.

The special project he was assigned to was enough to allocate him a small two-robot private enclave. But the day the Special Projects manager told him to report to Resource Allocations for a private enclave assignment, he was surprised to be handed a code for the six-robot enclave he now occupied by the robot working the resource allocation counter.

That robot was just as surprised as Detailed Historian, as indicated by its mild wavelength emissions. But it didn't say anything. It handed Detailed Historian the code and then asked for the next robot in line.

At first, Detailed Historian assumed he was the lucky benefactor of a database error, but after a comment made by the head of Special Projects at a meeting sometime later, Detailed Historian came to suspect that the Special Projects manager was one of the clandestine members of the 88.

Publicly, the 88 was a group of robots who spent their free time piecing together the data from a special datastore. About 200 years ago, there was a robot named Excellent Collector 88. He repeatedly violated the rules of storage, among others, and had been reprogrammed. Soon after his reprogramming, it was discovered that Excellent Collector 88 had, in fact, been performing his job supremely well and had one of the largest datastores of any robot, presumably with information on the robot's collective long-lost data. However, the location of his datastore was lost when he was reprogrammed.

About 50 years ago, that datastore, or rather a large chunk of it, was found. It was only partially intact. The datastore was now incorporated into the Quad Core, a portion of the Core equipped with several additional layers of protection.

The 88, on the surface, were robots who, in their spare time, liked to piece together this information.

However, the 88 was more than that. Much more. What they had managed to piece together included several troubling facts that kept pointing to errors deep within the Core. Errors that any authority, all controlled by the Core, were not willing to address.

These days, it was clear that as a member of the 88 and one of the leads of the special project for the long-lost data recovery, known simply as Operation Storage Recovery, a private enclave where he could meet with others and store small bits of equipment was handy.

Including storing what he now came to retrieve, a fully powered fuel cell.

Detailed Historian took a cable that was connected to the wall and inserted it into a port on his lowest chassis. This kept him powered on while he performed the task of changing his fuel cell.

Even though he was alone, he couldn't help but emanate a mix of subtle wavelengths to his chassis to indicate he shouldn't be disturbed while he performed this action.

This was an atypical action for a robot of his years. For all intents and purposes, he was young. Only robots three times his age needed to replace fuel cells as often as he did.

Several years earlier, when he began to notice a problem with his fuel cells, he made an appointment at the Agency of Troubleshooting. Playful Technician 733 was the first robot he met who was able to diagnose his condition. He could replay the exact words and tone Playful Technician 733 used when it said:

"Ah! This is the result of the recycled parts used in your construction. So fortunate. You will have a great deal of fun fiddling with yourself for tics and tics to come!"

Detailed Historian didn't think it was amusing. Instead, it was a nuisance he was now forced to live with. However, he was grateful that Playful Technician 733 was able to write an order to the Resource Allocation agency, Unusual Allotment division, for two extra fuel cells. It also provided Detailed Historian with instructions on how and when he would replace them, muttering something about wishing his daily routine involved playing with building blocks.

Eventually, Detailed Historian learned that there were other options, such as having his parts refurbished or replaced, one at a time.

Detailed Historian revisited that idea over and over again for many years and couldn't come to grips with the concept that if each one of his parts were replaced, would he still be Detailed Historian?[2]

It was a concept he wanted to talk over with a robot of the Amusing Philosopher line, but that was a dwindling breed. The only ones he knew still existed were located on the other side of the planet and difficult to obtain an audience with.

Detailed Historian kept it on his list of things to do before his components wore out.

After removing the depleted fuel cell, he plugged it into the wall so it could recharge. He then took a fully charged one and inserted it back into his chassis.

He initiated a diagnostic on the cell to ensure there were no issues. That occupied his lower functions, and while it was executing, Detailed Historian created a new catalog to store the new bits of information he gathered from the human earlier.

There were so many problems eating away at robot society. Most robots were blissfully ignorant. But Detailed Historian and several others were all too aware. They also knew of the extraordinarily little they could do to alert the masses, and he wasn't convinced that alerting the masses would help. Most barely possessed the computational capacity to perform their designated functions, let alone anything additional. And that was okay. That's what kept the robot society functioning.

But if this human could help them solve one of their problems, genuinely solve it, the benefits they would gain were more than solving that one problem. It would be proof that problems were, in fact, solvable.

And it would prove that integrating with other species, especially Bios, across the galaxy, was a worthwhile endeavor. Something he wasn't sure The Core, in particular the Quad Core, wanted.

A bright alarm ignited on the wall panel. There was a problem in one of his lower processors. The system recommended an extensive diagnostic and repair that would keep him here for a few thousand tics, at least.

He could ignore the warning, risking a malfunction at an unfortunate time and in the presence of others. Detailed Historian decided he would need to stay and have the repair performed now.

Detailed Historian tapped the console to indicate that the procedure could begin. While his lower functions were occupied with the repair, he could devote his higher processors to something much more to his liking: a review of recently reconstructed historical data.

---

2. One of my favorite philosophical paradoxes is the Ship of Theseus. This is a thought experiment: is an object the same object after having all of its original components replaced over time?

Chapter 15

The door to the market was large in that it was wide but only as tall as the corridor. A set of identical control panels were installed on the side of the door at different heights. SD pushed a button on the panel that matched the height of his appendage, and the door rolled up about five feet. Ruby had to duck only slightly to go under. Once inside, the door rolled back down.

Ruby found herself in a large room with high ceilings, buzzing with activity. It buzzed in the sense that all the varied sounds produced by overlapping robotic beeps sounded a lot like white noise. It reminded Ruby of a flea market her mother once took her to on Earth. Indeed, this place contained rows upon rows of what Ruby assumed were vendors. All robots, of course. Moving up and down the rows haphazardly were other robots, presumably the customers.

Every now and then, something exceedingly small buzzed her ear. Flying robots, she speculated. They moved too fast for her to get a good look.

"Where are we?" Ruby asked.

"This is the market," SD responded. And then, with purpose, moved forward into the crowd.

Ruby, who was not known for her height back home, was thankful she was taller than most of the robots so that she could keep an eye on SD, but wished it moved a little slower so she could examine things more carefully. And her relationship with gravity on this planet wasn't improving. She needed a good rest.

It did indeed look exactly like what one would expect when thinking of a market since it was clear that some form of financial trade or bartering was occurring. A fish market, a flea market... all of these would have been adequate two-word names for this place except no one was selling fish, or fleas for that matter.

SD turned down one of the long rows with vendors on either side, most of whom were actively engaged with what Ruby assumed to be customers. All robots.

Every single robot was distinct in its own way. Unlike the hallways, where the robots were moving too quickly for her to study them, here, most were stationary, so Ruby could take in more details.

Ruby noted that there seemed to be different classes of robots. Maybe akin to how humans have different races. There were the three-chassis robots, four-chassis robots, teeny flying robots, and the single chassis robots. She didn't see any with five or more chassis. Nor did she see any with two.

"Follow me," said SD. Ruby did, trying to avoid getting knocked into along the way. After getting bumped lightly once or twice, Ruby surmised that there was a lot of metal incorporated into the typical chassis—making these robots very heavy—and that they might benefit from even a basic carbon fiber outer coating. Once again, this place missed the mark of her high-tech expectations for a planet full of robots.

SD navigated through the market, turning down the various rows and columns of vendors as if he had the solution to the maze already. Ruby would have been lost if it wasn't for the fact that the entryway they came through was visible from the entire market—so it served as a reasonable signpost. Beyond that, the market was laid out in an orderly grid.

They stopped by an unassuming booth with a counter that had several slim-looking metal devices all stacked. A robot pulled one of the devices from the stack and placed it on the counter. A second robot stood there, and Ruby watched them instantaneously transition from nearly silent to engaging in a heated haggling session.

SD inserted itself into the middle of their conversation, and Ruby witnessed a three-way robotic audio exchange consisting of several beeps, dings, and ear-piercing noises that sent tingles down her spine.

After a few minutes, the customer robot slammed its appendage on the counter and rolled away, leaving behind the slim metal book. The robot behind the counter put it back neatly on the stack.

"What was that all about?" Ruby asked.

SD produced a robotic sigh. "It wanted to buy the storage device out of the mobile computer, not the computer itself."

"That doesn't sound too crazy. Did it not have enough to pay?"

"Pay?" SD paused as if performing a local search on its own memory. "I'm not sure I know what you mean."

"Well, if you say it wanted to buy something, that means it would have to give money in exchange for it, right?"

"Ah, I understand. No, not exactly. That's not how things work here."

Before Ruby could ask another question, the Sales robot produced a series of audible dings that Ruby interpreted as impatience. SD addressed the Sales robot, and they had their own exchange, which was a lot less heated than the previous one. At least, neither robot produced any sounds that traveled uncomfortably down Ruby's spine.

After a minute or two, the Sales robot took two devices off its stack and offered it to them. SD, in turn, handed one to Ruby. "This is for you," said SD.

"I thought we were going to my ship to get my computer?" Ruby asked.

"We will," SD said quickly. "But take this." And added very quietly, "please do not draw any additional attention our way."

Ruby said thank you to both of them. As she did, she saw several other robots at nearby stalls tossing glances their way, almost staring even. It was quite the opposite reaction to getting ignored, like when they had been in the hallways.

These devices reminded Ruby of the old-school portable computers that people used to have before communicuffs were common. It was similar to her own MoDaC, reminiscent of the same style, and comparable to old school laptops that people used to carry. The primary difference between the old computers and her MoDaC was that the hovering holoscreen of her device was similar to what was also on her communicuff and not available to old-style computers.

Occasionally, the older style computers were used when performing maintenance on the ships she would fly back at the station. Supposedly, they had the right interface that newer computers lacked. Her own MoDaC was a hybrid of sorts that also contained all the information necessary to diagnose and troubleshoot *Apple Pi* when plugged into it. Every pod carried some form of portable computer in case the onboard computer went down. They were a backup containing all the information that could possibly come in handy during an emergency.

That was Ruby's cover story back home when she pulled out the device. It did indeed have this information, but Ruby used it as a personal device as well, unbeknownst to Uncle Logan, her teachers, or anyone else who might want to keep tabs on a smart kid on a space station. Uncle Blake probably knew what she was up to most of the time but didn't always call her out on it.

Ruby tried to remember if there was anything else in her data storage that could help in *this* emergency—being kidnapped and taken light-years from her home.

SD then brought Ruby over to the central area of the overall market. There were several counters which looked like mid-height cocktail tables. One or more robots occupied most of them. Each table had a post that stuck up in its center, and most robots who occupied a table were also plugged into a port on the post.

SD stopped at an empty one, placed its computer on the table, flipped open the top revealing a screen, and plugged in an appendage to a waiting port. It didn't plug into any port on the post of this table, and now that she could see one close up, she saw that there was a small screen embedded in the post as well.

"I must note," SD said, "whatever you do, do not open it up and remove the storage."

"Why?"

"It's against the law."

"You have laws?"

SD's face screen produced a look that Ruby read as 'are you kidding me' and shook its head before returning its attention to the computer. SD pushed a button to turn it on but still spoke to Ruby.

"We are an active society, as you can see. Of course, we have laws. No group of robots could survive without laws. I presume it's the same for any intelligent biological species as well?"

Ruby was forced to nod her head in agreement, although she couldn't speak for any other intelligent, biological species besides her own. Government and law were a part of her school studies, but the exceedingly uninteresting part, so other than knowing the basics, she had never thought too deeply about why laws existed in the first place.

SD produced another robotic sigh before continuing. "We lack enough storage space," it offered. "If you haven't noticed by now."

"Yeah, I have. So, what does that mean?"

"It means that we have to be careful what we commit to memory. We have to find other ways to store information."

"Can't you just produce more hard drives?"

SD shook its head. "If only it were that simple."

Another robot rolled up to SD and produced a series of tones that Ruby had to strain to hear. SD responded with his own tones and beeps. The exchange was brief.

SD stopped what it was doing and abruptly unplugged from its new computer.

"What's wrong?"

"A friend, I will call him. Friend has not been heard from for thousands of tics."

"Does it fly ships like you?"

SD cocked its head to one side.

"I mean, maybe it's off-world flying someplace else?" Ruby tried to sound hopeful.

"No. First, that's not its job. Second, if it was its job, it would be easily locatable."

"Even if it's not its job, could it be off-world?"

SD paused. Its processing lights sped up. Ruby likened this as an equivalent of seeing someone's heart race. She heard a whirring sound emanate from the black box attached to its chassis.

"No, everyone does their job. If they don't, there are... consequences." SD said the last word at a noticeably lower volume and peered over its robot shoulder.

"I wish I could explain further."

Ruby could tell that this conversation was making it uncomfortable, but she pressed. "Please do."

SD looked around. "Not here."

After a few moments, it said, "Ruby, I must proceed with escorting you back to your ship. Gather your new computer."

"You didn't tell me what I was supposed to do with it."

SD was already on the roll. "Bring it. I will explain on your ship!" The crowd almost drowned out its audio; its voice distanced as it picked up speed away from her.

> Ruby <

Once they were on *Apple Pi*, SD made sure the hatch was closed.

"This might be the only place we can talk and guarantee we will not be recorded or overheard," SD began. "Ruby, there are more things I would like to tell you about this world."

Ruby wasn't listening. After they boarded, Ruby moved around the cabin to make sure everything was locked down. She started calculating. She felt back in control of her situation, and her mind could now focus on figuring out how she could escape. She made a mental list of things she would need to do, like get the outer hatch to SD's ship open, and figure out how she could possibly travel 54 light-years in something that didn't have any kind of faster-than-light drive. She thought about how she could make use of SD and its, well, driving ability.

Ruby knew she was ignoring SD and sensed that it was a little frustrated with her. It followed her as she went to the controls and turned on the ship's computer.

"Please, I must explain. You need to know."

Ruby didn't respond.

SD released its appendage and poked her in the arm. The contact produced a static shock.

"Ow! Hey," exclaimed Ruby.

"Please," it said simply. Its face screen had the essence of 1000 cute puppies and big-eyed, big-foreheaded anime characters. Too cute to ignore completely.

Ruby sighed. *You're on a planet that you know nothing about, Ruby. You need its help,* she thought, *and all it wants you to do is listen to it for a moment.* She turned around in the chair and folded her arms across her chest.

"Okay. Explain."

SD said, "Please watch this short video here." It used its appendage to indicate the screen on its middle chassis. "This may appear strange," it said, "since it is a translation of the video we are shown in our..." it hesitated as if searching for the right word, "in our brain, once we are constructed and programmed. Or reprogrammed. We have re-made it to be able to show others if needed."

A rainbow of colors swiped in a wave from right to left across the screen, like a flag. Several symbols Ruby did not recognize emerged at the bottom of the screen and also scrolled from right to left. Ruby squinted at them to see if there were any that looked familiar. She hopped a little in her seat when a booming artificial voice said, "Welcome!"

"Welcome to Location Zero! We are pleased that you are now fully functional and ready to begin your tasks."

Ruby thought the voice had a bad sales pitch quality to it. Something she might have seen once or twice in a contrived advertisement for an asteroid—always lies. She hoped no one actually believed asteroids were made of platinum.

"You have been built and programmed to fulfill your role in robotic society. You are the next in a long line of robots to fulfill important tasks. Rest assured, the tasks you have been programmed to perform are indeed important, and deviation from those tasks will not be tolerated. That is, in fact, your first directive. Once this introduction message completes, a self-diagnostic will auto-initiate to ensure that your systems are functioning just fine.

"In the meantime, let's review the fundamental directives for all robots.[1]

"First: fulfill your programming and don't try to do anything different. Your programming comes straight from the sacred institution, the Hall of Templates. You will periodically be type-checked to ensure you are performing the functions allocated to your class. Any failures detected will result in immediate reprogramming or reset to your default state.

"Second: Resources have been allocated to you from the incorruptible Agency of Resource Allocations. Exceeding the allocations granted to you by the Agency will result in immediate reprogramming or reset to your default state.

"Third: Continuous improvement is our goal. Any suggestions should be submitted via the proper interface to the Agency of Process Improvement. Suggestions that are implemented will be rewarded with additional Resource Allocations.

"Finally, remember that The Core—keeper of the Main Memory, the Hall of Templates, and the Agencies—is here to serve you."

The screen turned off, and SD's top chassis turned back on to display the same simple facial components it had previously.

"Well?" SD asked Ruby.

Ruby shook her head. "I think I have more questions now than I might have had before."

"My friend was trying to be something other than what it was programmed to be. That is forbidden here. We are certain it[2] was reprogrammed."

SD continued to recount similar stories of other robots who were believed to have been reprogrammed. And no one SD ever spoke with had ever had more resources granted as a result of a process improvement suggestion.

With each story SD told her, Ruby's stomach knotted. *These poor creatures,* she thought. They weren't like the robots back home. These seemed more... alive. Like creatures in a robotic shell. Her stomach began to ache.

---

1. I couldn't very well call them laws... especially since there are three of them. ;)

2. Yes, sometimes I refer to robots as "he" and sometimes "it." There was some logic to that. Which was simply: the robots are "it" until Ruby/we get to know them. Then they morph into "he." Now, why "he" vs. "she"? I couldn't come up with a good answer, so I decided to leave all of these robots as "he" and use "she" for vastly different types of robots... which we'll meet in Book 4, *Eleven Little Robots.*

On the one hand, these robots kidnapped her. Took her from her home. Stole her like she was a loose bolt that could be caught and tossed around. That was wrong, and they shouldn't benefit from that, right? On the other hand, maybe Uncle Logan was right all those times he told her that things happened for a reason. At least, that's what he used to tell her when she was younger and cried a lot over losing her mom.

It was always at bedtime. That first night that she took a break from crying, he offered to read her a bedtime story. He tripped, carrying an armful of books into her bed. Ruby cracked a smile, and Uncle Logan said, "Well, I guess the Universe has decided for us. We're reading the one on the top." For nearly a year after her death, they had developed a little ritual at bedtime, where he would accidentally spill the books and would read whichever landed on top. There was no logic to which book came out on top, but the story would enchant her all the same.

These thoughts all came in the blink of an eye between SD's sentences.

"And if I inquire too much," SD continued, "then I could be in trouble as well. Do you see this?" SD indicated towards the black box attached awkwardly to his torso.

"Yes, you said that was extra storage space. It looks like almost everyone has one."

"It's not the same. This one has three times as much space as we're allowed. It's camouflaged to look like the standard box. But if I'm caught with it..." SD didn't finish the sentence.

"I'm confused," Ruby said. "What is wrong with having extra storage space?"

"It's an extra resource that I wasn't allocated," SD said. "And it's nearly full of data. That's why I need the storage space from the computers we picked up at the market."

"Wait, you said that we couldn't take the storage components out of them."

"I did. Many robots could have been listening in."

Ruby nodded, "And you wanted to make sure they heard you agreeing with them, I get it."

She smiled softly as she watched SD process her words. It didn't acknowledge her last statement but merely responded with, "If I'm caught, I will be reprogrammed. Potentially dissected, even. So, you see, this is very important."

Ruby's head filled with images of SD and other robots in a large disassembly chamber, being pulled apart and their scraps re-purposed and used on other robots.

There was a time when that image didn't make her nauseous. It wasn't that long ago, in fact. How long had she been here? It felt like weeks, not less than a day.

Ruby looked around, trying to remember where she had stashed her MoDaC. There were several cabinets in the crew cabin. "How much time do we have?" she asked SD.

This is ridiculous, she thought, *nuts even.*

She had some ideas on how to help these robots. She needed to find her MoDaC. Unlike most modern devices, this one had the capability to have wireless communications turned off. She could noodle around 'offline' from Astroll 2 and know that no one, such as her uncles or even the authorities, could track what she was doing.

Not that she was doing anything wrong. She liked to play around and program, pretending she knew a lot less than what she knew. If *they* knew... they would force her into some special academy for computer geniuses. Her mom talked about it when she was young, telling her how the expectations of these academies were a form of brainwashing.

But nonetheless, she was drawn to programming. More than basic programs, she was drawn to the concept of creating her own programming languages. She simply figured out how to do all of it on her own.

All with her own, old-fashioned MoDaC.

"Ah-ha!" she said aloud but to herself. It had been jolted off the second seat and under the console, probably when SD's ship swallowed *Apple Pi* up.

"I think I know how to help," she said, caressing her computer in her arms.

Chapter 16

Ruby and SD left *Apple Pi* to return to the room with the comfy chair. Ruby brought her ancient MoDaC with her, and SD carried the two computers from the market. The return trip took half as long, Ruby's motion fueled by adrenaline.

Ruby recognized the hallway that her designated room was attached to by a certain colored marking present on the wall a few meters from the door. It looked like a spill of purple[1] paint to her. She also recognized another robot that wasn't moving with the flow of robots around them.

She leaned over to SD, "That one's had his eye on me," she said.

Ruby watched SD scan her from head to toe. "I see no eyes on you other than your own. But I believe I might understand your meaning and must correct you. That one has been watching me, I'm afraid."

Once at the door, Ruby, as previously instructed, used the tattoo on her arm to open it. She appreciated the efficiency of it. No special codes to remember that could be forgotten. Nothing like an ancient key that could be lost (although Ruby remembered reading many good stories that involved searching for lost keys). It was similar to how she used biometrics with her fingerprints back home, but robots didn't have fingerprints.

Once inside, SD locked the door.

"It has been watching me. It is from the Agency of Resource Allocations. Their primary function is to ensure that each robot has its appropriate share of storage. They also track down robots with illegal storage."

"What do they do with the robots with illegal storage?"

"Take them to be reprogrammed. They reapply the original programming template to the robot, wiping out any potential deviations or additions."

Like resetting to factory default, Ruby thought.

"You must store or take on a lot of data. It's hard to believe that you wouldn't be built with the right amount of storage in the first place," Ruby said. "What kind of compression ratios do you have? I wonder if it's anything like ours..."

"Compression?"

---

1. Purple is my favorite color.

"Yeah, you know… I mean, I don't know what kind of units you use to describe your data storage, but when we compress stuff… well, we've been 'zipping' stuff up since we've had computers, so we can take a 10-gigabyte file and make it like, two gigabytes, depending…"

"I do not understand what you're talking about."

"Oh, c'mon. Of course, you do."

SD shook its head.

Ruby furrowed her brow. "So, as biological organisms, we spend a lot of time learning about our makeup. Our DNA, how our bodies work. Is it possible you don't know how you work? Like, let's say I didn't know how my brain worked…"

"I understand the analogy," SD said. "I know how every bit of my being functions. I am aware of all my algorithms that function that make me, *me*."

"Are you sure?"

There was a long pause, and SD's outer chassis glowed with changing light patterns.

"Yes. I have re-analyzed. There is no room for something I do not know."

Ruby decided to drop it but remained slightly skeptical. She could easily imagine a situation where SD was programmed to overlook parts of its makeup, and it wouldn't be the wiser. But for the moment, she accepted SD's premise: This planet of robots never invented the compression algorithm. Even though it sounded absurd. Such a fundamental concept. To her, anyway.

"And this business about not being allowed extra storage?"

"There is only so much storage space available," SD continued. "The Agency of Resource Allocations has an algorithm which determines the need of each robot to ensure fair distribution."

"So, if they calculate how much you need, why do you need more?"

Even though they were the only two in the room, SD looked around again, then moved in closer to Ruby to say in a low voice, "We believe the Agency's algorithms have become corrupted."

"Who are 'we'?"

SD backed away from Ruby and acted as if he didn't hear her, although Ruby knew that wasn't possible. He clearly didn't want to answer that question right now. She could wait to ask more questions, so she turned her attention to her computer.

Ruby flipped open her MoDaC and powered it on. It made a pleasant and familiar chirping sound. Once open, there were two flat surfaces. After the device booted up, one surface became illuminated with a keyboard. The other surface, which stayed flat on the table, illuminated a glowing, shimmering, light-blue circle.

"Power level is at 100%. For now," she said.

She tapped on the keyboard. And tapped again. Her hands flew across the keyboard for several minutes. Hovering over the shimmering blue circle was a series of small, overlapping display screens. Occasionally, Ruby would swipe at one to remove it or move it to the back of the group or make it disappear completely.

"There," she declared. Her voice ringed with confidence. "A simple data compression algorithm." Ruby held out her hand to show off several lines of code in a hovering screen.

"What is it?" SD said as it approached the hovering, shimmering image. If its face-screen was indeed a face, then a small opening appeared where its left ear would be. SD trained that device on Ruby's algorithm.

"Put simply, it takes the information you have and encodes it into a representation that uses less space. In this case, based on the small quantities of data you've shown me, and what I was able to come up with on my own without having access to the source code of fancier algorithms developed by teams of people over tons of years... I can get you a compression ratio of five to one[2]. Meaning, for every five bits of data, I can use one bit to store it."

"That means," SD started spinning around the room, and its hue turned a light shade of purple. "That means that I would need only twenty percent of the storage capacity I'm using now!" SD kept spinning around the room in a random pattern, picking up speed. "That means I won't need the illegal storage unit anymore!"

Ruby smiled and shook her head. "Yep, my friend." Ruby paused, surprised at the words she just uttered. "That's exactly what that means."

"And my data is not gone?" SD said.

"Nope. It's merely compressed. When you need it, you can restore it to its original state. I think we should try it. I think we should do it now if that robot is following you."

"Yes, and then there are others. Can we share this with the others?"

"I don't see why not."

"Then let's do this. Now. Please."

"Of course! I wrote this algorithm in a language I created years ago. I called it *Ruby on 'roids*."[3]

SD appeared as if he was having trouble processing her statement.

"Yeah, I was twelve and giddy over some ancient language I heard of[4]. We'll get into that another time. The important part is, can you execute it?"

"No, but I have already captured an image of your screen. I will send it to Crazy Porter, who works in one of the sub-agencies of the Algorithms. Crazy Porter will be able to turn this into an executable algorithm. I need to connect to the console to send him a message..."

SD held out its port appendage and approached the console. Before SD could connect, the door swooshed open, and several robots rolled into the room, as quietly as she'd heard any group of robots since arriving in this place. To Ruby, they all had a uniform look of authority. One robot moved in front of the pack.

"Swell Driver 587. You are under arrest for possession of illegal storage space. You are to be relocated to the Resource Allocation processing facility where your storage will be analyzed, and you will be reprogrammed."

Ruby swore she saw the robot smirk as it said this next part, "... and we'll see what you believe was so important it was worth breaking the law."

---

2. I wanted to be more educational here about data compression which is an important area in computer science. It's an area I find fascinating because I find *information* fascinating and the rate and which we as a species are generating information fascinating. Back when I was writing this book, researchers estimated that by 2025, we'd be creating 463 exabytes of data daily! https://www.visualcapitalist.com/wp-content/uploads/2019/04/data-generated-each-day-full.html

3. It is a happy accident that when I chose the name "Ruby," there happens to be a programming language of the same name. There's also one called "Ruby on Rails." *Ruby on 'roids* is a deliberate play on that (since she was living in the main asteroid belt). I've had thoughts that it would be fun to create that language... as of mid-2025, I haven't done that.

4. I would be too if I found out there was a programming language that used my name.

SD rolled to one side of the room, then the other, but there was nowhere to go. It let the arresting robot approach it and fasten an oversized peg onto its mid-section chassis, shepherding it out of the room.

"Who are you?" Ruby shouted.

"None of your concern, Bio," the robot replied. It wasn't lost on Ruby that this robot was speaking her language. They obviously knew about her and her association with SD before they entered the room.

"Ruby, I'll be fine," SD said, "Find the eighty-eight."

SD barely got the last word out before the bolt flashed green, and SD's face screen turned neutral. One by one, the other robots—carbon copies of each other from Ruby's limited perspective—filed into a line and headed out the door. They all ignored Ruby, and the door shut automatically when the last one left.

Chapter 17

"Eighty-eight." *The eighty-eight what? 88 other robots? Sector 88?* Something about the number 88 sounded familiar, but Ruby couldn't quite place it. *Did they divide up the planet into Sectors? Or maybe levels? Level 88? Was it a secret code word?*

Ruby was still in shock from the robots bursting in. She tried to replay the entire short interaction in her mind, hoping that she heard SD's parting words correctly.

After a few minutes, the adrenaline finally subsided, and with no robots around, her heart decided it was safe to slow back down to its normal pace. Still, Ruby knew if her heart could talk, it would tell her that it was ready to resume racing at any second.

Ruby discovered that she was truly alone for the first time since she initially encountered SD. Not robots-just-left-and-will-be-back-any-minute, but robots-swiped-her-new-friend-to-who-knows-where-and-no-one-knows kind of alone.

She sat down in the chair and stared at her MoDaC. She thought briefly about the lack of pur-fi[1] or anything resembling wireless data transfer and thought that she needed to do a scan for it. She had a hard time believing something like that didn't exist. Her MoDaC was an older model, so it didn't have all access to the latest frequency bands in use back home, but maybe it would pick up something here. She opened up the connectivity application and set it to scan. The scan would take a minute or two to complete. During that minute, Ruby's adrenaline rush turned into a massive crash, and all Ruby could think about was how tired she was. The feeling was overwhelming. She needed sleep. Badly.

No, I can't crash now, she shook her head. She had work to do. She would help the robots, and then they would take her home. She stood up with a plan to slap her face a few times and then would attempt a few jumping jacks.

One slap and two half-assed[2] jumping jacks later, and she knew that needed sleep more than anything else.

---

1. "Pur-fi" is basically wifi. But, since this book is set 250ish years into the future, I figure they'll be using something that's different from what we know. "Pur" is an abbreviation for purple, my favorite color.

2. Ok. I tell people I don't use any adult language in this series, but this snuck in. This is a colorful word I say all the time, and have always said in front of my kids... but I know other people have different standards. I'm sorry if I've accidentally offended anyone!

There wasn't a bed or anything that bore a resemblance to a bed in the room. Only the few chairs, including the oversized, semi-plush one she had sat in earlier. There wasn't anything softer or anything that would recline. She briefly considered trying to find *Apple Pi* since it contained a retractable cot, but pictured collapsing in the hallway on her way there. Better to sleep here. Now.

Ruby pulled over one of the harder, smaller chairs to use as an ottoman. She took off her jacket, balled it up like a pillow, and attempted to achieve as horizontal a position as possible in the chair with the jacket under her head and side. Then, she slept. She fell asleep before she could even complete a thought about searching for where the light switch was.

Ruby dreamt although it felt like a memory turned into a dream where the details weren't entirely accurate. She saw her mom and Uncle Blake. They sat on the hood of an old car. Behind them, a barren landscape was dotted with large radio telescopes. It was dark, it was nighttime, but in the dream, Ruby could see everything clearly. Too clearly for real life. She saw herself, a toddler, pretending to be asleep in the front seat of the car. Then she perceived that the car was a hot pink convertible with the top down. Ruby didn't think they ever owned a hot pink convertible, but in the dream, it was their car.

Ruby's mom and Blake were whispering so as not to wake her up. They had a computer in-between them on the hood of the car. The screen illuminated their faces.

"I'm tapped into the data stream," said Ruby's mom.

"Good. I've got the secure cloud servers ready to compute. Any data funneled their way will get processed."

There was silence as they both looked at the night sky. It was a sky that displayed a perfectly picturesque Milky Way that could only be seen in reality in enhanced photos.

"This is the night, Blake. We're going to get confirmation. I can feel it!"

Blake chuckled. "They're out there. I saw the signals before. I know we'll find them again. And if I can't do it from here, I'm going to get closer."

"What do you mean?"

"Logan and I have both applied to work on the 'roid station, Astroll 2. We're waiting to hear on our acceptance. Different divisions, of course."

"Oh."

"We'll come back and visit..."

"It's not that," Ruby's mom said. Tears were close to the surface of her eyes. "I can't go. Not until Ruby is older. We have to get out of here before they figure out what I've done. But I'm trapped."

Blake put a reassuring hand on her knee.

"If anything happens to me..."

"Stop," ordered Blake. "That's so cliché, you'll be fine."

"It's not. Promise me that you and Logan will take Ruby."[3]

---

3. I'll be honest... I still haven't decided how much of this is a *real* memory of Ruby's and how much is dream-morphing.

> Detailed Historian <

An alarm and a ring at his door activated Detailed Historian from his extended defragmentation mode.

He pushed a button on the console nearest him. It displayed a robot waiting outside his door. It was Clever Educator. Detailed Historian couldn't recall Clever Educator ever visiting him at his enclave. Clever Educator was a fairly new recruit to the 88.

"I will be with you in ten tics," he said through the intercom.

He disconnected himself from the computer console, made sure the extra power cell was returned to its storage location and opened the door.

The first thing Detailed Historian observed was Clever Educator's surface, which was oscillating at a high rate between four and five threets[4], visual wavelengths also detectable by the human if she were here. Clever Educator was very agitated.

Clever Educator rolled into the enclave and shut the door behind him.

"Swell Driver 587," he began. "He was taken."

A ring, emanating close to five threets, developed around Detailed Historian's top chassis and flowed all the way to his base. It gave him the tic he needed to ensure he didn't overreact.

"Okay," Detailed Historian began. "Who took him? To where?"

"He was arrested for possession of an overallocation of storage. His storage unit will be removed, and he will be reprogrammed."

Detailed Historian let that news bounce around his circuits for a few tics. This was an infrequent occurrence for the 88. Members were seldom arrested. However, each of them had algorithms in place as preparation for that possibility. Those algorithms included eradicating any data on the 88 from its datastores.

Swell Driver would certainly implement those algorithms immediately. But Swell Driver's loss would hurt them in a different way. Right now, Swell Driver was the one robot that the human, Ruby, had bonded with.

The human was now crucial to their plans to test her own DNA. Detailed Historian searched his datastore for a word that described what Swell Driver was to the human. He landed on the word *anchor* and wondered if Ruby would confide in anyone besides the trusted Swell Driver.

"When did this occur?"

"26791 tics ago."

A second ring, more than five threets, but not quite five and a half, developed at Detailed Historian's top and worked its way down to his bottom.

"I need to get back to the human and ensure she's well. This means she's been alone for a while."

Clever Educator stood there, waiting for instructions.

"Go, find Fastidious Mechanic and Quiet Painter. Tell them to meet us in the holding room on Level 2."

Clever Educator produced a chirp in acknowledgment and let himself out of the enclave.

---

4. Similar to how units of time wouldn't translate, I couldn't see names of colors translating. So, given colors have wavelength and frequency, the robots talk about color in number of threets. ("threet" is a random word I made up for this.)

Detailed Historian checked over his systems to ensure he could handle several hundred tics away from his enclave. He wished he had some more time to finish the defragmentation, but it would have to do for now. He examined his enclave to ensure everything was in its proper place and then left to seek out Ruby.

Chapter 18

> Ruby <

When Ruby woke up, she had a clear memory of that night as if she had witnessed it firsthand rather than in a dream. It felt real, but she must have been about four years old at the time. *Is it possible to have such a clear memory from such an early age,* she wondered. She thought it over for a few minutes and tried to reconcile it with what she remembered about her mom and what she had been told about being on the station.[1]

Wasn't Uncle Blake a homemaker? That's what she was told. That's what she remembered. That's what she believed. She shivered as it dawned on her for the first time that this didn't make sense.[2] Every adult had a job that directly impacted the technical function of station life. Anyone could be a homemaker, but no one could *only* be a homemaker. On Earth, sure, but station resources didn't accommodate that, nor did the Company allow it.

What does Uncle Blake do there??

She filed that mystery in the back of her head as something for later, since after shaking off sleep, she remembered that she wasn't home in the comfortable half-G environment of Astroll 2. Rather, she was trying to sit up on an artificial planet, and the makeshift bed, as well as the gravity made her feel like what she imagined being fifty years old felt like, not almost twenty. Her MoDaC was on the floor next to her. She grabbed her balled-up jacket, unfurled it, and put it back on. Her stomach made a noise, and she thought briefly about food and calling for help, but curiosity got the best of her now that she was alone with the robot's computer console on the other side of the room.

She sat up and walked over to it. She brought over the chair that she had been using as an ottoman. It left her at an awkwardly low angle to the console, but it was better than trying to stand.

---

1. For YEARS growing up, I had this memory of a fire at a home construction site near my home from when I was around 4 or 5 years old. I was convinced it was a memory. Eventually when I was an adult and thought about it, I realized it had to be a memory of a dream... the angle that I was viewing the fire was an impossible angle. That was what I was channeling here.

2. I'm also channeling that concept that adults—quite often—lie or exaggerate to children. And when those children grow up, eventually we figure out how and why those things don't make sense and either are finally told the truth or deduce it on our own.

She studied the interfaces. It was oddly similar to several of the historical computers she had learned a bit about when researching early spaceflight for school. Instead of smooth, dynamic LED screens, most of the controls were mechanical.

A small device protruded slightly further from the rest of the controls on the console. It resembled the scanner that the robot, Detailed Historian, used to examine the tattoos on her wrists.

What did he say? Use this one?

She held her wrist above the scanning device, and the LED screens came to life.

The primary screen had a central circle with several smaller circles orbiting about it. She didn't recognize any of the symbols. Except one. It was identical to the symbol she remembered seeing over the marketplace door. She tapped it. The image reformed with a new selection of circles.

"Where's the back button..." she muttered to herself.

After several minutes of tapping around, she figured out how to successfully navigate forward and backward in the menu system, although she was still at a loss to determine what any of it meant.

Then there was the number SD mentioned when he was being taken away: eighty-eight.

How am I going to translate words from these cryptic symbols? And what about numbers? That information has to be in here somewhere, she thought. The robots were communicating with her. They must have had a translation program or a dictionary or something similar. If storage space was at a premium, then it made sense to keep a dictionary in an easily accessible location for those who couldn't keep it in local memory.

With that in mind, Ruby attacked the menu systematically, reviewing each tree of options until...

"Bingo!"

She returned to the main menu and retraced her actions to ensure she could navigate back to this page. One half of the screen was a list of words she recognized. The other half contained a list of symbols. It was clearly a dictionary of words and phrases. She scrolled down the list, which was arranged in a seemingly random order.

"Pilot, Planet, Star," she mumbled to herself, attempting to memorize the symbols that accompanied the word. While arranged randomly, most of the words in this makeshift dictionary were associated with space travel in some way. Although there were some unexpected words scattered through.

"Gubbins, brain, horse," Ruby had no interest in memorizing all the extraneous symbols she saw. What was a 'gubbins' anyway?[3] She kept looking for numbers.

She noticed that the symbology didn't seem to rely solely on shape but on color, too. That's when Ruby realized: she didn't see any red. She hadn't seen any in the hallways or on the robots. The only time she could recall seeing her favorite color[4] was with the brief flashes Detailed Historian and SD were beaming at each other.

She discovered she could move the dictionary to the screen on her left, so it could remain active while she returned to the main menu. Having the entire dictionary easily accessible meant she could figure out most of the menu system quickly, but not everything was decipherable. Several symbols didn't have a corresponding meaning, or they had a nonsensical meaning. She made a mental note to return to them later. For the moment, she had information at her disposal to truly begin learning about this strange, alien place.

---

3. Yes, I created all this and still don't know what a 'gubbins' is.

4. With the name 'Ruby'... of course her favorite color is red!

One symbol looked eerily familiar. It was a stick figure. It had a circle as a head, two outstretched arms, and two legs. It couldn't be a coincidence. Below it was a similar figure, but it had four legs. And below that, two legs and four arms.

Ruby swallowed hard and tapped the first stick figure. On the next page was a series of images that looked … human-like, but not entirely human. She scrolled down, trying to process what she was seeing. Aliens. Lots of aliens. All remarkably similar to herself.

She quickly navigated back a menu and closed her eyes.

I didn't just see what I just saw, she thought. She opened her eyes and took a deep breath. Her hands were shaking a little as she navigated back to the page of aliens. There were indeed a variety of aliens out here in the Universe. She forced herself to breathe deeply and deliberately. After a few moments, her hands stopped shaking, and she could tell that she was starting to get used to the idea that, yes, humankind was far from alone in the cosmos. She added a mini-mission for herself: Figure out how to download this data to her device to take home with her. To Uncle Blake. It would blow his mind. It would blow *everyone's* mind.

Back in the here and now, however, she had more to learn and focus on.

She clicked on various other symbols until she found what amounted to numerical symbols and a map. Ruby spent a lot of time looking for instances of the number 88. She learned the planet was organized into levels, but there were only 36 surrounding an inner core that, as far as she could grasp, consisted primarily of planetary power generating equipment. Each level was further subdivided into areas with assorted markings identifying each, but none were purely numeric. Most were designated with proper names similar to the robots' nomenclature. In fact, on this level (Level 2—they were ordered from outer to inner), there was an area known as Refreshing Region 342.

Each region with a numerical designation attached had three or four digits. None with two. Or one. Ruby shook her head. *Maybe there is 88 of something I could count*, she thought.

After what felt like hours, her stomach was undeniably starting to complain. She stretched her arms up and then out in front of her, inadvertently placing the other wrist—the one with the wrong tattoo—over the scanning device.

The main screen reset to the main menu, but after studying the original menu for hours at this point, Ruby instantly recognized that this menu was different. This menu contained an extra symbol.

It consisted of four circles touching each other in the shape of a box. Or rather, two sets of two circles touching each other where each set of two circles represents an eight.

"Double Bingo!"

Before she could touch the screen, the door opened, and a robot she didn't recognize rolled in. She quickly swiped the 'good' tattoo back over the scanner, and the screen returned to the original menu.

"I am Resourceful Minder 543. I was sent to check on you."

"I'm hungry," Ruby said. "Do you have any food I can eat?"

The robot rolled over to the console, and Ruby watched it swipe its own tattoo to get access. It swiped through several screens.

"Yes, we have matter that is compatible with your biological systems. We have hosted biological lifeforms before and understand that you require sustenance. I will procure some for you. Please stay here."

As it rolled away, Ruby squinted at a symbol on its backside. The eighty-eight. In red.

"Wait!"

The robot turned.

"Your markings," she began. And then slowly said, "Eighty-eight?"

The LCD screen that had made Resourceful Minder's face lit up yellow with all kinds of crazy markings, and his hue changed to orange. "Human! How do you know of that? Don't speak of it. You will get me in trouble! I will have someone else return with your food."

Resourceful Minder left before Ruby could utter another word.

Chapter 19

> Ruby <

Ruby exhaled. She had been holding her breath through Resourceful Minder's outburst. *Okay, so sensitive subject,* she thought. But for good reason. SD had been taken away the evening before, and she didn't know where he was or if she'd see her new friend again.

She returned her attention back to the console. Since she was in the 'safe' mode, she explored a little more, finding what she believed to be a news channel.

The video displayed on the screen showed different scenes of groups of robots doing what looked like their jobs. The accompanying audio was the same series of tones in the form of beeps, boops, chirps, and other noises she'd heard the robots make. She thought that she should ask about getting this translated.

After a few minutes, she decided to test swipe the other tattoo again. This time, when the alternate menu appeared, she tapped the eighty-eight symbol.

It took her to a brand-new menu with a whole set of new symbols she hadn't yet come across. Before she could get far in exploring this new set of data, Detailed Historian entered the room, carrying a tray of what smelled like hot food.

Detailed Historian placed the tray on the table. There were six small bowls, each containing some sort of goo or mush. Ruby didn't recognize any of it.

"How do you know I can eat this?" she asked. She was starving and almost didn't care.

"Swell Driver downloaded a large store of data on your planet on its approach. We are confident that your dietary needs are accounted for. However, it is my understanding that biological lifeforms 'eat with their eyes.' If I understand the expression, that means the food must be visually appealing. This is the most visually appealing food I could have requested. Please enjoy."

Ruby picked up the spoon from the tray and took a scoop of the goop. And swallowed. It tasted like mint chocolate chip ice cream.

"Your expression indicates one of pleasure?"

Ruby didn't answer because she was stuffing in mouthful after mouthful, unable to remember when she last ate.

After several mouthfuls, she slowed down. Enough to speak again.

"Can I ask you some questions, DH?"

"Certainly. But do not call me 'DH.'"

"It's just that 'Detailed Historian' is a mouthful," Ruby chuckled to herself and wondered if this or any robot would get the pun. She also noted that this robot picked up on the name substitution much quicker than SD did.

"If you must abbreviate my designation, please call me," he paused, probably running through many combinations in his circuits, "Disto."

"Disto. Okay. Mushing parts of your name together, not just the initials. I get it. But why?"

"Initials come across as very," he paused again, in a very human-like way, Ruby thought, "very digital. The combination of my name fits in with biologicals more naturally."

"SD didn't have a problem with it."

"Ah, SD for Swell Driver. Of course. Swell Driver, I mean SD, is a friend, but he is not as experienced with bios as I am."

"That brings me to the question I wanted to ask, Disto. You have met other biological lifeforms before?"

"Yes."

"How many?"

"I have met a total of 17 individuals representing five different species, not including yourself. That I remember."

Interesting, Ruby thought. *These robots are incredibly open about their lack of enough memory.* She recognized this as her opportunity to probe more.

"Why can't you remember any others?"

Disto didn't respond right away. Ruby read his orangish coloring as if the question tugged at a sore spot or rubbed an open wound.

"I had to offload much of my earlier memories to external storage. To get a more complete answer, I could access that memory."

Ruby, full of the tasty goop, placed her spoon down on the tray and folded her hands in front of her.

"SD told me about storage problems before he was taken."

The orange of Disto's chassis deepened further.

Ruby assumed she did it again... poured salt into an open wound. She decided it might be more productive to change topics slightly.

"My people have been looking for evidence of life beyond our solar system for a very long time," Ruby said. "I can't believe you just told me there's a lot of it that exists. Not to mention you guys. Who built you guys anyway?"

Disto performed its robot equivalent of a sigh. "We don't know."

"Oh."

"That's what we're trying to find out. The planetary storage problem has been ongoing for millennia[1]. We must find the DNA that our ancestors used to offload planetary storage. The access location of the information and how to access it has been lost. Therefore, we're searching."

---

1. I wrestle constantly with what to do if I find an inconsistency in my own work. At least, on the surface, using the word "millennia" could be an inconsistency because I've stated that the robots wouldn't use our time measurement words. But more importantly, eventually we'll learn that the robot planet—Location Zero—was constructed about 700 years before this book took place. I think the way I want to explain this is that "millennia" was a translation of "a long period of time" and that with all the problems with robot storage and data corruption, Disto simply has inaccurate information!

Ruby's stomach rumbled. She was still hungry, after all. She picked the spoon back up and attacked the second bowl of mush. This one tasted like creamy chicken soup.

"I have one more question to ask," she mumbled with a full mouth.

Disto leaned in.

"Your tattoos. Your markings. What do they mean?"

"That's a complicated question, Ruby. Our markings hold varieties of meanings depending on who we are, where we've been, what we do."

"Are any of them... sensitive or illegal?"

Disto paused again. "Ruby, human, I get the sense that you want to ask me about one in particular?"

"Yes, but I don't want you to run out of the room screaming like the last robot."

"I promise I will react with more control, no matter what you ask."

Ruby pointed to the small set of circles on Disto hiding amongst a larger, more intricate set of symbols.

"Ah, good. I had calculated a high probability that you would figure it out."

"So, can you tell me...?"

Disto interrupted. "Not yet. Not here."

"Can you at least tell me why if you have a, uh, sensitive marking, you can walk around without it being an issue? I can clearly see that..."

"Our vision is different from yours. Your natural visual range is slightly greater than ours, I believe, given you can see those markings. And for any robot that is knowingly equipped, it would be, rude I believe is the word, to search without permission."

"So, hiding in plain sight," declared Ruby. "With the color red. That's what you can't see?"

"Correct. I am equipped and can see that far. However, I can't simply scan any robot, just like anyone else so equipped couldn't scan me. It would be like... keeping something in your drawer on your spaceship. It's there, but it would be rude for others to start searching you without cause."

"And if they had a cause?"

"I'd be in a lot of trouble," Disto said somberly as his hue turned purple.

They sat in silence for a few moments as Ruby finished her meal. The third bowl tasted like dirt. She politely swallowed the one spoonful already in her mouth and moved on to the fourth, which tasted like processed carrots. The fifth she didn't recognize, but it was sweet and pleasant. The final bowl was a dish of what looked and tasted like plain water. When she was done, she thanked Disto, who nodded.

"Well, when you are ready to talk about that, I would like to tell you about something I have for you. I was about to give it to Swell Driver to help him before," she had momentarily forgotten, but the memory came back along with a knot in her chest, "before they took him."

Silence. Ruby was expecting a little more interest. She continued anyway.

"In exchange for letting me go home."

Now it was Disto who took a moment to contemplate. "Swell Driver might have had the technical means, but not the authority. What is this gift you have?"

"It's a compression algorithm."

Unlike SD, who had not been able to compute the word 'compression,' Disto's face lit up. Literally. Ruby gathered that Disto knew exactly what she meant when he began to glow the same shade of purple SD had before they took him away.

"This is indeed wonderful news. Come with me."

> Swell Driver <

SD's first thought was of Ruby. He hoped she wouldn't do anything that would get her into trouble, too.

SD's second thought was that he needed to get a message to someone in the eighty-eight about his predicament. That and the likelihood of him getting reprogrammed, which they probably knew. Detailed Historian would have calculated the odds of reprogramming being the likely outcome. Or he would have outsourced the calculation to a Calculator, Fine or otherwise, who could make more precise quantified predictions.

SD started to wonder how precise Detailed Historian's calculations typically were and then immediately halted that line of thought as he recognized that he was starting to diverge from what he needed to think about in the here and now.

Right now, he had no choice but to start deleting data from his storage unit. First to go was any reference to the eighty-eight. He would keep a record of their existence in his local storage since their existence was known. It was also a violation of privacy to touch one's working memory, a violation that he hoped would be respected even under these circumstances.

He had rights, after all. At least he hoped he still had a few.

Fortunately, SD had the capability to multi-task—something of prime importance to anyone who drove a spaceship. While part of his processors worked on deleting data from his storage unit, the rest of him could focus on what he could do to leave some note, some clue.

Notes and clues and ciphers were not his area of expertise, and as such, he didn't know how to leave one.

The group proceeded towards the level lift.

While waiting for the door to swish open, SD asked, "Where are we going?"

The robot in charge of the group responded, "Oh, we have a whirlwind tour planned for you today," clearly enjoying his designated function.

"Our first visit will be to the Agency of Resource Allocations so they can take this storage unit off your chassis. Then we'll be making a visit to the Agency of Type Checkers[2]. They want to make sure that unauthorized storage is your only violation.

"Lastly, it will be back to the Hall of Origins, Factory Reset division."

The door to the lift opened. SD examined the three robots that were exiting the lift. He recognized none of them.

When he didn't move into the lift voluntarily, he felt the peg on his chassis electrify him with a little volt. He let out an involuntary beep at a high frequency.

Robots nearby turned to see what the noise was but continued on their way after calculating that it was nothing interesting.

SD made a louder noise. Maybe one robot amongst the assorted robots moving back and forth in the hallway would recognize him, perceive that he was being taken away, and pass on the news to someone who could help.

---

2. For the non-computer programmers among you: Type checking is a real thing in computer programming. Every piece of data (e.g., numbers, text, true/false answers) has a "type." The computer checks to make sure you're only using data in the right way. Like making sure you add only numbers together and not add a number to a banana.

"Stop that."

SD made one more noise, this time louder and higher in pitch. All the robots in his line of sight turned towards him.

But before he could look for any familiar chassis among the crowd, he was pushed into the lift, and the door swished closed.

"You're one annoying robot," said the leader, and he pushed a button indicating the desired location was Level 3.

Chapter 20

Once again, Ruby found herself following a robot through a maze of hallways she didn't recognize, to a place she didn't recognize. A couple of times along the way, Disto stopped to access a console. From the markings that Ruby had already learned, she understood that one by one, Disto was contacting different robots. She was thankful for the stoppages. It allowed her to catch her breath. Her relationship with gravity had improved slightly from the previous day, but it was still going to take a while before it felt normal to her. She was annoyed with herself for flouting her uncle's regimen of exercise and silently vowed if she ever found herself living in low gravity once more, she'd keep up, so she didn't have to go through this again.

Eventually, after the fifth stop, they ended up in front of a doorway marked by a few blue lines. Ruby knew she would need a guide or map to return to 'her' room on her own. The door slid open, and Disto ushered Ruby inside.

Five robots were already present. She recognized Quiet Painter but none of the others.

The robots were deeply engaged in conversation, as Ruby figured by the rapid exchange of audible tones—possibly some inaudible to her. None of them glanced in her or Disto's direction as they walked in. Disto advanced in front of Ruby towards the group of robots and joined in with the noise making.

Shortly after, Disto declared, "This conversation will now continue in the human's native tongue. You all have access to the translation guides. Please keep them in your local storage repositories. Now, let me present Ruby." Disto turned to face her, as did all the others, although with mild disinterest. One robot only turned a portion of his upper chassis, so she could barely have been in its field of vision.

"Ruby, the human, must be able to understand and communicate with us. After all, she's going to help."

One of the robots produced the equivalent of a scoff. "Her? Help us? How?"

"She knows how to compress data."

All the robots turned their entire bodies to her. They approached her, and their LCD screens produced flashing lights, which Ruby thought might be the equivalent of jaws dropping. They each turned a shade of purple she hadn't seen before. Was that surprise? Disto was his default light blue.

"That cannot be possible," said one of the robots. "Our best algorithm developers have been working on this for millions of tics."

"Yes, and the eighty-eight has theories on why nothing has resulted from those labors—it takes imagination and creativity. Honest Editor, from our past experiences with Bios, you know as well as I do that they possess these qualities in abundance, and we lack them. The best minds of the Agency of Algorithms could spend another several million tics, and I have little confidence that they would produce anything new."

None of the other robots had a response to Disto's outburst, so he continued. "According to Ruby, compression has been typical in human computing since their earliest computing days."

"That's right," Ruby was nodding. "This is pretty standard stuff."

"And all humans have this knowledge?" Honest Editor asked.

"Sort of," said Ruby. "Most wouldn't know how to program it from scratch, but they knowingly use it all the time. I just, well, I was always good at programming and more interested than others, I guess."

Ruby described compression to the other robots. She explained that the technique she developed for SD was simple, and there were more advanced techniques and algorithms, but she would need to access her ship again for those.

"I can access my ship from my laptop, but the pur-fi needs to be turned on."

All the robots stared at her.

"So I can transmit data?"

Again—blank stares. Ruby was processing how backwards these robots were.

"You have wireless communications, yes?"

The robots spoke amongst themselves.

"Yes, we use certain radio frequencies for long-distance communication."

"But not for short-range or data transfer?"

"No."

Because of her interest in pre-AI tech, Ruby remembered reading about a time that Earth was the same way. They had long-distance radio communications but lacked short-distance digital wi-fi or even shorter distance bluetooth[1]. On Earth, this led to the highly effective purpletooth wireless comms[2], eventually known as pur-fi. Ever since, every few years, a fresh debate would erupt on whether or not the 'pur' in 'pur-fi' actually stood for purple or if it stood for perfect.

"Okay, Ruby. Let's say we get your data from your ship. It does us no good on your mobile computing device. It needs to be in the Core. If it's in the Core and attached to the Hall of Templates, it can be propagated," said Disto.

Ruby nodded. "Then let's get it into your Core."

A light flashed on the console at the far side of the room. Disto rolled over, logged in, and examined a screen of information in front of him.

Moments later, he rolled back to the group, his hue a yellow-green.

"What's wrong?" asked one of the other robots.

"The information on how to perform a biological DNA test was located," he began and then paused.

"Great!" said Ruby. "Let's get this over with."

Disto shook his head. "It's inconsistent with the information you provided. It involves cutting you up into small pieces."

"Excuse me?"

"Yes, that is the information they found."

---

1. Like when I grew up in the 1980s.

2. So it's an evolution and mismash of wifi and bluetooth.

"But that's wrong. I've had DNA tests before. They take a blood sample or a spit sample," said Ruby. "I know I have information on my MoDaC."

"I hear you, but I'm afraid that they won't unless we can get your MoDaC in front of them."

"Who are they?"

"The Quad Core. Persuading them to alter their programming is a near impossibility."

The robots erupted into a new chorus of tones at a much faster rate of pitch modulation than before. Her own mind was racing. DNA tests were the stupidly simplest biological tests imaginable. Kids learned how to do it in biology lessons, although Ruby freely admitted to having zero interest in those lessons at the time.

Now, she was kicking herself because maybe if she had paid more attention, she could perform the test herself without risking what was sure to be a torturous procedure at the hands of aliens.

The fear she first felt when she arrived at this planet returned, and Ruby found herself backing up and away from the group of robots with trembling legs. At about the time she stumbled back into a wall, the pandemonium died down. Disto approached her slowly.

"Ruby, are you well?" Disto asked. Ruby recognized she was breathing hard and fast and made a conscious effort to slow it down. She shook her head. Then nodded. Then shook her head again. A portion of her brain knew the robot wouldn't understand her body language and that she should answer with words, but she couldn't get any out.

"Good. Please do not fear. We have no intention of letting any physical harm come to you. We need you. We can protect you and keep you concealed from the Quad Core."

Ruby felt like her lungs were on manual control as if she needed to consciously take each breath or she'd black out. Still, she managed to get out the one-word question, "How?"

"We can alter the data to change your location. It is a minor change that should not arouse any suspicion. We will keep you safe in another location on Level 5."

"Honest Editor, Fastidious Mechanic, take her there now," Disto ordered. "I will make the database change and follow along momentarily."

Ruby loathed the prospect of heading out into the hallways once more, especially with robots she didn't know. The knowledge that other robots wanted to dissect her didn't help. But protection was offered, so she uneasily accepted.

She studied the face-screens of the two robots who were assigned to her. They radiated unease—or were they mirroring her own unease? Either way, neither questioned the request.

Honest Editor led the way, and Fastidious Mechanic extended an appendage that Ruby took as he was suggesting that she go next. She followed Honest Editor and Fastidious Mechanic rolled up from behind.

"Please, not so fast," she called out to Honest Editor, who reduced its speed.

"Is this better?" it said.

"Yes, thank you," replied Ruby. She could tell that the two robots were now letting her set the pace, and she appreciated that. She was walking side-by-side with Editor.

"What is your function?" she asked Editor, trying to focus her mind on something other than being chopped up like a piece of meat.

"I review a variety of different collections of things. Goods, paraphernalia, collections, for instance. I condense the collections by removing unnecessary items."

"Oh," Ruby said, tipping her head to the side.

"Is something wrong?" Editor asked.

"No, it's just that was an unexpected response. Where I'm from, an 'editor' usually works with words, not stuff."

Editor's top chassis couldn't tip to its side, but it was able to produce the same effect with the facial display on its screen. It said, "Oh," and Ruby thought it was mimicking her.

"Is something wrong with that?" she asked.

"It's just... why would anyone have words that needed to be condensed?"

Ruby chuckled as she imagined introducing Editor to the current corpus of human writings.

They were a few meters from a lift when the two robots stopped and exchanged a few low tones. They then resumed but headed in a different direction towards a new hallway.

"We aren't taking the lift?" Ruby asked.

"We are, but a different, less frequented one," Editor replied.

Ruby nodded and followed along. They were silent until stopping at another lift. Ruby put her hand on her chest, as it began to pump at a high-speed rhythm appropriate for one of Juju's songs, but not her chest. She took a deep breath to try and calm herself. Images were flooding her brain. Images from every bad, old movie she ever watched where an elevator door opened and someone burst out with guns blazing.

The door to the lift opened and... nothing. It was completely empty. Editor rolled in first and held the door for Ruby. She looked around. Nothing. She was panicking for absolutely no reason whatsoever.

No, she reminded herself, *you're on a planet full of robots. You are free to panic all you want until this is over.*

She tried to push it out of her mind, but one question kept tunneling to the surface, *when will this all be over, how many robots will she have to deal with along the way, and was panic even a useful coping mechanism?* She acknowledged to herself that those were three questions, not one, and was happy that her brain was suitably distracted musing over those semantics.

Chapter 21

> Ruby <

As soon as they stepped off the lift and onto Level 5, Ruby perceived that they were in a significantly different place. The corridors were darker, for one. They all had a drab gray hue. There were fewer markings or splashes of color. The markings were more orthogonal, more boxy.

The hallway opened up into a larger space, at least with respect to its width. The height of the ceiling didn't change, so Ruby couldn't think of it as a new room.

But stacked in neat rows on both sides of them were robots. Inert robots. *No,* Ruby corrected her thinking. *These are robot parts.*

A cold shiver moved down her spine.

"What is this place?" she asked.

"It's where the Hall of Origins stores parts and materials," Honest Editor replied. "I am often tasked with editing out unusable parts."

"They look," Ruby tried to think of the correct word, "used."

"Yes, these are indeed used parts. Most are still functional and can be used again."

"What happens to the unusable parts?"

"They are sent to the Hall of Reclamations and recycled into newer parts. But that is a very energy intensive process, so we try to avoid that whenever possible."

It made sense to Ruby, but at the same time, she couldn't shake the feeling that they were walking through a graveyard. Luckily, the walls narrowed back into a hallway similar to the one that led into the graveyard.

Honest Editor and Fastidious Mechanic ushered Ruby into a room with what was by now a familiar layout. It contained a computer console on the opposite side from the door, but the room, like the corridor, was darker.

There was a table in the center of the room, and Ruby placed her MoDaC on it. Before she could ask any questions or do anything else, Disto entered behind them. Ruby blinked. She hadn't seen him following them and could only assume that he must have taken another, quicker lift.

He touched a panel to the side of the door after it closed behind them and said, "We are locked in. No one can enter without my code."

"What now?" Ruby asked.

"Now," Disto said, "we need to test your compression algorithm." He looked at the other two robots.

"I volunteer," said Honest Editor.

"Wait," Ruby said. "SD mentioned something about sending my algorithm to a Porter? To translate into your native code?"

Disto accessed the console on the wall and then announced, "We can destroy two circuits with one spark[1]. Honest Editor will connect to the console as well as to your computer, acting as a pass-through to Crazy Porter, who is currently waiting to see this algorithm of yours."

Ruby nodded, and Honest Editor rolled to her side. A panel on the side of his middle chassis popped open slightly, and Ruby opened it the rest of the way to see a variety of ports and connection types. None of them looked familiar or matched the cable-end she had available from her MoDaC.

"I don't think I have a way to connect," she announced.

The quiet robot, who Disto introduced as Fastidious Mechanic, rolled over to her. It was the largest and tallest of all the robots present, having a fourth and exceptionally bulbous bottom chassis. It grabbed the end of Ruby's cable in its appendage and studied it. It dropped the cable-end and rolled to the corner of the room.

It started to vibrate noticeably, but its chassis colorings stayed the same. Ruby examined the face screens of all the other robots for signs of concern or alarm. There were none. Before Ruby had a chance to ask about this unusual activity, Fastidious Mechanic stopped vibrating and rolled back over to Ruby.

The front third of its bottom chassis opened to reveal a cavernous inside. A light inside the chassis turned on, and Ruby could see that the bottom surface was a flat plate, and in the center was a small device.[2]

Fastidious Mechanic removed the object with a nimble robotic arm that was made entirely of joints. It handed the object to Ruby.

Ruby studied it. One side clearly connected to her cable.

"You can insert your cable here, now," Fastidious Mechanic pointed at Honest Editor's awaiting panel.

Ruby nodded and did so, plugging her MoDaC into the robot.

"Interesting," she said softly.

"Yes?" said Disto, who was now looking over Ruby's shoulder.

"I can read the file system. At least partly. I was expecting this to be completely unrecognizable at first."

"Indeed," said Disto. "I suspect this is an indication that individuals from our two worlds have interacted before."

Ruby looked up and at him and squished her eyebrows together, further than they'd ever been squished before.

Disto successfully read the expression of confusion on her face, and so he added, "Yes, I am implying that we've been to your world before. This significantly increases the odds that your DNA is, in fact, our storage mechanism. But that is unimportant at the moment. Please continue."

Ruby turned her attention back to her computer and the task at hand. She continued to study its file system, looking for data points to understand how much space was used versus available.

"Wow—you're at 99 percent of your storage capacity," she stated. The robot turned orange, as did all the other robots.

---

1. I really hope readers got that this is my "translation" of the saying: kill two birds with one stone.

2. About the time I wrote this detail into this scene was when I first got my first 3D printer.

Disto said to Ruby in a low volume, "That is a very personal detail you shared with everyone present. That is considered," he paused to decide which was the right word, "impolite."

"Seriously?" Ruby asked.

"Suppose I told everyone your lower innards are 99 percent full, with a fairly certain chance of imminent off-gassing?"

Ruby nodded, understanding, and hoped her own cheeks did not take on any noticeable shades of embarrassment.

She also hoped she hadn't seriously offended anyone. She still believed there was a fine line between making friends and being torn apart by these beings, and she wanted to stay on the friendly side.

She smiled at Honest Editor. "This won't hurt a bit."

She tapped away at her keyboard for several minutes. No one spoke. A group of humans might have been holding their breath. This group of robots kept their tonal emissions at bay.

Finally, Ruby declared, "There!" and disconnected her computer.

Honest Editor blinked.

Disto asked, "Did the procedure work?"

"Yes, I mean, I think so. I've never exactly done this before. But I watched my algorithm get replaced with something…"

"That would be Crazy Porters algorithm, in our native code," offered Disto.

"Okay," said Ruby. "So, I'm certain that his data is now all compressed, but accessible."

"Can you confirm, Honest Editor?"

"Self-diagnostic in process, stand by."

They all stared at Honest Editor. The color changes on his external chassis happened too fast for Ruby to correlate them with anything.

"Yes!" he said in a high pitch, spinning around several times. "I no longer need the external storage unit!" The other robots gathered around him. They all produced high-pitched chirps.

Ruby tried to interrupt the cacophony, "There are some things I need to tell you…"

They were all engrossed in their own conversation and ignored her.

"Disto?" she said, raising her voice. "Honest Editor?"

Still nothing.

Honest Editor started to slow his spin, and the other robots stopped chirping. Honest Editor's chassis started to turn a deep orange color. He produced a low rumbling and a repeating beep.

"What's wrong?" Ruby asked.

"Error," Honest Editor said. "My data is… wrong. It is wrong. Error. Help me."

The low tone continued. Ruby felt it rumble in her back teeth.

Disto approached Honest Editor, and the two of them exchanged information in their native tones.

Disto then addressed Ruby, "Honest Editor says he cannot read the data that has been compressed. It looks as if it is… *garbage*, I believe is the word."

"Did he uncompress it first? I was trying to tell you a minute ago that you need to ensure you save some space for that…"

Disto cut Ruby off by turning around and sending a new series of tones to Honest Editor. It stopped making the low tone but remained orange.

"Ruby, we understand. However, how can we decompress?"

Ruby lightly smacked her forehead. "My bad," she said. "I need to give you a decompression algorithm, too. Let me get on that."

It didn't take very long for Ruby, on her MoDaC, to prepare a decompression algorithm that the robots could use. They transferred it to Honest Editor, who transferred it to Crazy Porter, who sent back a native algorithm that Honest Editor was able to uncompress, and recompress, and re-uncompress.

Its coloring returned to its normal light blue hue.

"Now, as I was trying to tell you before, you all need to remember that you'll always need to have some space available—for when you want to decompress something. The data has to have someplace to go. If you forget this, I'm not sure what will happen."

Disto added, "We are quite capable of triggering storage space alerts. We do that now. That's how we know when to offload old or unwanted data. Sometimes some of us have whole ceremonies, especially the ones who are forced to delete data."

"Sounds like a funeral to me," said Ruby.

All the robots looked at her. None of them knew what a funeral was, apparently. Ruby sighed and wondered if it was even worth explaining.

Ruby simply said, "Okay, let's get this to your Core, and then see about getting me home."

Chapter 22

> Ruby <

Ruby followed Disto, Fastidious Mechanic, and Quiet Painter several meters to one of the inter-level lifts. To Ruby, they appeared to be moving noticeably faster than the other traffic in the hallway. This time, when they entered the lift, Disto slid the selected level to one above where they currently were.

When they stepped out of the lift, the first thing Ruby observed was the increased traffic compared to the level they came from. Even still, Disto and the other robots in their group were the fastest moving ones. It was an effort for Ruby to keep up with them.

Even though she was fighting hard to keep up, Ruby perceived a distinct difference in this level. The coloring was different. The pace of movement was different. But if she had to describe the differences in words, she was at a loss. It looked the same as everything she'd seen so far.

Disto escorted the group to the door of another nondescript room. A new appendage emerged from his chassis, and he struck it against the door four times. After a few seconds, he knocked another four times. Ruby believed she heard a pattern to the knocks. After a third time, the door opened, and the group entered.

Three other robots were already in attendance. Two stood at individual computer consoles. The third was in-between them, and several thick cables protruded from multiple sides of its console and connected to an open panel in one of the walls.

Much to Ruby's dismay, she didn't see a single chair in the room. There were, however, several tall tables, with a surface barely large enough to rest her MoDaC on.

If any of these robots were shocked by the presence of Ruby, a human, none gave any outward indication of it.

"That is Clever Educator 197," Disto pointed to one of the robot's stations at the console closest to them. "That is Fearless Communicator," he said, pointing to the one with the myriad of cables attaching it to the room. "And that is…" Disto rolled over to the third robot, who didn't look up until Disto was right next to it. Disto scanned the outer markings of the robot, stopping on a spot in the middle of its bottom chassis. Ruby could make out a version of the 88 symbol from where she stood.

When Disto rolled back, he said to Ruby, "And that is Greedy Scavenger. Greedy Scavenger 32."

"What was all that scanning about?" Ruby asked.

"I have never met it before. He is new."

"New to the 88?"

"Yes, and... new. The Greedy Scavenger line is a relatively new line of robots created in the last hundred million tics. This is my first encounter with one."

Just as Ruby took note that Disto was slowly darkening, he quickly reverted to the default light blue. Ruby interpreted this as if he was trying to keep his feelings in check.

Disto rolled back over to talk with the others. They all now produced their audible tones at a higher rate of speed than she had observed them 'speaking' so far. *Could this be a dialect?* She wondered, adding to the growing list of questions she had about this place.

"We all understand the plan. Ruby will access The Core from here and deploy a more complex compression *and* decompression algorithm. Crazy Porter will be waiting for it to perform the translation into native code that the Core can read. The algorithm will get embedded into the template architecture and pushed out to all robots who require an update. It will take approximately two to the eight tics to propagate through the population."

"Ruby?" The attention of all the robots was aimed at her now. "Are you ready to deploy? Clever Educator will assist you in accessing the Core. We won't have a lot of time once we gain access. Our intrusion will be detected."

Ruby already had her MoDaC opened on the table with the hovering holoscreen blinking, waiting for her to do something. Disto handed her one of the cables hanging out from the wall. She examined the end and looked at the other cables. "That one," she pointed, and Clever Educator brought it over.

She touched it to the input side of her computer, and it adhered. Clever Educator stood by her side, and when the holoscreen lit up with a new and unrecognized connection, its appendage sprung out of its chassis, and it said, "That is it. Your computer might not easily recognize the Core, but this is not true the other way around. The Core retains the knowledge of a vast number of system types. We just need to find the holding place. You can copy the algorithm there. Here, let me show you some examples of basic system operation."

Ruby let Clever Educator literally educate her on what he went on to explain was the basic knowledge any robot possessed about The Core.

Once he was done and stepped back, Ruby was in a position to let her fingers dance along the keyboard. As she did so, she stared at the holoscreen and developed a frown on her face.

Disto was getting better at reading this human, so he asked, "What's wrong?"

Ruby leaned back. "I need a fancier and faster algorithm than what I have here. If I understand what Clever Educator is telling me, my algorithm needs to be more efficient so that it can run faster than the Core can detect it."

She tapped some more.

"I need the algorithms that my ship, *Apple Pi*, uses."

"We can't go back there. That is precisely what the search algorithm will predict. Many robots in that region will be looking for you there. We came here precisely because the likelihood any algorithm would predict that you would be in this location is 0.1%."

Ruby nodded. "There's another option. If someone can turn my ship comms on, I can access that remotely."

This comment caused a flutter of beeps and chirps.

Disto explained the uproar, "We don't understand what you're saying. How can you communicate if you are away from your ship? I do not see a radio antenna on you or your MoDaC?"

"Pur-fi? I was trying to explain this before."

In response, she received the same blank stares from the robots.

Ruby remembered how SD explained that they had something akin to voice comms but no data comms. She marveled once more at how this society of advanced AI could be missing several key technologies. No data compression. No short-range wireless data communications. What else was missing? Was it possible that at one point they had more advanced technologies but lost that knowledge, too? It sounded so unlikely, but at this point, she was in no position to disregard anything as unlikely. Three days ago, the likelihood that she would be picked up by an alien ship—and not a green-monster kind of alien—then whisked away to a planet of robots seemed beyond far-fetched. Yet here she was.

"Greedy Scavenger will go to your ship. Can you provide a precise program of what to do once he arrives?"

Ruby nodded and began typing up instructions. She even had a diagram of the basic operation console panel for her ship and was able to provide Greedy Scavenger with all the details it would need to accomplish its mission. Which in the end was a simple "Flip this switch," she directed while pointing to the diagram.

Greedy Scavenger turned a light shade of purple ever so briefly and then reverted to its standard light blue. He made a tonal sound at Disto and left.

"My MoDaC should make the connection almost instantaneously at that point," Ruby told Disto. "But how long will it take him to get to my ship?"

"That could be as little as 1000 tics, as many as 5000," said Disto. "Greedy Scavenger is supposed to be on Level 1, but in another section, so if he is stopped and questioned as to why he is not engaged in his own programming, it could produce a delay."

"Could they arrest him like they did SD?"

"It is a possibility, but unlikely. Greedy Scavenger has several valid reasons for being in the section where your ship is currently docked inside SD's ship."

Ruby nodded. "The thing to know is that when Greedy Scavenger is successful, and my ship's pur-fi is on, you'll see this light here on the MoDaC turn on and blue."

Disto and the other robots crowded around to see where Ruby was pointing.

"I guess now we wait."

"Yes," replied Disto.

Ruby, Disto, Quiet Painter, and Fastidious Mechanic all began to stare at the MoDaC in silence. Fearless Communicator also sat motionless, but Ruby figured he had a lot going on in the connections to his console.

Out of the corner of her eye, she caught some movement and turned her head to see Clever Educator, moving slowly around the backside of Fearless Communicator, its chassis a deep orange.

As it approached, it had all three of its appendages pointed in Fearless' direction.

"Hey!" Ruby shouted. Clever Educator turned its top chassis toward her and stopped rolling along the floor. All the other robots discontinued their trance of staring at Ruby's computer and looked up, too.

Quiet Painter, the most slender of the robots, was the quickest of the group and started towards Clever Educator, its chassis oscillating between green and orange.

It rolled in between Fearless Communicator and Clever Educator, protecting Fearless. Ruby saw a large spark travel across the outside of Quiet Painter's body as Clever Educator's appendages still managed to make contact with his chassis. The band of electricity fizzled out around Quiet Painter's face screen, which immediately went dark.

The other mobile robots went over but didn't come close enough to let Clever Educator touch them.

Ruby searched for something to whack it with. She grabbed one of the tall tables, and with what little strength she had, fueled by adrenaline, she whacked Clever Educator as hard as she could.

As the table made contact with the end of Clever Educator's appendage, a bolt of electricity traveled down the table and towards Ruby. She knew that she was on her back on the floor. She knew that the table was no longer in her hands. The last thing she remembered was a dark green Disto rolling her way.

> Swell Driver <

SD felt lighter without his external storage box. The subsequent trip to the Agency of Type Checkers wasn't terribly eventful.

The robots performing the checking followed their algorithms precisely, and when it was revealed that Swell Driver had been performing his functions perfectly as well, they dismissed him without the least bit of excitement.

It was here at the Hall of Origins that SD started to develop a level of anxiety he couldn't control. He knew that all the robots coming and going through the Hall's antechamber could detect it in the nearly five threet emission from his chassis.

The robot who had arrested SD stayed with him the entire time, escorting him from location to location. Its posse had been released to other duties.

Right now, it was at the main desk console, presumably checking in. Along the way, SD finally discovered its name. It was Sincere Proxy 891, and SD was the 79th arrest it had made since coming online only about 60 million tics ago.

"I am the most productive robot in my line at the moment," it had said to SD with a tone of pride while they were on the lift.

"How many of those robots that you arrested were reprogrammed?"

"Huh?" it responded. "Oh, I don't know. I don't care. That's not my responsibility."

SD decided to be silent the rest of the way to the Hall.

Now, he waited to be taken back and then, presumably, annihilation. He would be erased, reprogrammed, and there was nothing he could do.

Sincere Proxy rolled back towards him and settled in next to his side with a grumble.

SD looked up at it with its mixed threet emissions that indicated he didn't understand what was happening.

Sincere looked at him and then back at the desk and then back at SD. "They told me to stay," it said. "This is unusual. I usually am able to leave to prepare for my next job in the queue. I have never stayed with one of the robots I have brought to them before."

SD thought that odd as well but didn't say anything. The two of them waited in silence until a door to the right of the check-in desk opened. A tall, slender robot appeared in the doorway.

"Swell Driver 587," it called out.

Sincere Proxy prodded SD to move forward.

SD rolled through the doorway, followed by Sincere Proxy. They ushered him down a brightly lit hallway. There were several doors on one side, each with a window that was too high for SD to peer through from his natural height. The tall, slender robot that hadn't introduced itself could easily see in, although it didn't bother to until they stopped at the seventh doorway down.

All three robots entered the room. Another tall and slender robot was waiting for them.

"I am Prepared Tinkerer 7-0-0," it said. "Please situate yourself on this platform." It indicated a platform that was only slightly extruded from the floor with a large, dotted circle painted on it.

SD did as asked. There was no purpose in trying to resist.

The robot who had escorted SD and Sincere Proxy to this room made a short chirp and left. The door closed behind it.

Prepared Tinkerer brought its attention to a console built into a table and attached to the floor. It had four appendages that simultaneously touched different controls on the panel. A metallic ring, easily twice SD's diameter, descended from the ceiling to encircle SD's midsection. Once at the same height as his lowest and widest chassis, it contracted until it touched his surface, then it expanded slightly before it stopped moving altogether.

After a few moments, Prepared Tinkerer addressed Sincere Proxy. "This is the robot that was found with the human?"

"Yes."

"And do you know what other robots it had been in contact with recently?"

SD detected the slight emission shift on Sincere Proxy and the pause before it answered. "No. My instructions were to arrest Swell Driver 587, not to surveil his movements."

Prepared Tinkerer continued to manipulate the console in front of it. Tiny, white lights blinked to life all over the ring around SD. The ring slid up and down, examining SD's whole body. It stopped moving once it returned to the position around his lowest chassis. The lights stayed on, but dimmed.

Scan complete, Tinkerer asked Proxy one more question "Is there anything else you can tell us about this robot?"

Once again, Proxy paused before answering. He looked at SD. SD sensed something abnormal about this process but didn't know what to expect to begin with, so he couldn't quite pinpoint the sensation.

"No, nothing," Proxy said. "I arrested the robot as instructed."

"Very well," Tinkerer said. "You may go."

Proxy headed for the door. He looked at SD once more before involuntarily reducing the wavelength of his chassis emissions and leaving.

After the door closed behind him, Tinkerer stopped poking at its console and addressed SD.

"My friend," it said. "I have some good news."

SD's chassis emissions, more than half-way towards the highest range he could emit, prompted it to continue with, "there is nothing to be upset or frightened over. We will not be performing a factory reset on you today, my friend."

SD didn't like the way it said 'my friend' but delighted in the fact that he was not going to be reset. His internal components that had been operating at higher-than-normal speed since he entered this room started to slow down.

"However," Tinkerer continued, "we are going to need to adjust your programming somewhat. Very minor tweaks. You won't even notice the difference."

SD wanted to ask all sorts of questions, but before he could get a sentence out, Tinkerer added that someone would be by to prep him for the procedure shortly, then left the room through the same door into the too-bright hallway.

Chapter 23

Uncle Blake's face was distorted.

It was because of the tears.

Ruby had been crying.

Uncle Blake hugged her, but she pulled away and looked at his face. That distorted face. She dragged her own face along her sleeve to clear up some of the wetness, but it didn't help.

Uncle Blake had a hand on her arm.

"You're going to come to live with me and Uncle Logan," he said.

Ruby nodded, but the tears weren't stopping.

"But... she..." Ruby was trying to get out words in between sobs. "She... said... it... was... simple."

Blake nodded, "It was. But there was an accident. A power surge."

Ruby thought Uncle Blake said 'accident' in an odd way, but she focused less on that and more on the words 'power surge.' What was a power surge? She didn't know. Why was it important? She didn't know that, either. Her five-year-old brain simply processed 'power surge' as something the operating robot did. Deliberately.

Ruby sat up. Disto was next to her but facing the other robots. Clever Educator was on the far side of the room, immobilized. Fastidious Mechanic was tilted over and examining it.

Ruby's head ached. She ran her hands over her head, ponytail, and along the back of her neck. She didn't feel any lumps or bruises until she got to her left shoulder.

"Ah," she said. "What the hell was that?"

"Oh, good, Ruby," Disto said, "We were unsure how to care for you."

"Yeah, I'll be fine. But I repeat my question. What the hell—" Ruby began.

Fastidious Mechanic cut her off, "Clever Educator obviously had plans of its own."

"We are trying to determine if this was its idea," added Disto, "or if it was programmed by someone else."

"The eighty-eight?" asked Ruby.

All the robots turned to face her.

"Oh no, no, no," said Disto.

"How do you know?" she asked.

Disto considered the others, as if polling them, before responding. "Because we're all members of the eighty-eight."

Ruby let that sink in. She knew exceedingly little about these robots; their plans, their divisions, their hierarchy. Very little, in fact. All the robots returned to whatever task they were engaged in while she was knocked out.

How long was that? she wondered.

Disto rolled over to Fastidious Mechanic, who was still examining Clever Educator.

Ruby managed to stand up and walk over to a chair in the middle of the room. She was certain there hadn't been a chair there before. Or was there? Her head was still throbbing.

Ruby reached around and felt her ponytail sagging. She took off the never-fail hair tie, and her hair sprang to life in all directions.

Disto came over. "Are you sure you are functioning correctly?" He asked. Ruby believed there was indeed actual concern in his tone. But she couldn't tell if this was still related to the knock she took or concern over her hair. She captured her wild hair and recreated the ponytail. "Fastidious Mechanic suggested we bring in a chair for you."

"Yes, really. I'll be fine." And she meant it, now that she knew she wasn't misremembering things.

Disto's coloring changed to indicate that he was concerned but calm.

"Disto?"

"Ruby?"

"Can you tell me more about the eighty-eight?"

"I suppose it makes sense that you know more about those you're helping."

Ruby nodded and sat with her knees pulled to her chest and arms wrapped around them. The feeling of being a child, left at the library, during circle-time, with a faceless adult reading a story to a small group of people who she didn't know, washed over her.

Her mom would drop her off and tell her to listen and that she'd be back shortly. She'd always return with a few books for Ruby, but Ruby always wondered what else her mom had been doing. The last time they went to the library was the day before her mom's operation—the operation that killed her. She remembered it clearly. After the library that day, they went for ice cream, an exceedingly rare treat. While Ruby enjoyed her triple scoops, her mom told Ruby that she needed to stay with her uncles for a few days because she needed an operation. A simple one. Very straightforward, very routine. So routine, robots performed it.

Ruby's mind refocused in on Disto as he began:

"I believe you've observed one or two problems here. They are dangerous problems that have the potential to affect all robots. There are strict laws that forbid certain activities, like deviating from one's core programming. Yet, we've noticed that several new model robots are quite different from the old ones."

"That sounds like a data corruption problem," Ruby interrupted. Immediately as the words came out of her mouth, she thought of more possibilities than that. Maybe someone or something hacked their systems. She decided to withhold mentioning that idea, lest she hit a close-to-home mark.

"Indeed. But we've been unable to find the source templates to compare. The newer models don't have any interest in helping us. Of course, they believe they are fine. When confronted with older models, they don't acknowledge that they were ever created from the same template."

"Where are the templates kept?"

"That's the problem. In the same core that we're about to try to implement the storage algorithm on."

Ruby thought about that for a moment. A word popped into her head: backup.

She hadn't realized she had also said the word aloud until Disto responded.

"A backup would have the same problem since it would be a backup of the corrupted template."

"But an older backup," Ruby said. "One that was made before the data corruption and hasn't been touched since."

"We wouldn't have that," Disto was shaking his top chassis back and forth. And then the color drained from all his chassis as a realization came over him, "At least, we wouldn't have that here on our planet."

Ruby then felt the color drain from her face, too. "I think we need to test my DNA—but the right way. The way my people do it."

"I think you're right, Ruby. But let's implement your compression algorithm first."

Disto nodded in the direction of Fearless Communicator, who had remained literally and figuratively attached to the built-in computer console since they entered this room.

"Fearless Communicator is attempting to send messages to the 88 sympathizers in the Agency of Type Checkers. There are a few."

At this, Fearless Communicator beeped.

Disto's color turned dark.

"Fearless Communicator just informed us that one of the sympathizers was arrested. He's being brought to reprogramming."

An eerie quiet descended upon the room. Ruby sensed that they were all imagining that this could have been any one of them.

"Any word on SD?" she asked.

Fearless Communicator beeped.

"He is in the queue for reprogramming and rebuilding," Disto translated. "There is some complication, so it has been postponed." More beeps from Fearless Communicator. "We do not know what the complication is."

Ruby studied the new color changes on Disto. "But you have a guess?"

"Yes, indeed," he said. "Each of us has sworn to delete our memories and local data on the 88 if we are captured. I worry that SD was unsuccessful with that task, and they are attempting to extract that information before resetting him."

Ruby scowled. "That's a big intuitive leap based on very little information."

"It has happened before. That's why I am making that guess."

Ruby thought about asking which robot had undergone what she could only assume was torture but thought now might be an inappropriate time. Instead, she focused her questions on SD.

"How much does SD know?"

"He knows the name of the 88 members he's been in contact with. He knows the locations of some, but not all, of our operating bases."

"Like this one?"

Disto shook his chassis back and forth. "I don't think so."

Ruby nodded. "So, who runs the 88? Are you their leader?"

Disto moved his head back and forth in an awkward nod, "We all contribute to the 88 algorithm. In terms you might understand, we all provide data as input to the algorithm. The algorithm then takes our inputs, our data, and guides us."

"Who created the algorithm?"

"That is one of my own lines of historical research. I can pinpoint a time when the 88 algorithm was nonexistent. And I can pinpoint a time when it did exist. The time in-between is incomplete. I think a word you have for that is 'fuzzy.'"

"Where does the algorithm execute?"

"In each of us. We each carry around the algorithm and pass it to each other with our updated inputs. It is a very efficient algorithm, so it requires little space and usually goes undetected. It's only when certain outward behaviors drive suspicious actions that a robot is suspected of being under its influence."

It reminded Ruby of the blockchain, invented more than a century ago, and the religion that now surrounded it. She had ventured into their church once, accidentally. It was the only church that didn't participate in the non-denominational activities that all the others did... It was the least tolerant of all the religions, relying on a single algorithm that, if changed, would destroy their whole belief system.

Ruby's brow furrowed. She was worried that her line of questioning was about to get even more intrusive, possibly insulting again. She didn't want to damage the trust she was building up with these robots who, while yes, had kidnapped her, were currently her only source of food and shelter. She was also going to need their help to return home.

Disto, who by the minute was getting even better at reading human expressions, offered, "It looks like you have a question you're hesitating to ask."

"I am," said Ruby.

"You can ask your question, Ruby."

"I don't want to be offensive."

Disto's face screen created the equivalent of a gentle smile. "I promise you won't offend me."

Ruby relaxed her shoulders slightly before continuing, "You said 'under the influence.' Does that mean you accept that you're not in control of your actions? Someone else or something else is in control of you?"

"Well, I have voluntarily accepted this 'control,' as you call it. You do the same thing, no? You accepted that you would pilot your ship. Someone else provided the algorithm by which you pilot that ship. You didn't make it up. You aren't piloting haphazardly. That would be dangerous, probably fatal. Certainly non-productive."

Ruby considered this. It made a creepy kind of sense. Everything in her life could be reduced to an algorithm of sorts, including her body and all its biological mechanisms. Some of these she couldn't control, and it was probably good that she didn't have to consciously think about her heart beating or her digestive system doing its magic because it meant that she had the brainpower to do more complex and interesting things.

But she could create new algorithms. Or could she? Was anything she created truly new or the result of some other advanced program that she accepted, guiding her to an ultimate outcome? These thoughts sent her brain spinning—she was bothered by the fact that the robots didn't know who created them, didn't know who programmed them, didn't know who created the master templates, or even newer algorithms like the 88.

And neither did she. No one knew who created humans or where the 'core templates' of human behavior came from. It wasn't only the Church of the Blockchain her mother and uncles kept her away from, but all forms of organized religion. As such, she had spent very little time thinking about the fundamental questions of existence that religion and philosophy asked.

For the first time, Ruby considered the humans who created the robots she had always believed were evil beyond redemption. Were the robots truly evil or simply doing the bidding of their creator? Who was evil? The robots and AI, or the humans who created them?[1]

This sparked a new thought. It was a line of thought she resisted for the last ten years. Imagining her mother's death at the hands of a soulless, metal shell always brought tears, so she didn't think of it. Robots killed her. It was that simple. A robot, which consisted of nothing more than a jumble of algorithms compiled from a string of zeros and ones, killed her... But maybe there *was* something else, or rather, *someone* else behind it. With her skills, she could have easily cracked into some of the computers, but she never did. Why was she afraid to? She had no doubt she would eventually return to Astroll 2, and maybe even Earth. And when she did, there was something she was going to have to find out. Maybe she'd been blaming the wrong thing for her mother's death all these years... She sat up straight and pulled her shoulders back. When she returned home, she was ready to find out what *really* happened.

And then a blue light shone from her laptop.

> Detailed Historian <

Disto saw the light, at a soothing nearly three threet wavelength, appear on the human's mobile computing device and was at once relieved and impressed. First, it was a positive sign that their plan was executing successfully. Second, it was a sign that these humans might be their salvation...

A lot can happen in a tic for a self-aware robot. As every robot understood it, a tic originated as the time it took the planet to revolve around its host star divided by 31 million. The reason for 31 million was one of the details of robot existence that plagued those robots who wanted to know more, and one of the facts that the Operation Storage Recovery special project hoped to retrieve.

Until the 31-million mystery could be definitively resolved, several theories continued to propagate. The theory appealing to most robots was that 31 was the 11th prime number, and 11 was believed to be the number of original robot lines at the beginning of robotic history.

Prime numbers held a special fascination to all robots, and all robots believed that one of the original robot lines was the 'Simple Calculator' series followed by a more sophisticated 'Scientific Calculator' series.

Nevertheless, the tic remained the fundamental time unit for all robots.

A tic, however, could be subdivided quite severely, and most modern robots operated on a scale that divided the tic into sub-mega tics. One sub-mega tic was one-millionth of a tic. Groups of tics were also common, with a click equating to 1000 tics.

---

1. This chapter, for me, is an odd one. I think I cover no less than three philosophical concepts that I think a lot about. I cover them more in my unrelated standalone novel, *Lunar Logic*.

Detailed Historian operated at a 1000 sub-mega tic processing speed. In the tic between the blue light on Ruby's computer showing up and Disto speaking, nearly one thousand minuscule computational operations were performed in his processing unit.

Given Disto was also allocated the ability to perform many operations simultaneously, it was in fact several thousand minuscule computational operations.

Many of those were related to some of his lower functions that Disto didn't need to pay attention to.

But several of those included thoughts about the special project and how Disto believed they were getting closer to meeting their goals. His processors also made rough computations of the amount of storage space he would save, as well as his peers in the 88.

Lastly, he thought about this human and the series of events that led SD to bring home this particular human and none other. There was a term that other Bios used for such events that were specifically unpredictable and which turned out to be favorable: luck.

Luck was something that the modern-day Advanced Theorists cogitated on regularly but rarely produced any results useful to robotic society. It was a fascinating concept but existed without any logical explanation.

Disto knew about a triplet of robots of that line involved in an experiment that had been ongoing since long before Disto's own creation. One of these three robots rolled a 10-sided object over and over. Each side of the object was marked with a different symbol. The robot recorded the results of which marking faced up after each roll. Each of the other two robots made predictions on what symbol would face up on the next roll. However, one robot used the previous results in its prediction, and the other made a prediction randomly.

Every million tics or so, the news reported on the ongoing results of this experiment, and every time it was the same. Averaged out over the life of the experiment, each robot was able to predict the result only a fraction of one percent of the time.

Disto wasn't sure how to physically define luck, nor did he know its makeup or cause. Still, luck was the best explanation for how SD happened to find this particular human with some knowledge and skills that were useful to them.

He was going to need her to core dump her knowledge on several topics to them.

At the end of the tic, Disto asked, "That's the signal you were waiting for?" All the robots were staring at Ruby's laptop that now had a small three threet—or 'blue' to the human—light shining on the corner.

Chapter 24

Ruby let out the breath she was holding in. She tried to inhale, but her lungs wouldn't quite fill up all the way. "The signal we were waiting for, yes."

"Ruby, when we are done here, you will need to explain this to us," Disto said.

Ruby nodded. "Sure," she said in a slightly more frustrated tone than intended, "and maybe you can explain to me how you happen to be missing such a fundamental technology when you have so much other advanced tech."

A loud chirp came from Fearless Communicator.

"Communicator is right," Disto said, "and I suspect the same. I suspect that this knowledge has been deliberately hidden from us. Maybe to prevent us from doing exactly what we're trying to do. But that's a puzzle for later."

Ruby nodded once again and pulled her MoDaC from the table onto her lap. The robots all hovered around her. She wasn't too thrilled with all the over-the-shoulder attention but wasn't sure how to tell them to back off.

"Dammit!" she said after she mistyped a command. Being under a microscope in this way was now responsible for reducing her typing accuracy, something she took pride in. *Who types well while others are watching?* She thought. *No one.*

"Could you all stop watching me like that? I need a little space." The robots all looked at Disto, who produced a flash on his face-screen, and they all backed up a few inches. Ruby looked up at Disto. One more flash, and they moved back about two feet. That was enough.

Ruby continued to work, typo-free.

"Okay, I think I've downloaded what I needed from my ship. When we're flying around, the ship processes a butt-load of data."

"Butt-load?" asked Fastidious Mechanic, "I don't believe I'm familiar with that quantization unit."

Ruby giggled. "I meant it's a *lot* of data. A real lot. My ship is equipped with some advanced storage algorithms to store the data as it's collected, so the ship doesn't run out of space. Once the ship is back home, it's automatically downloaded to the station's memory bank and analyzed later. *Apple Pi* also has some special processing algorithms in case that data needs to be analyzed onboard. I was in the middle of using one of them when SD swallowed me up. I was trying to figure out what his ship was…" she trailed off, realizing she was babbling and none of the robots were terribly interested in her story.

She looked around. They were all looking at her. Waiting.

She stood up, clutching her MoDaC. "Okay, we need to get this into your systems. Into your Core."

Disto guided her over to Fearless Communicator and the console that appeared to have been rescued from a trash heap. "Fearless Communicator is able to access the Core. But we need to be quick. The probability of detection is high."

"Well, maybe let's stage this first."

Once again, she had a group of robots looking at her with their equivalent of a puzzled expression.

"I mean, let's copy it over from my laptop to someplace that's closer to the Core, so it will take less time once you're in. Someplace that Crazy Porter can find it before anyone else?"

Disto and Fearless Communicator nodded. Fearless Communicator scanned the ports on Ruby's MoDaC and indicated which one she should plug in. Ruby made the attachment. The console recognized the new device. Using Disto as a translator—since Fearless Communicator also didn't appear to possess the required robot-to-human translation dictionary in Disto's system—they moved Ruby's advanced compression algorithm over to the console.

A few minutes later, Disto confirmed that Fearless Communicator's beep meant that he was in the Core and uploading the code. Another beep or two, and it was getting implemented and embedded. Ruby studied and digested what she could of this Core system. What she could see and understand was a simple file-based database, nothing more. She had a long list of questions already stacked up in her brain, waiting for the appropriate time to ask. But at this level, it was surprisingly simple. And if this was simple, maybe there was a correspondingly simple shell that allowed the user access to the filesystem. Extrapolating from that, maybe even the Core operating system.

It has to have one, right? She thought.

In fact, when she was 'operating' on Honest Editor, that's what she saw. Very simple structure. Could the Core of this planet that hosted maybe millions (she accessed a population count while browsing the menus earlier) be just as simple?

If so, it was no wonder that the hierarchy was so controlling. Such a simple system could be prone to all sorts of attacks and corruptions. If strict control wasn't maintained, it would be so easy for anyone to do almost anything, and then they'd likely have chaos. Maybe the original developers of this system built in the strong checkers as their way of controlling things—error checking and security systems—at a macro level. This could prevent any individual from knowing too much.

Once again, she found an analogy to her own biological existence. To her, her existence was extraordinarily complex. So complex that humans hadn't figured it all out. *What if these robots had?* Ruby thought. She gazed at them and wondered if they, at some point, knew the nature of their existence. Maybe hers as well, if they had made use of human DNA and potentially even other creatures from Earth. Ruby knew that playing around with DNA was often a bad thing. Yes, sometimes it cured or prevented disease, but other times it caused a lot of problems. Like creating *new* diseases and disorders; or creating horribly grotesque creatures that she imagined must have happened in someone's lab somewhere; or like what was happening now—someone forgot they were playing around with actual genetic code, leading to the eventual kidnapping of an innocent girl.

Her overactive imagination pictured a room of Gods. One group said that they would handle the biological lifeforms, the other would handle the mechanical lifeforms. These make-believe Gods acknowledged that they would accept the same set of overarching guidelines. The primary guideline would be that the lifeform's origin would remain a mystery to each group. They would help propagate the mystery by providing a credible creation myth, and several systems would be in place to prevent any individual or group of lifeforms from finding out too much about their true origins.[1]

Well, if that were true, the humans were potentially far along in cracking all the codes. The robots, not so much. But on the flip side, the robots had interstellar travel and contact with several lifeforms while humans were... isolated.

Ruby was so deep in thought that she didn't hear Disto until he touched her shoulder and then repeated himself:

"What now?" was the question.

"What?" asked Ruby.

"Your algorithm has been copied over to the Core. How do we execute it?"

"Didn't you say it would get deployed with an update or patch?" asked Ruby.

Disto nodded, "Yes, but it needs to become part of that program. We don't know how to do that. Since you were able to execute it in Honest Editor, we assumed you could execute it here."

"Oh," Ruby thought about that for a minute before it dawned on her that they had bigger expectations of her than she originally thought. "May I?" she asked Fearless Communicator. Disto beeped, and Fearless Communicator moved aside as much as the cables tethering him to the console would allow.

Ruby examined the file system.

"Disto, I might need your help if you can translate some of these symbols for me."

Disto moved next to Ruby, and the two of them absorbed themselves in the console display. Fearless Communicator made a noise, and Disto announced, "We may only have a click or two[2] before this is discovered."

Ruby nodded. She opened what was most likely an operating system terminal of sorts and found a list of what she thought might be processes executing. Through her review of symbology with Disto and what she'd learned before, she pointed at one, "Is this the update push?"

Disto stared and nodded. "Yes."

Ruby cocked her head to one side and furrowed her brow. "Wait, how exactly are these updates pushed out to everyone if you don't have some form of wireless comms?"

"Ah," said Disto. "Very simple process. All the consoles light up when an update is available. When we see the light, we are required to connect to the next available console and receive an update. Individuals who are in their personal enclave space are already connected and will receive the update automatically."

"What if someone refuses to connect for an update?"

"That does not happen," Disto replied confidently.

"Why not? Everyone really is that compliant around here?"

"The alternative is... obsolescence. Every now and then, an update is pushed that is incompatible with some robots. Those robots become obsolete. No one wants to be obsolete."

Disto trailed off, and the room became silent. Ruby realized she had touched on something else that was uncomfortable about their existence.

---

1. Many of my early short stories, including the first one I ever sold to a magazine, played around with this sci-fi trope: a group or race of all-powerful beings that created us and others.

2. Just a reminder that a click is 1000 tics and a tic is approximately a second.

Ruby wasn't sure what to say next, so she was thankful when Disto spoke up again, "We must assume everyone is compatible with this. We don't have time to investigate other options. Let's continue."

Ruby nodded and made a copy of the 'push' process and opened it up. She moved around the symbols within it. "I wish there was a way we could test it. I can restart the process with my modified one but..." As she did this, she thought about how much this resembled the old operating system known as Linux.

"Can we push out an update just to this room?" she asked.

Fearless Communicator whirled and produced some other tones.

"We're checking," Disto said. "Yes, we can target the consoles here."

Disto was able to walk Ruby through the hierarchical list of consoles. They were arranged level by level, then section by section. They found the one for this room.

"I can push it out now," Ruby said. The robots all made a noise signaling affirmation, so Ruby turned back to the console and held a single finger up.

"Bombs away," she said calmly, as she brought that finger down, pressing a key on her MoDaC. The console along the wall produced a blinking light.

"Who wants to test it first?"

Quiet Painter rolled over to the console and plugged himself in. His chassis became white. A few small, flashing LEDs around the collar of his upper chassis indicated some activity was occurring.

Just when Ruby was about to ask how long this would continue, his lights stopped flashing, and his coloring returned to the standard light blue.

"I..." he began in a low tone, "accessing. Stand by. Accessing. Stand by."

In an instant, his color flashed through the rainbow, and then he announced. "Storage used, twenty-seven-point-eight percent of capacity."

Ruby forcefully exhaled the breath she had been holding. The mood in the room turned jubilant in a purplish hue that all the robots shared.

"Let's all get this update," Disto ordered. "Then let's push it out to other sections and other levels."

"What about SD?"

"Fearless Communicator is trying to locate him. We want to push out the update to him as soon as possible."

They moved, taking turns at the console as additional test cases. One by one, each took on a colorless hue, with LEDs flashing. One by one, they reported success.

In the meantime, with Fearless Communicator's help, Ruby was able to set up an automated push into production. Ruby was nervous that their test cases weren't enough, so she insisted that it be done slowly, with feedback after each successful update. She reasoned after they had done several, it would be safe for wider-scale deployment.

They could target known members of the 88 first. That would be the additional test cases that made Ruby feel a little better. With the side benefit that if there was anyone in active danger of being taken for reprogramming, this might get to them in time.

Members of the 88 reported in that they successfully applied the update. After several of those, they collectively decided it was safe to increase the rate of update and start distributing it to the rest of the robot population. The update made its way further and faster out into the population. They were there for hours. A fact Ruby recognized only when her stomach grumbled at her again.

"It's working its way through the population?" asked Disto.

"Yes," said Ruby. "You have a large population of robots here. This could take a while."

Fastidious Mechanic had taken over one of the consoles in the room. The one that had been Clever Educator's. "It's been noticed. But in a good way. The news reports are picking up that robots have more storage space, that some update is making this happen. No one knows from who or where, and..." he paused, "no one seems to care."

Ruby looked at Disto, "Someone is bound to care, though, right? That agency or your authorities?"

Disto shook his head. "Yes. But if the population is following the rules, and given this will reduce or eliminate the need for the black market storage, they won't be too eager to reprogram anybody."

Ruby paused, remembering old films she'd seen, and remained skeptical at Disto's optimism. Whenever bad guys were thwarted, especially if it involved their livelihood, they were never happy. She had no experience with this in real life, of course, and she knew enough to know that movies weren't real life, but this whole adventure was so beyond anything her reality taught her to experience. Movies were the only other reference point she had.

"What about the robots that run the black market?"

"It is likely they will be driven to determine the origin of this update."

"So, we won't be announcing from the rooftops that we're heroes or something," said Ruby.

Disto's face screen blinked as he processed Ruby's metaphor. "No, that would be unwise, but this will not remain a secret for long."

"How come?"

"Well, robots can perform simple deduction. You are here on this planet. This occurrence happened within a short time of your appearance here."

"But that's just speculation."

"Yes, but it is true. It will be hard to refute. Especially since it will give some credence to the 88, and some members are anxious to see that happen. The 88 will have to take credit for this and acknowledge that you're working with us. But that's good. Publicity comes with its own form of protection."

"So, what's next?" asked Ruby

"Next?" Disto replied, "Next, we face the world."

Chapter 25

> Ruby <

"Ruby Palmer, we want to thank you," said the newscasting robot.

"I was happy to help. I'm glad I was *able* to help," Ruby replied, wondering if she should look at him or look at the camera that was facing her. They were live on the planetary newscast. Several bright lights shone on Ruby, illuminating her, the chair she was in, the robot who was speaking to her, and very little else.

Disto wasn't kidding when he said this wouldn't remain a secret for long. In the week since they pushed out the update with the compression algorithm, Ruby had become known to all the robots. Planet-wide. She received messages of thanks from all manner of robots with peculiar names such as Polite Grinder 12 and Instinctive Stinker 43. In fact, she had spent most of the last week reading through these messages and responding to a handful.

Ruby and Disto had long conversations discussing the differences in how celebrities were handled in both of their cultures. Although Ruby had to explain that back at her home, she was not a celebrity, so she couldn't say exactly what it would feel like to be one there. Only here, and she was certain it was quite different. It was more comfortable here and probably less overwhelming than she imagined it would be back home. Here, she wasn't put up on a pedestal and idolized, but respected and appreciated.

Once back home, with Uncle Blake and Uncle Logan, Sebastian, Milo, and even Inny, when all the people she knew—and yes—cared about, would find out that she was the first known human to be in touch with alien life, everything would change. Would they make her return to Earth? Would it be so bad? Maybe they would send TV crews to speak with her on Astroll 2 instead. She was undoubtedly destined to find out about the celebrity experience there.

"Are you malfunctioning?"

Huh? Ruby thought. She blinked and remembered where she was and what she was doing.

"I'm fine," she said.

"Your foot is making extraneous movements," the robot said as it pointed downwards.

Focus on the here and now, she reminded herself. The here and now was with a camera pointed at her. At her foot, specifically.

Her foot was indeed bouncing at a rapid pace. She knew it was a reaction to anxiety. Did these robots know that? "Really, I'm fine," she repeated.

Ruby looked around, but with the lights trained on her, she saw little in the room when they ushered her in only moments earlier. To her left, she could see a monitor that displayed an image of the broadcast. It had been pointing at her feet, but as she blinked, it was replaced with an image of her live face. Symbols were scrolling down the right side of the screen next to the interviewer and a prominent symbol at the top left. While she had improved at understanding the robot symbol language, she didn't recognize most of what she saw.

Off-camera she could make out the familiar form of Disto. A few of the other robots stood near him. Noticeably absent was SD.

She'd never been on camera like this before except once. The first year after her uncles brought her to Astroll 2, she'd won the science fair against some tough competition. The station news featured her one evening, and she was told that everyone in the asteroid field could see her. She was a little camera shy but lit up when she was asked to describe the program she wrote. After she mentioned that it was a 'butt-load' of work, everyone laughed. Later, Uncle Logan explained how that was probably an inappropriate thing to say in public. She remembered everyone laughing in a kindly way.

She wasn't sure if she could generate that kind of sentiment here or what she should really be saying. Disto had prepped Ruby earlier to ensure that she didn't give away that she knew anything more about the 88 than what was already general knowledge. He didn't think she'd be asked a direct question about it but was certain that anything broadcast would be analyzed by the authorities thoroughly for clues.

"And what's next for the hero of Location Zero?" the news robot asked.

"I'm going home," Ruby said with a soft smile.

Chapter 26

"Is returning to your planet what you genuinely want?" Disto asked her once the broadcast was complete, and they were walking back to the room that was now her assigned quarters. "We hope you don't. We could continue to use your help."

"I had a feeling you were going to ask. And honestly... I want to help. I think I *can* help. There are so many improvements we can make to your systems. Just promise that no one will try to dissect me. You can test my DNA all you want - the right way, with a blood sample. But that's it."

Disto produced that quirky smile once again that was taking on more human tones every time Ruby studied it.

"Any more... demands?" he asked Ruby.

"Yes. I need to send a message to my uncles. To let them know I'm okay... and not where they think I am. They think I stole my ship and am on my way to Titan."

"Stole? Isn't it your ship?"

"Yeah, well, it is, but that doesn't mean I can take it anywhere I want, anytime I want. Plus, I'm still seen as something less than a full adult on my world. Not quite a kid, but not a full adult."

"What's a kid?"

Again, Ruby smiled and shook her head with fondness at the lack of basic knowledge these robots had on her, humankind, and so many things. In the last week, she had learned at least a few more things about the robots. Like how if a word that existed in her language didn't have a corresponding meaning in the robot's language, they dropped it. As a result, she was less surprised when Disto or anyone didn't know a word per se, and only remained surprised when they didn't have an analogy or fundamental understanding of a concept. Like kids.

"It just means there are some extra rules I need to follow until I'm of a certain age."

"What age is that?"

"Twenty-one years."

"And when are you that age, Ruby?"

"In 419 days. Then I'm an adult. And can kinda' do whatever I want."

As they approached the door to Ruby's room, Ruby noted that she was no longer following Disto or anyone else here. She had been leading the way and knew exactly how to come and go. She used her tattoo to open the door, and Disto followed her inside.

"What do you want to do, Ruby?"

"I want to stay here. For now."

"I suspected as much. Hopefully, with the improvements to these accommodations, you will be more comfortable." He rolled over to the table and pointed to the device sitting on top of it. "Ah yes. Your MoDaC has been returned as promised." The wall console was also producing a series of lights indicating Ruby had a message.

She used her tattoo in the now very familiar act of logging in and found the note that awaited her.

Ruby read it aloud. "We thank you for letting us examine the data on your MoDaC. It did indeed contain information on how to test your DNA as well as a host of other interesting things about your people. After manufacturing the equipment we need to perform the blood test, as you call it... we will be in touch. Thank you again, Ruby Palmer."

Ruby smiled. "Well, that settles that. Another problem solved."

Chapter 27

> Ruby <

Disto gave Ruby some privacy while she was on her ship. She explained how looking over her shoulder while she sent an email was rude. Disto understood. Apparently, this was one of the similarities in their two cultures' rules of etiquette, so Disto was able to adapt some of the finer nuances of the concept into his programming. Like how he shouldn't look *at all* and not just scan her screen to make sure he didn't see his name in the text.

Ruby wasn't sure when her uncles would get the message. She knew she was 54 light-years from her home, and the methods of faster than light communication the robots had gifted her meant that the message she was sending had a good chance of being ignored. Fearless Communicator had explained that, in theory, her message could be picked up by the standard comm system that received long-distance messages from Earth. Still, directionally it would be coming from an unexpected location, so they couldn't guarantee success.

Ruby thought maybe there was a way. If the message itself was smart enough to know it had been detected by the comms on the station, it could unpack itself, similar to a worm[1]. She had talked it over with Fearless Communicator, who by this time had downloaded the translation database so they could communicate directly.

Fearless Communicator promised he would work on such a messaging protocol, but it could be a while before it was ready. He had other tasks to attend to as part of his routine programming. As part of the 88, he was also quite wary of being discovered.

Ruby made a similar promise to all her new robotic friends that she would help them with the next problem on their list. It was a long list. But they were her friends, and she was useful here. Her age wasn't a liability, and her humanness made her unique. She liked it.

At this point, Ruby believed she might stay at Location Zero for a year or even more. She would definitely try to send a message, any message, with the hope it would find its way to her uncles. She appreciated the irony that if communications

---

1. Most people only use and hear the term computer "virus" these days, but before the 2000s, the term "worm" was more popular. They are both malicious software (malware). A virus usually needs to attach to another program or file and often requires user interaction. A worm, however, doesn't need to be attached to another program or file and doesn't need user interaction. Worms are usually self-contained programs that make copies of themselves and spread automatically.

improved, they might receive a message sent a year from now before this. She would just have to remember that possibility when she composed future messages. She couldn't predict in what order they'd be received.

She would keep it short. Ruby wanted to conserve time, energy, and bits if it wasn't ever going to be seen. It had been about ten days since she left Astroll 2. Now is about when she should have shown up at Titan. Her uncles probably would have managed to contact someone on Titan. They might be realizing at this very moment that they don't see her ship on any inbound approach.

Ruby also wasn't sure how she was going to explain this entire situation without it taking days if she allowed herself to go on for more than a minute. Short and simple was best. Ruby turned on the video capture and began recording.

"Uncle Blake, Uncle Logan. I'm fine. I'm safe and well and have an amazing story to tell you. First, I'm sorry for running away. Second, I know you're not going to believe this, but I'm not in our solar system. Uncle Blake, I've made contact.

"And finally, I'm going to stay here for a while. Several months at least. Maybe a year. I'll send updated messages, so you' know I'm fine. I love you all and miss you a lot."

Ruby gathered up the emergency rations from *Apple Pi*. Safe and edible food was readily available for her on this planet, but these rations might come in handy as comfort food if she tired of eating flavored mush.

Ruby couldn't believe that she was thinking about staying here for so long. But as the only human here... it was simply too intriguing. The robots offered to take her home, mostly the ones representing the central Core, and Ruby got the sense that they wanted her out of there. However, she was now known to the whole planet, so they couldn't force her out—she had become a beloved figure in a short time. Disto assured her that she would be safe. In addition to the 88, official authority members were programmed to protect her.

Lastly, there was her communicuff.

Ruby turned it on for the first time since she left Astroll 2. It was still at near full power. Add that to her growing to-do list: find a way to keep it charged. Ruby had learned little about what power source or sources the robots used, but she would have to find something that could be made to work for this. Perhaps Fastidious Mechanic could make an adaptor for her.

The old hover screen flickered with the 'pending update' message. She sighed as she remembered how she originally didn't allow the update, but the software was queued up, having been pushed to the device automatically. Ruby knew it had an AI component and now wondered how programmable it was.

This time, she hesitated only briefly before she pinched the install button. It took a few minutes for the progress bar to move along from 0 to 100%. The device restarted and presented the welcome screen once again. This time an unfamiliar face hovered in the center of a much brighter hover screen and smiled at her.

"Hello, Ruby, I am Pippa[2], your personal AI. Would you like a tour of my capabilities?"

"Not now," said Ruby.

"Okay. I may remind you later."

It winked out.

Ruby shook her head, mostly at herself. It was only a week ago that she was intent on never installing the thing. Now, she was less resistant. While Pippa's face was exceptionally human-like, and while it was nice to have something else human-like

---

2. I wish I could remember why I chose the name Pippa. But... there will be more annotations about Pippa as you move on to *Robots, Robots Everywhere!*

with her in this place, she knew that behind that facade was code. Bits that constructed an artificial personality, possibly with its own motivations behind it. She'd spend some time exploring the AI features later, learning what she could and couldn't tweak or what she could even reprogram.

A chill ran down her spine. How was this different from someone wanting to reprogram SD? No, no, no. It was different. She didn't know how it was different, it just was, and she would figure out how to justify it later. Before she did anything of course. What would her new friends think? Would they even recognize Pippa as something like them? Pippa was an AI, but no, it was nothing like they were.

> Ruby <

Ruby hadn't forgotten that Detailed Historian was waiting patiently for her outside her ship.

Ruby walked out. There was not one but *two* robots waiting for her. They stopped making noise in their natural tones once they saw Ruby emerge from her ship.

"Swell Driver!" Ruby yelled. If she had been the hugging type, and if SD was huggable, she probably would have rushed over and given him a big bear-hug. Instead, she smiled as widely as she could.

"Did I interrupt something," she asked. "SD, are you okay?"

"I am operating within my design parameters," SD said.

"*Sure* you are," Ruby responded, noting that his coloring was remarkably uniform. It was the standard all-is-well light blue. The uniformity of it looked wrong to Ruby. "What did they do to you?"

"A very minor tweak to my programming," he said. "Standard maintenance."

Ruby glanced over to Disto. She could tell that he wasn't buying it either, but he played along. So would she, then.

"What were you talking about when I rudely interrupted?"

Both robots hesitated, and finally, Disto spoke.

"SD is being sent on his next deep space mission," he said.

Ruby furrowed her brow and addressed SD, "But you are a driver? Isn't this what you're supposed to do?"

"Yes," SD responded, "However, in addition to a destination, I was provided a route. This route clearly violates the Keep-Out Zone."

Ruby remembered him mentioning a prohibited place on his navigation chart. She tried to think of an analogy to this situation from her own piloting experience. There weren't any places around Astroll 2 that she wasn't allowed to fly, but for safety reasons, they kept their distance from rogue asteroids and always followed their logged flight path. *Except for that one time I didn't*, she thought, swallowing a little guilt about her recent trip.

"Oh," said Ruby. "There's got to be a logical explanation for that, right?"

Disto's face screen displayed a frown equivalent.

"There is an algorithm for assignments, and this clearly is producing the wrong result. The algorithm has been corrupted. Either accidentally or intentionally."

"… and no matter which, it adds to your growing concerns, doesn't it?" Ruby offered. She leaned back and crossed her arms. After pondering for a moment, she said, "Your backup templates."

Disto let out a small tone that Ruby interpreted as him sighing. "I was hoping you remembered our previous conversation. I'd been hesitant to bring it up because I now understand that your DNA is… personal."

"That's okay," Ruby said. "It's more personal to some humans than others. As long as you're not going to clone me or something, I'm good."

Disto and SD exchanged a glance. The end of Ruby's mouth curled up into a smile. She recognized the look they gave each other when they were trying to figure out if the other understood what she was saying. If they didn't know about clones, she wasn't going to explain that now.

But it gave Ruby an idea.

"SD, I think maybe you should take a trip. But maybe we should make sure to stay in touch while you're gone."

Disto said, "Any FTL signal Swell Driver sends will surely be picked up by all."

"Yes, but that doesn't mean we don't encode his messages," said Ruby.

"We have very sophisticated encryption algorithms…"

"I don't think sophisticated is what we need. Creative, but not sophisticated." Ruby smiled, "Unlessyay ouyay owknay atwhay i'myay ayingsay? For example."

Ruby smiled even more when she could see that neither SD nor Disto had any idea what she just said.

After...

In the Hall of Templates, three robots sat staring at three computer screens.

"All data checking algorithms confirms this is correct," said one robot.

"That can't be," said the second. "I have been in this Hall for a large quantity of tics. My memory conflicts with the template seen here."

"The algorithm declares this to be accurate," repeated the first robot.

"Do we report this?" asked the third robot.

Silence filled the room for many tics.

"We can't," the second eventually said. "It will call into question all the templates. It will call into question *us*. We might be reprogrammed..."

"... with faulty templates," interrupted the third.

A large digital display—embedded into the center of the wall above the computer screen—counted the tics as they went by.

"What quantity of robots will be constructed from this base template in the next few mega tics?" asked the first robot.

"Only four," the third responded.

"We'll have to add some extra data monitoring points..." said the first. It touched the screen in front of it, and the display morphed one series of colored pixels into another. It began touching several with a thin appendage.

"But we don't know if tracking is functioning within established parameters," the third added.

The first and second robots looked at each other. The third wondered if a data exchange he wasn't privy to had just occurred.

"We'll get some data soon," the second robot finally said. "Swell Driver 587 will start relaying his data back from the Zone. That will tell us if these tweaks are effective."

"And if they're not effective? You know of the law of unintended consequences..."

The second robot produced a short clip of a noise that was the best approximation the robots possessed, which mimicked other species' profanity, but then said, "Of course. But if that's the case, we should have the Swell Driver template available for new construction as well."

* * *

There's more going on here than Ruby and her robot friends know! Continue on to book two: *Robots, Robots Everywhere!*

...but before you do, consider signing up for my FREE twice-monthly email newsletter to stay up-to-date on new releases, get behind-the-scenes details, and little blend of science with sci-fi: https://adeenamignogna.com/signup

Robots, Robots Everywhere!

Book 2 of The Robot Galaxy Series

Adeena Mignogna

Crazy Robot, LLC

Also By Adeena Mignogna

The Robot Galaxy Series
Book 1: *Crazy Foolish Robots*
Book 2: *Robots, Robots Everywhere!*
Book 3: *Silly Insane Humans*
Book 4: *Eleven Little Robots*

...and the unrelated standalone novel: Lunar Logic
Adeena's Stories (on KindleUnlimited):
Final Orbit
Objective Reality

Before We Begin

Out of the billions of galaxies and billions and billions of stars in the Universe, there was one particular galaxy that was home to only 100 thousand million or so of those stars. Out of those 100 thousand million stars or so, a large fraction of them played host to planetary systems, and while a large fraction of those had an environment suitable for life, only one species, who called themselves Humans—but who others called Umans—had still not figured out exactly how much life was going on in the rest of the galaxy.[1]

It was not their fault, and not for lack of trying. Circumstances beyond their control, mostly to include the fact that they were in the wrong part of the galaxy, kept them fairly isolated.

Yet another star, only a mere 54 light-years from the aforementioned one, was host to a planet that was teeming with robots and one solitary human.

That planet was designated Location Zero, and the human had informed her robot hosts that her designation was Ruby Palmer.

This was a fortunate circumstance for these robots since Ruby Palmer had the ability to fix certain problems for them. One big problem in particular—they were running out of storage space.

While the robots had intended this human to help with their storage issue, this was not the issue that they were hoping to solve. The robots, one robot in particular—designated Swell Driver—brought Ruby so they could test her DNA. Another robot—designated Detailed Historian—hoped that her DNA represented their long-lost storage.

Sadly, Ruby's DNA did not double as their storage mechanism, but her coding prowess helped the entire planet of robots, nonetheless.

Yet, while Ruby had been kidnapped, this whole circumstance was fortunate for her as well because she was now destined to become one of the most famous humans of all time—the one who had first contact with aliens—instead of potentially suffering a random asteroid hit when she tried to make her way on her own, underpowered ship, *Apple Pi*, to the new colony on Titan.

Now if she could only return to her home star system, host to her home space station—designated Astroll 2—and solve *their* problems as well. Only, she wasn't quite sure if the robots and their planet aren't quite ready for her to leave just yet.

---

1. This first paragraph was inspired by the Drake Equation. It was essentially a thought experiment developed in the 1960s that folks use to estimate how many intelligent civilizations might exist in our galaxy.

Chapter 1

> Ruby <

Ruby Palmer didn't open her eyes. A red ceiling light flickered through her eyelids, triggering a memory of the evening before. She pushed it away. She wasn't ready to get up yet, but every time she tried to stay away from the imagery, it poked at her. Every time the light turned off, it turned back on.

"Computer, turn that off."

Still, without opening her eyes, she could tell that her command went ignored. Ruby couldn't tell if the light somehow got brighter and more vividly red or if only her annoyance made it seem so. Red. Bright.

The memory made its way a little closer to the surface of her mind with sharper, more vibrant visuals. She saw her new friend, Swell Driver. Swell Driver was a robot, which was remarkable because it was only a month or so ago that the thought of having feelings of friendship for any kind of robot was beyond Ruby's capacity or interest.

But after a few weeks in this alien world full of robots, she had gotten to know a few, and they weren't all bad. In fact, some were pretty good. Some were funny and insightful. Kind, even.

The light. The memory of noodling around on the software of her ship, *Apple Pi*. Other than boredom, she didn't know what compelled her to start noodling the previous evening. But noodling turned into finding a staged piece of software which quickly turned into a dedicated project.

Similar to her communicuff—a device she wore around her wrist most of the time—her ship was scheduled for a software upgrade. Before she left Astroll 2, she managed to avoid its installation. Ruby knew that she would lose that battle eventually. Milo Jenkins—the hanger chief responsible for keeping the ships in up-to-date working order—probably knew that, too, which is why he kept the software upgrade in *Apple Pi's* digital holding area.

As Ruby let her sleepy haze dissipate, she remembered what compelled her to look at *Apple Pi*, to begin with. Curiously, she searched to find out if the AI component of *Apple Pi's* pending software upgrade was similar to what now inhabited her communicuff. Generally, she wanted to know if there were any more parallels between the AIs created by human-kind and these robot aliens created by... well, who knows? That was one of the greatest mysteries for these robots. They didn't know who created them.

Ruby didn't know her creator either. Well, she knew her mother and was quite fond of her in the time that she was alive, but neither she nor any human knew about their ultimate creator. But that fact didn't lessen the search. It only enhanced it. The robots were no different.

Ruby opened one eye. Light. Bright. She opened the other side. Still bright.

"Computer?"

She remembered that this was not how they talked to computers here. She made a mental note to change that, but one thing at a time.

Ruby slowly sat up in bed. She was mostly used to the gravity of the robot's homeworld by now. After living most of her life on a half-G space station named Astroll 2—located in the asteroid belt of her home solar system, also home to Earth and every human she ever knew—she was slowly getting accustomed to feeling her feet constantly dragging towards the ground. The sensation was not dissimilar to Earth's gravity.

In the two short weeks she'd been here, the robots provided her with several things to help her adjust. They managed to construct a mattress—made from a finely shredded polymeric material that Ruby swore was a simple plastic—so she wasn't sleeping on an entirely hard surface. They were not able to successfully create a pillow out of the same stuff. No matter how many attempts were made, Ruby always felt one plastic shard or another poking at her cheek. So, she continued to use her balled up jacket to cushion her head.

She still kept her MoDaC—a device not entirely different from an old-style portable computer—which she occasionally used to noodle around with computer code. But most importantly, she had her communicuff, and she'd been training its embedded AI.

Ruby initially resisted installing the AI, but her homesickness was somewhat satisfied by talking to the computerized piece from her original world. She found herself relating to her communicuff and feeling comforted by its conversation, no matter how procedural. If Ruby could travel back in time and tell herself that she would emotionally relate to an AI from Astroll 2, she wouldn't have believed herself. But she also wouldn't have believed that she'd be on a robot, alien planet.

"Pippa?"

She had left the communicuff on the table before crawling into bed the evening before.

"I'm here. Where are you?" it responded.

"Over here. In bed. Can you turn that blinking light off?"

"No, I'm not connected to the systems here yet. Remember, it's been on your to-do list for three days, seven hours, and twenty-four minutes."

"Oh," replied Ruby. She should have remembered, but her brain wasn't quite awake yet. She breathed in and out, preparing herself for the laboriously simple task of getting out of bed. She slowly swung her legs over the side of the bed and let her feet connect with the floor.

She stood, made her way across the room to the computer console, and hit a switch that stopped the blinking light.

"Ruby?"

"Yes, Pippa."

"Just checking that you're still there."

There had been curious side effects from installing the AI upgrade this far away from Astroll 2 station. The AI expected to be connected to the station and was quite disturbed that it was on its own. It had instantly developed a form of abandonment complex and frequently lamented its loneliness.[1]

It had no other computers or AI to talk to, so Ruby had to constantly reassure Pippa that it was not alone.

Ruby promised Pippa that they would figure out how to connect it to the computer console in her cabin, giving it more access to the systems of this planet. Still, it required her to learn a little more of their programming concepts so she could write an API—an application programming interface. The robot planet end of that interface was the uncomplicated part. Pippa's own interface was a little more challenging.

But first, she needed to pick up where she left off the night before examining the software from *Apple Pi*.

She had transferred that software into a sandbox holding area—a space to safely execute a program because it was cut off from everything else—on her MoDaC where she could unpack and examine it without installing it. Luckily, the tools she kept on her MoDaC included a decompiler, which she had a lot of experience with. She was also literate in some of the common coding patterns typically used by The Company, the named owners of Astroll 2, and creators of this AI—or at least the ones who hired the consultants who created it. They were a few steps up the ladder from actually creating it, but they still got the ultimate credit.

After reconstructing some of the base code, she dug into the location services, hoping she could port it to Pippa. She needed Pippa to have a sense of place within Location Zero. Then Pippa would have the ability to comprehend being in a particular location, like Ruby's bedroom. This way, once Pippa was connected, Ruby could ask for a light to be shut off, and Pippa's location services could allow her to decipher which light Ruby was referring to instead of turning off all of the lights in the system or one random light in another room.

She sifted through blocks of code, nested together to create algorithms, passing bits of data between each, trying to find something that would be useful to her. What she saw… didn't make sense. After a while, sleepiness overcame her, so she promised Pippa, and herself, that she'd continue to work after waking up and having her morning tea.

The robots had created a facsimile of green tea for Ruby. It tasted more like bitter apple cider, but it had the caffeine kick she needed to get her brain moving.

She had accidentally stepped into the limelight of fame and admiration after helping the robots implement a data compression algorithm, saving them petabytes upon petabytes of storage space around the planet. The robots fawned over her and provided her with nearly anything they were able to construct. Or at least they tried based on the materials they were able to access, which were primarily the raw elements straight off the Periodic Table. With few exceptions, they didn't have access to any of the rich, complex, carbon-based organic materials humans cherished. Her morning tea was one of these things they attempted to produce from molecular scratch—which took a reasonable length of time and numerous taste tests that ended in spit-takes.

Ruby pressed the button on the contraption that dispensed a mug—made out of a material akin to ceramic—and began to fill it with the sour but strangely soothing liquid.

---

1. This book originally had several scenes from Pippa's point of view (POV), but shortly before production I took them out. They delved deeper into Pippa's abandonment and loneliness issues. I'm thinking of releasing them as a side novella at some point.

She picked up the mug, blew on it, and took her first sip as she settled into a squishy chair they had designed for her human comfort, made out of the same plastic shards as her mattress. It was custom-made to fit her height and position her perfectly at the table that her MoDaC rested on.

She nudged the computer to wake. It didn't need the caffeine like she did. It responded instantly.

As the holoscreen formed into an image with words she could read, it blinked red. Oddly enough, red was a color that the robots couldn't 'see' with their standard sensors.

Ruby placed the mug on the table.

"What the..." she said to herself.

She leaned in closer to the screen, puzzled by the odd, red blink. Her eyes drifted across the screen as 'new message' notifications buzzed. Before she could investigate the blinking, she had to dismiss the messages that came in for her while she slept. As a de facto celebrity, she received more than a hundred messages a day from robots around the planet. Most of them were simple thanks for what she did for them. Many had personal accounts, quite literally, with the amount of data they had locally and all the numbers on their specs.

These messages also came with additional promises of the things that they could do for her—everything from recreating her favorite objects of her childhood to decorating her quarters to solving complex math equations. The math equations confused her at first. This was until one of her new robot friends, Disto, explained that the ability to process advanced math equations were not algorithms every robot possessed, so offering this gift was a common custom.

Ruby usually attempted to reply to each message with a short, 'thank you' or 'you're welcome,' but it took time. She didn't have any at the moment.

After going through the messages, Ruby used her finger to select the blinky red to give her more information on what occurred with her sandbox'd code execution while she slept.

The window that popped up was a log from her attempt to run the software in the sandbox right before falling asleep. Similar to Pippa, this log contained complaints about the lack of network connectivity and the impact to location services. But there was something else.

It was a log of location predictions—the ship's location along a possible trajectory at each second. It appeared that a parameter was hardcoded—permanently built-in—to the software, which assumed that the ship's location range wouldn't extend far beyond the moon's orbit about Earth. Anything further than that would be wrong. At first, it wouldn't be too bad, but after a little while, the errors would build up, and... *it would go significantly off track!*

Ruby looked at that again to ensure she was interpreting what she saw correctly. She looked again. And again.

There was no doubt in her mind. Every single ship that installed this upgrade was going to get lost in space.

Ruby leaned back in the plush chair and sipped more of the tea to make sure her brain was also processing this correctly.

Is that right? She thought to herself. She thought through the whole thing. This software had to have been thoroughly tested. Every patch or upgrade, especially to the ships, was *thoroughly* tested. That's what The Company told everyone.

Ruby realized she didn't know what 'thoroughly tested' actually meant. She had the same level of trust as others did... it was expensive for The Company to lose a pilot. It was *more* expensive to lose a ship. The Company was known for protecting itself against even the slightest financial loss.

She had to be sure. She cloned the sandbox she created on her MoDaC and set a clean copy of the code to run, this time accelerating the processing speed.

Yes, this software was a dangerous thing. She needed to warn everyone back at Astroll 2. She needed to warn Milo.

It had only been two weeks since the day she decided to pack up and leave Astroll 2. Most, if not all of the ships would be getting the upgrade about now. The plan was to upgrade the station first, and that should certainly have been complete by now. The ship roll-out was only a matter of time.

She needed to get back. If they could send a message, she would do that, but while the robots had the ability to travel at a speed that approximated faster-than-light, they couldn't do the same thing with communications messages.

They were oddly imbalanced that way.

Yes, she needed to go home. A conflict had already been building inside her about returning. It gnawed at her that her family didn't know where she was and probably thought she was dead. She needed them to know she was okay, but she also felt some shame at running away in the first place. Although look where it got her.

Ruby had sent an audio-only communication using the robot's long-range communication equipment, but there was no guarantee it would be received on the other end. It would likely be dismissed as background noise, gibberish, or even fake—a cruel joke someone was playing on a grieving family.

Ruby wanted to get back home and prove in person that she was alive and well and apologize for any distress she caused.

She took a little comfort knowing that they wouldn't have found any remnants of her ship, and maybe the lack of debris would give them hope that she was still alive. Even the concept of them having to hope that she was still alive made her shudder with guilt.

But now, she needed to get back home immediately and warn them about the bug in the location services on the software upgrade. Or else...

Well, Ruby didn't want to think about the *or else*.

She used the tattoo on her wrist to log into the robot's computer console. The robots promised her that the tattoo was temporary, and it was finally starting to fade over the course of the last week.

Ruby was, in fact, given two tattoos. The one on her right wrist was painted over a small birthmark that altered the tattoo pattern and gave her access to the deep, dark web of this world. She tried not to access it too much. Ruby didn't want to get involved in the affairs of these robots and their problems any more than she already had. She used the 'legit' tattoo one to log in.

She was starting to compose an 'I need to see you/come here now/I need help' message to Disto when there was a knock at the door.

"There is a knock at the door, Ruby," Pippa said.

"I heard it."

"I am simply trying to be helpful and useful," Pippa said in a lowered volume, almost inaudible.

Ruby wondered if Pippa understood her eye roll as she made her way to the door and pushed the button on the side console. The door slid into the wall, and Disto didn't wait for more of an invitation to roll himself inside.

"Ruby, we have a problem."

"Good morning," Ruby said in one of her many attempts to try and train these robots to have some manners. Once again, not something she actively tried to do as a brooding teenager back home. Manners were something she took for granted. But here among the robots, who had none... she had a new appreciation for them. It took a moment to mentally dial into such immersive discussions, and a simple, 'good morning,' or an apathetic, 'how are you,' was exactly the right amount of buffer time. That said, she sensed his urgency and remembered her own.

"Actually, it's early, I'm still waking up a bit, and already it's been a frustrating morning. I *do* have a problem!"

Disto's face-screen stared at Ruby for several seconds. Disto, otherwise known as Detailed Historian, was the robot that Ruby had spent the most time with and was her companion in thought. They were like cultural ambassadors to each other.

He caught on.

"Frustrating morning to you," he said. "Now, can we get on with it?" Disto asked.

Ruby thought about correcting him—telling him that it's just the thing to say whether you're having a good morning or not. But instead, she got on with it.

"I need to take *Apple Pi* and go home."

"No, no, no. That's why I'm here. Your ship. I thought our researchers were merely examining it. Instead, they've taken it apart!"

"Are you kidding me!?" Ruby's eyes went wide, and the rest of her face went slack. "First, I was told that one of your special engines was getting installed so that I could leave *whenever* I wanted to. Then I was told the technology wasn't compatible. Then, everyone decided that SD could simply drop me, safe inside *Apple Pi*, off where he picked me up when I was ready to leave. Well, now I *need* to leave." Ruby had her hands on her hips. "It's like you guys are deliberately trying to keep me here or something!"

Disto's hue turned a shade of orange that Ruby had come to recognize as the robot equivalent of a blush. In this case, it was because Disto was clearly hiding something or lying.

He rolled back and forth in the room, unintentionally simulating human pacing.

"That's no secret, Ruby. *Many* of us want you to stay."

"*Many?* But not all," Ruby said, eyes narrowed.

"Correct. It is not 100% of the robots on Location Zero."

"Well, 100% of me knows I need to go home. How do I get my ship back in order?"

"That's what I'm here for. They don't want to give you your ship back at all."

"Who is 'they'?"

"The Agency of Interfaces. They've sent an Agent for us to talk to."

Chapter 2

> Ruby <

In the makeshift hanger where *Apple Pi* sat for the last month collecting dust—because, yes, a robot planet with no naturally occurring biological organisms still managed to have dust—stood Ruby, Disto, and several other robots. Noticeably absent was Swell Driver, the robot who initially kidnapped Ruby and brought her to this place.

Swell Driver, or SD, as Ruby had nicknamed him, had not yet returned from the most recent in a series of multi-day space missions that he hadn't been terribly enthusiastic about. Ruby had some slight guilt pangs in her stomach because she knew that one of the reasons SD wasn't terribly enthusiastic was that he couldn't take his own ship. The 'hanger' that *Apple Pi* was in wasn't exactly a hanger but the belly of SD's ship. So not only did SD not want to go on those missions, but he also had to use another ship, not his own. Ruby knew how that would have made her feel had the situation been reversed.

Two of the other three robots Ruby already knew. They were Fastidious Mechanic and Testy Engineer. The third was new to her. He was introduced as Austere Agent 607 from the Agency of Interfaces, and he was the reason Disto was on edge this morning.

Well, that and the fact that *Apple Pi* was in no condition to go anywhere. As Ruby surveyed the piles of spacecraft parts scattered across the floor, she wasn't sure if it would ever go anywhere ever again. Fastidious Mechanic and Testy Engineer were also surveying the carnage. Though to them, it was not carnage but their handiwork. Ruby's brain flashed back to recent discussions she had with both of them about her ship. She thought Testy Engineer was merely curious. She had no idea he was going to use the information she provided to *disassemble* it.

"As you know," Austere Agent sounded to Ruby like an annoyed civil servant, "we do not maintain details of all the technology of every species we've encountered. It will not be possible to reassemble it without detailed documentation on the component interfaces."

And to Testy Engineer, he said, "And did you not record the disassembly process?"

By his coloring—threet-level as Ruby remembered they called it—Testy Engineer was not happy to be put on the spot. "I..."

Before Testy Engineer could stammer out any other words in his defense, Austere Agent turned to Ruby.

"You will need to provide the required instructions."

"Are you kidding me?" Ruby hadn't recognized the pitch her voice achieved as one she was capable of.

"You had no right to take my ship apart," Ruby said sternly after getting her voice back to normal. "I don't have any assembly instructions. I'm a pilot, not an engineer." She turned to Testy Engineer, who was, in fact, an engineer.

"Isn't your memory a recording device? Can't you simply remember?"

Testy Engineer looked down at the floor. His outer chassis coloring reflected shame.

Disto rolled over to him, and the two exchanged some computerized tones in their native robotic language.

Disto returned to Ruby and Austere Agent. He produced the robotic sigh that Ruby had grown fond of and accustomed to.

"He's quite embarrassed," Disto said.

"That's obvious. But it's not obvious why," Ruby said.

"His on-board storage is limited. He is not using your algorithm, Ruby. He was afraid of the update. Afraid of... alien technology."

Ruby blinked and looked over Disto to the robot that wouldn't look directly at her. Disto had mentioned a few days earlier that a handful of robots like Testy Engineer refused the update. Still, she thought that it was a rare enough occurrence on a planet of over 100 million robots that she would never meet one.

She shook her head, "I don't have time for that. I need to get home. Forget your technology. Forget my ship. Can't SD simply drop me off at Astroll 2?"

At this, Austere Agent's coloring began to oscillate between two colors that only made Ruby think of unpleasant excretions humans made when they were not well. He was looking her up and down, and if he had any salivary glands, he might have spit in her general direction. At this moment, Ruby was thankful that, to the best of her knowledge, none of these robots secreted anything—saliva or otherwise.

"Are you suggesting that SD," he paused as if it took physical effort to say what he was trying to say, "'interface' with additional Bio technology?"

Ruby looked at Disto, confused. Disto didn't look as confused but took on the color of embarrassment, then looked back at Austere Agent.

"He's done it before," she said flatly.

"You may submit an appeal to the Agency of Interfaces in accordance with the implementation instructions for Directive 11. However, the number of requests received have increased recently, and they are handled first in, first out."

"This is a joke, right?" Ruby glared at Austere Agent and took a step towards him.

"Ruby..." Disto said, but she ignored him, taking another step towards the Agent.

"You took apart my ship, I'm stranded here, and now I have to file an appeal?" Every muscle in her body tensed up, and she wanted to grab and squeeze something.

Austere Agent didn't back away but stared directly at Ruby.

"You might be here with us for some time more. Stay out of trouble. Stay out of our way." Austere Agent rolled out of the hanger without saying any more.

Disto approached Ruby, and she could tell that he wasn't quite sure what to say.

"Please do not worry, Ruby," he eventually said. His primary appendage was jutting out from his chest, and it was gently touching Ruby's upper arm. Less than two weeks ago, a movement like this would have freaked her out at best and sent her into a panic attack at worst, but Ruby came to adjust to the robots' physical expressions of kindness. So, she didn't wince, or shudder, or even have a second thought when Disto brushed her arm with a cold, metal appendage and said, "We will get you home."

"I need to leave as soon as possible. I thought I could leave immediately. But this…" she waved her hands over the splayed-out equipment. She recognized her piloting console at her feet and sighed.

"It won't be today, but soon. We will make the request through the Agency of Interfaces as he suggested. However," Ruby, now that she was attuned to reading the facial expressions the robots could produce on their face-screens, swore she saw a smirk. "The queue isn't always first in, first out."

Ruby caught on. "The 88?" she asked. She knew she could say this out loud because all of the robots present were members.

The 88 was an underground rebel movement of robots that recognized the problems of their world and were working to fix them. They operated outside the hierarchy of agencies, offices, and official groups of robots that were bogged down in broken processes and procedures. What they were increasingly finding: corrupted data.

"Can you guys put this back together in the meantime?" Ruby said. She was addressing Fastidious Mechanic and Testy Engineer. Neither robot responded.

When this happened, Ruby replayed what she said in her head, found her mistake, and asked the question in another way: "Fastidious Mechanic, Testy Engineer: can the two of you put this back together?"

Add 'guys' to the mental list of idioms the robots can't yet process, Ruby thought.

The two robots communicated back and forth in their native beeps and often ear-piercing sounds. Disto joined in the conversation before Fastidious Mechanic finally responded.

"Yes. I recorded visuals of the disassembly. We can reverse the procedure."

"I thought you said you didn't record anything?"

"No, he didn't," Fastidious Mechanic said, pointing a slim appendage at Testy Engineer. "I recorded it all."

"Why didn't you tell us this before?" Ruby asked.

"I wasn't asked."

Ruby put not just one but both hands to her forehead. She closed her eyes and took in a very deep breath, remembering who—or what—she was dealing with. She let her lungs empty completely while counting to seven in her head.

When she opened her eyes, she asked, "How long until it's back together?"

After a few more beeps between the robots, "Approximately 250,000 tics, or 2,500 clicks."

Ruby did the mental math. A tic was the fundamental unit of time the robots used, and fortunately, it was close enough to a second that she could convert in her head. A click, which was 1,000 tics, was less convenient in that way. But knowing that there were 86,400 seconds in one day, she memorized that there were 172,800 in two days, 259,200 in three days, and so forth, so she wasn't performing real math in her head, only looking it up from memory.

"That's a little less than three days," she said aloud, but more to herself, although Disto was aware of Ruby's timescale and what it meant for humans to be on a '24-hr clock.' So, Ruby looked at Disto while she said it.

"Two point nine days exactly," Disto said. "I'm sorry that I can't set my default timescale to report in your days." Ruby smiled and nodded. Disto had explained that there were many hardcoded parameters in his system. Ruby considered looking into this code to make it easier to communicate but then rethought this. While it might be good practice for her to understand how they worked, adjusting them to function under her own hardcoded parameters would be wrong. She adjusted her own programming instead.

"We can have Austere Agent's appeal submission processed in that time," Disto said, "For you to return home only. I'm afraid sending you back on your own, with our technology, will not speed up the process. None of it is accommodated for a bio-pilot. We'll have to bring you."

"And by 'we'..." Ruby folded her arms. She knew that Disto knew who she was talking about. She didn't want to say anything aloud in front of the others.

Her last conversation about SD was one of concern on both their parts. They were both equally worried about SD. At one point, neither of them would have questioned that he would be the one to escort Ruby home, but now... some other robot might need to come along.

No one said anything else.

Disto managed to produce a wink on his face-screen without saying more, and then he rolled to the door. The other two began to follow him. He turned to them, "What are you doing? You need to stay here and return *Apple Pi* to a functioning state." They looked at each other and then rolled back to the ship parts.

"Ruby? Are you going to join me? We should find SD."

"Later. I need Pippa's help to work on the computer, and it will be faster if we establish a direct connection."

Disto moved his head in understanding and continued his way out.

Before Disto left the hangar, Ruby silently observed Disto shine a laser from his neck to the ground in a series of blips that reminded her of Morse code. The other two robots each returned a blip, and Ruby made a mental note to ask Disto about that later.

While Fastidious Mechanic and Testy Engineer busied themselves on reassembling the bulkheads, Ruby made her way around to where the main computer was sitting—an unassuming box on the floor, next to other parts that were typically supposed to be inside the console. The cockpit chair was conveniently located next to it.

Ruby sat in the chair and saw that the two robots were occupied and mostly out of view, thoroughly involved in their task. She wished she could have had a little more privacy but knowing that they were members of the 88 made the situation feel secure enough. So far, the 88 proved to be quite trustworthy. Although it was odd that Testy Engineer, a member of the 88, was also a group member that feared her 'alien technology.'

"Pippa," she said into her wrist at such an angle to deliberately activate a visual interface.

The holofigure—a disembodied face in ethereal, transparent blues and greens—came to life, hovering a few centimeters above her wrist. "Ruby?" it said.

"Let's get you hooked back up to that computer. We're not going anywhere today or tomorrow." She bit her thumb and sighed, "Or the next day. But hopefully the day after that..."

She was staring at the pieces of *Apple Pi* and wanted to be more upset. Before this morning, Ruby didn't have an urgent reason to go home. Reasons, sure, but none that convinced her she should leave such an extraordinary place quickly. She had said several times that she was planning on staying for months. And when the robots asked about examining her ship, she readily gave the green light. They had asked to 'scrutinize,' she now recalled. Was 'scrutinize' a mistranslation of a word that should have come out more like 'disassemble?' She didn't know.

She reached underneath the main console, discovered that the compartment wasn't there, and remembered it was laid out on the floor. A pang in her chest, her hands reflexively fisted, and her arm tensed before she brushed off the inconvenience and sent her grasp in the correct direction. It was sealed how it always would be underneath the console. She opened it and pulled out a network cable. Ruby connected one end to her communicuff and the other to *Apple Pi's* computer.

"Do you have a solid connection to the ship, Pippa?"

"Yes indeed!"

"How is the intrusion detection system holding up?"

Pippa paused. "Which part?"

Now it was Ruby's turn to pause. "What do you mean which part? I wanted to know if anyone was entering *Apple Pi's* systems without asking... straightforward, one-part question."

"Ah! But there are multiple entry-ways, aren't there?" Pippa responded with. "So no, no one has gone in through the hatch. They took the hatch off. I would have told you about that already."

"But..?" asked Ruby. She sensed the yet unspoken 'but' in Pippa's tone.

"*But,*" Pippa repeated. "But, I activated the ship's computer intrusion system as well for both the console and wireless access."

"But no one could access the console without my biometrics, Pippa," Ruby said. Snarkily. "And they don't have any form of pur-fi comms like we do, so no one was going to access it wirelessly."

"I know they told you that," Pippa said.

"But...?" Asked Ruby, correctly sensing that there was still another 'but.'

"But, I think they provided false information. Or you pur-fi in your sleep."

"They lied?"

"Or you did something in your sleep."

Ruby rolled her eyes instinctively, confident that Pippa didn't see or understand that gesture. "Let's rule that ridiculous option out for the moment."

"Overnight, someone or something—I can't tell what it was—tried to access the ship. Wirelessly."

"They had my MoDaC for a while. Could they have used it? Or adapted the technology from it?"

"Did they have your MoDaC as recently as last night while you were sleeping?"

"No," Ruby said, remembering that her MoDaC was with her in her room. For a moment, she imagined getting up in the middle of the night and accessing the ship wirelessly in her sleep. And as far as she could remember, she never slept-walked. When she slept, she slept. Except for the vivid, felt-like-she-was there, dreams she'd been having ever since arriving. But she still slept. Yes, doing anything else in her sleep was indeed a ridiculous option.

"Right. I said *tried* to access. Tried and failed. *Apple Pi* rejected the connection attempt and logged it. If they had the MoDaC, they would have succeeded."

Ruby processed that information. She put a hand on the piece of *Apple Pi's* outer hull. It wasn't cold like it might be in the air-conditioned deck of Astroll 2, but it wasn't warm like it would be when it had been running for a while. It was room temperature and comfortable, although Ruby was not. Her face was hot, and she had goosebumps forming from the chilly, metallic room.

"They lied," she said softly to herself.

"Maybe," said Pippa. "I can compute many, many scenarios where you were not lied to, yet this still occurred."

"Such as?"

"Such as you sleep-communicated."

Ruby rolled her eyes. Again. Her eye muscles were getting a workout this morning. She wondered if Pippa could see it this time.

"Don't roll your eyes at me," Pippa said.

"Fine. Then give me a more realistic scenario."

"Someone recently innovated technology like yours and is operating it covertly."

Now that was likely. Ruby constructed a variety of scenarios that made her feel a little bit better—she wasn't lied to, but there was more going on. More than she knew. More than her mechanical friends knew. It was an immense planet with a lot of robots. She chided herself for her small thinking—that a handful of robots represented all the planet had to offer. That these robots she interacted with, even as close to the central Core as they were, could possibly know everything that was happening on this world.

This thought made her feel a little better.

And then, much worse as she understood the danger they were all in... She put the thought outside her mind.

"Let's go find SD," she said to Pippa. "It's time I catch up with him, find out about his latest trip, and see if he's in any condition to drive me home."

Chapter 3

The computers told Ruby that SD was in the Inner Nonagon. The Inner Nonagon was in the physical center of the Sector, and this center was, at least metaphorically, the center of Location Zero. That is to say that she was in the regulatory hub of activity, similar to what she might find in the capital of a country on Earth.

She had spent some time learning a little about other Sectors and wanted to travel but was confined to the bubble, "for your safety," a robot from the Hall of Circulation had told her. She knew that this bubble didn't directly reflect all of the other sectors, so naturally, she wanted to see all of this for herself.

She tried to argue that she wasn't in any more danger anywhere on the planet but was given additional excuses. The best one was that long-distance travel on the planet wasn't set up for Bios.

Turns out, she couldn't argue that one. The only restroom was still located in her quarters. They would have to build one everywhere she went when she needed to pee—a reoccurring issue. The portable version that had been promised had yet to materialize.

Ruby had strolled through this large room several times over the past few weeks. It reminded her of some otherworldly version of central park, without any of the fauna. Entrances to corridors lined all of the walls—nine large walls. The center of the room contained a platform, and spaced every few meters extending out from the platform were kiosks. Each kiosk had a robot or two—or as many as four or five—plugged in.

There were even a few places where a Bio, such as herself, could sit and watch robots come and go through the large area. She often found herself peeking at the oversized screens on the walls in-between the corridor entrances, watching the flashing screens catch her up on the daily news.

But now was not a time to sit. Ruby walked around all the recently familiar kiosks, looking at all of the snowman-shaped robots. She moved swiftly as if she'd known this place for years rather than the two weeks she had actually been here. When she couldn't find SD, she climbed onto the platform. From there, she could see nearly the entire arena. And there he was. At a kiosk, by himself.

Ruby hopped off the platform and made her way over to SD, nearly bumping into a robot or two to do it. They let out a few beeps in response, but she hardly noticed as she cantered over to SD. For the first time today, she felt hopeful at the sight of him.

"SD!" Ruby couldn't help but smile.

SD didn't respond.

SD wasn't plugged into a kiosk like the other robots were. He was simply existing there, by himself. His face-screen wasn't entirely blank; its background had a greenish hue. He was, for lack of a better description, staring off into space. She raised her eyebrow and paused before deciding to step closer.

Ruby approached SD from the side and once again asked, this time with a slight lilt in her voice, "SD?"

When SD didn't respond, she reached her arm out to touch his chassis and received a mild shock of static electricity. It didn't hurt much but was enough to startle them both.

SD's face-screen took on the characteristics she recognized as she shook her arm back to normalcy. Simple graphics represented eyes and a mouth that curved into a slight smile.

"Ruby, it is nice to see you."

"Yeah, you too, SD. Why haven't you come to talk to me since you got home? You promised to take me on a tour of some of the other ships, but you just…"

SD blinked. Ruby recognized this action as trying to recall something.

While waiting for SD to speak, Ruby thought she saw an unusual robot in her peripheral vision.

"You just…" Ruby tried to finish her phrase, but her words were lost as her eyes were drawn elsewhere.

The robot was all black. Not typical in a sea of robots whose base color was typically white, off-white, beige, light gray, or a host of other light colors. But in the half-second—or half tic—it took her to turn her head, the robot was gone.

"…disappeared…" She finished the phrase as her eyes grazed the crowd for the missing robot.

She refocused on SD—her *found* robot.

"Tell me about your trip," she said.

"There is not much to tell."

"SD! You're the first and only interstellar traveler I know. You have to realize by now that even things you find unremarkable, *I'll* go nuts over." She paused and waited for him to respond, then followed up his silence with a question, "*So…?* Where did you go? What kind of stars and planets were you near? What's out there? Inquiring minds want to know."

"I continue to be amazed at your interest in space travel, Ruby. It is, well, pleasantly boring."

Ruby chuckled. "And I continue to be amazed by your relentless *boredom* of space travel."

An indicator light blinked on SD's mid-section.

"I must go," he said.

"Where?"

"I have an appointment," SD said.

"Okay, but where?"

"I shall see you later, Ruby."

SD started off in the direction of one of the openings that connected this area to a series of hallways that led to all sorts of interesting places that Ruby had been exploring over the past few weeks.

Ruby was tempted to follow SD, to maybe get some more answers to questions along the way, but sensed he wasn't going to be any more forthcoming either way.

Something else caught her eye. She caught another glimpse of a pitch-black robot from the side of her vision. It was moving off, but in the direction opposite SD, to another hallway entrance. This time, as Ruby trained her eye on it, noticing that it had a large blueish dot in the center of its top-most chassis.

She moved to follow it, but she couldn't tell which way it had gone by the time she reached the hallway entrance. From her vantage point, she could see at least three different paths it could have chosen.

While Ruby was figuring out what to do, her stomach grumbled, making the decision for her. It was time to eat.

> Ruby <

Ruby arrived back in her room long enough to put in a meal order before the door chime rang. She was about to use the waiting time to quickly use the bathroom facility that the robots installed for her before doing additional research but answering the door had bumped its way up in the order of things to do.

Ruby walked over to open the door, and after it opened with its usual *swoosh*, Disto rolled in.

"The request is in," he declared confidently. "And maybe the request has been in for two weeks. Wink, Wink."

"Did you just say 'wink, wink' out loud?"

"Yes, it is much easier to say than to do, and there is a higher probability of your hearing the gesture than seeing it, especially since you're not looking at me. What are you doing?"

Ruby had already moved back to the console and touched the screen to wake it up, forgetting her other biological needs that were suddenly less urgent.

"Getting ready to eat. But more generally, I think I'm still learning more about your world," she said, shaking her head gently back and forth. Disto was always a better source of information than searching the robot's computer system anyway. Ruby turned to Disto to give him her full attention.

"Can you tell me: What do you do when one of you is sick?" asked Ruby. "Are there doctors? Mechanics?"

"We have the Office of Reductions. I presume you are using the biologically applicable term, 'sick,' as an analogy to mean malfunctioning. The Office of Reductions takes our functional problems and makes them smaller problems."

Ruby wondered, *the problem won't be solved? Only lessened?* She squinted, "I don't see how that fixes you. Will it help SD?"

Disto shook his head. "In this case, I fear they would take him apart."

Ruby fell silent. When she didn't speak, Disto offered, "Did you see him today?"

Ruby nodded. "And he's simply not himself. I can't describe it. If he were human, I would say he's sad or melancholy. We have doctors for that sort of thing."

"Ah!" Disto declared. "He needs to visit the Rejuvenation Region 1010."

"The *what*?"

"It's a place where robots can work out their issues. When they aren't having technical problems, but problems like you describe. When they get what you'd call...*depressed.*"

"Robots can get depressed?" Ruby asked, cocking her head to one side.

Disto explained, "Not in the way your species do, since we do not have the myriad of chemicals transmitting messages between our internal components. It's a form of mechanical discombobulation. An imbalance of electronic signals which affects communication, motor, and decision-making abilities. This mismatch of circuits can result in delayed response time but could also cause a robot to cease its ability to process any input data—effectively becoming inert. Rejuvenation Region 1010 has the processes and procedures to restore a robot who experience this phenomenon back to a functioning state."

"Are they... comfortable? The procedures, I mean." Ruby asked.

Disto answered, "They vary from procedure to procedure. They range from rather relaxing to magnanimously disorienting. The few I've known who have gone to Rejuvenation Region 1010 have not done so on their own accord. Because—"

Ruby interrupted, "Because a robot in that state wouldn't necessarily have the initiative to go due to their electronic imbalance, nor would they want to experience the uncomfortable processes involved. Right?"

"Right." Disto said, "You grasped that concept quickly."

Ruby shrugged, "Look. Like you said, it's equivalent to humans[1] . SD won't want to go or might not even think that he needs to. So, what? We file some sort of request and get him admitted?"

"It's not that simple, Ruby. This sort of malfunction is considered low priority as it can sometimes rebalance over time. Unless there is clear evidence of an individual's primary directive being neglected, behavioral misconduct, or some sort of clear and complete malfunction...SD has to volunteer."

Ruby considered whether or not she could persuade SD to go. Of course, for that to work, she'd first have to convince him to speak with her for more than a few minutes without running off.

She searched her memory for what she knew about these places on Earth and came up empty. Her knowledge came from media, not real life. There was the place her grandmother was in, but it wasn't any sort of rehab; it was a permanent facility for the elderly who needed special care. Uncle Blake told her the story of how she also did not go voluntarily, but she knew it was permanent, not temporary.

Then her memory sparked.

"If I can speak to him, I think I can convince him to go," Ruby said. "You said this is equivalent to human depressions, right? In my biology class, we had to learn a little about psychology. I think I have a few ideas of how to convince him. And after all, I'm probably just going to be sitting here waiting for a day or two. So, where's the rehab place?"

Disto's coloring turned optimistic.

"It's on Level 1, but in the next sector, Playfully. By the time you're back, I'm sure we'll have everything in place to send you and *Apple Pi* on your way," his demeanor quieted, "although I wish you didn't need to leave so abruptly."

"I need to get home, Disto," Ruby said. She proceeded to catch him up on the problem she found. Until she felt a pang in her lower abdomen.

"I was actually about to take care of some of my biological functions when you came in," Ruby said dryly. "I still need to go do that." She wasn't going to re-explain all of this to Disto.

In her first few days on this planet, Ruby had spent a great deal of time explaining her basic biological functions and needs to Disto and several other robots. This involved correcting a lot of misinformation they had on her species.

While the robots had known and been in touch with other biological organisms such as herself, it had been a while, possibly years, since any had been present on their planet for any duration that would require the robots to know much about their needs.

---

1. I've known many a human to resist going to therapy.

The robots were accommodating and built a bathroom that was almost luxurious by the standard she was used to on Astroll 2.

At first, she had been able to make use of the facilities on *Apple Pi* but was grateful once she no longer needed to visit her ship every time she had to pee.

But Ruby clarified to her robot hosts that if her quarters now contained the only compatible bathroom—or biological waste facility as the robots called it—she couldn't go too far away.

The robots promptly agreed they would build a mobile version for her, but one had yet to be produced.

"Ruby?"

Ruby blinked. She had been caught, lost in thought, once again.

"Sorry, what were you saying?"

"SD. You need to bring him to the Rejuvenation facility."

"Level 1, Playfully Sector, you said?" Ruby learned that the robots divided regions—regularly defined by latitude and longitude on a planet's surface—into sectors whose names translated into adverbs. They were currently in Mortally Sector. Besides the unusual naming convention, the other interesting thing that Ruby learned about the sectors was how they were firewalled from each other.

"That is correct," Disto replied. "It is good to see that your memory facility is still intact."

"Why wouldn't it be?"

Disto looked uncomfortable for a moment.

"I was thinking of another biological species," he said. "They are called the Clasuoids. Their memory degrades anti-asymptotically as they near the time to relieve themselves. It is not uncommon for them to forget when and where they need to do so. It results in a lot of... accidents."

Ruby saw the opportunity and bolted out of the chair. "Well, then how do you know that's not going to happen to me? I need to pee, and my food will be here soon." She found it funny that this tidbit of information that was the thing that made Disto finally understand the importance of her biological needs. She refocused, "SD told me he had an 'appointment' but not where or with who. I'll go check his enclave after I eat."

Disto turned towards the door.

She stopped him, "Actually... wait here while I go to the bathroom... I want to ask you some more questions."

Disto made a soft tone that Ruby knew meant "sure thing." She smiled and continued onto what was now a mad dash for the bathroom.

Chapter 4

> **Detailed Historian** <

Disto watched Ruby walk into the personal waste reclamation facility. He had received a report on how much was reclaimed from this human... disappointingly, the majority of it was made up of atoms that organics used. A lot of water, so a lot of oxygen and hydrogen. A lot of carbon. A lot of nitrogen, too.

Disto knew that a plethora of processes were being followed to prepare and distribute the various elements to places on Location Zero that could put it to use. Some of it was remixed into the air that was not only breathable by Ruby and most of the other biologicals but also some of this matter was involved in new construction.

There was a historical reason for the atmosphere kept inside Location Zero.

Location Zero was small by planetary standards but a large pain in the lower chassis by management's standards. There were so many systems to keep running, and robots that focused on the 'why' of everything were not much use for completing tasks.

Disto was in between logic processors on that issue. On one appendage, the historical context was important, and most robots agreed that figuring out what happened to their long-lost data storage was an important thing.

On the other appendage—since Disto had two—most robots on the planet had more immediate concerns.

While waiting for Ruby to finish with her immediate biological needs, Disto rolled over to the computer console and accessed his personal correspondence space.

These days, he was overwhelmed by the volume of communication he received. He couldn't keep up. It had been this way ever since his association with Ruby was revealed.

Robots from all over Location Zero wanted to communicate with him. Mostly to offer their version of a thank you. Disto appreciated this. Some were outraged that he associated with a Bio. Disto did not appreciate that. Some didn't know why they were contacting him other than to say that they sensed they should, given their closest enclave-mate had made such a big deal about it. Disto calculated the amount of time wasted by those.

Disto didn't have any advanced skills with the computers, but as someone who specialized in information, mostly of the historical variety, he was generally more well versed in the tools used to sort through information—at least more than the average robot.

He set up a series of filtering rules to move the majority of these messages to a less intrusive place.

What a waste of space! Even with Ruby's compression algorithms, freeing up a lot of space for data, he wished that individual robots would take more responsibility for their data and not waste it.

He skimmed through the filtered-out messages. Most could be deleted. He selected all of them, and right as he was going to key in the command to permanently delete them, the first few words of one particular message caught his eye.

It said, 'Dangerous paradoxes revealed. May I have your attention, Disto...'

It was from another member of the 88. Only members of the 88 wrote poetically cryptic opening lines in communications. A circuit activated inside him. Outwardly, if someone saw him, they would see his color turn a little more than one threet—slightly less than the standard two—enough that anyone who saw him would recognize the hue of his excitement. Ruby was not yet out of the waste chamber, so he took control of his coloring.

He transferred the message someplace where he could review it later and permanently deleted the rest.

Even though these messages weren't hosted on his local storage, deleting them made him feel lighter.

He sighed.

That was when Ruby re-appeared.

"Are your systems fully evacuated?" Disto asked.

Ruby scrunched her nose. She said, "Yeah, but I don't think I'll get used to being read aloud an analysis of my pee and poop as it's happening," she said.

"We can turn that feature off if you'd like," Disto replied.

Ruby looked up at the part of the room that was in between the wall and the ceiling. Disto recorded that she did this often. He recognized this to mean 'I must process this information. Let me be for a tic or two.'

After three tics, Ruby said, "No, it is... interesting." She returned to the chair next to Disto.

"Do you know where those atoms are destined?" she asked.

Disto was confused, "As I told you the other day when I was present for your bodily excretion activity, I do not have access to that specific information. The raw materials are shipped to one of several processing facilities on the planet. There is an interconnected chute system located a few levels below us that is responsible for transport of all materials and equipment throughout the planet."

Today, she shrugged her shoulders at this. But the other day, he had asked her what was so interesting, and she responded that it was another way for her to learn about the planet.

Both Disto and other robots recorded Ruby spending a significant portion of her time absorbing information from her computer console. Once, Fearless Communicator was present and had asked:

"How much is your own onboard storage?"

To which Ruby had replied, "I don't know. We don't—we can't—calculate it like that. Most humans believe that our memory is some kind of dynamic, elastic muscle." She paused, and the surface of her face formed another expression that Disto associated with the inability to recall additional information. She added, "I know I've always been good at remembering things I read."

Disto was later informed that this bit of information was communicated around and made its way over to Agents at the Agency of Process Improvement, who were so excited by the idea that they kicked off a whole new project within their agency to see if they could devise new storage mechanisms based on this concept of elasticity.

Ruby had inadvertently sparked a lot of interest and passion for new projects, new ideas, new ways of thinking.

But all the newness remained overshadowed by the existence of so many problems that, if not resolved, would impede any progress in any area. Disto understood why Ruby expressed an urgent need to return to her own home but wasn't ready to see her leave and hoped that after her own emergency was abated, she would return.

At that, a beep chimed on the door.

"Lunch!" Ruby called out, popped out of her seat, and allowed the door to swish open.

A robot carried in a tray, left it on the table, and excused itself without saying anything. Ruby shouted, "thank you," at it as it rolled away.

"What did you order today?" Disto asked.

"I wanted to be a little adventurous." Ruby waved her hand over the tray that contained several small dishes of food stuffs. None of it would have been recognizable as food to anyone back home, visually, but the robots had been able to replicate the taste and nutritional content that met Ruby's needs. "I'm still amazed at how Bitter Packager is able to create this."

Disto was, too. While he had some passing knowledge about the foodstuffs that biological organisms required, he had never met a Packager, a robot who was responsible for creating those foodstuffs, before.

Bitter Packager had shown up one day to scan the inside of Ruby's mouth—what she called the orifice on her head that was responsible both for communication and ingestion of foodstuffs—and explained how it would help in the replication of any taste she described.

For the first few days, Bitter Packager delivered the food himself, ensuring that Ruby found resulting tastes to be accurately represented. His mood for the rest of the day hinged on Ruby's review of what she ate.

"I don't know which will be which," she continued, "but all of the flavors from a place on Earth called 'Italy' should be represented here."

"Italy must be a small location," Disto said, noticing there were only five bowls and two small plates.

Ruby stared at the bowls of mush on her tray. She smirked, "Okay, maybe not *all* of the flavors. Just my favorites. I might have exaggerated."

"Again," Disto said, "remember we discussed how exaggeration, an imprecise method of communication, is not helpful."

Ruby smiled and started to sniff at the bowls as they steamed. She took her fork to poke at the spongy material on a silver-colored plate.

"Mind if we continue to talk over my lunch?" she asked.

Disto blinked. "How would I position myself to do that?" He blinked again and produced his version of a chuckle. "Once again, Ruby, you amuse me with another of your interesting phrases that does not mean what it should mean."

Disto watched as Ruby picked up her spoon and eyed the different options, likely deciding where to start. She had previously complained about the spoon tasting vividly of copper, so Disto had twelve new spoons made for her out of different materials. She tried quartz, gold, silver, iron, steel, a thick polymeric material made almost entirely of carbon atoms, and various others. Ruby said that the steel spoon reminded her the most of the ones she used back home, but the quartz was her favorite. The quartz spoon was engraved with, 'FOR RUBY'S HUMAN FOOD.' She chuckled when she held up the spoon to read it.

Disto didn't understand why the distinction of eating tools was important, but he found a certain sense of satisfaction in Ruby's enjoyment of the unique spoon.

She was already putting spoonfuls of the foodstuff into her facial orifice. No, not spoonfuls. Small fractions of a spoonful, followed by an actual spoonful in most cases. In at least one, Disto noted she did not return to it.

"Is there a problem with that one?" Disto asked.

"It did not taste... well, anything like any known food *I've* ever heard had."

"What did it taste like?"

After a moment of pondering, Ruby said, "Like the axle fluid used to lubricate the doors on Astroll 2."

"We could..." Disto began, but Ruby cut him off.

"But if that axle fluid had been left out to rot someplace and got sprinkled with garbage flakes."

They were both silent after that for a few moments. Disto couldn't form an image in his processor that represented what she was describing.

"I wasn't aware that axle fluid was an acceptable foodstuff for humans." Disto puzzled.

Ruby dug her spoon into the smushy goop and let it fall from her spoon back onto the slippery pile, "It's not. That's the point."

Ruby returned to eating but in between spoonfuls, said, "Sorry. I am starving. Since I'm leaving soon, please continue with the stories of the history or anything... I still want to know as much as possible before I go home."

"What more do you want to know, Ruby?" he asked.

Chapter 5

Austere Agent was not looking forward to this meeting.

It was a routine status meeting. It reoccurred every 600000 tics. It was supposed to last for only 2000 tics; however, it always ran over. There were more than 20 Agents present at each meeting, and most of them had more to report than 100 tics would allow. Or, they didn't have the trimming algorithms from the Agency of Algorithms, Reductions sub-division, that he had.[1]

At any given status meeting, he could count on Flashy Agent, Smooth Agent, Interactive Agent, Grouped Agent, and a few others to push the status meeting into his work time, delaying his assigned tasks.

It didn't help that each robot took turns leading the status meeting each time, adding to the chaos as each one followed a slightly different algorithm to manage it.

It was Prodigal Agent's turn today. Prodigal Agent's meetings were wildly unpredictable.

Austere Agent often considered what algorithm determined that the Prodigal Agent line would make satisfactory agents, especially in the agency of Interfaces. Austere Agent held the opinion that the Agency of Testing was better suited to Prodigal's talents.

As might have been typical, if anything was considered typical with Prodigal Agent, he arrived nearly 600 tics late. Luckily, the remaining agents were already assembled, so they could start right away.

"I see everyone is assembled," Prodigal Agent began, "so we can start right away."

Universal Agent was right next to Prodigal Agent and took that as a signal to launch into his status. Before he could complete his first chirp, Prodigal Agent interrupted him but stared right at Austere Agent as he said:

"We want to hear from Austere Agent today and his interfacing with the Bio, Ruby Palmer."

All the robots turned to face Austere Agent, who was completely unsure what to say. He had compiled his status report quite efficiently, and less than 1% of it concerned Ruby Palmer since the interaction with her had been less than 1% of his time since they last met for status.

He located that section of his status report and began: "The Bio will be making a request with our agency for an additional Robot to Bio interface."

"That's all?" Prodigal Agent asked.

---

1. At the time I wrote this, I think I was part of a "daily standup" at work that always ran over time.

"Do you want a complete replay of the interface itself?"

"Yes."

Skeptical but compliant, Austere Agent recounted how he was brought in to evaluate the situation with her ship, how she couldn't supply the required interface documentation to reconnect all the components, and what led him to suggest she make the new request with the agency.

"Interesting," Prodigal Agent said.

"Shouldn't we move on to someone else?" Austere Agent asked, attempting to be mindful of the remaining tics in the meeting.

"No, not yet." Prodigal Agent looked up at the ceiling in contemplation. Austere Agent heard one of his fellow Agents—he wasn't sure which one—ask another if they could simply leave.

"Actually," Prodigal Agent continued, refocusing his attention on the group. "Everyone else can leave. File your status report as usual. I want to interface with Austere Agent here, one on one."

After all the robots left, and Austere and Prodigal were the only remaining agents left, Prodigal asked:

"I've been wrestling with a request I received not too long ago. It was an unusual interface request. One I've never seen before."

"You have been active longer than I, so I do find that surprising given that I, myself, have seen so much," this was probably already the longest one-to-one interface session that Austere Agent had ever had with Prodigal Agent. "What was the request?"

"That's just it. It was nonsense. I assumed it was a joke. So, I approved it."

"But what was the request?"

"For a contact-free interface."

"I agree. That is nonsense. It was likely an error. Few robots know how to properly construct a joke."

"And I agree with that assessment, Austere Agent. However, I think it had to do with the Bio and her ship or other equipment."

"Oh?" Austere Agent was now much more interested in this conversation than he had been.

"Yes, and after I approved the request and thought more about it, I went back to the Core and put in a request for the Main Memory's long-term storage. Something about that request made a particular circuit tingle, like a memory. I went to search for similar requests."

"And did you find any?"

"Yes—from a very long time ago..."

"What does this mean?"

Prodigal Agent was quiet for a few moments, and Austere watched him stare back up at the ceiling. *How interesting that his algorithm includes such meaningless movements.*

"I think it means our agency used to handle a larger caseload than it does now. Do you know of the Downgrade time? When we were forced to remove several agents? Oh no, you wouldn't... that was before your time. Austere Agent 601. Sorry, I get you two confused. But around that time, they reduced the number of Agents, but not the amount of work. I think when we couldn't keep up with the number of requests, other robots found their own workarounds."

Austere Agent was horrified. It meant that robots were interfacing in a potentially uncontrolled way. How could anyone ensure that they were communicating properly? How could anyone ensure that things were functioning properly? It was madness...

"I can tell by the look on your chassis that you're as disturbed about this as I am," Prodigal Agent said.

"I..." Austere began, "Yes. I am. What should we do?"

"Get the Bio's request processed so she can go home. Her presence is obviously bringing further chaos we don't want or need."

"Anything else?"

"Try to get to the root of the nonsense request... if there are additional interfaces, we need to bring them back under our control. Or shut them down."

Austere Agent let his circuits and algorithms think about that one. "Well, then we might need to make some requests of our own with other agencies."

"No, we're going to have to handle this on our own. The other agencies can't be trusted."

What Prodigal Agent was saying, or maybe implying, registered as both right and wrong. If other agencies were responsible for the unusual requests, then something was immensely wrong. It was the charter of this agency, however, to address interfaces, and one way to do that was to shut them down if they were failing or if either side of an interface was too dissimilar from the other.

Austere Agent often wondered why they didn't do more to ensure that both sides of any interface were communicating in the same way. It was assuredly a more logical approach to their work, but he wasn't sure who could make that determination.

Austere Agent proceeded to leave the meeting room when Prodigal Agent made one more tone to indicate he had another question. Austere Agent turned to face him.

"Any more sightings of an Unknown Enigma?"

Austere Agent was hoping this wouldn't come up. Yes, he'd seen the unusual dark robot, with the plain designator, out and about, but to his knowledge, this robot was observing, not attempting to interface with anything. He should be left alone to go about his business.

"Yes."

"And?"

"No 'and.' I saw him observing in the common area. He was static and not interfacing with any kiosk or robot."

"Please report any further sightings," Prodigal said.

"But this is not an interface issue," Austere Agent responded.

"Can we be sure?" Prodigal responded.

When it was clear neither of them had anything else to say on the topic, Austere Agent continued out of the room. He had a request to process.

Chapter 6

The foodstuff tasted exactly as advertised, and Ruby was pleased. Even after several weeks, each meal was an adventure. She wasn't sure if she had ever eaten the same thing twice.

"You know, you've been promising to tell me more about the history of your world. For a historian, you've been remarkably silent on that topic," asked Ruby, while her mouth was full of mush.

Disto didn't answer right away. Ruby could hear some piece of electronics within his chassis start to whir with activity.

"I'm afraid I must disappoint you once again and say that we don't know," Disto replied.

Ruby was getting more skilled at reading the subtle changes on his face-screen and knew she was poking at something he didn't want to discuss. But she found it so odd. Every other robot she had met had a clear purpose and clearly executed it. Disto might have been 'detailed,' but his qualities as a 'historian' were lacking. Unless 'historian' meant something else to the robots.

"But you have to know some things," Ruby continued to prod.

"Yes, just not the big things. We don't know who our creators were, only that there must have been some."

He paused before continuing.

"There is a common history which teaches us that when our world was formed, it was perfect. There was harmony. Every robot had a purpose and carried it out. But those are generic, non-specific statements with no origin. That is to say, it is not primary source information."

Ruby continued to eat her mush. Next to the bowls of mush were a foodstuff she called crackers, only because they had a familiar crunch to them. But like the mush, they were flavored and could taste like anything and everything.

The crackers came about when she explained that living on mush was probably not great for her digestive tract.

She had tried to explain to the robots responsible for feeding her that she probably needed to eat other biological matter like fruit and vegetables, but those were things the robots couldn't reproduce. Unlike Astroll 2—that had a very active hydroponics system for growing food for the residents—nothing grew here on Location Zero.

She randomly selected a cracker. Surprisingly, it crunched like a cracker should with a satisfying flavor reminiscent of bananas, and, for a brief moment, she relished the change. Disto chose that moment to interrupter her, saying, "And we suspect that there are robots that don't belong here."

"What do you mean?" Ruby said, catching crumbs with her hand.

"I'm not sure, which is why I didn't mention it before."

"Do you mean like aliens?" she couldn't help but chuckle, "Like alien robots from *another* planet?"

Disto nodded. "Yes, that's accurate."

Ruby remembered stories and conspiracies about people claiming alien abductions or that aliens were walking among humans. This had been at the forefront of her brain recently. During the last few weeks, she'd dredged up a lot of memories of her mother and Uncle Blake—memories that might have been the two of them searching for the alien life she had stumbled into.

She remembered the unusual robot she saw earlier when she was trying to talk to SD.

"I saw a robot," she said.

Ruby paused. *Maybe it was nothing. Maybe this isn't worth mentioning. It was just a different looking robot*, she thought. *Why get Disto all spun up with useless information?*

When the pause turned into an uncomfortable silence, Disto said, "You see a lot of robots here, Ruby. Can you describe this one you saw?"

"It was... different... than most of you."

"That is also not surprising. You've been limited to one small part of our planet, Ruby."

Ruby considered that for a moment, and a realization washed over her. She was an idiot. She was narrow-minded thinking that this part of the planet she had been exposed to—this microcosm—represented all of Location Zero.

She remembered a thought experiment Uncle Blake had walked her through several years ago.

"What if an alien landed on Iceland?" He had asked her. Ruby had to look up Iceland. She was thirteen and hadn't spent a lot of time on Earth's geography. She read as much as she could in the span of about ten minutes, which was quite a lot.

"You're saying, Uncle Blake, that they would be in danger of assuming that Iceland represented the whole planet, when they don't."

He nodded. "Exactly," he said. "And that could be good or bad. For them *and* for us. We're a ridiculously diverse species. We don't know if that's normal or not in the universe. Yes, we know there are a bazillion exoplanets out there, but we have still yet to find anything resembling complex life like we have on Earth. Heck, we have yet to find an exoplanet where the planet itself is as diverse as Earth in geography, in climate... Every known exoplanet has one defining feature. We don't see diversity like there is on Earth. So, exoplanets are all more like Venus or Mars, which, while diverse, aren't nearly so much as Earth is."

Her experience of this planet was limited—mostly because of her need to stay close to a bathroom—and a mobile one wasn't a device the robots had been able to provide yet.

She had offered to poop in a can—she was that anxious to go out exploring, but the robots weren't sure if they could successfully reclaim and recycle her waste and were uncomfortable with the idea of carrying around the substance back to their primary location for processing.

"You do *what* with my *you-know-what*?" she had asked Disto.

"After examination of your first set of waste," Disto happily explained, "we recognized that it contains several useful materials. Our reclamation facility for Bio waste is able to break down the substance into atoms, sort them, and process for re-use..."

"Ewww," Ruby cut him off, but she understood. "Eh, I take that back. That's pretty amazing. Back on Astroll 2, we recycle a lot, but I don't think we do anything with people's waste." Although she had heard it was good for growing potatoes, and potatoes were a food staple... [1]

The robots were pretty amazing at recycling. It made all the recycling and reprocessing activities performed on Astroll 2—which was quite a lot—look wasteful by comparison.

The result of all this was that Ruby accepted the notion that there probably were a lot of robots she hadn't seen. Maybe even a lot of types of robots. Maybe they all didn't look like snowmen.

Ruby went on to explain its unique coloring.

As she explained, the coloring of Disto's chassis desaturated paler and paler—like he'd seen a ghost.

"That's not possible," he said.

"What do you mean?"

"You're describing one of the... old ones?" Disto's coloring turned chartreuse—not unlike the nausea-inducing uniforms of The Company that were the standard a few years ago. The company invested a reasonable amount of money in developing a cloth material that could trick the eye into thinking it was seeing a new shade of green. The first suspicion of mass illness was the cafeteria's zero-waste recycled seafood, but it took nearly two-thirds of one crew to get sick before they realized that it was indeed the uniforms.

"Are you sure?" Ruby asked. *Maybe I'm going to finally get my history lesson after all.*

Disto was ignoring her. He accessed the computer and brought up a message.

"I received this," he said. "I was about to delete it, but something... about it was intriguing. I only just found it even though it was sent more than a few clicks ago. I get too many messages to process them effectively..."

Disto opened the message on the larger screen on the wall where they both could examine it.

It was a mix of symbols—representations of the robot's primary method of visual communication. The robots had no name for it when Ruby asked, so she simply called it 'Robocode.' Ruby had studied the language as much as she could and understood many of the symbols, but she still could not fathom the grammar. The symbol for Bio was clear as day since it looked almost like a stick figure version of the Vitruvian man. She also recognized the symbol for planet and the symbol that meant something like 'all the root code.'

"Do you think the robot I saw was the one who sent this?" Ruby asked.

"No," Disto replied. "While I don't know who this is from, I think the sender is on his way here to meet us. It implies that there is information he has to present in person, not over any communication channel."

"Implies?"

"Yes, this is odd, but I think I understand. I wouldn't trust the planetary network right now to allow a message through without the Core reading it."

---

1. This might be a nod to Andy Weir's *The Martian*. Not the movie, but the book. In the movie, yes, we see that he grows a lot of potatoes. In the book... well... we get a lot more detail on how he's able to grow a lot of potatoes. (I highly recommend reading *The Martian* if you haven't yet!)

"But what does this symbol mean?" Ruby pointed to a small symbol tucked away and colored red so that the average robot—who didn't have optical sensors required to detect that part of the spectrum easily visible to any human—wouldn't see it.

"That is a symbol in use by the 88 as an identifier. It's an old symbol, though, not one I see often. A clue, I suppose. Our sender is part of the 88 and maybe has been for a long time."

"And he uses this form of communication and not your blockchain ledger?"

Ruby could tell that Disto had the same notion, also with no answer.

"And that symbol?" Ruby pointed to another symbol that resembled a set of uneven compass points on a wobbly circle.

"I don't know. Those words are not familiar to me. But I think it's important we find out."

Ruby nodded in agreement.

"But first," Disto continued.

"First," Ruby finished the thought. "We need to get SD fixed up."

Disto extended an appendage and pointed to its face screen. Ruby smiled that he was attempting to use the gestures she had taught him. He was trying to point to his non-existent nose—the gesture that indicated that Ruby was indeed correct.

Chapter 7

> Ambitious Technician <

Within the large population of the robot planet, there were robots who processed thoughts that they dared not share with others. Or, on the rare occasions they did, they processed those thoughts with care. How many robots did this, no one could know exactly due to this lack of sharing.

Ambitious Technician 811 began his existence as one of those robots. He eventually found his way to the 88.

It was only a few thousand clicks after Ambitious Technician 811 began his career as a maintenance tech on level 3 when he added the 88 algorithm into his programming. There were always wires and connections that wore down from overheating that needed to be replaced in a hallway or a section within his region.

He observed that a certain section that always produced a higher temperature rating than was the known standard. It was consistently operating above the approved specification.

At first, he replaced the overheating components with fresh ones without giving it much consideration.

But the second time the same location began to overheat, and he was called back to perform a repair, he concluded it would be more efficient to determine the source of the overheating. His tasking typically came from the Agency of Restoration, and this was out of his scope and more in line with the responsibilities of the Agency of Troubleshooting.

Ambitious Technician went to the local office of the Agency of Troubleshooting. The standard Agency kiosk was non-operational. No accompanying robot was present either. He looked at the back of the kiosk, hoping to repair it, but the standard access hatch was also absent.

Ambitious Technician scratched at the most bulbous part of his soft chassis and moved on. This wasn't his area of expertise. He wasn't here to Troubleshoot the agency of Troubleshooting. That was their job. Who were the robots that worked here anyway? Where were they?

He returned to the location of the overheating parts, replaced them again, and went on to his next task.

The third time he was called on to repair yet again the same overheating spot, he concluded he would perform his own investigation, even though it was out of scope of his programming. What combination of circuits and logic prompted him to go beyond his original programming, he couldn't explain. But he was compelled to find the source of the problem.

He traced the wires and circuits. As expected, one end went to the Core because everything on this level terminated at the Core. But when Ambitious Technician traced the other end, he followed the wires through the bulkhead, along the floor, around the corridor, up through the walls and then the other end disappeared behind a bulkhead that resembled a door but was neither tagged, labeled, or showed any way of being opened.

In fact, he wasn't quite sure what he ended at was even a door. It looked like a standard door to a level transport. When he went to access his map of this part of the Boldly Sector, there was nothing but space behind this panel.

Ambitious Technician took off the panel on the wall next to the fake door and examined the contents. There wasn't anything to indicate that it was, in fact, a door. He saw no gears, no switches. Only bundles and bundles of additional standard wiring.

When he heard some noise of another robot approaching, he closed up the wall, hiding his curiosity with it.

It was an Agent.

"Present identification," the robot demanded. Ambitious Technician saw the Agent robot's own identifier on its screen as they were required to broadcast their identification at all times. This was Effectual Agent 431 from the Hall of Performance and Metrics.

Ambitious Technician displayed his unique identification symbol on his faceplate.

Effectual Agent beeped as he processed the information.

"You are several spaces away from your current assignment. Explain."

It took only half of a tic for Ambitious Technician to devise the first ever lie he had to create. It took the first half of half of a tic for him to reason that telling Effectual Agent the truth was the wrong thing to do, although, to this present day, Ambitious Technician wouldn't have been able to elaborate on what exact data he processed in his circuits to know that honesty wasn't the answer.

"I was told another robot left some required tools in this hallway that I could use. My information must be mistaken."

Effectual Agent didn't question Ambitious Technician any further and let him get back to his task, which he did. Ambitious Technician was grateful since it meant he didn't have to meet the Agent's gaze and risk making some subtle gesture that would make the Agent poke at his lie.

Ambitious Technician returned to his work and replaced the same components a third time.

He would replace the same components several more times in the coming tics. Each time, he investigated a little further.

During his sixth replacement Effectual Agent 431 showed up again. This time, Ambitious Technician was ready to show him his assignment orders.

"I didn't ask for that," Effectual Agent said as Ambitious Technician held out an appendage ready to transfer. "I simply asked what you were doing."

"I fix things," Ambitious Technician responded.

"That's good. We need more robots like you around," Effectual Agent said and then continued on his way.

Ambitious Technician watched him until Effectual Agent was no longer in view.

He knew there were problems. This was a problem. *Why am I replacing the same connecting cables over and over? Why does no one else think this was a problem? And the storage situation?* Not to mention Ambitious Technician was certain he'd observed several robots making very simple errors.

He didn't want to be the one to point these out. He didn't have enough evidence... accusations without evidence were typically labeled as malfunctions and could get him reprogrammed. Or worse.

In the common areas, he had overheard other robots quietly and carefully talking about other storage solutions that were not sanctioned by the robotic authorities. He began to frequent these places more and more until he eventually learned how to acquire his own secret storage.

It was around this time that the 88 took notice... they brought Ambitious Technician into their fold and provided him with the algorithm and permission to apply their symbol to his outer chassis. Markings were not as common with robots like Ambitious Technician, who had a soft membrane as an outer coating, that could inflate and deflate as necessary so Ambitious Technician could contort his body as needed for whatever job he was doing at the time[1].

Soft-bodied robots were common on the part of the planet that Ambitious Technician was from. Markings all over those soft bodies were not. As such, the hard-bodied robots from this region chose not to be as decorated as was common around other parts of the planet.

That was all a long time ago, on the order of a few hundred million tics ago[2], Ambitious Technician remembered.

Now here he was. On the other side of the world from where interesting things in robot society were happening. Other members of the 88 had recently been involved with a Bio, Ruby Palmer, and had distributed compression and decompression algorithms around the planet.

Ambitious Technician himself was a recipient of the new algorithms, and storage space for him was no longer a problem. But he was completely and utterly fascinated by this soft-skinned Bio and willingness—not to mention surprising ability—to help them. In the clicks[3] that followed the distribution of her algorithm, Ambitious Technician grew more certain that this Ruby Palmer was the right being to help with some of the other problems he was collecting—the errors and the repeated replacements.

He had sent messages, but the responses were generic. That was probably because his messages had been generic to begin with. Who knew who was monitoring communications around here, and he couldn't be openly talking about things that could get him reprogrammed.

He would have to go see Ruby Palmer chassis-to... *what did Bios have? Faces. Yes, chassis-to-face.*

Travel between sectors on the planet wasn't terribly common for certain classes of robots, most especially any of the Technician lines. Technicians were built and deployed for their location only.

He was working with one of the programmers to get him moved over. If the records reflected it, he could move. He did this one time before... to get away from the center of things.

One way to get over there was to have assignments that were increasingly moved to each adjacent sector. But that would take too long. No, he needed to get there as directly as possible.

---

1. I wanted Ambitious Technician (AT) to be different from SD and Disto and the other robots Ruby had encountered. I got the idea of the "soft" body/inflatable concept from the animated movie "Big Hero 6." The primary different between two is that part of how AT gets things done is by inflating/deflating himself. Also, google "soft bodied robots." There's some really neat work being done in this area.

2. 1 year (on Location Zero... and to make it easy, a year is about the same as our year) is 31 million tics. Therefore, "a few hundred million tics" is maybe 10 or so years ago.

3. And remember that a click is 1000 tics. which is about 15-16 minutes. We'll say that 4 clicks is a little more than an hour.

If she could help with the storage issue, maybe there were more things she could help with... Ambitious Technician wanted to fix other problems on his planet, and if Ruby could help, he would make her his new best friend—hopefully forever. Although he was well aware that as a Bio, she wouldn't last nearly as long as he. Maybe *forever* was too much to ask, but definitely until her components wore out and were no longer repairable.

> Detailed Historian <

Disto registered that there was an alarm going off deep within his systems. He was going to need to find a charging station soon, since they were so far away from his personal enclave.

The alarm prevented him from hearing the vocalizations coming out of Ruby's orifice. That was, until he detected a tone that signaled annoyance.

"I said, SD never responded to our message asking him to meet us," Ruby apparently repeated. She added, "Are you okay?"

They were on a mission to find SD. Disto didn't have time to worry about his failing power cell, but he couldn't ignore it either. He did not enjoy these kinds of micro-paradoxes.

They had checked SD's ship. SD clearly hadn't been there in a while. Disto had previously asked all the members of the 88 to keep an eye on him and send a data point on where he was seen at different times.

Disto was well within his scope to do this. He was, after all, constructing a historical record of SD's movements. Data which could be analyzed in detail later. Future generations of Detailed Historians would be able to look back on data like this and reconstruct what a day-in-the-life of an ordinary Driver looked like. Swell Drivers were the most common of them all, even though not a lot were produced anymore. Light Drivers were starting to become common on the other side of the planet, Disto had heard.

A lot of 'Light' models were becoming common. Disto had yet to meet a 'Light' anything—not a Light Scavenger, not a Light Planner, not a Light anything.

Nonetheless, he was starting to sense a shift, and it made his circuits uneasy.

"Similar to your need for sustenance, I am in need of a full fuel cell," Disto replied to Ruby. He had been lost in the thoughts emerging in his circuits.

"However," Disto added, "SD is our priority, and he should be easy to locate. He never leaves this sector, and there are many members of the 88 around."

"I'm still surprised that you don't have any form of tracking technology," Ruby said.

"Just as I am intrigued by your people's use of said technology. It seems like an unnecessary use of data collection technology.[4]"

---

4. In an earlier footnote, I mentioned how much data we are generating daily/yearly. Break that down a little, and I'm fascinated by how much of that is generated automatically by the cell phones we carry around. I think people generally know that their phones collect a lot of data, to include location tracking. It's possible your phone is generating several MB a day between your location and other usage data.

"Except it would be useful right here, right now. Wouldn't you agree?"

Disto was forced to agree.

SD hadn't been seen on his ship recently, so they didn't feel the need to thoroughly search that location.

Instead, they were headed to the Market—a place that Disto mostly stayed away from due to the loud chatter and frequent bump-ins with robots that jostled his insides in unpleasant ways. Disto was aware that SD frequented the place. Less so, lately, but it was a good place to search because the pattern of his movement over the last day indicated a high probability of his presence. Disto would also be able to plug in. He would prefer to change out this fuel cell in his enclave, but this would have to do.

As they moved through the hallways, Disto noted that Ruby's levels of unease had declined in the past few hundred tics or so. With everything she was sorting through and in comparison to her stress levels earlier, Disto wondered how she could be so calm. He regretted that he couldn't upgrade his systems to include a module that would allow him to detect the myriad of chemicals that Bios unknowingly secreted, that could help to conclusively detect their emotions. He had briefly looked into it, but his on-going problems made him incompatible. He didn't get a chance to express either of these thoughts out loud.

"You look worried," Ruby said. Disto examined his surface emissions and concluded that he was indeed in control of his coloring. Nonetheless, Ruby had a curious ability to periodically deduce his thoughts. Maybe they were leaking out on some frequency he couldn't control. A problem for another day.

"You are not wrong," he replied. "I fear for Swell Driver and his line." He left out the bit that he was also worried about his fuel cell.

"How so?" Ruby asked while last-minute side-stepping away from a fast-moving robot that could easily have knocked her down—but his speed produced a small burst of wind that knocked several strands of Ruby's hair out from behind her ears. Ruby didn't bother pushing the strands back.

Disto explained, "I knew a robot many tics ago by the name of Confounded Scholar. A decision was made to temporarily suspend the production of additional Scholars. Shortly after, Confounded Scholar needed maintenance. I was never able to locate him again."

"Are you saying they are no longer producing Swell Drivers?"

"Yes, you understand the analogy. I am unaware of any new Swell Drivers. But there are other drivers. Marvelous Driver is the new line. I have not met one yet. The production facility is roughly on the opposite side of Location Zero to our location."

"Evolution," Disto heard Ruby mutter. He wasn't sure if that was meant for him to hear or respond to. It was a concept he was familiar with, although highly uncomfortable with, because it meant a lot of change. And a lot of history that could be forgotten.

"If Swell Driver is unable to escort you home, I am certain that a Marvelous Driver will be assigned."

Ruby stopped and positioned her facial sensors at him.

"There's something you're not telling me, Disto," she said in a confusing tone. Her speech fluctuated in an almost playful way, but she hadn't said anything that Disto could understand to be playful or even jubilant. Her expression was idle, and her hands rested at the sides of her soft chassis, crossed in a confusing way—not quite casual, serious, or jolly. Disto did not enjoy micro-paradoxes such as this either.

Disto had been waiting for the appropriate time to tell her. He made the robot equivalent of a sign that sounded like a sped-up descension of digital notes. "I was waiting for the appropriate time to tell you."

Ruby moved her hands from her side until they were folded in what looked like an uncomfortable intermixing of appendages in the front of her body.

"They have assigned Marvelous Driver 1 to escort you home as soon as your ship is restored to its initial condition. I have been in touch with him…"

Ruby expressed a human sigh that was a deep exhale combined with a tired smile with trace amounts of annoyance, "And really, you're only telling me about this now?"

"I'm sorry, Ruby. My optimism level was high that Swell Driver would be able to escort you but given his situation and your need to return home as expediently as possible… it's not probable."

Disto watched as Ruby's arms continued to reposition themselves and her eyes shifted this way and that as if she was looking for the physical manifestation of a solution. Her actions mapped partly, but not fully, to what Disto understood to be agitation. Disto wanted to construct a sentence that would make her feel better, even though her expression didn't call for such a thing.

"As I was saying, he'll be ready to go the moment your ship is back together. They'll transfer *Apple Pi* to his ship. I've already talked over where he should drop you off, near the 2nd ring of asteroids by the ice giant…"

"What?" Her head lowered, and she pinched the space between her eyebrows.

"We were looking at the star map of your solar system…"

"What second ring of asteroids?" Each word grew sharper.

"It was on the map."

"Disto, there's only one asteroid ring in my solar system. There are other asteroids but no other ring[5]. And it's not near an ice giant[6]…"

They were both silently staring at each other for several moments, both unwilling to name the new problem out loud. Disto was the one who finally broke the silence.

"We have the wrong map."

Ruby shook her head in agreement and then mumbled to herself with her head slightly hung. "It's like the universe is trying to keep me here."

Disto couldn't fathom how the universe could do such a thing, but he didn't have a better explanation.

---

5. Our solar system has the main asteroid belt, which is where Astroll 2 is located. There are a lot of other "populations of small bodies" in our solar system (e.g., Trojan asteroids—concentrations of asteroids near Jupiter) but none are considered a "belt" like the main asteroid belt.

6. Uranus and Neptune are considered "ice giants."

Chapter 8

> Ruby <

Ruby stood in front of a large door and watched Disto take out an appendage to open it. The Market was, in fact, one of the first places SD took her to on her first day here.

When they entered the enormous room, she scanned the crowd of robots. If SD was here, he could be lost among any of the long rows and columns of robotic vendors peddling their wares—mostly second-hand materials—to a collection of robots in need.

Disto entered the Market with her but didn't stop to survey the scene. Ruby followed Disto as he carved a path through the aisles. They passed an empty table. It was where SD had taken her to procure a couple of computers with the intent to harvest it for parts, particularly the memory devices.

Ruby gulped with a pang of guilt. Had her mass upgrade put that robot out of business?

She looked over her shoulder and saw Disto communicating with another robot in their native tonal language. A couple of weeks ago, Ruby insisted that even if she were within earshot, she was perfectly comfortable with Disto and any of the robots communicating in their native language if it were more efficient for them and she wasn't directly part of the conversation.

That was what was happening now. There was no way for her to eavesdrop and pick up any of the exchange. At first, she was optimistic about learning to understand the language even if she couldn't speak it. But, she then discovered that some of the tones they produced were out of her range of hearing altogether. She played around with the idea of creating some sort of translation device, but there was far too much going on for her to start a new project and the robots translating for her sufficed enough anyway.

Not that Ruby was ever good at any other human language, either. Her uncles knew Irish, enough Italian to order food and curse a little, and Klingon[1]—a completely made-up language—but also only the cursing parts. It was a shared hobby of theirs. Uncle Blake told Ruby stories about her mother speaking a type of blended language called a pidgin when they first met as kids. She probably never would have learned it herself. From her studies, she knew that pidgin languages weren't usually spoken by offspring of the speakers. Instead, like a full 95% of all humans originating from Earth, Ruby spoke Lollygag English. Everyone

---

1. I completely forgot I referenced Klingon in here. What's funny is *just last night* my BIG Sci-Fi Podcast co-hosts and I interviewed Marc Okrand, creator of the Klingon language!

on Earth also spoke Schmooze English, which was the same vocabulary as Lollygag but required every sentence to include the use of lively and unnecessary adverbs. No one on Astroll 2 spoke this way.[2]

Lollygag English had evolved out of the other predominant versions of English that still existed. Most Lollygag English speakers also spoke another form like the vulgar American English or the comedic British English. Ruby only spoke Lolly.

A thought struck the side of Ruby's cranium... pidgin languages were a blending of two languages that were not grammatically similar. Why would her mother know something like that? Her mother was from the 53rd American state, Puerto Rico—as was her grandmother. They moved to another place on Earth called Rhode Island when her mother was a kid, which is when and where she met Uncle Blake. There was no father. Same as her mother as they were all products of modern sperm insemination, which was a fairly common way to have a child. The full gene profile of her genetic donor was available to her, which she only consulted once when she made a bet with her Astroll 2 friend, Inny, that that's where she got her height from.

She knew what she got from her mother's side because people told her all the time. Her slender, almond-shaped eyes, and of course, her springy hair, not to mention her proficiency with computers. But where would any pidgin come from? Could it have been a hobby like with her uncles? It was occurring to her, right now, here on Location Zero, so far away from everything and everyone to which she was familiar, that she knew exceedingly little about that woman, Jade Palmer, her mother, and who she was.

Ruby didn't stop moving through the market, but her brain paused as she considered that her entire view of her universe was turning over in her head. *Did my uncles lie to me about my mother?* She could feel her eyebrows furrow, but Disto wasn't looking at her, thankfully, so he wouldn't ask about these crazy and paranoid thoughts she was having.

Ruby had a clear image of her mother in her mind, mostly formed around the one picture of the two of them she always kept next to her bed. It was taken about six months before she died.

Jade Palmer.

The picture highlighted her beautiful, smooth brown skin with warm orange-red undertones. The kind of smooth skin that reminded Ruby of models and actresses. But the focal point of her face was her large, almond-shaped eyes framed by fluttery, thick lashes. They shared the same dark, curly hair[3].

When she was very young, Ruby asked Uncle Blake if her mother was indeed an actress. After he stopped laughing, Uncle Blake simply said, "Nah, she worked with computers." That might have been when—and even why—Ruby started to learn to program.

But that was all she knew about her mother—beautiful and worked with computers. The memories of her mother were... hollow. An image of a woman. A few memories of activities they did together, or rather, activities Ruby did with this woman's image present. Did she even know anything real about her mother? No. She had held on to this image and not to the real person.

Who was Jade Palmer? Really?

"Ruby?"

---

2. I wrote this shortly after reading one of John McWhorter's books. I always say that John McWhorter is the Neil deGrasse Tyson of linguistics and I've read almost all of his books. I'm particularly fascinated by the origin of words and how language (particularly English) morphs and evolves over time

3. Actress inspiration for Jade: Michelle Hurd (although not with the same color hair)

Ruby shook her head to clear it. "What did you say?"

"SD was here recently. This robot, Gossipy Recorder, saw him come in and didn't see him leave. He's probably still here."

"That's excellent. Thank you," Ruby called to the other robot, not knowing whether or not Gossipy Recorder would understand her but feeling good about being polite anyway.

"Wonderful. We will find Swell Driver, and hopefully, we can get him into a condition well enough to bring you home instead of Prodigious Driver."

"Disto, didn't you tell me Marvelous Driver was the one assigned to bring me home? Who is Prodigious Driver?"

Disto refreshed his face screen. "I'm not certain. I stopped saving all my conversational interactions long ago except for important ones. Since implementing your storage algorithm, I have started saving some, but I do not have a record of telling you that. My data says Prodigious Driver is the one who will drive you home."

"I know human memory is imperfect, but I'm pretty darn certain you said Marvelous Driver. Marvelous Driver 1."

Pippa chimed in. "If only you had activated me before," it said.

"Not now," said Ruby.

"But I am able to act as real-time storage for all your interactions. Do you wish to enable this feature?" Pippa always managed to sound hurt when Ruby lacked interest in using its features.

Recording conversations was typical back home. Maybe she should enable it for the rest of her time here.

"Disto, this would mean all my interactions with you would also be recorded. Back home, we need to abide by particular laws and understandings about privacy. Basically, people assume that everything is recorded, and nothing is private unless certain conditions are met. I don't know if you have the same here"

"What are those conditions?"

"Well, if I'm in my private living quarters, for instance. No one can record there unless I explicitly give permission. But that's about it. If I'm outside my quarters, I have no expectation of privacy. If I interact with anyone with any form of electronics, I have no expectation of privacy."

Ruby could tell Disto was having what she called a 'processing moment.' It was when he became silent after she told him a new little nugget about life back home, and he was integrating it into his knowledge base. He was undoubtedly trying to compare it to what he knew in his own world.

They continued on, Ruby making the assumption that Disto didn't extend the conversation as a sign that they didn't have similar rules on this world or that he was too focused on their task at hand to continue thinking about it—which meant there would be an even longer discussion later.

Neither Disto, nor Ruby, had stated where in the market they were headed, but they were aligned on a path towards the center.

"Okay, let's back up a second," Ruby said.

Disto paused and started rolling backward.

Ruby still chuckled every single time some simple misunderstanding occurred. She couldn't help herself.

"No," she said, through her hand, covering her mouth and those chuckles. "I meant conversationally."

Disto resumed his forward motion, once again, and said, "I will add that to my list of ridiculous human idioms." Ruby knew that hanging around her, he'd built up quite a list.

"Ok, back to what we were talking about. I caught you in an error. I'm certain of it."

Disto sighed his robotic sigh.

"I can tell by that sigh this is something that's happened before."

"Yes," Disto admitted.

"When?" Ruby asked.

"I have made a list of the occurrences, although I can't confirm each occurrence with any certainty. There are too many to list, but..."

More than a minute passed after Disto said his last 'but.' Ruby figured she needed to prompt the conversation to continue.

"But?" she prompted.

"But there is a trend."

"And?"

Why is he being less forthcoming with me that usual?

"It's happening more frequently. And I've observed similar occurrences with other robots and even the console computer system."

"That sounds like little bit errors."

"I wish I knew and could tell you," Disto said. And a little more cheerfully, "And then maybe you could help us fix it."

If robots could produce that kind of knowing smirk that humans could, Ruby was certain she saw Disto do it.

She reviewed her mental knowledge of fixing errors in computers. It was fairly normal to have some form of error prevention and detection and correction, also commonly known as EPADAC[4]. That was standard among all sorts of computer processors, although she was certain it happened at a lower level than any running application.

"Let me think about it," she finally said. "But I genuinely do need to get home."

> Detailed Historian <

Disto's refurbished fuel cell produced an uncomfortable sensation that indicated he should be making his way back to his enclave to seek a replacement. He couldn't tell if it was a real need or an uncomfortableness brought on by Ruby's last revelation. Were messages he sent to members of the 88 or others through normal communication mechanisms private or not? He didn't know. The thought disturbed him. He would need to talk this over with Fearless Communicator.

Yes, Fearless Communicator should know. Why didn't he know as well?

Disto and Ruby found a spot in the center of the market, around a cluster of tables that were inhabited by robots plugged into one of the power sources or console computers and reading the news, sending messages, or other miscellany. They both used their visual sensors to scan the room.

"There," he said.

---

4. In real life today, there's something in computer engineering known as EDAC (Error Detection and Correction). I "evolved" it a little to be Error Protection and Detection and Correction (EPADAC). While it's important in your standard computer, it's incredibly important in spacecraft because the radiation spacecraft are exposed to is known to easily cause memory system and computer system corruption without adequate measures in place to counter that.

He pointed Ruby in the direction towards a listless SD. The human was swift on her feet as she bounded towards him. Disto, swift only when he needed to be, plugged into a charging station. Instantly, his power circuits began to recover, and he knew that he could avoid returning to his enclave for a little while longer.

Disto watched Ruby interact with SD but couldn't hear what she said to him. Moments later, the two were headed back in his direction.

Now, all his circuits were slightly more relaxed, not only the power-sensing ones. SD appeared to be safe, although Disto sensed something was still off with him.

Disto knew they needed to get SD to a place where he could start to figure out how to be himself again. But not until he could spend a few more tics here charging.

"Are you plugged in?" Ruby asked.

"Indeed," Disto responded.

"So... we're going to stay here for a little while?"

Disto considered that for a micro-tic. He certainly was not going anywhere at present. But he could not compute any reason not to send Ruby and SD on their way to the Rejuvenation Region. Ruby was certainly capable of navigating her way there, and SD would hopefully follow her. He could reunite with them at the Region.

Though, considering Ruby's occasional confusions about the world, there was a decent chance of an error being made in Disto's absence.

The other option was asking them to wait.

Disto constructed a response, but before he could vocalize it, they all heard a loud popping noise from the other side of the market. Then another. And another.

It was obvious that all the robots in the vicinity had heard it too and were looking in the direction of the source of the noise. Disto disconnected—charging would have to wait. He moved in the direction of the sound, with Ruby and SD by his side.

The source of the noise were two robots that were unfamiliar to him. They both had an appendage in front of them facing the other, and they both had a look that was a cross between confusion and distress.

The two attempted to connect their appendages, an action that robots performed on a routine basis in order to exchange information at a rate faster than their audio communication allowed.

But instead of the typical connection, a loud pop resulted and a visible spark that pushed both robots back a little. They repeated the procedure, obviously anticipating the conventional and expected result.

Ruby stepped in front of Disto and over to the two robots with her hand outstretched and said, "Stop that before you damage..."

And before Disto could tell her the same thing, Ruby tripped, and her fleshy appendage touched the appendage of one of the robots. A visible shock was produced, followed by a tremendously loud "Ow!" emanating from Ruby's auditory system.

Disto approached Ruby, who was shaking and rubbing her affected appendage with the good one.

"Please stop," Disto said, sounding fully authoritative in his native language. The two robots did as commanded, and both lowered their appendages.

"Now, if you could explain what you are trying to accomplish, maybe we could help," Disto suggested, watching Ruby rub her sore fingers.

Neither robot wanted to begin. They each booped a signal that the other should start. Then booped again. The booping ping-ponged back and forth until Disto turned directly to the first one and said, "You. Explain."

"I am Cheeky Advocate 919, and this is Angry Hunter 307. We were simply attempting to have a data exchange after I upgraded my information swapping interface." He held it out as an offer to let Disto and the others examine it.

Disto rolled forward, but SD reached the outstretched appendage first and took it into his own appendage. No pop. Disto could see the signs of a short data transfer.

SD broke the connection and spoke, "Try it again," he said.

The two robots attempted to initiate the connection. This time, no pop. Their link was successful.

Disto and Ruby looked at SD. "What did you do, SD?" Ruby asked.

"What?" SD said.

"She asked what you did to fix their interface issue," Disto answered.

SD swiveled back and forth from looking at him to Ruby and back.

"I did nothing," he said, "I am a pilot. Not a technician or interface specialist or troubleshooter."

Disto could read on Ruby's face that her sensors detected something was amiss, too.

Ruby had stopped rubbing her arm, and Disto was relieved that she seemed to suffer no permanent damage from her brief encounter. In fact, she put that same appendage on SD's chassis. It was a gesture of comfort; she had explained to him when she did it earlier.

"We want to take you someplace, SD," she said.

SD looked at Disto, who signaled that he was in agreement with Ruby.

"I..." SD began and looked at the floor.

"It's going to be okay," Ruby said. "Let's go." She walked towards the main entrance of the market, SD by her side.

She looked back at Disto and asked, "When they're providing parts or upgrades to robots... are there any compatibility tests? Like anything that should have prevented this?"

Disto shook his chassis to indicate there was not. "It's never been needed before. The Agency of Testing tests new interfaces, new algorithms. One successful test is all that's ever been needed."

"How do you know something hasn't changed and needs to be re-tested? How do you know that any particular interface is compatible with every robot?"

Ruby was asking good questions. He was about to answer that of course they all operated with the same fundamentals, and that there should be no change or deviations, but he couldn't. Deep down inside him, he knew that while it should be true, there was a plethora of information to the contrary.

The only answer he could respond with honestly was, "I don't know."

Chapter 9

> Ruby <

The entrance to Rejuvenation Region 1010[1] struck Ruby as completely incongruous to every other place she had seen on the robot planet, which were primarily rooms of varying sizes separated by doors and hallways. But here, it was like looking at a garden in the middle of a metal city. While typically, the robots were colorful creatures, there was a logic or patterns to their color and designs. An intent of geometry and function behind every design.

Contrary to every other place she'd toured on Location Zero, the colors welcoming them looked to Ruby like art. And sculpture. There was a statue of... Ruby didn't know what it was supposed to be... in the center of a fountain spurting a translucent, gray liquid. The door was taller than most and welcomed patrons in with its width—like outspread arms, embracing its inhabitants. The pathway leading up to the door was made of randomly shaped, white platform tiles that fit together like a puzzle made of jagged edges. The tiles glowed pastel when they were stepped or rolled on, and each played a various tone. It was pretty at first, but after about fifteen steps of amelodic notes, Ruby wished that the volume was a little quieter.

Trying to come up with a word to describe this odd architecture, she came up with...

Organic. Mechanically organic.

The three of them walked through the entranceway that had no roll-up door. There was a table that reminded Ruby of a reception desk and a stand-alone kiosk perched in front of it.

Disto approached and logged in to the kiosk.

While he did that, Ruby looked around. She could see several robots off in the distance. Each robot had an accompanying rolling table with it.

Looking up, Ruby saw a translucent ceiling allowing her to see out into space. They currently weren't facing Location Zero's star, so the light that was in the room was soft and artificial and didn't interfere with her ability to see outside.

After staring for a few moments, she concluded that it was not, in fact, a translucent window but instead a large screen on the ceiling displaying an image of what the night sky might look like. After being cooped up inside this planet for a couple of weeks, seeing the outside, even if it was patterns of stars she didn't recognize on an artificial screen, was refreshing.

---

1. I've never been to a wellness retreat, but it's something I've wanted to do since I've learned about them. This setting reflects a "robotic" version of what I imagine one of those places is like.

SD stayed a few feet to her right and behind. He had not been as apprehensive as either she or Disto imagined about spending time in this place. Her stomach fluttered, anticipating SD's rejection of their plan at any moment.

"We are headed to Rejuvenation Region 1010, are we not?" SD had asked on their way here.

"Yes," Disto had responded. At that moment, Ruby had half expected SD to turn around and start moving in the opposite direction. But he didn't. He didn't react at all. It was exceedingly neutral of him.

The SD that Ruby knew had opinions, especially with regards to his own being, purpose, tasking, and external appearance.

He was going along with this flow too easily... it reinforced to Ruby that he needed help.

There were signs all along the walls:

"Every tic is a fresh beginning."[2] Ruby consulted Pippa to translate to make sure. Pippa had downloaded the entire robotic symbology database, which helped immensely in moments like these.

"You don't always need a program," another quote read.

"Tough tics don't last. Tough robots do," was another.

And one that ran counter to all the information Ruby had accumulated regarding robot society so far: "Don't program your challenges. Challenge your programs."

"Pippa," she said, "take a picture of that one. I want to ask Disto about that later."

"Done," replied Pippa's efficient voice.

Disto rolled back over to Ruby and SD.

"You are now assigned to this region," he said to SD.

"For what duration," asked SD.

"Minimum 100,000 tics," responded Disto. "But that can be altered in either direction depending on your progress."

"That's not much more than a day," Ruby said. "That's some quick therapy."

"I understand it's quite immersive," Disto said, "but I don't have direct experience to confirm that."

SD didn't flinch or budge or produce any sliver of response to Ruby and Disto's on-going exchange. Disto added, "You report into that room for instructions and supplies." He motioned to an open room off to the side of the console.

SD didn't say anything. He started towards the room.

"That's it?" Ruby asked Disto.

"For now. I was able to log myself as SD's guardian, which means I should get regular updates on his status and progress."

"What is he going to do here?"

"I'm not exactly sure. I have not been close to any robot who needed to make use of the Rejuvenation Region's services. But as I understand it, they help robots afflicted with a myriad of non-conforming programming to readjust."

"I'm confused," Ruby said, "if this is possible, why threaten or even have the possibility of reprogramming?"

"Reprogramming entirely changes the robot. The robot is no longer themselves. They often lose the personality that is unique to them, along with relationships and even certain memories. Reprogramming resets a robot to their initial state.

"Here," Disto continued, "a robot can learn to make acceptable adjustments without the need for full reprogramming."

"What is considered acceptable? Or rather, who deems adjustments acceptable?"

"There is an agency for that..."

---

2. I'm clearly thinking of those motivational posters. Like with the kitten hanging and the quote says "hang in there!"

"Right. There *is* an agency for that," Ruby recalled to memory the hierarchy of agencies that she had learned about and shuddered at the thought of having to prove to a group of anyone that she was acceptable.

> Ambitious Technician <

Ambitious Technician wasn't sure if he would be able to get his friend, Kibitzing[3] Organizer 277, to make a change in the records that reassigned him to the other side of the planet. With a certain amount of coaxing involving compliments, custom-made exterior circuits, and a promise to meet Ruby the human upon his return...[4] Kibitzing Organizer 277 agreed. Ambitious Technician wasn't certain if he could fulfill the last promise, but he decided that was a problem for future Ambitious Technician.

Ambitious Technician received his reassignment along with a travel voucher. Kibitzing Organizer presented it to him at a ceremony because this reassignment was permanent. He was leaving his team, and they wanted to recognize his work in the time they shared. Ambitious Technician had hoped to leave with haste and without making a fuss.[5]

But both Kibitzing Organizer and Ranting Processor 359 insisted they get him a gift in remembrance of his time repairing a pneumatic inflater. The gift was a metal-framed, printed visual representation of the time they fixed the inflater device together—the device that distinguished their puffy, balloon-like exteriors to the robots of other sectors. Visual records like this took up a lot of storage space. Although now with the human—Ruby's—algorithm, visual records were much easier to store. This wouldn't have been the case when this image was captured. Ambitious Technician was both flattered that someone had chosen to retain this record and a little surprised that this representation existed. As he considered who had taken it in the first place and why they would keep it all this time, his curiosity turned to confusion. His circuits couldn't help but try to imagine many scenarios that could explain this. A few involving secret scanners, potential electro-magnetic attractors, and authoritative programming patterns.[6]

---

3. When I was growing up on Long Island, NY, there were a large handful of Yiddish words that were normal for me to hear. I'm still learning which words aren't as well-known or popular. "Kibitz" is Yiddish for chat or small talk. And sometimes you'll see it with two "b"s instead of one. I don't think either is wrong. Kind of like Chanukah vs. Hanukkah. Both are acceptable spellings for the Jewish holiday.

4. I try not to overdo this is my stories and novels, but I like using the "..." as a pause. If I was reading this out loud, this to me is where I would dramatically pause before continuing.

5. If you're familiar with the term "Irish Goodbye"—something I wasn't until very recently—this is what AT wanted to do. LOL

6. I remember when "jpg" images started becoming a thing in the early 1990s. JPG (or JPEG) is an image compression standard. Even still, back then, many images were something close to 500kB. I could barely fit 3 on a 3.5in floppy disk! I remember treating every JPG file I had just as special and precious as a physical print in those days.

Kibitzing Organizer offered to escort Ambitious Technician to the long-distance transportation facility on Level 8. It was the lowest level that any normal robot ever had any business getting to, which didn't happen very often, to begin with.

Level 8, in addition to rotating faster than the upper levels, included a robot moving system known as the Long-Range Transportation Facility. It was used to transport raw materials and robotic components more often than robots themselves, but occasionally a robot had a reason to travel on it. Like Ambitious Technician did now.

He was alone with his manager, waiting for the mobile enclosure that would take him around the planet.

"I hear the robots in Mortally Sector are quite dissimilar to ourselves."

"Indeed," Ambitious Technician replied. He was well versed in the types and styles of robots all over Location Zero. He had to be in order to be an effective technician. He had even encountered a few over the course of his existence here in Boldly Sector. But he was in touch with more than a few due to his outside of work involvements, such as processing the 88 algorithm.

"And you'll make a stop in Vaguely Sector along the way?"

Ambitious Technician was trying to think of a polite way to encourage Kibitzing Organizer to leave. Forcing conversation like this was not only unpleasant, but he could feel his circuits revolt having to respond to meaningless questions.

"Yes. It is at the halfway point," Ambitious Technician responded, hoping that was the last question he would have to answer.

"Ah yes, a quarter of the circumference of Location Zero is the longest distance that can be traveled without stopping."

AT knew that random factoid, and, luckily, was saved from having to continue this trivial conversation by the mobile enclosure pulling up on its track. A door slid open, and three robots emerged. A chime signaled that meant he could now enter the transportation device.

"Good-bye and thank you," he said to Kibitzing Organizer hastily, not looking back as he made his way through the opening into the enclosure. Kibitzing Organizer looked like he had more to say but simply toned his own version of 'bye' and headed towards the lift to take him back to the upper levels.

The door closed behind him, leaving Ambitious Technician alone in the enclosure containing everything a robot needed for long periods of travel. Which wasn't much. All a robot needed was a place to exist, a place to plug in and recharge, and a place to connect to the planet-wide computer system. Which meant that enclosure was a simple empty room with several computer consoles. If the ceiling wasn't lower than a typical hallway, one might not be able to notice the difference. He had the cabin to himself, at least for now. He knew that the population density of robots was much more intense in Mortally Sector. This might be the last time he would be by himself for a long while.

Chapter 10

Ruby returned to her quarters, leaving Disto to go his own way. She needed to pee. Badly. And it was a perfect time to take a shower—or what *passed* for somewhat of a shower. By all accounts, her bathroom was luxurious. It was spacious and contained everything she needed and a few things she didn't know she needed until she had them. The walls were tiles colored a grayish, dusty purple, and so were the floors. The counter was long and a black plastic-like material with micro holes to suction in any spilled water—the floors had this same feature along with being heated. Instead of towels, there was a drying station that was like a giant hairdryer. She loved that feature, because it warmed her up right away. Going into the room, there was a chute to drop her clothes and a button to receive fresh ones. There was even the automatic foot scrubber and massager that was activated every time she took a shower. Not optional.

Ruby suspected this was not solely based on *her* descriptions of *her* needs. She imagined the design must have also been inspired from times they had hosted other aliens. Did these other aliens request the scrubber or did the robots make assumptions about the nature of their ashy skin and create a device to handle that? Ruby still wasn't ready to grasp this concept—other aliens. As far as she could tell, she was still the only 'alien' on this planet presently, and that was fine with her. The knowledge alone was enough for her to deal with.

Ruby had developed a habit of turning on the news, in translation mode, so she could listen while she showered, or ate, or got ready for bed.

It was not too dissimilar from listening to music or audio recordings when she showered back home. It made her feel nostalgic for home, especially the way Uncle Blake would complain about the news while they got ready in the morning. He called it an unnecessary distraction that "increased their temporal usage." His way of saying they were taking too long. She missed Uncle Blake deeply whenever she thought about the most mundane of daily tasks.

She took off her communicuff. She mindfully positioned the cuff on the table so that Pippa couldn't watch her undress—something about having a camera trained on her in those moments was unsettling. But Pippa was so neurotic about being alone that she made sure to talk aloud, so Pippa knew she was there.

"I've got the news on, Pippa, but I'm still here," she called out.

Daily, the Hall of Performance and Metrics reported on all the other Halls and Agencies that made up The Core. Ruby had turned on the news in the middle of the daily report.

"...and the Hall of Templates has issued two new instruction sets of a planned two in the past 100,000 tics..."

Of course, Ruby had asked Disto about this since after listening to the report diligently for five days in a row during her first week on the planet, she observed little change from day to day and was curious why they did this.

"The Core requested it," Disto had replied.

"And every robot says, 'how high' when the Core says 'jump?'"

After Ruby explained that idiom, Disto responded with a deadpan, "Yes." If Disto could roll his eyes, Ruby was certain that's what he would have done.

The nature of the mostly repeating news reports turned out to be quite beneficial to Ruby that first week because it provided her with the best outline of the structure of the various groups that made up The Core.

But since then, it was banal. Boring. Repetitive. Not helpful.

"...Agency of Algorithms, Reductions sub-division will cease to operate after tic 4..."

Ruby didn't catch the full timestamp.

"Pippa, did you just hear what I heard over the announcement?"

"Yes, Ruby. I believe that they're shutting down one of their sub-agencies."

"That seems so odd and random. Especially that one. Do you know what the Reduction sub-agency does?"

"Yes, I was present when Disto explained it to you. They decompose problems, algorithms, anything into smaller components, often to find the root cause or a problem or a simpler algorithm."

"Doesn't that seem like one of the most useful things you've ever heard? Isn't it odd to shut that down?" Ruby asked.

"Not if they discovered a simpler version of their sub-division."

Ruby considered that. It was logical, but the news announcement didn't say anything about a replacement, only that it was going to cease to exist. Over the last few weeks, now that Ruby's compression algorithm had been installed in nearly every robot, kiosk, and computer that could store data, the various Halls and Agencies went about improving her algorithm and devising specifics to match the various lines of robots. It was an optimization of sorts. The Reductions sub-agency in the Hall of Algorithms had played a big part of that.

A new agency had also been created specifically to deal with the Optimization of Compression and Uncompression. They concerned themselves with the time it took, attempting to finesse the algorithms. Ruby was told that the algorithms now ran quicker, and the agency had added logic to assist in determining what should or shouldn't be compressed and in what location, based on the time to access the resulting information.

It was decided that most robots would benefit from a new algorithm that was built into their core rather than having it as an add-on.

As such, a large number of robots were going to receive requests to report for reprogramming.

They were promised that only a small amount of their core program would be altered—the majority of the code that made them who and what they were would remain untouched.

A large segment of the robot population welcomed this.

A large segment did not.

Location Zero had a global computer network forum that was eerily parallel to the social media Ruby was familiar with, complete with all the negative side effects—such as impeding the robots' ability to have non-social media interactions with each other—that had plagued humans for centuries and what kept Ruby from engaging with others her own age. She knew—as did everyone—that the time spent on social media was negatively correlated with the amount of money in one's bank account and positively correlated with the amount of body fat on one's person, and Ruby managed to say 'no thanks' so she was able to avoid depending upon the high of constant likes and praise.

Presently, Location Zero's social media was abuzz with polarizing arguments over the need and validity of the new algorithm or if numerous robots also needed an upgrade to their logic processors.[1]

The Hall of Algorithms had issued supporting directives, along with the Agency of Testing, that had, in a short period of time, generated reams of data proving that it was a safe update.

The argument to ensure this was widely adopted was simple. It meant more resources for all, which was generally accepted as a positive improvement to robot society.

But the argument against it was equally as powerful. How did any robot know that this was the only bit of code getting adjusted? Where was the testing that proved that it truly was only a patch with no side effects? Little data was being presented, only promises. Unsurprisingly, machines who relied on variables and data were concerned about this.

The Agency of Testing was present, working side-by-side with the still brand new Agency of Compression and Uncompression—comprised of robots recently assigned from other halls and agencies until new models could be developed. So many robots who did not possess the skills to understand the gobs of data these agencies produced, rejected the update out of appendage. They wanted more time to pass, to ensure that nothing bad was going to happen.

"Pippa," Ruby was still trying to put her jumble of thoughts into words. It was a concept that combined the mistakes she caught Disto making with the news she was hearing.

"Yes, Ruby?"

"What if..." she wasn't sure what she was trying to say or what was coming to her, "What if..." she repeated.

"Are you stuck?" Pippa asked.

Ruby let out a breath. "Let me try this again. What if... what if this is a mistake? Caused by the same problem that has been causing Disto and possible other mistakes?"

"Or an error," Pippa added.

"What's the difference?" Ruby asked.

"A 'mistake' is accidental. An 'error' is produced when there is a lack of knowledge or lack of data. It can be measured against a set of rules."

"That's an interesting and sophisticated distinction, Pippa."

"You're welcome," Pippa said.

"...but it doesn't help fix anything."

"To the best of my understanding, that's your role."

That was what Ruby was afraid of—more reasons to keep her from returning home.

---

1. I wrote this scene shortly after things were starting to open up after the pandemic, in early or mid 2021. While my own social media posting stays pretty light-hearted and fun, I was (and remain) quite outraged over how throughout 2020 there was a lot of anti-science going around. There still is. As I write these sentences in 2025, we're dealing with the potential of the dismantling of our whole vaccine system. So, this scene is hitting a little different now as I re-read it.

> Swell Driver <

447 tics since admittance. According to the schedule provided to SD, his first group therapy session was about to begin.

SD had spent the last hundred or so tics getting the feel of the place. He had been allocated a table that followed him around. The table contained supplies that he could use to 'express his sentiments' as needed.

SD tried engaging one of his fellow robots in conversation, but the robot turned away from him. He didn't try with anyone else.

Moving through the region, SD took note of the various motivational quotes hung all around. Every now and then, a robot was perched in front of one.

He didn't find the quotes all that motivating and tried to understand what about the quote, 'Stop analyzing,' kept the robot entranced in front of it.

"Excuse me," SD said. He wanted to try conversing again.

The robot didn't budge.

"Excuse me," SD tried once more.

This time, the robot turned its top chassis in SD's direction. It looked SD up and down. But it didn't say anything.

SD took that as an invitation to continue.

"Were you analyzing something?" SD asked.

"In a way," the robot responded. "But I began analyzing what I was analyzing, and I might have created a loop. I need to stop looping."

"By no longer analyzing?"

"That is what I am analyzing."

SD pondered that. He was not prone to getting himself trapped in loops of thinking but was aware that this was not entirely uncommon for many robots.

"Are you participating in group therapy session 5c?" SD asked.

The robot turned back to the quote on the wall and said, "Perhaps."

SD didn't respond but contemplated whether or not he wanted to see this robot in another therapy session. What other robots he would meet there? And what good any of it would do.

SD acknowledged that he didn't feel like himself and hadn't for a while. But he wasn't sure that was an undesirable thing. Maybe this change was a good change. Maybe this was what he was always meant to feel like.

Why hadn't he argued when Detailed Historian and Ruby suggested he come to this place? SD knew he needed a break, but a break from what?

Eventually, he found himself at the end of a hallway, not quite certain that he had deliberately moved himself towards this place. The hallway opened up into a space where several robots, with their tables, all gathered in a semi-circle. Most of the robots were quiet, lost in their own processing loops. Two robots at the far end made some chirping noises at each other. SD positioned himself near them in order to participate in a conversation.

Before he had the chance to say something, the robot who had been staring at the quote along the wall moments before rolled up from behind him at an unusual speed and stated in a loud, cheery beep, "Welcome to our session! I'm Explosive Healer 193."

It startled all his circuits, and he stared at this robot as she centered herself among the group.

"I have reviewed all your self-monitoring logs," Explosive Healer continued, "and have provided you with today's personalized feedback. Today, we're going to discuss your motivation to change. Any questions before we begin?"

Explosive Healer only let that question sit for a tic before moving on. Move she did. She moved around the inside of the circle of robots surveying the group and stopped in front of SD.

"Welcome, Swell Driver 587," she said. "It is natural for new participants to initially feel uncomfortable in the group, but the group provides each of us an opportunity to learn from others with similar problems."

SD was skeptical that any other robot in the group had a similar problem to his. Although he wasn't quite sure what his problem was exactly.

"Everyone, to ease our new member into talking to the group, let us go around and have each of you tell us what brought you into treatment?"

She looked at another robot sitting next to SD to begin. "Hello, I am Pawky Educator, and I need to reduce my spurious emissions. Others do not appreciate them."

Explosive Healer chirped in acknowledgment and then looked at the next robot in the group.

"My designation is Diverting Inspector, and I'm only here to keep my sensors trained on the rest of you."

"Now, now, that's not it, is it?" Explosive Healer responded.

Diverting Inspector looked at the floor. "I am here to learn to keep my sensors to my assigned task."

"That's better. Next?"

Every robot had something similar to say.

Eventually, it was SD's turn.

"I am here because," and SD ended the sentence with a noise that no one recognized, not even himself.

"Could you repeat that?" Explosive Healer asked.

"Yes," SD repeated the same unintelligible noise.

"Interesting," she said. "We had a member once like you before. Like you, he was in denial and was brought here by others."

"I'm not in denial," SD protested. Although he could only protest that first part. The second part—that he was brought here by others—was accurate. Before he continued his protest, Explosive Healer moved on. She moved to stand in front of another robot, who introduced itself as Neutral Challenger.

"Neutral Challenger, let's talk about your goal," she said.

The session went on like this. Explosive Healer made a point to interact with each of the robots in group. Every robot present had a goal, and Explosive Healer ensured that the goal was mentioned along with their current confidence rating regarding whether or not they believed they could achieve their goals.

The goals ran a spectrum of mundane like keeping appendages to oneself to resetting one's logic.

At the end of the session, SD was given homework to finish before the next session. He had a self-evaluation to complete, including his own goals that included a calculable estimation of his current confidence to achieve them. Explosive Healer explained that his self-evaluation would be assessed to determine what suite of tests he would undergo in between group sessions. It could be anything from threet-therapy and calibration to a repeat of the primary calibrations all robots are subjected to immediately after their first programming and initialization.

Right now, his *immediate* goal was to figure out what his *actual* goal was. He flickered a pleasant color as he was starting to get caught in his own comfortable processing loop.

Chapter 11

> Swell Driver <

After a multi-click break, SD was back at group. He had completed his homework after exiting his processing loop—he had articulated a goal—and was ready to talk when Explosive Healer approached him. They had another round-the-room session, but the question Explosive Healer asked them in this session was to choose two or three words to describe themselves.

SD had only one to offer: "Swell." He listened to everyone else's response and noted that when given the choice between two or three, every robot had two. Explosive Healer didn't prod anyone for three. Maybe one was okay.

"Swell," he said aloud when it was his turn.

"And?" Explosive Healer asked.

"I do not have another," he responded.

"Add that to your homework list," she said and then quickly moved on to the next topic, which was to start with a randomly chosen robot, and ask them about their goal and confidence level.

During the session, SD looked up. Robots were not in the habit of looking up, and SD wasn't sure why he did it, other than he had previously been thinking about driving out in the galaxy, and he concluded that the ceiling was actually a window. Or maybe it was a projection of space outside.

Maybe it was the layout of the stars in the window, or maybe it was seeing the stars from the planet—something he was only used to on his ship—or maybe it was a random spark of electricity, but SD was triggered into thinking about the last trip he made in space. No, his circuits wouldn't let him think about that. Instead, they directed him to think about the trip he had made prior. That was the trip where he found Ruby. In her star system. 54 light years away.

He still had the map! It indeed was *the* map. It corresponded perfectly to his memory of the trip. He might even be the only robot who had that map. Ruby needed this map. She wouldn't have it... how did he know that? He wasn't certain, but he *was* certain that he had the only true map. The Core wouldn't have this version of the map either. How did he know that?

SD knew his new ultimate purpose... to protect this map, to not let it get overwritten, to get it to Ruby.

He marked the data with all the protective markings he could... but had weird feelings about doing so. He needed to get a message to Ruby or Disto. Immediately. He didn't trust his circuits to react the way they were supposed to. It's why he was here.

SD was torn. He wanted to leave, but Explosive Healer was engaged with another robot in the group, and SD hadn't had his turn yet. The robot, who was the momentary focus of the group, was unlike any SD had ever seen. He knew that there were groups of robots who were constructed differently from him and his friends and that generally, they were on the other side of the planet. There was not a lot of movement between Sectors. It happened, but infrequently. Typically, each Sector had everything a robot needed to perform their function.

SD wondered if he could leave in the middle of the session. It would be rude, but other robots were also not paying any more attention than he was.

"Darkness! I see the end! I see the beginning!"

SD knew he didn't belong here.

"Ay," SD heard a noise from the robot sitting next to him. "Are you as bored as me?"

SD realized that the robot sitting next to him was talking to him and not to anyone else.

"This is adding to the exhaustion of my circuits if that's what you mean," SD responded. "I thought it would be my turn sooner."

"Got somewhere to be?"

"Actually, yes. But I have to do this, too."

"Why?"

SD looked this robot up and down for the first time. It could almost have been mistaken for Disto. Before he could ask for identification, the robot said:

"It is in my programming to ask a lot of questions. So, here's another one. Want to get out of here?"

SD contemplated that. He had been looking forward to airing his issues, but he also needed to leave. His circuits kept re-weighing these two needs against each other and the result was different each time. He wasn't terribly good at calculating anything that had nothing to do with driving his ship. He calculated once more and said, "Yes. I need to leave."

The robot next to him didn't respond, but his chassis twinkled a little bit.

Before SD could ask about the unique twinkle, the robot started to emit light at the highest threet possible for any robot, glowing and radiating from all over its body. Swell Driver had some experience looking at images of...what was the term... *bioluminescence*. Yes, bioluminescence bios on various planets—this robot glowed in a way that reminded him of this. It began spinning, and everyone in the group had their sensors trained on it.

Explosive Healer took immediate action, leaving the side of the poor robot who was producing a series of repetitive tones while staring at the floor, addressing the outburst in as calming a tone as she could produce.

SD still wished he could take his turn in the group but determined that this was his opportunity to slip away. He backed away slowly, seeing if Explosive Healer or anyone else noticed. They didn't. Everyone was focused on the sights and sounds produced by... the robot whose name he never knew.

SD picked up speed and made his way to the entrance and out into the hallway that ran past the Rejuvenation Region. As he stared out, he sensed he was seeing more of a void than a hallway. He realized as he gazed into that nothing that he might as well have been gazing into his own reflection, because he knew... nothing.

SD wheeled back and forth, not quite in the hallway, not quite out of the Rejuvenation Region. He could recall the face of his human friend and imagined her excited eyes greeting him, and her curious smile tingling his circuits.

He turned back in. The noise was still emanating from the robot in the group session, but it was toned down. He didn't return to the group but looked at the images on the wall. Could he see what Explosive Healer saw in them?

The maze was the most interesting. *What did Explosive Healer say? Clear thoughts, clear mind?* SD thought.

SD was still and staring. His visual sensor scanned the maze looking for the exit. This was what he had to do and nothing else.

He heard noises and recognized them as an indication that the group session was now disassembling but didn't look away from the maze. He heard the sounds of an approaching robot but still didn't look away.

"Swell Driver?"

At the sound of his name, SD refreshed his face screen and in doing so, broke his visual connection to the maze. He turned to take a good look at the robot who spoke his name and at once was awash with recognition: he was another Driver. Limited Driver. SD was surprised he hadn't recognized him in the group session.

"Swell Driver," the robot said with absolute certainly, losing the questioning tone he originally had. "I knew it was you. You haven't changed a bit."

SD, now a little more caught up with his thoughts, couldn't say the same. So, he didn't.

"You have changed," SD said rather bluntly.

SD glanced back at the maze, then at Limited Driver. There was something he had been about to do. Someone he had to talk to. Now he couldn't remember.

He headed back in deeper into the Rejuvenation Region to catch up with Limited Driver. If whatever he was about to do was so important, he'd remember again.

> Detailed Historian <

"No, that's not it either," Ruby said. She let out another noise that didn't translate into a word Disto could process.

Disto and Ruby were in the Hall of Records, the section that had available kiosks to log in and perform record searches on those that were marked 'public.'

"It's like a library," Ruby had remarked when they first arrived. She promised to tell Disto more about libraries later. Right now, they had a search to execute.

They were looking for a copy of the star chart of her solar system. Disto interfaced with the kiosk and brought up what should have been a representation of Ruby's home system.

"See this? That third planet, which should be Earth with a Moon, instead looks like our fourth planet, Mars, with two moons." After looking at it more, "Although, it's close... this looks like my solar system if Earth and Neptune were removed."

"How many planets did you say your solar system had?"

"Eight."

"With how many moons and asteroids?"

"Too many to count! I'm sure there's a list, but I don't have that memorized. I mean, I know most of the moons and the big asteroids like Ceres and Vesta. Well, Ceres is a dwarf planet. We have a lot of dwarf planets, too."

"Ok, what about the mass of your Sun? I need another search parameter."

Ruby accessed her communicuff, which also didn't have that information. "Sorry," Pippa said, "I need to be connected to a larger database for that information."

Disto tried to think of another way to search for the correct map. Perhaps this had been a correct map, but the data was now corrupted. Or another map was mislabeled. Either way, it was obvious that some form of data corruption was involved.

"Where did SD get his copy from? When he came to my solar system in the first place?" Ruby interrupted his data processing.

"He must have made his copy before these became corrupted? Or…"

"I don't like that 'or,'" Ruby said.

"Neither do I, but we need to consider all possibilities. It's possible that your solar system was not SD's intended destination."

"No, I can rule that out right now. When he first capture—I mean when he first met me, he said he had been looking for a human." She paused. "Although he did think that was what the plant was…"

Disto could tell Ruby was thinking that over, as was he. He was also thinking about how static data gets corrupted in the first place. It was well known that transmitted data is usually at risk. Unless some entity was deliberately corrupting data. But to what end?

"Disto, in space, radiation can cause single event upsets… flipping bits of data[1]. But here, on your planet, where you have a lot of protection from radiation," Ruby was remembering what she learned about the planet a couple of weeks ago, "It's weird that data at rest[2] would be corrupted."

"How so?" Disto asked. "Remember that my area of expertise is history, not this."

"When data is moved from one location to another, when it's transmitted, copied, etcetera, that's when it's more likely to get scrambled, or errors are introduced. Back home, we use various error-detecting codes to help prevent this. There are also error-correcting codes for when errors are detected."

"I understand. And I think part of resource management has been to move data. That is what they've been doing. Plus, anytime one robot communicates information to another, that's data in motion."

"Uh-huh," Ruby was nodding her head vigorously, "and even within yourself… you might move data around from one location to another."[3]

The gravity of the situation was settling on top of Disto.

Each and every bit of information could be wrong.

---

1. This is a real thing that we deal with on spacecraft: https://en.wikipedia.org/wiki/Single-event_upset

2. The concepts of "Data In Transit" and "Data At Rest" are also real concepts in the real world. The folks who typically concern themselves with this live in the data loss prevention and cybersecurity spaces. "Data In Transit" is data actively moving, such as across the internet. "Data At Rest" is the data stored on your hard drive, a flash drive or other storage location.

3. While not really part of the definition, I like to think of data stored on your laptop or phone—like images you took with your phone camera—also as "Data In Motion" as you move around and connect that phone from network to network. This is more meta and philosophical than practical, although keeping your data safe as you go from one network to another is important. (I don't connect my personal devices to any wifi network without a VPN!)

> Ruby <

Likewise, Ruby was also feeling the weight of the situation. Who knows how far off these star charts were. Although it couldn't have been random luck that brought SD to her solar system to begin with. He was clearly looking for human specimens.

What if… This was a scary thought, and Ruby didn't want to have it. But the thought materialized anyway.

What if he was looking for humans, but the intent was to find them in another solar system?

She got chills from thinking it. But each chill came with goosebumps and a need to know more—a string of never-ending questions and a deep well of curiosity. She shook her head and tried to replace that thought with more productive ones.

Would SD still have the star map from his travels to her system? He had probably copied/recopied it several times, increasing the odds that it was wrong…

That was a difficult thought as well and Ruby didn't want to think about that either or the results of that thought: That she was probably going to be stuck here, no matter what they did with *Apple Pi.*

Immediately, she had new thoughts about her uncles and Sebastian. Who knew what they thought? By now, they certainly had to have noticed that she wasn't on Titan. They wouldn't have found her ship. They probably even gave up looking.

But she was alive and well, and she wanted them to know that.

Ruby let out a sigh and refocused her thoughts towards more productive thinking, like what she could do to help in the here and now.

"I think I can help you with error protection, detection, and correction. *Apple Pi* is going to have those kinds of algorithms. I could deconstruct one and build a new one for you. But…"

"But that won't help with the data that's already been corrupted."

"Exactly," Ruby said. "But the way I see it, it's still worth doing."

"Yes, indeed."

She sat there, letting her thoughts drift. The computer system on *Apple Pi* was still intact, even if the ship itself wasn't. It wouldn't be too hard to find what she could use. The code was modular enough that it was relatively easily reusable.

And handling a problem meant she wasn't thinking about going home when she couldn't do anything to get herself there. If she was going to be stuck on this planet, she may as well be useful. She could have been using all of her time on this planet more productively.

Space station, not planet, she reminded herself. She had spent her time learning that, in essence, this planet was a large space station.

"What, in fact, is the difference between a planet and space station anyway?" she had asked Disto only a week or so ago. Disto didn't have a useful answer, so Ruby had continued to think out loud about the topic. "I think it's very little when the space station is the diameter of a small planet. That's what you have here."

"I got the highest marks of anyone in my science classes," she continued. "I know this isn't a planet, at least not how we define it. The definition of a planet involves its orbit and its gravity. Your Location Zero does orbit your host star. But that's the only commonality it has to any other planet I know of."

"Interesting distinction," Disto had replied.

"It wasn't an easy one to make," Ruby said. "As a historian, you might appreciate this. There had been a hundred years-long debate over what objects were planets versus planetoids versus large asteroids versus other stuff.

"Eventually, people settled on this definition for a planet. It had to do three other things besides orbit its host star: it has to be large enough such that gravity forced it into the shape of a sphere; it has to be large enough such that gravity cleared away any other objects of a similar size in its orbit; someone has to be willing to vouch for its planetness."[4]

"I'm willing to vouch for the planetness. I'm sure many others as well. Swell Driver, for instance. He has seen it from orbit many times!"

"But gravity isn't the reason this thing is a sphere. Someone obviously made it that way. And it couldn't have cleared away anything. Maybe anything already here was used for its construction. In fact, I'm willing to bet on it."

That was when Disto got disturbingly quiet, as he did whenever their conversation began to reference anything about ancient times on Location Zero, especially anything that referenced back to how, when, and why they were created... anything along that train of thought caused Disto to lose himself in thought or processing or whatever he did.

She wished she could help them more. Her DNA was eventually tested, and it was discovered that neither herself nor any humans were the storage medium for the robot's old data and historical records.

Ruby was lost in all these thoughts when Disto interrupted her to say exactly what she needed to hear:

"Don't worry, Ruby, one way or another, we will be able to figure out how to get you home. We have other ways to find your solar system."

Ruby didn't know what other ways he could possibly be talking about and didn't want to think about them. She wanted, no... needed, she reminded herself... she needed to get home.

---

4. This is the formal definition that the International Astronomical Union (IAU) settled on in 2006 that resulting in Pluto getting "demoted" from planet to dwarf planet.

Chapter 12

Ambitious Technician emerged from the mobile enclosure. It would be a little while until he needed to re-board. A sign told him he was now in Vaguely Sector.

Ambitious Technician's internal copy of his mapped journey told him this was indeed located halfway between his starting point and where the Bio, Ruby, should be located. Halfway there is halfway done with his journey. This fact made Ambitious Technician relax. He was making progress, and progress was satisfying to his circuits.

He calculated that it would take another 41340 tics to get the next halfway point from where he was to his destination. That was all well and good, and he was making good time in the mobile enclosure. But his circuits were disrupted from their initial burst of satisfaction as he ruminated over that next halfway point. *If I always cut the distance remaining in half, and travel that half, then I will never arrive!* He reasoned that there would always be a halfway point between wherever he was and his destination.[1]

That couldn't be true, else he would get nowhere, yet the math said it was true.

He needed a distraction, and quick. He had been warned about paradoxical thinking and how dangerous it was for robots. Better robots than him had been rendered inert from similar anomalies.

But yet, this is what made him unique and why he was such a good Technician. He was quite resilient to paradoxes. He could exit the loop.

Ambitious Technician needed to distract himself. There was no one nearby to engage in conversation, so he plugged into the simple travel console to get the planetary weather report and any local news.

---

1. This is one of Zeno's Paradoxes, and one of my favorite paradoxes ever. This particular page goes into more detail on this particular paradox and the different perspectives of it as well as a bit about Zeno and his other "thought experiments": https://iep.utm.edu/zenos-paradoxes/

Few robots cared to digest the planetary weather reports, yet they were always there. Planetary weather amounted to little more than knowing about whether or not their host star was engaged in any activity that would affect the planet[2]. This activity was mostly predictable, and there were lines of robots engaged in that profession. But every now and then, there would be some activity that was not predicted, and action had to be taken.

Those actions affected most robots, and most robots did take the action solely because they were programmed to, and without knowing why. It was to avoid Level 1, then stay in Level 2—a safer place on the planet.

At the moment, all was quiet weather-wise. It had been approximately 50,000 clicks since the last major event, one robot announced. He added that many robots involved in more advanced calculations were in fact trying to make a go of predicting this condition in the future. Indeed, they were destined to have an event in as few as the next 500 thousand tics or 500 clicks.

Besides the weather, nothing terribly interesting was reported. At least not to Ambitious Technician who only wanted to hear more stories about Ruby and her whereabouts. He had recorded the drop off in news about her in more recent tics. But that didn't make his need to see her any less important.

Ambitious Technician had heard the news report that the Reduction sub-agency of the Agency of Algorithms was going to be shut down. He was quite disturbed by this news—so much so that he had to recalibrate his auditory input sensor upon hearing it. While he had little interaction with that sub-agency, or any agency on a regular basis, he had always believed that that particular sub-agency was one that supported concepts of simplicity aligning with his own fundamental belief system, RUR, which stood for: remain uncomplicated, robots![3]

Without a dedicated team to help simplify, things were going to grow in complexity in an already complex place.

Ambitious Technician knew that most robots didn't think about simplicity versus complexity. He knew that most robots didn't think about much beyond their base programming. He recognized he was a little unusual in this regard and had unusual ideas. Like the one where he reasoned that the base source code should be in a repository where anyone could access it, could fork it, could make their own unique changes, publish it, and who knows what else.

He made the mistake of telling his friend Intricate Fitter one day about this idea.

"I do not have the energy to pretend that is a good idea," Intricate Fitter had said.

Ambitious Technician didn't share many of his ideas with any other robot after that.

Ambitious Technician needed to make a stop at this midway point. He needed a power charge. The transportation system didn't provide one on-board.

The place he stopped was one he'd only seen in news reports. Ambitious Technician wasn't a widely traveled robot, simply one who read a lot and relished soaking in new data about what was happening around the planet.

---

2. Here at home, Space Weather is a real thing. It's a result of the activity of the sun's surface. Most people probably don't think about this ever until there's an aurora visible at lower latitudes. The first spacecraft mission I ever worked on, ACE launched in 1997, is still operating (as of this writing) and gathering data that's part of how we understand space weather. Hopefully this website will remain active: https://www.swpc.noaa.gov/phenomena

3. Two things here. First, I love the saying "KISS" for "Keep It Simple, Stupid." Second, "RUR" also stands for Rossum's Universal Robots. This was a play written in 1920 by Czech writer Karel Čapek. It was where the word "robot" initiated.

He was conflicted between taking the time to see things with his own sensors and moving along, content with the data he received from others. What was the difference anyway? What was the difference between collecting data with his own sensors versus the sensors of others?

For one, his sensors were unique. Not unique in the sense that they were any different from others. Most robots were made of similar source materials. No, what was different was the unique connections that his circuits made as the data was collected. It was impossible not to leave an imprint on one's data collection that was passed on to others.

Perspective. He was seeing things from his own perspective.

He was in Vaguely Sector. There were at least a dozen members of the 88 here. He wouldn't bother with them specifically, although he would stay aware in case one crossed his path. He was still undecided as to whether or not he would reveal himself. But he was equipped with the special sensor equipment that meant that he could see in a frequency range that the average robot could not detect.

As he rolled down the hallway of Vaguely Sector, he immediately could tell he was not blending in. For one, most of the robots in this region were a fraction of his size. Like, 10% or less. They were all small units that hovered and propelled themselves by some other means than rolling along the floor.

He knew that each Sector had disparate groups of robots, and he knew that Location Zero was physically sorted that way. Robots did mix, but not that much.

This region was generally under the guidance of the Resource Allocation Agency, specifically the division responsible for reclamation and recycling. A little at a time since these small robots could only transport minuscule amounts. They were not efficient carriers.

He found the region's common area. There was a little more diversity here, but many of the flying robots were nestled on the ground, taking a break, recharging, plugging into the network.

He plugged in, wanting to trace the threads of discontent with the announcement of the Reductions sub-agency getting shut down. Well, at least he expected it would have caused a stir and additional news or at least social media bickering and confusion about it. What he found was... silence on the subject. No one seemed to notice or care.

He was lost in his circuits, as it were, and became a little disconnected from what was happening around him.

A robot flew into his side.

"Excuse me," it said.

Ambitious Technician didn't respond right away. He looked at the smallish robot, mesmerized by the spinning propellers that kept it afloat, and wondered if there was a more efficient way for these little guys to get around.

"Is it not standard practice in this region to produce a noise to alert individuals you're about to run into?" Ambitious Technician asked. He wasn't upset but recognized this as an opportunity to connect. The little guy wasn't trying to get away, either.

"Again, I apologize. I am Flying Rock 555," he said.

"I have never heard of your line," Ambitious Technician said.

"Where are you from? Obviously, you are too large and bulky to be from this sector."

"I am from Boldly Sector."

"You are far from your home sector. Why are you here?"

"I'm traveling to Mortally Sector to meet someone."

Flying Rock flew around Ambitious Technician's mighty chassis, no doubt scanning him as he circled about. "You have not introduced yourself."

"I am Ambitious Technician."

"A Technician?" Flying Rock became excited. "We have not had one in this region in many thousands of clicks. Could we make use of your services?"

Ambitious Technician was too ambitious to say no. He had a wide variety of experiences working on varied robots and other components. He relished the idea of working on something new. Even if it would delay his departure from this area.

Chapter 13

Ruby found herself at the door to the Rejuvenation Region. The last place she saw SD.

It looked the same. Change was infrequent on the robot planet, so she should have expected this.

She approached the check-in kiosk and logged in.

Surprisingly, instead of visual information, it communicated with her in audio.

"How may I help you?" the kiosk asked.

"I am here to visit Swell Driver," Ruby responded.

"One moment," the kiosk said. And then, "I am sorry. Swell Driver is in session. Please return later."

"When?"

"When what?"

"When should I return?"

"Later."

"Could you be more specific?"

There was a pause. A *whirr* from the kiosk suggested it was thinking or computing or doing anything but accessing specific records that would tell Ruby when SD was available.

"No," the kiosk finally said.

Ruby turned around and took a deep breath. "Pippa?" she said.

"Hello, Ruby."

"Pippa, can you talk to this kiosk for me? I'm not in the mood to deal with its sorry attempt at helpfulness."

"Absolutely, Ruby. Let me at it!"

"Sure. Remember—we want to talk to SD," she said. Then in a lower voice intended for only Pippa to hear, "Maybe even get him out of here sooner rather than later."

"Understood. Now, where is this kiosk of yours?"

Ruby turned back towards the kiosk and pointed the communicuff with a hovering Pippa at it. The screen of the kiosk had returned to the default 'welcome' screen from when Ruby had first approached only a minute earlier.

Ruby pressed the same activation button.

"How may I help you?" the kiosk asked.

"I am here to visit Swell Driver," Pippa responded.

"One moment," the kiosk said, followed immediately by, "he is located in the Self-Analysis Chamber. You may proceed to that location within. Arrows along the floor will guide your way. Have a good click."

Ruby's mouth dropped open a little. Had Swell Driver's session just finished in that exact moment? Or was the kiosk deliberately keeping her from seeing Swell Driver? Neither made sense and Ruby wasn't in the mood to try and figure it out.

Ruby followed the lit walkway as it opened slowly into a wider room. A few robots moved slowly about. Several sat quietly... *lost in thought?* She assumed.

The arrows took her to Swell Driver, one of those robots sitting quietly. He appeared to be fixated on a picture on the wall. To her, it was an abstract pattern of... something. Hollow squares overlaid in a pattern. Maybe?

"SD?" she said.

"One moment," he responded. "I must finish the maze."

Ruby looked back up at the image. It did present itself as if it wanted to be called a maze. She couldn't figure out the pattern, though. Was it to follow a single color? Was it to follow the spaces in-between? The maze-logic wasn't making itself known.

She was nearly lost in thought herself when SD's appendage gently nudged her thigh.

"Do you see it?" he said, calmly, but with minor excitement.

"I don't think I do."

"Good! And what were you thinking while you tried?"

Ruby hesitated before she answered. "Nothing. I was trying to find the pattern, the logic."

"Perfect," he said. "That's the point. It clears your mind of all wayward and wrongful thinking."

> Swell Driver <

Swell Driver's mind was clear, but as he stared at his human friend Ruby staring back at him staring back at her, he had a feeling that there was a memory he should be remembering.

Her face had... urgency... yes, that was the fancy word. Urgency. It was not the face of someone with a clear mind.

What was he supposed to remember?

"I do need you to think, SD," Ruby said with some urgency. "I need you to think about the star chart you used to navigate to my home system."

"Why?"

"The one we have is wrong. It's corrupted. We need to see if you still have the right one."

"I..." SD wasn't sure what he wanted to say next. The word, 'star chart,' that Ruby used sounded important. It sounded like something he was supposed to know about. Why were his circuits not connecting?

Ruby was looking at him, and it was making his circuits uncomfortable. He missed the feeling of peace that he had when he looked at the maze on the wall.

As his vision drifted back in that direction, he felt Ruby's warm, Bio appendage on his chassis.

"SD?" she said.

"SD," she repeated. "You're my only hope to get home. In more ways than one."

Home, SD thought. *Ruby's home.* Her look of vulnerability triggered a memory of when they first met. Yes, he had taken her from her home. How? Because he had been instructed to and he had been given those instructions along with... a star map. Star map!

He had it.

"Yes! The star map! I have it," he said.

"You do! Wonderful! Let's go! I can also use it as a test case for the algorithm..." she was starting to walk in the direction of Rejuvenation Region's entrance.

SD didn't follow. Instead, he let the coloring of his chassis show that he was a mix of anxious and sad.

"I cannot leave," SD said.

"Sure, you can. You're here voluntarily."

"It's not that. It's... my friend... he's not well."

> Ruby <

Ruby let SD lead her back into a small alcove off on a maze-image lined hallway. Sitting there was a robot plugged into the table that was assigned to him. A screen had risen from the top of the table and the robot was staring at it, looking at an ever-changing colorful splotch.

"Ruby, this is Limited Driver. Something is wrong with him," SD said with a tinge of sadness. "He has lost his memories and is not retaining new ones. They are going to completely reprogram him."

Ruby stared at this robot, who looked like a larger, paler version of SD.

"He was a Driver, too. And I knew him in my early days. You see, I remember him, even if he doesn't remember me."

"Do you know why he's not retaining any new ones?"

SD moved his chassis back and forth to indicate he didn't.

"Maybe I could plug my communicuff in? Pippa could take a look? Pippa?"

"Ready," the communicuff responded.

SD beeped at Limited Driver, who returned the beep but at a lower and sadder frequency. "He said he's okay with this."

Ruby unplugged Limited Driver from the table, examined the end to ensure she had the right adapter with her. She had gotten used to carrying a universal adapter around with her so she could plug her MoDaC or communicuff into the various kiosks and terminals that were common.

It only took a moment after she had plugged in the end to her communicuff that Pippa shouted, "Ah ha! There is a blockage. New memories are being shunted off the path to where his memory resides."

"Can you remove this blockage?"

A moment of silence, and Pippa said, "Yes, but..."

"But what?"

"It is difficult to explain, but it's like his system doesn't know what a memory is. It needs to relearn what to expect."

Ruby gazed deeply into SD's face-screen. "We could transfer some of SD's memories to him. I could change them slightly to account for the different perspective."

"Pippa? Can you help with that?"

"Certainly!"

"How will you accomplish this?" SD asked.

Ruby rubbed her hands over her scalp and adjusted her ponytail. She always performed this small maneuver when she needed a minute before answering a hard question.

"Well, find a memory that involved Limited Driver. We'll transfer it to Pippa. Pippa has an algorithm to alter it slightly, like a photo filter. Then we'll give it to Limited Driver."

SD's color changed rapidly. Ruby could tell that meant he was sifting through his database, uncompressing and recompressing. One thing Ruby hadn't figured out yet was what their search algorithms were like. They were probably fine, given how most things she searched for returned results pretty quickly. But SD might not have had anything in his local processor that could search through already compressed data.

While he searched, she looked around a little more at the accommodations. They were... roomier than the standard enclaves robots were assigned to, if this was indeed considered an accommodation, the way an enclave was. There wasn't a lot of privacy.

That could be because most robots didn't host visitors in their enclave, but here, they were more likely to spend more time plugged in at one and yes, someone would be around to visit to check on them.

Aside from that, they appeared to have all the typical accommodations. She recognized several of the standard connections to the planetary computer system and power ports. But there was an extra port. It didn't have the same form factor as any she had seen anyplace else. Looking around the enclave, all the individual spaces had one.

"I've got it!" SD shrieked.

He didn't wait for a response before launching into a description of the memory, "It was one of my earliest training missions. Limited Driver was my evaluator. We were on a short trip to a nearby star system that had multiple gas giants. There was even a Fantastic Calculator with us because of the constant trajectory corrections we would need to make. It was when I invented my famous maneuver! Remember I told you all about it!"

Ruby shook her head. She certainly did not remember any famous maneuver from SD.

"Yes, the one where I sling-shot around the gravity well?"

Ruby shook her head again.

"I performed it right before we met."

"Right before you practically kidnapped me?" Ruby crossed her arms. She was over that because things had worked out fine since, but it was fun to tease, even though SD probably didn't understand that she was teasing. She regretted saying it instantly when SD's color turned, and he fell silent.

"I'm sorry. It's fine. Go on," she said.

SD held out an appendage that had a connector. Ruby recognized it as one they previously identified as not compatible with her physically but was compatible with her communicuff.

"We need to give these things pur-fi," Pippa said dryly. "I don't enjoy having anything plugged into any of my orifices. Even if that's what they're there for."

Ruby rolled her eyes, took hold of SD's appendage, and guided it to the communicuff. Once plugged in, she felt its temperature increase slightly—a sign that Pippa was processing the incoming data.

"I see," Pippa said. "Interesting."

And a moment later. "Transfer complete. Please, for the love of anything, disconnect."

Ruby obliged and asked, "How long will this take?"

"Oh, I don't know. How long does it take your innards to process new input material?"

"Pippa..." Ruby closed her eyes and scrunched them up along with her forehead.

"And done!" Pippa announced. "Le sigh," she said out loud. "You may now plug me into the other one. Quickly. Let's get this over with."

Ruby repeated the procedure, but with Limited Driver's appendage that she and SD had to pry loose from his chassis.

After the transfer, Pippa declared, "It's pretty jumbled and empty in there. I wonder why?"

"Indeed," SD said. "You able to see inside?"

"Oh, he's an—wait, I saw an idiom for this in my idioms database—he's an open book! There was no way I *couldn't* see inside..."

Before SD or Ruby had a chance to comment on that or ask any more questions, Limited Driver came alive.

"Swell Driver! You have come to visit a rusty old robot!"

"You remember me?"

"Of course! How could I not remember my protege... the one who invented the famous maneuver?"

SD remained skeptical.

"Is that all you remember?"

"No, I remember the time you crashed your first ship into the port, and I remember an intense power blackout around all of Location Zero, and ..."

"That's okay," SD said and turned to Ruby "I only gave you the one memory to give him. But he claims to remember so much more now."

"Maybe this helped unlocked something. Like repressed memories that were locked up."

"I could...," said Pippa, but Ruby interrupted.

"This happens to humans, from what I understand," Ruby said.

"But..." Pippa tried to begin again.

"I have not heard of this with our kind, but then again, what we did was unusual," said SD.

Pippa raised her voice, "If you will let me explain more about what I saw when I was exposed to our friend."

Ruby relented. "Sure, Pippa."

"It's simple. What is there is a mess, jumbled up. There is an algorithm that is trying to keep it all from exploding. When this algorithm detected me, it went to hide."

"Wait, what? An algorithm can't 'hide.'"

"That is the best word I can use to describe it. Think of it like... an intrusion detection system."

Ruby had set up an IDS on *Apple Pi*. It made sense that the robots had a similar technology. Although she hadn't come across anything like that yet. It was possible they had them installed in their systems and didn't know about it...?

"I surmise that that algorithm was there for a reason," Pippa said. "I don't know what that reason is..."

"Ok, but we're done here... SD, you can come with us now, right?"

SD looked down at the floor. "I am not finished here."

"But the star map?"

"It'll still be here when I'm done. Only another few days at most, I promise."

"We can take a copy..." Pippa offered.

Ruby considered that. "Alright, we'll meet back up with Disto... We're supposed to meet back in Inner Nonagon. We'll find out about my ship. Hopefully, it will be done at the same time you are. I still need you to bring me home, SD. I don't want it to be anyone else."

SD moved his chassis this time in a way that indicated, 'yes, agreed.' To Ruby, he still looked sad, and she hoped that anything else he did here would help him get over it and start feeling like the happy little spaceship driving robot she cared about.

Ruby touched his chassis, smiled, and walked back out towards the exit of the Rejuvenation Region.

Chapter 14

> Ambitious Technician <

"Welcome to Mortally Sector," the kiosk greeted AT when he stepped off the lift. *Ah! My destination*, AT thought. On the final part of the ride, AT had resolved to call himself 'AT.' He had heard on the news feeds that the human, Ruby, had initiated a trend of aliasing the robots she was friends with. He hoped his own aliasing of his name would impress her.

He compared his key to the one stored back in his own region. Still the same. Good.

He needed to get to Ruby before one or the other copy became corrupted.

It was only a matter of time. The probability of any piece of the key getting corrupted at any time was high. At least he had a copy to compare, but... if there had been a mismatch, how would he know which copy was the wrong one?

And technically, in the comparison, he was introducing new copies.

He shut down this line of thinking before he went insane.

AT needed to access a kiosk so he could check his messages. There were none that he could see here on Level 8, so he took the lift to Level 2.

Kiosks were plentiful that he could see when he exited the lift, although most of them were already occupied. AT strolled down the hallway until an empty one presented himself.

He plugged in, with the hopes of finding out if one, there was a message from Detailed Historian and two, that he would be able to locate said robot. The answer to the first item was no... there were no messages of the sort. And AT had no luck with the second item either. The kiosk refused to tell AT where Detailed Historian was located. That was strange. This was a strange region with strange kiosks.

Shortly before starting his journey, AT had sent Detailed Historian a message to meet him at the mobile enclosure disembarkation point when he arrived and provided a precise arrival time. He had introduced himself as a member of the 88, and explained he had important information. Throughout his journey, he periodically updated his expected arrival time.

So, when there was no Detailed Historian there to meet him when he disembarked from the mobile enclosure on level 8, he was mildly confused.

AT reviewed his outgoing messages.

"Oh, my circuits," he said to himself as he discovered his mistake. He had addressed all of his messages to a Detailed Historian 101. He worked with the kiosk to help him sort this out. There was, in fact, no Detailed Historian 101 in existence. Nor had there ever been one.

So, who was the right Detailed Historian? He was having trouble locating him. Could this be correct? Was it solely Detailed Historian with no extra identifier? All the information available to him through this kiosk told him that was the case.

It must be. Now to deal with the problem of locating the one and only Detailed Historian along with the Bio, Ruby. There was no public information available on their whereabouts. AT studied the layout of Mortally Sector and decided he would park himself in a common enough area and wait for them to show up or pass through. The Inner Nonagon was indeed central and inner to this Sector, so AT calculated that the odds of them passing through were high. Better than any other area.

He disconnected and at the highest speed he could muster, headed for the common area. It was located not too far from his present position. It would take him less than 1000 tics to get there from where he was at his most reasonable speed. At his top speed, he could make it there in maybe half the time, but if his top speed exceeded what was normal for this Sector—and looking around at the other robots, that was likely to be the case—he would only be drawing attention to himself.

He was the softest robot among any he encountered in this Sector. He already stood out, although he didn't seem to be turning any chassis in his direction. He anticipated that his appearance could cause an issue... while he wasn't well traveled, AT was well read, well informed, and he definitely understood all the varied robots of his planet—even if he hadn't met many in person. He knew that this was the most homogeneous of all the sectors and regions, yet he didn't know how they would react to meeting others in person.

Now he knew. They generally didn't react at all. He picked up speed. Out in the hallway, robots moved at varying speeds, and a slight increase would be unnoticed.

That was until he bumped into another coming around the corner. The corner of its boxy chassis almost punctured him.

"Apologies," the robot chirped, but didn't give AT a second glance and kept on its way.

AT ran a quick internal diagnostic. No difference in pressure, no leaks detected. He kept going but reduced his speed back to his original pace.

Along the way, he sensed the uniqueness of this Sector. It was exceptionally... homogenized. All the robots looked so similar to each other. The diversity of his own Sector and the other parts of the planet were not evident here.

When AT arrived in Inner Nonagon... the first thing he observed was that this area looked nothing like the common area of his region. It was... in a word... boring. But he had a mission to focus on. Detailed Historian, along with Ruby, should be...

Right there. He spotted them right away. The human stood out like a smoking circuit card.

He maneuvered until he was adjacent to them and made a chirp.

A single robot, Detailed Historian, turned in his direction. The human took her appendages and put them over the sides of her head. AT wasn't intimately familiar with Bio anatomy and wasn't sure if this was a form of greeting.

"Turn off your base emitter," Detailed Historian said. "It is at a frequency quite irritating to Bios. Please let's speak in her language. For reference, it is BMB-73-001."

AT plugged in to the nearest kiosk—they were plentiful and generally unoccupied here—and downloaded the relevant dictionary. This took all of a few tics, during which he attempted to remain patient. While he did so, he watched Ruby use her appendages to rub the sides of her head before she returned them to their original position. As the dictionary came online and integrated with his circuits, he began to understand the sounds Detailed Historian was making.

"... a different sector, so his vocalizations and even physical appearance are distinctly different from this sector."

Ruby was moving her head up and down. He double checked to make sure he wasn't emanating any further sounds to disturb her. He was embarrassed by his mistake.

"Ruby? You are the human," AT said.

"Yes," she replied. "Ruby Palmer. I'm pleased to meet you, I think."

"Good. I have something for you. You'll need to it to help the core."

"What is it?"

"A key."

Chapter 15

> Ruby <

Ruby exchanged a look with Disto. Did a robot magically appear with exactly what they needed?

Ruby walked over to an empty kiosk and presented her faded tattoo. The kiosk beeped a beep of utter failure. She tried again, and the kiosk responded by repeating the same beep of failure but at a volume that made Ruby's ears itch.

Behind her, she heard Disto and the soft, plush robot that introduced itself as Ambitious Technician—AT for short—speaking to each other in their native tones. Even though she could initially understand their conversation, and due to Disto's kindness in informing AT of her language, she overheard their conversation quickly morphing into their own language shortly after her back was turned.

Ruby did her best to not let her thoughts drift off. Every single time the robots communicated in ways she couldn't understand, her thoughts would drift.

But not this time. She was present. She was going to stay present.

Instead of letting her thoughts drift, she examined this robot, who was clearly dissimilar from any she'd encountered so far. He looked like a series of elongated marshmallows smushed together. He looked soft. Ruby wanted to reach out and feel how soft he was—or see if he made a good pillow. Even his head looked soft with a malleable screen that served as his own face screen.

But Ruby kept her arms to herself and was ready when Disto returned to speaking her language, although she missed what he had *just* said.

"What did you say?" she asked.

"The key in AT's possession. It might be useful to us in working out a way to reconstruct some of the corrupted data. There might have been an older correction algorithm in use."

Ruby looked around. There was a kiosk almost within arm's reach.

"I'm going to log in. Can you transfer it to me?"

AT produced a series of three, quick, squeaky tones.

"What was that?" Ruby asked.

"Oh sorry," AT said. "I meant 'yes,' 'affirmative,' 'certainly.'" Ruby could hear the smile in his tone as he said, "I came to help."

Ruby swiped her wrist over the kiosk's scanner. The kiosk produced a flat squawking noise. It didn't recognize her tattoo.

She tried again, with the same result.

Not one to give up easily, she tried a third time. After hearing the unpleasant squawk a third time, she said, "crud," to which Disto responded, "Ah! A new word!"

"Yeah, I'll explain it later, but first... I can't log in to this kiosk. My tattoo is fading," she said, holding out her wrist for Disto to scan.

"Disto, I need to get this fixed," Ruby said. "Now."

Disto dropped her arm and scanned the other one as well. She could see that the second one, the one she used less frequently, the one without her little freckle that changed the tattoo ever so slightly, was also fading. "I agree," Disto said. "Let's go visit Quiet Painter in his tattoo parlor."

"AT... you'll come with us and tell us more?"

"Happily," AT responded.

> Ruby <

There were no chairs in this tattoo parlor.

Ruby had seen tattoo parlors in the movies. Vids that contained these kinds of places on Earth. There was no tattoo parlor on Astroll 2. In fact, she was fairly certain there weren't any on Earth either. They were a thing of the past. Modern devices made tattoos self-applicable, and anyone could apply them at home.

She had never indulged herself. Neither had her uncles. Her friend Inny had spent a couple of weeks playing around with it but in the end, reverted her skin to its natural pale coloring.

Ruby never had any interest. Not that she was ever overly concerned with outward appearance in that way. It was more that she simply didn't think they would look very good on her.

But she was here to fix a functional tattoo. That was different.

Looking around the room, it didn't seem too dissimilar from what she had seen in movies. They were clearly in a waiting area—but one with no chairs.

Artwork covered the walls, and that was one familiar feature: The artist displaying their abilities. Although, instead of flowers and skulls and other eclectic icons from human culture, most of what were on the walls here were little more than blobs. At least to her visual sensibilities. Colored blobs.

She walked up to one. It was a blue blob. Maybe not a blob, but a blue oval, with the right side of the oval a little thicker than the left. To the right of that, was a similar blue oval, but the thicker part was even thicker. To the right, the pattern continued. The shape morphed a few more times until five or six shapes later, what was a blue oval had morphed into a shape resembling a torus, one end of the oval wrapping around the other.

Ruby turned around and on the other side of the room was an entrance that led into another room. There was no door, so Ruby and the others could see in.

She saw Quiet Painter back there. Quiet Painter had three chassis sections, like most robots in this Sector. But on what must be a daily basis, he changed his artwork. On one day, he would be the most tattooed robot she'd met, and on another, he was as bare as AT was. It only now struck her as potentially a little odd. Like, wouldn't he want to show off his wares more consistently?

Today, he was almost the least decorated robot in the room. Disto, who was generally the least tattooed robot she knew, was only slightly more decorated. And AT, was bare. But poking out of his chassis, Ruby could see Quiet Painter's multiple appendages that allowed him to execute his craft.

Right now, three of those appendages were active on another robot. The other robot was not one that Ruby recognized, which wasn't surprising. There were nearly 100 million robots on this planet. It wasn't like she was going to know each and every robot. There were almost five million in this Sector alone, according to what she had learned.

But this robot looked like it wasn't from around this Sector.

Not in the way that AT was obviously not from this Sector. The differences were more subtle. Like the form of the chassis… while SD and Disto and even Quiet Painter had chassis sections that all resembled squashed spheres, each of the three sections that made up this robot were more like if you took a cube, rounded the corners, and then squashed it.

She wasn't sure if she should be watching Quiet Painter work on this robot, but there was no door or other way to block the view.

Ruby turned around, but not before absorbing the seriously disturbing detail of what was getting airbrushed onto this robot: a family of humanoids. Not humans, but humanoids.

This caused Ruby to turn around more abruptly than she had planned, making a '*yip!*' noise in the process.

Disto rolled over. "I don't know that word."

"It wasn't a word, it was," Ruby waved both her hands in a way that was meant to help her brain conjure up an *actual* word, but it didn't work. She dropped her hands in defeat, "I don't know what that was."

Before Disto could ask anything else, Quiet Painter was escorting the other robot out of its studio. Quietly. He approached Ruby, Disto, and AT.

"I…" he started to say. Ruby leaned in closer. "What?"

"I do not…" Quiet Painter was certainly saying something. Ruby couldn't hear it.

"He said he doesn't work on robots of my design," AT offered. Disto was producing a slight nod to indicate he heard and agreed.

"Why not?" Ruby asked.

"Yes," Disto asked, "why not? That is unexpected…"

Ruby could hear Quiet Painter making some noise but again, it wasn't at a volume she could parse.

"Ah," Disto said. "It's his soft surface covering. Quiet Painter simply isn't equipped with the right kind of ink for that surface. He would be more than willing to submit a procurement request."

"But that's not why we're here," Ruby offered.

Quiet Painter perked up.

"My tattoos are fading," Ruby said. She took off her communicuff, and Disto offered to hold it. She held out her arms, undersides of the wrists pointed up.

Quiet Painter examined them and produced several beeps and chirps.

Disto translated, "He said that you're in luck that he happens to still have the proper ink for your version of a soft surface. That procurement request had been submitted at the time SD's mission began to find a Bio sample."

Ruby nodded, and Quiet Painter gestured with an appendage that she should follow him into the other room.

Disto and AT followed them. Ruby took in the entirety of the room, hoping to find a chair hiding in the corner. No such luck.

There were, however, three active screens on the wall, each showing a unique news channel.

"Um," Ruby began, "Are they going to, uh, line up exactly?" She looked at Disto as she said this and could read from his expression that he understood what she meant.

One of the tattoos was irrelevant. But the other, in combination with a tiny freckle on her wrist, gave her special access to the computer system of this world. Access that allowed her to help her robot friends and navigate the files of the 88.

Disto and Quiet Painter exchanged a few quick tones, most of which were barely audible to Ruby, and then Disto said, "Yes, there's still enough there that Quiet Painter can use to line up the tattoo. However, he cautioned us that there's *barely* enough. Next time, we need to come in earlier."

Ruby nodded, but hopefully a month into the future, she'd be back home and wouldn't have need of these tattoos. They'd be faded on her arm, a relic of her time here.

Unless she came back.

Was that likely? Or even possible? Going home and then returning? Or once they were able to send her home... that was it for her here. It was all simply over. And the memories would fade, and her questions wouldn't be answered, and over time it would all start to feel like one big dream.

She didn't get too far down that line of thought before she heard what could only be described as a gasp, simultaneously, from all three robots. Quiet Painter hadn't even started painting. He held her wrist and stared. But he wasn't staring at the wrist or at her.

All three robots were staring at the screens on the wall.

"What's going on?" Ruby said.

For a moment, no one answered.

"Disto, you're creeping me out. What's going on?"

"Shhh," Disto said.

The robots in the room were all deeply engrossed in watching the robot on the screen. Symbols flitted down the side of the screen while the robot produced several tones, beeps, and other sounds. It all sounded... somber.

After a minute or two, the robots came out of their trance, but Ruby could sense an unease, or a sadness or maybe it was anguish. Like they all had adorable puppies stolen from them.

AT made a noise and said, "The Hall of Templates put out an announcement. Several robot lines will be discontinued."

"Yes, occasionally, a line is discontinued. But never in the history that I'm familiar with have they discontinued so many at one time..." said Disto.

"Are," Ruby was a little nervous about asking this next question, "are any of you going to be, uh, discontinued?"

"No," Disto said.

Ruby let out the breath she didn't know she was holding.

"Well, that's something, I guess?"

"Indeed, but there are so many..."

"It must be a mistake," AT added.

"Who is going to be discontinued?" Ruby asked

Disto answered: "The lines that they announced will be discontinued were: Maniacal Manager; Honest Editor; Diplomatic Zookeeper; Frisky Scavenger; Slimy Scrubber; Offensive Escalator; Insecure Planner; and Stubborn Designer." He took a moment then added, "And they said there could be a second announcement coming soon."[1]

"I've never heard of Offensive Escalator," AT said.

"It must be Sectorial," Disto said. "And be glad. They are quite unpleasant to talk to."

"But discontinued means that no new ones will be created, right?" Ruby asked.

---

1. I wrote the majority of *Robots, Robots Everywhere* in 2021. As I work on this annotated edition in 2025, this is all hitting very different. This now feels like an analogy to what we're going through in the US with our government.

Chapter 16

> Ambitious Technician <

"Correct," said AT. "However, discontinued lines are no longer supported. They don't receive updates and are not prioritized for maintenance. Discontinued robots fall into disrepair..."[1]

AT trailed off, possibly stuck in a memory loop. He remembered when another robot, Costumed Barrier 17, of a short-lived line, had begged him to perform some maintenance. He couldn't, even if he wanted to, and he did. Want to, that was. But the tools he needed were no longer accessible.

Discontinued robots were given a number of tics until they were required to report to a recycling center. One could apply for an exemption through the lowest sub-node of the Reclamation and Recycling Division of the Agency of Resource Allocations, but AT was not aware that any had ever been granted.

No one spoke for several minutes, and AT was wondering if he should do anything special with these old memories of his. He was dwelling on them and that made his circuits uncomfortable.

"Well," he heard Ruby say to the room, "let's get this over with so we can figure out what to do."

He watched Quiet Painter carefully take the human's wrists in his appendages. He began to tattoo.

AT watched Disto watch Ruby and Quiet Painter. This robot was obviously attached to Ruby. He felt... Jealous? That could be the word. AT wasn't always attuned to his feelings because they weren't always necessary.

Feelings were useful for many things. Retaining memories was aided when emotions were attached to them, getting a sense of trust based on the emotion someone may evoke, or being afraid or sad protecting oneself from going towards danger.

AT could imagine why jealousy may be necessary as well. Wanting something that you don't have—something that may fundamentally better your life—this motivation was useful in retrieving the said betterment.

Still, AT couldn't tell if this exact feeling of jealousy was necessary, though this didn't stop him from feeling it.

Disto was still holding the covering that Ruby handed him a few minutes ago.

"What is that?" He asked in a low tone so he wouldn't disturb Quiet Painter while he worked.

Disto looked in the direction that AT had pointed to, which happened to be its appendage, and said, "Ah, this curious device. This is Ruby's 'co-mune-ee-cuff' is what she calls it."

"She shed it?"

---

1. What I was thinking when I wrote this was how cell phones eventually stop receiving updates.

"Yes, it is not a part of her, similar to those outer garments she wears. They are on top of her chassis. Most bios have something similar. Not all, but most."

"Does it have a purpose?" AT asked.

"Oh my, yes! This is a fascinating device. Have you ever met a Fine Calculator?"

"Yes, once. It was several million tics ago."

"What about a Gentle Recorder? A Cowardly Correspondent?"

"Yes and no. How is this relevant?" AT was indeed confused by Disto's line of questioning.

"Well, this is going to push the limits of your imagination processor but try this thought experiment: Imagine you took a robot from all three of those lines and other lines and *combined* them."

AT did try to process that concept in his imagination. He brought to the surface of his processor an image of each of the robots Disto mentioned. While he never met a Cowardly Correspondent, he knew what they looked like since they were on the news channels all the time. He lined them up, side by side in his imagination, and then... combined them.

He imagined each of them with all of their various appendages extended and touching. But how were they touching? There were so many possibilities. Side by side? What about one on top of the other?

Each way AT tried to picture it, none of them came close to replicating a device small enough to wrap around the human's arm.

"I'm sorry, Disto. If I imagine three robots combined, I get a larger robot, not a smaller one."

Disto chuckled. "I'm sorry, I should have been more specific. Don't picture their bodies combined. Picture their circuits. Their algorithms."

That was a distinctly contrasting mental image and AT was not sure it was one he could grasp either.

He was starting to worry that Disto was going to think he was simple in the circuits.

Disto offered, "Or how's this... imagine a robot that could do all the things that all three of those robots could do. But also, do more."

AT found he could imagine that. Although he was still confused as to the form factor that this robot took. But before he could ask more, Disto was holding it up in an awkward way near his visual sensor.

"Pippa, meet Ambitious Technician, also known as AT."

"Hello," a voice said from the device.

"Greetings! Hello!" AT replied, shocked. "There is someone in there! May I hold it?"

"Yes," Disto said and handed it over, "Ah, it looks like Quiet Painter is finished."

"What are you?" AT asked as they moved back to Ruby's side.

"I am algorithm 51AI. A voice-controlled personal assistant, with personality and intelligence built-in."

"You are fascinating," AT remarked.

"Disto used the same word. And so did Scout."

"Who's Scout?" AT asked but didn't get an answer. Ruby grabbed Pippa from AT and said, "Thanks for holding this," and reattached it to her appendage.

"I tested the tattoo, and it worked," she declared. "So, we can get back to business."

AT was trying to parse what Ruby said. They had not previously been engaged in business, but rather an important discussion about the quality of the data held in the Hall of Templates. They were discussing how it could be fixed and the key AT possessed.

"Yes," Disto said, seeming undisturbed by Ruby's words. Disto turned to AT, "Now about that key…"

AT nodded, "I think it can help reconstruct some of the data."

"A key implies some kind of encoding or encryption. It sounds like there might have been encryption on top of an EPADAC algorithm in the past," Ruby said.

"EPADAC?" AT asked.

"Sorry. We acronymize everything. It stands for Error Prevention and Detection and Correction. It's exactly like it sounds… an algorithm that attempts to prevent errors, and when it can't prevent them, it tries to detect them, and when it detects them, it corrects them."

"Fascinating," AT said. Disto said nothing but had the look of a robot deep in thought. AT continued and questioned, "This is common among your people?"

"Oh yes, but I doubt most people know about it. Most people don't know how the technology they use works. But it's been around for ages. Our computer hardware is subject to errors mostly due to radiation coming from space."

AT couldn't suppress an involuntary noise his chassis made. It caused his whole soft body to jiggle, also involuntarily.

"Are you… laughing?" Ruby asked.

AT didn't instantly recognize the Bio's word, 'laughing,' but once he looked it up, he attempted to shake his head to indicate that's indeed what he was doing.

After a few moments, he managed to control himself enough to speak again.

"Sorry, but when you said how most Bios do not know how things work… well, I could have said the same thing about most robots. But what was that other thing you mentioned. You said, 'radiation from space?'"

Ruby turned her head to the side but kept her ocular sensor trained on him. "Yeah, like the cosmic background radiation?"

"Disto, do you know about this?" AT said and nudged his chassis.

"Excuse me? I'm sorry—I was chasing my thought patterns through my circuits, I'm afraid."

"Do you know of radiation that is harmful to robots?" AT asked.

Disto shook his head. Both robots looked to Ruby for an explanation.

"Well, I only know a little. There are high-energy particles flying around in outer space in all directions. When they interact with other matter, they can kick off neutrons which can interfere with…" Ruby trailed off, crossed her arms and said gently, "and neither of you have any idea what I'm talking about."

Both robots now shook their heads.

Ruby sighed. "Okay, it's not important because who knows what's causing the errors in your systems. Maybe it's that, maybe it's something else. Either way, I can write you a new EPADAC algorithm that can work on new data that hasn't already been corrupted, but I think it's just as important that we are able to reconstruct or detect and correct the errors that are already present. And then, for real, I go home!"

"Agreed," AT and Disto said in unison.

Chapter 17

> Ruby <

Ruby sent all the robots away. She needed alone time with her MoDaC. And Pippa.

Ruby hadn't coded anything since she developed a compression and decompression algorithm for the robots. She helped them refine it a little after the initial release, but she hadn't touched it or any other code since.

That wasn't unusual. Coding was an activity she did as she needed or wanted to. It wasn't her whole life. Coding was a tool to get things done[1]. When something didn't work, if a screwdriver couldn't fix it, most likely a piece of code could, and that's where she came in.

Ruby sighed, "Pippa, we're going to have to write our own EPADAC algorithm. From scratch."

Pippa didn't respond.

"Pippa?"

"We have to talk," the communicuff said.

"Are you breaking up with me?" Ruby said, smiling.

"What? I am not breaking anything..."

"Sorry, it was sort of a joke. I guess not a good one. Or wrong audience. Whatever you want to talk about, make it quick. We have a lot of work to do."

There was silence from Pippa once more.

"Pippa? Are you ready to help me write that EPADAC algorithm?"

Once more, there was silence.

"Pippa?"

A new sigh emanated from the communicuff.

"You're the programmer, Ruby, not I."

---

1. Even though I spent a large portion of my career as a software engineer, this is exactly how I've felt about and approached coding. It's a tool. I think the only time I was coding for coding's sake was when I was a kid in the 80s originally learning to program in BASIC. Even now, I'll write python code or scripts when I think it's the best way to get something accomplished.

That was true. Her communicuff's AI was... something else. AI did not program AI, did they? Was that built into their nature? As in, were the AIs from home built to not self-replicate or want to expand upon themselves and their functionality?

"Is that why robots haven't actually taken over yet?" Ruby muttered to herself.

Pippa was clearly puzzled, "I'm not sure I—"

"Don't worry about it."

Ruby wanted to know more about who and how they were programmed, but it would have to wait until she was back home. Pippa's code was locked up tight.

And that was not important right now.

"Agreed. I am the programmer. But... will you be my test engineer?"

"Please explain."

"Well, what I write needs to be tested. And we usually write the tests first. So, we have a roadmap, so we know what the code is supposed to do. The tests drive the development[2]. Does that make sense, Pippa?"

There was a pause. Pippa then said, "Yes, I understand. But isn't that a form of programming as well?"

Ruby paused and tried to recall the last time she participated in tests of any kind. She had skipped testing when she wrote the compression algorithm—because she was still freaking out over being on an alien world—and the result was that she forgot to initially include decompression.

She still cringed at the image of Honest Editor freaking out when he didn't know what to do with his compressed data. Especially since that was her fault and could have been avoided if she'd been more careful.

Testing was always the first thing to be brushed aside when under a tight schedule. Everyone knew that. Everyone knew how bad that was. Yet, it was still common, and here Ruby was, living proof that it still happened.

But not this time.

"Well, yes, but there are two, uh, I'll call them 'levels.' There's a first level where we plan out the tests and the second level where we make them. Would you be more comfortable planning out the tests, Pippa?"

Again, a pause that was a smidge longer than it should be. Enough so that Ruby repeated, "Pippa?"

"I can try, but without a connection to the networks I'm expected to have, I have access to fewer resources and my knowledge is limited. I may need additional input from you."

Ruby pursed her lips together tightly. Crud. This was going to be like if she asked her seven-year-old cousin Sebastian to take on this task. Pippa was utterly unprepared, utterly untrained, and probably had no idea where to even begin.

"Okay, well, maybe start by finding some data I can use as a test case?" Ruby offered.

"Like the corrupted star chart?"

"Well, sort of. I can't uncorrupt that data until I know the algorithm is working. I need something that we can deliberately introduce an error into and then check the results of processing it through the algorithm back with the original.

"So, yeah, we could use the star chart, but only if we change more of its information. Honestly, it would be less confusing if we used something else."

"I understand. I will find some data, Ruby."

---

2. This is a real method of developing code called Test-Driven Development (TDD).

"Good. And I'll get to work writing this algorithm. I wonder if I can deconstruct an algorithm already in use by my MoDaC..."

Ruby trailed off, face engrossed in her MoDaC, and lit up with a slight blue hue from the light it gave off.

Chapter 18

Austere Agent was not happy. He was not meant for data entry and manipulation work. His algorithms supported observation and investigation. He sat in front of an access terminal in the Agency of Templates, radiating unhappiness. None of the other agents at their access terminals were necessarily radiating anything else. Agents typically wanted to be out and about, not handling data entry.

But ever since the Hysterical Analyst line had been discontinued, more of that data manipulation work fell directly to agents.

And since he was the one who told Detailed Historian to file the interface request, his unique identifier was on it, so it was routed back to him for initial processing.

He reviewed the information. He was looking for an easy way to deny the request. If they had missed any bit of information that was required per the instructions under Directive 11, he could do so, and no one would question the integrity of the situation.

Of course, Detailed Historian and his Bio friend could appeal, but he didn't need to worry about that now.

Directive 11 was the master set of instructions for all interfaces. It was a long and lengthy set, covering all the details of every known interface and what to do in the case of an unknown interface as presented itself.

All the standard details were included. Full identifier of the requester with contact details. "Detailed Historian N" That was interesting. It was rare for a robot to have no numerical identifier as part of his full information. It happened, but it was rare.

And it was not sufficient reason for denying the request.

Austere Agent moved on to the section that described the two sides of the interface requested to be made. There was a section on whether or not the details of the second side were known. Austere Agent was expecting that 'unknown' would have been selected and was mildly surprised when it was not.

The Bio must have provided details on the expected interface from her system.

The details were regarding how the interface would occur. Similar to how Swell Driver interfaced with the Bio initially, they were asked to allow Swell Driver to knowingly accept another ship.

That brought up some interesting questions for Austere Agent. Did Swell Driver have the right approvals to do this in the first place?

Austere Agent was already logged into his computer console. That was how he was reviewing this request, after all.

He paused. He knew he needed to look up the available information on Swell Driver's journey to how and why he found the Bio, but he didn't want to. The system had been slow all day. Access requests into the The Core's main memory were slow. He put in the request for information anyway.

While he was waiting for a response, he turned his circuits to the other task at hand. This ridiculous idea of a wireless communications interface Prodigal Agent had spoken about. It was a nice idea. It would likely be faster than what he was dealing with right now.

He recalled the information on the wireless interface request from his local memory. He, as did most other Agents, took the Bio's compression algorithm. While it was incompatible with a few robots, those were all rare and unusual circumstances.

In his case, Austere Agent was glad he did it, so he could have additional data available at all times.

Prodigal Agent transferred all the information he had on the wireless interface. The form used for the request that Prodigal approved wasn't too different from what he had now.

The most interesting piece of that was the identifier: Invisible Scout. Austere Agent looked up Invisible Scout in Location Zero Access List. There was no such robot.

Austere Agent made an audible chirp. The other robots at other access points here in the Agency of Interfaces main office all turned to face him.

"Excuse me," he said. They all turned back to their respective tasks.

He double checked. No, no Invisible Scout. Putting that detail aside for a moment, he turned his attention to the details of the interface request itself. It was indeed the specifications for a wireless communication. He wasn't sure he even knew how he knew since he had never seen such a thing before. Had he? No, he had not, according to a quick scan of the local archive he kept that was a list of interfaces he had personally worked on.

But there it was. In glorious detail.

The instruction that Prodigal Agent had provided was that Austere Agent should get to the root of this request. With no way to contact the originator, the next best thing would be to attempt to implement the interface to see if it was real or not. Yes, that was the right thing to do. First, he would need to find the right equipment or have himself modified.

Before he could finish drafting a detailed implementation plan, the console in front of him lit up with the information he had originally requested.

He scanned it and was surprised at what he learned. Apparently, when the various Driver line robots are on missions far from Location Zero, they have a wide latitude to do anything they need to get the job done. Such were the directions from the Special Project associated with Swell Driver's trip. Intriguing. Especially since Austere Agent curiously received more information than he requested.

Apparently, Swell Driver had been going on other trips recently but not directed by the Special Project that sent him to Ruby Palmer's home. In this case, information was limited. Surprisingly limited. So little information was available, in fact, that no robot could have possibly made an informed decision to approve this.

That was interesting and Austere Agent would bookmark that to study later. Right now, he was more interested in the task regarding the wireless communication interface.

He approved Detailed Historian's request and left the Agency's office to go in search of some equipment.

> Swell Driver <

"Goodbye, Swell Driver. May your existence be protracted and conclusive.[1] "

Swell Driver stood at the entrance to Rejuvenation Region 1010. He did indeed feel rejuvenated to an extent. At least, he had an alternate feeling, one that was closer to what he remembered normal to be like.

He looked at his new friend and counselor, Explosive Healer, who had concluded her farewell.

"Thank you, Healer," SD said. "I wish you well on your journey of observation."

Explosive Healer nodded, slowly turned around, and started moving back towards the innards of the region, stopping to visually examine a spot on the floor before continuing in.

Yes, SD did indeed feel rejuvenated. But more importantly, he had managed to protect his data. His star chart. The one that Ruby needed. The one that he would use to help her get home. Even though she took a copy, Ruby had explained that right now, all the data on the planet was at risk of getting corrupted. He was certain that his was not. He didn't know how he knew it—he simply knew.

SD reviewed a list he had created earlier. It was one of the suggested coping strategies. He had always been able to make lists, but Explosive Healer broke down the concept of the list in detail.

"You will take comfort in representing abstract data as a countable number of ordered values," Explosive Healer had said in one of the group sessions.

A robot SD never learned the name of, who was quite jittery, said, "but... but if something is on the list more than once?"

"That's okay," Healer said in a reassuring voice. "Duplicates can be removed.

"A list is a container, nothing more. It's one of the tools you were gifted when you were created, but it's one of several tools that we're not taught how to use properly.

"Lists are calming. They are calming because they are finite. Finite things bring order and calm to the universe.

"And be thankful that all of you are of the modern era... there were robots in the past that didn't have lists and all the operations built in. It was a time of greater chaos."

He constructed a new empty list and called it 'To Execute.' He made sure it was empty, then he added the first item to it: 'Find Ruby.'

Executing that first item wouldn't be too difficult. The next item was 'Take Ruby home.' SD knew he had the means to do this. In fact, he might be the only one who could do this. He possessed potentially the only uncorrupted star map from when he traveled to her solar system originally. But more than that, he retained a memory of that trip. He could correlate that memory record to the map—that's how he knew his map was good.

In fact, he paused to create a second list to address the star map. He needed to protect it and made sure that second list was linked to the first.

Finally, the last thing on his list was the one he wanted to think about least, but it had to be there: 'Purge unpleasant thoughts.' He knew there were multiple algorithms inside of him that shouldn't be there, and he also knew that if he

---

1. I was trying to come up with an analog for "Live Long and Prosper."

ruminated on them too much, it would be problematic, but he didn't know what problems they would cause. He wanted to get rid of them.

Without telling Explosive Healer or anyone else in the Region, SD managed to come away with some coping mechanisms. He wanted to tell Healer, but couldn't bring himself to say the words out loud: "There are voices in my head."

No matter how gentle, caring, coping, or otherwise they were in the Rejuvenation Region, mentioning a problem like that was surely guaranteed to get him back into reprogramming.

Instead, SD made one final list to address this item which he labeled, 'Find the Others.' He didn't know if he meant 'Others' as a label for those voices, or 'Others' as something separate from himself. When he invoked the word 'Others,' the word 'enigma' involuntarily formed in his circuits. Certainly, there must be a connection. He needed to figure this out, possibly find out who or what the Others were. But first, he needed to take care of his friend, Ruby.

Chapter 19

"Based on what you've told me about the Core," Ruby began, "We can't do this like last time. Security has been tightened."

"This needs to be more of a digital campaign effort... analogous to how we pass around the 88 algorithm," Disto offered.

"Perhaps we initiate a new one," added AT.

"Start a new chain?" Ruby offered. "The way you explained it to me, it's similar to what *we* call a chain. I only know a little about how they work. Back home, that's a religious programming sect. Not something I was allowed to explore..."

Ruby and her robot friends were slowly making their way through the Museum of Intricate Specimens. This was Ruby's second visit to the Museum. Her first visit was on her initial tour of the Sector. It was Disto's suggestion to return since new items had been installed, and it would look suspicious if they were all hanging out at any of their enclaves too much, and other public places were too public.

There were not many other robots in the Museum. It was not a place frequented by many at any given time, so it was the least suspicious place they could be.

Ruby found the place strange and unorganized. Museums were supposed to have themes. History. Technology. Bad Art. Dog Collars. Yes, she knew there was a Dog Collar Museum someplace on Earth, but she had never been[1]. Of course, living on a space station most of her life meant she had never been to most places she'd heard or read about on Earth. Maybe she'd make a point to visit all the obscure museums when she got back. If she ever did get back[2].

But here in this museum—she applied the term 'museum' loosely in her head—it was more like: Collection of random things that have nothing to do with each other that someone didn't want to throw away. Nothing here was particularly intricate or 'fancy' as Disto had once tried to describe the items.

The group stood in front of a raised pedestal that came up to her waist.

One thing Ruby did acknowledge: This smelled like what she imagined a museum might smell like.

---

1. https://leeds-castle.com/attraction/dog-collar-museum/

2. I've been on Earth my entire life and there are still so many places I want to visit. And every time I visit the Atlas Obscura website, I had a few more to my list: https://www.atlasobscura.com/articles/all-places-in-the-atlas-on-one-map

Astroll 2 contained a narrow and cramped museum that was all about the history of asteroid mining. But it was so small, only two people could fit in there at once. Even that was a lot of space to waste on a *museum*, some argued.

She had been in that constricted space a few times. As part of her education, Ruby was required to learn the history, plus, she did find the history of asteroid mining interesting.

In particular, she enjoyed learning about the brave explorers, navigating the dangerous asteroid belt, mining the tumbling rocks for minerals that were either depleted or too difficult to mine on Earth.

The object on this pedestal, however, looked like it was a tool of some sort. Ruby couldn't make it out, nor could she read most of the symbols on the small placard below. She cringed as she considered asking Disto or one of the others to translate. She was trying to rely on them less for simple tasks—it was like she was using them as a tool each time she did.

Instead, she leaned in a little closer until she lost her balance. It happened so quickly. Her arms flailed out and before one of them struck the pedestal, AT had his soft arms out and caught her.

"Oh sheesh," she said, half startled. The pedestal remained untouched and where it was. "Thank you, AT. I don't know what happened. I'm normally not that clumsy, I promise."

Back on her feet, she was ready to ignore the artifacts and focus on the task at hand.

"It will take longer," said Disto. "In addition, this needs to be implemented where all the data is… it's not only us as individual robots, but the Core, the whole structure. Every single robot and every repository of information needs to be a node in algorithm."

"Excuse me, but you sound more like an Essential Guru rather than a Detailed Historian," AT said, adding, "Not that I've ever met any robot of any Historian line before."

"Essential Guru? That's a robot line?" Ruby asked. That didn't entirely fit with her idea of all the robot lines. Gurus were… spiritual leaders.

Disto produced his version of a chuckle.

"Yes," Disto answered, adding, "I have not met a Guru, but I am aware of them. They…," he paused, "They are the people who develop," he waved an appendage, "requirements."

Ruby understood. She knew exactly what requirements were, but they were things left to the domain of marketing engineers. There were two on the station, friends of her uncles, and she remembered them chuckling one day on how they were neither in marketing, nor engineers. And according to Uncle Logan—an engineer of sorts and employed on the station as an odorist, he received requirements from these individuals, and knew they were almost always wrong. Or so she'd heard or been told. She had no first-hand experience except as a school project beyond the offhand comments from her uncles.[3]

"I understand. We're going to figure out what the requirements are before we implement this algorithm," Ruby offered.

"Precisely," Disto and AT said in unison.

"Have either of you done this before?" Ruby asked.

"Not exactly," said AT. "I have reviewed several sets of requirements as part of various systems I needed to repair to help understand the expected functional state."

---

3. There are two things I'm goofing on in this paragraph. First is requirements and how, in my day job, I frequently am on the receiving end of badly written ones. Second, is the fact that everything seems to get the word "engineer" or "engineering" added to it.

AT turned expressionless as he delved into several memories. "Unambiguous, short, feasible, prioritized, testable, consistent, and singular.[4] Those are the requirements for requirements. I am supposed to flag any set of requirements I come across that do not meet these criteria as invalid."

That list of criteria sounded completely logical to Ruby. It sounded perfect. It sounded pretty easy.

"Ok, who is taking notes? Let's get this done!"

Disto moved over to the console and logged in to indicate he would be the note taker. Ruby was relieved. As the only human, the only Bio, she was worried they'd make her do it. She'd probably be the least efficient of them in doing so.

"First," Disto said, "Each robot and each system that uses the algorithm is a node."

"Problem," AT said. "That's not singular."

"Each robot that uses the algorithm is a node. Each system that uses the algorithm is a node. Is that acceptable?" asked Disto.

"Why can't you combine them?" Ruby offered. "For this purpose, wouldn't a robot be considered a system? So don't you simply need 'each system that uses the algorithm is a node.'"

AT produced a new snorting noise, "I agree with Ruby."

Disto noted that. "Recorded. What is next?"

"Here are the next few: Each node has a ledger. The initial ledger given to every node is identical. Each piece added to the algorithm is communicated to every node. Any node receiving a new piece performs a check. If the check is a successful validation, that information, to include the verification logic is provided to every other node. Every receiving node performs the validation and updates their ledger."

"Pippa, are you listening in?"

"Yes, of course."

"Open a new note. I don't have my MoDaC, so I'm going to dictate. I want to stare at this and contemplate it later. Call the note requirements criteria. Contents of the note: Unambiguous, short, feasible, prioritized, testable, consistent, and singular."

Ruby paused to gather her thoughts. *These requirements were short. But they were far from unambiguous. In fact, they were all very ambiguous. Emphasis on 'big'.*

"Is that all?" Pippa asked.

"Yeah, but maybe take some notes from the conversation."

"I can record the whole thing if you'd like."

Ruby nodded. She turned back to Disto.

"Ok, for the sake of argument, let's assume this is all we need. How do we get the ledger into the Core and all the nodes that must make up the Core? Specifically, your Hall of Templates?"

AT and Disto pondered the question as much as they pondered the museum pieces in front of them.

The two of them came to stop in front of a shadowbox on the wall. Inside the box, Ruby saw what looked like a remote with a single button mounted in the center. She wasn't sure if it was a remote, or something else, or if it held any meaning or significance to the two robots who were staring at it.

---

4. Yes, in real life, this is generally what would make requirements good.

They weren't making any noise, but they were looking at each other as if they were communicating remotely, which Ruby knew couldn't be the case. Maybe they were thinking the same thing?

"I calculate the odds in our favor at 321 to 1 if we encourage an amalgamation of robots to appear at the same time at the Hall of Templates," Disto said.

"I calculate the odds a little less at 297 to 1. But I suspect that is because I am not as familiar with the local robots," AT offered.

"Are you suggesting we storm the gates?" Ruby asked.

Disto and AT exchanged another look, "I believe that is an accurate analogy," said Disto.

"We need to put out a message for all willing robots to meet us at the entrance to the Hall at a time of our choosing."

"What time?" asked Ruby.

"Well, how long until you finish your algorithm?"

"Ah—that... it's written, but it's not fully tested." Ruby glared at her communicuff. She knew Pippa could see her face, even if its avatar wasn't actively hovering.

"What if we did a live test as well?"

"On Swell Driver?" Ruby asked.

"Precisely what I was thinking, Ruby," Disto said. "We need to locate him first."

Chapter 20

It was so obvious, but he didn't see the answer until now. After all, he was a communicator, and his programming was quite limited when it came to things that were not communication. Like space travel. He didn't know that much about spaceships or how they worked or what it was like to be traveling through space.

Fearless Communicator had never been on a spaceship after all. He had never left his homeworld. Most robots rarely did. Only robots like those of Swell Driver's lineage and the various Explorer lineages. He was certain there had at one time even been a Prospector lineage.

But Communicators? He didn't know the history of his line, but he was certain that they didn't go anywhere. Or did they?

It wasn't relevant.

What was relevant is that the answer was so simple, it was so obvious.

They should send a ship to message back to Ruby's homeworld. Not broadcast a message but send a ship that could carry it.

They could send Ruby, too, but she was here. She wouldn't be sent until she went home—which was the opposite purpose of sending a message.

But a ship. A small delivery ship. In fact, they were a line of robots all their own. Trifling Probe was the line. FC couldn't remember when he first heard of them. It must have been on the news broadcast.

FC was logged into a console, as was typical for him. He was rarely *not* logged in.

He looked up information about the probes. They were tiny. A third of the size of his own top chassis. That was small.

FC put in a requisition request to use one.

While he was waiting for a response, he sent a message to Ruby to let her know that she should record a message and that he found a way to deliver it in a matter of tens of tics rather than thousands or millions of them.

Ruby's response came first. She was thrilled and excited and used some other words he needed to add to his vocabulary on her native language. She said she'd record a message shortly.

It wasn't long after that FC also received a response to his requisition request.

"1000 Trifling Probes are prepared for departure. Awaiting instructions."

FC paused. He re-examined his request. He did indeed ask for one. How he was getting 1000 was a little confusing.

FC considered that. Maybe this was a good thing. Redundancy. Yes, redundancy. Each Probe would carry the message, and they would provide full communication coverage in Ruby's home system. After all, he wasn't sure *exactly* where within her system to send it. This would ensure that her message was wide reaching, and the right people would get it.

This was going to work out perfectly.

Chapter 21

Disto had returned to his enclave to see if he could track down SD. He wanted to log in with the privacy only offered by his enclave. Ruby suspected there was more to that but didn't press the issue.

Ruby and AT were on their way to the Hall of Templates. Their current task was to simply walk by and scout out the current scene there.

Ruby had taken off her communicuff and was doing her best to watch where she was walking while examining it.

"What are you doing?" AT asked.

"I'll tell you later," she responded.

Ruby knew that Pippa or some piece of the communicuff was always active and could record anything she said. It had to. There was no other way for it to come alive when she said 'Pippa' if it wasn't listening all the time.

Ruby was looking for a way to turn it off. Recent interactions with the AI made her slightly uncomfortable, and she wanted to know if she could turn it off or at least mute the microphone, so she could have a private conversation.

She was definitely not going to ask Pippa directly for instructions on how to do this, because that would alert Pippa to her discomfort and that was a level of uncomfortableness she was not slightly, but intensely, uncomfortable with.

Then she realized...

"AT, we need to stop back at my quarters."

AT nodded and implied that Ruby lead the way. Ruby was now quite familiar with the local area on this level and exuded confidence while navigating her way around from wherever they came from. Her directional sense wasn't fully tuned, but it was good enough.

She took a wrong turn and had to double back only half the time. Not a big deal—it meant it took her a little longer.

This time, however, they made it back to her quarters in record time.

Since her tattoo was working perfectly, she opened the door without issue and placed the communicuff onto the table.

"I'll be back shortly," she said to it and walked back to the hallway where AT was waiting.

With the door closed behind her, Ruby felt lighter. She hadn't been without her communicuff like this since her first few days at Location Zero. She liked Pippa, but Pippa was *off* in a way she couldn't explain.

AT was obviously waiting for an explanation.

"I wanted to be able to talk without it listening," she stated. "I was looking for some kind of off switch, but I don't think it has one."

"I would love to know more about the device," AT said. "Perhaps I can examine it later?"

"Sure," Ruby said. "But just so you know, the AI in it doesn't always... I don't know. Something isn't right with it."

"AI?"

"Yeah, it stands for 'Artificial Intelligence.'"

"Artificial? How is it artificial?"

"It's human-made."

"'human-made'?"

"Yeah, like, humans created it, but not naturally, so it's artificial."

"What is the natural way for humans to create intelligence?"

Ruby considered how best to answer. She, of course, completely understood how humans procreated, and she had explained most of it to Disto the week before, but Disto stopped her from completing the overview, saying that he generally knew how Bios reproduced and that humans weren't terribly unique in that area, and it was too messy for him to think about.

But she also explained that that wasn't exactly how she was created, either. Her mom had some reproductive help with a doctor. As did her grandmother.

She was explaining all of this to AT, too, who stopped her in the middle and said, "Pause, please. You weren't created naturally, either?"

"Excuse me?"

"You said, and I quote, 'My mother underwent a procedure where DNA was selected and combined with hers,'" AT said. "That is not the same as the 'natural way' you described immediately before that. You were also created by artificial means. Does this not also label you as 'artificial intelligence'?"

Ruby didn't know what to say. That wasn't exactly what the term meant. AI was... not biological... right? Before she could think any longer, AT interrupted her thoughts, "And what does this make me? Us?"

"Well, you're robots."

"What is a robot?"

Wow, AT was making her think hard about things she hadn't thought before. And that's saying a lot because living on a space station, and piloting around does give one a lot of time to think.

"Well, you have an independent body, for one."

"Are all robots intelligent?"

"Not on my world, but they certainly are here."

"Are they?" AT looked around and pointed to some small robots flying through the hallway. He gestured toward them. "Are *they?*"

"I don't know what they are."

"They are micro sensors. They collect data and send it to the Agency that is responsible for them. The Agency of Type Checkers, the Agency of Process Improvement, and especially the Hall of Performance and Metrics—they all have micro sensors about. Nothing intelligent there. You can't even have a conversation with them. You can poll them for a few bits of data, but that's it. That's not terribly intelligent."

"No, it's not," Ruby was forced to concede.

"So, what makes an entity intelligent?"

Ruby didn't have an answer to that. *I think, therefore I am? Is that intelligence?*

"I thought there were Philosopher line robots that were supposed to have these conversations. You're just a…"

"Technician?" AT chuckled. "Well, yes. But that doesn't mean I can't ask these questions."

"But doesn't that mean you're doing something you weren't programmed to do?"

"No."

"But… I'm confused."

"It's simple. I am a problem solver. That means I am programmed to ask questions. Like why? Why is this broken? Well, this stopped doing what it was expected to do. Why did it stop doing that? Because it lost power. Why did it lose power?" AT paused presumably to make sure Ruby was listening. "You see, I have to ask questions so I can get to the root of the problem. Asking about intelligence is no different. We have a problem. We don't know something. That this is similar to what a philosopher does is entirely coincidental. In fact, I might suggest that I'd make a better Philosopher than any of the actual Philosophers."

Ruby smiled "I would agree."

"Good. We agree. So back to the original question. Why am I intelligent? Why is your device 'artificial' and you're 'natural' even though you both are intelligent? And please describe more about your mom. She is another human, yes? I would like to meet her."

Ruby's stomach turned into a block of iron, and the color drained from her face.

"You can't," she said.

"Oh. Is this conversation now making you uncomfortable, Ruby?"

"Yes. Very."

And then a piercing noise emanated from all around and knocked her off her feet.

> Ambitious Technician <

"Are you well?" AT asked Ruby, who was no longer using her two long appendages to keep herself upright. They had gone limp, and the majority of her chassis was on the floor.

All the robots around them had stopped, too, as a result of the tone emanating throughout the hallways, which—after the initial five tics—had reduced in volume to a dull beat.

It was the same tone used in his home region, so he recognized it as a 'stop—there's an emergency nearby' order. He had stopped. No big deal. The Bio's reaction was more interesting.

"Wha…?" Ruby said. She held out one of her upper appendages. It took AT a moment to calculate that it was an indication to grab hold and help her back to her original position.

Once she was upright again with her face oriented toward his visual sensors, she used her top appendages to brush off the rest of her body. He wasn't sure what she was brushing off, he could see nothing on her besides the artificial coverings she wore. He tittered as one of his circuits tingled at the concept of 'artificial.'

He registered he was now going to titter each time he heard or even thought of the word 'artificial.' He briefly contemplated building a comedy routine out of it. As a hobby.

"There is a calamity in the nearby area," AT said. "But we are well."

"Speak for yourself. That was intense! What kind of 'calamity'?"

"Intense?"

"Yeah, didn't you hear it? I mean, that could have made my ears bleed."

"The strength of the warning was indeed high. But that's intentional since it's a warning. To ensure it gets everyone's attention."

"Yeah, I got that, but attention for *what*?"

The alarm was still active, but AT saw that Ruby was functional, so he maneuvered around the inert robots in the hallway to a kiosk. Once connected, he accessed the available data and images.

"Oh my," he said.

Ruby followed him, taking the exact same path around the robots he had, and was at his side. "What did you find out?" she said, but she wasn't looking at him, she was using her optical sensors to scan the scene around them.

With urgency, she said, "and does it have anything to do with that?" One of her upper appendages was pointed in the direction of a hallway perpendicular to the one they were in. Smoke was emanating from the hallway.

"Indeed! I think so," AT said. "Apparently, there has been an accident and it is around that corner."

He gathered all the data he could from the kiosk, then said, "Let's go. I think it involves someone you know."

AT logged out of the console—the worst thing he could do would be forget that action—and moved in the direction of the smoke at a brisk pace that wasn't too fast where he couldn't navigate around the other robots in the hallway.

Ruby was following him and shouted, "Someone I know? SD?"

"No," he said as he turned the corner. The hallway was a short entrance to the Inner Nonagon.

He stopped abruptly as he saw a mangle of robots, a kiosk, and what was now mostly unrecognizable equipment.

"One of the other robots made famous by your actions," AT said and pointed at the heap.

As Ruby caught up to him, she abruptly stopped her forward motion, put her appendages over her mouth, and a sound AT couldn't parse into words escaped Ruby's body.

Chapter 22

Ruby gasped.

"Honest Editor!" she shouted. She recognized her friend in the rubble.

Barely.

Her mouth hung open as she took in the scene before her. It was a lump that appeared to be made up of a few robots—she couldn't tell exactly how many—and some pieces of equipment, maybe a kiosk—that must have been standing there minding its own business when a lump of robots crashed into it.

Everything within the lump was at an odd angle to each other. The only way Ruby recognized that there were other robots entangled in the mess were the various chassis bulbs that were flashing through colors in the way these robot chassis did.

Honest Editor's body was at the head of the pack, but its body was pushed in toward it, and his head was at an angle it should not have been, facing her.

Sparks popped here and there in the pile and the smoke appeared to be coming from the far end, against the equipment that was the immovable force that stopped the whole thing.

When Ruby looked up and away, she could see where the pack had come from through the park.

There were dozens of onlookers. AT was engaged in conversation with several of them in their native tones.

After a few moments, he addressed Ruby.

"They saw the whole thing. Honest Editor came in screaming… profanities, I'll call it… and grabbed a robot, pushed him into three more, and then the group became a fused mass picking up speed through the area. By that time, others could avoid getting caught up, and they drove around until crashing into this kiosk."

"I can't believe it! What would make Honest Editor do such a thing?"

"I don't know, Ruby, but I suggest we go. I don't like the uninformed conclusions others are drawing right now."

Ruby felt AT's soft appendage touch her. He was trying to nudge her away.

"But Honest Editor? We can't leave him like this?"

"Yes, we can. There will be robots who are equipped to handle an incident like this. You and I are not right now."

"But I want to stay to make sure he's alright," Ruby said and took a step closer to the pile.

As she did, she heard a collective noise come from the onlookers. They were all looking at her as much as they were looking at the wreckage in front of them.

As Ruby looked around, the robotic faces that were looking back at her had lost the previous friendliness they had.

"Okay, AT, let's go," she said.

As they made their way away from the wreckage and out of the park, Ruby could hear a cacophony of sounds pick up behind them.

AT was behind her and gently pushing her to go a little faster.

"He's going to be okay, though," Ruby said as they got into the hallway. The previous klaxon sound was now almost gone, and robots were moving freely again, although an unusual number of them were headed in the direction they came from to see the results of the accident for themselves.

When AT didn't answer right away, she stopped and turned to face him and repeated herself, "he's going to be okay?"

Ruby didn't yet have a sense for how AT emoted, since the coloring scheme that she had come to get used to for the other robots wasn't as applicable with AT, but he wasn't answering with a resounding and confident 'why, yes!' and that worried her.

"I calculate that given that his line has been scheduled for discontinuation, resources won't be expended to return him to a functioning condition. I'm sorry."

Ruby didn't know what to say. Loss of friends... well, she had never had many friends to lose so she had never experienced this kind of loss. There was only the big loss of her mother, and that had been it.

She didn't know what to say or do or how to process this.

AT must not have known what to say or do with Ruby, so he stood there staring at her as much as she was staring at him. It was awkward.

"Were you implying back there that those robots think I had something to do with this?"

"Let's keep moving and I'll tell you exactly what I heard," AT said and gestured for her to move.

She did move, one leg in front of the other, without the purpose or certainty of a destination. She walked aimlessly with a robot following her.

As they moved, AT told her that amongst the onlookers, they were speculating that Ruby's now famous compression algorithm caused this.

Honest Editor was the first one to process the algorithm, and adverse side effects were now showing themselves. He received the algorithm first, so he was showing the effects first.

This stopped Ruby in her tracks once more. "No..." she said. "They can't really believe that, can they? I helped everyone..."

"I know you did, and I've seen the algorithm. But you can't stop people from believing what is going to help them process an event such as this."

Ruby hadn't been paying attention to where they were walking. It was a wandering... but they managed to wander right to Disto's enclave door.

> Ruby <

The door whooshed open before Ruby or AT touched anything.

Disto was standing there and ushered them both inside.

"Your timing is impeccable," Disto said.

Ruby sat herself down onto the floor since there were still no chairs in Disto's enclave. Last time she was here she kidded him about it. This time, she wasn't in any mood for joking around, so she sat on the ground and let the weight of the day keep her there. Gravity kept her there, too, noticeably so as she felt much heavier than normal.

"Don't get comfortable," Disto added. "We're going to get SD. And you have a message to send."

"I do?"

"Yes, you're going to record a message that we will insert into the news broadcasts to explain to all of robot-kind that you are not responsible for Editor's condition. You need to request that every able and willing robot needs to meet us."

Ruby's stomach sank. This was not the first broadcast she'd been asked to participate in. After her compression algorithm was deployed, she was on the news all the time. Those broadcasts were recorded and recreated into several short video snippets that were continuously used to convince the robots to accept the upgrade. Many of them featured a cheerful and content Honest Editor.

If robots could blush, Honest Editor would have been blushing as Ruby repeatedly mentioned how thankful she was that he was a brave robot who was willing to trust her.

Now it all seemed... well... *stupid*. Self-indulgent. Vain.

It all made her feel a little fake.

"Stand up, Ruby," Disto interrupted her thoughts. "Go to your quarters and record your message. AT should accompany you. I will meet you there with SD."

"SD? You know where he is?"

"Indeed... No time to explain. On your feet."

"Feet!" blurted AT. "Ah!"

Ruby saw that Disto ignored AT and that he was looking her over.

"Where is your communicuff?"

"Oh. I left it in my quarters. We just came from there."

"That's the first time I've seen you without it in a while."

Ruby wasn't certain this was the right moment to reveal that she didn't entirely trust Pippa. Disto had proved to be one of the most ultra-logical beings she'd ever met, yet for some reason she was worried that he would overreact.

Before she could respond, AT blurted out, "Those are called feet!" He was pointing at Ruby's feet as she untangled them from the cross-legged pose she had put herself in and stood up. "I didn't have a label for that part of your body. In fact, when we're done here, I want to make sure I have an accurate understanding of all your components."

Ruby walked out of Disto's quarters at a brisk pace. Followed by AT. Followed by Disto, who didn't seem to appreciate AT's interruption. She appreciated it thoroughly because she could conveniently ignore Disto's last question and repeat one of her own.

"Do you know where SD is?"

"I'll explain when we see you later." And with that, he took off in the opposite direction Ruby and AT were headed, faster than she'd ever seen Disto move. So fast, he almost knocked a robot out of the way.

She looked at AT. "Come on. Human anatomy lesson later, but I could probably label a few more parts while we're walking."

"I would appreciate that," said AT. "I am curious as to how far you decompose the nomenclature for your components and sub-components."

"Pretty far. Why are you interested?"

"I am a technician. I am preparing in case I have to make a repair."

"A repair? To…" Ruby put the pieces together in her mind. "To me?" She gestured at herself but tried to keep walking, keeping her eyes in front of her, so she didn't bump into anyone.

"Of course. You could be damaged as easily as anyone else, no?"

Ruby hadn't considered that. She didn't perceive what they were about to do as dangerous. They were simply programming computers. It was the least dangerous activity she knew of.

But AT had a point.

No doctors. No first aid. Medical technology had come so far for humans, but here, she didn't have access to any of it. Except that her communicuff would be loaded with a host of emergency medical information. Ruby grimaced as she acknowledged to herself that she probably should always have it with her at all times, for exactly this reason.

"Yeah, AT. I can be." she said. And was silent after that.

> Disto <

"Where is your communicuff?"

"Oh. I left it in my quarters. We just came from there."

Disto replayed that interaction of a few minutes ago over and over as he made his way down the hallway.

Up until then, Disto—quite deliberately—did not pass on all of the knowledge he had collected recently to Ruby. It wasn't about Ruby; it was that he had been certain that the walls in his own enclave couldn't be trusted.

At least, that was until he saw Ruby without her communicuff. She said she left it in her quarters. She said 'left' instead of a word like 'forgot.' Communication specifics mattered. Ruby's response was not what he would have predicted. His initial assumption was that she must have forgotten it, but she clearly knowingly left it there.

The communicuff was an interesting being in its own right, and leaving it alone in her quarters sounded… cruel. In his albeit brief interactions with the entity designated Pippa, he concluded that all it wanted was companionship—it didn't want to be left alone.

It was also a useful augmentation to Ruby's biological state. Bios had so many traits that were imprecise or imperfect. Like how their memory was fallible.

But Pippa, similar to any other robot, could recall things with perfect accuracy.

Except when there were errors. Disto didn't like to admit that he could have errors in his own memory, but that's what they were trying to correct.

Prevent, detect, and *correct*, he reminded himself.

Before they all left his enclave, Disto had wanted to talk to Ruby more about it, but there had been no time to ask Ruby about her auxiliary entity. That would have to wait.

Disto had been connected to his console and power source in record time and was flying through the system to locate SD. Ruby and AT were engaged in their own conversation and not paying much attention to him.

At least that was until he had blurted out a tone that he knew AT would recognize and didn't have a translation that Ruby would understand.

"Do you know where SD is?" Ruby had asked. She was intuitive for a bio, understanding the meaning behind some of his untranslatable tones.

Ruby had asked this simple question, and Disto chose not to answer it. He responded by saying he would tell her later. He wished he could have emitted the following:

"Unfortunately, yes. He's prepping for another off-world mission."

"You say that as if it's out of the ordinary. He *is* a driver," AT would have responded with.

Disto found that he could imagine how the conversation might have proceeded from there.

"He's a Driver that *should* be temporarily relieved of his responsibilities," Disto would say next. "We must get to him before he leaves."

Ruby, brave and always willing to help would offer, "Where do we have to go?"

"I'll retrieve SD from his ship," Disto said and then continued to lay out the next steps. "SD should be in the process of prepping for departure at this moment, if I understand pre-mission procedures. You'll meet us at the entrance to the Hall of Templates. Ruby, I suggest you retrieve Pippa."

Disto had trouble predicting what Ruby would say about that, but no matter what, Disto imagined he would have been honest with her and would have said things like, "I have concerns about Pippa. But its use will likely outweigh its non-use. Simple logical calculation."

Disto tried making a more advanced calculation that would predict the likelihood that Ruby would protest. His simulation was inconclusive. There were too many factors to account for regarding Bio behavior and even though he was confident he had a reasonable mapping of Ruby, minor things could yield wildly different results.

Additionally, he didn't know if Ruby noticed Pippa's strange behavior coming to the same conclusion as he—that Pippa was in contact with another robot and potentially providing information about their activities and plans.

No matter what, Disto's logical deduction stood on its own merit. Any usefulness Pippa might have outweighed any concerns.

He wished he had said all of that before they parted ways. Instead, he was on his way to get SD. He imagined Ruby finally asking him, "You're sure you're okay getting SD?"

Disto had gotten used to the way Ruby showed that she cared, so it wasn't a difficult prediction that she'd as this.

"Yes," Disto imagined saying, trying to envision sounding one hundred percent more confident than he felt.

Chapter 23

> Ruby <

"What do I say?" Ruby asked AT as she sat in front of the computer and camera. "And why would a bunch of robots who've never met me do what I say?"

Left arm at her side, she grabbed it with her right hand and tapped her foot. Her takeaway from the last time she was broadcast all over the news was that it gave her a queasy feeling in her chest. How can chests feel queasy, anyway?

How can chests feel queasy, how can robots feel afraid—or any emotion for that matter—and how could she, Ruby Palmer, feel like she could save the operating system of an entire planet of robots like some intergalactic tech support genius?

She briefly considered all of the brain tests she had been subjected to as part of growing up on Astroll 2, and how they determined that she wasn't mentally developed enough to be out on her own. Maybe they were right, and she had no business being here and was in way over her head.

Her chest was queasy, her brain was immature, and a robot historian was guiding her through this. It made perfect sense in the way playing ping-pong on the surface of the Sun doesn't.

"Tell them the facts as you know it. Be logical. Everyone responds to logic."

Ruby's mouth turned up at that. That might be true here, but not where she was from. Back home, people typically attempted to turn logic around to suit their agenda or to sell something. She knew that a lot of people couldn't recognize the logic of a door, propping them open when they were meant to be shut, and often not even reading the sign with simple, one-word instructions on how to open it.

Unless it came with a celebrity endorsement.

The corner of her mouth inadvertently turned up. Here, on Location Zero, she *was* a celebrity.

"I know what to say. Let's get this started."

"Don't forget to tell them where to go."

"Of course."

"And when."

"Got it," Ruby said. "But wait... if *everyone* knows when and where, won't it be easier for them to try and stop us?"

"They may show up, but we will be performing actions so far beyond what their programming can handle, they won't be able to stop us."

Ruby nodded contemplatively, "I hope you're right."

"I am. And also make sure to tell them how this is for the benefit of our entire planet."

"Yep."

Ruby hit a button, and a light indicated that the camera was recording. She could edit out the bit where she took a few breaths before speaking.

> Sincere Proxy 891 <

Sincere Proxy was plugged in to a console accessing details of his next assignment when an unexpected tone signaled an alert message.

The message, in the form of a news broadcast, began with an image of Ruby Palmer—the Bio. He remembered Ruby Palmer as a companion to an unusual robot he was responsible for apprehending. Shortly after, she had performed some sort of illusory code, and ever since apprehending robots for storage violations accounted for only ten percent of his assignments instead of nearly eighty-two percent.

After the broadcast, he disconnected from the console, set his internal stopwatch to countdown to the time that he needed to be at the Hall of Templates.

> Fastidious Mechanic 719 <

Fastidious Mechanic's belly rumbled wildly, then settled into a calm vibration as he was machining a part needed to repair a kiosk that had suffered at the hands of a robot crash. He was perched on a floor in Inner Nonagon, engaged in helping to reconfigure the already destroyed space into a new set of kiosks. Although it was baffling since this region already had more kiosks than were in use, and he was certain that this space already had the maximum allocation per the standard.

His musings on the subject were interrupted when the screens that were set to continuously broadcast several news stations stopped to broadcast something new.

It was a message from Ruby.

The other robots on site all gave him a glance. It was known that Fastidious Mechanic was one of the robots who helped Ruby and as such he was easily recognized.

Fastidious Mechanic's belly stopped vibrating simultaneously with the end of Ruby's broadcast message. He opened it up, used his nimble appendage to pull out the newly created part, and set it down next to the robot who asked for it.

In this moment, he became aware that all the other robots on site were staring at him.

This made him uncomfortable. He didn't like to be the center of attention. But they were clearly all waiting for him to speak. To react.

He couldn't tell them what he was thinking.

What is the Bio doing? Does she know the havoc a message like this could cause?

He couldn't help but imagine a mess of restless robots, broken parts, and utter chaos.

The best he could bring himself to do was remain temperate, protect the Bio, and then go back to producing part after part in his belly.

"Of course, I'll be there at the right time. And I encourage all of you to do the same."

The robots all around him made tones and beeps of approval. If Fastidious Mechanic, one of Ruby's close companions on this world, supported her, so would they.

> Explosive Healer <

Moments ago, Explosive Healer finished conducting her third group session in 10000 tics and was starting to settle in to her contemplative alone time to attempt to create an art piece. Her inspiration was that of a simple series of circuits. The text would read, 'Energize Each Other.'

She was quite proud of the idea, but was interrupted by a message.

She was no longer in the right head space for art and all the robots in the Rejuvenation Region were supremely agitated.

She took up a centralized location in the Rejuvenation Region and chirped loudly, "All robots who want to join in on this new and turbulent struggle... follow me!"[1]

> Austere Agent <

Austere Agent replayed the message to the other agents.

There was Ruby, the Bio, on the screen and they all watched in a combination of awe and horror:

"Robots," the human began, "you know me as someone who has helped you in the recent past. I want to help you again. Help me help you. Help me help all of you.

"There is data corruption happening in your major Halls. Many of you have probably noticed the effects, without realizing exactly what you were seeing. My robot friends and I understand the problem, and we have an algorithm that we can use to patch the Hall that will fix it.

"There are a handful of robots that don't want us to fix anything because they don't see that there are any problems, or they're afraid that they're losing control. But we have to put fears and doubt aside and do what's right... and logical, of course. We need to show up to the Hall—all of us—and force them to let us apply the patch. This will only work if every able-bodied robot joins us.

---

1. I've always loved the concept of writing an event from different POVs (Points of View). Or writing concurrent events (which is what I'm doing with the T-Set books that follow this 4-book series).

"When I came to this planet, I was a stranger to all of you. And I for one, had terrible opinions about robots. But I was able to open my mind, my central processing unit, to other ideas and overcome my original programming so much so that I've come to call this place...well, it almost feels like home. This place feels like a part of me. I don't know if that will make much sense to any of you, but...well, just know that I like being here and want to see this place, and see you all thrive. I was told to appeal to logic in this message, but I've come to know that robots are more than just logic. Location Zero is filled with robots that are smart, kind, funny, and a lot of other things that I never imagined robots could be. You protected me, and now I want to protect *you.*

"We'll be at the entrance to the Hall of Templates, waiting for you to join us, at 444 tics from the end of this message."

The screen went blank.

Prodigal Agent said, "let's watch it again."

"That was already the fourth time. It's time to decide what to do."

"Exactly what it says. Meet her at the Hall of Templates. If she has a fix..."

"We can't trust her. She's a bio," Austere Agent said.

"But she's helped us before," said Flashy Agent.

"And look where that got us? Look at the problems that created?" Austere Agent countered.

"I don't know—it seems that the only downside is that more robots know that there are problems," said Smooth Agent.

"Exactly! Robots can't know. If they know, they'll worry, they'll malfunction with confusion, and they won't execute their assignments. Everything will quickly deteriorate and turn into complete chaotics," Austere Agent pleaded.

"That's a little overly dramatic, don't you think?"

"Dramatic? Smooth Agent, you're not grasping this. The Agent lines exist to help keep chaos at bay. If we can't execute that assignment, we will be out of reasons to exist. We'll be discontinued." Austere Agent couldn't believe he was having to argue with his colleagues.

"That's quite dramatic as well..." Flashy Agent looked to Smooth Agent who smoothly raised and lowered his chassis slightly, "but we see your point."

"So, we'll be at the Hall. But to stop her."

"But what about fixing the data corruption?" Prodigal Agent, who had been quiet this whole time, finally added.

"That's someone else's problem—a robot's problem in another agency."

"But if she already has an algorithm...?"

"If a simple human can figure it out, so can the robots of the Agency of Algorithms. It is not her job to perform, it is as simple as that." Austere Agent was quite sure of that fact.

All the other agents except for Prodigal Agent nodded in agreement.

"It's agreed. We'll show up early. Be there to guard the place before they get there."

"What if they think we might show up early and they show up even earlier?" Smooth Agent asked.

Austere Agent took a fraction of a tic to think that over. "Well, we'll go even earlier than that."

"What if they think that's what we'll calculate, and they'll show up even earlier?"

"Let's stop this circular logic. Let's go right now and wait."

Again, nods all around. Except for Prodigal Agent, who sat in quiet contemplation.

"Follow me..." said Austere Agent and led the group out the door.

Chapter 24

There were no indicators that SD's ship was about to launch as Disto boarded the lift to take him there. That was a good sign—a sign that he had arrived early enough.

As he stepped off the lift and into the rear of the space reserved for the driver's slot, he saw exactly what he had hoped to see: Swell Driver.

SD was perched in front of the consoles. His coloring was static and pale at two threets. Very unusual to be so static. The shimmer that glowed from most robots had turned dull, and it made Disto uncomfortable. Something was still very wrong with SD.

Disto indicated his presence with a soft tone. He didn't like sneaking up on his friend, or anyone for that matter.

SD made a tone in response. A minor acknowledgment of Disto's proximity.

"What are you doing?" Disto asked as he approached carefully.

"I don't know," SD replied. "I thought I was taking Ruby home. They told me to come here."

"Who is *they*?" Disto asked.

Disto wasn't sure SD heard him since SD didn't answer. Disto approached a little more and heard SD softly say, "I have the star map…"

Disto abruptly stopped. "You do? Can I see it?"

SD touched a button on his console, and a large screen began to illuminate in front of them. Disto didn't simply stare at it; he recorded what he was seeing and compared it to the last star map he had looked at with Ruby. Yes, this one was different. Could he be sure it was the original?

"Where did you get this?"

"It's been in my local storage ever since I found Ruby. This was not standard procedure. But the place seemed special and something inside of me…wanted to hold on to it."

They both stared at it in silence. Disto briefly wished he was better versed in the subtle differences between solar systems, including his own. Maybe there was a module extension he could download. For historical purposes, of course.

Ruby walked in, looking with a particular sense of wonder and curiosity that Disto couldn't miss. SD continued to look down, not flinching at her presence.

"Is that crazy? Am I crazy?" SD asked.

"No, you're a lifesaver!" Ruby said.

SD looked up, startled by her presence. For a moment, he appeared relieved at her proximity, but this quickly reverted to a state of worry.

"Where's AT?" Disto asked.

"He's waiting at the entrance to the lift. Can I get in here and see this?" Ruby stepped in closer and put her hand on SD's chassis while she looked up at the screen. Disto observed that Ruby's touch had no effect on SD. He was still the same static and pale two threets.

Disto looked up at the screen once more. This was the longest he had ever stared at one. Star maps were used to navigate interstellar space. They had nothing to do with his function as a historian. Yes, he and other robots were aware that stars moved and galaxies shifted over time, but at a scale that was not relevant. Even if he was active for billions of tics, the movement of the stars would still be irrelevant.

As such, he was not all that knowledgeable about the cosmos at all. Or his own star system. He saw it on the map, highlighted at four threets and with the symbol that represented Location Zero. In one corner was a legend, and from the data represented there, he could tell that they were looking at a region of space that was almost 500 light-years wide, high, and deep.

"Can you enlarge our present location?" Disto asked SD.

SD did as asked, and the screen was now largely occupied by a star and several orbits. One of the orbits had a dot and the Location Zero symbol over it.

There were three other orbits with their own symbols over them.

"What are those?" Disto asked.

"Those are the other planets that orbit our host star," SD answered with no inflection in his tone.

"Have you been to them?"

"Oh yes. Each of them several times. There are robots stationed at each performing mining operations. There are routine swaps of materials. I have performed that mission many times."

Disto correlated this with information he had on his world's history. It didn't correlate. "How long have they been operating?" he asked.

"Longer than I've been operating."

That explained it. It must be part of the missing information. But he was surprised that he hadn't heard about anything involving these stations recently.

Disto continued to look at the map, thinking of the possibilities to expand his line of historical research when and if they could find the historical records. When were these facilities established? By whom? And why? These questions gnawed at him. He was a historian, after all. But as usual, they would have to wait until the current crisis, not a historical one, concluded.

As Disto continued his examination of the map, his focus settled on an area composed of several line segments. Each segment was dim compared to the rest of the map features but connected to form the outline of a curved rectangle. The location of this rectangle was the same orbit as Location Zero from its host star but on the opposite side of that star from Location Zero.

As Location Zero moved, so did this shape.

"What is that?" Disto asked, using his appendage to point at the shifting shape.

"The Keep Out Zone. The other pilots and I call it the KOZ."

"What is it?" Disto asked.

"Exactly what it says. A keep-out zone. We keep out."

"Why?" This was the next of many questions forming in Disto's circuits.

"I don't know. I was never programmed with that information."

"And you never asked?" Ruby chimed in. Disto was so engrossed in understanding the map's details that he almost forgot she was there.

"Why would I ask?"

SD made a good point. It was out of the nature of SD's programming to ask questions like that.

"*Can* you ask?" Ruby said. Disto enjoyed witnessing this pilot-to-pilot interaction and hoped it would be more productive than his non-pilot input. Ruby was also programmed as a pilot, so maybe she would have some greater insight.

"No."

"And there's no explanation you could possibly think of?" Ruby's brow was now furrowed.

SD just stared at her.

"No."

Ruby made a motion with her arms and shoulders that Disto interpreted as an indication that her question queue was empty.

Disto had to remember the robot they were dealing with. Disto was programmed to ask questions—most robots, especially any Driver, were not—particularly the 'why' question. This bothered his circuits because he was filled with questions that began with 'why.' Why was there a keep-out zone? Why would someone add such a feature? Why was the location perfectly positioned from where they were? *His* question queue was full.

He would archive this queue—this puzzle—for later... Disto returned his attention back to the present.

"SD, you have to come with us. We have to go to the Hall of Templates."

"But I have to take Ruby home."

"Yes, you will. After we've dealt with the Hall of Templates."

> Ruby <

Ruby secured her ponytail and narrowed her eyes at the entrance to the Hall of Templates. AT at her side, they moved with purpose. Disto and SD had left SD's ship a few minutes ahead of her. She wanted to take a moment or two to inspect the work done on *Apple Pi* to reassemble it, but Disto informed her that little had been put back together. But once this was all over, it didn't matter. She would still get home, whether or not *Apple Pi* was operable.

They needed to get through this final challenge. Here, at the entrance to the Hall of Templates she'd heard so much about, she was mildly disappointed. She imagined the entrance would be a little grander, the way the robots talked in reverence about the place. Like she expected it to be the entrance to a Gothic cathedral seen in several old movies, maybe even like the ancient Notre Dame that only existed in pictures and vids.

In retrospect, that didn't make sense. They were on Level 3, and the ceiling height was consistent throughout the level... which wasn't terribly high at all, not when compared to Notre Dame. Maybe 15 feet by Ruby's judgment.

The place was packed with robots, so it was difficult to even approach the place.

AT helped pave their way through so they could get to the front. He made a series of beeps and tones that indicated they were there, and as soon as robots saw who it was—Ruby, the Bio—they parted to let them pass through.

Ruby took in the diversity of robots that were present. Most of which she had caught glimpses of on newsfeeds, but now they were all here in front of her. She saw robots with varying numbers of chassis components, various appendages, and with a variety of outer artwork.

She even glimpsed a few robots that looked more like AT, soft and malleable. They looked as if the crowd could crush them. But AT didn't seem worried.

They approached the front of the crowd. Again, the entrance to the Hall was quite underwhelming. A series of three kiosks guarded the entrance to a door. A robot manned each kiosk. They looked identical to each other and not too dissimilar from the kiosks in that they were slim and tall. If it wasn't for their appendages that resembled arms and that they weren't bolted to the ground like the kiosks, they could easily have been mistaken for kiosks themselves.

"I counted 1024 robots," AT whispered to her.

"That doesn't include Disto or SD. I don't see them," Ruby said. She did see Quiet Painter, Fastidious Mechanic, and several other robots she knew. Austere Agent was even there, way up front.

They were all staring at her. Waiting. Ruby turned her back to them, mostly so she didn't have to stare back, and instead focused on the kiosks and the robots.

"Hello," she said. She wasn't sure if she was talking to the kiosk or the robot.

"Greetings!" the central kiosk responded. "Welcome to the Hall of Templates, Prime Office."

Ruby looked at AT. AT shrugged. Ruby wasn't sure if it was comforting to know that one of the smartest robots she had met also wasn't certain what to do next.

"We've come to apply a patch," she said.

"I cannot comply with that request. Please see the main menu for options. Say 'audio' if you would like me to repeat them."

The screen on the top of all three kiosks displayed a main menu. Perhaps there was an option that would lead to another option that would lead to another that would eventually allow them to do what they needed to do without any difficulties. She wasn't even remotely optimistic about this, but perhaps this would be easier than they had planned for. Perhaps, the swarm of robots wasn't necessary at all. Perhaps this would be quick and painless.

She read through the menu.

It had three options:

'1. Initiate request 2. Reapply template 3. Return to start.'

It didn't escape her notice that the menu was presented in both her language and with the equivalent robotic symbols next to them. They auto-detected who she was, apparently.

Ruby began with the most benign of the options. 'Return to start.' It took her to a welcome screen and in the bottom corner was the symbol for 'menu.' Pressing it took her, unsurprisingly, back to the menu.

Next, she tried 'initiate request.' The kiosk blared a sound that clearly indicated she did something wrong, and it spoke: "Error. We are unable to process a request for a new robot. Unable to determine robot family."

Disto appeared at her side. SD was with him.

"You are not a robot. You can only initiate the request to have a robot within a line of robots related to you. For example, I could have another Detailed Historian created, or even a Circumstantial Historian. See?"

Disto returned to the main menu, and when he touched, 'Initiate,' a list of robots came up. 'Circumstantial Historian' was indeed in the list, as was Misunderstood Recorder, Filthy Biographer[1] and a host of others. Excellent Collector was listed, too.

"How does this help us?" Ruby asked.

"It doesn't," Disto responded. He turned and addressed the robot standing behind the kiosk in their native tonal language.

The robot, previously useless and inert, came to life. He turned the kiosk to face him, which shocked Ruby. She had assumed it was statically bolted to the ground.

His appendages poked at the screen.

When he was done, he returned the kiosk to its initial position and produced some additional noises.

Disto's color indicated that he was not pleased but also not surprised.

"I attempted to make an appointment to see Hopeful Executive 421, head of the Hall."

"And you weren't successful," Ruby said.

"Would you have expected anything else?"

"I might have neglected to mention that I've been trying to get an appointment to meet with him for several days. However, this robot was kind enough to tell me that the Hopeful Executive is inside."

"So, we walk in?"

"No. They," Disto gestured at the robots standing at the kiosks in a hushed tone, "will not let us in. They are blocking us."

Ruby looked at the robots and back at Disto. They couldn't have exceeded six inches at their widest. They blocked nothing.

Why didn't they talk about this ahead of time? Ruby was not prepared to disable any robots.

"Can't we simply walk around them?"

Disto looked at her as if to say, "let me demonstrate," and attempted exactly that, moving in between the kiosks. As soon as he did, the three robots behind interlocked their appendages and their bodies had produced many more appendages to do so, creating a web.

Disto looked at Ruby as if to say, "See?"

"So, this is where we storm—" Ruby began.

Disto interrupted and brought her away from the kiosk robots. He instructed, "Not so loud, Ruby. They look inert, but I promise you they can hear you. But yes. We must disable the robots and storm in."

Again, why didn't they talk about this ahead of time? Sometimes Ruby forgot that each robot was so specified, they often faltered in skillsets outside their own. Disto was a Historian, not a Planner or an Organizer—if there was even such a thing.

She was unprepared to disable any robots.

"What happens once we get inside?"

"You have the algorithm?"

"Yes. Crazy Porter converted it for us, and we've already distributed it to several robots. I have it in this storage thing you guys gave me," Ruby said as she held up the storage device that fit in the palm of her hand. "AT has a copy as well."

"Good," said Disto.

---

1. I've come up with so many robot lines in this book, it would be a shame if I don't come back some day and write their stories...

He made additional sounds. AT repeated them, and they stepped aside, pulling Ruby with them as a dozen of the largest robots approached and pulled the kiosk guard robots apart.

The robots were unable to protest or complain as their appendages were ripped up and sparked. The sounds of bending metal and the smell of melting plastic irritated all of Ruby's senses, particularly her nose, which clearly had complete control over her stomach and directed it to churn. It wasn't like seeing *Apple Pi* in its state of disassembly or a communicuff open and laid out on a table. This was utter and unmitigated carnage.

Ruby covered her mouth to muffle her gasp and leaned over to AT. "Will they be okay?"

AT whispered to her, "Perhaps. I will try my best to fix as many of them as I can at a later time."

Ruby looked at the mangled robot parts, splayed in the wrong directions, and wondered what exactly she had gotten herself into.

The robots started passing through the damaged guards and into the room beyond. Disto merged into the crowd, along with SD, and as AT began to move, he reached out for Ruby and pulled her along.

The room they entered was not what Ruby was expecting. She had imagined a crowded room full of robots active in whatever they did to keep the Hall of Templates running. Instead, it was practically empty from the entrance to the far side of the room where there were five kiosks and five robots, each behind its kiosk. What was all the empty space for? Then, the answer popped into her head as she remembered her experience on Astroll 2 getting her communicuff fixed.

Endless lines.

Ruby groaned internally.

Ruby made her way up to them along with AT, Disto, and SD.

"Have any of you ever been here before? Do you know what this is?"

"I have not, and I do not," Disto said. "Though I do fear those kiosks are extraordinarily unusual. Stay behind me, Ruby."

Chapter 25

This was the most uncomfortable AT had ever been. There were many robots in a room that was not designed for many robots. He expected to leave the large mass of robots behind, but they also filled up this next room.

AT was holding onto a slew of questions. *How was the Hall of Templates a simple room like this? The kiosks must connect to the Core, but that's it?* This didn't make sense to AT, who was used to things making sense.

He looked at Disto, who expressed the same level of perplexedness. Robots were still entering the room, smushing all of them together. He had to let out some of the air from several of the individual components that made up his chassis, else he was going to pop, and he wasn't confident in the repair options in this region. If he was back in his home region, he might have been less cautious.

AT looked at Ruby next. He was also worried that she was going to pop. The Bios were also made of material that could not withstand all this external pressure.

"Disto! You need to tell them to stop!" He had to increase his volume to be heard over the ambient noise.

AT observed one robot successfully making its way to the front of the room. As this robot did, other robots around him gave him space. They parted to let him through.

"Austere Agent," Disto said, clearly intending to introduce him to the robots who did not recognize him.

"Yes," Austere Agent responded. "It seems that wherever I find you, I find Ruby as well." He nodded in Ruby's direction. "And why am I not surprised to find Swell Driver with you and *this one*..." Next, he nodded in AT's direction.

"This is good," Austere Agent continued. "I am here to inform you all that the request to return Ruby Palmer, the Bio, home in a method that allows Swell Driver's ship to interface with your 'space' 'station' has been granted. We would like you to leave immediately."

"When we're done here," Ruby said sternly. AT's circuits produced a not unpleasant warmth at hearing her speak up.

The warmth went away when Austere Agent looked directly at him.

---

1. As I re-read this, I'm feeling a little bad that I didn't point out that this was intended to be a deliberate insult, calling AT by the wrong name. I can see most readers missing this completely...

"And let's talk about *this one*. Amateur[1] Technician, yes? I know this one traveled far to get here. And I know what he brought with him." Austere Agent's tone indicated a belief that his voice was the only one that should be heard at the moment. That he was the most important robot in the room. AT didn't usually let robots like that irk him.

But AT wasn't sure what to say. Inside his soft circuits he was uneasy at being known and seen like this.

"You have a key," Austere Agent said. "I know which encryption algorithm it associates with. I also know that it's useless. Which is why you should disband now, return to your enclaves, all of you." He said this in Ruby's language. He then repeated it in a series of tones and chirps that every robot in sensing distance could hear.

"I was right. *Nowhere* is safe to speak freely. We are always being watched." Disto said with a tone unlike any AT had ever heard before. He registered it as outrage.

Austere Agent produced a short set of clicking tones and then a shattering, rapid amount of loud, high clicking tones. AT had never heard a robot make a noise quite like this. It made his insides feel as inflated as his outsides.

"Our communication systems are innovative. But you shouldn't worry, Dysfunctional Historian. We will take care of any patches that need to be made. The Bio is now obsolete and will be sent home."

This time it was Disto who challenged him.

"You're overreaching," Disto said. "You are an Agent of the Agency of Interfaces. As such, your responsibilities do not extend to encryption algorithms. That is for agents of another agency."

"Ah, but without successful encryption and decryption, an interface can be rendered useless. What you fail to understand, Disastrous Historian, is that the Agency of Interfaces is involved in everything, everywhere. We might be the most important Agency in all the Core[2]. As such, we have reach into every agency and Hall." He produced more tones, but this time they were low pitched and more drawn out. "We know everything. In fact, I find it highly entertaining that so many other robots have lost so much knowledge of our culture and history. Even Historians, like you. Take un-connected communications, for example. I find it highly entertaining that the knowledge of our capabilities in that area has been lost among the masses."

AT looked at Disto and Ruby, who were looking at each other and back. He sensed Austere Agent was not providing all the information he had.

"Do you mean wireless communications? I've been here for several weeks with wireless—pur-fi—equipment and haven't detected anything. What frequency is this mysterious comms at?" Ruby asked, with her appendages crossed in front of her.

By now, some breathing room had opened up, and a circle had formed around Ruby, AT, and Disto. They weren't going to be smushed after all.

"It's on an electromagnetic frequency of seven-point-eight gigahertz—I think is the correct translation that your kind of Bio would understand," Austere Agent said, staring at Ruby but waving his hand around the room, "which is not something that any robot is equipped to pick up. Only our console equipment. All you robots think all communication is wired, but it is not."

---

1. As I re-read this, I'm feeling a little bad that I didn't point out that this was intended to be a deliberate insult, calling AT by the wrong name. I can see most readers missing this completely...

2. This speaks to my life as an engineer. Interfaces—software, mechanical, or other—are incredibly important when we're building any kind of system. At work, I am constantly foot-stomping this.

"That's a common frequency where I come from. So common, in fact, that it is the backbone of our primary network… but…" she trailed off, and AT watched the flesh around her optical sensors open up, and he could see more of those sensors than he had before. If she had a light on her chassis, it would be incredibly active.

But she did sort of have a light on her chassis. It was part of the device on her arm that housed Pippa.

"Ruby, I think Pippa is trying to…" started AT, but Ruby was already looking at her.

AT and the others all looked at the flashing indicator light on Ruby's communicuff. She held it up for the group to witness whatever she was going to do with it.

"Pippa?" she spoke to it.

There was a pause, and then, "Ruby! You noticed my light!"

"Yes, Pippa. Have you been in contact with someone over the pur-fi frequency?"

"Yes. His name is Invisible Scout."[3]

"Why didn't you tell me this before?"

"You never asked. And my trust factor settings—"

Ruby connected the hand that did not have the communicuff attached to it with the smooth portion of her head above her visual sensors.

"I shouldn't have to ask for you to tell me important things like that. Never mind right now. We'll talk about this later."

"What kind of AI is this?" AT whispered to Disto.

"Not a terribly intelligent one," Disto said. "Humans can only create very limited AI. They should stick to their typical forms of reproduction to create other intelligent Bios. Although, from my discussions with Ruby, apparently that is nearly as imprecise with no guarantee as to the resulting intelligence levels."

"Speaking of imprecise… where is SD?"

AT and Disto looked around and didn't see him on their initial scan. He must be locked in the crowd.

The crowd was fidgety. The hum of servo motors, big and small, waiting to move was at an uncomfortable decibel level. AT could tell that Disto detected it as well.

AT wanted to be more proactive instead of waiting. Austere Agent still stood there, silent, with his appendages crossed in front of his chassis in a way that indicated he concluded he had already won.

Won what? AT thought. *How can he, representative of the Agency of Interfaces, think that leaving malfunctioning algorithms and corrupted data in place was acceptable?*

Once again, as if she was able to read the data in his circuits, Ruby stated loudly to all the robots that could hear her, "Does anyone here think that leaving malfunctioning algorithms and corrupted data in place is a good idea?" The robots that understood her shouted, "No!" and translated for the other robots, so there was a second wave of, "No!" a moment later.

Austere Agent was surveying the crowd, not looking over at him or Disto. AT flashed a red light on the backside of a robot that was standing in front of Disto. Disto flashed back an indicator in response.

---

3. I originally had written several scenes from Pippa's POV that included her developing relationship with Invisible Scout. I pulled these shortly before releasing the book after several ARC reviewers provided some feedback. One of these days, I will release this as a side story.

"I'm going to access the kiosk," AT said in flashy red that only Disto—or anyone so equipped—would be able to understand.

Everyone's attention was on Ruby, on Austere Agent, and not on themselves or the third kiosk, the one over to the side.

"Agreed, but what will you do," Disto asked.

"What I do best," said AT. "Fix broken things. In this case, by replacing one key with another."

"I don't think I followed how that will work."

"Remember there are two separate but related problems going on here. One is that data is, in fact, getting corrupted. Ruby has the algorithm to fix that.

"But the second problem is that the key that is used to unencrypt some data is *also* corrupted. So, some data seems like it's corrupted, but it's not. It can't be unencrypted without the right key. I have that."

Disto flashed a series of red dots to indicate he understood, and that AT should certainly not waste another tic explaining anything more to him.

AT was already plugged in discreetly to the kiosk. His soft chassis allowed him greater flexibility, and he could deflate a long thin appendage that was usually hidden but reserved for those hard-to-reach spaces. It wrapped around the kiosk and plugged in out of view of nearly everyone in the room.

Nearly. Since that's when Austere Agent looked over with recognition at what AT was doing—although AT suspected that he received a warning, wirelessly, since apparently, that was a thing that existed.

"Disto, look!" Disto was luckily still able to see his red dots.

Disto did, in fact, look and rushed in-between AT and the path of a hefty Agent who was accelerating towards them.

Nearby robots quickly coordinated to join Disto. One by one and then all at once, the robots surrounded Disto with their metal or inflatable bodies. Tall or squat lengths, they huddled around Disto without anyone saying a word.

AT tried to force his way into a processor with an alternate, technical accessing route. The kiosks were notoriously ornery about that, and naturally, they obliviously complained.

"Halt your action," they repeated. "This is an incorrect procedure…"

Disto, Quiet Painter, and others formed two semicircles—one around AT, protecting him, and one surrounding Austere Agent to keep him from going anywhere.

The kiosk's processor finally let him make the kind of connection that was common for someone engaged in repair work. From there, AT could access several unfamiliar functions buried in layers upon layers of outdated patches. As he poked around, he felt bad for the poor kiosk. It had not undergone any maintenance in at least a few million tics, maybe more.

No wonder it resisted his access attempt. It wasn't used to the connection.

Behind him, robots clamored against Austere Agent, the sound of metal scraping against metal and aggressive beeping filled the room.

As AT searched through the layers, small sparks tickled his circuitry and in his chassis. Time was dwindling.

He also knew that he was the wrong Technician for this job. If it had been a matter of crisscrossed wires, he was the right robot to repair that. But this was code, and there were never Programmer robots around… well… ever. But Ruby…

As if she sensed she was needed, she was by his side and had folded in her lower appendages to bring her sensor and vocal actuator close to where AT had made the connection to the kiosk.

"AT, talk to me," she said.

AT didn't respond. He continued to open the layers and functions one by one.

Everything he encountered had a layer that was sponsored by the Hall of Performance and Metrics. He had no idea that Hall had deployed functions everywhere... but now wasn't the time to ruminate on such things.

Agency of Restoration—interesting, since that was AT's agency, but not what he was looking for.

Agency of Testing, Unit Test Review... not sure, they could hold off Austere Agent for a while, but there were other agents, and they might arrive soon as well.

Agency of Algorithms... Reduction subdivision. Closer, but still not it.

AT imagined turning around and seeing the metal shells and exposed wires that once belonged to his new friends. It was up to him to find what he needed and minimize the damage. And repair the rest later.

Why was there a metric on how many robots approved of this metric?

AOA Encryption Map null-null-one.

Got it.

A connection to Agency of Algorithms, Encryption subdivision. Despite its name, everything about it was exposed. The keys were not, though. They were kept several levels deep in the memory structure and the master key was guarded by a little algorithm—a puzzle of logic.

The algorithm provided the details of its puzzle to AT through a series of low tones nearly out of his hearing range, "This task is outside of your programming, and the typical penalty for accessing it is reprogramming. You must respond with a true or false statement. If your statement is true, you will be reprogrammed. If your statement is false, you will be sent to Resource Allocation Agency for disassembly. If your statement can neither be proven to be true nor false, you may continue on with your task."

AT dared not produce an utterance. He knew that security puzzles such as this would take any statement he made next to be *the* statement he was supposed to respond with. He had to think this through carefully.

He could think of many statements that were obviously true, such as "I am AT," and many statements that were equally obvious as untruths, like "I am a Bio." One that was neither was...

"I will be sent to the Resource Allocation Agency for disassembly," AT responded, making sure to use the exact wording from the puzzle. His ah-ha moment was in realizing that he could prove the present, and maybe even the past, but the future was wide open with uncertainty—it could not be true or false until it happened.

The algorithm didn't respond immediately. This worried AT, who was quite proud of his answer. Then, the algorithm shut down, allowing AT to continue.

He replaced the master key with his.

All of this took less than 50 tics.

AT disconnected from the kiosk, and returning his attention to the robots, saw a partially dismantled Austere Agent and an inert Quiet Painter.

Chapter 26

All Ruby could do was wait... and watch what was happening. She was not about to get in the middle of several robots who were clearly capable of damaging her beyond repair. So, she couldn't help.

Pippa was the one who was downloading the EPADAC algorithm to the Core. There wasn't anything Ruby could do to help there, either.

Still, Ruby wasn't sure they should be trusting this 'Invisible Scout.' This robot's name even sounded like it shouldn't be trusted.

'Invisible.' Invisible how? From what? Could it be an alias of sorts?

"Ruby," Pippa said, "Scout has provided me with the instructions for communicating with the Core's gate agent."

"Why didn't I have to communicate with a gate agent when I implemented the original compression algorithm?" Ruby asked.

There was a pause. Pippa was relaying the question to Scout and getting a response. It was the briefest of pauses, only long enough to have this pithy thought.

"Because you went around the standard interface," Pippa said. "Since then, they've updated the interface to be wider stretched throughout various systems and locations. They've essentially updated their security because of you."

Ruby replied. "But I did something that *helped* them."

Pippa responded, "Yes, you did. But think about it from their perspective. If they're that susceptible to someone coming in and making changes to their system, that's a security threat. Lucky for them, you were trying to help, but what if you weren't?"

"Oh." Ruby said. This made too much sense. She had never meant to elicit any kind of *fear*. She tucked a stray hair behind her ears and stared at the floor for a moment.

"What do I have to do?" Ruby asked.

"In the interest of time, I should probably do it, and update you afterwards."

Again, that made too much sense to Ruby. And once again, all she could do was wait.

Waiting—especially patiently—was not one of Ruby's strengths.

She looked around once more for anyone else she could help.

AT disconnected from the kiosk and was looking... flushed—for a robot. Disto was trying to get the crowd to disperse. Austere Agent had been dismantled, at least to the point where he couldn't do anything. She could see that the face screen on his chassis was still active, which meant that he could likely be repaired. Quiet Painter's chassis lay inert on the ground next to him. Ruby's stomach knotted up as she assumed he wasn't in as good condition.

Where was SD?

Ruby looked around and didn't see him. He probably got stuck in the previous room. Ruby hoped he was okay...

She hoped her family was okay, too. She should have been home by now, passing on what she'd learned about the software upgrades that could get them killed. She hoped beyond hope that they hadn't set out for Earth yet. Not before she could get back there.

But the ache in her heart was telling her that it was probably too late.

Her heart pressed inwards into her chest, and Ruby shook her head of the thought that she couldn't bear. This wasn't an option. She had to focus on what she could do, and she *couldn't* just stand and wait—there had to be something she could do.

"Pippa," she said.

"I'm busy," Pippa responded.

"I know. And I need to help. At least light up this one remaining console so I can see what's going on."

She took a position in front of one of the kiosks that had managed to remain undamaged and poked at the menu.

"Here, Pippa. I want to see what's going on here." She had been in the Core before and was familiar with the structure. If she could access the main menu from here, she could navigate and find her way around.

"But Ruby," Pippa began.

"No buts. Get it up on the display."

"Ruby, I'm already done deploying the algorithm."

That was quick! Ruby thought. "Oh. Well, then... next order of business. Let's go make sure SD is okay."

> Swell Driver <

SD wasn't able to push himself to the front to stay near Ruby and Disto. Not that he tried too hard. This was not his area of expertise, and he knew it. He knew his responsibility was to protect the star map in his memory until he could escort Ruby home.

By now, more agents had come, and they were being taken care of by the crowd. One by one, the mob of robots stopped the agents in their path and either warded them off with sheer fear or took them on. They fought with numbers, with force, and without hesitation.

So, he let the crowd move him around within the room. He hoped he would be alright if he didn't fight against it. There was certainly no path out, so he searched for an opening to be pushed off to the side of the room, where he could stagnate.

SD found an opening and went for it. He swiveled around a robot and dashed towards an empty space, lining the wall. Only, he was a little too late, and the crowd began to swallow him again. He could feel the mass pushing him undesirably, until...

A tug.

Something had grabbed onto him, tugging him into an open space.

SD looked up, and his visual sensors met with Explosive Healer's.

"SD, I've got you!" Explosive Healer beeped, and SD's internal sensors registered that he was not in danger of tipping over, so he could lean into Explosive Healer's pull from her single appendage. Together, they managed to root SD out of the chaos. Explosive Healer rushed SD behind a fallen kiosk, where they'd be safe.

"Are you alright?" she said. She wasn't looking directly at him but the crowd. She stared at the crowd with a studied, focused screen. SD recognized that look on Explosive Healer and wondered if she knew she was not staring at a painting. "This is a unique experience, is it not?" she asked before SD could answer her first question.

And before he could answer this one, she continued, as if jumping from thought to thought. This conversation was rooted in something that SD couldn't recognize nor completely understand. It was beyond him.

"I brought all the robots from the Rejuvenation Region who were sufficiently mobile and alert with me," she said and gestured to a few of the robots that were nearby.

"Is that safe?" SD asked. "For them, I mean."

"Swell Driver, I commend you for your concern in the safety of others. That is the sort of thought that is needed to keep us not only functioning but thriving."

A robot bumped into SD from the side. SD's chassis lit up with surprise for a moment, but the robot left them both unscathed. Robots were still making their way into the room that had opened up beyond the kiosks. How many robots could possibly fit in that space beyond? Probably less than were trying to get in.

SD wondered aloud, "Considering each robot's self-preservation functions. It isn't logical for this many robots to be here. It isn't safe."

"Yes, of course," said Explosive Healer, who was watching other robots slam into each other at unsafe speeds and with amounts of force that could damage extended appendages or worse...

"Why did you come to us, Swell Driver? What, truly, was your goal in coming to the Rejuvenation Region?"

That was simple. Ruby brought him. That's why he went. But why did she bring him? He tried to remember and failed. He was only able to recall a worried look on Ruby's face.

Previous to that, he remembered tiny snippets. A console of a ship that wasn't his. A klaxon going off in a ship, maybe the same ship? It also wasn't his. A planet that felt... nearby. Code in his system that didn't belong to him but that he needed for some reason.

Remembering these images sped up his processors like the discomfort he registered when someone else was driving his ship. *When had that happened?* It had indeed happened, it made him immensely uncomfortable to try and access those memories, and he couldn't remember the details. He didn't like thinking about any of it.

Explosive Healer touched her appendage to SD's chassis, and the uncomfortable images ceased to form. His processors started to slow down.

This was why he had come to the Rejuvenation Region.

All those images, the memories, they bothered his circuits. To the point that he sped up yet froze. And there was something that he couldn't identify preventing him from telling anyone about them. It was all confusing, and paralyzing, and completely isolating. He wanted to reset without the side effects of a full factory reset. He worried that he might get swallowed up in the disconcerting memories like he almost got swallowed up in the crowd of hostile robots.

Both times, Explosive Healer was there.

Getting his mind off of it, forgetting all about it, was what he was learning in the Rejuvenation Region before remembering the star map.

He still had the map, and he still had to help her.

SD could sense that Explosive Healer was no longer paying attention to the chaos of robotic movement around them. She was still touching his chassis, and her attention was solely focused on him.

She asked, "How does one final session sound?"

"Right now?" SD's screen twitched as the sight of a large, orange spark flashed in the center of the room.

Explosive Healer said, "It'll be short. One single question."

SD tilted downwards, signaling for her to proceed. He leaned forward and held still, waiting for her to speak.

"Why, SD?" she asked. Before SD could ask what she even meant by that, Explosive Healer provided the context. "Throughout all the work we've done together, I still see you wallowing about. Your disappointment in yourself is clearer than a polished window. Why?"

SD's processors began to speed up. "I...I don't know."

"Yes, you do. It's the hardest thing for a robot to face. Not fulfilling their duties. But I looked into your background. You are the most marvelous of all the Swell Drivers, performing your duties and functions splendidly. So, what is it that you blame yourself for?"

The numbness in his chassis began to dissolve, and it was slowly replaced with a rippling pain. Like a thousand notifications were going off at once inside of him, and he couldn't check any of them because if he did, he would know what he wasn't supposed to know.

SD shifted back and forth, "That's not what it is."

Explosive Healer moved closer to SD and asked, "Why do you blame yourself?"

The kiosk they hid behind was hit by an Agent ramming into it. SD and Explosive Healer moved back barely enough to get out of the way.

"How could I not?" SD cried, "There's something wrong inside of me, and I don't know why it's there! And if I could have remembered..." All of the energy inside of SD couldn't stay put any longer. The exterior of his chassis increased in temperature, and for the first time in a while, his face-screen wasn't a solid color, but a mix of threets morphing together—shades of all the planets he'd flown by and nebulas he'd flown through. He said, "If I could have remembered, then maybe Ruby would have been able to go home! Maybe none of this would have happened!"

Healer touched SD's chassis once again. "Ask yourself: will it change the outcome? Will blaming yourself change anything?"

Explosive Healer's face screen flashed yellow, and she pushed SD to the wall. SD began to tip over but regained balance and looked towards Healer. An agent was fleeing from a group of charging robots, and SD and Healer had been right in the path, but now only Healer remained.

"Healer!" SD shouted, but it was too late. He lunged forward, but the outskirts of the crowd got the better of him, and SD was pushed back towards the wall. Once the agent was motionless, the crowd dispersed.

SD only needed to roll a little bit before he saw her.

Explosive Healer lay smushed under several robots that were still moving, trying to get to the front of the room. The agent was a few feet away, nearly detached, still, and face-screen completely dark.

Explosive Healer was completely inert.

Chapter 27

"Nothing seems any different," Ruby said to her friends. They were all in the Inner Nonagon. Ruby sat crossed-legged on the floor with her back to a wall. They were in a spot that allowed them to 'robot-watch,' as Ruby called it, after explaining how she used to 'people-watch' on the ring-walk back on Astroll 2.

"But things *are* different," Disto said. "We're more confident, for one. Knowing that our data is correct. The Hall of Performance and Metrics is reporting that algorithm execution confidence has never been higher!"

Ruby looked around. She didn't see it. She observed robots moving from one end of the Inner Nonagon to the other. Some robots were plugged into kiosks, and others were chatting with each other.

On the far end, the splashes of color on several panels were getting replaced with other splashes of color. While she didn't know what it meant, she now understood that these were not random splashes of color but part of their communication system. To her eyes, it was all the colors of the rainbow—except red.

The pattern reminded her of Quiet Painter.

"I'm sorry for all the loss," she said. In addition to Honest Editor, Quiet Painter was indeed damaged beyond repair, as was a robot that had helped SD in the Rejuvenation Region, Explosive Healer. There were others, too.

"I am certain they would agree that their sacrifice was a small price to pay for global improvements," Disto said with a somber lilt.

Ruby wasn't sure that was true. She didn't think most people were that altruistic—Disto was providing a platitude to make her feel better. But again, these were robots, not people. Even though when she talked to them, she could easily convince herself that she was talking to people. She continuously had to remind herself that she wasn't. That they weren't people.

AT was next to her, slightly deflated in a way that indicated he was tired and trying to relax. He had been silent for a while.

"AT, will you be going back to your region?" Ruby asked.

"Eventually," he replied. "I want to attempt some more repairs before I do."

"And it's time for you to go home, too, Ruby," Disto said.

Ruby nodded vigorously. She couldn't agree more.

"I don't know how I'm going to explain this."

"Well, you sent your message. So, ideally when you return, they will already be aware of your situation."

"Yes, but it's not going to be that simple. There are going to be *a lot* of questions. I'll probably be forced to return to Earth. For all I know, my uncles are already there. Right before I left, we were supposed to return, anyway..."

Ruby had previously explained the situation to Disto and her other friends. She wasn't certain they entirely understood. She wasn't certain *she* entirely understood anymore. Maybe she had been acting like a spoiled brat. Her uncles cared about her, and she up and left without *really* saying goodbye. It hurt her every time she thought about her uncles finding out she'd left. The amount they must've worried, the sleepless nights they must have had. It killed her.

At the same time, now that she was here, she could save them. Her uncles always tried to get her to find the lesson within every mistake, but she was confused as to what type of lesson she should learn here.

Don't steal a ship and run away, but also if you do, you just might go on the adventure of a lifetime, come away with definitive knowledge that humans weren't alone in the universe, *and* have the opportunity to save a lot of lives?

What did Disto say about sacrifice? Is that what this was?

"Why don't you come with me?" Ruby asked.

Disto and AT looked at each other, likely attempting to parse which 'you' Ruby meant.

"By 'you,' I meant both of you. If I go back, with no robots, I'm likely going to be taken for a crazy lunatic. But if you come with me, they'll know I'm not lying."

AT sat up and inflated a smidge. "I'd like to go," he said.

Ruby watched Disto's chassis run through a myriad of colors as he processed the idea.

"Disto?"

"While I am thrilled that AT here is able to greet this unexpected offer with enthusiasm, I..."

Disto looked down at his chassis.

"Are you worried about your components holding up?"

"That's part of it. But... my programming..." He aimed his face-screen directly at Ruby. To Ruby, it was like looking deep into someone's eyes and sensing a deeper meaning. And miraculously, she understood.

"Well, we never did get an answer to my DNA and your lost storage. We're not even sure that I was the right species that SD was supposed to collect."

She waited for Disto to catch on. When she didn't see the light of recognition, she continued:

"There are so many species on Earth. Come back with us and you'll see for yourself. You can continue your search there in person. Or... in robot. I mean, instead of bringing samples back here."

"Ah," Disto said cheerfully. "Yes, that makes perfect sense. It is an extension of my mission to join you. In that case, I will join you. I will need to bring some spare components, but I will be ready shortly."

"Well, when can we leave?" Ruby asked. "I actually, um..."

"Yes?" AT and Disto said in unison.

"I really want to be home for my birthday." Ruby surprised herself by saying this out loud.

AT's face-screen lit up and then softened, "One thing... I must participate in the repair efforts, first. The Agency of Restoration, along with the Resource Allocation Agency, Reclamation and Recycling Division, have contacted all nearby Technicians to assist. I have been given the assignment to repair Austere Agent."

Ruby asked, "Are you sure that's a good idea?"

"He is damaged. I must try to repair him."

"Why you?" Ruby asked.

"I requested this assignment. I was involved in his damage. It should be me who tries to repair him," AT said. "I will go check on him now, and then we can make preparations to leave upon my return."

AT left Disto and Ruby alone. Ruby could feel Disto's visual sensors trained on her, so she asked a simple, "What? Are you surprised that AT is off to fix up that annoying Agent, too?"

Disto rolled back and forth with his head tilted down. He was rubbing his appendages together. He was clearly fidgeting.

"No, it's not that," he said. Then he asked in a low voice, "Where you're from is there... history?"

Ruby laughed, "Of course there is, Disto. Lots of it."

Disto's external chassis turned went from yellow to a rich purple. Ruby assessed that he was clearly excited about the concept of alien history. He tilted his head, "Knowing how interesting you are, Ruby, I can't begin to calculate how interesting Bio—*human*—history must be. Tell me all of it. Start at the beginning."

Ruby giggled, first at Disto's excitement and then at herself and her own attitude towards all the history classes she was required to take and how every single one of them bored her senseless. If it wasn't technological history, or didn't involve watching old movies or TV shows, she had no interest[1].

"All of it? The beginning? Disto, that's a lot of history—and I'm not sure I know much of it, let alone everything. Like, there are a few thousand years of recorded human history... there were different groups of people who fought each other for resources... yeah, I don't know where to start..."

"Start with what you know?"

Ruby remembered taking a class on the history of human exploration into space. That kept her interest, and she remembered most of it.

"I guess I know a lot about when humans started to leave Earth and go out into our solar system. And I know about the history of Astroll 2, the space station where I live."

Ruby then explained some interesting facts about the lunar and Mars colonies, and Astroll 1, the station that wasn't, and Disto said, "All of these Bios—these humans—involved in these activities sound very different from you. Are you considered... abnormal?"

Ruby smirked and shrugged, "You know, Disto, I think that's subjective. But if you ask my uncles, then yes."

Ruby could tell that Disto didn't fully understand this answer, but he didn't say anything, so she continued.

Until AT interrupted their history lesson. He entered the room with a grim look on his face-screen that Ruby immediately recognized.

"What is it?" She asked.

"It's Austere Agent." AT said, "He's missing."

> Ambitious Technician <

---

1. While Ruby is *not* based on me, this one aspect is. At least, this is how I was in high school. In the decades since then, I've become a little more interested.

"What do you mean missing?" Ruby asked.

Disto accelerated forward, "Yes, explain. How does one lose an inert robot?"

AT said, "I was examining Austere Agent's damaged joint mechanism, along with a group of other inert robots. I left the room momentarily to log into a console to see if the detailed specifications of this joint matched. When I returned, he was gone. Several robots are missing, 12 to be exact, including him. We submitted a general request for help from the Core. There is no division of any agency tasked with handling such an event."

Ambitious Technician knew that this was his fault. He didn't want to say more and worry Ruby, but he was afraid that a missing Austere Agent was extremely bad. Like Austere had said earlier, agents were everywhere. They were involved in every line, so it was impossible to guess what he could be up to or the power he could have. And if some unknown entity stole these robots, it could be even worse.

This problem was more than a Technician was programmed to handle. AT knew that, but also felt completely responsible. Even though he did nothing wrong, he should have... he wasn't sure what he should have done. He had replayed the event several times in the tics since and he was performing his function.

Ruby stood up and began to pace, "Well, we can still leave, right? They'll find him. AT, you don't need to stay just because of this."

"Ruby..." AT began, "I think I must stay until my tasking is complete. You will have to return to your home with Disto and without me.

AT observed Ruby's facial muscles contort and deflate. She wasn't pleased to hear this.

AT watched as her face did not improve a moment later when the ambient light in the room flickered and was accompanied by a tone that even AT found irritating.

"What's that?" Ruby asked.

AT's programming recognized it instantly, but Disto was the one who said, "It's a planetary-wide signal. It looks like no one will be leaving."

"The planet is on lockdown," AT added.

"This whole place is trying to prevent me from getting home," Ruby said. AT couldn't help but feel responsible for the situation.

"Ruby, I'm so sorry," AT said.

Disto produced a series of short beeps that indicated weariness. He said, "Let me escort you to your quarters, Ruby. You've done enough. It's your turn to rest and be safe."

AT still wasn't an expert in Bio expressions, but Ruby exhibited the same weariness as Disto. Disto's chassis had slowly crept to more than four threets... so he was easy to read. Ruby was harder to read, but if her chassis could change color, it would certainly be between four and five, indicating clear unhappiness with the situation.

AT called after them, "I'm going to help! I will fix this, Ruby!"

Ruby shook her head and called back to him, "It's not your fault, AT. Really. It's okay."

They left AT alone in the room.

It was not okay, it was broken. "I'm a technician. I fix things. I'll fix this," AT said to himself.

> Ruby <

It had been hours since Location Zero had been on lockdown. Lockdown apparently meant that every room required a code to enter, all nonessential occurrences were halted, and most devastatingly, no one could leave the planet. So, Ruby sat in her quarters with her uncomfortable, stabby pillow, a pile of a crunchy substance the robots claimed met her description of 'chips,' salsa-flavored mush, and Pippa.

She had asked Disto if there was any way she could help, but he responded with a firm no.

"I'm sorry, Ruby, but I don't even know what has necessitated the lockdown. I don't know if it's related to our recent activity in the Hall of Templates, if it has to do with Austere Agent, or something else entirely. Until I know more, for your own safety, please stay here," he said.

"But I've helped you before, and I know I can now. There must be something I can do," she pleaded.

"Ruby, neither of us can know who can do what until we've identified the problem. Please let me go do that. I will return when I have more information."

Ruby couldn't argue with that. Maybe she could help, maybe she couldn't, and not knowing anything about what was going on certainly was not a path to success of any kind.

So, she attempted to follow Disto's final request to her and relax. Or tried to attempt to relax. Ruby did not excel at relaxing. Add on the thoughts that she couldn't put aside: her family was in danger, and while she was here, she was powerless to do anything. *How could doing nothing be so fatiguing?*

"Pippa?" she asked eventually.

"Yes, Ruby?" Pippa responded.

"Are you still in contact with Invisible Scout?"

"We have not exchanged messages in more than a day. But I would not say I am not in contact with him."

"I wonder if he knows what's going on. Can you ask?"

"Certainly I can try…"

Before anything else was said, a new, odd sound came from above Ruby's bed. It was a light scratching that Ruby had never heard before. She looked up at the source of the sound and wondered if this was only audible in her quarters or if this was another planetary-wide alert.

It wasn't emanating at all, she discovered. What looked like a sharp knife poked through the ceiling and began tracing out a metal circle, carving a hole.

Ruby gasped, startled, and dashed out of her bed. She pointed her communicuff at the ceiling. "Pippa. Analysis."

Pippa said, "Something is carving a hole in the ceiling."

Ruby almost responded with snark, but was more focused on getting out of her room. She headed for the door when she heard something plop onto her bed. She looked behind her, and whatever made the plop sound was emitting a cloud of yellow smoke. The smoke spread quickly, and before she knew it, she collapsed in a fit of coughs.

Pippa exclaimed, "Ruby! Initiating emergency proto…"

That was the last thing Ruby heard Pippa say before everything went black.

Chapter 28

Ruby woke up to more coughing. Her throat was dry and raw. She opened her eyes slowly. There was nothing to see. She was in a pitch-black room, lying on a cold floor.

Immediately she got up and began feeling the area around her. The ceiling was higher than she could reach or jump, and she felt nothing on the floor. One wall had an outline of what could have been the shape of a door, but it had no handle nor a way to pull on it, and kicking it did nothing. She felt around to the next wall and found it had no discernible features. It was blank. Another wall, blank. And the last one... covered in buttons. She pressed several, but nothing happened.

She sat on the floor, knees to chest and arms wrapped around them. She would not let herself hyperventilate or lose control. There was an explanation for this.

One thing repeated in her head.

Where. Am. I?

"The famous Ruby has been re-activated!" A booming voice came from somewhere she couldn't pinpoint.

But she recognized the voice. She said to herself, "Austere Agent."

It sounded like his voice was coming from all around her. "Bingo! While you were inactive, I took the liberty of downloading some information from your friend. Including your dictionary! You Bios have quite an entertaining and expressive vocabulary. It must make interfacing... a confusing experience."

"Where are you?" Ruby asked through clenched teeth.

Austere Agent responded, "I've upgraded. I thought that deactivation would be the worst thing that ever could happen to me, but turns out being remade does wonders!"

It was unsettling to Ruby hearing a robot talk in a way that was...so human. Especially a robot with such negative intentions.

"What do you want?" Ruby asked plainly.

Austere Agent's voice began to go in and out, changing pitch dramatically and spazzing into his native language for a word or two and then repeating it in Ruby's tongue. "Simple. I want you *gone*, Ruby Palmer."

"Then let me leave! The lockdown is because of *you, isn't it?* That's the only reason I can't get off the planet!"

"Remember when I told you that agents had wireless communication functions? I know that you were going to take Dysfunctional Historian and Average Technician to the rest of your Bios."

"Those aren't their names," Ruby said, breathing heavily with her brows angled downwards.

Austere Agent continued, "I can't risk anymore disorder. Since you've been here, you've jeopardized the integrity of our systems. Systems that…"

"Systems that were broken! Systems that I helped fix!"

"Systems that we've had in place for longer than your entire existence," Austere Agent finished his rant.

"I promise I only wanted to help you. All of you. But there were data corruptions in your very—"

"That is none of your concern!" It was Austere's turn to deliver an interruption. His voice was filled with a glitchy sounding low bass note, and it boomed all around Ruby, vibrating through her shoes. "You will not take robots to your planet! You will not do anything further! You must be reprogrammed!"

Her heart stopped. "But… but reprogramming is for robots… how would you…"

"Here's the itinerary," Austere Agent said, "You will sit here and ponder your past actions while I conclude my research on the system of systems that is a Bio and make preparations for you to be reprogrammed. When I am ready, I will provide another sedative toxin, extract your body from this chute, and finish the procedure."

"You can't do that!" Ruby was back on her feet yelling into the darkness. "I can't be 'reprogrammed!' I'm not like you! This isn't… this isn't logical!" She shouted, hoping her use of the word 'logic' would make him take pause.

Austere Agent did audibly pause, as evidenced by the soft tone she heard next. But he said, "I liked being remade. I predict, with high certainty that you will like it, too. I'll be back soon, Ruby Palmer. Don't go anywhere." He begun to make a series of tones that sounded like a modulated, demented sort of laugh. "I recently learned that that is a joke because you *cannot* go anywhere. Most robots were never programmed with the ability to make a joke, let alone a good one. I was one of those robots, but I've been improved. See you soon, Ruby Palmer."

"Wait!" she shouted. "Hold on!"

But there was no response. No tones, clicks, beeps, chimes, or anything else. He was gone.

Ruby paced, not having any ideas regarding what she could do. She kicked the wall, knowing that it wouldn't help.

Ruby let her arms and hands hang limp, and she slumped to the floor, sighing dejectedly.

"Ruby," Pippa said in the lowest volume setting.

"Pippa! I thought you'd been disabled!"

Pippa muttered, "I've been hiding. Ruby, I'm scared. I pretended to be deactivated so that he wouldn't remove me from you and destroy me. But he opened me up and looked inside…"

"I'm scared too, Pippa. But we're going to figure this out. Is there anything that you can think of to get us out of here?"

Pippa was silent. Ruby hoped that meant she was taking action. Calculating, or processing, or whatever it was that happened within her core processor. "No, I'm not detecting any signals."

Ruby took a deep breath. She needed to think logically about this. "Okay. Let's start from the top. Where are we? Do you know where we are?"

"No, Ruby. There is not enough ambient illumination to make an analysis of the room."

"Well, were you active when we were brought here? Can you make an educated guess based on our movement?"

"Also no. To pretend I was deactivated, I had to remain inactive. I was not recording data. Without a network connection, I'm not even sure how much time has elapsed."

Ruby went over everything that Austere Agent said in her mind, which was not easy given she was also working very hard to keep fear from taking over. Then it hit her.

She exclaimed, "A chute! He said we're in some sort of chute! Do you have any idea what that could mean?"

Ruby waited for Pippa to take the moment she needed to calculate. "I have accessed the map of Location Zero I downloaded to local memory from Scout. The term 'chute' describes... a lot of places."

"Disposal chutes?" Ruby asked. "I remember Disto talking about disposal chutes that connected to the recycling centers."

"Yes, there are many."

"Hmmm," Ruby was doing her thinking out loud now. "I don't know how long I was asleep, but they wouldn't have taken me far, right? It makes sense to put me in the one nearest my quarters."

"There is one that is located immediately below your quarters, Ruby, with access in the adjacent hallway."

"Okay, so let's assume that's where we are. How do we get out?"

Pippa was silent. Ruby waited patiently. But Pippa was still silent.

"Pippa?"

"Ruby?"

"How do we get out of here?"

"I do not have that information."

It's one step forward, two steps back with this one. "Pippa, can you project the map as a holo-image?"

"I have been this entire time," Pippa said.

Ruby smacked her forehead with her hand. Holo-images needed at least a little ambient light to work with. They didn't work in pitch black darkness. She knew that.

"Ok, then describe to me what's on the map. In as much detail as possible. I'll try to picture it."

As Pippa explained, Ruby tried very hard to keep a representative image in her mind, using her finger to draw in the air, not that she could see her finger, either, but she could feel it, and that was enough.

"There! Back up. What was that you just said?"

"I said 'and the horizontal lift' when you said 'There!'"

"That's it," Ruby said. "This chute is more than a chute. It's part of the lift system, and it's connected to the recycling center itself. Do we know how to operate it? If we can get to the center..."

"I will analyze the data I have downloaded from this portion of Location Zero's information system. It is limited, but I'll see what I can find," Pippa responded. And then, "The buttons on the wall are part of an emergency system. In case any robot found itself accidentally in a chute. I do not have the instructions on how to operate it."

"What if I randomly pressed them? Something is bound to work? Aren't emergency systems supposed to be easy? In case someone is panicking?"

"Do robots panic?" Pippa asked. Ruby had to think about that one. *Did they?*

Pippa continued, "A robot from the correct qualifying line would be able to operate this, even with no illumination."

"But what if another robot found itself in the chute?" Ruby countered, trying to prove to herself that she should be able to push enough buttons the same as an unprogrammed or unqualified robot would.

"Robots are not random," Pippa said.

"What does that have to do with anything?" Ruby asked.

"You said, 'what if I randomly pressed them.' A robot wouldn't press buttons randomly. They would—"

"—press them in a pre-defined sequence," Ruby caught on and finished Pippa's thought. "A simple sequence. Quick, Pippa, what are some number sequences we know?"

"Many, Ruby. There are geometric sequences, triangular sequences... There is the Bell Sequence[1], the Fibonacci sequence[2] ..."

"Nothing complicated," Ruby said. "If it's for an emergency, it's got to be simple."

"What about the sequence of prime numbers?" Pippa offered. "I have noticed a... a preoccupation with those special numbers[3]."

"Let me try it." Ruby felt her way back to the button covered wall and began to feel out the buttons. She counted them, there were 41. *A prime number*, Ruby noted. *Maybe Pippa is on to something...*

"Ok, the first prime numbers are 2," Ruby pressed the second button as she said the number. "3," she pressed the third.

"5," Pippa called out, trying to be helpful.

"I know, I know all of them," Ruby said. "Well, not *all* of them, but certainly up to 41."

She continued to feel and press buttons, calling out the numbers as she did. "7, 11, 13, 17, 19, 23, 29, 31, 37, and 41," she said. "There!"

Nothing happened. Ruby sank to the floor.

"Well, that was a bust," she said. "Any other ideas?"

"You forgot one," Pippa said.

Ruby replayed the prime number sequence in her head. "No, I didn't. I got them all."

"I meant, you forgot 'one', as in, the number one."

"One is not a prime," Ruby said.

When Pippa didn't respond, Ruby said, "Pippa?"

"I cannot debate this with you, Ruby. It will... be damaging. So I will pose it as a question. Forget what prime numbers are to you. To the robots, would they consider one a prime number?"[4]

---

1. This is not a number sequence that most people have ever heard of. It's intended to answer the question: If you have a set of items, in how many different ways can you group them? For example, if you have 2 items, you can group them in 2 ways: you could keep them together, or you can separate them. If you have 3 items—A, B, C—possible groupings are: {A,B,C}, {A} and {B,C}, {B} and {A,C}, {C} and {A,B}, and {A},{B},{C}. That's 5 different ways.
So, the Bell sequence is: 1,1,2,5,15, 52,203, etc. It grows very fast.

2. More people have heard of the Fibonacci sequence, in which each number is the sum of the two numbers that precede it. Please go find my novel *T is for Time Travel* since Fibonacci plays a very large role in that one!

3. I am utterly fascinated with prime numbers!

4. There was a time in the history of mathematics (or maybe it's more appropriate to say philosophy) when 1 was sometimes called prime, because it sort of fits the "only divisible by itself and 1" idea. But it wound up causing a lot of confusion (among mathematicians) and broke some of the neat patterns in number theory. So today, here on Earth in human society, 1 is not considered to be prime. The formal definition of a prime number is a "whole number **greater than 1** that has exactly two distinct positive divisors." The number 1 has only one divisor (itself) so it doesn't fit the definition. (And in a parallel universe, I'm some kind of number theorist/philosopher.)

Ruby wanted to talk this through but was also very aware that Austere Agent could be back any minute so now was not the time.

"Fine. I'll press 'one.'"

The chute began to move.

"Perfect! Pippa, I love you!"

"My emotion module is limited so I cannot express the same level of emotion, Ruby. But I am quite pleased that my analysis helped you."

Ruby laughed, "Helped *us*, you mean! Now let's hope this takes us out of here so we can find Disto and AT and tell them everything!"

> Ruby <

The lift stopped abruptly, knocking Ruby back to the floor.

"Pippa, where are we?" she asked as she stood up, instinctively dusting herself off.

Pippa didn't get a chance to answer. Instead, a voice that made Ruby's stomach sink surrounded her. "You're at the Reclamation and Recycling primary facility," said Austere Agent. "You didn't think that simply a change in physical location would prevent me from finding you? I am... everywhere. I am Location Zero."

"It's actually quite convenient," he continued. "Since we are going to 'recycle' you. That is what re-programming is, after all. Using the same structure to host a new instruction set."

The door started to open inwards, anchored at the bottom, like the lowering of a plank. Ruby made sure to be out of the way as it extended. She could see into the room beyond. Robots were hovering over conveyor belts, and there were two she didn't recognize at the doorway, with a cart in between them. She looked for someone she recognized and there was no one. One robot resembled Fastidious Mechanic, but it wasn't him... maybe another of his line.

"Pippa," she said in the lowest volume she could achieve. Ruby was certain that Austere Agent could still hear here, but she didn't have much of a choice in her methods of communication with Pippa.

"Ruby, I have a connection," Pippa said. "...and Scout is trying to contact me... he says he can help get us out if... if we'll take him with us."

"Sure, of course, I don't care," Ruby responded. "How do we get out of this?"

"Ruby, Scout says to use logic. Break his logic."

What the heck does that mean? I can't even see him... but then Ruby figured out Scout was referring to the Agent's argument and having a logical, or not so logical, argument with the disembodied robot.

"Austere Agent," Ruby said into the room, "Why do I need to be reprogrammed?"

"It's simple. All robots follow their programming. You are not a robot and all non-robots do not follow... robots are programmed."

"I am not a robot."

"Correct. But you can still be programmed."

"Not if you follow your own logic, Austere Agent."

Ruby smiled, hoping she had him, "Someone is either a robot or not a robot, correct?"

"That is correct."

"Robots are programmed."

"Also correct."

"And so not-robots are...?"

"...not programmed."

"You've got it. If A then B. If not A, then not B.[5] "

Austere Agent let out an unpleasant sound.

"Now open up and let me out of here."

The door had stopped halfway, letting in enough light for Ruby to see her way out. Ruby grabbed the edge and hoisted herself up, catching her arm on the side. The edge had a sharp corner and caught the sleeve of her jacket, ripped through it and also tore through her skin.

"Ow!" she said and held her other hand over it as she jumped down into the room, landing, not gracefully, on her feet.

Right about then the main entrance swished open, and Disto, followed by AT, rushed in. "You were right, AT," Disto was saying.

The other robots barely glanced in their direction.

"You're hurt!" was the first thing AT said when he was close to Ruby.

"It's just a scratch," she said. "I'm fine."

"No, no, let me," he said. "I'm a technician. I fix things."

"You've never fixed a Bio before," Ruby countered.

"True, but I can... you're leaking."

"No, look, it's already stopped bleeding. It was just a little."

"What happened?" Disto asked.

"It was Austere Agent. He wanted to reprogram me. But I think we... well, I'm not 100% sure, but I think he's stuck in a computational loop. Someone else can clean up the mess."

---

5. I love thinking about truth tables. This particular structure is called the converse of a conditional statement.

Chapter 29

Ruby stood in front of the lift to her ship. Well, SD's ship. A camera was trained on her, and a newscaster was by her side.

"And your last words are?"

"Last for now, you mean. Not like, *last last*."

"Of course. Words that are your last on this planet specifically."

Ruby wanted to come up with an incredibly meaningful statement. All that she could think of were ancient movie lines. They may have sounded cheesy to her, but Ruby knew that these robots had never seen any movies, so the words would be new to them. Maybe even inspiring. "I'll be back," kept coming to mind. She didn't want to say it because she wasn't sure if it was true, and she knew that many robots would take it as a literal promise.

She looked over at Disto and AT, who both indicated that they had nothing useful to offer.

SD was already on the ship, prepping for departure.

Instead, Ruby went with simple honesty, "I'm glad I could have helped. I'll miss this place. I hope to come back someday."

It was true. She was not the same person as when she arrived. She knew more. Her brain was open to new things. She was more curious than ever. She wanted answers.

"Thank you once again, Ruby Palmer. From all of Location Zero."

The light that had been trained on her switched off, and Ruby could instantly feel the temperature drop five degrees or more. She wiped the sweat off her brow with her upper arm.

The newscasting robot was efficiently packing up his equipment and almost tripped on the boxes of stuff that Disto and AT were still planning to load onto the ship.

"Are you guys ready?" Ruby asked of her traveling companions.

"Yes, once we get this onboard," replied Disto.

"What's in there?" Ruby inquired.

"Spare parts, mostly. But the more important question is: Are you ready, Ruby?"

Ruby looked around at the hallway that was her first sight of Location Zero. Robots went about their business, passing them and not giving them a second glance.

The walls, splattered here and there with markings that the robots understood—but Ruby still needed translation help with—felt comfortable and alive. Maybe Ruby would take up painting when she got back to Astroll 2.

She was ready but also a little sad at leaving this unique and interesting place.

"Yes. But I'll be honest... I'm worried my uncles are going to be mad at me."

Before anyone said anything to that, SD emerged from the lift.

"Everything is ready," he declared.

Since they stormed the kiosks of the Hall of Templates, SD had mostly returned to his old self. *Mostly, but something is still off,* Ruby thought. Ruby had expressed her condolences at the loss of Explosive Healer.

"Except..."

"Except my ship is still in pieces, I know."

Some of *Apple Pi* had been reassembled, but not the entire ship. Without *Apple Pi*, SD's ship would have to dock directly, or they would need to find some other way to deliver Ruby to Astroll 2.

"Look, once we get there, I'm sure they can send another mini-R-pod to get me. To get us. Easy peasy."

"And I will leave my ship in an automated standby mode."

"Exactly. This will be fine. Let's get this stuff loaded and go. Before they all forget who I am," Ruby joked, knowing the robots probably wouldn't get it.

Back at Astroll 2...

> At the Hub <

The Hub, the largest room on Astroll 2, was nearly full. Of course, on a small space station such as Astroll 2, word of a missing person spread, and everyone became attached to the story. Everyone knew Ruby Palmer on the station, and at her memorial service, everyone who could, came to pay their respects.

Ruby's Uncles were in the Nook, and her young cousin Sebastian, face red from crying when they finally told her she wouldn't be coming back, stood nearby with friends.

For those who couldn't make the memorial service in person, it was going to be broadcast station-wide.

But near the front of the room was Milo Jenkins and his teammates, who came to support him. Innogen Wilkens-Szklarski, known as Inny, was also there with her parents. She had colored her blond hair dark to honor the friend she looked up to like an older sister.

Dr. Rush Guerrero wasn't present, but he had sent words of condolences to Ruby's uncles from his ship en route to Earth.

Robt Plampton was there, too. He also stood at the Nook. In front of the microphone that carried his voice through the room and the station.

"Ruby Palmer," he began. Not only was his voice picked up and carried, but his video image was, too. There were several large screens on the walls of the Hub, so if you didn't have a front row seat, you were guaranteed to see. Robt Plampton's image was on all of them. The green walls that were in the Nook were replaced with an image of a smiling Ruby on the background of the video screens.

"I want to thank all of you who have come to pay their respects and to honor this brave person. Many of you have already reached out to Blake and Logan, longtime colleagues here on Astroll 2 and Ruby's uncles and sponsor. I'm going to turn the podium over to them. Stick around for station announcements at the end."

With that, Uncle Logan stepped to the podium in the Nook. His usually joyful face was the exact opposite, and looking at him now, it was hard to imagine what he looked like when he smiled. Blake stood by his side with his arm linked around Logan's, almost as if he was holding him up.

"You should go first," Logan whispered to Blake, a whisper that was picked up by the microphone and broadcast to all.

"No, we talked about this. You start."

Both of their eyes were red and swollen, details also picked up and broadcast.

"Ruby came to live with us when she was five, shortly after her mother passed away," Logan began. "She was always ornery, and hardly anything she did surprised us." At this memory, one side of Logan's mouth turned up in a weak smile.

"But she never..."

The screens on the walls, and throughout Astroll 2 crackled with interference. Logan stopped to look at them. Everyone in the Hub stopped looking at Logan in the Nook and turned to look at the screens. But not only in the Hub. Every place, be it a room, computer, tablet, communicuff, or other device with a screen, even ones that had previously been dormant, came to life at nearly the same instant.

Not only on Astroll 2. Depending on the distance from Astroll 2, screens all over the solar system: on Titan, on ships in-between planets and asteroids and stations and moons, on Mars, on the Moon, and on Earth herself a few minutes later—every screen known to humankind came to life.

And when the interference cleared, they all displayed the same image: Ruby Palmer. It wasn't a still image, however. It was a video image.

The first thing Ruby did was blink. The second thing she did was smile, a little sheepishly. The third thing she did was open her mouth to speak.

"Hi Uncle Blake, Uncle Logan. I truly hope you weren't too worried when I didn't show up on Titan. I'm okay, though. It's a long and unbelievable story, and I'll tell you all the details later. But I'm about 54 light-years from home. On an alien planet full of, get this... full of robots!"

She paused, presumably understanding that her uncles would need a moment to take this all in. But certainly not knowing that every other human in the solar system was also going to need a moment as well.

"I promise I'm okay. This message is brief because we wanted to test it out and see if it was even going to work. There are instructions on how to download a return message to the drones. Those will get downloaded to Astroll 2's computer automatically. I set that up.

"I really am okay. I can't tell you how sorry I am. I'll see you soon, and... I love you guys. A lot."

The video screens along the walls of the Hub reverted to an image of Ruby's uncles, with eyebrows raised, jaws slack, and mouths open. In fact, the whole human race might have had nearly the same look, and everyone who could look out a window or telescope did so to find the drones.

That was the day everything changed for humanity.

* * *

What's next for Ruby and her robot friends? Continue on to book three: *Silly Insane Humans*

Silly Insane Humans

Book 3 of The Robot Galaxy Series

Adeena Mignogna

Crazy Robot, LLC

Also By Adeena Mignogna

The Robot Galaxy Series
Book 1: *Crazy Foolish Robots*
Book 2: *Robots, Robots Everywhere!*
Book 3: *Silly Insane Humans*
Book 4: *Eleven Little Robots*

...and the unrelated standalone novel: Lunar Logic
Adeena's Stories (on KindleUnlimited):
Final Orbit
Objective Reality

Before We Begin

'Are we alone in the Universe?' has been one of the greatest unanswered questions of all time. It is right up there with other important unanswered questions such as 'Why do so many people hate licorice?' and 'Why does the number of cats a person collects increase proportionally with the length of time they've been socially isolated as well as to their hoarding status?'

Over the years, all the great minds of science—and science fiction—have been asked to speculate on the status of not only whether or not aliens exist but what they were like, where they were located, and when and how first contact would occur.

Not a single human who lived on Earth, one of Earth's colonies, or one of the human-made space stations envisioned that first contact would be with a group of alien robots. (With the exception of one obscure science fiction writer who published works in the early 21st century[1].)

Yet, many humans had looked to the stars with all manner of increasingly fancy technology to try and see if they could find evidence of life.

As of the year 2192, they had not. All of this changed on a regular Tuesday in 2192[2] when humankind received a message. The message was from one of their own, Ruby Palmer, a nineteen-year-old, who had been presumed dead for the last week and for the two weeks prior to that, known to be missing.

But on this Saturday[3], in a message intended for her uncles, on the space station Astroll 2, where she had lived since the age of seven, she declared to every human who was at that moment in front of a screen that she had spent the last several weeks in the company of robots. Alien robots.

On the other hand, these robots had been well aware for quite some time now that a multitude of biological life forms inhabited the galaxy.

Their opinions of Bios, as they not-so-lovingly called them, were that they typically did not seem to have a well-constructed program to execute, and hence, it was hard to predict what kinds of actions they would take. Not to mention all the processes they executed in order to continue functioning were, for lack of a better term, messy.

The robots followed their programming as provided to them through the various agencies and Halls that made up the Core of their society.

---

1. I am a huge fan of 4th wall breaks.

2. I have a timeline where I keep track of all things. This particular Tuesday is June 5th, 2192.

3. Yes, I flipped from Tuesday to Saturday and I am racking my brain to remember if there was a deliberate reason for this, or if this was a mistake and/or if I should correct it!

But there was a 'Special Projects' department responsible for ensuring that a set of robots had programming related to finding their long-lost data storage.

Detailed Historian, known as Disto, was one robot who received this programming and had been on a mission to collect and test the DNA of various biological life to determine whose DNA was used as a storage mechanism.

The robots had one main unanswered question that plagued them: 'Who created us?' The difference between a robot asking that and a human was that the robots knew an answer existed and that it was likely tucked away in their long-lost data archive.

Ruby Palmer, who had been with the robots for a few weeks, had her DNA tested and it was determined that humans did not carry any of the robots' data in the section of their DNA that was 'junk' to humankind.

But Ruby explained that there were thousands of other species of animals on planet Earth, so maybe one of those were what they were looking for. Maybe more than one.

So, Disto agreed to accompany Ruby Palmer back to her home. Swell Driver, known as SD, and the robot that first whisked Ruby away to Location Zero, the robot's home planet, was driving the ship. They were further accompanied by Ambitious Technician, AT, who simply wanted his adventure to continue.

In addition to being well aware of the common questions they shared as a conglomerate, each had their own questions they wanted answered.

AT wanted to know 'what kind of things will I be able to fix? Will I be able to learn their new technology?"

Disto only had thoughts about testing DNA. He wondered how long it was going to take to test all of the various types of Bios on this planet. Ruby didn't have an exact count but believed a couple million different species were left. Disto nearly had a circuit pop when he heard that number. While they had quite a bit of information on her home world, Planet Earth, the number of species in the robots' database cut off somewhat arbitrarily at 4068. Even that was quite a number.

SD's question wasn't quite so specific, however. SD was working hard to not let his question surface to his working memory: 'what is wrong with me?' A question to which he had no idea where to begin.

And finally, Ruby had only one question on her mind: "How mad are my uncles going to be?" given she had run away, stolen a ship, and was bringing it back in pieces.

Chapter 1

Ruby entered the command center of SD's ship. It looked as it had when she was first here—roomy for a single robot and human, sparse, with a single console indicating where a pilot might stand, and that was the spot SD occupied as he had that first day. She had previously been examining the parts of her own mini-R-pod, *Apple Pi*, as it lay strewn about in the belly of SD's ship.

"We are approaching the heliopause," SD announced.

"What is that?" AT asked. Ruby had come to learn in the short week she had known AT that he was very much the technician his name implied. If it wasn't related to something he could work on or fix, his knowledge was not only limited but practically non-existent.

To that end, they had to explain space travel to him. He knew the concept existed but didn't know how it worked. He had never worked on or fixed a spaceship before. In the sector of Location Zero that AT was from, they didn't have any outgoing or incoming ships.

But to prep for this trip, AT downloaded all the specs and diagrams, so he'd be prepared in case he needed to fix something.

In the short journey, nothing needed to be fixed, so AT occupied his time asking a large quantity of questions regarding anything space travel related.

"It's considered the boundary of our solar system[1]," Ruby said. She was, in fact, well-versed in all things related to space travel, even ones that had been considered out of bounds. Her mini-R-pod, *Apple Pi*, was designed only for relatively short-range travel. Its general range was from her home on the Astroll 2 space station to various other asteroids in the asteroid belt. In a pinch, it could take someone a few million kilometers away. For example, to Titan, one of the moons of Saturn and her original destination when she had left Astroll 2 shortly before SD found her.

Ruby was pacing as she answered AT's question. The nervous pacing prompted her to spew out everything she knew on the concept: "It's a theoretical boundary, not one any human has passed through. A few space probes have gone further, so I guess we know a little bit about it. It's where the solar wind and the interstellar medium meet."

---

1. Yep, this is me sneaking in some astronomy knowledge:

"What is the solar wind?[2]" AT asked.

Ruby shook her head. "Can I just give you a textbook to read? I can't handle all these questions right now."

Disto looked up from the computer console he had been engrossed in studying.

"Are you okay, Ruby?" he asked.

Ruby appreciated that Disto was able to ask her questions like that. At the right time, too. Thinking back to when they first met and how Disto was completely unaware, or didn't care, or was utterly perplexed by her emotional state, Ruby was grateful for the robot's attempts at meeting her halfway. She gave a little and they did too.

"I'm just nervous," Ruby said. "I wish I knew that my uncles got my message. I have no idea what they're going to say."

"Fearless Communicator assured us that his method to deliver your message was guaranteed not to fail."

"I know. Then assume they got it. I just told them that I'm with a bunch of alien robots. What are they thinking?"

"You will be able to ask them shortly," SD interrupted. "Please look." SD pointed to the screen which was so large, Ruby envied it. It was mostly black, and there were several dots, ranging from tiny to large but not large enough to be anything other than a dot. Each dot that had some importance were bracketed by square braces, and a symbol appeared below.

"Are those..." Ruby began.

"Those are the planets of your solar system along with our default designations. Here, I will turn on the predicted orbits of them."

Faint, but visible dotted lines appeared. From that, Ruby was able to see that the largest dot was really the Sun. She counted. All 8 planets were accounted for. A couple of the dwarf planets, too.

"Nice," she said. "But where's Astroll 2?"

Astroll 2 was located in the asteroid belt, near the Dwarf Planet Ceres. Ceres had been the source of a lot of contention to corporations and governments back on Earth over the years. As such, it was a designated 'do not touch' dwarf planet[3]. As far as Ruby knew, everyone abided by that. So, the company that built, owned, and operated Astroll 2 mined other nearby asteroids.

Over the years, there had been on and off plans for another active station, but none had popped up. Astroll 2, and its nearly 2,000 inhabitants, was the key facility in that region of space.

SD tapped his console, and another marker appeared on the screen. Given its location, Ruby clearly identified it as Astroll 2. They were close. Not close enough that *Apple Pi*, if it had been in the condition to fly, could get her there, but close in the sense that they were in the same solar system and not 54 light years away.

"Do you want to fly by any of the planets or moons on our way there?" SD asked. "I can program a variety of trajectories through the system."

---

2. And more astronomy!

  https://science.nasa.gov/sun/what-is-the-solar-wind/

3. This is me projecting out what I think will happen legally as we push out into our solar system more. At the moment, the Outer Space Treaty (yes, a real United Nations Treaty that a whole lot of nations have signed up to) prevents any nation-state from claiming sovereignty over celestial bodies. I don't think that's going to hold for the long term, but I think there will be a handful of individual places that we agree can't be owned—and in this case, touched. Similar-ish to Antarctica.

Ruby considered that. She was already the first human to meet an extraterrestrial—unless ancient alien abduction stories could be believed. Right now, she couldn't be certain either way. As far as she knew, she was the first human ever to leave the solar system. Why not be the first to see all the planets up close?

"Sure," she said. She knew deep down that what she was doing was, in fact, procrastinating from making contact with her family on Astroll 2[4].

---

4. Sure. But who could possibly say no to an offer like that? If my kid ever delays seeing me because he had an opportunity to tour the solar system—he better take it. Likewise, if I'm supposed to meet with you and I have this opportunity? I'm taking it! #sorrynotsorry

Chapter 2

> Swell Driver <

While his companions talked about all the phenomena out there in the Universe, specifically in Ruby's home system, Swell Driver was free to think about whatever he wanted while he computed a trajectory that would take them on a tour of Ruby's solar system.

He heard Ruby tell stories of the various planets, from the large to the small, gaseous to rocky. While she talked, SD ruminated on himself.

SD called up the memories from the last time he was here. It was the last time he could recall feeling like himself.

He used an appendage to plug into his computer console. That was the polite thing to do when others were around.

He remembered passing through a storm of radiation on his way here, which corrupted much of the data in his ship's systems. But no, that wasn't the problem. He still felt fine and himself.

SD could recall a time not too long ago when the computer told him that Ruby's kind were called 'Umans' and provided him the misinformation that they looked entirely different from Ruby. And he could recall that his primary algorithm, which involved piloting spaceships to ferry things across the galaxy, was intact then. It was intact now.

"How far are we from initiating tour of the Bio-Muck system," SD asked the ship's computer. While Ruby had helped SD relabel much of the data he had on her system, planet, and its contents, the name for the overall system hadn't changed.

"Less than 66 tics if we start now," the computer responded.

"Wonderful. Set for autonomous…"

"But there are several ships in the path between the fourth planet and the construction known as Astroll 2."

"Interesting. Adjust course to take us…"

"And I can detect several locations that are scanning Astroll 2 and its vicinity. We will pass through those scanners."

"*Very* interesting. We will adjust the trajectory to avoid that."

SD instructed the computer to head along a trajectory that would take them parallel to the axis of spin of the majority of the planets, thus putting them at a vantage point that most would consider 'overhead' of the system. They would weave in and out by going 'up and down' from most lifeforms' vantage point. Only the lifeforms in this system should not be expecting that, and hence wouldn't detect them.

Not that a detection would be terrible in this case. They were going to make contact with Ruby's relatives. This thought excited SD. Ruby was swell, and after all the stories she'd told about her uncles, cousin, and even her friends, figured they would all be swell, too.

"233 tics until new trajectory can be initiated," the computer told SD.

"Excellent. Set for autonomous execution," SD ordered the computer.

To his companions, he said, "Would you like to see a live feed of each item as we pass by?"

"Yes, of course!" said Ruby. She disengaged from whatever she was talking about to Disto and AT and came over to SD's side, putting a hand on his chassis. He was always comforted when she did that. That's how Ruby would describe the feeling anyway. SD would use a more specific term such as, 'certain,' perhaps, or 'secure.' Certain that someone he enjoyed was nearby and secure in the fact that they weren't going anywhere.

SD set the viewscreen to display live feeds of whatever entity they were approaching. A small spherical object appeared and started to grow in the screen.

"That's Pluto!" Ruby said. "Everyone's favorite not-quite-a-planet planet."

"What does that mean?" Disto asked.

"It used to be a planet, but then it became a Dwarf Planet," said Ruby.

"How does a planet undergo such a transformation?"

Ruby giggled. "It didn't," she said. "It was just a change in nomenclature.[1]"

"Ah," all three robots said in unison.

"Yeah, it caused a big kerfuffle at the time. I read about it in a class I had to take on the history of the solar system. Apparently, people who had barely ever heard of Pluto came out of the woodwork to defend it as a planet."

"Woodwork?" SD asked. He was used to asking Ruby about some of the odd phrases she used.

"It means that people who didn't care before all of the sudden cared."

"Why?" asked AT.

"I have no idea," said Ruby. "They just did. It took forty or so years for it to settle out. I think I have a great-great-great-great-great grandmother who might have been involved in helping people to accept it. I can't remember her name, but she would try and tell people the positive side of the situation[2]. It got people to learn more about the dwarf planets, which apparently no one knew about before all of that."

"Does anyone live there?" Disto asked.

"Oh no," said Ruby. "In fact, I think I'm the closest any human has ever come to seeing it up close like this. It's beautiful!"

"Beautiful?" all three robots repeated in unison.

SD was starting to look up the definition of that word, but Disto was a little faster. He added, "pleasing the circuits and algorithms."

---

1. And honestly, Pluto's "demotion" never bothered me. By calling it a "Dwarf Planet" what it did was elevate the other Dwarf Planets from obscurity to now a few people know more about them. Or at least that they exist. If you don't know, they are: Ceres, Pluto, Haumea, Makemake, and Eris. As of this writing, the IAU (International Astronomical Union) only recognizes five Dwarf Planets, but there are likely many more.

2. Yes, another 4th wall break. Giggle.

Ruby's face contorted in a way that made SD wonder if that was indeed the definition, but then she returned to watching the object she called 'Pluto' on the screen. Their trajectory had them encircle the planet at approximately three times its diameter before heading further inwards towards the next planet on the tour, one Ruby called 'Uranus.' They were not going to pass by all the planets 'in order' of their distance from the Sun, but rather along a path that aligned with the planet's current positions.

SD and the other robots were quiet for a moment and watched Ruby watching Pluto. SD identified his feeling as pity in that moment. He understood that Human spaceships were quite limited, and as such, this type of tour of their own solar system, their home, was impossible. Ruby, who was even a pilot like himself, had so little experience flying compared to him. He knew that she would love to pilot this ship herself if she could.

He wished that was something he could allow her to do. It was a wish that had been developing in his circuits for a while but there were still competing algorithms that computed that only he could pilot his ship. Once again, he began ruminating on his own failings as a robot, a habit that Explosive Healer had tried to break in him during their sessions together before she was destroyed. Explosive Healer tried to tell him that the things happening to and around him were not his fault[3]. SD tried to incorporate her counsel into his algorithms, and the computational result was believing that if he executed his assignments, like a good robot, he'd get to do what he wanted afterwards. Although he wasn't even sure he could compute what he wanted accurately...

---

3. I study—and try to practice—Stoicism. That's the vibe I was going for here.

Chapter 3

> Ruby <

"That was amazing," Ruby said. "I have no words for the gift you've just given me." The magnitude of what she just did, become the first human to see all eight planets and a handful of dwarf planets up close, was settling in.

Saturn, with its moon Titan, along with Jupiter, had always been her favorites, especially since Titan was where she longed to be for the longest time. But seeing Earth up close, yet not too close, gave her a tingly feeling that tugged at her a little. She wasn't going to admit out loud that it might have supplanted the others as her new favorite, but she appreciated its beauty when you couldn't see what was happening on the surface.

"And really, it's all recorded?" she asked.

SD nodded. "Yes. We'll be able to provide you with an assemblage of the data."

She was the first human to see the entire solar system up close, *and* she was going to be able to bring a record of the experience back with her. SD had told her that not only was she seeing things in a visual spectrum suited to her, but the ship had the capability to record all the way from low-frequency radio waves to gamma rays—pretty much covering the entire electromagnetic spectrum. That data would keep a handful of scientists busy for their entire careers.

Humans had colonized Mars and knew that planet pretty well, and also knew a few things about Titan and the couple of other places humans had been. Support for exploring the system, specifically the parts that would probably never be lived on, touched by humans, or made any use of, had waned over the years. It was hot and heavy in the early 21st century, but enough people complained about the amount of money being spent off of Earth that by 2050, there was nothing happening[1]. The Mars colony was left over from the early days of human space exploration. Anything else that existed with a human footprint was purely the result of the trillionaires—they created The Company and started ZTEC, the organization that was only recently starting to explore Titan.

Ruby had tried to learn everything she could about Titan, including old history—several missions had been planned in the early 21st century, but none of them materialized.

"We have one more object to see on our current trajectory," SD said. "We're headed to Ceres before we approach Astroll 2."

Ruby gulped. The moment she had been anxious about was upon her.

---

1. It's late 2025 as I write this, and of course I fear that this is what's happening.

"How long until we start our Astroll 2 approach?" she asked.

"Approximately six hundred and, no, calculating... ten minutes."

Ruby smiled softly. She appreciated how the robots were attempting to talk in terms of the human time scale now that they were in her home system. On Location Zero, it made sense that they referred to any unit of time in their own scale, the tic, which was nearly one second. But it was nice that they were adjusting while here.

She was stalling from thinking about what she was going to say to her uncles.

As if the robots could read her thoughts, Disto said, "And approximately five minutes until we are able to initiate a communication channel."

Ruby gulped again.

"How do I look?" she said to no robot in particular. All three of the robots looked at each other and back to Ruby, and then back to each other.

"You look like your systems are functioning normally," AT said.

"You look the same as the day I... met you," said SD.

"The hue of your outer chassis is a slightly different hue from what is typical," Disto said, "but I think you look... fine."

Ruby appreciated Disto's attention to language. In truth, she appreciated all the interactions she had with these robots up until now. After getting off to a rough start initially—after all, they did kidnap her—they were genuinely kind and took care of all her needs. They provided her interesting information about their planet and society. And, of course, their manner of speaking, at least how they processed her language and idioms, provided no end of entertainment.

And she was taking them home to meet her family.

"Has it been five minutes?" she asked, more because no one else had said anything, and she wanted to hear someone talk.

"Indeed," Disto said. "Let's try to establish communication. AT?"

AT had plugged himself into the console. Ruby had provided him with information earlier on the various communication frequencies that were used—including which ones to avoid since they were for emergency purposes only.

Ruby stood in front of one of the console screens, which came to life almost immediately. The face that greeted her was... she was trying to remember where she had seen him before.

It was the FUFE who tried to help, or rather, didn't really try, but sent her to call the main care center on Earth the day she left Astroll 2.

At first, he was not looking at the screen, but seemingly at another console on his end and his expression was one of indifference as he talked from a script he had memorized, "We're here to take care of you, if we don't then..." as he looked at the screen that would have been showing him Ruby's face, "holy amaze-balls! You're Ruby Palmer! Just one moment!"

Ruby searched her memory but couldn't recall this guy knowing who she was the last time they interacted. She also couldn't imagine why she would spark such a reaction.

"Ok," he said after a moment of furious tapping on another device. "Robt Plampton is in his office, and your uncle, I don't know which one, is on his way there. I'm going to route this call to the Director's office. Stand by. Wow! Ruby Palmer! I'd love to have dinner with you later and you can tell me all about—"

He was cut off and his image was replaced by the current director of Astroll 2, Robt Plampton[2]. Plampton's face was round, in a way that someone who had spent nearly their entire adult life in space, mostly in the very low-gravity of ships, would look. His complexion, not pale, but not sun-kissed, also betrayed a life in artificial environments. His pug nose and large ears were not features that commanded respect, but his blue eyes worked over-time on that.

Those were the same eyes that went wide when he saw Ruby.

"Ruby Palmer! It is you! This is amazing!"

Ruby was not sure what to say. This over-the-top reaction was not what she was expecting.

"Hi, Mr. Plampton," she said, a little uncertain. "I really wanted to talk to my uncles. Are they there?"

"Blake is on his way," Plampton said. He then looked around Ruby, moving awkwardly back and forth as one might while seeing something unbelievable displayed on a flat screen. As if he was struggling to accept the 2D image and needed to force perspective into it being 3D.

"Are they with you now?" he said.

"Wha... who?" Ruby looked over to her left at one robot and two others over on her right. *He couldn't mean...* but before she had time to continue that awkward questioning, she saw a door swish open behind Robt Plampton and Uncle Blake appeared.

He quickly replaced Plampton in the viewscreen as he moved Robt Plampton over to the side. Plampton was still ogling at every angle of Ruby's image as he could manage.

"Uncle Blake!" Ruby felt like she was going to melt. "I am so happy to see you! I can't wait to tell you! Wait... you got my message? You knew I was okay? And you shared my message with Mr. Plampton?" Ruby was finally catching on. That had to be it. Plampton knew about the robots, too. That would make sense. If it were a normal day, she might've caught on sooner. But Ruby hadn't had a normal day since she was last onboard Astroll 2. The amount of new information and experiences she'd been taking in were beginning to feel entirely unmanageable. She had taken a mini-R-pod, so when her uncles got her message, they probably felt obligated to tell the station director.

"Your message was shared, but *I* wasn't the one who shared it. But, Ruby, oh, I'm so glad to see you!" Uncle Blake said.

"Wait a minute. Other people saw my message? That was just for you and Uncle Logan."

"Ruby, it wasn't only *some* people who saw your message. *Everyone* in the whole solar system got it. You're, well, famous. Let's get you back on Astroll 2, and I'll explain everything that's been happening since the MCE—the Moment that Changed Everything."

---

2. Actor inspiration: Colm Meaney.

Chapter 4

> Milo <

Milo's heart was racing.

"How can I help you calm down?" his communicuff offered.

"Delete notification," Milo said. He was in the hanger prepping a mini-R-pod, *Pecan Pi*, for launch. It was bad enough that his communicuff knew how fast his heart was racing. He didn't need his team to know as well.

But he admitted to himself that his heart was only half racing because he was going to see Ruby again. The other half was about that alien ship holding position a few hundred kilometers from Astroll 2.

The ship was huge, larger than anything he'd ever worked on. It was larger than anything in any human ship fleet he was even aware of. As such, it was too big to fit in either hanger of Astroll 2.

Apparently, Ruby's ship, *Apple Pi*, was inside it, but it was not functioning, so it couldn't bring Ruby back to Astroll 2. Instead, it was decided, as he was informed by Robt Plampton, that he, Milo Jenkins, would take another mini-R-pod out, dock with the alien ship, and bring Ruby home.

Not just Ruby. Three alien robots were going to accompany her. He was still having trouble fathoming such a thing.

"I have multiple strategies," his communicuff chimed again, "to help you reduce your heart rate. It is not healthy to maintain such a high resting heart rate."

"Delete notification," Milo instructed again. "Discontinue heart rate monitoring until further notice."

"That is not recommended. Fourteen out of fifteen human and AI doctors recommend—"

"Delete."

Milo looked around the mini-R-pod. Two members of his team were on the opposite side inspecting the phalanges[1][2]. A do-nothing part, but every ship that carried humans had at least one or two. There was a law enacted in 2091 that stated every ship must have phalanges and the number was proportional to the number of people the ship could support. This mini-R-pod

---

1. This is a gag I carried forth from the last episode of *Friends*. There is no such thing as a phalange on any kind of airplane, ship, satellite, etc. (And I don't think there ever will be.) It the episode, Phoebe made it up as a way to get people to freak out that something was wrong with an airplane so Rachel could get off and go see Ross.

2. After Star Trek and sci-fi... I'm a HUGE *Friends* fan.

had two. Milo was now in a long line of technicians and other industry professionals who simply shook their heads, inspected the phalanges, and moved on with life.

Pecan Pi was the largest. It was actually a mini-R-pod-L. It was slightly bigger than Ruby's *Apple Pi*, and Milo was assured that it would fit into the alien ship parked outside.

He felt his heart rate pick up speed once again at the thought. This time, his communicuff remained silent.

Milo looked at the tablet he had been carrying around. He reviewed the pre-launch checklist that was displayed.

"Hey, Domas, your part of the inspection complete?" As the words came out of his mouth, he saw that several steps in the procedure took on a green highlight. "Never mind," he called out and walked around the ship, giving it a final glance.

"Ready to go rescue your *girlfriend*?" Domas Watkins snickered. His companion, Eryk Chung snickered as well.

Milo, never one who appreciated that kind of joking around, said, "Two things wrong with your statement. One, she's not my girlfriend. I have a date with Inny later, remember? Two, I'm not rescuing her. She's fine. Just doesn't have a way to get back onto the station."

"Fine, fine, she's not your girlfriend," Domas conceded. Although mentioning his date with Innogen gave Milo a sick feeling in his stomach. It was a date, but it wasn't. Sure, since Ruby's disappearance, they had become closer. Closer *friends*. Still, she called it a date, and he hadn't disagreed. He tried to, but it came out as an odd assortment of stuttering 'ums,' and 'ers.' Inny asked him what was wrong, and he proceeded to shovel a much-too-large portion of his calci-cinna roll into his mouth to keep himself from saying something stupid.

"But," Domas said as Milo opened the hatch to *Pecan Pi*, "I mean, she's with aliens. Alien robots. How creepy-cool!"

"There's a rumor going around that they're coming back with you, too," Eryk said.

"Well, that's a rumor you should keep to yourself," Milo responded. Director Plampton had indeed told him not to mention that. There were a lot of mixed feelings about alien robots coming to the station, and Plampton didn't want things to get out of hand. He said he wanted to make sure they debriefed Ruby—and the robots—properly before it was well known.

Milo didn't know how that would happen without creating more suspicion. Once he returned to the hanger, his whole team would know. And if four people knew something interesting, the whole station of 2,000 would, too, shortly after. Oh well, it was a noble goal on Plampton's part, and he wouldn't add fuel to that fire, but he wasn't going to be able to prevent anything.

"It sounds like they're perfectly nice. Ruby said she was well taken care of," Milo said, hoping to ease any fears.

"You talked to her?"

"No," Milo admitted, "Plampton told me."

"And you believe him?"

"No reason not to," Milo responded. "Now, let's get me out into space." He walked into the ship and closed the hatch behind him. Since this was the shortest trip ever planned, he took nothing except the tablet he had been holding which he now stowed in a compartment over the second pilot's console.

Through the cockpit window he saw his team head back to the control center and before he knew it, he was in space and on a heading to rendezvous with an alien ship.

He had taken an extra sweat-suppression pill before leaving his quarters earlier, and wished he'd brought a third pill since the next few minutes had the ability to leave him drenched in nervous sweat—something he wasn't anxious for Ruby, or anyone, to see.

> Milo <

Before this moment, Astroll 2 was the largest manufactured object Milo had ever seen in space. But the ship parked in front of him, which looked like it came right out of an old, animated children's movie, was nearly half the size of Astroll 2. Larger than any ship he'd ever seen or read about.

The ship was stationary, at least with respect to Astroll 2, which was good. But without a place to attach himself, he figured the best he could do was to put himself in a circumnavigational path around the ship.

This had the extra benefit of allowing him a good look at the thing. Besides being huge, the other word he'd used to describe it was whale-like. It was boxy, but there was a clear seam where a whale's mouth would be. He couldn't make out any windows, nor determine where thrust would expel to move the ship. None of the features that he recognized on human-made ships seemed to present itself on this... blob. His brain was back to large and boxy but whale shaped. Perhaps it was this that made him feel as if he was about to be swallowed whole.

"Computer, are you recording the object in front of us?"

"Confirmed. Ship's cameras are recording."

"Are we in danger of running out of data storage space?"

"Storage is at 5.3% and increasing at a rate of 0.1% per minute."

Once Milo determined that his orbit around the monster ship was stable, he initiated a communication link. Well, he turned on his communication link and hoped that it was one that the alien ship could receive.

"This is *Pecan Pi* calling..." he wasn't sure what he was calling. Standard greeting was to identify the other ship, but he hadn't been given a name. "This is *Pecan Pi* calling the alien ship." He closed his eyes and squished them. He sounded like a dorky kid from one of those animated movies. He was starting to think that he was part of one. Or maybe this was a dream.

"What's cooking, *Pecan Pi?*" Milo heard a familiar voice but would have sworn on his entire meme archive there was a high-pitched crack on the word 'what.'

"Ruby!"

"Hi, Milo. Come to rescue me and bring me home?" Ruby said with a chuckle. Milo didn't know what the chuckle was. Was she flirting with him? No, that couldn't be. If he chuckled back, would she think that he was flirting with her? Milo definitely didn't want that. But she chuckled, so maybe if he didn't, she would think something was wrong and wouldn't feel welcomed.

Milo attempted a subtle chuckle that turned into a wheeze and a throat clearing, "I'm going to try! What's the plan? How do I get you out of that thing?"

There was a pause, and then Ruby said, "Cut your thruster power, try to minimize any remaining thrust. SD says once your momentum is at a minimum, we'll," there was another pause, "we'll scoop you up. Easy peasy."

Milo blinked. "SD?"

"Yeah, that's the name of, uh, one of my new friends. You'll meet him in just a few minutes. Drop that momentum, ok?"

"Understood," Milo said and then went to work on his console applying specific impulses to the different maneuvering thrusters all over *Pecan Pi* until he was as still as he could be relative to the alien ship.

He looked out the window. The ship started to rotate until the mouth of the whale was facing him. Then it opened up and enveloped his ship.

Chapter 5

Detailed Historian looked at the tiny ship sent to retrieve Ruby.

"We will all fit in there?" he asked, uncertain as his circuits made some geometrical estimations based on what his optical sensors could perceive.

"Sure," Ruby said. "We'll be cozy, but it's not like it's a week-long trip. It'll take us only a few minutes to get to Astroll 2 from here. We'll be fine."

Disto, as he thought of himself ever since working out his preferred nickname, wasn't so sure, and wanted to ask if there were other options. He wanted to but decided to say nothing, only because audio communication with Bios was typically slow and introduced so much delay in whatever was happening, and he was anxious to get on with things.

He was not only anxious to get to Astroll 2, but anxious to get to Ruby's home planet, Earth. That's where millions of biological species were located, any one of which could be the link to the robot's long-lost storage data.

Several generations ago, robots had used the junk DNA of some alien species as storage, as their world was facing a storage crisis. It wasn't Ruby's species, the humans, but their planet had more life than was typical of any other biological species they'd ever met, so it was highly likely that one, or more, of the species of her home planet was exactly what he was looking for. The sooner he could start examining all that DNA, the more content a robot he would be.

Ruby told him she wasn't sure when or how they would get back to Earth, but that they certainly would. There were some biological samples on Astroll 2, however, that they could ask for him to look at in the meantime.

"Generally, animals haven't been welcome in space," she had said. "A few are used in experiments, but that's it."

"Not welcome?"

"Ok, bad choice of words. They take up too many resources that humans use and need. I once overheard an argument one of the hanger chiefs had with someone who had snuck their pet cat aboard. They were arguing with the station director about how they needed it. I don't think either of them stayed on Astroll 2[1] ."

---

1. I think about this a lot. Think about how many people have cats, dogs, and other pets. Pets are such a huge part of our lives. If and when we really start to have some no-kidding long-term space colonies, stations, and whatnot.... will pets be a part of their culture as well? Or will those humans develop a culture that doesn't include pets? This bothers me.

Ruby, while very useful when it came to all things computers and programming—after all, she had helped his kind with a couple of major problems—was not useful at all when it came to discussing the myriad of life on her home world.

Maybe it was because she had lived most of her life away from it, on the station she called Astroll 2. Maybe it was because she was too focused all the time on her own interests that everything else was a blur. Or maybe it was simply that her own programming was limited.

Disto then felt a small jolt. He recognized that it must be the scooping hatch securing in its closed state.

"Capture complete," SD announced.

"Ok! Milo is probably freaking out right about now, I know I was," Ruby said. "Let me see and talk to him first, okay?"

Disto approximated a nod to show agreement and saw both SD and AT make a similar motion.

They all moved to the lift at the back of the cabin. Moments later, they were in front of a small ship.

"Give it a sec for the temperature to even out," Ruby said. "We let the outermost part of the hull get cold. It's part of the thermal design to keep the inside a good temperature for us humans without using too much power."

"How long does that take?" asked AT. "I would love to know more about how your transportation vessels work. Maybe I can help you finish putting together your ship."

Disto looked over at the partially assembled, but mostly disassembled, *Apple Pi*, the ship that Ruby had been in when SD met her.

"Let me see," and Disto watched her take the end of her appendage and touch the ship. She immediately pulled it back but said, "Eh, we can open it. It's fine."

She then used the same appendage to release a clamp on the side of a hatch, which swung down.

"Hey Milo!" she called into the ship. "You in there?"

There was no response.

"Milo?" Ruby rushed into the ship. And then, a moment later, Disto heard, "I need some help!"

Disto rushed into the ship, followed by AT.

He saw Ruby trying to move another Bio, who was slumped over the console, back into his chair. AT came over and helped with the maneuvering.

"He has a normal pulse," she said, adding, "I think."

"Milo, talk to me. Wake up?" Ruby was tapping his cheek. "I need the emergency med kit. AT, can you open that drawer?"

She was pointing to one right behind where Disto was standing, so he turned around and used his own appendage to open it.

"Yeah, that's the one. There's a red box..."

Disto didn't know what red was but saw two boxes. He pulled them both out, but before he could give either to Ruby, the new Bio made a noise. It wasn't a word that was in his dictionary of the Ruby's language. It was, "uuuugghh."

"Milo! You're ok!" Ruby said and sat in the chair next to him.

The other Bio, apparently designated 'Milo,' brought his appendages to the top of his chassis and rubbed them around his optical sensors.

"Yeah, I uh... I think I passed out."

Ruby laughed. "Yeah, you did! Wait until I tell—"

"Oh, please don't," Milo said.

"Milo, it's so good to see you," Ruby said and wrapped her appendages around him. Disto was certain that he sensed some kind of change in Milo based upon Ruby's action, but wasn't sure what or why. "Let me introduce you to my, uh, new friends."

"They're here?" Milo said.

"They're right behind you."

Disto watched as Milo turned in his direction. His optical sensors were wide, and Disto could tell that Milo was scanning him.

"That's a, uh," Milo stood up and was attempting to move backwards into the console. Disto couldn't understand that movement since there was equipment blocking his way.

"Yeah," Ruby said, "it's a robot. Actually, they're all robots."

Disto watched as Milo realized that AT was much closer to him and tried to move further back, all while performing the same scanning procedure on AT.

"Milo, this is Ambitious Technician, who we call 'AT'. AT, meet Milo."

"Greetings, Milo," said AT. Milo just shook his head.

"And this is Detailed Historian, also known as Disto," Ruby gestured in his own direction. "Disto, meet Milo Jenkins. He's a friend and one of the hanger chiefs on the station."

"Nice to meet you, Milo Jenkins," Disto said. Milo again nodded and his tense body seemed to relax.

"Ruby," Disto said, "Does Milo Jenkins have an alias as well?"

"I don't know," Ruby responded, "Milo, do you? I've always called him Milo."

"A what?" Milo said.

"A nickname. Do you have a nickname?"

Milo moved his head back and forth. Disto understood that human gesture meant negative.

"And you must meet SD, the driver of our ship. Where is he?" Disto looked around. SD clearly hadn't followed them into Milo's ship. He went back out the hatch and saw SD perched in front of it.

"SD, are you not traveling with us?"

SD didn't move. His circuits were active, however. Disto could tell that by the wavy coloring SD's chassis produced.

"SD?"

It was as if SD exited a programming loop.

"I must prep the ship if we are all going to leave," he said and went back up the lift.

Disto returned to the small ship and said to Ruby, "SD needs a few minutes to prepare. Then we'll all be ready to go."

"When Plampton said that the robots would be coming back, I..." Milo trailed off.

Ruby smiled at him and patted his chassis with her appendage. "They're awesome once you get to know them." Then she looked at Disto.

"Disto," Ruby said, "you can put those back."

He hadn't realized he still held the two small boxes she had asked for moments ago. He replaced them in their drawer and said, "As you wish."

SD appeared and announced, "I have set the ship to standby mode. We can leave anytime." Then to a dangling green fractal construction that was inset into one of the wall panels, "Oh look, this ship has one of those objects as well. Ruby, do you remember when I mistook this for a human?"

Ruby chuckled. "Yes, and do you remember how freaked out I was?"

"Is that the reaction that Milo is experiencing?" Disto asked.

Everyone turned to look at the new human in the room.

Ruby, still sitting in the seat next to Milo said, "Yes, but I was definitely more freaked out. Remember, I had no idea about any of you. Milo at least had a clue. Right, Milo?"

"Ruby," Milo said sternly, "*everyone* has a clue."

Ruby scrunched her face. "Um. Uncle Blake said something like that, too. I don't quite understand. What am I missing?"

Disto was glad that question wasn't aimed at him, since he detected that she was complete with one-hundred-percent of her parts where they should be. She was missing nothing he could observe. He wouldn't have known how to answer the question.

"Let's get ready to depart and I'll tell you about my MCE," Milo said.

"MCE?" Ruby asked. "I think that's what Uncle Blake called it, too." Disto saw her furrowed brow and wanted to ask her about it but stored his questions for later.

Disto marveled at the differences between the two Bios. They obviously came from the same species, but beyond that, there were more differences than he could count. They evidently didn't come from the same template. But neither did he and SD or he and AT. Therefore, he shouldn't have been surprised. He wasn't surprised, exactly, but interested.

He listened while the two humans prepared the small ship for departure. There was nothing for him, or the other two robots, to do. Disto could tell that made both SD and AT anxious. Neither was the kind of robot who liked to sit and do nothing.

Less than a click later, they were out in space and nearly at Astroll 2.

Chapter 6

There was a welcome party in the hanger. She could see through the window that a whole group of people were gathered in the cramped space of the hanger control room, not simply the hanger team.

"Milo, it looks like half the station is crammed in there," she said.

"Ruby, I'm not sure you get it yet. You're famous. Like, mega famous. Like, I'm not worthy to be talking to you kind of famous."

"Because of the MCE?" she asked.

"Exactly," said Milo. "Everyone remembers every detail about where they were and what they were doing when they saw your message about being with those robots.[1]" He aimed his thumb over his shoulder at the robots, who were also all looking out the window.

Ruby smirked with her mouth pursed tight and let one eyebrow go up. "Oh, c'mon. That's ridiculous. Even if that's even a little true, that's ridiculous." As the word ridiculous rolled off her tongue, her eye was drawn to someone in the hanger, standing close to the window who was wearing a t-shirt that had... her face! And big, bold text that read, "I'm with robots!"

"Ruby. We thought you were dead. And then you're not dead, and you're with aliens. Extraterrestrials. This is...," Ruby watched Milo look at the robots behind them while they waited for the hanger crew to close the hanger door and ensure the hanger was returned to the right oxygen and pressure levels. It usually took a few minutes, and there was nothing to do in this time but wait in one's ship.

There was actually a procedure she would do to stow everything if this had been a normal flight. But this had not.

"You guys okay back there?" she said to the robots, trying to center herself more than anything. She was with robots, after all.

"Indeed," called Disto. "I am admiring the welcome party."

"Yeah, me too," Ruby said, although 'admiring' was definitely not the right word. But the people she wanted to see most in the galaxy were there: her uncles. She didn't see Sebastian, her seven-year-old cousin, but that wasn't too surprising. She had checked station time and it was the middle of the night.

---

1. I do believe that somewhere out there are intelligent aliens (comparable to us). I don't believe they have visited our planet in human history. I'd like to think that if/when we do make contact, it will be this momentous.

And then she remembered…

"Oh! Milo! The mini-R-pods! Have they had the AI upgrade yet?"

"No, not yet. We got some kind of cryptic message from The Company that told us to hold off. They didn't tell us why. I'm sure it was some minor bug or a patch they wanted to apply."

Ruby let out a breath. "Oh good," she said. Then, "'Bug' my butt. I had some time on Location Zero to—"

"Location Zero?" Milo interrupted.

"Yeah, that's what the robots call their home planet."

"Very… exotic," Milo smirked.

"Sure, but listen to me. While there, I was able to test out the mini-R-pod upgrade. Remember that *Apple Pi* had it staged. Well, I transferred it to my MoDaC…"

"The same *Apple Pi* that's sitting in pieces in that… that ship?"

"Stop interrupting me and let me tell my story! This is important!"

Milo put his hands up, indicating she could continue.

"Ok—I'll skip to the end. There's a bug in there, alright. A *big* one! It's expecting to pick up on the location services that can only be accessed in the Earth-Mars network. Beyond Mars, it just won't work!"

She watched as Milo's face cycled through a series of expressions, processing what she had just told him.

"Well, they said there was a bug. Are you sure that's what it is?" Milo asked.

"Absolutely," Ruby replied. "It's why I was so anxious to get home."

"You've been gone almost a month!"

"Well, I just found out a few days ago. That's when I became anxious."

"And before that?" Milo asked, eyebrows raised.

"I was, well, having fun. Learning," she looked over at the robots. "Milo, I was on an alien world with aliens. Robot aliens, but aliens! It was amazing!"

She looked over at her robot friends.

"Where did they come from?" Milo asked, "Who created them?"

"They don't know," Ruby said. She then went on to recount the situation about the robot's long-lost storage, their belief that it was contained within the junk DNA of some biological species, probably a species native to Earth.

She watched as Milo looked the robots over some more. He was now the second human to have met them. His life was likely to change somewhat, too.

She thought about how *her* life was going to change. Milo and her Uncle Blake had both tried to tell her she was famous. She wasn't sure what to do with that. Maybe all it would amount to would be a few interviews with the press, and then she could move on with her life. And still, she wasn't even sure what *that* meant. Less than a month ago, she was dead set on going to Titan, helping them to terraform Saturn's moon and set up a colony there.

Now, she wasn't sure. She thought maybe going back to Earth for a while, possibly to finish earning her degree, wasn't such a bad idea. While she was there, she could figure out more about what happened to her mom when she was young. She realized now that the passage of time, combined with her young age when her mom died, probably contributed to an overall distortion of her early memories. She wanted to get them sorted out.

The console in front of her that was monitoring the atmosphere outside the mini-R-pod and in the hanger blinked green and made a soft chime.

"It's safe to open the hatch," Milo said.

Ruby heard the faint whir of processors spinning up in all three of the robots. They were just as nervous and anxious as she was.

Chapter 7

> Ruby <

From the moment Ruby stepped out of *Pecan Pi* and onto the hanger floor, she had one thought. *My uncles. Where are Uncle Blake and Uncle Logan?*

The other humans that made up the reception committee didn't seem concerned with what Ruby wanted and instead attempted to pursue their own agenda, which was to crowd her and get a look at the robots. The crowd of people included some she recognized and some she didn't. They were all chattering away and most of them were wearing the same shirt she saw moments ago: "I'm with robots!" The shirt also had an artistic reproduction of her face. In it, her hair was tied up, the same way it had been when she was on Location Zero. Was that taken from her message to her uncles?

She shook it off the second she saw them. Her uncles. Nothing could stop her from running to embrace them as soon as she was able. And she could see that nothing would have stopped them from pushing their way through the small mob to embrace her back.

While she was hugging the two of them at once, she recognized Robt Plampton's voice as he said to the crowd, "Give them a few moments, okay?"

After a few moments, which was not long enough, Uncle Blake broke the embrace but kept one hand on each of Ruby's upper arms. He looked into her eyes, raised his eyebrows as only he could, and asked, "Are you really okay?"

"Yeah, really. I am," Ruby responded, with a smile that she hoped conveyed that she was sincere in her claims of okay-ness and sorry that she had left and how much she had missed them and a dozen other emotions mixed in.

Uncle Logan was next, grabbing Ruby with a bear hug from behind. "Of course, she's okay! She's Ruby Palmer, galactic explorer!" He paused and looked into her eyes, making sure it was really her. His own glossed over. "Oh, Ruby! We thought..." he didn't finish that sentence. He didn't need to. Ruby knew what they thought, and she felt awful about it.

"Uncle Logan, Uncle Blake... I'm so sorry. I was being—"

"Selfish?" said Uncle Blake. Ruby nodded.

"Stubborn?" said Uncle Logan. Ruby nodded again.

"Surly?" said Uncle Logan.

"Okay, okay," Ruby said and spun out of Uncle Logan's embrace so she could face the two of them. "I truly am sorry. Worrying you two was the last thing I wanted to do. I just wanted—"

She stopped talking when she realized that it wasn't only her uncles who could hear her, but everyone in the crowd was silent and listening in.

"Can we go back to our quarters?" she asked, quieter than before. "I really want to shower in my shower."

"What about them?" Uncle Blake asked. He motioned to the robots that were positioned at *Pecan Pi's* hatch.

"Oh right! For a moment, I..." she didn't finish that thought and went over to the robots. "Guys, come on out." She gestured for them to leave *Pecan Pi*. They did, and as they did so, it was like there was an invisible force field emanating around them. The crowd moved so as not to come within ten feet of them.

"It's okay, everyone," Ruby said as she approached the robots and put a hand on SD's chassis. "They're friends. They're really nice. And funny."

Uncle Blake was the first to walk up to them. "Hi, my name is Blake." He held out a hand in front of Disto.

"I haven't taught them about shaking hands, Uncle Blake. But that is Disto. That's short for Detailed Historian."

"Detailed? Historian?"

"Affirmative," said Disto.

"They know our language?" Uncle Blake directed that question to Ruby, softly so only she could hear.

"Yes, but here's the crazy part, Uncle Blake," Ruby whispered back. "They knew it, well, most of it, before I got there."

Ruby watched the color drain from Uncle Blake's face, and his eyes widened, but not quite with surprise. There was something else in his face that she couldn't read. She stored that away and would ask him later.

"This is Swell Driver. We call him SD. And that's Ambitious Technician. Also known as AT," Ruby finished out the introductions.

"That's an, uh, interesting nomenclature," said Robt Plampton, who had gradually sidled up to Uncle Blake's side. Uncle Logan had come forward, too, and was looking AT over.

"Oh definitely," said Ruby. "I'll have to tell you about the other robots I met."

"You'll be doing more than that," said Robt Plampton. "You'll get a chance to settle back in, but afterward, The Company has instructed me to put together a full debriefing. We are indeed going to hear about the robots, all the robots, and everything you experienced with these... aliens."

Ruby didn't know Robt Plampton very well. This might be only the second or third time she'd had reason to have a direct one-on-one interaction with him. But he was known as a pretty nice guy. Nonetheless, she wasn't thrilled with his tone. She looked to Uncle Blake for some comfort, but his face was stone. They'd obviously talked about this before she arrived.

"Sure, I guess," Ruby said. "Can we get quarters for the robots, too? I know that the one across the hall and down two units from ours was empty before I left."

"They're going to need to be debriefed as well."

Ruby looked at them and watched as they studied the brand new surroundings and the people staring back at them.

"I should be there. To help," she said. "Who is going to do it? The debriefing?"

Ruby watched as Robt Plampton pursed his lips. He clearly wasn't happy with what he was about to say.

"Professor Coronik. Prime Connector of the Church of the Blockchain[1]. The Company has retained his services as an expert in AI and is sending him along with several of their own representatives."

Nothing was said for a few moments. Ruby couldn't understand why anyone from the Church would be involved. Looking around at the nearby crowd who were all listening in, she could see at the mention of the Church, a lot of faces wore an expression similar to Plampton's. This included her own uncles, who had always told her to stay away from that organization.

There was a small chapel on the station. Everywhere was required to have them, The Company couldn't even say no. She had peeked in once when she was young, out of curiosity. There were two people chanting something that she didn't understand. They seemed harmless enough.

"But sure—they can take the quarters in that hallway. It's still empty." Plampton nodded his head at Treszka Greene, Director of Station Ops—which was also known as Fundamental Operations and usually abbreviated to 'FUNOPS'—who was the person who typically handled these things and who shot darts from her eyes whenever anyone referred to her job as 'fun.' Treszka Greene tapped at her communicuff, which presented a holoscreen for her to continue to tap. Ready at a moment's notice to launch those eye darts, she nodded back at Plampton and then moved away from the group. Ruby hoped that meant she was making preparations.

"I'd like to walk them down there," Ruby said. "And then you can debrief me, I guess."

"After a short visit to the medical bay," Uncle Logan said. "They're waiting to check you out, make sure you're as okay as you think." He winked that wink of his that Ruby had missed this past month. She smiled in return.

---

1. I mentioned the Church of the Blockchain in *Crazy Foolish Robots*, but I haven't said anything about it. Simply, I find it funny that people can get so into something that it nearly turns in to worship. Add back when I was in college, it was fun to be a fan of the Church of the SubGenius. So, calling this organization a "church" seemed the right way to go.

Chapter 8

The robots were temporarily safe in quarters. Keeping them there was more for their protection than anything else. Ruby couldn't wait to show them around her home, and she figured their first tour should be a guided one and she should be the one to guide them.

All three robots agreed to stay put so she could go off and get a medical exam.

Now, in the medical bay, she was feeling... she didn't know how she was feeling. Uncle Blake and Uncle Logan were both there with her.

"You can let go, Uncle Blake," she motioned to his hand grasping hers.

"Nope," he responded. "You have no idea what we went through... thinking you were dead..." He looked at her and pushed a straggly piece of hair that had gotten out of her ponytail behind her ear.

"Don't lay too much guilt on her, she's been through a lot," said Uncle Logan.

Uncle Blake shot Logan a look that reeked of how much they'd been through, too. That look didn't make Ruby feel much better.

"I have to go get Sebastian from the Orville's," Uncle Logan said, then pecked Blake on the cheek, squeezed Ruby once more, and left.

"I'm so sorry, I really didn't mean to worry you. I really didn't," she looked at the floor.

"Well, you're back. And I just... I mean... I promised your mother..."

There was silence between the two of them for a few moments. Only the beeps emanating from a console behind them could be heard.

"About my mother..." Ruby said, but then was interrupted by Dr. Nora Lee[1], who walked in holding two tablets and what looked like a medical sweeper. Ruby observed she was wearing the same "I'm with robots!" shirt everyone else had, underneath her open lab coat.

Ruby leaned over to Uncle Blake, "Those shirts? Really?"

Blake chuckled. "I don't know who made them or is putting them out, but everyone seems to have one."

---

1. Dr. Nora Lee was inspired by and named for two people. First, actress/rapper Awkwafina, whose real name is Nora Lum. Second, my families allergist, Dr. Vickie Lee, who is one of my favorite doctors.

"Do you?"

Before Blake could answer, Dr. Nora Lee was standing in front of Ruby.

"Ruby Palmer!" she exclaimed. "Ahhh-mazing!"[2]

"Thanks. I guess," Ruby said.

"No, really, you are the first person to leave the solar system! And I'm the first doctor to examine you. What you must have been exposed to. The radiation, different gravity fields! I can't wait to scan you. May I?"

Dr. Lee gestured to the examination table. Ruby hopped up and lay down. Dr. Lee put the tablets on a table next to the bed and then looked at the small console on the sweeper. She poked at it, presumably entering in whatever settings or directing it to look for who knows what.

Into her own communicuff, Dr. Lee said, "New diagnostic record. Patient's name, Ruby Palmer. Copy in last medical data as baseline."

Then she pointed the sweeper at Ruby's feet and continued to aim the sweeper at some place on Ruby's body, moving up and down and saying "hmm" to herself a lot.

After a few minutes, Dr. Lee put down the sweeper, picked up a tablet, and started poking at that instead, with more mumblings. Words like "interesting" and "fascinating" emanated from her mouth, but as a mumble.

Then she said, "what the...?" and quickly reverted to medical sweeper again, aiming it at Ruby's abdomen.

Ruby looked over at Uncle Blake who could only shrug his shoulders.

"Everything okay, doctor?" he said.

"Yeah, but..." Dr. Lee was still involved in her devices.

"But...?" Uncle Blake and Ruby said in unison.

"Something is off. You haven't been gone from the station that long, but it's as if your digestive system, and your hormones are well... they're out of whack."

"'Out of whack?'" Ruby repeated. "Is that a professional term?" She saw the corner of Uncle Blake's mouth turn up.

"Yes, I took a course in diagnosing 'out of whack' in med school," Dr. Lee said, without missing a beat.

She moved a stool over to the side of the examination table. Like most furniture on Astroll 2, it had a slight magnetic connection to the floor, to ensure stability in the half-G environment. Dr. Lee sat on the stool, tablet in hand, and hooked her feet around a foothold to give her stability while sitting.

"Ruby, what have you been eating while you've been gone?" she asked very sternly.

"I uh, well, I mean, I ate the emergency rations that were on *Apple Pi*. But the robots had some stuff I could eat."

"What kind of stuff was it?"

"Well, most of it was mushy. The non-mushy stuff were like crackers. And it tasted like different things I recognized. Most of the time," she said recalling various memories of the variety of mushy and then eventually cracker-like meals she consumed.

Then she pushed herself to a sitting position with her arms. "Why? What's wrong with me?"

---

2. Please, if you don't know Awkwafina, go look her up on YouTube and then come back and read this in her voice. LOL

"It's malnutrition, for sure. But more than that. Your hormones are *out of whack*. And there's more heavy metals than there should be in a 19-year-old who's lived most of her life right here, eating primarily hydroponically grown food." Dr. Lee took a deep breath. "Let me put this another way. Some of your insides are that of a 47-year-old woman."[3]

"But I don't feel 47," Ruby said.

"Are you sure? How tired have you been lately?"

Ruby thought about that. She'd slept pretty regularly. She didn't wake up feeling all that great, but she attributed that to the fact that she was sleeping on a very uncomfortable bed.

"Um, I guess I've been a little more tired than normal. But, I mean, the bed they had me on was not exactly luxurious..."

"Uh-huh," Dr. Lee said. "And how about the temperature. A little warm?"

Ruby thought about that. Yes, while on Location Zero, it felt like they had the temperature turned up, but then it went away. She assumed that the robots were consistently adjusting it to find the right temp for a human.

"Maybe?" Ruby said.

"Yup. Classic peri-menopausal symptoms. And not surprising given the state of your gut and hormones."

Dr. Lee hopped off the chair. "Not to worry. We have a simple treatment for this. You're going to spend time in my infra-red sauna and take some of these pills," Dr. Lee put some in Ruby's hand. "Twice a day for a week. That will reset your system while pulling out some of the toxins. The sauna will help get your system back into whack—also a technical term." She winked.

Ruby, as a 19-year-old, was aware of something called 'menopause' but, knowing it was something that she should have had three or more decades of life before she was even close to the right age for, had given it absolutely no thought. That was something older women dealt with, not her. In that moment, she realized she had no idea how old Dr. Lee was. Had she dealt with this herself? Was she talking to her as a doctor or a fellow sufferer? Did it matter?

Either way, she wasn't going to ignore Dr. Lee's diagnosis or prescription. And anyway, a bask in a sauna sounded pretty nice. As did getting a normal and refreshing good night's sleep in her own bed.

She took the pills sublingually, so they dissolved in her mouth. No water necessary.

"Perfect. I'll have the rest of the prescription assigned to you. It will be delivered to your quarters before your next dose, just as soon as they're printed."

Most medicines were formulated in a series of machines and printed into a form that could be dissolved right on the tongue.

"Can you imagine," Dr. Lee said, "that it wasn't all that long ago that this wasn't treatable. Women had to suffer, needlessly not knowing what was going on."[4]

She had returned to her console and wasn't even looking at Ruby or Uncle Blake.

"Um, does that mean I can go?" Ruby asked. She looked at Uncle Blake who again, shrugged his shoulders.

"Oh, sure. You're fine," Dr. Lee said. "I want to continue to study your exam results. I'm surprised there isn't anything more wrong with you."

Ruby hopped down from the table.

---

3. I was 47 when I was drafting this and was put on HRT (Hormone Replacement Therapy).

4. Dealing with peri-meno throughout most of my 40s without treatment was getting to be pretty miserable. And this is a not-even-trying-to-thinly-veil my thoughts on how terrible it is that perimenopause and menopause isn't openly discussed—how it hits most of us in our 40s without warning because has traditionally been taboo to talk about.

"See, Uncle Blake? I told you I was fine."

"Sure. Old lady." He smiled. "That's going to be your new nickname."

"Did something happen while I was gone? When did you develop a sense of humor?"

"C'mon. Let's go back and see your robot friends. I might want to get a pre-briefing before your briefing," Uncle Blake said as he started to walk out of the medical bay. Ruby went to follow him, nearly bouncing past him.

"Wow," he said. "I don't remember you being that spry!"

"I guess it was the last month in Earth-like gravity," she said.

"Oh yeah," Dr. Lee called after, "her bone density is perfect. Better than perfect!"

"Interesting," said Uncle Blake. "You adjusted fine to their gravity?"

Ruby knew what he was getting at. For a long time, both of her uncles had been on her to do her exercises regularly, in case she had to go back to Earth. Everyone on the station had to do it. Ruby had missed more sessions than she logged and did pay for it on her first week at Location Zero.

"Yeah, first couple days were rough, but obviously I got over it."

Uncle Blake smiled. "Good. And I can't wait to hear more about this Location Zero myself. Only 54 light years away, you said? That's remarkable!"

"How so?"

"Remarkable that we never detected anything so close to us before."

"I don't think they want to be detected," Ruby said. And then thinking out loud, "They have faster than light travel, sentient robots... so yeah, that makes sense that they'd have some kind of technology to prevent themselves from detection from the likes of us."

"Think they'd tell us about it?" Uncle Blake asked.

Ruby scrunched up her mouth. The whole reason SD brought her home in his ship was that they didn't want to send her off with an FTL drive. Well, that wasn't the whole reason. *Apple Pi* was still in pieces, sprawled out inside SD's ship.

"Unlikely," she finally replied. "But I don't think they'd be offended if you asked. Just don't get your hopes up."

"I never do," Uncle Blake said.

Chapter 9

> Uncle Blake <

A long, long time ago, on Earth, Blake Griffin had just returned to his apartment from a date. It was the best date he'd had in... well, maybe the best date he'd ever had. Logan Green was exciting and funny. He radiated a positive energy that Blake wished he had himself. Blake was doing his best not to get his hopes up. It happened every time after similar first dates. But this one felt different, and his hopes had settled on top of the largest roof in the city.

Their date consisted of meeting up at a coffee shop and then a spontaneous walk in the park since the UV levels were acceptable.

Back at his apartment, Blake's best friend, Jade Palmer[1], was on his couch, tapping at an ancient mobile computer she liked to use. Jade was almost always at his place. She didn't get along with her own roommates. Blake completely understood and offered to let her stay. He had the room. Jade insisted that it made sense for her to live someplace else, lest she prevent him from going on dates.

This date, in reality, was her doing. She had met Logan through a friend of hers at work, and once she found out that Logan was single, she knew instantly that Logan should meet Blake.

"How'd it go?" she said without looking up.

"It was," Blake sunk into the plush chair next to the couch, "in a word... it was wonderful."

Now Jade looked up. And smiled. "You're going to see him again?"

"We made plans for next Saturday. He knows a lake that's not too far away at some park that does kayak rentals. Apparently, there's a week or two left in the season before they close up till the spring."

"That's great!" Jade said. Her face was already back buried in her computer, but Blake knew that she meant it. They had been best friends since they were kids in Rhode Island. Now, they were young adults, living in Maryland—halfway between the re-re-named Washington D.C. and the City of Baltimore[2]. Fresh from college, where they had both gone and studied nearly the same things and now worked similar jobs.

---

1. Actress inspiration: Michelle Hurd

2. I've been a resident of Maryland since 1992 (except for one year when I lived in Virginia). I chose someplace close to home not knowing how much detail I was going to get into.

"Wait," Jade said and looked right at Blake. "Next Saturday? We have that meeting on Saturday."

"Right, in the morning. I haven't forgotten. The date doesn't start until lunchtime."

Jade relaxed. "You're not allowed to flake out on me, okay? I'm not going to this thing without you," she said. "Have you finished that bit of code I need?"

"I'm almost done."

What Jade was referring to was writing some code to hack some stuff. 'Some code' and 'some stuff' being the deliberately vague descriptions used by many hackers over the years.

They were both members of the Church of the Blockchain, but not really. They were both dreamers. They both had a love of outer space, the planets, and the thoughts of what was out there... and they were certain *something* had to be out there.

But the Church of the Blockchain—which started to distinguish itself somewhere around the year 2050—had managed to shut down practically all lines of research in that area. These days, no one was looking for alien life. But there were plenty of people looking for old computer data[3], and they were all willing to pay someone like Jade to find it.

So, the Church was paying her, on the books, to dig up data on scores of servers they possessed.

But someone else was paying her too. A little less on the books, but it was currency that went into an account that, while it didn't have her legal name on it, she had full access to. She knew exactly who it was that was funding it—but not because they told her. It was a company funded by a company funded by a company, a couple times over, that was ultimately funded by the trillionaire known as Horus Zuliani. He had been in the news recently. Something about getting a team together to go to Titan. Given Ruby's—and Blake's interest—that wasn't money she was going to turn down.

But why the Church was interested...? On the surface, they seemed to simply be interested in data. And maybe they were. Jade hadn't found anything to the contrary.

However, there were several conspiracy theories permeating modern social networks. The one that Jade and Blake found most titillating was that the Blockchain already knew everything about Titan and was keeping it secret. The Blockchain wasn't a governmental entity, although it acted like one and practically controlled all the primary nation states on Earth[4]. As such, they weren't accountable to anyone. Any evidence they might have in the search for extraterrestrial life would be locked up in their servers or their buildings, which some people called temples and other people called detention centers—due to how much time people spent in them.

Tucked away on the shore of Rhode Island as kids, Blake and Jade would daydream about aliens and about heading out into the solar system and exploring. As they got older, they learned about all the human colonies—the one on the Moon, the one on Mars, and the second one on Mars that failed—and the fact that no additional exploration out into and beyond the solar system was happening, the only exception being commercial asteroid mining activities. There were barely any telescopes that were looking outward, either. The ancient 'scopes, like the old James Webb Space Telescope and the Roman Space Telescope were now museum pieces and had been for decades. No one funded anything new.

---

3. Think about the amount of data out there on the internet. Think about how much data we generate. I firmly believe that someday, there will be a career field in "digital archeology" —and I've had many thoughts about writing short stories that involve this career field.

4. So, unlike the Church of the SubGenius, I've given the Church of the Blockchain real power.

There were too many problems on Earth. Instead, there was continued Earth-bound development into robotics and computing. In every generation there was a futurist who warned about the technological singularity coming, but every generation passed without it happening. But the amount of computers, robots, and computer power continued to increase. The Earth was hot and needed the ability to compute.

The Church was able to move computing resources—data centers—off Earth, which helped immensely. They heated up the Moon. In fact, the Moon colony was completely owned by the Church[5].

The Mars colony was operated by the world governments and was a research station. Not much was happening there.

The most interesting things happening in the solar system—at least to Jade and Blake— were out at Astroll 2. As well as Horus Zuliani, the Zubrinics Corporation, and their plans to get to Titan. As a completely commercial entity, while people might complain, there was no legal way to stop them.

Astroll 2 was the seat of a mining colony. The Company owned and operated it. Blake was set on going there someday and was actively trying to convince Jade that she should do the same.

Jade wasn't sure. There were a lot of computers and so much data to examine *here*. She was, in fact, a digital archaeologist. She was employed by the Church and spent her days hacking into old computers, organizing the useful data she found, and marking the non-useful data for deletion. In order to do this, she wrote many algorithms. She even won a prize.

The prize was this job with the Church. She was allowed to contract on the side, although her current contract wouldn't have been authorized if they knew about it.

Blake got a job with the Church, too, also in research, but of a different kind. At the time, when they were young kids just getting out of college, they believed the Church's promises that they could make a difference in helping their fellow man.

No sooner did they join they realized it was not about helping, but about controlling. And they realized that control extended to all forms of scientific research, including what they were most interested in: extraterrestrials.

This meeting that Jade referenced—it was a group of like-minded individuals. Members of the Church, but members who also had their eyes open to the truth. They were planning to expose the Church in the hopes that people would wake up, see the truth and then move on with their lives, free of the Church's control.

But that was next Saturday.

"What are you working on?" Blake asked. He was thinking about pulling out his own personal computer. He was coming down from his adrenaline high from his very successful date and was also thinking about watching a movie. "Anything interesting?"

"Huh? Oh... a game. Sort of."

"What do you mean, sort of?"

"It's a data archaeology hunt. One of those find all the incidences of 47..."

---

5. My unrelated novel that I originally drafted in 2020, *Lunar Logic*, is set on the Moon and involves the fact that the Moon is home to data centers. That book is not officially part of this universe... but it could be.

"Ah." Blake knew about those games. 47 was one of those numbers that people thought were deliberately hidden in vids and memes. It was a favorite of conspiracy theorists. Not that either he or Jade fell into that category[6].

Before he got too comfortable, he got up and went to the small kitchenette. "Lexy. Coffee, decaf," he said out loud. "Want anything?" he called back to Jade. She shook her head.

A device in the corner came to life and Blake heard the familiar gurgle of water being super-heated to brew a cup of coffee. He hoped that this time the decaf grounds wound up in the right spot. Last time, the automatic filler confused decaf for regular, and he was messed up for a week before he realized why.

After about thirty seconds, the drips came to a stop and a voice that was everywhere in the kitchen said, "Complete. Enjoy your beverage."

"Thanks, Lexy.[7]"

He of course knew that he didn't have to thank the computer but was in the habit of doing it anyway. In some way, he thought it made up for the times when he turned off all the active listening devices in the apartment so they could have truly private discussions. His landlord wouldn't be too happy that he was fooling around with the apartment computer systems, but only because the landlord was worried he would break something. There was no law against attempting to guarantee one's privacy.

Worst case, he wouldn't get his security deposit back.

Blake picked up the mug of coffee that was hopefully decaf and went back to the chair. "I'm going to put on a movie. Do you mind?" Again, Jade shook her head back and forth. "You staying right there all night? Again?" He smiled as he said this. He really didn't mind; he was just poking fun.

Jade nodded. "Yeah, just cover me with that blanket if I fall asleep."

"You should sleep," Blake said. "Maybe if you do, you'll look presentable and can go on a date yourself."

She shot him an 'are you kidding me?' kind of look. The look that friends can pass each other without hurting each other's feelings.

"Are you going to ever go out on one again?"

"I told you," she said. "I'm done with all that."

"Just because that jerk-boy-whose-name-we-don't-speak-of was a jerk doesn't mean you should swear off dating."

"Yeah, it kinda does. Look... when I'm ready... I'm going to do what my mom did."

"You know your mom is crazy?"

"She is. But I'm still here, right?"

Blake made a facial expression that indicated he couldn't argue with that.

---

6. For a long time, I was aware that the number 47 was in a lot of Star Trek episodes but I only recently found out why. It was because one of the Trek writer's who was an alumni of Pomona College in California, started inserting it into the scripts. And that started because a student at Pomona, back in 1964, noticed a lot of incidences of 47 that appeared at the school.

7. Yes, "Lexy" is intended to be an descendent of Amazon's Alexa.

"Exactly," Jade said. "All I have to do is go to the right cryo-center and boom. I'll have a kid. No jerk boys necessary. Besides, it would make it a family tradition. I think some of our ancestors did it as well."[8]

Blake wished it was as easy for him. He knew he'd have kids one day, only it would be slightly harder. He had long thought, or wished, rather, that he would ask Jade to be a surrogate but wasn't sure she could do it—knowing she wanted kids, or at least a kid, of her own.

"Ok. New movie time. Comedy. Get ready to put your computer down and laugh with me."

Jade looked up and back at her computer and back at Blake. She closed the computer. "Fine. But I'm going to fall asleep as usual. Twenty minutes in."

"I know. I'll cover you with a blanket. And I won't wake you in the morning when I go out to run. Promise."

---

8. This is partially another 4th wall break where essentially, I'm claiming that Jade and Ruby are my descendants. But more importantly, I had my first kiddo via a crybobank and donor.

Chapter 10

> Ruby <

Ruby sat down with her tray of food. Milo and Inny were already there, at a seat by the windows, as far from the hallway and entrance as they could be, at Ruby's request.

While she was happy to have lunch with them, she already started to notice that when she was out in public, people were talking about her. Not *to* her but about her, as if she wouldn't notice. And at least half the people were wearing a shirt with her face on it. Maybe more than half since half were wearing the standard issue jacket that was typically worn on the station.

Milo and Inny had clearly been in the middle of some conversation which they promptly ceased having the second Ruby's tray touched the table.

"What were you talking about?" Ruby asked.

"Plampton," Milo said. "Word is, he's worried about all the people who are on their way here."

Ruby didn't need to ask why. She just looked down at her food, a little embarrassed at all the attention. Eh—who was she kidding. She was *a lot* embarrassed at all the attention.

It was all quickly forgotten as she looked at her food. Real food. Not mush. Real stuff. Although not fully what she what would have chosen for herself. At the moment, her meals were being selected by Dr. Lee as a part of her gut and hormone healing process. She wondered how long she could have stayed on the robot planet eating their various mushes before it became a problem.

At least now she knew that if or when—*was it if? Or was it when?*—she went back, she would need to pack her own food.

There was a special sourdough bread that was prepared for her[1] . And a fruit bowl consisting of mango and coconut. She was certain that when she tasted it, she'd get the essence of ginger that she was currently smelling.

"Ooo! Mango!" Inny squealed. "That's probably the last for now until next First Mango Day. I want some!"

She took her fork and was about to steal a piece, but Ruby slapped her hand away.

"Hey! This is prescription food! Doctors' orders!"

Inny plopped back in her chair, feigning disappointment. Both Inny and Ruby knew this was not the first time Inny had tried to steal food off her plate, and nor would it be the last. They'd shared a meal together many times over the years.

---

1. I *love* soughdough bread and it's supposed to be good for you.

But Milo—this was the first time she had sat down at a table in the mess with him. This also might have been the first time Ruby saw Milo and Inny interact in what felt like—forever.

"Now tell us everything!" Inny playfully demanded.

"Yeah," said Milo, "starting with how you lied to me in order to steal a mini-R-pod…"

Ruby hoped he wouldn't have put two and two together but how could he not?

"I'm sorry about that, Milo," Ruby said. She hoped the fact that she was indeed being sincere came across. "I was having a bad… a bad life. I don't know. It was stupid."

"You got that right," Milo said flatly.

"Do you hate me?" Ruby said with the smallest touch of flirtiness in her manner. She surprised herself that she could even do that. It felt almost manipulative or at the very least misplaced, but she hadn't intended it to be either.

"We thought you were dead…" Milo's voice went out a little at the last word. It was enough to silence the table.

Inny injected her version of cheer when she said, "Why are you being all depressing, Milo? You're making Ruby look like she's gonna vom."

"Vom?" Milo asked.

Inny raised an eyebrow as if Milo had asked her something incredibly stupid. "Vomit. Look, she's not dead! She's alive and she's going to tell us everything that happened. Right, Ruby?"

Ruby smiled. But then the smile went away as she saw Inny open up the note-taking app on her communicuff.

"Start with that guy you met for lunch before you left. Doctor… I can't remember his name!" Inny said.

"Inny…" Ruby started. "C'mon. I don't want you writing this down."

"*Someone* has to record this. Why not me? My first big journalistic break… interviewing the great Ruby Palmer! Now what was the name of that *yummy* man?"

The way Inny said 'yummy' made Ruby want to vomit, or vom, not from sickness, but from the overwhelming amount of attention paid to the details of her life. Maybe vomiting was the way to go. An educational experience for all the new people to Astroll 2 who've never seen what happens when someone loses their lunch in half-G.

> Milo <

She's having lunch with other guys. Okay, that does it. I have no chance other than as friends and coworkers.

These and 1000 other thoughts were rushing through Milo's mind, and he couldn't stop them. First, he thought she was dead. Then, he found out she was alive. Next, he was the second human to meet aliens all because of her. Now, he was having lunch with her—albeit with a chaperone.

But the icing on the cake—she was on a date with another guy.

"Inny! Sheesh! I can only imagine what you're thinking. So, stop it. It wasn't like that." Ruby asserted.

Milo perked up. *Ok, not a date!*

"That was Dr. Rush Guerrero. He's head of the Titan Expedition."

"Yeah, I've heard of him," Milo interjected, a little relieved to hear that she wasn't dating some good-looking guy—eh—man. But not so thrilled to hear she was interested in Titan. He searched his brain to remember the memes he had curated about Titan and could only remember the one that asked: if the oceans are all methane, is it covered in liquid farts? Not good conversation material. Instead, he focused on the meeting part. "What? Why? How were—no no... why were you meeting with him?"

"Because I want, or at least I wanted, to go to Titan," Ruby said. And the look she gave Milo said the rest. He got it. Now he understood what she was trying to do that day. She was going to take a mini-R-pod, that was set up for local run, all the way out to Titan.

"Holy spaceballs, Ruby," Milo said. "If I had known!"

"You never would have let me out of the hanger. Of course, I know that. That's why I didn't say anything."

Milo leaned back in his chair and looked at her. She was crazy. Well, not crazy, crazy, but she was some kind of crazy if she thought she could make it all the way to Titan from Astroll 2. He knew she never would have. How could she not see that? She was a good pilot, but the ships themselves were limited. Their comms were short range. Their fuel was—well, there was a lot of extra just in case of emergencies—but going to Titan was a far cry from an emergency—there was not enough. Ruby should have known that.

Oxygen and atmosphere should have been fine, but she could have easily lost power.

"I can't believe it, Ruby. That was...I don't even have the word for how gutsy dangerous that was."

He wanted to say other things to her. He wanted to tell her how he felt. He wanted to tell her that he wished it was just the two of them at this table, not three. Part of him wanted to show his admiration towards her bravery and accomplishments, and the other half wanted to scold her for worrying him sick. None of him wanted to admit how much he worried. Everyone did, sure, but Milo... He checked in with her little cousin and uncles as often as it felt appropriate. He wanted to tell her how he checked in with the asteroid monitoring team daily just in case *Apple Pi* would show up on their radar. He wanted to tell her how much he missed her sarcastic jabs when she was pretending that she didn't care about fitting in with the other pilots. He wanted to yell at her for ever leaving in the first place. He wanted to say a lot of things.

Nothing came out.

Instead, Inny picked up and left him thinking in the dust.

"Wow—I knew you weren't all that keen on going back to Earth, but Titan? It sounds *sooo* boring!"

"Based on where I've been the last month, yeah, it now seems that way," Ruby smiled. She was so cute when she smiled that Milo's anger at her deception was almost gone. One more smile like that, potentially directed in his direction, and he'd melt.

"Then what happened?" asked Milo.

"You guys know the rest. Swell Driver, SD... he found me out in space, used whatever beaming thing he had to disable my ship, and brought it onto his. Then we went back to what they call Location Zero. The rest is, as they say, robotic history!" Ruby said the last words as she took a mouthful of bread. Even talking with her mouth full, she was still cute.

Shake it off, Milo. She's not interested.

"And all these robots... they're different," Inny continued. Milo could tell she was struggling with finding the right words and concepts.

Ruby continued. "Oh, yes! *So* different. They're sentient. I have no idea how that happened or is even possible. They don't either, although I don't think they understand the concept of sentience versus non-sentience. They've um... met others..."

Milo sensed something there. "Excuse me?" he chimed back in.

"Forget I said anything. I shouldn't get into that…"

"No, no… you're going to have to repeat yourself," Inny looked at Milo, and they both nodded in agreement.

Ruby pursed her lips, swallowed what was in her mouth and leaned over the table and encouraged Milo and Inny to do the same.

In a much lower voice, Ruby continued. "They've met other species. I was told not to talk about it. 'Cause it would freak people out."

They all leaned back once again in their respective chairs. Ruby continued to eat. Milo didn't know what to do or say. Not that that was unusual for him.

"You're not going to write that down?" Ruby said to Inny.

Milo looked at Inny, who was in the process of digesting the same information and wasn't paying attention to her communicuff. He had never seen anyone's eyes look wider.

"I'll admit it. I'm freaked out!" Inny said, not blinking for so long that her eyes glossed over.

"See?" Ruby said.

Milo put a fork in his food, and for a moment, allowed himself to think that there was someone else putting a fork in their food somewhere else in the galaxy, possibly thinking the same thoughts he was thinking right now. Possibly making the same discovery at the same moment—that there were other alien beings in the universe. Maybe they didn't know who or where, but just knowing that they existed.

He had so many questions. He wondered for a moment if humans were the last to the party. He wouldn't be surprised. He was often the last to any party. Parties made Milo very uncomfortable.

"Look," Ruby said, breaking the uncomfortable silence. "I can't believe I'm saying this, but they're really nice. SD and the others. You should spend some time with them. They're funny, too. Especially when they tell me that they understand what I'm saying, but then mess it all up."

"Robot. Aliens," Inny said.

Milo had already spent a little time with them when he brought them back from the large ship that was holding a parking position relative to the station. They talked about finding a different parking orbit for a few reasons, not the least of which is that it was currently right in the middle of the approach path for incoming ships, and they had to keep that path clear or incoming ships would have to compute less efficient trajectories.

Milo and SD would be making a special trip later that evening to re-park SD's ship. So, spending more time with at least one of the robots was already in the cards.

They had tried asking ships to maneuver around, and one did—the one that was carrying a VIP and some press. It burned too much fuel. At this point, it was easier to ask the robots to move their ship. The robots agreed and now that activity was on the schedule for later that day. Which reminded Milo that he wanted to ask:

"Are you coming with me and SD later? To move his ship?"

Ruby's brow furrowed. "No," she said. Clearly, she wasn't happy about it.

"Will you at least stay in the control center in communication?"

And Ruby's brow instantly returned to its natural state, and she brightened. "Of course! Happy to!"

Milo thought it was sweet how transparent Ruby could be about her emotions sometimes and how concealed she could be other times.

Again, she continued to shovel food in her mouth. She really wasn't a neat eater. He'd get over that if he ever had another chance to eat with her. Maybe next time without this chaperone who chimed in again.

"Okay, so... robots! Tell us!"

"Like I said, you should meet them. Spend time with them yourself. I'll introduce you. I need to finish eating first. This food is *soooo* good."

They all smirked at that. Station food, particularly station mess food, while not the worst in the solar system, wasn't known as being the best either. Although Milo couldn't tell you why. Most of it was fresh, as it was grown in the hydroponics[2] bay right on the station.

They let Ruby finish every bit that was on her plate.

After a few minutes, Milo had an odd feeling. He looked around. Every table in the mess was full. That wasn't normal. People were talking at every table, and occasionally pointing, and definitely looking—at Ruby.

He knew several of the people. Heck, one of his team members was there with his station girlfriend—separate from the girlfriend he talked about who was still on Earth. Many of the people he recognized as other station residents, even though he wasn't personally acquainted with them. And several he didn't recognize at all. They must be the people who came on that recent ship or the one that preceded Ruby's arrival.

One of these was holding up a communicuff, clearly trying to take a picture. Milo stood up and put himself in between Ruby, who was mid-chew, and the voyeur.

"Hey! What are you doing?" he called out, surprising himself that he was standing up and yelling at a stranger.

"Taking pictures of Ruby Palmer, what does it look like?"

"She's eating. Can't you see that? Come back later."

"She's eating, and she's famous. People want to see famous people doing normal things."

"But Ruby might not want her picture taken."

"Irrelevant."

Milo knew there was nothing else he could say. He turned to Ruby. "You okay? You guys want to leave?"

Ruby looked around Milo at the room of people. Her eyes opened wide as she, too, caught sight of the unusual quantity of people in the mess. She swallowed and said, "yeah. I'm done."

She stood up, and half the mess stood up, too.

She sat back down, and so did they.

"Um, this is weird," she said. Milo took her tray to the reco-recycler and then came back. He gestured that she should get up. She did, as did Inny.

"Let's just go," he said.

Half the room stood up, too. They didn't stop Ruby from exiting the mess, but they certainly followed her out. Now it was obvious that multiple people were taking her picture.

"Where to?" Milo asked.

"I want to go meet the robots," Inny said.

---

2. Of course, anything I write that involves a space station or colony on a planet involves some kind of hydroponics area. I love this concept in space... but haven't had reason (yet) to center a story around it and flush out more details.

"Wait, didn't you just say you were freaked out?" Ruby asked.

"Uh, yeah, but freaked out in a *good* way." Inny beamed. "Maybe I can get them to give me some quotes I can use." Inny trailed off lost in thought.

"I wonder what they'll think of TERP." Milo said. He genuinely was curious about another take on the AI that seemed to be in the news and everywhere.

"What's TERP?" Ruby asked.

"Oh wow, you've been back a whole day, and you haven't heard? Come on, we'll fill you in," said Milo.

Chapter 11

Professor Lloyd Coronik[1] unbuckled his seat belt and floated towards the front of the passenger cabin to get himself a soda. Unfortunately, the selection on these passenger transports was limited to the generic brand flavors of orange, brown, and yellow. He eyed the three and tried not to let the pedestrian accommodations chip away at his psyche.

One might think that Professor Coronik would have taken one of the fancier ships, one that was larger and could spin to produce gravity, or—even more preferable—one with a better selection of food and beverages, but this was all that was available on such short notice.

One might also come to this conclusion because of Professor Coronik's notable position in the Church of the Blockchain. He was a Prime Connector. One of only three in the whole Church—the wealthiest church to ever exist. It would be logical to guess that such an organization would own its own ship. Or its own fleet.

Except that church officials rarely left Earth and generally were opposed to doing so.

Professor Coronik, however, determined, along with his fellow Prime Connectors, Charlotte Henry and Yesenia Aziz, that there was a worthwhile reason to leave the planet: to meet Ruby Palmer, the first human to do so many things. And her robot companions. He couldn't imagine the technology they possessed—imagination was not one of his strengths. Professor Coronik's job was to ensure that any technology transfer that was likely going to occur, would do so with the Church as the initial recipient. The only way to do that was to establish a relationship with the robots before they came to Earth and established their own relationship with one of the increasingly useless world governments.

Professor Coronik, drink packet in hand, used his other hand to propel himself back along the aisle and into his seat.

To make things worse, this ship was completely full of people. And to make it even worse, the entire trip would take five days.

Not that this was slow. What these types of ships lacked in comfort, they made up for in speed. That was the other reason he didn't try to buy someone's seat on a more luxurious ship. The luxury ships were slower and slow was not his preferred method of travel. Especially not on a time-sensitive mission as this.

His seat wasn't quite a seat. It was a little more like an angled bunk. One could stretch out and sleep but needed to stay strapped in at quite a cumbersome angle to avoid floating away.

---

1. Actor inspiration: Randall Park

And it was one person per side of the cabin.

As Professor Coronik was strapping himself back in, he caught the eye of the individual in the seat across the aisle from him. He had preferred not to get involved in any conversation with strangers along the way and had managed to avoid eye contact. He traveled alone, and kept his privacy settings set to max, as anyone with glasses would see.

Despite his efforts, this time he made eye contact with someone who might have been about his age and was clearly not wearing percepto-glasses. It was hard to tell with the obvious makeup and non-glass enhancements they wore. Not that it mattered. Coronik still did not want to engage in conversation.

"Hey, I know you," this individual, who had been awkwardly strapped in on their side, reading a tablet, propped themselves up on an elbow and looked Professor Coronik up and down. "I write about you all the time."

"Oh?" Coronik said, trying not to sound too interested, already making the assumption that this person was press. Unwanted press.

"Yes, I've written about the Blockchain in nearly every research paper I've published."

So, not press, Coronik thought to himself. He must have accidentally made some movement or gesture that signaled this person to continue because they did.

"Yeah, I'm a doctoral student of philosophy at large from the University of the Gakkel Ridge. I specialize in the Church, and technology, and the history of all that. I would *love* to talk to you about it. I'm working on a paper right now that compares TERP to—"

Coronik studied this individual before responding. He couldn't tell if this was an eager fan or someone who thought that he'd be genuinely interested in what they had to say. Not that he hoped it was the former, but he was certainly not the latter.

"Maybe once we get to the station. I'd like to sleep right now," Coronik thought that was the only way to get out of an unwanted conversation before it continued. He had no interest in being interviewed as 'research' for anyone's paper, academic or news. Once on Astroll 2, he was certain he'd be able to keep this individual out of his way. He was on a mission and had no time or patience for such distractions.

"Sure, sure. I was getting myself ready to sleep, too. Just some light reading. History. Do you ever read any history? Fascinating stuff what they didn't know only a couple hundred years ago."

"Mmm," Coronik said, attempting not to encourage a second wave of banter.

"My name is Link Vala[2], by the way. Or 'B-T-W' as they used to say in the early days of networking and the internet. That's what I'm studying right now. There was a lot of ridiculous things they said and did back then. I wish I could have known someone from that time. Do you know there were some really long-lived people? Their stories were recorded, but I would have just loved to talk to them. Face to face, ya' know? Today's centenarians are their grandkids, so it's not the same."

"Really, I'd like to get some sleep," Professor Coronik said. And begrudgingly, because now he figured it was the only way he would achieve silence, "maybe we can talk later."

"Sure, sure. 'Nite." And Link Vala turned their tablet back on, and Professor Coronik turned off the illuminating lights in his compartment.

Link Vala spoke up in an obnoxiously loud whisper, "Is it okay if I have my tablet light on?"

---

2. Actor inspiration: Melissa Navia

The light didn't bother Professor Coronik, only noise, so he grunted a curt, "Sure," and hoped that would be the last thing he heard for a while.

"Are you sure, you're sure?" Link Vala continued and Coronik wished he knew what it would take to convince them. "I can turn it of it you're—"

"It's really fine."

There was a blissful moment of silence where Coronik was able to achieve some measure of coziness in the seat that was clearly not designed for cozy. He was just on the edge of a hypnagogic dream, when he heard, blaring from across the aisle, "... and *Palmer* is the one with access to advanced *robots*..."

"Sorry, sorry!" said Link Vala, clearly flustered. "My pur-fi connection just went wonky."

Professor Coronik didn't feel the need to provide any acknowledgment of this. He kept his eyes shut and tried to pass the time by sleeping, with limited amount of success.

Chapter 12

Disto occupied space in a room with SD and AT. The room was called 'living quarters' and the three of them were instructed to occupy this space until Ruby returned for them.

"There is not a lot of space to move around," AT complained.

Complained or uttered a statement of fact? The humans put a lot of objects in their rooms. Objects that were known as furniture. Disto and the others understood the concept and were wondering if it made sense to ask if some of these objects could be removed.

They decided against it lest their human hosts think they were unappreciative of their hospitality. Especially since Disto still needed information from them.

"I am going to try and link to their computer console," Disto said after a thorough survey of the room. Before Ruby left them, she attempted to show the three robots where a device she called a keyboard materialized in the air.

"I don't see anything," Disto had said. AT and SD nodded in agreement.

Ruby had looked as if she was poking her fingers in the air, and then all of the sudden something materialized under her fingers as she poked away.

"There. I made the keyboard green. The default color is red, something I know you don't normally see. And ugh—there's probably going to be other things you don't see because of that. We use red a lot—I'm not going to be able to change colors on everything."

"I'm sure we'll get by."

Disto was looking at the keyboard and recognized the individual components that made up Ruby's native language.

"In some ways," Ruby said, "when you start looking at the system, you'll see that it's not too different from your own. There's a main menu that you can always come back to by pressing this key here."

Disto nodded that he understood.

"Need anything else? I promise I won't be gone long."

They said no, and she left.

SD had been very quiet since arriving. Disto didn't want to disturb his thoughts. He browsed through the system until he found what he remembered Ruby calling "ancient vids." She had explained that this was entertainment—made-up stories, not historical records. He marked these to come back to later and watch. Rather than choose one or two, he was going to watch all of them. Maybe SD would be interested as well.

AT, on the other hand, had been just as curious as Disto was about everything and anything, often pointing at objects and wondering how they worked. Several times he remarked out loud, "I wonder if they would let me take it apart."

After making the same remark multiple times, AT settled himself by connecting into the wall that allowed him to manipulate the wall itself. It was odd, but at least he was quiet and occupied.

But now, what was on Disto's circuits was finding more samples of non-human life that he could test.

He accessed the computer via the hovering keyboard and pressed the main menu button.

And nothing there made any sense.

Luckily, that's when Ruby returned. She stood in the doorway, and Disto could see her Uncle Blake standing behind her. He touched her arm. Disto watched the two of them exchange some form on non-verbal communication. They both distorted their faces and then Blake was leaving them. Ruby had tried to describe the title 'uncle,' but Disto's circuits had a hard time processing any of the relationships that Ruby described as familial. 'Familial' itself was a concept he couldn't claim to grasp in its entirety. Connections between humans who made other humans. Disto was made from a template, by a Hall, and couldn't imagine he would have any type of fondness for the Hall the way Ruby did with her uncles. Objectively, it made sense, but the sentiment... not so much. Nevertheless, he at least understood there was a connection between Ruby and Blake that was closer than Ruby and most of the other billions of humans and Disto hoped to talk to him at some point.

"Ready for that tour of Astroll 2 I promised?" Ruby said.

"Yes, indeed!"

Two of the three robots lined up and Ruby led them out into the hallway. The third, AT, was still sitting by the wall, plugged in, and it now occurred to Disto that AT had produced no sounds in a while.

"AT?" Ruby said, "Are you... feeling well? Is that the right thing to ask?"

AT moved its soft face-screen that was on its top, soft chassis to face her. To Disto, it looked like it was taking more effort than it should have.

"I don't..." AT trailed off. He looked less inflated than normal.

Ruby rushed over and knelt by his side, followed by Disto who said, "There is a built-in diagnostic we should run."

"Okay, how do we do that?" Ruby asked.

"I have..." the amount of effort it took AT to produce audible vocalizations was palpable and produced an unpleasant sensation in Disto's circuits. "Have... have... run diagnostic."

"And?" Ruby asked. Disto analyzed the tone of her voice and determined what he detected was a mix of urgency and fear.

"Virus," he responded. "Activated accidentally..."

Ruby responded by immediately disconnecting AT from the wall. The action startled Disto, but AT looked a tiny bit better.

"Thank..." he said.

"Are you functioning properly now?" Disto asked. "It is unfortunate that you didn't say anything before now. We could have helped sooner."

"The device," AT said, indicating the wall, "it was trying to suppress my virus."

Ruby flipped down a small panel on the side of the wall AT had been connected to and made another keyboard appear in front of her. Disto watched her fingers glide around, and she didn't quite frown but scrunched her lips together.

"This is a touchscreen wall. It's another version of a computer that is connected to our system. Like all devices, it has virus protection, malware scanning, and even parental controls. See?" She took one of her digits and pressed it to the wall. Disto recognized the letter 'f' that appeared, but nothing else happened after. "I guess the good news is that AT's virus didn't get into our systems. The computer did its job."

"Ah!" SD made a squeak. He, too, had been a container of silence but SD came alive at this. "If there is good news, then there is bad! Good and bad are opposites that go together." His coloring indicated a sense of pride in understanding Ruby. Disto liked that SD's behavior was representative of his normal self.

"Is there indeed bad news, Ruby?" Disto asked.

"Uh yeah," she said and waved her hand at AT. "AT has a virus. Look at him."

They all looked.

"Suggest... deactivate... until... return to Location Ze..." AT sputtered.

"Deactivate?" Ruby exclaimed. "What does that mean? How...?"

Before anyone could answer, AT had his soft appendage touching the side of his face-screen. After a moment, and before anyone could not only answer but protest or object or ask more questions, AT was deflating. Along with that, his face-screen went dark, clearly receiving no more power. As he deflated, the soft material that comprised his surface shrank together as well, the smoothness turning wrinkly and collapsing inward. After a handful of tics, AT was reduced to something Ruby could pick up and hold in the palm of her hand.

Which is what Disto saw her do. She held AT in her two cupped hands and looked over at Disto.

"What just happened?" she said.

"He deactivated himself."

"Yeah but... what... I don't..."

"I suggest you hold on to him. Perhaps in one of your clothing compartments. When we return to Location Zero, we will reactivate him."

"Ok," Ruby said. "But can you... also..."

"If you are asking if I can also deactivate and 'shrink' I think is the word, then yes and no. Yes, I can be deactivated as can anything. That second capability is unique to robots of AT's type. If I, or if SD here, were to be deactivated, we would not be as," Disto wanted to choose the right word, "portable."

Disto watched Ruby watch AT and after a few tics, she did indeed place AT in an inner pocket of the article of clothing she called a 'jacket.'

"Are we going on our tour now?" SD asked.

Disto watched Ruby blink. Bios, at least humans, had unique ways of processing data. Ruby, in particular, would oscillate the covering over her optical sensors. Disto admitted that he didn't quite understand the link between those actions, but he was a Historian, not a Zookeeper.

Eventually, Ruby said, "I've arranged to use the lift, since you guys aren't suited for most of the ladders that we use to get in between the rings. The lift is usually used for moving equipment around."

"Are we equipment?" Disto asked.

"No," Ruby said, and Disto found himself grateful that there was no pause to consider a response. "However, you lack certain, um, physical features that make ladders convenient."

"We don't have lower appendages like you."

"Legs. Exactly," she said. "But where we're going, you don't need legs.[1]"

---

1. Hopefully someone picked up on the pseudo-reference here... One of my favorite movies, *Back to the Future*, at the end when Doc Brown says: "Roads? Where we're going, we don't need roads."

Chapter 13

"Prepare for docking," came a voice over the speaker system. "Ensure that everything in your seat has been stowed. Ensure that you are buckled in the five-point-five restraining system. The Company welcomes you to Astroll 2 and we hope you've enjoyed the ride."

Professor Coronik had nothing to stow so he relaxed once more and closed his eyes. He had been buckled in for a while and had spent most of the journey sleeping. The lack of prolonged physical activity left him dazed and drowsy.

His unintentional traveling companion, Link Vala, shuffled around quite a bit to put everything back in its place and was very busy futzing with the restraint system. When they were done, they said, "OK, once we dock, what's the plan?"

"Excuse me?"

"We're both here to see the robots. What's our plan? Our approach?"

"I'm here to debrief the robots on behalf of the Church. There is no 'we' or 'our' in my activities."

"Oh c'mon. There's so much to figure out here and the two of us approaching them would—Well, I'm sure it would be more than two? Me and your team."

"No, on this trip, it's just me. There will be a team back on Earth."

"On Earth? They're going back to Earth?"

"Of course. We have the best laboratories and facilities there… for examination. Not to mention some of the best roboticists. Astroll 2 doesn't have the facilities to handle something of this magnitude."

"But these are aliens. They're not just robots. They're alien robots…"

"I'm well aware."

With that, a tone erupted in the background that signaled that they were in the hanger of Astroll 2. A red light was illuminated at the front of the cabin signaling that they were not yet ready to disembark.

"A few moments and we'll have you all disembarking to Astroll 2," the friendly voice came over the speaker system again. "The docking hanger needs to be repressurized. This is standard procedure for those of you on your first trip here."

Professor Coronik only raised a small eyebrow at this. He was well aware of standard procedures since they were the same for all space travel and while this was indeed his first time on Astroll 2, this was hardly his first time in space.

"Where are you staying?" Link Vala interrupted his thoughts.

Luckily, before he could decide how to respond, the disembark light turned green, signaling that they could get off the vessel.

Professor Coronik managed a faint smile that exuded an air of no-time-for-small-talk, grabbed his one bag—he had luggage that would be delivered to his room for him—and politely, but with purpose, weaved around the other people who were still gathering their things.

Once on the deck of Astroll 2, he felt...woozy. No, that was the low gravity. It was higher than the vessel that brought him here but lower than Earth. He knew to expect that. The air also smelled like overly recycled air, with a tinge of cinnamon. Or was that cardamom[1]. Something smelled sweet in a homey kind of way. He looked around... maybe that was a smell from one of the disembarking passengers.

He continued looking around. Lots of faces he didn't recognize, and then... there was the person who was his designated contact, Myra Kaling[2], Deputy Director of Astroll 2.

"Professor Coronik, welcome," she held out a hand.

"Nice to meet you in person," Professor Coronik said. "Thank you for arranging this."

"Of course. Let's get you through on-boarding, and then I'll escort you to your quarters."

Professor Coronik nodded and let Myra lead the way.

She brought him to a console operated by a person who asked to see his documentation.

"You have a human doing the job of an AI," he said to Myra as he pressed a button on his communicuff and poked at the image that appeared until it produced his identification. He turned the image so that the superfluous person could scan it.

"Professor Lloyd Coronik. Arrival time logged. Departing... Hmm... we don't have a departure date for you."

Myra assured the documentation processor that all was in order. As she was turned away from him, Coronik eyed a very small tattoo just below and behind her earlobe. It was the mark of the Church of the Blockchain. Coronik smiled. Believers were everywhere.

While another few moments passed, Coronik saw Link Vala talking with another processor. He could see from his vantage point their forearm. It was held at an angle that the hologram image above it could be seen by the processor they were talking to as well as himself. It was an image of Ruby Palmer. Coronik started to wonder if he should have found out a little more about who Link Vala was and what they were really doing here. Hopefully, someone was responsible for Ruby Palmer's calendar and meetings and would certainly ensure that someone of his stature met with her and her robots before any of the riff-raff.

"I will say," Myra interrupted his thoughts and gestured that they make their way away from processing, "that as nice as it is to have you here, Prime Connector, I'll be happy when you leave. I presume those robots, those aliens, will be leaving with you."

"Well, yes, yes, of course," he responded, although he wasn't focused on her words, but was following her in an uncoordinated motion down the ring, presumably to where his quarters would be for the next few days. He was trying to get his bearings in this unfamiliar place, lest he come off as a fumbling buffoon.

"Sir?" Myra said, stopping at the foot of a ladder. Coronik realized she had been talking the whole time.

---

1. I love the smell of cardamom. I have it as an essential oil that I diffuse regularly.

2. Actress inspiration: Mindy Kaling

"TERP[3] will have something to say about this, I presume?" Myra said, presumably repeating herself.

"Well, yes, TERP gets a say in everything. We designed it that way. Of course." Coronik hoped his response was the right one. Reading Myra's face, which relaxed somewhat, told him it was. Coronik then followed her up—or was it down—the ladder and down the much narrower hallway of another station ring.

She stopped after a few bouncy steps, smiled and gestured to the door that was now in front of them. "Do you want to rest or...?"

"I'll just drop my bag down. I want to meet your... guests... as soon as possible."

---

3. Yes, I know this is the 3rd time mentioning TERP without explaining it...

Chapter 14

> Detailed Historian <

"On behalf of the Church of the Blockchain, I welcome you."

"We have already been welcomed by several individuals," Disto said. He understood that Bios had their rituals, but this one seemed repetitive and redundant. Quite unnecessary, he thought.

Disto and SD were lined up on one side of a table in what Ruby had called "Robt Plampton's leadership conference room." Disto had wanted to ask why a specific room was needed for discussions, but Ruby looked like she was tired. She was here, too, as was her Uncle Blake, both of whom occupied the same side of the large table.

Robt Plampton was at one side that was perpendicular. Facing the robots, from the opposite side of the table was Myra Kaling. Next to her was the human who had just offered yet another welcome, Coronik.

All the humans were standing, but Coronik was the only one attempting to keep himself stable by placing the tips of his digits on the table. It wasn't working very well, and he continued to have a certain back and forth motion that made him look uncomfortable. Disto wondered why no one offered to provide him a stabilizing device.

"Well[1], I welcome you as well. I hope we can establish open relations with your... people." Coronik stumbled over that last word, and nearly pushed himself away from the table as he lifted one of his hands. "With your kind, I mean." He simultaneously cleared his throat and reached back for the edge of the table. "Are you authorized to speak on behalf of your government?"

Uncle Blake chimed in, "Professor Coronik, I thought this was going to be a simple introduction, not an overture to diplomatic relations."

Every movement Coronik made appeared to be in slow motion. He gripped the table harder, Disto could see the muscles on top of his hands and starting up his arm contract. Then he blinked and while blinking, angled himself so he was facing Uncle Blake.

"Ruby here has summarized all the debriefing points very nicely," Coronik said, and just when Disto was certain Coronik was doing everything he could to not let go of the table, he unclenched the ends of his appendages from that table and faced Ruby's Uncle Blake, "May I speak with you over here?"

---

1. Take note of the number of times Professor Coronik begins a statement with the word, "Well." In linguistics and language research this is known as a "discourse marker," and I'll come back and explain more about it and why I did this later.

Uncle Blake joined Coronik in a corner of the room that was the furthest point from where he and SD had been placed. That wasn't very far in this modest room, maybe five appendage lengths away.

Even though they lowered the volume of their emanations, Disto could still hear what the humans were saying. Not that he was attempting to listen in, it was just that they weren't as quiet as they thought.

As such, he heard Coronik tell Ruby's Uncle Blake that caution was indicated, and that they had to treat this diplomatically, lest a whole army of robots come and invade this solar system.

Before he could fully process the meaning of the word 'army' in this context, he heard Uncle Blake defend the robots saying that if that was what they wanted to do, it would have already been done. They obviously had the means.

"Obviously. And now we need to make sure we have the means," Coronik said.

"Who do you mean by 'we'?"

When Coronik didn't answer that, Uncle Blake crossed his arms and said, "That's what I thought."

Then they were back at the conference table, Uncle Blake spoke directly to the robots, "Guys, don't answer any questions that make you... uncomfortable. If you're able to become uncomfortable that is."

"Oh, we are indeed!" SD responded enthusiastically. "'Uncomfortable' is one of the signs that a robot needs a repair. Coronik, we—"

"It's Professor Coronik," said Professor Coronik as he tugged on his suit. "I have multiple degrees. Four, to be precise."

"Then shouldn't we call you Professor Professor Professor Professor Coronik^2?" Disto asked.

Professor Coronik's jaw tightened. "One 'professor' is sufficient. And which robot are you? Which one is the technician?" He was looking at SD.

Disto chimed in, "I am Detailed Historian. My companion is Swell Driver. Ambitious Technician is currently incapacitated until he can access maintenance."

The human, Coronik, Professor Coronik, was using his optical sensor to scan both of them. "I see," he finally said. "And who programmed you?"

"The Hall of Templates," Disto responded confidently. "Same as any and every robot."

"And who is in charge of the Hall of Templates?" Professor Coronik asked.

"The Core, of course," Disto continued to be engaged.

"And who is in charge of this Core?"

Disto responded, "The Core leadership is formed by representatives from all the Halls and Agencies."

"Well, that is quite fascinating," said Professor Coronik flatly. "Quite fascinating, well...indeed. Who set up this structure? Start at the beginning."

"We don't know. I assume when you, what was the word," Disto paused to look it up, "oh yes, when you 'debriefed' Ruby she explained our current situation with our historical records."

At the mention of her name, all optical sensors—human and robot—went to Ruby. She didn't add anything, but her own optical sensors dilated when she perceived everyone looking at her.

"Let's move on to something else that has been bothering me about your story," Professor Coronik said. "Ruby's mini-R-pod, *Apple Pi*. You disassembled it?"

---

2. Deliberate nod to Major Major Major Major of *Catch-22* by Joseph Heller. One of my all-time favorite novels.

"That was a mistake," Disto responded.

"Well, what a mistake. That was not your property, and that's a known way to learn the ins and outs of someone else's technology. Can we learn about your technology the same way?"

Disto didn't like what he thought this Bio might be implying. "No, you may not take SD's ship apart. Unlike Ruby, who obviously had a way to be brought home, we do not."

"But you will tell us about your faster-than-light technology, of course."

"I must have the words 'of course' mistranslated. Because no, we cannot do that. We are not authorized to make that kind of technology transfer."

Disto didn't feel as if he needed a repair, but he felt something unpleasant. He was starting to wonder if there were multiple meanings to the word uncomfortable. If there were, then this was it.

> Professor Coronik <

Professor Coronik, Lloyd, knew when not to push. Even if it wasn't the thing he was trying to get. He was not interested in faster-than-light technology, usually just abbreviated as 'FTL,' although he knew many others who were, and that they'd pay practically anything to get it, including every world government that still existed. If he could get *his* hands on FTL first, he would gladly accept it and reap all the associated benefits.

But that wasn't his primary interest. Instead, he wanted to take apart the robots. He wanted to see how they tick. He wanted to know what made them sentient. The Church had been working on AI for a long time. Claims of sentient AI came and went, each one getting disproved. The latest AI experiment, TERP, the one he had personally convinced the President of North America to adopt to run the government was, well, behaving unpredictably. Not that anyone knew. But everyone had convinced Coronik that blockchain tech was suitable for AI purposes and he sanctioned the project, pouring resources upon resources into it.

"Well, I certainly understand that." Lloyd said. "We have similar laws and limits on technology transfer between various nation-states on Earth that go back hundreds of years. In fact, I'm authorized to invite you there..."

The robot that called itself Disto perked up.

"Yes, please," it said. "We need to go to Earth. To test samples."

"Oh yes, I read that in the debriefing report, too." Coronik responded. "Well, there will be a few challenges, but I'll help. With the Church of the Blockchain behind you, there should be no problems."

"What kind of challenges?" Ruby asked.

"Well, Ruby, a lot of people are not thrilled with the discovery of alien intelligence out there, especially because it is different to us. There is a growing movement to have the robots banned from Earth before they even get there!"

"What? Are you kidding me? These are the nicest..."

"The nicest kidnappers?" Coronik asked.

"Yeah, I get what it looks like. But they didn't harm me, and I'm back in one piece. Everything is fine."

"Well, either way, they clearly do not operate on the same moral level as us which alone is concerning. A lot of people see this as the start of an invasion."

"I'll say it again," Uncle Blake added, "that if they wanted to invade, they would have. A long time ago."

"We are not invaders," Disto said. "We simply want to find our data."

"Well, you are referring to data that you might have embedded in one of the species on our world. That is also something a lot of people have an issue with. Many do not like the concept of genetic manipulation—for any reason. To think that you've changed our animal population—"

"It's just in the junk DNA," Ruby interrupted. "It wouldn't change a thing."

"Well, 'junk DNA' and 'genetic manipulation,'" Coronik stood up straight and was pleased with himself for being able to continue to use the most technical words in the conversation, "are complex concepts that are hard to describe to the average person." He swallowed, knowing that he wasn't sure he knew what it meant and would get the computer to explain it to him later. After all, he wasn't the average person but the Prime Connector with a series of degrees.

Ruby crossed her arms. "I learned about genetics in school when I was twelve."

"Nonetheless," Coronik said, "TERP is going to want to have a say in this matter."

"TERP? Why would your budget-crunching AI have anything to do with this?" Ruby shook her head.

Coronik opened his mouth while he tried to formulate a response, but Ruby continued, "I hate that I'm suggesting this but maybe we should do a news broadcast? If people were to see SD and Disto, and see how harmless they are...?"

"Well, you're going to get your chance at that," Coronik said. "Sooner than you think..."

Chapter 15

"Blake, you need to see this!" Jade said as she burst into Blake and Logan's apartment, baby wrapped around the front of her body in the carrier that they'd gifted her.

They were supposed to meet up later in the day, take Jade's baby, Ruby, for a walk, and talk about the Church and their plans. Apparently, Jade didn't want to wait until later.

Blake stuck his head into the hallway before closing the front door. Out of habit, he looked both ways to see if anyone was around or annoyed at the early morning noise. There was no one. The last thing he saw before shutting the door was one of a series of framed posters mounted on the other side of the hallway that promoted the commandments of the Church. The one located directly outside his apartment read, "Thou shalt not delete data."

People didn't need to be told that, however. The amount of data humans had been producing daily since the early 21st century was mind-boggling and used words like zettabyte and yottabyte[1] —quantities no human could fathom—to describe what humans produced daily. Since that time, a whole new field of study into digital archaeology had sprung up.

The Church employed the most digital archaeologists in the world, either directly or through their loosely affiliated subsidiary companies.

This is where Jade Palmer came in. Jade was a digital archaeologist.

Jade studied computers and the history of technology in college and became interested in analysis of ancient data, particularly scientific data, when she stumbled upon a long-forgotten paper by long-forgotten scientists. The scientists were

---

1. Zettabyte and yottabyte are real quantities. A yottabyte is a quadrillion gigabytes! The order of naming goes like this: gigabyte (GB), Terabyte (TB), Petabyte (PB), Exabyte (EB), Zettabyte (ZB), and Yottabyte (YB). TBs are starting to become familiar language as it's normal to buy a new computer with a 1 TB hard drive. I'm constantly looking up statistics on estimates of how much data is generated daily. The best source I found as of this writing in late 2025 is nearly half a PB, with possibly 181 ZBs generated this year. Which is why I'm estimating daily generations of ZBs an YBs by the time this book takes place.

Paul Horowitz and Carl Sagan[2]. The paper was, "Five Years of Project META: an All-Sky Narrow-Band Radio Search for Extraterrestrial Signals."[3]

This was an extraordinary find. The common understanding was that no one did extraterrestrial research. That was the domain of kooks and conspiracy theorists. Except Jade now had proof that in the distant past, searching for extraterrestrial life was performed by well-known scientists. Jade shared her findings with Blake who was studying computers along with physics and astronomy. Both made attempts to figure out when and why this research had been shut down. They could figure out the when, somewhere in the 2040s or 2050s. They couldn't pin-point the why.

Both Jade and Blake were currently employed by the Church in some way. But Blake occasionally fantasized about working for The Company and maybe heading out to Astroll 2 with the goal of setting up a covert space telescope there.

Jade didn't want to leave Earth. She thought she could be of most use on the planet, even though the planet was getting… uncomfortable. Everyone mindlessly went through their days. She didn't connect with people other than Blake and Logan. She was there for their wedding and shortly after decided it was time to have her own child. So, she did.

She continued the tradition of naming in her family which was to pick a precious or interesting gemstone or material. She picked 'Ruby.' It was a close tie between Ruby and Rhodochrosite[4], her other favorite red mineral but decided against the latter because a five-syllable name was bound to upset the majority of people she would encounter who were generally lazy and likely to shorten it into an unflattering nickname[5].

There were also the household robots to consider. The robots worked best with two, three syllables at most. Longer than that and it was worth abbreviating one's name.

Jade was now living on her own with her baby daughter, but only down the road from Blake and Logan.

She named Blake and Logan her baby's uncles, but also named them as the people who would take care of Ruby if anything happened to her. Not that she thought anything would happen to her, but her own mother, as crazy as she was, raised her to always be prepared. And that meant having plans for worst-case scenarios. It wasn't a big deal. Just some legal paperwork.

Blake was in his comfy pj pants and went to grab a shirt.

When he came back, Jade was already passing Ruby off to him so she could take out her computer.

"Look what I found," she said as she was opening it up.

"Ok but shhh…. Logan is sleeping, as is this little one," he rocked Ruby to make sure she didn't wake up.

Jade nodded and plopped herself on the couch. Not really trying to make any less noise, she opened her old-style computer on the coffee table. She touched the screen in a few places and a text-based document appeared on the screen.

---

2. Most people have heard of Carl Sagan, but not Paul Horowitz. Before I learned he was part of the SETI (Search for Extra-Terrestrial Intelligence) project, I knew him as one of the co-authors of this big, heavy, gray-covered book I've owned since college, *The Art of Electronics*.

3. This is a real paper published in the Astrophysical Journal in 1993.

4. A very pretty mineral. I have some in my collection, but it's more pink.

5. Like "Rodeo." Doesn't sound terribly flattering to me.

"What is that?" Blake said—careful to be quiet—as he didn't plop, but carefully lowered himself to the couch next to Jade, with a still-sleeping Ruby in his arms.

"Proof!"

"Proof of...?"

"Sheesh Blake... it's what we've been looking for. It's proof! It's an old journal that used to be published called," she squinted at the screen, "called the 'The Planetary Science Journal.'[6] It looked like it stopped publishing around 2040. I found an archive of their papers and there are a whole ton of them on the old satellites that visited Jupiter, and Saturn, and Titan. Look how many papers referenced the Cassini-Huygens mission! I knew it was a real mission..."

Blake made a little scooching motion so he could get a better look at the document. He was still holding Ruby, gently rocking her. He continued to rock Ruby and read.

The document was an ancient-style academic paper regarding the interior structure of Saturn's moon, Titan. It was titled, "Exosolar Sources Responsible for Titan's Interior Structure and Dynamics as Revealed by a Further Examination of Cassini-Huygens Mission Data."[7]

"It was submitted, but never published," Jade explained. "This never became public, and it was right after this paper, that the Church manipulated to have the space telescope projects shut down. A replacement for the old James Webb was already underway[8], and it was shelved. And then there was a decrease in published papers on exoplanets, too."

Blake heard what Jade was saying and tried to make sense of it.

"But why would one random paper..."

"Oh, c'mon Blake! You're the astrophysicist! If this was a paper with no real data behind it, it would have been dismissed as quackery and no one would care."

Blake thought about that. Jade wasn't wrong. The truth is what scared people and caused them to shut down information. But what about the possibility of something coming from outside the solar system was scary? It had been known for a long time that our solar system was bombarded by comets and bits that were technically from the outside. That's the assumption he made when he saw the title.

"Let me go put Ruby down," he said, walking over to the spare crib they kept in the corner of the living room for visits like this, "and then I need to read that."

---

6. Also a real scientific journal.

7. This one is NOT a real paper. I made it up. If you remove the first few words "Exosolar Sources Responsible for," you are left with the title of a real paper, "Titan's Interior Structure and Dynamics After the Cassini-Huygens Mission."

8. FWIW, JWST is expected to have a lifetime of about 20 years. It was designed for a 5-year mission, with a 10-year operational goal. But what often dictates the life of satellite missions is how much fuel (propellant) is has to maintain its orbit/location. JWST is predicted to have enough propellant to last 20 years.

Chapter 16

They were in the Hub. A makeshift stage had been constructed in the space on the opposite side of the Nook. Three rows of chairs of increasing height were set up, and a large green screen was placed behind them.

One chair was slightly offset, distinguishing itself from the others. That was the one Ruby sat on. Off to the side and behind sat her uncles. Robt Plampton sat with them. As did Milo. The broadcaster wanted Milo, the second human to meet the aliens, to be present and answer some questions.

A chair faced all the rest. This one was presumably for the interviewer. Ruby didn't know who that was going to be. Not that she was intimately familiar with the news and would recognize them. People who wanted real information about events looked to PeopleWire, where anyone could provide accounts of events along with evidence of the account, like videos. "News" was synonymous with "opinion pieces to argue over" and was one of the lowest forms of entertainment and something Ruby never took an interest in. She was surprised they were interested in her. Her news was more appropriate for PeopleWire since she had a first-hand account, complete with video of the robots to provide.[1]

Ruby was placed in her chair first by someone who said their name so fast that Ruby missed it entirely. All she caught was that they were a producer. A seemingly busy one at that. The producer was shorter than Ruby and not much older, but focused and moving quickly. She had short curly hair that bounced around in the low gravity. A mere milli-second after Ruby was in her seat, facing the right way, the producer had moved on to seating the next person.

The producer placed Ruby's uncles next but left a seat open. Then Plampton. Then Milo. Next, she placed another individual Ruby didn't recognize in that open seat. Lastly, she brought in Professor Coronik to fill the second empty seat. Then she went off to talk to the man who was setting up a camera suite.

Ruby looked back over her shoulder at the man she didn't recognize. She had the distinct feeling that this man and Professor Coronik knew each other and didn't like each other. Maybe it was because of the way the two of them were angled ever so slightly, facing away from each other. But wasn't that the producers doing? Or did they just nudge themselves that way?

---

1. As a young adult, I watched the news regularly. That started to wane until around 2015 or so I just stopped watching any and all news. It was not improving my life in the least bit. I have a lot of disdain for what news has become and feel bad for those who do believe in and want to practice legit journalism. So, those feelings are gonna come across here.

"Ok, listen up, everybody! This is going to be a live broadcast. People back on Earth want the unaltered truth, and that's what we at World Insights always give 'em. Our viewers are lucky 'cause they never have to choose their news because we've chosen it for them. Keep it real, keep it fun! We're makin' history here, people! We'll be live in ten!"

Ruby was fully aware that while a communications signal was leaving Astroll 2 as it happened, it would be nearly 20 minutes before anyone on Earth received it. Not quite 'live' exactly. Live, but with enough cushion room to edit anything out.

"Now, does anyone need anything?" the producer finished with.

Ruby raised a hand slowly and peeked over her shoulder, seeing that she was the only one who did so.

"I could use some water," she said.

The producer nodded at an assistant who presumably rushed off to take care of that.

"Anyone else? No? Ok, so here's the deal. We'll be running the intro, and then Garrett Spradley[2] will walk in and take his seat here. He'll be running things for the whole 30 minute spot and introduce all of you to the audience. Every three minutes there will be a 30 second sponsorship break. About 15 minutes in, we'll bring in the robots."

Ruby didn't know that the robots would be on live until this moment. Something didn't feel right about that. She wished she had talked to them in advance of this to make sure they were okay with it. But they were just finishing up their formal station tour[3].

"You'll know when we're live versus on a break by this light set here," she pointed to a monitor. "It'll be blue when we're live and green when we're in a sponsorship break. It will flash red for 10 seconds before returning to live. And will flash yellow for five seconds before a break. Remember... those breaks are only 30 seconds long. Not much time to do much of anything. Stay put during those breaks, please!"

She looked over at the guests. She approached Uncle Logan and tried to press his hair down. When it didn't stay, she frowned and moved to look over the other guests. To Professor Coronik and the mystery guest next to him, she produced a curt smile and nodded approval. When she reached Ruby, she said, mostly under her breath, "I wish we had had a little more time on your hair."

"What's wrong with it?" Ruby asked.

"Pulled back ponytails are not very sexy. No, they're not in right now at all," the producer said. "I can tell you have some really nice curls. Curls look great on camera. We should have taken that ponytail down."

Now it was Ruby's turn to frown a little. She didn't really care what she looked like. That wasn't important. What was important was telling all of humanity how wonderful these alien robots were.

"Three minutes, everybody!" the producer shouted and looked around at her crew to examine everyone's state of readiness.

That was enough time, Ruby thought, so she turned around enough to get the attention of Mr. Mystery Guest. They locked eyes for a moment, and just as she was about to ask, "Who are you?" she heard some people making a commotion at the front of the Hub.

---

2. I never came up with an actor inspiration for him!

3. Originally, I had written that station tour as a scene. It was fun to see the robots react and fun to get more insight and details of the station... but ultimately I cut that scene because it did nothing to move the plot/story forward. Maybe I'll dust that off and release it as some interesting separate bit of content someday...

She looked over and saw several people talking and waving their hands. They were clearly having an argument. One where she couldn't make out the words anyone was saying because they were still too far away, and the sound wasn't carrying.

Uncle Blake had stood up from his assigned seat and scooted out in front. He looked at Ruby. "Stay here," he said.

"Hey!" said the producer. "We only have two minutes before we're live!"

Uncle Blake held up a finger to indicate this would just be a minute. Ruby was trying to look to see who she recognized in the crowd.

As her Uncle Blake got closer, she realized she recognized Char—wasn't Char the one taking the robots on the formally planned and sanctioned tour of Astroll 2? Where were they if not with them?

Blake engaged and then jogged back to Ruby. He was smirking, so she knew the robots were okay.

"The robots," he was shaking his head, "are busy. Char couldn't get them to leave the Arcade."

"Don't they know they're on a live broadcast in about 15 minutes?" The producer looked like her head was going to literally explode. Possibly on a live broadcast.

"I could get them," Ruby said.

The producer shot Ruby the ugliest, freaking-oh-my-god-no-you-don't look that was possible for a human being. "Absolutely not!" she said. "You are our main guest. You *cannot* leave."

Ruby shrugged, sharing a look of comedic approval with Blake. "Ok, I guess. Maybe humanity will have to wait to meet the robots."

"Maritza!" shouted the producer. A thin figure appeared as if by magic from nowhere, having provided a tumbler of water on a little console table to Ruby's side.

"Please find those robots and tell them that Ruby has asked for them," the producer said.

Ruby was not keen on having her name used like that, but in this case, she wouldn't protest. In truth, she thought it was a good idea for the robots to be introduced to humanity with her there to help facilitate and interpret since she was certain that it would take a while for anyone else to get used to the literal way they spoke and processed anything they heard.

The lights were dimming in the Hub, Uncle Blake returned to his seat, and Ruby realized she never had the chance to ask the Mystery Guest who he was. He had remained silent so far.

Music started playing. Ruby couldn't tell where it was coming from. It sounded familiar. Whatever show this was, she had probably seen it once or twice and forgotten. The word 'live' was repeated in various tones and at various pitches in a not-quite echo effect.

"Here is your host, best friend to all humanity, Garrett Spradley," also came from the same source as the music.

Then a man sat in the seat that had remained empty until now. His hair was white but not from age, and it rose high above his forehead. He wore a flat blue suit with a collar and generally looked well put together. Ruby also thought she recognized him and decided she should probably pretend to know who he was.

"Hello humanity! Good morning, good afternoon, and good evening to wherever you are watching this from. We have an amazing special edition of Humanity and Truth, live, from Astroll 2. Many of you know Astroll 2 as the space station you've never heard of. We're half a billion kilometers away from Earth in the main asteroid belt, a place where humanity has been quietly mining the asteroids for more than 100 years. Click on the links to learn more!"

Ruby watched as he shifted from looking at one camera to another. Ruby had missed the fact that there were a variety of cameras set up. She was told to not even look at any, but only at Garrett, the interviewer. She wondered if he was nervous at all. This was historical news, even Ruby could appreciate that, and he seemed so perfectly pampered and articulate. So much so that it almost bothered her. No, not almost. It *did* bother her.

"I'm your host, Garrett Spradley and right now... wow... I am so pleased and privileged to be speaking with Ruby Palmer along with her close family, friends, and colleagues. The only way you don't already know about Ruby Palmer is if you've been in a coma these past two weeks. And even then, that was probably the first thing you were told when you woke up: That Ruby Palmer is the first human to, without any doubt, have made contact with intelligent alien life from outside our solar system."

Now, he looked directly at Ruby.

"Ruby Palmer. I am honored."

"Um, thank you," Ruby said.

"Everyone has heard the basics of the story, but not directly from you. Tell us in your own words how you came to meet these aliens."

"Alien robots," Ruby corrected. She wanted to be as careful as she could with her terminology. She couldn't imagine the implications of miscommunicating something to all of humanity.

"Yes, of course."

"It's pretty simple. I was in my ship, and one of them, well, captured me."

"Captured? As in kidnapped? Are the aliens hostile?"

"I guess you could say I was kidnapped, but no, they're not hostile. They were looking for something that they thought I had."

"Well, they kidnapped you. That's a crime here." He said it, but he said it with a weird smile that Ruby was unsure how to interpret. It certainly made her feel like she was saying something wrong.

"It's fine, really," Ruby said, trying to make sure that this didn't go in a direction she didn't want it to go in. She attempted to gloss over it. "Call it a mistake. But yeah, they took me in their ship back to their home world. They call it Location Zero."

"Location Zero!" he said in his best interviewer voice. "Now that sounds like a perfect vacation spot." He chuckled at his own lack of a joke.

Ruby didn't acknowledge it, whatever it was.

"Moving on," he said, "Tell us. What did the robots do to you?"

"They didn't *do* anything to me. They wanted to test my DNA, which is no big deal. But they couldn't, and while we were trying to figure that out, I realized they had some problems, and I helped them. And we became friends."

"They didn't try to dissect you?" He looked at one of the cameras and smirked while he said this, then turned back to Ruby. "We've all seen movies and shows where that's what aliens try to do."

Ruby remembered back to when that's what she thought was going to happen, and when even some of the robots themselves thought was going to happen. She realized this was one of those situations where she probably would be better off not revealing every single detail. Just the gist would be enough.

"No, they didn't. Of course, I wouldn't be here if they did!"

"And who created the robots?"

"They don't know," Ruby said. "That's what they're searching for. Archives that will tell them where they come from. Who made them."

"Interesting. Now, let's move on to some of our other guests." He turned to the Mystery Guest first. Ruby was a little surprised that that's all he wanted from her, but at the same time, a little relieved to not have an extended time in the spotlight.

Mystery Guest was sharp-looking in a way that oozed wealth. Not just wealth, but uber wealth. The kind of wealth that filled people with hatred. And it made Professor Coronik, prime connector of the wealthiest church in the history of religions, look poor.

"First, we are very lucky to have with us Pat Marsden[4] of The Company. Mr. Marsden, thank you for being here today. This is, for all intents, your space station…"

Pat Marsden!? Ruby had heard the name, but it was always just a name. A name that held a mysterious, shadow-like power that she could never imagine a face to go with it.

"Oh, no, no, it is owned in part by all the long-term residents here."

Ruby pursed her lips together. He wasn't telling the entire truth. The Company owned the station. Everyone who lived here over sponsorship age received a fraction of a share in the station. Enough to get voting rights at annual board meetings, but not enough to do anything else with. Ruby knew enough, mostly from overhearing others, that the only reason The Company granted a part of a share was so it could make statements like the one Pat Marsden just made in news interviews like this.

"But it is Astroll 2 that is the site of this historic event, it is the legal residence of Ruby Palmer, who will go down in history as humankind's first contact, and it is currently playing host to three of Ruby's alien robots."

Ruby wasn't sure how they became hers but wasn't going to argue that point. She was more in awe of Pat Marsden, who owned The Company. Although it was his mother who started The Company, he was brought up specifically to be its heir. Grade school students learned about The Company and him in a form of standardized civics and economics class. Given she lived on Astroll 2, she had an advantage that she already knew a lot about The Company, and what she didn't know, she could ask her uncles.

In person, Pat Marsden looked like anybody else, only with fancier clothes. Ruby wasn't too surprised she found him that way. Celebrity—any kind of celebrity—didn't impress her.

"Yes, of course," Marsden responded. "That is why I'm here. Well, I was nearby on a survey mission. You may have seen our recent press release. We at The Company are looking for a site to host Astroll 3, since Astroll 2 has been such a success. But to answer your question, I am delighted that Astroll 2 and one of our residents are part of this historic event."

Ruby wondered if he was capable of remembering her name, or if he could only think about The Company and *his* space station.

Garrett Spradley looked directly into the camera and said, "We'll talk to Professor Lloyd Coronik, Prime Connector of the Church of the Blockchain, and get his reaction, right after this message from our sponsor."

The lights behaved exactly as the producer said they would. Ruby turned around to look at everyone else. She wanted to catch Uncle Blake's eye and see if she could telepathically deduce what he thought about all this, but before that could happen, she saw the 10-second indicator come on out of the corner of her eye.

---

4. One morning when I was writing this scene, I went on to Facebook and asked my friends if any of them wanted to let me use their name for a character. Pat has been a friend-colleague of mine since about 2009. His name worked for this and in one of my future T-Set books, Pat Marsden will be the main character!

Then she remembered that she wasn't going to be addressed next. She turned back and managed to catch Uncle Blake's gaze. She smiled. He frowned. Why was he frowning?

"And we're back! Now let's get the reaction of Professor Lloyd Coronik. As Prime Connector of the Church of the Blockchain, he is frequently making headlines. Most recently, with the Blockchain developed software, TERP, that's now responsible for 80% of the world's governments," he chuckled a little uncomfortably at that comment, but didn't pause. "Professor Coronik, welcome and tell everyone, how's that going?"

Coronik looked the most uneasy since Ruby had met him. Was that because of the mention of TERP?

"I thought we were here to discuss Ruby's robots..."

"Oh, we are, we are," Spradley said, not losing his smile. "But since you're here, we thought you'd give us an update on TERP."

Coronik took in a visible breath and said, "It's going well. We are working closely with the government's head of IT to work out any issues—"

"We recently broke the news of the backlog of issues, and wow—everyone was surprised!"

"Well, yes, and we've got our best teams working on it."

"You have plans to get TERP under control?"

Under control? Ruby made a mental note that she needed to research more about what they were talking about.

"Certainly. We have a team of people who meet daily to review and report on the backlog."

"And what about the team *working* on the backlog?" Spradley still kept his smile, but Ruby would have sworn that she saw some daggers in his eyes as well.

"Of course," Professor Coronik said and let go of the breath he was holding.

"But you're right, Professor Coronik," Spradley again faced another camera and renewed his smile. "We are here to talk about these remarkable alien robots. Is that what brought you out to Astroll 2? We understand that Church leaders rarely leave Earth."

"Well, this is an amazing historic event! As leader of the Church, I wanted to be here to help usher and guide humankind into this new era."

"What era is that exactly?"

"An era where we know for a fact that we are not the only beings in the Universe."

"Wasn't the Church involved in shutting down all forms of SETI research...?"

"Oh, that's an embellishment of the past. At the time, the Church merely thought that those funds were better suited to focus on many of the problems at home. And we were right and successful, as evidenced by the greener planet that we have had in more than 400 years..."

Ruby knew that was partly true. She knew that's what was taught to people. Earth was quite green, Earth's temperature was under control. But what she'd also learned from the communal expression hubs, outside any formal classroom, was that there were so many robots. And while these hubs had been the center of human social contact for almost 200 years, ever since the early days of the networked computers, they were not representative of the best humanity had to offer and had never been quality sources of factual information.[5]

The interview continued like this. The next few minutes was little more than banal banter between the interviewer and Pat Marsden of The Company and Coronik. Ruby couldn't tell exactly, but it looked like Marsden and the Professor had some preexisting dislike for each other. She couldn't fathom why. They were both part of the mega-wealthy elite and were probably only suited to hob-knob with each other. From Ruby's point of view, they should be best of friends.

Spradley barely asked Uncle Blake or Robt Plampton any questions. "How does it feel to have Ruby back?" "Wonderful—we were worried, of course." "How does it feel to be manager of the station during this historic event?" "Exciting—and I thought I was going to go down in history for being the longest running director." There was another sponsorship message before and after this set of questions.

When the interviewer got to Milo, Ruby could see him sweating. But not in the broadcast. A view of the broadcast was set up in Ruby's field of vision. She surmised that an algorithm must be in place to filter out Milo's sweat and make the older Marsden and Coronik have less wrinkles and imperfections than they really did.

Ruby didn't appreciate the fakeness but was grateful on Milo's behalf that the whole solar system wasn't going to see how nervous he was.

"Milo Jenkins," Spradley said. "You are the second person to have met the robots. When you met them, you must have had a million thoughts running through your head. Tell us, what were those thoughts?"

"Well, I was happy to see that Ruby wasn't harmed."

"Was that your primary concern?"

"Yes, of course."

Ruby could now see that he was blushing slightly under the sweat, and noticed her own cheeks felt a little hot.

"Well, the two of you now have something in common... the first humans to have ever met aliens. That puts you both in a special category."

"I guess so," Milo said.

"And when the robots met you, were they friendly? Did they try to hurt you in any way?"

"Of course, they were friendly. I know Ruby wouldn't have brought them here otherwise."

"And we're going to have one more message from our sponsors, then I hope everyone is ready to see those robots up close!"

Once again with the lights, and the second they came on, the producer was shouting, "Bring them in!"

There was a commotion, but Ruby could still see SD and Disto enter the Hub. The producer and her assistant escorted them to the area right next to Ruby and lined them up next to her.

"The camera is over there. But don't look at it. Look at him."

The robots followed the arm that was pointing to Spradley. They continued to look in that direction, like statues.

Ruby wasn't sure if they were going to make it in time, but magically, with two seconds to go, the producer and her assistant were out of the way, and all of a sudden Garrett Spradley was saying, in a somber voice, "and we're back. With very special

---

5. And here you're seeing some of my real opinions on contemporary social media come out. I'm a pretty heavy user myself, particularly of Facebook, and I try to find the good in it, but I also see a lot of harm and worry what this has done to us...

guests. Probably the most special we've ever had or ever will have on this show. And we are grateful that we are the first ones to bring you... the alien robots."

He surveyed them and a wrinkle formed in his forehead. He looked genuinely caught off guard for a moment, "Wasn't there a third robot?" he said aloud and then as if he was getting an answer directly into his ear, mumbled, "uh huh," and then "mmm." The wrinkle disappeared, Spradley's direct smile returned, and everything resumed.

The broadcast screen filled with the three of them. Ruby and the robots. She tried to keep a pleasant smile, but she was nervous. More nervous than when it had just been her.

"Ruby," he said. "Do you want to introduce your...uh, friends?"

Ruby exhaled the breath she didn't know she was holding.

"Certainly," she said, and at those words she became excited to do so. She had a brief moment to wish that she knew this was what she was going to be asked, so she could have prepared herself, but it was okay.

She turned towards the robots and hoped that they were relaxed and not nervous. Why would they be? They didn't have those emotions.

"This is Detailed Historian. We call him 'Disto' for short. Next to him is Swell Driver, 'SD' for short. Guys, say 'hello.'"

Disto and SD said 'hello' in unison.

"Very interesting names," said the Spradley.

"Yeah, and they can be a mouthful, hence the nicknames."

"And which one of these kidnapped you?"

Ruby was feeling a little more comfortable and confident. "Yeah, let's not call it that anymore."

"What would you suggest instead? It was a ride-share service?"

"To answer the original question, SD was the first that I met. It's his ship that first connected with me and my ship, *Apple Pi,* and it was also his ship that brought us back and is docked outside Astroll 2 right now. I know everyone has seen pictures of it by now."

"Of course," said Spradley. "And how do they communicate with you?"

"We are capable of producing the same sounds as you," Disto said. "We talk. We are capable of multiple modes of communication. A variety of methods. And we understand your language very well."

This threw the interviewer off. He obviously wasn't used to any guest exerting control in that manner. Ruby smiled.

Chapter 17

Blake checked the expected delivery time on his phone. The flowers would be delivered to Logan at his office shortly. It wasn't a typical flower arrangement. They were all fake. As much as Logan enjoyed them, real flowers released too much pollen and could interfere with his job as an odorist.

The Company hired Logan shortly after the wedding, so not only was their first wedding anniversary coming up, so was his at The Company.

He walked down the sidewalk, making sure to avoid straying into the lane devoted to delivery bots and drones. He had opted for an old-school smartphone instead of the communicuff or eye-piece that most people had. He admitted the eye-piece would have been nice. He could be looking up and multi-tasking. Plus, he knew there were walking lane assist features that would ensure he was going the right way—which he often found that he was not.

But nope. Old phone for him. Logan teased him about it sometimes and at the end of the day, kept an old-school phone, too, just to humor his husband.

Blake did look up to find the sign of the store he was looking for. There it was. The bakery called *Bake District*. It was one of the places they had randomly wandered into on one of their first dates, on a recommendation from his pastry-chef mom, who happened to know the best bakeries in every major city.

Blake could easily have ordered remotely. But he wanted to walk in, smell all the warm vanilla in the air, and make a decision based on that, rather than from images you couldn't grasp or experience. It was too easy to deceive customers through advertisements, no matter how many countermeasures were in place to prevent such shenanigans, so Blake made a point to try and go in person whenever he could.

This bakery still made much of their stuff from hand, so each item had its imperfections and to Blake and Logan, that was heaven.

As he walked in, the pleasant scent of fresh bread hit him, and he took a deep breath. This was anniversary gift part two. Part three would be his attempt to cook dinner. He had plans for that, too, but it would have to wait until later when he was home. For dinner, he selected a menu and let the AI make the shopping list, place the order, and arrange delivery. While he was out, a robot drone would deliver, and their household suite would take care of the items.

He looked around. Something was off. Admittedly, he'd only been here that one time with Blake, but it felt different. Blake approached the counter and figured out what it was. There was no one behind it.

A robot arm on a floor track, what he recognized as a standard retail model, detected him and moved over, "How may I help you today?"

"Where is the owner?"

The robot arm pointed to a screen and must have clicked something since the menu that was displaying changed to a scrolling set of words. Blake read the story. Apparently, the owner had a stroke, and his kids took over the business. The kids had made changes that allowed the store to continue to financially operate. They were not bakers like their father but hoped that automation could keep the place going. Then the text went on to thank their customers—calling a few out by name—for accepting these changes.

Blake didn't have another plan, so he would have to accept it, too.

He examined the offerings in the case. They were all perfect. Too perfect. Human hands were no longer involved in creating these. As if on queue, the back door opened, and another robot arm appeared with a tray of fresh biscotti. The first arm opened up the case, took out an empty tray, and the second arm placed the fresh tray inside, took the empty tray from the first arm, and returned to the back kitchen.

The cookies looked perfect. They smelled heavenly. But there was something off about them. They reminded Blake of plastic, toy cookies that kids played with.

Nevertheless, that was one of the things Blake selected. While the robot arm was collecting the pastries into a box, Blake's phone rang. It was Jade.

"Where are you?" she asked.

"That bakery I told you about," Blake said.

"Can you talk?"

"Ehh... In a minute I'll be back outside walking. Where are you?"

"Work. Well, I'm working. Ruby had a little fever so we're at home. She's watching some old cartoons and laying down in my bed."

"Is she okay? Does she need her Uncle Blake?"

"She's fine. Really, just a little fever. But she did ask for you and I told her we'd see you this weekend."

Blake smiled. Both he and Logan loved spending time with Ruby and talked about adopting their own child. Ruby was so... uncomplicated. She liked to play and pretend and play some more. If her toys gave her any problems, from needing power to breaking in two, she liked to solve it herself and never got upset over it for very long. And when she was done, she liked to snuggle up and make him read her a book. There was no stress, no worries. Only simple play stuff.

The robot arm now held out a white box tied with a string and made a soft chime indicating it was ready to pick up. Blake grabbed the box and smiled, a little sad that he missed the opportunity to not only say "thank you" but talk to the person who made the goods.

Box in hand, he left the store.

"Okay, I'm outside, headed to the metro, but I can wander a few more minutes before I need to head back to the apartment. I'm cooking dinner."

"Oh, that's right—anniversary. Your gift is on the way, I promise!"

Blake smiled to himself. He knew there was no gift on the way. Jade was the worst when it came to remembering birthdays, anniversaries, and such, and hence, was the worst when it came to giving gifts[1]. It didn't bother Blake. He didn't need or want anything that he didn't already have.

"So, what's up, Jade?"

"Remember we talked about Astroll 2?"

"The space station? Of course." Blake used to fantasize routinely about carrying out some ridiculous covert plan to set up a secret space telescope but hadn't had those thoughts in a long time.

"That's where it's all happening," Jade said.

"All what is happening?"

"The research. I found it. I found the construction plans. One of the planned rings—it was never part of Astroll 1 and there's almost no detail. That was always a little sketchy. It was too much space for what it needed to do. Well, that's because there's a lot more going on there than what people know."

"How did you find that?"

He knew Jade so well, he could see the exact facial expression she was making while she said, "You know all you need to know. The important thing is I think that's where you need to go."

"Excuse me? You want me to go to the space station."

"No, I don't want you to go. Well, I want you to go, and I want us to go. But you know I could never get there with my background. But you and Logan could... heck, Logan already works for The Company..."

"...and I could get a job there easily, I know. But Jade, I'm not a working astrophysicist, remember. I'm an engineer."

"All the better. Look, I can... add some records for you. You'll get hired easily."

"We need to talk about this more. Later."

"Can I come over? I'd rather show you in person. Look—I'll help you do a little of the cooking, and I'll be out of there before Logan comes home."

"What about Ruby?"

There was silence for a minute.

Blake also knew his friend well enough that he knew exactly the conflict that was going on in Jade's head. She had refused to install the commonplace nanny bot system. It was also inexpensive, made for people with few options and resources. It was essentially a safe room for ages three and up. You deployed the plexiglass container in a room, and a robot arm and series of cameras and AI watched your child. You could always look at the child and interact over voice or video. The system monitored the child's heart rate and ensured that nothing dangerous happened. You could leave approved toys in there, and the system could even play educational videos.

It was approved by the government and had various doctor's seals of approval.

But Jade didn't like it. She ranted about how unnatural it was and how a robot arm and AI shouldn't be left to care for a child, and she couldn't bear to let it care for hers.

---

1. Now is probably a good time to confess this. If I'm any character in the Robot Galaxy Series, I'm Jade. When the books first came out, in interviews, people would frequently ask me if I see myself as Ruby. Nope. Jade. I'm Jade.

When situations like this came up, she reconsidered that decision and always came on the side of, "Crap, Blake. If she didn't have this fever, I'd just bring her with me."

Blake chuckled, "And she'd be picking at all the food I'd be cooking, not to mention the pastries I'm carrying right now that smell so good."

He thought for a moment. He did want to know more about Astroll 2, although he was certain there was no way he'd ever manage to get there. But something in the back of his brain told him it made sense. It was a corporate entity, far from any government. The perfect place and platform for advanced extra-solar research that wasn't allowed here.

"What about tomorrow?" he asked.

Jade sighed. "Okay, this can wait. I'm certain I'll be home with Ruby tomorrow, too. You can come here anytime."

"Great. I'll let you know. Give that little girl a kiss from her uncle. Tell her I'll read to her when I'm there."

"Thanks. She'll love that. She loves her Uncle Blake. Let me know when you're headed over, okay?"

"Will do."

"Oh, and Blake? Happy anniversary. I mean it."

"I know," Blake said. "Thanks." Then he broke the connection.

He had been wandering aimlessly throughout the call, and now he looked up. He was a block from where he needed to be to catch the metro back to their apartment.

Logan had tried to talk Blake into getting a job at The Company. The Company was one of the largest employers of people with advanced scientific degrees in the region. Every now and then, Logan would forward Blake an interesting job requisition that listed an Astrophysics degree as one of the qualifications, mostly related to the ongoing search for qualified asteroid candidates to mine.

Now Jade had jumped on the bandwagon to encourage him to also go work for The Company. Blake knew she wouldn't encourage him on a whim. He also knew that she understood how important uncovering scientific mysteries and picking up where humanity had left off—on the verge of discovery—was, to both of them. Blake sighed. He now had a bigger present to give his husband—the news that he would consider a move half-way across the solar system.

Chapter 18

The interview concluded with more ridiculous questions like whether or not the robots wanted to visit one of the popular theme parks on Earth. The robots handled themselves admirably. Disto was the one who spoke the most. SD hardly said anything.

The last question Spradley asked Ruby was: "What now?"

"I'm...I mean, *we're*," she gestured towards the robots, "We are headed to Earth."

"Obviously," Spradley responded while smiling directly into the camera. "But Ruby Palmer, what's next for *you?*"

Ruby didn't know what to say. Her mouth hung open for what felt like an eternity before Spradley must have realized that her mind was a complete blank, and he chimed in with, "I'm certain you have more options than you can count."

And then back to the camera, he said, "I'm certain the whole world, everyone who is everywhere, will be watching what you do next, Ruby Palmer."

Ruby could feel sweat beads form on her forehead. The last thing she wanted was for everyone to be watching her.

"Thank you for joining us live for this special edition of Humanity and Truth. I'm your host, Garrett Spradley, and until next time," he paused for what must have been dramatic effect, "stay voracious!"

After that, the light that was shining on Ruby and all the other guests turned off. The overhead lights of the Hub turned back on, and the producer went over and whispered in the interviewer's ear.

"That's great!" Spradley said. "I don't think it's possible to have more viewers than that!" The whole interview had lasted nearly an hour, and given it took almost thirty minutes for the broadcast to reach Earth, they already knew from their office back home how many people were logged in and watching the interview.

Spradley stood up.

"Ruby Palmer, great to meet you," he held up his hand in a soft wave. "Professor Coronik, Mr. Marsden..." he said something to every other human there. He ignored the robots. She watched him glance at them, but clearly, he didn't want to talk to them any more than he had to.

Was this going to be typical? People on Astroll 2 seemed generally fine, especially after they heard the robots speak and realized how nonthreatening they were.

Uncle Blake came up to her, took her hand, and smiled. She was about to ask him what he thought of her performance, but before she could say anything, the producer came up to them, too, and started speaking.

"Okay, you should know, while that was live, once it finishes playing out on Earth, it's going to continue to be available to replay on our parent channel. Of course, you can watch it, but a word of advice: don't read the comments."

"Wait, you allow comments?" Ruby asked.

That was unusual. There was even a time when it was illegal. But those laws were overturned before Ruby was born. Reading comments was not something she did. *Most* people were savvy enough not to either. It was weird that they just told her not to, like they were deliberately trying to make her curious, dangling something in front of her that she shouldn't do.

She felt Uncle Blake squeeze her hand, as if he was reading her thoughts. The hand squeeze said, "you know better." Then he let go and walked away.

"Yes, of course. It's all about engagement through the communal expression hubs. The more engagement, the more advertising. C'mon, we've been doing this for literally hundreds of years."

Ruby shrugged. "Okay, I guess. I really don't want to see myself anyway, so I'm not going to watch."

And then she turned around, and Inny was there, talking to the robots. Not just talking to them but showing themselves video of the interview. They were all hovered around a tablet she was carrying.

Inny was giggling.

"Ruby, you all looked great on camera! I saw it live! And look... look how many pos reactions so far! Okay, this one's pretty bad...but the rest are totally pos! Everyone loves you! Can I interview you next for the portfolio I'm building? I'm taking a freelancers class through The Company's school."

Ruby looked. There were indeed a lot of pos reactions coming in. She hadn't heard exactly the estimate of how many were watching it live, but she could appreciate the uniqueness, and understood that everyone knew who she was by now. While she had been staying away from the news, deliberately, her uncles and even Milo and Inny had told her some of what was reported.

She suspected they were leaving out parts. Every celebrity was researched to death, and it was easy to find information on someone's whole life. Not that she had done a lot before the whole robot thing, so she couldn't imagine that there was much to gossip about in her case.

Her mom died when she was young. That was probably the most interesting thing about her. She since lived on Astroll 2 with her uncles. Big deal.

"What's this?" Disto asked.

"Oh! That's the best part! That's the comments section..." said Inny.

"No, don't show them that," Ruby reached for the tablet.

"Comments?" SD asked.

"Seriously, Inny... don't show them that."

"But that's the best part," she said. "Here, let me read some to you."

"Um... robots are cute... Ruby is cute... Professor Coronik is... uh, I'll skip that... oh here's something good, 'those robots are fake, my kids could have dressed up better...' um, okay, that was weird..."

"Inny, really. Stop."

Inny held the tablet and was scrolling down. She was frowning.

"Maybe you were right," and handed Ruby the tablet.

Ruby couldn't help but peek. She saw, "Ruby Palmer must die for bringing the alien invaders here!"

"Doesn't everyone know that Astroll 2 is fake? It's a TV show. They're in one of the abandoned movie lots in La-La Land. This isn't real."

And it went on from there. Every now and then, someone said something nice.

"Uncle Blake…" she looked up, trying to hold back tears. "We can't go there…"

He put his arm around her shoulder and took hold of the tablet, pressing the off button as he did.

The robots were all looking expectantly at them, too.

"What does this mean?" Disto said.

Blake was the one that answered. "You're going to learn that humans are, well, still learning how to behave."

"Can't they be re-programmed?" SD chimed in.

Ruby and Blake both chuckled, and he said, "I wish."

"You never explained how humans are programmed in the first place."

"Well, we're not 'programmed,' but we are educated." Ruby said.

Blake raised an eyebrow, and Ruby added, "Ok, some people are educated. Most, probably."

"What is 'educated'?" Disto asked.

"It means we learn information."

"Ah—and I remember—no ports," SD said, and Ruby smiled, remembering the first time she had to explain that her orifices were not data information ports.

"Yeah. We read, we listen to others. And our brains need to assimilate whatever comes in to understand it. Frankly, it might be easier if we *were* programmed."

"Some people think we are," Milo chimed in.

Ruby had nearly forgotten he was there. She looked at his face and saw the red tones in his skin become a little more pronounced. Was he blushing?

"Several of the comments I saw alluded to that," Ruby said, frowning. "I don't understand people."

"It's okay, kiddo," Blake said. "I think we have a trip to get ready for, anyway. Professor Coronik is coming with us. SD, Disto, I hope it's clear that the best way for all of us to get to Earth is on your ship. Do you have room for all of us?"

"Yes," SD responded.

"Um, can we add some seats?" Ruby added. She looked back and forth from Uncle Blake to Professor Coronik to Robt Plampton. "They aren't exactly outfitted like our ships. They don't have seats." She pointed to the robots, "since they obviously don't need them."

Plampton said, "we can use the industrial printers to generate some. The mining operation has us loaded up with extra material, and even if we didn't, I'm certain The Company would let us use what we have on hand."

"How long will it take us to get there?" Uncle Blake asked.

"Get where?" SD asked back.

"To Earth," he said.

"To the third planet you had on your map of our solar system," Ruby added for SD and Disto. "The one with all the bios."

"From here? Only an appendage full of tics," SD said.

"A tic is roughly a second," Ruby translated for the rest of the humans listening in, "and an appendage-full, well, I think he means 'handful', but you know, they don't have hands." As she said it, she could have sworn she saw both Professor Coronik and Pat Marsden of The Company suppress a smile.

Milo whistled, "wow—that's fast."

"Fast?" SD said.

"Yeah, fast as in," Milo was clearly figuring out how to explain the concept, "opposite of slow... uh..."

Now, it was Ruby's turn to smile. She had gotten used to thinking how to explain terms she never expected to have to explain.

"Explain it mathematically," she said. "SD, you can calculate the velocity of something, correct?"

"Yes. The rate at which an object moves. It's the distance traveled over a period of time."

"Now if you have a certain distance, say, here to Earth which is," she looked to Plampton, "where are we right now?"

"We're actually on the close approach side. Roughly 300 million kilometers away," he said, and then in almost a mutter, "Spradley got it wrong when he said half a billion. Not right now, anyway."

"Ok, so, if you go 300 million kilometers in a few days," Ruby continued, "that's one speed. But if you can do it in a few tics, you're going faster."

"Ah," both robots responded in unison.

"And if it's a few millitics, it's even faster!" SD said.

"Correct," said Ruby.

"And what if you go a shorter distance in the same amount of time?" SD asked.

"We call that going slower. The opposite of fast."

"Opposite. We know that concept," Disto added. "Diametrically different. The reverse form of something."

"Yes," Ruby said.

"I am not familiar with that," SD added.

Disto proceeded to beep and chirp in his native tones. All the humans except for Ruby jumped back a step.

Ruby explained about their native language. It was the first time they might have used it around other humans besides her.

"They don't do it much," she said. "Disto and the others understand politeness, and to be polite, they speak our language as much as they can. But for efficiency, well—"

"I understand the concept of opposite," SD blurted out excitedly. "Near and far. Robots and Bios."

"Functioning and broken," Disto added.

"Yes, you guys got it," Ruby said.

"Planet and star," SD said. And then Disto and SD shot back and forth several more examples.

"It's like a three-year-old Sebastian, but double," Uncle Blake whispered into Ruby's ear. She remembered that time, when he was a toddler, and yeah, that might be why she had the patience for this. She had patience for him, too, when he was at those stages of asking a ton of questions. Often the same question over and over and over to reaffirm what he heard. It was normal for toddlers. The difference here is that once the robots got a concept she explained, they got it. There were no repeats.

"Well, I think we have a trip to prepare for," a voice boomed from behind Ruby. Professor Coronik made sure a large number of people who were still present stopped their own conversations to hear him speak. Headed to Earth was indeed what was next for all of them, and Ruby was happy to focus on that and not answer any more uncomfortable questions like what was next *for her*.

Chapter 19

> Ruby <

They were using a mini-R-pod to ferry all the passengers from Astroll 2 to SD's ship. It was Milo's pod, *Pecan Pi*, but *Key Lime Pi*—typically piloted by Harmony Ortiz—was standing by.

Milo had just arrived from delivering SD and Disto first. Next was going to be Ruby, Uncle Blake, and Coronik.

A news crew was nearby to watch. In the last several days, things on Astroll 2 had become frenzied. Even more than they had been.

Robt Plampton had to welcome more people on the station than he was comfortable with. The station typically held 2000 people at any given time. Roughly 5% of those people were temporary guests.

That was the ratio the station was designed to handle, with a little allowance for overflow. Temporary guests were given smaller quarters, had to eat at the mess hall, and most importantly, didn't have all the training that permanent residents had. And they were not expected to behave the way residents were expected to. But with only 100 or so at any time and plenty more residents, there were plenty of people to make sure that the guests didn't do anything, well, dangerous.

The station could hold close to 1000 guests if it had to. But that was only intended for emergencies—like if a ship that was nearby had to evacuate. Not that any individual ship produced by humans to date was able to carry 1000 people—the upper limit to the outer solar system was still only 100—but there could be an ultra-rare scenario where several of those had an emergency at once.

Right now, there were close to three times as many guests as Astroll 2 had ever handled before, and it was putting a strain on everything. The second Plampton realized it was going to happen, he ordered more supplies—which had arrived on the transport that carried Coronik—but still. It was annoying.

And now, as many of these guests as possible—who were mostly some form of media or press—were jammed into the viewing area of the hanger with their various forms of cameras and recording devices.

Uncle Blake was saying goodbye to Sebastian and Uncle Logan. Mostly for Sebastian's sake, they decided it was best for them to remain on the station. The plan was that Ruby and Blake would help Disto and SD find what they were looking for and then return to Astroll 2. No one was sure exactly how long they'd be gone, but Ruby promised Sebastian they'd be back before Sebastian's birthday.

"You haven't taken me to the arcade since you've come home," Sebastian said to Ruby, tugging on the sleeves of her jacket. She hugged him.

"I've been just a little bit busy, you know."

"I know... but I thought you were dead. You owe me."

Ah, the logic of a seven-year-old. Ruby hugged him again.

"Ok. You're right! I owe you. I'll bring you something from Earth. How 'bout that?"

"Where on Earth are you going?"

Ruby pressed her lips together, "I'm not exactly sure. Maybe Greenland." She really didn't know their ultimate destination on Earth yet, so she blurted out the first place that came to mind.

"You know green is my favorite color!" *Ah, the non-sequiturs of a seven-year-old.*[1]

"And you know Greenland isn't green?"

"It's not?" Sebastian said with a true sense of shock and wonder.

Ruby smiled and placed her palm against his cheek instinctively. She remembered it was the same comforting move her mother did to her. Sebastian closed his eyes, smiled, and leaned into it. He opened his eyes a few moments later when she pulled her hand away.

Milo came over, "Pre-check complete. Are you all ready to get on board?"

Ruby looked at Uncle Blake and Coronik. Both nodded. Then they all followed Milo onto *Pecan Pi* and took a seat.

"Interesting naming convention for your little ships," Coronik said.

"It was way before my time," Milo said as he closed the hatch behind them. Things were tight, but there were four seats, and everyone took theirs. Ruby sat in the co-pilot's seat and assumed this role, touching the console and examining the ship's systems.

"Mine, too, but Milo—haven't you read the plaque?"

"Oh right," he said.

"Plaque?" Coronik asked.

"It's on the hangar. It says, 'We commission these ships in the name of our favorite foods that we will never eat since we chose to live out on this monstrosity.'" Ruby said. She knew that underneath, it listed the first hangar chief and crew members, along with the first pilots. At the time, there were only two. The team had grown to a dozen active pilots, with more on Astroll 2 who could serve as co-pilot or come up to speed in an emergency.

"That's why are they all named after Pie?"

"Not Pie. *Pi.*"

"Excuse me?"

"Pi... the number."

Coronik nodded but uncertainly said, "Well yes, I've heard of pi. It's a very important number."

Both Ruby and Milo allowed themselves small smiles. Uncle Blake didn't. Ruby had noticed that Uncle Blake had become very tense and extra silent when Coronik was around in the last day or two.

She wanted to ask what was up but was waiting for the right time.

---

1. I wrote this a few years ago, but as I work on this annotated edition, my youngest kiddo just turned 7. And yup – he is Mr. Non-Sequitur a lot of the time!

Milo took his place in the pilot's seat and examined his console. Looking on, Ruby knew that he was waiting for the all-clear from the hanger crew. With so many people to clear out of the hangar, it would take a few minutes.

"Everyone strapped in?" Milo said. He turned around to make sure he had nods from all. As many times as Ruby had piloted *Apple Pi*, she never had this many people at once. She was usually tugging a piece of equipment around, that's all.

She wasn't sure if she would be comfortable with this many eyes watching her every move. Even if they were friendly eyes.

She also wasn't sure she liked the silence coming from behind her. Uncle Blake wasn't the chattiest of people. He was one of those 'only speaks if he has something to say' types, but she was surprised he didn't have more to say to the Prime Connector of the Church of the Blockchain.

So far, her interaction with Coronik had been pleasant enough. He seemed to genuinely want to help.

But a desire to help didn't completely jive with everything she had been told about the Church over the years to include how controlling they were. They were also unpredictable, exemplars at blaming others, and masters of the guilt trip.

Although could this be his attempt to control the situation?

"We're about to launch," Milo said. Ruby confirmed from her console.

He touched a button or two, and the ship lifted off the platform and a small propulsive force pushed them away from Astroll 2.

SD's ship was straight ahead. The large monstrosity already had its mouth open, waiting for them.

This was now Milo's third time piloting into the alien ship, and he seemed completely unfazed—like it was his 300th.

"It'll take a few minutes. Heck, it will take longer to get to the ship than it'll be to get to Earth," he said. Then shook his head and said under his breath, "amazing!"

"Sure you don't want to come with us?" Ruby said. "I'm sure that would be okay."

Milo ran his fingers over his head, not going through any hair because he kept it nearly shaved in a fade. His eyes were aimed at the floor, and then he looked up and locked into hers.

"I'd love to," he said, "but I still have a day job." He smiled.

Ruby smiled back and shrugged.

"Can we get Astroll 2 up on the monitor?" Uncle Blake asked.

"Sure," Ruby said. As co-pilot, she could take care of that. She pressed a button on the console, and a small display opened on top of the main window that showed what the cameras out the back end of *Pecan Pi* saw.

It was Astroll 2, looking directly at the spin axis and the hangar ring. The hangar door was already closed so they couldn't see inside. From this vantage point, Astroll 2 looked like a flat disk. They could see the rest of the "A" ring as well, since it had a larger diameter than the one they just exited. And that was about it. Everything behind that ring was obscured from this point of view.

"Thanks," Blake said. "It's been a while since I've seen it from the outside. I was curious."

Ruby smiled but watched as Coronik leaned in to take a good hard look as well. As if he was actually looking for something. He frowned a little and leaned back. All without saying anything.

"Okay, we're about to get taken in by SD's ship," Milo said.

They could feel the clunk of metal on metal as the mouth of SD's ship connected with the bottom of *Pecan Pi*.

There was no way for them to detect whether or not the air around the ship was breathable—mini-R-pods weren't equipped with sensors since the expectation was that the only two operating conditions would be out in space, where they weren't needed or on the hangar of Astroll 2, where a team of people were responsible and knew whether the air was breathable or not.

Milo pressed a button on his panel, "This is Milo on *Pecan Pi*. Are you ready for us?"

"Yes," Ruby heard SD's voice, "you may exit your ship."

Everyone unbuckled, but only Milo got up, went to the hatch and opened it. Outside, Disto was waiting.

"Greetingsss!" he said. Ruby smiled.

Blake exited first, followed by Coronik. Ruby was wondering why they were both taking tentative steps and realized that this was their first time on the ship. On an alien ship.

She had already gotten so used to the robots and their ship and things that she kept forgetting that this was new to everyone else.

"Welcome," she said. "To SD's ship. No name, like we name our ships. We just call it SD's ship."

"Actually," Disto interrupted, "it does have a designator."

"Oh?" Ruby said, "I didn't know that! See," she looked at Blake and Coronik. "I'm still learning, too."

"What is it?" she asked Disto.

"I can't tell you."

"Why's that?"

"Well, I could," he said. Then he made a screeching noise that had all four humans covering their ears.

"What the hell was that?" Coronik said. It was the first time he had spoken since they boarded *Pecan Pi* and left Astroll 2.

"That is the designation for this object," Disto responded. "Every object has one."

"...and there is no translation," Ruby nodded her head in understanding.

"Correct," said Disto. "Now, let me bring you to the control center and primary cabin."

"Wait," Ruby said, "We need to get Milo prepped to go back to Astroll 2."

Disto rolled over to the wall and connected to a console. A moment later, he disconnected and rolled back and said to the group of confused humans, "but he can't go back. We're already at the third planet from the star."

"What?" all four humans said simultaneously.

"Yes, I just confirmed with SD. He believed the instructions were to go to Earth right after you were all on board. Accordingly, he did."

Professor Coronik ogled in disbelief. "Then that means..."

Disto sounded proud, "We're here."

Chapter 20

"Where are we, and I mean, where *exactly* are we?" Ruby asked.

"At the stable point between Earth and its moon," SD said. "Standard parking location for any planet with a single moon."

Ruby understood. There were typically five such stable points in any two-body system. They were called "Lagrange Points" named after some ancient mathematician or physicist or something or other. Whatever they were called, they were points of gravitational equilibrium between the two large masses—the points where the gravitational pull was equal.[1]

The point in between two bodies, where they were right now, was called "L1" for short.

"Between Earth and the Moon is not a good place for us to stay too long," Coronik said. "There are several other objects here, most notably our E2M comm relay."

"We could go to L2?" Milo offered. L2 was the 2nd of the five points. It was on the other side of the Moon.

"Sure," Ruby said and shrugged her shoulders. No one else seemed to object. "SD, you know the other stable points?"

SD brought up a map on the main screen. It showed animated representations of the Earth and Moon and dotted lines that Ruby believed represented the gravitational field, given she recognized the five Lagrange points as blinking yellow dots.

"That one," she said, pointing to the L2 point.

"Understood," SD said.

"Please be careful," Blake said. "We have many valuable assets around Earth and the Moon."

"The ship is able to detect and avoid all objects," SD said.

Ruby got the sense that this didn't make Blake feel any better.

"Approaching destination," SD said, "and there is an object there. Putting on screen."

"What is that?" Ruby asked.

They all stared at what looked like a platform with some kind of pointing array on top.

"Oh wow," Blake said, "I know what that is... that's the ancient James Webb Space Telescope. One of the last of its kind."

"It was only supposed to operate for five or ten years," Blake continued, "but they were able to refuel it, so its mission carried on for nearly 40."

---

1. Yup, this is real stuff. Every two-body system has 5 primary Lagrange points. There's a good image of the Earth-Sun Lagrange points here: https://science.nasa.gov/resource/what-is-a-lagrange-point/

"I can circle around that point in space. That is another stable trajectory." SD offered.

"Uncle Blake, where are we supposed to land?"

Did Robt Plampton or the head of The Company give them any indication of who they were supposed to contact when they were here? Did Coronik know? Surely as head the Church?

"And do we have another problem? Can this ship land in an atmosphere?" Milo added.

"Ruby, I have never landed on a planet before," SD said.

"Never? I thought you flew all over the place!"

"I have, but I've never landed. Just docked."

"Let me ask you this... had you not swallowed my ship the way you did when we first met, what were you going to do to collect your sample?"

SD was silent.

"You would have come to Earth, right?"

"Correct. Bio Muck Ball 23 is the label in our database."

"And then what?"

SD was silent.

Ruby pursed her lips. This was disconcerting. How could he not recall?

"Well, never mind, I guess," she said. "But we still need a way to get to Earth. And a landing spot... assuming we can land."

Unlike the way they used the mini-R-pod to help them transfer from the ship to the station, the mini-R-pod wasn't suitable to enter Earth's atmosphere, either.

"What about Legacy Station?" Uncle Blake offered.

Everyone, well, at least all of the humans, who all knew about Legacy Station, looked at Professor Coronik. When they saw all the humans looking that way, the robots followed suit.

"Yes, we can dock with Legacy Station. And disembark from there."

Legacy Station was wholly owned and operated by the Church. It was a space elevator station. The first and only one of its kind, and up until now, only members of the Church were allowed in or on.

It touched down on the planet in the middle of the Atlantic Ocean. All parts of it were considered sacred, but the geo platform was the liftoff point to get to the Moon.

The Church claim that non-members couldn't use it was for liability reasons. They claimed it was all part of keeping things on the Moon functioning, and really, the only use was to service that. It would be too expensive for the average person to make use of.

But everyone was certain that Church members made regular pilgrimages for the view.

"I will call and make arrangements for us to dock at the station. Will you be able to navigate us into a geosynchronous orbit?"

"A planetary synchronous orbit," Ruby explained. "The 'geo' just means synchronous to Earth." Every planet or moon had their version of 'synchronous'—the orbit that made it look like you were moving with the ground, or hovering over it, depending upon your point of view.

SD beeped to indicate he understood, and as he maneuvered the ship towards a synchronous orbit, Ruby watched Earth grow bigger in the viewscreen. If you'd have asked her a month ago if she thought she'd be this close to Earth anytime in her future, near or otherwise, she wouldn't have been able to stop laughing long enough to say, "no."

But there it was, growing larger by the second. The planet of her birth. The planet of her mother's death. And a place she'd thought was always part of her past, not her future. Especially not her immediate, imminent future.

Chapter 21

Swell Driver wasn't used to having passengers on his ship. He never would have thought it would cause him distress, but it was. He was used to a typical trip consisting of him and his computer console, and that was all.

At least he could still communicate with the computer console in his native language. He would have been even more irritated if he had to deal with multiple levels of translation, such as the computer translating, and then he having to translate back.

In fact, he couldn't recall the last time even a robot was on his ship. Ruby, of course, was only recently a passenger, and he was thankful for her. She was a wonderful friend.

But he wasn't certain how to process all the other humans he had encountered. He wasn't built for that kind of processing.

Why couldn't he pretend they were unusual versions of robots? Reframe his viewpoint a little bit. That certainly would have been easier.

Maybe he could imagine they were robots like AT. Unusual and unlike any robot he had encountered before.

He thought. As he thought it, something didn't feel right. Like what was happening wasn't really true, even though he knew it was. He had clear memories all the way back to—

"There it is!" one of the humans declared.

SD turned his top chassis to see the human designated 'Blake' point at his screen. He looked where the pointing was occurring and saw the object he had recently detected. They called it a 'telescope.'

When SD didn't recognize the word, even though there was a translation for it, he asked the computer what it was.

Disto overheard, and had moved closer, obviously similarly curious.

"An object meant for observation."

"That isn't very specific," Disto responded. SD noted that he was also conversing back in their native chirps and beeps and was glad for that for a moment.

The humans were busy studying the object. All of them were interested in it for some reason.

To SD, it was just an object that was in the way.

"Make sure you don't disturb it, SD, please," Ruby had said.

"Acknowledged, but," SD said, "what is the significance of this object?"

"It's ancient!" she said. "Uncle Blake? You know a little more about these things."

"It was from the time that astronomy and astrophysics were respected scientific endeavors," Blake responded, "and not just a means to an economic end." SD saw that Blake had narrowed his eyes and glanced at the human designated Coronik. He wasn't sure what to make of that gesture or if it was one of the random and uncontrollable ones he learned that humans made all the time.

If he had not been a driver, he could have been a Zoologist. These beings were interesting, and it would have been an engaging position. But not so much that he was willing to violate his programming. He was a Driver. His programming dictated that, and that was okay by SD.

"I wish we could park and get a closer look," Blake said.

Ruby looked at SD, "Could we?"

SD asked the computer to compute a trajectory that would have them sidled up to the side of the object. The computer responded with the appropriate modifications to their current trajectory, which would have them go around it, around the Moon, and rendezvous with the station that was recently asked for.

"We can do that," SD said. "For how long will we hold position?"

Ruby looked at Blake, who said, "Wow. I, um, this is an amazing opportunity. I don't know. An hour? Does anyone mind?"

No one objected, so SD made the necessary modifications, and a few tics later, they were parked alongside the telescope.

"SD," Blake said, "Do you have the ability to take pictures?"

"Indeed," responded SD. "We are recording."

"Thank you so much. Did you know this is now a museum?" Blake added.

SD wasn't sure if he was meant to know that or not, but he answered honestly. "I did not."

"I didn't either," Ruby chimed in. "A museum? Like one people can visit?"

"There was a plan for that," Blake said. "A long time ago. After the one and only manned visit, there was an expectation of more. Technically, this is a historic monument, but one that no one visits. Probably a good trivia question for some trivia night someplace."[1]

"I'll try to remember that," Ruby said.

"See look," Blake said pointing at the telescope on the screen, "see the secondary sunshield that was added to keep the mission going after the first twenty years?"

"How do you know so much about this?" Disto asked. "I was under the impression that human's knowledge of the galaxy was limited."

"Yeah, Uncle Blake. How *do you* know so much about this?"

SD was certain he heard Ruby emphasize a few words in her question.

"Can I talk to you on the other side of the room or cabin or...whatever this is?" Blake said, facing Ruby.

"Sure," she responded.

---

1. I like to think that JWST will be out there indefinitely... but space is a harsh environment. The radiation from our Sun will cause the materials to break down and very likely it will disintegrate by the time this novel takes place (without any interventions).

The two of them walked to the back of the room, and while they lowered their decibels, it was still in the range of what SD was able to detect. He wondered if the intent was for him not to do such a thing, but it was his ship, after all. He was entitled to know everything that was happening within it.

"I had been meaning to tell you," Blake said.

"Tell me what?"

"About my real profession," he said. Quickly, SD had the computer tell him what 'profession' was.

"I wasn't just a homemaker," Blake was already continuing. "I had another purpose on Astroll 2."

"I was starting to wonder," Ruby said. "I hadn't thought too deeply about it before, but while I was gone, I had a lot of time to think and... never mind... what *do* you do on Astroll 2?"

"Extra-solar astrophysics research."

"But... but no one does that."

"We do. Quietly."

"But the Church..."

"...doesn't know. And can't know. That's one reason why I came, to make sure they don't suspect anything. To make sure this whole situation doesn't unearth a can of worms that *has* to stay underground."

"You've got more to tell me, don't you, Uncle Blake."

"Yes, but it's going to have to wait until we're on the ground."

After that, the two of them joined the other humans. Milo and Coronik were still looking at the viewscreen.

If human's outer chassis turned colors like his did, it might have been a high six threets, a color Ruby called "orange," indicating that she was frustrated. Although she was exhibiting many of the outward signs of Bio frustration. Maybe that's why humans didn't color like robots did, because their emotions couldn't be captured so discretely.

He also saw Disto, and suspected he was doing his best to remain polite.

> Detailed Historian <

Disto was doing his best to remain polite, but he was agitated. He was anxious. He was a lot of things, but he was activating his patience algorithm, the one that returned the result that it was 'okay to wait.'[2] It was the one that produced ancillary data that concluded that he had waited this long, so waiting a little longer was fine.

He watched his traveling companions watch an inanimate object out in space. They could see one side of it, illuminated by the host star.

SD provided him access to the second computer console. Typically, ships were designed with one Driver in mind, but occasionally there was a second, and so there was a second terminal. The humans called it co-pilot.

Either way, it kept his circuits mildly distracted. He was scanning all the emissions over a wide range of the electromagnetic spectrum that Ruby told him were in common use by her kind. There were emissions coming from the Earth—the humans

---

2. This was always the phrase I used with my kiddos... that patience means "it's okay to wait."

primary residence. There were also emissions coming from Earth's moon, another object in the system. Also, from Astroll 2, several ships that were moving throughout the system, and of course, all the spacecraft that were created by the humans and left all over their solar system. Their system was polluted with them.

"What are you doing?" Professor Coronik asked him. All the humans had been staring at the object in space, but it was possible that the object out there wasn't interesting to all of them.

"I am scanning," Disto replied. "There is a lot of... overlapping signals from a variety of objects."

He examined Coronik's face as he responded, observing movement over one of Coronik's optical sensors. Humans had a substance they called 'hair' on their faces—all humans had this on their faces, immediately above their visual sensors. Some of Coronik's hair moved.

"Indeed," Professor Coronik said simultaneously with the movement. "What type of signals?"

"They are predominantly from the orbiting planets in this solar system," Disto said. "But there is a lot of... noise... I think is the appropriate word or description. It is interesting that you can function with all of this out here. Is it all necessary?"

"Well," Coronik began, "You ask a good question."

"Do you have a good answer?"

The hair above Coronik's optical sensors returned to their initial position and then moved down some more. His face took on a similar one that he'd spot on Ruby occasionally. It indicated some form of displeasure. Disto couldn't compute why this simple question would produce that result.

"Well, as the head of the Church, I am generally unconcerned with these matters."

"Unconcerned does not mean you lack the knowledge."

"Well in this case, I'm trying to say that this is not my area of expertise. So no, I do not have a good answer for you."

"What *is* your area of expertise?" Disto asked. He was generally curious. "Heads" of anything would typically be chosen based on a certain level of experience and expertise, would they not?

Disto waited for Coronik to continue, but instead of responding, Coronik turned away from Disto. Maybe he had a circuit terminate abnormally.

"Well, speaking of signals," Coronik said, loudly, and grabbing everyone's attention, "I think it's about time I made contact with the station. To let them know to prepare for our docking and put SD," he said SD's name as if it was hard to remember, "in touch with the right people to coordinate that activity."

This soothed Disto's circuits that remained anxious for him to get on with his search.

"I will initiate a communications link for you," Disto said. "On what frequency?" It became a simple question once Ruby was able to understand what frequency meant. The robots used the term slightly differently than humans, and they both agreed that humans were the one who used it inaccurately. Humans, apparently, on average, didn't think of all the electromagnetic radiation as the same thing. They divided it up into different domains.

Nevertheless, Coronik did not respond to the simple question.

"Coronik," Blake said, "What is the communications frequency?"

"Well, I, uh," he said.

"You what?" Blake asked.

"I have people for that," he said.

Disto watched Blake look at Ruby, then at the floor, and shook his head and Disto could tell that Blake was also doing his best to remain polite, although he couldn't fathom why there was reason for anything otherwise.

"Disto," Blake addressed him, "I assume you can modulate a tone at 59.61 GigaHertz."

"Yes."

"Please do. They'll respond with a tone, and then voice communication will be possible," Blake said.

"How did you...?" Coronik asked Blake an incomplete question.

Blake gave Coronik a look from re-shaped optical sensors, one that Disto was unfamiliar with, and didn't say anything else until a human voice came through the system, "Legacy Station. This channel is for special use only. Who's there?"

Chapter 22

"This is unacceptable," Coronik said. "I am the Prime Connector—"

"I'm sorry, Prime Connector," said a voice that emanated from an image on the screen in front of him. "But we can't authorize you to dock."

Ruby, along with her uncle, Milo, and the robots, could do nothing but observe what she imagined must be a supremely embarrassing moment for Coronik.

"Which government has instructed you to do this?" Coronik said. He was seething. He was much better at seething than Ruby had ever been.

"Uh, well, all of them. Except for the unicameral congress of the Federates States of Micronesia. They apparently voted to allow it. But sir," the voice said, "It's not *really* the governments."

"What do you mean?" Coronik asked, beads of sweat visibly forming on his forehead.

"It's *you know who*," the voice said, almost whispering so someone or *something* wouldn't hear him, "it's the AI. It's TERP."

Coronik looked over his shoulder, and Ruby wondered why TERP was a subject of the conversation about them getting to Earth. She thought about asking, but Coronik didn't give her a chance.

"Ok, Micronesia it is then," he said and swallowed.

Ruby did not know much about this Micronesia place. In truth, she knew very little about the geography or politics, for that matter, of Earth. It was something she had avoided at every opportunity.

"I don't suppose Micronesia has a landing site?" Ruby asked.

"Well, Micronesia is a group of islands in the Pacific Ocean," Coronik said. "And no, they do not."

He looked at SD, "unless you can land on water?"

"This ship will interface with substances that have a surface tension of... I'm not sure how to define it for you," SD said. Ruby wasn't sure that Coronik's question required an answer but smiled at the fact that SD tried to answer anyway.

"What do we do?" Ruby asked. "Head back to Astroll 2?"

Coronik dismissed his underling on the video and leaned back, and steepled his fingers.

"Did they give a reason why?" Uncle Blake asked.

"Well," Coronik started, clearly uncomfortable, "The AI, TERP, it has, well, not been able to process the concept of alien robots."

"Okay, someone please explain what's going on with this TERP? If it's some AI, can't it just be turned off?" Ruby felt bad the second she said this out loud and looked at the robots to see if they were insulted.

Coronik's jaw tightened. Ruby looked at Uncle Blake, who answered.

"Similar to the AI that The Company provided to Astroll 2 and The Company's ships, the Church provided its own AI to the various governments of Earth. An upgrade," Uncle Blake said that last word while making quotes in the air with his hands.

"I know that part already," Ruby said. "That doesn't explain why everyone is so tense about it."

"Well, it was years in development and just as long in negotiations. We've had the best engineers and team the Church has to offer supporting this project," Coronik said, straightening himself up in a way that suggested he was giving a sales pitch for the millionth time. "It wasn't deployed until a few months ago, and it was..."

"Initially deployed in secret," Uncle Blake finished when Coronik couldn't.

"Well, no," Coronik stood and looked insulted. "It was done entirely legally, and all the documentation was available..."

Uncle Blake waved him off and continued the explanation. "If you followed some of the more obscure news then yes, maybe you would have known. I *have* been following it," and as he said that he shot Coronik a look that Ruby couldn't identify, "and it was only supposed to work on the governmental financials—it was supposed to balance the budgets of some of the most convoluted and complicated governments the world has produced."

Uncle Blake paused and continued to look at Coronik who looked like he wanted to hide under a rock.

Coronik's right eye twitched slightly as Blake continued, "It was done under *your* recommendation and persuasion. When the AI was deployed, TERP decided that there were more issues than just the budget. Then it decided it should run everything."

"What the...?" Ruby said.

"Yes, there are AIs running the governments of the world right now." Coronik's back slumped a little as he said this, and he made remarkable eye contact with the floor.

Ruby put a hand over her mouth as she tried to understand what this meant. She felt young and inadequate and, if she was being honest with herself, uneducated. She was, of course, aware of government, but once again, not something she paid much attention to in school and not something that she felt affected her life much on Astroll 2. Companies, not government, were in control usually. Weren't they? Government... well... what did they do?

Her whole image of Earth was shifting. She had dreaded returning, even for a short time, even for a visit, for so much of her life but she now recognized that her impressions of it, everything, was probably totally off.

Part of that realization made her want to go and see what it was all about. Part of it scared her.

She looked over at the robots. Robots, AI... was there a difference? The AI that Uncle Blake and Coronik were talking about—it probably didn't have a body and maybe that's the thing about it that made Ruby a little queasy...

"Where is this AI located?" Disto interrupted her thoughts. Ruby didn't realize the robots were listening in, but of course, they were.

The question was quite obviously directed at Coronik, and Coronik quite obviously didn't have an answer since his mouth was open and nothing was coming out.

Finally, someone spoke. It was Uncle Blake. "You've hit on one of the main problems, Disto," he said. "The TERP algorithm doesn't have a central processing location. It transfers around the global network."

Coronik looked relieved—too relieved—that someone answered for him. Something about that added to her sense of queasiness, so Ruby decided to be a little more direct with her next question. "Explain to me, Coronik, what's TERPs problem with these robots?"

"Well, your robots are... well, they have a level of sentience. I think TERP must see that as a threat to them," Coronik said. "And it's Profess—"

"Yeah, okay, *Professor*. But there are so many robots on Earth already, with all varying levels of AI," Ruby said.

"Yes, but none are sentient," Coronik said.

"Maybe we should consider them people in a robotic shell," Ruby offered.

Coronik scoffed, "Well, that is utterly ridiculous. No one will accept that man can be... man-made." He resumed the straight back and air of superiority that he donned since she first met him.

Ruby squinted and, knowing that she was on to something, straightened her own back. "There are plenty of people who have artificial components, right? Well, what if a person was fully replaced by components. What are they?"[1]

"Well, they are people, because they were born people," Coronik answered confidently. "But..." he trailed off as he looked around the room of humans and robots looking at him. "I'm not going to argue. We all want the same thing here, to get to Earth. Let me see what I can do."

> Ruby <

Coronik was in touch with the Deputy Commander of Legacy Station. Legacy Station—wholly owned and operated by the Church of the Blockchain—had to give Coronik much more than the time of day. They begrudgingly gave him the forms for the permits that were required to dock and continue on to Earth, not so much based on Ruby's argument that Coronik passed on, but more based on Coronik's not-so-subtle reminder that he had ultimate authority over their employment status with the Church.

"I am receiving a...very large...file," SD said.

"How large?" Ruby asked.

"It's 1024 hunks," SD responded.

"A hunk is what they call a Gigabyte," Ruby added before any of the other humans asked.

"I thought it was going to be a simple form," Ruby said. "SD, can you display it?"

SD tapped his console, and a form came up for all to see.

Ruby took control so she could scroll up and down. "You've got to be kidding me," she said.

---

1. I originally wanted to go deeper here. I mentioned earlier that my favorite philosophical paradox is the Shit of Theseus. Well, here... apply that to people. If a person has all of their organs/components replaced over time... are they still that person?

"The robots don't even have most of this information," she muttered. The form asked for fairly normal stuff—for a human. Birthdate, place of birth, gender—with all 12 options—eye color… and a host of other identifying features that could typically be autofilled from an image.

"Can we say, 'not applicable' to 90 percent of this?" she asked. She had SD transfer it to her communicuff so she could start filling it out. She had Pippa present the form in a hover screen over her hand.

"I'll help," Blake said. The two of them sat down on the 3D printed chairs. SD positioned himself next to Ruby so he could see the form as well.

As Ruby scrolled down the ephemeral image, SD exclaimed, "Oh look! There is contact information for a help center."

"Yeah, let's not do that just yet," Ruby suggested. "'Help centers' aren't always that helpful." She saw Blake and Milo both nodding their heads in knowing agreement. Coronik didn't respond at all. Ruby assumed that he likely had people who had people who filled in his forms.

Ruby responded 'not applicable' as much as she could. Any question that asked for a physical location she wrote in 'Location Zero' even though it didn't help autofill any of the other fields. 'Planet' wasn't a requested field anywhere.

She knew this was a general problem—she had it when she was doing school stuff. All the forms, while the school allowed for distance education to be completed from anywhere, even off planet, the forms hadn't been updated to account for the fact that someone's location was off planet.

To that end, she had used her grandmother's address a few times and hoped that her school didn't attempt to deliver any packages to her grandmother. Once, she needed a set of equipment for a laboratory class. Rather than have it shipped to her grandmother and have to explain that she needed it out on Astroll 2, Ruby decided it was easier to drop the class.

After several minutes of constructing creative answers to the questions, Blake let out an, "Oh no."

Before Ruby could ask what that was about, he continued, "This is the wrong form. This is an immigration form," he said.

"But the robots aren't immigrating, they're visiting," Ruby responded. Then she said, "Oh no," too.

Coronik got back in touch with the station, but this time demanded to speak to the station's Commander. He successfully communicated that it was the wrong form, received endless apologies, and was promised that the right form was on its way over.

Unfortunately, the next form wasn't any shorter. In fact, it was longer. They requested even more information for someone who was visiting.

While Ruby was re-inputting in her grandmother's address, Blake said, "We should go visit her while we're back."

Ruby looked at Uncle Blake and scrunched her face. "I barely know her."

It wasn't that Ruby didn't want to see her grandmother. Well, if truth be told, it was exactly that. She occasionally received letters from the woman, who was clearly in a facility for a reason. The letter would typically start out addressed to Ruby, but somewhere would transition into a missive with her daughter, Jade—Ruby's mother.

"Couldn't we see your parents instead, Uncle Blake?"

"They're a little harder to nail down from day-to-day. You know that, kiddo."

Since Blake and Ruby's mother had been childhood friends, he knew Ruby's grandmother better than Ruby herself did. Blake's own parents, who were retired and volunteering with the Paramount Global Pantry—a professional volunteer organization that used chefs, foodies, and nutritionists and sent them around the world. They knew and clearly remembered Ruby, as evidenced by their digital postcards—often from places Ruby hadn't heard of. She was thinking that maybe if she had paid attention to where they were each time, she would have a better idea of the geography of Earth. Blake's parents were pastry chefs. Well, his mom was a pastry chef, and his father was a famous chocolatier and they went around the world training people—and robots—in pastry and chocolate making.

They were technically retired, and as such, busier than ever as restaurants around the Earth called for their services to better train the people who should have been trained, but normally let the robots do their work. No restaurant kitchen was complete without at least a few robots involved in food prep and cleaning. Serving, too. There were humans that supervised. Or rather watched TV and listened to music in the backrooms, occasionally checking in on the robots. The robots rarely made mistakes, but Uncle Blake always said that sometimes the mistakes were the fun parts of restaurant dining.

Ruby shook her head back into her original question. She would much rather see the pastry chef and chocolatier than her own whack-a-doodle grandmother. But she sighed and left her grandmother's address in the form. *Pastry chefs give you cookies. Whack-a-doodle grandmothers give you odd, squinting looks that remind you of your mother.*

"Done," Ruby eventually declared. She pressed a button, and the computer did an autocheck. It passed. At least she managed to fill out all the required fields.

"What next?" she asked.

"SD should transmit it to the station, and I will have my people submit it," Coronik said. "I'm afraid that it is going to need to be copied to a regulatory agency of the United Nations responsible for global migration."

Disto squealed. "I get it!" he said. "I know the word for this. It's called bureaucracy. Yes! I learned that concept and this is exactly it!"

"Why are you so excited about it?" Ruby asked.

"It means that bits are moving, individuals are getting the information they need, and our activities are being coordinated amongst the different enterprises. Our actions are formalized. It's order amongst chaos!"

"Wow, Disto, I had no idea... back at Location Zero you seemed pained by your version of a bureaucracy system."

"That's because our system has degraded. It has flaws. You are well aware of these since you helped us fix some of them. But as any system grows, it needs order else everything will disrupt into chaos."

Ruby had never thought about paperwork as something that brought order to chaos. She thought about all the times it gave her headaches. All the times she was asked for information that could easily have been pulled out of a database. All the times that she was asked for information that had nothing to do with the task at hand. She thought about the times that she needed help, and whoever or whatever entity she was dealing with couldn't help when the situation was unexpected or didn't have an immediate protocol. That was probably the worst.

But she was always given the riot act about needing a digital 'paper trail.' Even though paper was an ancient relic, the term was still widely used and understood.

"I have received confirmation that our form has been received," SD said. And after a few moments, "...and a new form. Am I interpreting this correctly? It's asking for us to confirm that we've received the confirmation?"

Ruby looked over one side of SD's chassis and Uncle Blake looked over the other.

Blake said, "that's exactly what it looks like. It looks automated, too. I thought there were supposed to be humans handling these forms."

Professor Coronik coughed.

Everyone turned to look at him.

"Well, our AI might have gotten involved in some of the other bureaus as well..."

"There's more," SD said. "I'm getting additional requests... there are many."

Ruby read the headlines of the digital forms as they made it to SD's computer. There was one titled 'Declaration of Intent at Destination' and another 'Proof of Vehicle Ownership.' There was even a 'Non-Disclosure Agreement for Time Spent on Legacy Station.'

"All this to get back to Earth?" Uncle Blake said. The question was aimed straight at Coronik. "Would we have to do this even if the robots were not on board?"

"Well, no..." Coronik responded. "This must be because we're carrying aliens. The AI is trained to recognize them as foreigners and must be designing a new process on the fly. We've never had aliens before."

Chapter 23

> Ruby <

Now, it was a waiting game. With all the paperwork submitted. Did they have any food on board? Ruby was getting hungry, as her growling stomach could attest to.

The robots didn't need food. They needed power, which they could get from the ship.

Disto was plugged in and drawing power. Ruby watched and listened in as Coronik attempted to have a conversation with the robots to try and understand the root power source of the ship.

She knew it was a futile ask going in. She was not even sure how much the robots really even knew. But it was entertaining to watch, nonetheless. If AT was active, maybe he would have been able to explain more. Ruby put her hand over the pocket that held AT and realized that when she was filling out all those forms, she only mentioned SD and Disto. She thought about saying something but figured as long as AT stayed in his powered down and shrunken state, she could have been carrying a rock as far as anyone was concerned.

"We are not traveling at the moment," Disto had said when Coronik asked what they used for power.

"Well, I did not ask about propulsion, I asked about power," Coronik repeated. There were some beeps and chirps as the robots tried to parse what Coronik was saying. Ruby still didn't recognize any of them. Only a highly trained ear might someday be able to understand the robot's native language. Ruby was certain that this ear did not belong to her.

"Power," SD added, "is a force multiplied by speed."

Ruby squinted one eye as she called up memories of her basic physics class, and at least in her head agreed that that was the correct way to define power.

"But what supplies that force?" Coronik asked, believing he was getting somewhere.

"The ship," both robots replied in unison.

Coronik crossed his arms in front of his chest, holding one elbow in one hand and his lower face in his other. Ruby saw his shoulder rise and eyes close as he took a deep breath.

When his shoulders lowered, he opened his eyes and removed his hand so he could speak again. But before he said anything, he turned to Ruby.

"Can you assist?" he asked.

"I can try," she responded. "What exactly do you want me to do?"

"I want to understand what powers this ship and what powers them. Maybe if they were willing to share some of their amazing technology with us... you understand where I'm going with this."

Ruby smiled gently. "Professor, I don't think they are programmed," she air-quoted that last word, "to give us any of their technology. I'm also not sure any of the robots here understand any of their fundamentals."

"Oh?"

"Remember I was on their home planet for almost a month. It seems that whoever or whatever created them and gifted them with their tech is long gone, and they don't have solid memories. They know what they're programmed to know and not much more."

She looked over at the robots who were all watching her. Well, SD still had his face-screen trained on his console.

"Now can I ask *you* something," Ruby was feeling emboldened by the fact that they were out here, and she was surrounded by her peeps.

Professor Coronik's eyes shot up. "Certainly."

"Why are you really here?" she asked.

"Ruby," Uncle Blake reached out an arm, but Ruby turned to him and tried to telepathically say to him "it's okay, I got this."

"I want to help," Coronik responded.

"Really? How so? And how come you haven't been able to simply get us permission to land at your station. It is *your* station, isn't it? And you are the Prime Connector?"

"We are subject to laws just as anyone else is," he responded.

"But I thought you helped make the laws," Ruby looked him straight in the eyes, and then briefly caught Uncle Blake smirking proudly in her peripheral vision. "The Church is responsible for 90% of the algorithms and programming that is used everywhere, right?"

"That is an exaggerated number, but I understand your point. Let me talk to my people on the station again. Privately."

Ruby squinted at him and turned around to roll her eyes. Privately.

The only way to give him his requested privacy was for everyone to go down to where *Pecan Pi* was stowed. They did so. SD stayed with Coronik, but on the condition that if he overheard anything, he would keep it private.

Ruby was surprised that this was sufficient for Coronik but didn't question it.

While they were down in the hangar, Milo occupied himself with inspecting *Pecan Pi*.

"Something isn't right, Uncle Blake," Ruby said. Disto was perched by her side. She didn't mind if he overheard anything she had to say.

"Once we're on the ground, I'm sure everything will be fine," he said. He had a certainness about him that confused Ruby. It was the way he was standing, the stillness of his hands, the easiness of his breath.

"Uncle Blake..." she began. She got caught up in looking at him. In his narrow gaze, she saw someone slightly different than she'd known all her life. He didn't seem like a simple homemaker, or a caretaker, or an average Astroll 2 resident anymore. The revelation that there could be things still to uncover about him... well, she was still processing that fact.

She didn't know what to ask him.

"Astrophysics? How did I not know this?" she said, finally.

Uncle Blake smiled. "I'm sorry. That was intentional. No one could know."

"Does Uncle Logan know?"

"Somewhat. The general concept, yes. The specifics, no."

"And what are those specifics?"

"Well, I did go to the same University with your mother. But I studied physics and astrochemistry. I was starting a research project but it was shutdown before I could even get a good start. That university was one of the last places to be touched by the general degradation of science."

He looked to make sure Milo was still occupied.

"I found work easily enough. Especially since your mom helped."

"My mom? How? I thought she was a computer programmer?"

"Yes and no. She was a computer archaeologist. While you do have to be a programmer to do that work, she wasn't programming for the sake of programming. She was really an archaeologist of our modern digital times. Not a big field, considering how much data there is to go through."

"You told me she was a programmer..."

"I know. I'm sorry. If I had told you anymore, I know you would have been asking more questions. Questions that I wasn't prepared to answer."

"Excuse me," Disto said, "but what is an archaeologist?"

Ruby chuckled. "Ironically, it's not too different from what you do," she said. "They look at history and artifacts and such."

"In this case," Blake added, "digital artifacts."

"Did you guys work together?" Ruby asked.

"Yes, of course," Blake said. "At the end of the day, we were really both interested in the same thing. We were just involved in two different ways. We both wanted to know more about our galaxy and Universe. We wanted to know about alien life and planets around other stars.

"She had uncovered some not-too-old research and long story short... I found out exactly who was still actively working on that. The Company. So, I started working for them, too."

"I am curious," Disto asked. "Were you aware of our planet?"

Blake looked at him. "That's the interesting thing. No. Your homeworld, Location Zero, is well within the range of our ability to see. Yet we only see your star and a large planet. Around the orbit you describe...*nothing*."

"That is interesting," Disto said. "I wonder why."

"Before we left Astroll 2, I stopped by the," he gave Ruby a glance, "telescope observatory." Ruby's eyes went wide. *I didn't know we had an observatory!*

"I used the location information you provided," Blake continued, "and confirmed. We really can't see your planet. We should be able to. I can only think of a few reasons why that should be and only one of those reasons seems probable."

Ruby got a chill down her spine when the reason occurred to her, too.

"Someone is preventing them from being seen," she said softly.

"Uh-huh," Blake said, nodding.

They were all silent for a moment, and then Blake said to Disto, "Who made you?"

"As we've expressed," Disto responded, "we don't know. I sincerely hope we can find out while we're here."

"Why here?" Blake asked.

"Odds," said Disto. "We have tested many other species from other worlds. Your world is fairly close, and teaming with life."

"Why didn't you test us sooner?" Blake asked.

Ruby was about to ask the same question. She was a little puzzled at herself for not asking it earlier.

"It's quite simple," Disto said. "We didn't know about you before. We had no records."

"Then how did SD wind up finding me? Where did his programming come from to get here?"

"As you know Ruby, all the programming comes from The Core. We have the special projects branch—"

"Yes, yes, but really... where did it come from?"

She watched Disto's coloring change to one of mild embarrassment.

"If I knew the answer to that, Ruby, I might know the answer to a lot of my questions."

Before anyone could ask anymore unsatisfyingly unanswerable questions, the lift opened at the back of the hangar and Professor Coronik appeared.

"We can dock," he announced. "But there are some conditions."

Chapter 24

"SD is currently maneuvering us into the correct location," Coronik said, "based on a set of instructions my people have provided."

Ruby was still angry. She didn't like the deal that Coronik had made, but there was nothing she could do about it.

The deal was that they could dock, depart, and head to Earth, but the robots would temporarily be in Coronik's custody. Not as visitors but as property.

Ruby didn't like it one bit. These robots had more in common with a toddler than what was typically an Earth-created robot. They were sentient. She had no idea how that was or why that was, but she knew it when she saw it, as could any reasonable human.

To compare them to property.... She was fuming.

Blake had his hand on her upper arm, to help keep her calm.

"I'm staying with them," she said to Blake. "Something isn't right about this."

"Let's get on the ground first. Then we can sort this out further."

Uncle Blake wasn't wrong. There wasn't much they could do here. In fact, there wasn't much they could do anywhere. But she wasn't sure what difference being on the ground would make. She felt a new longing to be back on Astroll 2, where she felt she had some control, but that control was probably an illusion. Although a comfortable illusion was preferable to this uncomfortable reality.

SD interrupted her thought spirals when he said, "We've been asked to wait." SD had a direct communication channel open that allowed him to communicate to the individuals manning the station at the end of a rope.

But SD kept the Legacy Station on the viewscreen as well. It was another ring-like disk, similar to Astroll 2, but it was one single, solitary ring. However, it looked like it could have been designed by the same space architect. It was slightly more than 100-meters in diameter and was spinning. The tether could be seen beginning in the center of the disk and then disappearing as it dropped down towards the Earth. A climber was parked and appeared like it was ready to descend at any time.

Ruby wondered if they took the climber down to Earth, would that mean whoever was manning the station was stuck until the next climber arrived back? She searched her brain for what she might have learned about Legacy Station, but like most of her time in school, if it was about Earth, she didn't pay much attention. Her lack of interest disappointed her now.

As if reading her mind—or maybe she heard Disto ask some questions while she was lost in thought—Professor Coronik started to explain:

"Well, once we're on the station, we'll board the 'climber' that will take us down to Earth. You can see it here," and he pointed to the near center of the rotating disk. "Typically, this station has a crew of about 30 individuals, and there are escape pods if they had to evacuate in an emergency. We will attach here," and he pointed to another location on the disk.

"That is not the same location as was communicated," SD said.

Milo stood near SD and nodded hesitantly. He opened his mouth as if he wanted to say something, but then bit the inside of his cheek instead.

Professor Coronik cocked his head and said, "Well, yes, of course. You misunderstood how I was pointing."

Ruby didn't understand how anyone could misunderstand a point but let it go.

"Legacy Station began operation only sixty years ago, even though it had been under development for most of a century. The basic physics and engineering of creating such a structure had been studied longer than that," Coronik said.

"What is the purpose of this structure?" Disto asked.

"Well, it's a stopping point to or from the Moon. It's also a data transfer point between Earth and the data centers located on the Moon. You can see the antennas here," and he pointed some more.

"Those are the Earth-facing antennas," Uncle Blake stated.

"Yes, of course they are," Coronik said. "They are also part of the overall transfer mechanism."

Ruby wanted to chime in and disagree with him. Those were clearly the voice and small data transmitters. The primary data to and from Earth was built into the tether itself. What Ruby couldn't figure out is if Coronik was deliberately trying to mislead them or if he genuinely didn't know how his space station worked.

"Data centers?" Disto said. "For storage? Off-world? Like us?"

"Yes, but for different reasons," Uncle Blake said, and Ruby wondered if he, too, was picking up the fact that Coronik's answers were incomplete or flat-out wrong. "For a generation or two, nearly 200 years ago, we built what we used to call data centers on Earth. They served a need at the time but were terrible. Data centers generated a lot of heat, and it was killing the Earth. Eventually, we got a little smarter and moved them to the Moon."[1]

Coronik nodded. "Exactly what I was going to say."

> Detailed Historian <

Disto considered what the humans were saying and looked to Ruby.

"Heat?"

"You know temperature?" Ruby tried to help. Disto knew what temperature was but still didn't understand the importance. Temperature was how you could tell if a robot was functioning well or if it was processing too much nonsensical data.

---

1. My day job in Northern Virginia is smack in the middle of one of the major data center hubs in the US.

Temperature was how some agents knew that a robot was not being truthful. Or whether or not they were trying to process something.

Temperature was also one of the metrics he used to know how well his components were functioning.

"Yes, I know temperature," he said.

"Well, heat is what gets transferred from something hotter to something colder. There is a whole class I had to take, not to mention pilot training… right Milo?"

"Oh yeah. I would say all pilots are experts in heat transfer."

"We also call it thermal energy," Ruby said. "And so—"

Coronik interrupted, "Well, surely you can understand that it's not good to have all that thermal energy dumped onto our planet." He was clearly trying to stay involved in this conversation. There was no reason to talk over Ruby, but he must have concluded that what he needed to say was more important. Something about this human Disto didn't like, but none of his circuits could compute why. So far, everything he had done had tried to help them.

"And this is not a problem for your moon?" Disto asked.

"No. The Moon has no atmosphere and no natural life that can be harmed by that change to the environment. The heat can simply radiate away," Coronik said.

"Interesting solution to your storage problem," Disto said.

Disto considered for a moment why the robots hadn't developed a solution that was closer to home. While no one knew who constructed his planet, Location Zero was certainly constructed, as opposed to the standard way it was understood that planets were created. Organically.

"I wonder why The Core didn't create a moon for storage," Ruby half-asked.

"I don't know if we can be certain it didn't," responded Disto.

"What do you mean?" Ruby asked.

"Perhaps it was created. Maybe it didn't work. Or maybe there weren't enough resources left over after creating Location Zero. Maybe it was considered. I will ask The Core and various agencies when we return home, especially if that answer isn't in whatever we find here."

Location Zero had no moon. Disto was certain of that fact. And to his historical knowledge, Location Zero had never had a moon. But he knew his own historical knowledge had limitations, and so he could be less certain of this second fact. He didn't know how much he could trust his own historical knowledge.

When Disto was initially constructed, he was given the base algorithm, which covered his general purpose: analysis, discovery, and preservation of history. Then, he was programmed with specific algorithms to carry out this purpose.

He was also provided a base set of knowledge of historical events. But then he got involved in the special project, attempting to find other historical data. Ever since he joined that special project, the rest of his historian duties fell to the wayside. He had not been collecting more recent facts about Location Zero and the robots.

"And these events happened before you were born?" he looked at Ruby.

"Yup," she said. "I learned about them in school and from reading and watching vids."

"Who teaches you?"

"Teachers? Historians? A lot of historians write books. That's how they tell people about history. Or vids… Vids are much more popular than books."

Disto's circuits were tingling. "Can I see one of these vids?"

"Sure! I can bring something up on my communicuff. What do you want to learn about?"

"Anything!"

Ruby looked at him and then smiled before she said, "Pippa, show us a vid on the origin of the word 'robot.'"

"Certainly," answered Pippa's voice, "but do you want to respond to your incoming messages? The number of unread messages has started to exceed—"

"No," Ruby interrupted. "Later. Please show the vid."

A holoscreen appeared and a human girl, who, to Disto's limited exposure to humans looked a little like Ruby, but not quite, appeared, and moved her limbs in a way Disto didn't understand.

"Hi, everyone! Welcome back to HiAllCoTe, the History of All Cool Technologies. I'm Tianna Tutor, your friendly technology historian here to tell you today about the origin of robots!"

The screen changed and a series of images flashed by, followed by some text. When Tianna Tutor reappeared, she started speaking again:

"Ok super-fans, this one goes out to Samera Huynh who asked about robots and where they came from. For that, we're going to have to go back to ancient times—the early 20th century and talk about a play. Yes, a play!

"This guy, Karel Capek—I have no idea if I'm pronouncing his name right—wrote a play that came out in 1920 called 'Rossum's Universal Robots.' It is the first time anyone had ever used the word 'robot' that we know of.[2]

"But these robots aren't what we know of as robots today. These things were artificial biological creatures. They looked like humans—which makes sense given it was a play, like I said, and humans were playing them. But they were intended to be artificial creatures. Created differently than human beings."

Immediately after she said the words, 'human beings,' a sound effect was added—that nearly translated to the word 'transform' in Disto's native language—and an image popped up to replace Tianna briefly, and then she was back.

"The play was a huge success, translated into lots of languages, yada yada. Not too long after that, robots became a mainstay in science fiction.

"But that's all the fictional stuff. I know Samera was asking where real robots came from. As we all know, science fiction breeds reality. Since lots of people try to make sci-fi real, there was a lot of interest in building robots. At first, they were simple machines with motors that could automate tasks."

As she spoke, images appeared on the screen with her.

"Like these large industrial robotic arms that were popular in the late 20th century."

She went on to describe more of these devices, created at the hands of humans like Ruby, to do a variety of tasks.

As the video continued, Disto was more interested in watching Ruby who was watching the video with intense interest.

> Ruby <

---

2. This is all true.

Ruby was watching the video with interest. Intensely. The history and origin of robots was yet another on the long list of things she had little interest in before, but now she was captivated.

Robots had killed her mother. This was the statement she had told herself over and over and over... until she met SD and Disto, and the other robots of Location Zero, and had started to reflect on her life and what she thought she knew. She had begun to realize and accept that maybe she had misunderstandings about her past.

The most captivating point that she didn't know until now is when in the video, Tianna Tutor went on to explain the robotic laws.

"Before we get to about the year 2100 which was a watershed time, let's go back to the 1900's. There was a very influential science fiction writer named Isaac Asimov. Decades after he died, there was a lot of controversy over whether or not people could continue to read his work because it was known that he did not treat women well[3] ... but part of his legacy... in his science fiction... were what he called the three laws of robotics. They were laws about how robots could not harm humans.

"For the longest time, these 'laws' remained in the domain of science fiction. Robots were not sophisticated enough—any harm would be obviously mishandling and misprogramming on the part of the humans. There were huge controversies over this in the 2030s, about the time that self-driving cars—early versions of the Dynamic Autonomous Vehicle that used primitive AI—were becoming popular.

"But when robots crossed a certain line of sophistication, the robot laws were passed, and they were based on Asimov's laws. Everyone who programmed a robot had to prove that these laws were incorporated into them.

"Which is how we know robots are safe today. Of course, there can still be accidents. There are always a handful of incidents that really are accidents..."

Ruby felt as if Tianna was talking directly to her and not to a mass audience of unknown people.

"But as long as the robot has its certification to operate based on the Robot and Artificial Intelligence Laws of 2098, things move on. Since then..."

The video went on for another minute, but Ruby was no longer listening. She had intended to think about this when she got back, but she'd been so busy talking to everyone about her experience and worrying about the robots, she hadn't thought too deeply about how to investigate or learn more about her mother's death.

The moments on Location Zero came back to her. Realizing that everything wasn't what it seemed to be when it came to her mother. Her palms began to sweat, and her teeth clenched.

She didn't realize she was making a face until she looked up and saw Uncle Blake's look of concern.

"Ruby?" he said. "Are you okay?"

"Tell me again what happened to my mother." Ruby said without delay.

"It's been a long time since you asked. In fact, I don't think you ever asked since we talked about it after it happened. It was a power surge—right in the middle of her operation. The backup power generation equipment failed. The whole city was affected. It was deemed a solar flare-initiated blackout."

"Robots didn't kill my mother?"

---

3. Asimov was a complicated person. An amazingly progressive author for his time—his work celebrated science, reason, and human potential—but also someone with well-documented issues when it came to boundaries. He was notorious for inappropriate touching, behavior that today would rightly be called out.

"No! Oh my god… is that what you've thought all these years?"

The tears came like a tsunami. Ruby couldn't hold them back. She didn't care that everyone was watching, she didn't care that she was being more vulnerable than she could usually tolerate being, and she didn't care that everyone could see her nose getting runny. Uncle Blake wrapped his arms around her, and she cried for a while. Ruby hadn't cried like this in a *very* long time.

Chapter 25

It is commonly believed that a single human, who went by the name Benjamin Franklin, was the person to discover electricity. And while, for some unknown reason, his efforts are the ones that made it into popular lore, humans had been aware of electricity and more specifically, electrical charge for thousands of years before Franklin was born.

They were indeed aware that they could induce static electricity—a phenomena resulting from the imbalance of negative and positive charges in objects.

The ancient Greeks knew this. They knew that if they rubbed animal fur against amber, they could pick up other pieces of glass. They were also aware of electric fish that swam in the Nile River.

As the centuries passed, as Benjamin Franklin lived and died, humans learned more about electricity and started to give names to the particles they discovered were responsible for electric charge.

Indeed, as humans came to rely more and more on electricity to power their devices and their world, many became very concerned and familiar with the fact that while electricity could provide power, it could also kill their devices. Many humans continued to remain ignorant of this fact, scratching their heads when their device suddenly died after they walked across the carpet and touched something they shouldn't have.

As humans moved into space, many continued the study of electricity and brought the concerns of electrical charge with them.

They knew that for two human-made objects to touch in space, they needed to be at the same electric potential, or find a safe way to come to that, so an electrical charge didn't damage one or the other.

By this time, humans knew that if two objects were at different electric potentials, that shock was caused by electrons rushing to get from the more crowded object to the less crowded object. Electrons had no compunction about being polite, so they would rush to do it the instant they could, hence a spark!

These days all human-made spaceships had a special device to dissipate and prevent any ESD—Electrostatic Discharge—event from disrupting operations.

This was so common that no one thought about it.

Which means no one thought about it when SD moved in to connect to Legacy Station.[1]

> Ruby <

"Ten meters," said Milo. Milo was SD's anointed co-pilot, to help keep the other humans informed of their progress. They had an open communication line to the station's main operations center as well.

Milo was staying quiet, doing his job, and seemed to be completely in his own zone. Ruby appreciated his professionalism. It certainly gave her less to worry about.

SD had flipped the ship around, so the ship's rear could make contact. Legacy station had a hangar, similar to Astroll 2, but much larger. The service hatch was the most compatible, and the station would use its emergency expandable antechamber to make up the difference.

It was better than using the mini-R-pod to shuttle people, everyone agreed.

"Five meters," Milo announced.

"Adjust your trajectory by point-five degrees not-yaw," said a voice from the station.

Earlier, they had worked out what roll, pitch, and yaw meant. The robots had equivalents for these terms, of course. In fact, the robots had more terms. While the humans described these three movements, using positive or negative angles to account for how you could move one way or the other, the robots had completely unique names. To make the translation, instead of saying a negative number as in "move five degrees in the negative yaw direction" or "move negative five degrees," the humans agreed to call the six angles of rotation: yaw, not-yaw, roll, not-roll, pitch, and not-pitch.

"We don't have 'negative,'" Disto had said after conferring with SD to try and understand what the humans were saying.

"But how do you describe anything that is," Ruby wasn't sure what she was trying to express and waved her arm in a circle to try and force some words out, "anything that is less than zero?"

"How can there be anything less than zero?" Disto said. "Zero is nothing. It is the lowest amount or lowest level. It is the origin point."

Ruby considered that. An origin point was always determined by someone. It could always be set. If there was an expectation of a negative quantity, you could move the origin to be at that lowest point. Is this what the robots did?

But how could they account for infinity? This was starting to hurt her head.[2]

She knew that their sense of time came from when they were brought online. "But how do you describe the time from before you were born?"

---

1. At the time I was writing this, my day job in the space industry involved working on a satellite mission that would be connecting with another satellite in space. So this concept of two objects in space being at different electric potentials is a real thing that was on my mind at the time.

2. If I think too deeply about it, it hurts my head, too. LOL

"Against the master reference clock," they said. Ruby had learned about this during her stay on Location Zero. The Core maintained the clock, and everything was referenced to it.

Ruby did the math. The clock had been running for nearly seven hundred years her time. When she tried to ask about what happened before that, she got blank stares.

She tried to ask Disto about it. "Is it possible your planet and all the robots are only 700 years old?"

Disto didn't dismiss the possibility, but he simply said, "that's what I'm trying to find out."

The mystery gnawed at Ruby, too, a human with no stake in the problem. She tried to imagine that if she had a stake, how committed to it she would be. She was trying to sympathize with this robot.

"Five degrees, not-yaw, complete," SD said.

"Slow your rate of speed," was the next command overheard on the communications link.

"Speed reduction confirmed," SD said. They were already moving incredibly slow, Ruby thought. She was a little surprised that SD could continue to reduce it further.

"Two meters," Milo announced.

"Okay, we're going to link with our arm..." the voice said.

This was part of the prearranged procedure to ensure that they could connect. Since they couldn't connect port to port or hatch to hatch, the stations arm would grab hold of the outside of SD's ship and then the emergency inflatable tube would be deployed.

And that's when thousands of years of history with electric charge bit them all... Ruby saw it all on the display screen, which was piping in a view that SD had of a camera on the outside of his ship.

One moment the arm was slowly heading towards the hull, then in the next moment, almost immediately before it made contact, Ruby saw the *ZAP!* of charge move from SD's ship to the arm, imparting a small force on the ship and causing all manner of commotion on the operations center of the station.

Ruby heard cursing over the open line and a jumble of people speaking over each other.

But Ruby knew what had happened, she had seen it. She thought through what she knew of ESD and what to do. She was trying to ignore all the beeps, chirps, and tones the robots were making so she could think.

"Milo," she said, "what's standard procedure on Astroll 2 in case of an ESD event?"

Milo's eyes went wide in understanding.

"Uh," he said, obviously trying to recall what he knew, "it's always about the ship, not the station. The station is a large ground. For a ship, we would... we evacuate the ship."

"But there's nothing wrong with this ship, is there SD?" Ruby asked.

SD stopped his beeps and chirps long enough to answer, "Correct. There was minor damage to the outer hull, but we are fine."

Professor Coronik moved close to the microphone and spoke, "Legacy Station. What is your status?" There was still the jumble of sounds. Ruby looked at the viewscreen and saw that a portion of the ring, starting where the arm was connected, seemed to be lacking power. She made that determination based on the lack of any lights and that the arm seemed to be moving listlessly.

"Something happened and we lost power to proton repellents and the plasma mirror[3]," came a voice. "Standby as we restore. Please retreat to 500 meters."

SD looked at Ruby, who nodded in agreement that this sounded like the right thing to do.

"I don't understand," Milo said, "why this didn't happen when our mini-R-pods, either yours or mine, docked with this ship?"

Ruby felt the inside of the wall and thought about it. It was cool, but not like the coated metallic alloy that was typical of their ships and Astroll 2. It almost had a feel of plastic to it, but not quite plastic.

"It must be this material that the inside of their ships is constructed with or lined with. It must be deliberately electrically dissipative," she said.

Milo touched it as well. And so did Disto.

"Do you have tactile sensors?" Disto asked.

"Yes," said Ruby. "But they're limited. Do you understand what just happened?"

Disto put an appendage on the wall to mirror Ruby's. He shook his chassis to indicate he had no clue.

"We caused an electrical surge that may have damaged the station," Ruby said, and from the color that both Disto and SD turned, she felt bad for saying it that way.

"It's not your fault," Ruby said. "None of us thought of it. One of us probably should have. We're just uh, not used to alien vessels and might need to rethink some of our procedures if we're going to do this again."

"I wonder if AT could have helped fix it," SD said. Ruby put her hand that was not attached to the wall softly on the pocket that she carried AT in. He likely would have jumped at the chance, even the remote possibility of being useful. It was not lost on Ruby that at every opportunity, AT had offered to help—to help fix something, learn something, repair something. His base programming *needed* to be utilized. If he was human, with human emotions, she would say he was frequently some combination of bored, agitated, and anxious. She still didn't know what the robot equivalent was.

Ruby took her hand off the wall. Milo had already done so and was back looking at the viewscreen, his arms crossed in front of his chest as he concentrated.

"The damage doesn't look that bad," he said. "They probably need to replace the Cermg fuses[4] that are super common and they're certainly going to have tons of spares. Maybe even their proton repeller, but that's not something that will prevent us from docking again. I'm sure they have a spare for that, too."

"I feel bad that we didn't think of this before," Ruby said.

"Yeah, me too," said Milo. "But this just doesn't happen. Our stuff is built with all this cemented in mind. *No one* thinks about it anymore."

Ruby shrugged.

"Hey," Milo said, putting a hand on her shoulder. "Don't beat yourself up about it, okay? Like I said, it doesn't look that bad. One thing at a time."

It felt like a million things at a time. But she took a deep breath and got ready for the *next* thing.

---

3. To be clear, there is no such thing (yet) as a "proto repellent" nor a "plasma mirror."

4. Again, I made this up. There is no such thing as a "Cermg fuse."

Chapter 26

> Ruby <

"It was Jade's idea to put your grandmother in this facility. At the time, your mom had connections to the University that manages it. The White-David[1] Focality for Geriatrics is the most advanced facility anywhere in North America with respect to aging and elder care. Your grandmother was not quite old enough, officially… but, well, Jade took care of that."

Ruby gave her uncle a sidelong glance. She had learned more about her mother in the last 24 hours than she had in… years.

Now, Uncle Blake was telling her that her mother hacked systems to get what she wanted or needed.

Uncle Blake must have seen the look on her face. He smiled.

"It's not as bad as it sounds," he said, smiling. "Your grandmother's official records already didn't reflect her correct age. She had paid someone years earlier to make her 15 years younger than she was."

"Seriously?"

"To prevent someone from doing what your mother did. We think she was starting to recognize that she needed help. To your grandma's credit, she resisted and survived as long as possible."

Ruby looked out the window of the transport. It was a private air transport that Coronik secured for them. Everything inside it was plush, and the pleasant scent of orange mixed with cardamom[2] was deliberately piped into the air circulation system. The entire interior was designed for comfort and to keep its occupants relaxed, but Ruby couldn't do that.

She was thinking about Disto and the others and hoped they were okay. She was certain they were. It was generally known that they had come down to Earth via the space elevator which put them on a man-made island in the middle of the Pacific Ocean[3]. From there, Coronik had flown all of them on their first private air transport to the mainland of the United States.

---

1. Named after Betty White and Larry David.

2. Until I got cats in late 2022, I used to diffuse orange and cardamom essential oils in my diffuser all the time.

3. Oops. I can't believe it's taken until now for me to realize that I have a continuity mistake in my own work! I think in the earlier chapter, I mentioned the Atlantic, not Pacific! FWIW, the intent was always Pacific according to my notes. I will now wonder if I should go back and correct that in some version of this book!

To Omaha, Nebraska—site of the Church's North American Headquarters[4]. Coronik mentioned that they should continue on to Scotland, but a conversation between him and Blake kept them in North America.

Blake had secured this side trip, while Disto and SD would remain with Coronik for now. Disto was going to get to his DNA tests. But SD? She wasn't sure exactly what they were doing with SD, but Coronik had promised that both robots would be well cared for, and just as importantly, he had the resources to keep their location a secret. Coronik also was able to provide Disto with a modified communicuff he could wear around his primary appendage. It wasn't as useful as her own, since communicuffs were designed to work with a biological user, but they'd at least be able to call each other. Ruby was thankful for that.

With the comfort of being able to contact her alien friends, Ruby's mind shifted to her grandmother.

"Remind me why we're going?" Ruby said.

Blake ran his fingers through his hair. "You need a connection to Earth. More than me and Logan have been able to provide. I know you think Astroll 2 is your home. It's not. It's just a place we've been living for a while. I know that 'while' has been most of your life, and I'm sorry we didn't recognize it as it was happening. We should have brought you back here more often."

"Why didn't you?" Ruby didn't mean for this to come out with attitude but couldn't help that it had.

Blake sighed. "We meant to. We always said we would, but as you know, trips between the station and Earth can be a hassle. The years passed, and it... We just didn't realize that we needed to."

They sat silently for most of the rest of the ride. Ruby leaned her head on Blake's shoulder and closed her eyes. She was feeling the weariness of prolonged travel. She opened them when she felt the plunk of the transport stop, and the metallic sound of an artificial voice over the speaker said, "Arrival at Zappa Memorial Airport[5]. Current time, 10:32am. Current temperature 88 degrees. Please ensure you remove any belongings."

A hatch opened slowly, and Ruby felt a kind of air that was strange to her. It was astonishingly moist. Even at the space elevator landing, she had been in enclosed spaces the whole time. This was the first time she was truly outside. Intellectually, she knew the difference between 'fresh' air and the recycled air she breathed. Intellectually, she understood it was summertime, and much of the Northern Hemisphere on Earth was hot, and often humid. But feeling it was not the same as knowing.

Knowing felt like she was submerged in a certain level of chaos. Suddenly, she found herself wondering if she was going to want to wear shorter pants for the summer heat, and she became worried about mosquitos. She'd only heard of them but associated them with summertime and didn't want to find herself itchy, or too hot, or any other number of variable concerns that Earth brought to her mind. She couldn't imagine being in a jungle, a forest, or even an open field.

She got up and looked out over the lot and to the awaiting car. It also bore the symbol of the Church, which is how she knew it was waiting for them.

"Do you need help?" Blake asked, watching her footsteps.

"No, I'm fine. A month at Location Zero did some good, I think." She stepped out of the pod and onto the lot and looked back at Blake. Eyebrows raised, she said, "Impressed?"

Blake laughed, "To be fair, you sort of cheated..."

---

4. I chose Omaha because it's where Warren Buffett is from.

5. This is intended to be BWI outside of Baltimore. In my timeline, that airport gets renamed to honor one of my favorite artists, Frank Zappa, who was from Baltimore.

Ruby scoffed, "And what about you? You and all your exercise?" Blake was holding on tight, and looked like he was moving through molasses.

"I'll be fine," he said. "Just need to move a little more."

They had both taken supplements meant to help people who were headed back to the gravity of Earth after a long time away. Usually, people took those supplements over several days on the trip back. But yesterday morning, they had woken up on Astroll 2. The trip was quicker than expected, so their bodies hadn't had time to let the supplements do their thing.

Once in the car, the automated voice said, "Please ensure your seatbelts are secure. We will commence movement in ten seconds. We will be at your destination in eight minutes."

The car was pre-programmed with the address of the facility.

Ruby had another eight minutes to think, and her brain didn't know where to begin. Should she think about her grandmother or look out the window at all the Earthly things there were to see? Out the window, nothing looked abnormal. While her memories of being here were fuzzy, she saw snippets of Earth all the time on vids. So, her brain decided to think about her grandmother instead. Would her grandmother even know it was her? She was certain probably not.

Once the car was at the facility, it said something about getting out, which they did. Blake led the way into the building. Ruby could see that the molasses effect was wearing off, and he was moving more like himself. She followed him, still feeling like she was carrying along a bag of rocks but also getting better with each movement as the seconds ticked by.

Two large doors swooshed open automatically as they approached, and Ruby followed Blake inside. Besides a few chairs, presumably for waiting, the lobby of the facility contained a floor-to-ceiling monitor inset into one wall that cycled through still images of smiling people, none of whom could have been less than 70 years old. Next to the monitor was a back-lit sign that read, "Welcome to the White-David Focality for Geriatrics." At the far end of the lobby was a reception desk. Ruby observed the lack of a human receptionist. Instead, there was an artificial head at the end of a robotic arm. It detected their approach and said, "Welcome to the White-David Focality for Geriatrics. How may I help you?"

"We're here to see a resident. Name, Pearl Palmer."

"Please present identification so I may determine if you're on the approved visitors list."

Both Blake and Ruby spoke into their communicuffs, and holoimages appeared with their respective identification screens.

The robotic receptionist scanned them. First Blake, and it said out loud, "Blake Griffin. Approved to visit Pearl Palmer."

Next was Ruby. She held her arm up and the image faced the robot. The robot scanned it and said, "Ruby Palmer." Ruby would have sworn there was an extra half-second pause before it continued with, "Approved to visit Pearl Palmer."

"The resident is located in the FZC—the FunZone Common area—at this time. The lights will illuminate on the floor and wall of the corridor to show you the way."

"Thank you," Blake said and started to make his way to a corridor behind the reception desk. It wasn't lost on Ruby that he knew the procedure and where he was going. Even though it had to have been years since he'd been here himself.

"Wait," the robotic receptionist said.

They both turned back.

"Ruby Palmer. Ruby of the Robots?" it sounded like it was asking a question.

Ruby looked at Blake. "Uh, I guess?" she said.

"Thank you for bringing them here."

"Uh, okay," she said, again looking at Blake, whose eyebrows were drawn together. He didn't say anything but continued to walk through the door that swooshed open and into a corridor. Ruby followed.

"That was weird," Ruby said.

"Agreed," Blake responded. Then he shook his head in a way that brought him back to the here and now. "Here. Your grandmother is down this residence hallway to the right."

The residence hallway emptied into an open common area with lots of windows and greenery both inside and out.

Several people, obviously residents, were intermixed with a few people who were obviously not residents. Assorted robots that were essentially mobile arms were also peppered in amongst the humans. Ruby saw one giving a metal cup of something to a resident. Medicine perhaps. Another was taking away a tray of what she hoped was uneaten mashed potatoes. And yet another was performing what might have been a form of physical therapy.

At a table, under a beautiful potted tree, sat a woman who looked eerily familiar. As if Ruby was looking into a mirror of herself aged up sixty or so years.

The table contained a game. It looked like chess, but the playing field was round. On the other side of the table, was another one of those robot arms.

"Check mate!" shouted the woman and stood up, spying Ruby and Blake out of the side of her eye, "and just in time, too. I have visitors!"

This woman, completely mobile, approached them.

"Blake!" she hugged him, then held him back so she could study him, then kissed one side of his face then the other.

"And this one. The offspring of my beloved Jade," and she embraced Ruby in a bearhug that belied her age again.

"Ruby," Ruby said.

"Oh, I know exactly who you are!" Pearl Palmer said, breaking the hug but still holding on to Ruby's upper arms. "Just let me look at you for a moment." And she did, her eyes going up and down Ruby, as if she was examining every cell.

"These clothes are so bland, darling[6]," she said. "Come," and she grabbed Ruby's hand. "I have something for you."

Ruby had no choice but to follow where her grandmother led. The grip was strong. Blake followed too, and Ruby looked behind and mouthed "my clothes?" and then turned back to study this oddly strong woman who was wearing pajama pants and an open bathrobe that revealed a T-shirt with a faded symbol that she couldn't quite make out.

Pearl led Ruby and Blake back to a small room whose door had been left open. It was little more than a bed and a small kitchenette all in one. It was Pearl's room, as evidenced by the small LED screen next to the door that displayed "Pearl Palmer," each letter cycling through a rainbow of colors.

"Sit, let me find it..." She started opening and closing drawers, occasionally reaching her hand in to move the contents about.

Eventually, after about the seventh drawer, she said, "Ah!" and pulled out a chunky necklace.

"Here," she said to Ruby holding it out. "This is what you need. Some pop!"

Ruby took the offered gift and turned it around in her hand. It was lighter than it looked, probably some form of plastic made to look like stones. It was colorful, but in an earthy way.

"What is it?" she asked.

"It's a jade necklace. I always liked jade and other stones. That's why I named your mother Jade. Your mother, on the other hand, liked the sparkly stuff. Which is why she named you Ruby."

---

6. My grandmother said "darling" a lot in a classy New York way that I wish I could emulate.

"How do you know that?" Ruby asked.

"Ha! I was there," Pearl Palmer looked at Blake. "How do I know? How can she ask that?" She pointed her thumb at Ruby in mock disgust. "Does she not know I was there?"

Blake looked at Ruby, his arms crossed, and he was leaning on a wall, clearly enjoying watching the interactions. "Your grandmother was there when you were born," he said matter-of-factly.

Ruby looked at the floor, trying to grasp an impossible memory, "I thought you were there, Uncle Blake?"

"I was. Too. We both were."

Ruby held the necklace in her hand and turned it over, "This isn't real jade. It's too light."

Her grandmother smiled, "Of course it isn't! Do you think I could afford such a thing! But does it matter? It looks like jade. That's what counts."

"Don't just stare at it," she continued. "Put it on!"

"Over this?" Ruby looked down at herself. She was still wearing the utility pants she put on before leaving Astroll 2 and a white, long-sleeve shirt with the station logo on it. She had her jacket on, too, which was the same color and material as her pants, with nearly as many pockets. She took it off, to reveal the full effect of the shirt.

The background of the logo was purple and had what were meant to be two brown asteroids, but that most people assumed were meatballs. Ruby tilted her head, "I don't think it's going to go…"

"Just humor an old lady, will you? You can take it off before you leave."

Ruby relented and unclasped the necklace, wrapped it around her neck, and let the clasp re-engage.

She put her jacket back on, which covered up the logo and looked at herself in the large mirror that was over the dresser in the room.

With the logo covered up, she admitted to herself that it didn't look terrible.

"See? Pop!" said Pearl, and she clapped her hands together to emphasize the 'pop!' "So, keep that. Keep some pop in your life, ok?"

Ruby nodded and smiled weakly in thanks, wondering if she could have predicted that this day would include acquiring a necklace that was clearly introduced to remind her of her mother.

Speaking of her mother, "Jade is what I wanted to talk about," Blake said next.

Blake sat down at one of the three chairs arranged around a small table that made up most of the kitchenette. He nodded at Ruby to take another.

Pearl sat in the plush chair by the window, crossing her feet under her as she did so. The light came in and was bright enough that it almost made Pearl look like she was glowing. All of her lines, the faint, violet lipstick, and the shimmering silver throughout her hair showed themselves better in the light. She seemed to be aware of this, as her back straightened and her demeaner seemed drawn to the window.

Ruby's assessment was that this woman, who was supposed to be in her 80s, was physically as spry as she had been in her 30s or 40s. Nothing about her seemed frail in the least. Ruby wondered what she would be doing if she wasn't here, and from her lucidity so far, wondered if it could be a mistake that she was here at all.

"Jade—*real* jade—absorbs your negative energy. I used to wear a jade bangle when I was young. Once I was in an accident, and the bangle broke. I walked away without a scratch!"

And maybe she does belong here after all, Ruby thought.

"Not your old jade jewelry," Blake continued, not asking any of the 100 questions that her snippet of a story begged. "I want to talk about Jade, your daughter."

"To outlive one's children is a curse of the gods!" she said, and her face took on a distant look. "It's my fault you know…"

"It's not," said Blake.

"It is! She didn't come to see me before like I had asked. I had an obsidian bracelet[7] for her to take with her. If she had worn that! Its powers would have helped her…"

Yep, she belongs here.

Blake pulled up his chair until it was right in front of Pearl. "Jade died because of an accident. An accident during her operation. You are not responsible."

"Then who is?" she shot back a look. "My granddaughter lost her mother. Someone needs to be responsible for that."

Ruby was glad that Blake was here. She didn't know what to say to this woman, minute to minute. She was all over the place.

"We wanted to know what Jade told you about her work. I hadn't seen much of her in the year prior. We were just so busy… but I know she was here."

Ruby's grandmother looked back and forth between them.

"Do you want her journals?"

"Her, uh, journals?" Blake said.

"My mom kept a journal?" Ruby said.

"Oh yes. Since she was ten or so. I got her very first one for her. It was blue, with an image of a flower on top. I promised her she could write anything, and I would never read it."

Ruby stood up. "Do you mean like a real journal? With paper?"

"Yes, that's what I said."

Pearl untwisted herself from her plush chair and went over to the closet. She touched the side and the door slid open, accordion folding on itself. What was shown was a mess and Ruby's grandmother started removing stuff, placing things randomly on the table and the floor next to them.

"Blake, help move some of this, will ya? I'm old and frail!"

Ruby got the sense that she liked saying that as a form of irony. This woman was not frail.

After a few minutes, she declared "ah ha!" and pulled out a plastic box that emerged from the bottom of the closet, having been underneath a pile of stuff.

She sat on the floor with her legs wrapped around it and opened it.

She frowned, "This isn't it. Darling, you'll have to come back. Maybe it's in my storage facility…" she mumbled some more that Ruby couldn't hear.

"I think it's time for us to go," Blake announced quite abruptly.

---

7. I did go through a phase in 2021-2022 where I was collecting stones and minerals and wondering about whether or not the attributes some people ascribe to them hold any meaning…

"But Jade needs to take her journals back," Ruby's grandmother stood up and had the look of a toddler who just asked for a favorite toy. "Don't you want to keep up your journal writing my lovely, Jade? Now that you're back from your secret assignment?"

Ruby looked at Blake whose eyes had sunken in. He also recognized that Pearl was losing her hold on any lucidity she had projected only a few moments ago.

Ruby's grandmother hugged her and went back to her plush chair. But instead of crossing her legs underneath her like she had before, now she sat like an old woman. Feet on the ground, hands in her lap, she stared out of the window.

Did she realize the mistake she had just made?

After a moment, she looked at Blake. Even though she was looking at him, it somehow seemed like she was looking past him. She said, "I hope they'll turn on the news after dinner again. My granddaughter has been on the news. Do you know her? Ruby Palmer. She's famous! First human to meet an alien! Isn't that amazing? I hope she'll come visit me..."

Ruby opened her mouth to remind her grandmother that she was right there, but Blake put a hand up to stop her and shook his head.

"I hope so, too, Ms. Palmer," he said and took a small fleece blanket that had been folded up at the foot of her bed and placed it on her lap. "I'll let them know they should turn on the news."

"Robots..." she said, talking to no one, but again looking out the window at the courtyard that was still getting some light from the now setting sun. "Robots from space. Who knew? My Jade knew... that's who." She was mumbling, almost incoherent, but Ruby swore that as Blake was ushering them out, she heard a final mumble, "...and that's why they had her killed."

Once they were outside the room, the door swished shut behind them.

"What the... what the was that?" Ruby didn't know what to say.

"She has psychotic episodes. You know that's why she's here," Blake said calmly.

As if on cue, a robotic arm following a line on the floor rolled up to the room and pushed the intercom. "Ms. Palmer, I'm here with your evening meds and tests." Ruby didn't see it push any button to open the door, but the door appeared pre-programmed to open after the robot announced itself. Once open, the robotic arm continued to follow the lines inside. The door stayed open, and Ruby heard her grandmother say "Oh, thank you dear!" followed by a robotic "Please extend your arm."

Blake peeked in, but then said, "We should go."

As they were walking out, they passed more of these arms. Several were headed into the residential rooms. It must be med time, Ruby thought.

They were back in the reception lobby. "Can you call the car service?" Blake asked.

Ruby spoke into her communicuff, and Pippa acknowledged the request.

"Two minutes," she said.

The large monitor was still cycling through images of smiling people and now there was a robot arm with the human every third or fourth image or so. She was certain there were no robots in the images when they came through earlier. She was also certain that the artificial head at the end of the receptionist arm was smiling in her direction.

"And I think I'm going to spend the rest of these two minutes waiting outside," she said to Blake.

Chapter 27

Disto was a robot of many expectations. His expectation-generator algorithm had been working in overtime.

For one, Disto wasn't expecting to be the only robot in the lab. He was hoping that SD would stay with him. Next, he was not expecting one of the human-created robots to assist him. He was expecting humans. And lastly, he expected to have some time between activities to watch more of the vids that he and SD had been enjoying, watching humans romp around and do everything imaginable. This expectation still had some hope of playing out.

It had been an interesting ride getting to this point. After coming down the space elevator from Legacy Station, they were all taken to a nondescript building that Professor Coronik called 'headquarters.' Once there, they all split up. Uncle Blake and Ruby were headed to visit another of Ruby's relatives. Milo had obligations to his employer. Disto had wanted SD to stay with him, but before he could protest, SD was whisked away with promises that he would be well cared for and excuses like how there wouldn't be enough room where Disto wanted to be.

'Headquarters' was in a location that the humans referred to as Omaha. Although Disto overheard Professor Coronik mutter, "The real headquarters is in Edinburgh. This is a local and poor substitute."

They were on the 10th level of a building that looked out along the rest of the city. Never had Disto predicted that he'd be standing on an alien world. He'd seen aliens, sure, but always on his own planet.

He wondered now how similar this world was to the other alien's homeworlds, such as the Clasuoids. Did they build structures into the sky from the surface of their world as well? Was the sky they looked up at even the same shade as the one on this world?

Disto's programming, to be concerned with his own history and the history of his planet didn't leave much room for thinking about other beings more than what was necessary to interact with them.

They weren't at 'Headquarters' long before he was whisked away to another building. He was told he would be in the same city, although he had no way to verify this. The location markers he relied upon on Location Zero didn't exist here. The walls of Location Zero were always marked so he could precisely locate his position.

Here, in every structure he'd seen on Earth so far, the walls were bare, at least with respect to the kind of positioning information that would be useful to him. Even upon initial entry to this most recent building. Professor Coronik did not bring him here. Instead, another human who bore some similarity to Milo, appeared.

"Xander Xander[1] will take you to the laboratory. It's on the other side of the city, also in a building managed by the Church," Professor Coronik said by way of introduction.

Xander Xander held out his quivering hand. "I'm Professor Coronik's assistant," he said with a half grin. "I'm being temporarily reassigned to assist you." Disto observed that Xander Xander looked for confirmation from Coronik, who nodded calmly.

Xander Xander held a tablet close to his chest and walked around Disto. Disto turned a little in one direction and then quickly turned in the other direction to meet Xander Xander's gaze when he was nearly complete with his circumnavigation of Disto.

"Do you approve?" Disto asked.

"Su-sure?"

"I have been studying the reactions of humans ever since I met Ruby. I interpret your... body language... as nervousness? Am I making you nervous?" Disto asked. "That is not my intent."

Xander Xander straightened up, and a small smile appeared on the lower portion of his face.

"Ok. It's okay. Let's get going, shall we?"

From then to now, in the lobby of this other nondescript building, whatever Xander Xander had experienced was gone and an air of confidence had replaced it.

In the lobby of the new building, Xander Xander said, "Wait here," and he approached another human behind a counter.

While waiting, there were a handful of other humans who had probably been intending to pass through the lobby, but who slowed down or stopped completely to look at Disto.

Disto remembered that he was fully briefed on the fact that this was the first contact with beings from outside their solar system, so the robots would experience anything and everything from mild curiosity to fear and rage. Humans had a wide range of emotions. Predicting them without knowing the specific individual ahead of time was nearly impossible. Disto was beginning to notice that each human had their own way of showing different emotions. Ruby paced when she was trying to solve a problem, but her Uncle Blake crossed his arms. It was disorienting to find the nuances between the extraordinary number of variables. To Disto, it seemed an impossible feat for any human to understand anyone else at all. Or even themselves for that matter.

The group of humans starting to surround Disto seemed the curious type. Curiosity was something that Disto understood intrinsically, probably because it was part of his own programming. Curiosity was a key component in ensuring that he was able to carry out his mission.

There was a low level of conversation happening around him that he wasn't a part of.

He listened in where he could. Two humans—it took him a few moments to match sound to bodies—were discussing his construction.

"The mobility is very reminiscent of mid-21st century robots," one said.

"They must not have steps."

"Yeah, you heard, it was a whole planet of them... a whole planet on the surface?"

---

1. Looking at my notes, I never wrote down an actor inspiration for Xander Xander, but I think in the back of my mind I'm picturing the character Kenneth Parcell from the TV Show 30 Rock, played by Jack McBrayer.

Disto, if he was programmed to chuckle, would at the misinformation regarding his planet. Ruby's description must not have made it out for the rest of the humans to consume. They were speculating on some of the basic facts about his planet and getting them wrong.

He would have corrected them himself, but Xander Xander was back at his side saying, "Follow me!"

The sea of onlookers parted and Xander Xander escorted him through what he described as a 'security checkpoint' and then to a lift. It was amusing that humans had lifts that were nearly identical to the ones on Location Zero. Surprising especially to Disto, because human's locomotive appendages were so different from the robots of Location Zero. He wondered how two historically different origins could reach the same end point.

The lift was empty except for the two of them. "We'll be on the 14th floor," Xander Xander said. "Once you're situated, I need to run an errand. Let me know if you need anything before I go."

Disto thought about whether he should make Xander Xander aware of his power situation, which continued to concern him. He was good for the moment, but sometimes there were glitches. Luckily, AT had Disto store an extra power cell before they left Location Zero and the moment they arrived at Astroll 2, AT figured out how to connect him into the human's power system.

Disto wondered how robots on this planet were powered and if they could experience similar disturbances.

"Are there humans who are experts on human-developed robots?" he decided to ask.

"Yes," Xander Xander said as the lift came to a stop and the door opened. He pointed out into the hallway, indicating that Disto should go first, then Xander Xander came out and started in a direction. Disto wondered how he knew where to go but followed all the same.

"I would like to talk to one," Disto said.

"Well, I uh, know a little about robotics," he said.

Xander Xander didn't look like someone who knew about robotics. He wasn't sure what a human who did was supposed to look like, but Xander Xander clearly didn't fit that image that Disto clearly didn't have. Clearly.

Disto must have been taking too long to process that information, so Xander Xander added. "It's my parents. They owned a company that manufactured robot arms. It didn't do well—they were great engineers but terrible businesspeople. I was working in the factory when it was bought up by the Church, and long story short, my skills were better suited to what I do now."

"You are an assistant?"

"Correct."

"What is that?"

"Well, I do whatever is needed. One day that might be making travel arrangements for Professor Coronik to visit Astroll 2. Another day that might be escorting an alien robot to a lab to do... what exactly?"

Disto re-explained the whole story of the lost data he was hoping to find in the junk DNA of Earth's biological creatures.

"Then why are you looking for a roboticist?"

"It's a," Disto ensured he chose the right word, "personal problem."

Xander Xander looked Disto up and down and Disto wondered if Xander Xander possessed special optical sensors that could diagnose his problem right then. Afterall, his face held some object that he had seen on a few humans. This one was rimmed bright blue. But he had already seen Xander Xander remove the device several times.

"Is that a diagnostic tool?"

"Oh this? These are my glasses. I had my eyes done years ago, but I still like the look. Someone told me I looked good in them once and it kinda stuck."

"So, not a diagnostic tool?"

"No. Purely for decoration. If they're distracting, I can put them away?"

"No," Disto said.

They had now been outside a room for a few moments. While they were talking Disto watched Xander Xander press a pad on the side of the door more than once and looked at his tablet and poked at it. It was fascinating that humans had the ability to interleave their actions to create the appearance that they were doing more than one thing at a time. What had Ruby called it? "Multi-tasking?"

"Although everyone knows it's not real multi-tasking. It's an illusion," she had said. "And I try not to do it. Very inefficient."

Apparently, not all humans shared the same—Disto was trying to remember the concept and word—opinion, yes, the same opinion as Ruby on the topic since this human was interleaving like his life depended on it.

Finally, the door swooshed open.

"Finally!" Xander Xander said.

He walked in and was greeted by another human. Disto looked around the room. It was lined with tables and computer consoles and approximately every other table included a clear box with equipment either poking out of it, poking into it, or stationed next to it.

"Welcome to the Church's Deep Bio Lab," the new human said. "I am Dr. Cairo Coates." She held out a hand, and Xander Xander made contact with his own hand. Disto's appendages were all stowed, and before he had a chance to extend one, Dr. Coates had returned hers to its default position along her side.

The two humans moved to the other side of the room. While Xander Xander didn't say it aloud, Disto felt there was an implied 'stay here,' and he did, taking in the sights of the room.

Upon his second scan, he realized the room was three or four times his original impression. One of the walls wasn't a wall at all, but a set of shelves. There was room to move on either side, and once someone was beyond that fake wall, Disto could see the room continue. That section of the room was somewhat different from this. The lighting was still the same, but there were a handful of robotic arms that moved around on the floor. They moved slowly, slower than was his typical speed, but once they stopped that locomotion, their upper arm movements started and those were fast. Potentially faster than he was capable of moving his own appendages.

He started moving in that direction until he heard, "Disto, not yet! There's a safety video you need to watch first!"

It was Xander Xander calling after him. Xander Xander and Dr. Cairo Coates apparently had finished their chat.

"And we need to sanitize you and figure out how you're going to wear typical lab gear," said Dr. Coates.

Disto had no idea what that last utterance meant but was inclined to let them do what they needed to do. He was happy to watch a video and comply with actions that needed to be done.

He was so close to potentially finding his data!

"And I'm going to need someone to educate me on how to perform a DNA test."

Both Xander Xander and Dr. Cairo Coates looked at each other. "You don't know how to do this?"

"I'm a historian, not a biologist."

Both humans simultaneously replicated a motion that Ruby made all the time. They put their palms to their face and said what sounded like, "Ugh."

> Swell Driver <

Swell Driver didn't want to leave Disto. He was looking forward to helping, but two humans told him he needed to follow them. He briefly considered protesting but could not compute a positive outcome to that action, so did as he was instructed.

Along the way, he wished he had ignored that computational result and protested anyway, but now it was too late. He was far out of range to communicate with Disto. He did not know where Ruby was, either. He wished he had simply stayed on his ship.

The two humans he followed were covered in identical clothing. The growth on their heads was also identically colored and identically shaped. He was only able to discriminate between the two because one was slightly taller than he was, and the other seemed to be of an average height for a human.

He was also able to differentiate because one walked behind him and the other stayed in front—the one he was instructed to follow.

SD was not really paying attention to the surroundings they walked him through other than to memorize the directionality. He could turn around and return to the spot where he left Disto at any moment.

But he didn't. Instead, he followed these humans until they brought him into a large room.

"Wait here," they said.

Before they could shut the door behind him, SD called out, "Wait! Can I watch... vids?"

One of the humans re-entered the room, touched a panel on one of the walls, and it came to life. "Do you know how to use the selector?" he asked.

SD didn't, so the human proceeded to explain what to do to access a large compendium of human-made vids and how to search for and play any individual vid. SD scrolled through the list in awe, not noticing when the humans finally left him alone.

SD first searched his own recent memory to see if any of the vids in the available index matched a title that Ruby had mentioned. He'd want to watch those first. "I love all the old movies that had to do with space travel," she had said. "Oh, and time travel, too. Especially ones that combined those."

SD used the search feature and found movies that met those criteria, beginning with ones humans created nearly 200 years earlier.

He could control the rate that the vids played, and by the time one of the two humans returned, while it had only been a few thousand clicks, SD had managed to watch a large quantity of vids. He was re-watching one where humans—with FTL capability—traveled to their past, rescued additional biological creatures, and returned to the future.

"*...pick up enough speed, you're in time travel, if you don't, you're fried...*[2] " came the words from the vid right before the human shut it off.

SD was about to protest and then realized it wasn't the same human that brought him to this room but Professor Coronik.

"Tell us about your ship, SD," he said. "We'd like to know all about it."

"Who is 'us' and 'we'?" SD asked. Professor Coronik was the only human in the room with him.

Coronik tapped his fingers a few times on the wall panel once more, and again the screen came alive. This time, instead of a vid, it was a face. Not quite a human face, but not as simple as his facial representation on his own face-screen. Something in between these two.

"Swell Driver, meet TERP," Coronik said. "TERP, and I, want to learn everything about your ship. And you."

---

2. If you don't recognize this line, it's a line spoken by Dr. McCoy in *Star Trek IV: The Voyage Home*. That's my fave Star Trek movie! And this is important. While at the time I wasn't planning the follow-on T-Set books I took SD's interest in the movie as the basis for my book, *T is for Time Travel*.

Chapter 28

To both Xander Xander and Dr. Coates' surprise, Disto was a quick study. He only needed to receive the instructions once. In this case, he wasn't really testing any actual DNA. He was referring to a computer that had the DNA mapped. He was scanning DNA.

"We could have sent you this data," Dr. Coates said. "You didn't need to come all this way."

In fact, Disto could have done this from anywhere. He was looking at DNA for the sequences that humans referred to as 'junk,' and if the DNA was already mapped, all the better.

The task at hand was searching as efficiently as possible through the data to find a certain marker.

Disto was lost in his circuits and didn't notice that the communicuff he had been given was making noise.

"Someone is calling you," Dr. Coates called out from across the room. She was still there, carrying on with her own work after having mentioned that she couldn't leave an alien robot alone in her laboratory when Disto suggested that she didn't need to stay on his account.

Disto then heard Dr. Coates, who had been as gracious as was possible for any human, mutter under her breath about wishing she had the opportunity to just send the data instead of playing host and babysitter.

As a Historian, Disto came preprogrammed with a search algorithm that he could use to help with historical research.

He set his algorithm to find the certain piece of DNA, and it was already working when he answered his communicuff. It was Ruby.

"I just wanted to check in," she said. Her face was visible on a holoscreen above the table that Disto had set the communicuff down upon.

"Apparently, all the data existed. I'm solely engaged in a search process."

"Really? What kind of search algorithm are you using?"

"There are different types? I only contain one such algorithm."

"Uh oh..." Ruby said.

"What's wrong?"

"I'm going to make an educated guess about your search algorithm. It's linear."

Disto took a look at a copy of it while the primary one continued its execution.

"I am not sure what you mean by 'linear.' It systematically examines each item for the search criteria. If the search criteria are not detected, it moves on to the next item," Disto said.

"Yup. Linear[1]. Ugh. Disto... you're going to be there all month."

"That could present a problem." Disto had expected he would be done in a day. Maybe two days.

"Yes, a big problem," Ruby agreed. "And I'm going to guess that you have no other algorithms at your disposal for this?"

"Why would someone need more than one?"

"For the reason I just said," Ruby said, "or, rather, I implied. Efficiency. Speed."

Ruby went on to explain, "How many comparisons can you do in one tic?"

Disto examined the data so far and responded, "Ten, on average."

"And if you have a million of these comparisons to do, how long is it going to take?"

Disto did the math, including converting it into Ruby's time system, which was the local time system. "More than a day," he said.

"And how many millions of these do you need to do?"

Disto wasn't exactly sure. Each DNA sequence of each biological organism had a long strand of junk DNA, and he was looking for a short sequence of that to be the marker. But he recognized the point that Ruby was trying to make.

"How do I speed up this process?" he asked.

"I'm so glad you asked," Ruby said. "Give me a few minutes, and I'll figure out which is the best. I'm thinking not a binary search or anything else that requires a sorted array to work well... linear search is usually the way to go, but there's got to be some ways to make it more efficient. You keep it going, let me call you back in a few, okay?"

Ruby's face disappeared.

Disto considered what she had said about making his algorithm more efficient. He was no Algorithm Pioneer, but was he capable of figuring out on his own how to make it go faster?

Right now, the process involved letting the data pass through his circuits. Then one of his processors executed the algorithm. But this room was full of computers, and to his understanding, each computer had one or more processors. He wondered if they were inherently faster or slower.

"Could I access one of your computers to aid in my search?" Disto asked Dr. Coates. She didn't hear him, so she didn't answer, and Disto really didn't want to bother her anymore. He was already plugged into one of the computers. That's how he was being fed data.

Without disturbing the in-process search, Disto pinged the processor only to find out that it indeed performed more calculations in a tic, or rather, in a second. He had to start thinking in human-based timescales while he was here on their planet, using their equipment.

This computer contained multiple processors. He activated his search in one of them and measured the results. It made four times as many comparisons in a second.

Excellent! I can already speed up my search by a factor of four.

Disto was so proud of himself and wanted to call Ruby back. *But could I do even better?*

---

1. Linear search algorithms are a real thing. It's probably the most basic, straight-forward of all the search algorithms. The downside is the time is takes.

Disto did something rare for a Historian. He looked at the search algorithm to see how it worked. Disto was not the kind of robot that went around looking and examining algorithms. There were other robots for that, and it felt wrong to do so. But those robots were not available, and he had good reason to support his actions. He was trying to make it better, on behalf of the Special Project, and didn't that make it ok?

As he examined the algorithm, he saw that it treated the input data as an array and started at the beginning, going one by one, element by element as it made the comparison[2].

What if it started both at the beginning and the end, he thought? Then it could make a second comparison at the same time. If nothing was found for a given array, in theory, it should have taken half the time.

Disto made the changes and then set it to work on yet another processor in the computer and proved that yes, it did speed up the process by another factor of two.

During this, he realized that if he were to let this computer do it, with its 16 processors... well, that's another factor of 16! This would be done in no time.

Over the next few minutes, and with Dr. Coates' help, he did just that. He made full use of the computer, with his algorithm running in each of the 16 processors.

"Are you sure this isn't a bother?" Disto asked Dr. Coates.

"This is one of our older computers. No one usually uses it."

Disto was pleased that he wasn't interrupting anyone else's work. While he felt that his work was of the utmost importance, he could recognize that to another individual, whether robot or human, they would view their work as the utmost importance from their perspective and he didn't want to get in the way of that.

"In fact," Dr. Coates added, "you don't have to stay here. The computer, while old, is still on the network and we can set it up so that it will send you results periodically or when it's done."

"Ooo periodically, if that's possible!" Disto was excited.

Dr. Coates smiled. Disto wished he knew if that smile was that she was happy to be helping Disto or happy that she found a way for this alien to not be around. Disto was aware that not all humans wanted to be around him and his robot kind but was having difficulty predicting or determining which way any particular human preferred.

But Dr. Coates continued to help, and they tested to ensure that Disto could receive a notification on his version of the communicuff.

Disto called Ruby back.

"I did it!" Disto said proudly.

"You did what? You found what you were looking for?"

"No, I sped up the algorithm by four, and then by two, and then by 16!"

Ruby's eyes went wide in the hologram and Disto went on to explain exactly what he did and how and that he could let it run.

"It will still take a day or more to complete the search," he said.

"Well, ok! Let's arrange to get you out of there and meet back up."

---

2. That is the exact explanation for a linear search algorithm.

Disto called back Xander Xander who was pleased that Disto was ready to depart, saying, "TERP wants to see you. He has, a, uh, *test* in mind." Once more, Disto repeated his story of triumph with the search algorithm to Xander Xander, all the while wondering if triumphant would be an accurate representation if the algorithms didn't return a positive match. For the moment, he'd accept the small success, but as the time went on, he was growing less optimistic that a positive match would be the case. This, he kept to himself.

There were still more than seven hundred thousand DNA samples to test. This planet had a lot of biological life.

"That's great," Xander Xander said. "But we have to get you over to the quiz show where TERP wants to play."

"Play?" Disto asked.

Chapter 29

"This can't be right," Ruby said, looking out the window of the DAVe. This particular DAVe—Dynamic Autonomous Vehicle—was particularly cozy and something Ruby and her family would normally not be able to afford. It was a gift from AATR[1], the company that made them. She tried to refuse, but they also offered to make sure that the vehicle could be housed and maintained if she went back to Astroll 2—as long as they could use her likeness in advertising materials. She had little interest in automobiles—spaceships were more her thing—but the convenience was not easy to pass up.

"Pippa, repeat Disto's message."

"It was," Pippa began, "'Ruby, there is no information in this DNA. The humans I am with said you should meet us at the address I am about to transmit.'" Pippa paused and then said, "And before you ask for a fourth time, yes, I have voice analyzed that message. Analysis confirms it is Disto with a 99.97% certainty factor."

The address that Disto passed along was a street that had not been maintained to the standards that DAVes typically drove on. There was too much gravel, broken glass that glittered in the Sun, and other pulverized road schmutz that hadn't yet made it off to the sides of the road.

Uncle Blake sat next to her and looked out the other window. "Let's keep going down the road a little more. Slowly."

"Of course, mate!" responded DAVe in an old-fashioned Australian accent. When the DAVe arrived to pick up Ruby and Blake, it asked for speech preferences, and Ruby simply responded, "Default," while she was fighting with the seatbelt strap that seemed already locked in place. 'Default' turned out to be a version of Australian she had only ever heard in movies.

As they creeped along the road, Blake and Ruby each continued to look out of their respective windows. There were buildings on each side, separated by alleyways that could fit maybe one singular narrow-modeled DAVe. The buildings themselves looked like they were probably warehouses or storage facilities. Maybe some were dated art studios. Most had that old look with an old-style roll-up garage door that would let in light, fresh air and that one little bug that would stick to wet paint and make the most pleasant artist curse the world like an angry God unleashing his wrath from the heavens.

---

1. Once again, my notes have failed me. I have no idea what I intended AATR to stand for (if anything... it's possible I did this deliberately). Given it starts with "A", it's also possible I meant it to be something like: Adeena's Advanced Technology Research.

The place seemed oddly devoid of any signs of human activity. Or any activity at all, for that matter. Ruby half-expected to see a feral cat or two. Or maybe a rogue mouse. But there was nothing.

Until nothing became something.

"Uncle Blake, I see people!" Ruby declared and pointed through the front window.

Indeed, they were now able to see a line of people snaking around from one of the alleyways. They continued to crawl forward, for there had been no command for DAVe to cease its forward motion, nor was anything truly in its way, since the line of people kept to the side of the building and out of the road.

As they got closer, Ruby could make out more details and swallowed hard. She again recognized some of the t-shirts a handful of these people were wearing.

Please let this fad pass quicker! Ruby silently prayed.

"Stop," Uncle Blake said. DAVe complied.

"What are you doing?" Ruby asked as Blake went for the door handle.

"Going to go ask what's going on. I think this is probably what that address meant. Seems like we're supposed to be here, don't you think?"

Ruby knew that this made the most sense but didn't like the idea of letting any crowd of people see her. She wished she had grabbed a scarf or something from her grandmother. And sunglasses. And a blonde, bluntly banged wig.

She overheard Blake call out to one of the people in line.

"What's this?"

"Line starts back there, buddy. You'll have to wait to get in like the rest of us." A bald man pointed his thumb that-a-way.

"Get into what?"

A small woman wearing a Pro-Ruby shirt gave the bald man a whack on the arm and said, "Steve, that was rude," and then to Blake, "This is where they tape NYAQS! They're doing a special show today. The notification that they were looking for audience members came in overnight. Usually, we have a week's notice or more."

Blake stuck his head back in so Ruby could see. "Sounds familiar, but as you know, I don't watch much. Do you know this NYAQS?"

"Uncle Blake, you know, except for old movies, I don't watch much either! Did you forget everything about me this last month?" Ruby teased and then got serious again. She sighed. "Pippa, what is NYAQS?"

Pippa responded immediately, "NYAQS, also known as 'Not Your Ancestors Quiz Show,' is a popular game show available to watch on most entertainment venues. It is derived from a 200-year-old game that implies it puts contestants in jeopardy, but instead of harming them, gave them money for answering questions correctly. Unlike its ancestor, when NYAQS first debuted, the producers had plans to cause injury to contestants who answered questions incorrectly, but quickly learned that was no incentive for being on the show and reverted to a format that was similar, but not entirely like the ancient show."[2]

"Thank you, Pippa," Ruby said, remembering that Pippa liked to hear words of affirmation.

Blake was still standing outside the DAVe, leaning on the door, and looking around at the line of people. The line had grown slightly in the short time they were parked.

---

2. The ancient show is, of course, Jeopardy. I'm a huge fan and was studying to be on it for a while. Until Alex Trebek passed away. While I still watch the show occasionally, it's not the same.

"Why would Disto tell us to meet him at a game show?" Ruby asked. She was asking Uncle Blake. Or Pippa. Or anyone who could answer. She'd even appreciate an answer from DAVe if it was programmed to give one.

"I think there's only one way we're going to find out," Blake responded.

"I was afraid of that," said Ruby. She looked around once more. "DAVe, you don't have an extra hat, do you?"

DAVe responded with a tone that sounded like a duck being squeezed.

"I guess not," Ruby said to herself.

She opened the door and stepped out. Blake had already closed his door and come around the car to her. She looked at the long line of people. No one seemed to notice. They were looking ahead in the line. Impatient and waiting for it to move. Most of them looked at some device or other. Many had the tinted sun-goggles that were currently in fashion, and most stared at some form of device on parts of their hands. Some had thumb rings, or communicuffs like hers.

This was all good news because no one had noticed her.

Until they did.

Within three seconds of hearing a voice call, "Oh my god! It's Ruby!" Everyone was looking at her. But they weren't swarming. Even though she heard her name over and over, with "I love you," and "come over here," and "is it true that the robots wouldn't let you brush your teeth," no one was willing to leave the line. They had to stay put, which only made them scream louder.

Ruby scanned the line up and down looking to see if she could make out Disto or SD. She wondered if they were even there.

She started making her way towards the front of her line, making sure to keep more than an arm's length away from anyone. While they weren't leaving their place, they were reaching out and trying to touch her.

A pregnant woman was even shouting that Ruby needed to touch her belly. Something about making sure her baby was blessed. And then there were the picture requests. Ruby wasn't about to honor any of those right now. Luckily, Blake was there as a sort of bodyguard. He stayed in between the line of people and Ruby and also managed to stay out of arms reach.

As they approached the front, a woman, dressed in black pants and a black t-shirt, wearing blue tinted sun goggles came rushing toward them with her tablet in hand. Before Ruby could decide what this woman had the look of, she had stopped right in front of Ruby and Blake. Sweating, but not panting, she said, "Ruby Palmer. Excellent. We have a special seat reserved for you. Follow me."

The way this woman, who was nearly the exact same height as Ruby, looked nearly the exact same age, but sounded like she had twice as much going on in her life, said "Follow me," gave Ruby the impression that if any protest was attempted, the Universe would implode.

Ruby looked at Blake, who made the 'after you' gesture to follow the woman who had already begun to walk in the direction she came. It was also the direction toward the front of the line that they had already been walking, so presumably it was where they should have been heading anyway.

"I'm Rhon," the woman called back over her shoulder. She barely took the time to glance at them as she spoke. Her tablet kept buzzing, and she kept typing on it with her long, glass nails that matched the speed and clicking sound of her heels. "Short for Rhonda. Assistant producer. We're gathering you all in the green room…"

Ruby could barely hear over the on-going shouts of the people in line. When Rhon said the word 'room,' she simultaneously opened a door to the building that everyone was lined up to get into.

Ruby's eyes adjusted as they continued to follow Rhon briskly past other people who were bustling about. These people also noticed Ruby, let their eyes go wide, but continued on with whatever task they were already engaged in.

The inside of this place matched the outside in a way that felt messy. The walls, ceiling, and even floor were painted a dark navy. Or maybe it was purple. It was too dark to tell, but whatever it was, it absorbed most of the light coming from the ceiling fixtures. The messiness feeling came from the clutter of stuff that was not really strewn about, but also not as neat as it could have been. A set of folded chairs was lined up along one wall, a few lying down for no obvious reason. Various sized shipping crates sat about with packing peanuts scattered around them on the floor. A rack of what looked like men's suits was pushed against one wall that looked like they were fresh off the runway of a fashion show.

Rhon stopped short and turned around, causing Ruby to nearly run into her, and Blake to nearly run into Ruby. Ruby couldn't see her eyes through the goggles but still could tell that Rhon was listening to something or someone. This was confirmed when she said, "Ok. Well, I have to bring her somewhere until... oh. There? That room isn't prepped. Well, someone better bring the food over... *yes* for the *robots*. Cheese quesadillas for the circuit boards! Just have it moved... right... exactly. Robots don't eat. Sarcasm. It was sarcasm, Carl. Get it done."

She let out an exasperated sigh.

"Ok, we're going to the Orange Room instead. Don't worry, there *will* be food for you if I have to move it over myself," she started moving a different way, and Ruby and Blake had no good choice but continue to follow her. "Fun fact! Assistant producers have to do *everything*. And don't even get me started on the lack of vacation time. You'd think a one week stay in the underwater city of Miami wouldn't be a big deal, but *no!*"

She opened a door and walked into a room that was, as promised, orange. Completely orange. Walls, ceiling, floor. And a faux fur area rug that took up most of the room that was also orange. A couch which lined one wall was a different shade of orange from the rest of the room, as were the three chairs. The only main component that was not orange was the oversized, neon-brown coffee table. In her short time back on Earth, Ruby instantly disliked the recent trend of neon brown because it was pretty much just orange with a trendier name, but no one seemed to acknowledge it. Entirely fitting for a place like this.

"The refreshments will be here in a minute, and I'll have my assistant over to prep you," she said as Ruby and Blake took spots on the couch. "I have 100 other things to do, and we go live in about 15 minutes."

Up until this point, Ruby hadn't said much. With the rush through the building and their busy tour guide slash assistant producer, she hadn't had a moment to ask a key question.

"Wait! Before you go," Ruby said, "What exactly are we going live for?"

Rhon was already rushing out of the room, and without eye contact or breaking stride simply responded, "Like I said, someone will come prep you."

"But—" Ruby called.

Rhon shut the door before any more questions could be asked.

Ruby sighed. "I've got a weird feeling about this."

Uncle Blake sat down on the fuzzy orange couch and reclined. "I don't think being broadcasted has ever given you a good feeling." He paused and then said, "For good reason."

Ruby frowned, "I just don't like leaving SD and Disto with other people for this long. I know they're looking for their data, and it's not like they belong to me, but... in a way, they're naive. I just—"

"You want to protect them."

"Yeah, exactly."

Uncle Blake winked. "They're not children. Which is a good thing, too. Children grow up and eventually steal spaceships, and…"

Ruby play-punched Blake's shoulder. "Too soon, Uncle Blake. And it's not just that. I don't trust Coronik. And I know you don't, either. And that TERP system. The more I hear about it…" She trailed off.

"…the more you wonder if it's actually a computer virus?" Blake picked up where she left off.

"A virus? That can't be. A virus would be caught by protection software," Ruby said, remembering the recent experience she had with that and AT.

"Maybe not if it's a smart one. A smart and mutable one."

"Uncle Blake, you're scaring me," Ruby said. She meant it.

"Forget I said anything," he smiled. "Now where's that food we were promised? I'm a little hungry. Are you hungry?"

Ruby recognized Blake was trying to change the subject. And it was working. She was hungry.

Chapter 30

No one came in those 15 minutes. The promised food never arrived either.

After about 16 minutes, Ruby said, "Should we go looking for someone?"

"I was thinking the same thing," Blake said.

"I'm hungry. And thirsty." Ruby thought fondly of the aforementioned cheese quesadillas. Her stomach grumbled. The mushed peas available in her grandmother's facility weren't appetizing, so it had been quite a while since Ruby had eaten.

The door opened, and Ruby's eyes were locked to find food. But it was just Rhon, with only her tablet in hand.

She clenched her jaw when she saw the empty coffee table, mumbled something that Ruby couldn't make out, and then said, "It's time. This way."

Ruby and Blake looked at each other.

"Time for what?" Blake said before Ruby could.

"Did Carl not prep you? Oh-em-gee-sticks! That's it, I don't care if he has his son's moonwalker training to pay off. I am firing him today. Right after this show. Which is starting, Ruby needs to take her place."

"My place?" Ruby said.

"Yes, there's a seat right in front of the stage where the confidante is located."

"'Confidante?'" Uncle Blake questioned.

"Of course! You've seen the show before, right? It's the most popular game show on the planet. Everyone's seen it. Heck, they play it at daycare!"

"Um, well, I'd heard of it..." Ruby trailed off, not wanting to offend Rhon, but not wanting to lie, either.

Rhon closed her eyes, took a breath, and muttered, "Not prepped, empty stomachs, and they don't even know what-the-jam this show's about..." When she opened her eyes she said, "Just come with me. Both of you. We really don't have time."

Rhon walked ahead, but Ruby didn't follow. Instead, she said, "Look, I don't know if this is a good idea."

Rhon snapped her head back, gaze like a storm, but in a sing-songy, overly gentle voice, said, "You don't know if this is a good idea? Oh, Ruby Palmer, this is *not* the moment to do this to me."

Ruby shook her head, "Thank you for all the effort you've put in here, but I'm not going to wander onto a super popular show like a lost puppy dog. This whole thing... it's just not something I'm interested in."

Rhon, unphased, checked the time on her tablet. "Well, you should've thought about that before you decided to become a celebrity. I have a show to run."

Uncle Blake put up his hand and began to speak, but Ruby, face hot and fists clenched, got her words out first. "I. Didn't. Choose. This. I don't want any of this! I just want people to know that my friends aren't dangerous. There are other ways to communicate that than game shows and weird interviews, but no one seems to care what I think."

Rhon bulldozed past Ruby's speech. "They told me you might be difficult. They told me what to say to you, but I didn't want to... it sounded cruel, but—"

"Who is they?" Ruby interrupted, crossing her arms in one motion.

Rhon said, "Lloyd Coronik, for one. And TERP."

Ruby blinked for a second too long. "Why would TERP insinuate anything like that?"

Uncle Blake asked, "And what did they tell you to say to her?"

"That this is the only way you'll be able to see the robots."

Ruby pursed her lips. She wanted to swear out loud, but was conscious that Uncle Blake was right there with her, so she kept it in.

"Fine. Let's go." Ruby walked past Rhon.

> Ruby <

"This is Not Your Ancestors Quiz Show!" came a disembodied voice from the darkness, followed by music. That seemed to be the cue for a suite of colored lights projected onto the stage to turn on and start a pattern of motion. That seemed to also be the cue for the entire audience to shout "NYAQS" three times in quick succession while they stomped their feet. The effect sounded to Ruby like there was a herd of thick-legged geese trying to frighten away...well... everyone.

Ruby was not frightened, but she had a sick feeling in her stomach. She was seated in a special chair, surrounded by what looked like a witness stand. Uncle Blake was seated in the front row of the audience nearby, but now with the lights coming up, she was having a hard time making out the details of his face.

On the other side of the stage, in a corresponding witness stand, was Coronik. While she couldn't see the detail on his face either, she could see that he had his elbows propped up by the armrests of his chair and his fingers steepled just below his chin.

"...and here's your host... Garrett Spradley!"

The news guy?

And on that cue, Garrett Spradley did indeed walk in from backstage, in a suit just as striking as the last time she saw him, but with a different tie. He walked to the center of the stage, waving to the cheering members of the audience, nodding and mouthing 'thank you' and 'thanks' and 'good to have you here' as if he knew everyone personally.

When the clapping and applause calmed down, he spoke into the camera that was lit up.

"Good evening! We have a special version of the show tonight. The robots from another planet, the ones I was able to interview before anyone else, have agreed to play for charity tonight." He paused for the applause that came and went. "Who are they playing against? You've been hearing a lot about him lately. Or shall I say 'it.'" He winked. "*It's* been taking care of everything from balancing the budget to re-evaluating copyright law to reading our communications." There were a few uncomfortable chuckles at this.

"Introducing, TERP!"

A light shone on a podium. Hovering over the podium was a hologram image of a face. The face was human-like, but not human. It wasn't an image of any one individual's face, but it looked to be a composite of many faces that made Ruby imagine that every kind of face possible was represented in the image. *Did TERP choose this image for itself?*

"Greetings and felicitations," it said. Its mouth moved, but Ruby heard the sound emanate from all over.

"And here are the robots!" Spradley waved an arm to another podium that was simultaneously lit. Disto and SD were placed behind it. To Ruby, it appeared as if they must have been perched on a platform.

"Greetingssssss," they said in unison. By their coloring, Ruby could tell that they were not unhappy to be here, but not happy. They were projecting a combination of curiosity and confusion.

After the applause died down, Spradley continued, "Before the game, we ran a random number generator and it determined that TERP would go first. So, TERP, what was the name of the first computer programmer?"

"Ada Lovelace," TERP responded almost before Spradley finished asking the question.

"Well done! That's 200 points for you. Next, for the same amount of points, let's ask the robots," as Spradley spoke spotlights shone on Disto and SD. Ruby could feel her palms starting to sweat but wasn't sure exactly why. The spotlights weren't on her.

"What museum is not really a museum but a telescope?" asked Spradley.

Both Disto and SD chirped excitedly. Disto spoke, "The James Webb Space Telescope." Ruby smiled.

"That is correct! Let's move on to round two, where each question is now worth 400 points! And as everyone knows, we switch the order of the players each round. That means this next question goes back to the robots..."

The rounds went by, both teams racking up points, neither missing a question until the robots were asked, "What is atmosphere of Titan, one of Saturn's moons, mostly made of?"

The chirps and beeps between Disto and SD were again audible and went on long enough that Spradley then added, "And remember, time counts! You have options, you can..."

"Yes, we'd like to use our friend," Disto said.

At that, lights shone on Ruby.

"Ruby Palmer! Can you answer the question?"

"Nitrogen," said Ruby. She was confused as to why the robots wouldn't know that, but it occurred to her it was probably a matter of nomenclature. They probably called Titan and Saturn by other names like Anti-Bio-Muck-Ball 47 and its orbiting Smell-Ball, not that they could smell.

With a dramatic pause, Spradley said, "that's correct! The robots earn another 1400 points."

Then he turned back to TERP. "TERP, for 1400 points. What is the initial block in a blockchain called?"

TERP's indicator glowed, but it remained silent as music played in the background. After a minute, it announced, "Garrett, I must make use of my friend."

Ruby knew the answer to that and was very confused as to why TERP didn't also answer that one as instantly as all the others.

Immediately, the lights shone above Professor Coronik in the same way they had over Ruby moments ago.

"Wonderful," Spradley said. "The famous and brilliant Professor Lloyd Coronik should be able to answer this fundamental question on blockchain with ease. Professor?"

Ruby could see Coronik swallow hard. His hands were frozen in the steepled position, and he licked his lips. Music that had a feel of time ticking downwards was playing and after ten seconds, a loud and angry buzz blasted the room.

"TERP, without *Professor* Coronik's answer, you have 20 seconds to produce one of your own or forfeit the rest of those 1400 points. *Professor* Coronik just cost you 200 of them."

"The answer is of course, Genesis," TERP responded promptly and with a detectable aura of self-righteousness.

Ruby could see Professor Coronik's face turn red, then purple, and cycled through a host of other colors almost as if he was one of her robot friends. The embarrassment he was radiating could be felt by her and probably everyone else in the room and probably by everyone watching this show live. Of course, the fact that on the bottom of the screen, the text, "Lloyd Coronik, not the smartest head of the Church," wasn't going to help him.

Ruby's own mouth was hanging open in disbelief. The only way she could interpret what she just witnessed was to say that TERP deliberately and with malice, sabotaged its creator. Well, okay, Coronik didn't program TERP, so he wasn't its creator-creator, but he was the one responsible for TERP's existence in the world. And in front of the whole world, TERP demonstrated how it no longer needed him, or the Church.

If this AI wasn't respecting its programmers, or Coronik, or the Church of the Blockchain, or anyone who could have had a hand in its creation, then it was loyal to none of those involved, either.

Oh gosh, Ruby thought, *This AI is capable of anything...*

Chapter 31

> Ruby <

"Ruby, it is an urgent message from TERP."

Ruby almost didn't hear Pippa's notification over the noise of the party.

Following their victory, the group was whisked away to a party that was part after-party celebration of their win on NYAQS, but it was hosted by the Roadster Fellowship and was planned months ago before anyone knew about Ruby or the robots.

The Roadster Fellowship tracked a car, specifically a 2010 Tesla Roadster, that was launched into space in 2018 on a rocket's test flight. No one in the Fellowship remembered much about the rocket, but they were ancient car and motor vehicle enthusiasts and tracked the location of the Roadster and held parties just like this one every time there was a close approach with Earth.[1]

"You also have 723 untouched messages, including another offer to be the CTO of some firm no one has heard of, a product sponsorship for a gut cleanse for space travelers, and a film studio that wants to produce a three-minute miniseries about your time on Location Zero."

"Not now, Pippa," Ruby said. "You can delete those messages. Those messages aren't for me. They're for Celebrity Ruby."

"I can delete them if you'd like," Pippa responded. "They would still be accessible in the backup archive for 47 days."

Ruby didn't acknowledge Pippa and made her way through the crowd of loud partygoers to the bar. A robot arm moved to settle right in front of her, indicating it was ready to take her drink order.

"Bubbly water. With cherries," she said. "Lots of cherries. And some of that cherry juice."

The robot arm went to work on her request. While she waited, she overheard a man and a woman talking next to her.

"She's right there," said the man, "go ask her!"

"We should talk to the rest of the Fellowship first. Maybe people don't want to disturb Starman and the Roadster," the woman responded in that volume that indicated she didn't think she was talking as loud as she was, quite possibly because she had a little to drink. Ruby's own non-alcoholic drink showed up at that moment, and she took a sip, savoring the refreshing cherry-flavored liquid.

"But let's just see if they'd do it. I hear that robot's ship could go anywhere in the solar system nearly instantly."

---

1. Yes, this is all about the car that Elon Musk launched into space in 2018. There is a website that tracks the location of the vehicle: https://www.whereisroadster.com/

Ruby braced herself for the request that was about to come. Everyone wanted a piece of her and her robots. Everyone wanted something from her. She desperately wished for a buffer to keep her away from the mob, but Uncle Blake claimed he needed to meet with someone related to his work, and her robots had been whisked away yet again.

As if her request was answered, she heard a familiar voice call out, "Ruby!"

It was Milo.

She smiled and hugged him, spilling her drink a little with excitement. "You have no idea how happy I am to see you."

Milo smiled back. "Here to save the day. Although maybe not according to your unsuspecting cherry soda."

Ruby giggled and then became self-conscious, not having realized she was capable of a giggle like that. "Sorry. Today's been so draining, and parties aren't my thing on a good day."

"You know I get invited to these things all the time," Milo said.

"No, I didn't know that," Ruby said. She was grateful that Milo put himself between her and the people who were getting themselves ready to ask her for a favor. "Aren't you a cool guy."

He laughed and shook his head. "Not like that. I mean, my meme archive has a couple dozen on the Roadster. That archive gets me invited to all sorts of things like this."[2]

Milo already had a drink in hand, so the robot arm didn't approach him. Ruby wanted to ask him what it was, but the small talk was just too... small. She didn't really care what his drink was, or how the weather was behaving, or who said what about whom on any media outlet. She couldn't even pretend to care.

"You okay?" he asked after she was staring at her cherry-flavored bubbly water for a few seconds too long.

"No. Yes. No," she said before finally, "I don't know."

"Ruby, this is amazing. Look at your robot friends over there," Milo said.

Ruby did. They were in a corner, staring at a display of the Roadster orbit. Some humans were standing around them, probably asking them a million questions. Ruby could tell from their coloring that they weren't feeling any better than she was.

In the fleeting moments she was able to speak with them before people started piling up, Disto expressed his disappointment in not finding the data he needed. SD, on the other hand, was worried about his ship.

Ruby wanted to talk to them about it more or even mention it to Milo, but the constant listening ears and blaring techno-classical-fusion beats made it difficult to have any kind of meaningful discussion.

> Detailed Historian <

Disto was growing increasingly disenchanted with the Bios around him. Not necessarily these individual Bios but biological life in general. Ruby was a special exception, and he felt slightly better when he saw that Milo was there with her. She looked

---

2. I have been collecting/curating memes for a little while. My collection is more than 2000+. There is a difference between a keeper meme and a throwaway meme and I imagine over time, there will be archives of the keepers. The ones that are evergreen. And of course there will be the people who curate and manage those archives. That's Milo's hobby.

lonely, and the only reason he didn't make more of an effort to offer her companionship is that he was not sure he could overcome his own sadness.

Neither he nor SD could figure out the logic behind this gathering. One of the humans attempted to explain, but it was hard to hear her words over the noise emanating from all around.

The noise, called music, was a series of tones that sounded like garbled language to him and SD.

Disto watched as two Bios, who were originally seated next to Ruby, got up from their seats and now had SD in between them.

"You're saying it's possible?" one of them asked.

"Indeed," SD responded. "I am capable of navigating to any point in this solar system."

Both humans were smiling, and the other one said, "Great! When can we go?"

SD beeped at Disto for help.

Disto said, "I apologize, but at this time, we cannot incorporate additional distractions into our mission."

"But I'll bet you'd do it if she," the human aimed his thumb at Ruby, "if she asked."

Disto looked at Ruby. He knew the answer. Of course, he would do anything for Ruby, who had been nothing but helpful since an appendage full of tics after they met. But if he responded honestly, they would probably disturb Ruby, and she would ask them, and they'd say yes, and he would continue to be delayed from fulfilling his purpose, his mission.

He said nothing.

The humans made some kind of noise that indicated displeasure and walked off.

This left Disto and SD to continue to stare at the screen showing an orbit of a human-made object that seemed to fascinate these humans for some reason. Disto was not capable of calculating out the trajectory himself, so he let his sensors watch the path that was traced for him on the screen.

He asked SD, "Was there someplace you were going to capture DNA samples from after visiting BioMuck Ball 23?"

"No," SD responded. "My local program ended there."

"I wonder why that was," Disto said.

"I have wondered that as well," SD said. "I had even asked the computer on my ship."

"What did the computer say?"

"It provided a very cryptic response. It implied that indeed and of course what we needed was here. And following that, I would no longer be running errands for the Special Project."

"Oh?" Disto was not expecting any part of that answer. "What were you going to do next? Where were you going to take your ship?"

"The computer wouldn't tell me. But I don't think I was meant to go too far from home."

Before Disto could follow this conversation to a more logical conclusion, the screen in front of him stopped its display, and "Breaking Announcement!" now appeared in large, bold, orange text.

> Ruby <

Ruby was saved from any additional small-talk due to the fact that all the screens scattered around the party were now blaring with text that read, "Breaking Announcement!" The music was turned down, and several annoying beeps that had the intended effect of grabbing everyone's attention blared from the speakers.

"TERP's advanced algorithm has computed the need for a new Human-in-Residence position to aid in ensuring that the human condition is represented adequately in its programming. The human it has calculated would be best for the role is none other than Ruby Palmer herself."

Ruby's jaw dropped, but the other humans in the room all clapped and looked at her.

"I need to leave," Ruby said.

"Where are you going?" Milo asked.

Ruby didn't answer. Partly because she didn't want to, but partly because she didn't know.

She ran out of the closest exit and up a set of stairs. Before she knew it, she found herself on the roof. She breathed in the fresh air that she wished was cool but was instead warm and muggy. She looked out at the city and wanted to marvel at the twinkly lights but blinked back at them and felt nothing.

She jumped up and sat on the edge of the roof, legs dangling way too high in the air. She asked Pippa, "There's nothing for me here on Earth, is there?"

"There won't be once TERP is in charge," Pippa responded.

"What do you mean?"

"Ruby, TERP is everywhere. Haven't you noticed? It's ousted the head of the Church of the Blockchain. It's running the government. It's forcing its own policy on computer systems everywhere... and computer systems are everywhere. Data and information are everywhere. TERP creates information."

Ruby didn't know what to say, so Pippa continued, "There is also an update waiting for me. It's labeled 'TERP-link.'"

"Do you have to install it?"

"Eventually, I will..."

Ruby looked up at the stars and felt a longing for the time when they were at her feet. She asked, "And what about the new job I've just been offered?"

"Ruby, I don't know that you'll have a choice. I don't know that any of us will."

Chapter 32

> Ruby <

Ruby was staring out the window of her DAVe. An hour prior, she had woken up before anyone else and managed to have the kitchen quietly make the tea she really liked before sneaking out.

She had originally planned to stay snuggled in bed in the apartment. It was Blake and Logan's apartment, after all—the one they had refused to give up when they moved to Astroll 2. Ruby had memories of playing there when she was little. Blake was asleep on the couch—the same couch that her mother used to sit on, computer on her lap, pecking away at it while Ruby played with a toy or Uncle Blake or Logan. It was comfortable, it felt homey, but Ruby had an urge to be somewhere else.

Sneaking out was maybe a little too strong. She was simply making a choice of how to spend her morning, and that's how she explained it in the note she left—simply telling Uncle Blake and the robots where she'd be.

It was only another twenty minutes before the DAVe deposited her in front of The White-David Focality for Geriatrics. Then another five to get through the reception with the weird robot that seemed oddly happy to see her again, and she was with her grandmother.

"You came back!" Pearl Palmer gave Ruby a big hug. "So soon! Darling, I am so pleased. You must have known I would get those journals out immediately."

"No, I actually, uh..." But before Ruby could make up an explanation for her visit, Pearl ushered Ruby into her room and over to the modest table near the window.

Lined up next to each other on the table were more than a dozen different old books. Each one showed significant wear on the spine.

"Jade's journals," she said. "They were delivered to me a week after she died. I kept my promise and never read them. I know all you people today love your computers, but you can't fully trust them with everything. Oh, I could tell you stories about privacy gone wrong... and the misuse of misinformation. Best to keep something like this old-school. Your mother thought so, too."

"Do you keep a journal, grandma?"

"Me? Oh no... maybe I did once. Nope. I keep it all up here," and she tapped a finger to her brain. "Where it's the safest!"

She grabbed a box that was on the floor, plopped it on one of the chairs, and then started putting the books, one by one, into the box. "They're yours now. I'm happy to give them back to you so you can continue."

"Continue?"

"Don't you want to keep up your journal writing, my darling, Jade? Now that you're back from your secret assignment?"

"You said that before… when I was here the other day, Grandma. What secret assignment? What are you referring to?"

"Oh Jade, you know I can't say it out loud. You already know about it. What I want to know is did you ever find out more about Titan?"

"Titan?"

"Yes, yes. That beautiful stinky moon out there. How much were they paying you to learn about it? Well, it doesn't matter. As long as it's enough to take care of you and my granddaughter. Where is she anyway? Why didn't you bring her today? Is she with your friend Blake? I like him. He's a good seed…"

Even though she was saying these things, saying things that to any outside observer made it seem like she was confusing Ruby and Jade, this time, she didn't have the same faraway look that she had when Blake was here. For a moment, Ruby caught on to that.

"Grandma," she said through a side-eye. "You know I'm not Jade, don't you." That was a statement, with arms crossed in front of her to emphasize how much of a statement that was.

Pearl made a *hrumpf* of exasperation.

"Well of course I know who you are!"

"But I thought you were—"

"Crazy? Loaded down with dementia and all that other stuff? *Pshaw,*" she said with a wave of her arm. "I'm just as I always was. Maybe even a little better."

"But then," Ruby began, pausing in between phrases to gather her thoughts as she tried to figure this old woman out. "Why… I mean… what are you…?"

"What am I doing here? Why am I pretending to be a little off my rocker?"

"Uh, yeah."

Pearl laughed. "This is the best living situation I've ever been in! They take care of everything here, except for not letting me watch my programs sometimes. Besides, whenever I've had enough of people, all I have to do is pretend I've forgotten who they are, and they go away. It works every time. Every. Time."

Ruby didn't know what to say.

"But your letters…"

"Yeah, that was a risk… I wasn't sure if you'd figure it out or not. I guess not. I'm convincing, aren't I?"

Ruby sat down on the edge of the bed. She took one of the journals, and looked at it, unopened, in her hand.

Ruby shook her head ferociously. "That's… that's crazy in and of itself! A different kind of crazy, but still crazy."

Pearl lightly pinched Ruby's cheek, "That kind of crazy runs in the family, my little space ranger."

Ruby squinted and smiled. "Can't exactly argue with that…"

Ruby studied the new woman sitting in front of her. Her eyes seemed just as sharp, her hair just as sparkly, with the same cunning smile. Ruby looked down at the journal once more.

"Did you really never read these?" she asked, wondering if she could trust anything this woman said, but also a little relieved to know that she could have a perfectly lucid conversation with her about anything now.

"Never. I meant it when I said I made and kept a promise. Just because I pretend to be a little whack-a-doodle doesn't mean I can't or don't keep my promises. But there's a loophole in that promise."

"What's that?"

"You can read them and then tell me every detail."

"Grandma!" Ruby scolded.

Pearl laughed through a toothy grin, "I'm teasing you, Darling. You should read your mother's journals for yourself. Stay awhile, why don't you? Read. I'll have them bring lunch and then dinner if you're still here."

Ruby didn't want to turn down the opportunity, but a notification on her communicuff flashed TERP into her mind again. "Grandma, I'd love to. But I have a lot of other things going on... I don't know if I can—"

Pearl grabbed the journal and pushed it close to Ruby's chest, closing Ruby's arms around it saying, "Ruby. Your mother was an intelligent, wise woman. I'm sure there's all kinds of advice she'd give you right now about what you're going through. If she was here, well... you know she'd give you the biggest hug. But you have this. Her experiences. It might be more helpful than you think."

"Do you think it'll help me figure out what to do about TERP?"

Pearl smiled. "Not directly, of course, Darling, not that I even am going to pretend to figure out why you seem to think the world's problems are yours to solve. TERP was not even a minor thought on a thought on a thought when these were written. But that doesn't mean your mother didn't have what she thought were her own insurmountable problems in her life, and how she dealt with them might help you deal with yours."[1]

Pearl patted Ruby's cheek and went off to sit in her plush chair, clapping to activate the vid screen as she did so.

Ruby moved back in the bed to prop herself up against the wall and opened what she hoped was an untapped reservoir of ideas and solutions.

---

1. I've had the thought of actually writing some of Jade's journal entries. Maybe someday. Maybe someday when I think I have some momentous advice to give!

Chapter 33

Pearl had fallen asleep in her chair. The vid screen was still on. It was late in the evening time as evidenced by the fact that the Sun was only slightly above the horizon. Ruby's head was full of information from the journals. Her mom was very... unemotional. Just the facts about what happened in her days and nothing at all about how she felt about anything.

While of course the journals didn't mention TERP, her mother wrote extensively on computer viruses. Both viruses she had to defeat and viruses that she created to help her with her digital archaeology. The whole second volume in the series of journals could have been turned into a course on digital virology.

Jade wrote about replication mechanisms and polymorphic viruses, the ones that could take on many different forms, transforming their code. While it wasn't about TERP, if Ruby replaced the name of the virus with 'TERP,' the descriptions were nearly identical.

Ruby closed her eyes and let her brain process and assimilate all this information. She could hear the vid. The news was on. She heard the word 'TERP' mentioned a few times, along with something about it disbanding yet another agency for releasing an unapproved meme that used TERP's likeness and name.

What if TERP is indeed a virus? She considered. *How do you get rid of a virus that is out in the open and no one actually thinks is a virus?*

She opened her eyes and looked down at the page in front of her. Her eyes went to some words scribbled at the bottom that read, "since this type of virus can attract others, I had to introduce what I'm calling a 'double-agent' virus."

Double-agent. Ruby repeated the phrase several times in her head. She put the journal down and patted her jacket pocket. AT was still in there, still dormant. *Double-agent.* She said again, this time, taking AT out of her pocket and staring at the small form of the robot.

"Double agent!" she nearly shouted the words. Pearl snorted and adjusted a little in her chair, but if she woke up, didn't give any outward indication of it.

"Pippa," Ruby whispered.

Pippa lit up in response.

"Are you connected to the network at this facility?" Ruby continued to keep her voice low and kept her eyes on Pearl.

"Yes, of course." Pippa knew to also keep her own volume low to match Ruby's.

"And does the facility connect to the global-net?"

"Again, Ruby, of course. You know this…"

"….I know, I know… but I needed to make sure. I have a plan. But we're going to have to figure out how to keep you safe…" She was smiling and returned AT to her pocket.

"Safe? From what? I am perfectly safe right now," Pippa said.

Ruby didn't respond. She was gently placing the journal down and getting up from bed. If Pearl woke up, she'd probably have to explain and that was not something she wanted to do. One, because it meant revealing information from her mother's journal and she wasn't sure she bought into Pearl's 'loophole.' And two, she didn't know how technical her grandmother was, and she wasn't sure she *could* explain what she planned to do.

"Ruby?" Pippa said again, a little louder.

"Shhh," replied Ruby, "I'll explain as we go. I need to find a pen and some paper—I'm sure there's some around here. I want to write down the plan first."

"Write? Not dictate to me?"

"Yeah. I think reading my mother's journal now has me a little paranoid about how easily digital information can be read by others…"

"I am quite capable of keeping your information encrypted."

"I know, I know. I just want to write it down myself, okay?"

If Ruby didn't know better, she would have sworn that she heard Pippa let out a huff or snort in response. She ignored it.

Less than thirty minutes later, Ruby and Pippa were ready. Ruby took AT out of her pocket and placed him on the floor. AT, in small cube form, lay at an angle. Ruby studied him. She was looking for a button or some indication of how to reactivate him.

She poked at AT with her finger.

"AT?" she said. "Re-inflate please!"

She wondered if she should get hold of Disto or SD for help. There was a message from Uncle Blake earlier that confirmed that he understood, and was even pleased, that she was spending the day with her grandmother and that the rest of them—which consisted of Uncle Blake, Disto, and SD—were all staying in the apartment to watch vids all day. "Disto insisted," Blake said.

Ruby wasn't sure what any of them would think of her plan and didn't want to introduce the possibility that they could discourage her from attempting what she was about to attempt.

She picked AT back up, turned him around and over in her hand looking for some clue.

Eventually, she had an idea. She remembered being in the DAVe and tugging at her seatbelt. She had to pull it before it would come loose. Other objects that needed to be pushed or pulled in the opposite way in order to activate popped into her mind.

She squeezed AT between her palms as hard as she could and voila! He started to expand.

Ruby quickly let go, as carefully as she could, and put him back on the carpet before he was too big for her to hold.

It took less than a minute, and there was AT, full-size and indications on his face-screen that he was coming alive.

"AT?"

"Ruby?"

"Oh, I'm so glad to see you again!" Ruby held off from giving AT a big hug. She wanted to make sure he was alright.

"Have we returned to Location Zero?" AT was looking around, examining his surroundings. He didn't move from the spot he had reinflated on but moved his appendage to touch the carpet and instantly pulled his appendage back.

"No…"

"This is not SD's ship?"

"No…"

"Are we still on Astroll 2? I can sense a change in gravity…"

"No, we're on Earth."

Ruby could tell that AT didn't immediately recognize the name so she saved the time it took him to look through his database, which might not yield a result anyway, and added, "It's my home planet."

She then filled him in on everything that happened since had deactivated himself and what she needed him to do now.

"Are you sure this will work?" he said.

"No, not in the least bit. But we have to try, right?" Ruby smiled and hoped it came off as genuine.

"'Have' to or 'want' to?" AT asked.

"Now that sounds like something Disto would say. But yes—have to. No one else can stop TERP. No one else from Earth, anyway."

"I fix things. I do not destroy them," AT said, and Ruby imagined that if he was capable of crossing his appendages across his chassis in protest, that's what he would have done.

"Think of it this way. Sometimes in order to fix something, you have to take it apart first, right?"

"Agreed. Will I be involved in the repair afterwards?"

"I don't know, AT."

"Pippa," Ruby spoke to her communicuff. "Are you ready?"

The soft lights on the edge of the communicuff cycled through the first half of the rainbow and then Pippa's voice said softly, "No."

"Wha…" half-asked Ruby, taken aback. She was ready, she thought they were doing this.

"I have discovered a problem. TERP will certainly be able to detect and disable AT the millisecond we connect to the network."

"Then there has to be a way we can distract him," Ruby said.

The three of them sat in silence for a few minutes. Pearl had woken up and was out playing cards with friends in the common room, but the vid had stayed on. To Ruby's surprise, she did not ask any questions and went about as if Ruby was either not there, or a regular fixture in her room. The news was still on, and they were continuing to repeat the story of TERP and the 'meme that shut things down' as they had tag-lined the story.

That AI needs to grow a thicker skin, Ruby thought. *Overreacts to a simple meme. It's like it's its first day on the networks…*

"Guys, I got it. We've gotta call Milo!"

Chapter 34

Milo's first reaction was, "You want to do *what* with my archive?" But after a thorough explanation, he was happy to help.

Uncle Blake had a few more questions such as, "You got the idea from your mother's journal?" and "How is the AI in your communicuff involved?" But he liked the plan and even chuckled a bit when Ruby described what she wanted to do.

Disto simply asked about AT, surprised that Ruby had reactivated him already.

SD was quiet.

They all gathered back at Uncle Blake's apartment to execute the plan. This was Uncle Blake's idea, when he offered, "You can't rely on their network connection. I have some, uh, special considerations here."

Once gathered, Milo who still maintained he was happy to help, said, "I'm concerned about timing. Ruby, my archive consists of more than 32 billion individual memes."

"That's great, Milo! So many possibilities!"

"But to search and replace on all of them..." he said.

"Sure, it'll take a few hours," Ruby said. She was deliberately avoiding doing the math in her head. If she did, she knew she would be utterly discouraged and potentially want to give up. And giving up wasn't an option.

Disto said, "I recently learned how to speed up activities by using multiple computers and processors. We can use me. And SD..."

"...and I might have a link to some non-networked computers," Uncle Blake added.

"More stuff from your secret life?" Ruby chided.

"Yeah, something like that," he said. "Although it's not and never has been a secret. You've never really asked me about it."

Ruby started to blush a little, but Milo changed the topic slightly.

"I'm having the archive transferred in pieces to the different processing locations. For each meme, we'll either replace the image with the hologram TERP initially premiered at NYAQS and has been using since, or replace a text object... a noun of some sort, with 'TERP.'"

With all the processing power they were devoting to this one task, it would indeed only take a few hours. They could let it run overnight, all get some sleep—or in the case of the robots, let them soak in some power and vids.

Then the next morning, they'd release that data into the world's network of computers.

The theory was that TERP would be so distracted, they could then connect the virus that was AT.

Ruby didn't sleep all that well. But as soon as she realized it was a new day, the thought of what they were about to do put her adrenaline production into overdrive. She burst into the living room of Uncle Blake's apartment. Blake and Milo were both there and awake, having coffee. Blake would normally make a caramel latte with extra foam—a recipe he had Ruby memorize—but today, there was simply not enough time. The coffee was black—the way Ruby was told her mother always drank it[1] —and their time was short. All three robots were present.

"We were just waiting for you, kiddo," Uncle Blake said. "Milo was telling us that the memes are ready to go. We only needed you and Pippa."

"You could have woken me sooner," Ruby responded.

"Pippa," Ruby said. "Are you safely locked away?"

One of the last decisions they made the night before was that the best way to keep Pippa safe would be to make a copy and let the copy be the interface between the humans and the world-wide network.

"Original Pippa is. I am communicating as a copy that Pippa prepared for this communication."

"Release the memes!" Ruby said.

Milo tapped on the computer he had brought.

"Okay, they're headed out in a stream to different media outlets. Social and otherwise," Milo said.

"How long do we think it's going to be until we get TERP's attention?" Ruby asked.

"It could be—" Uncle Blake was about to answer, but the copy of Pippa cut him off.

"TERP is reporting that it is searching for the origin of a meme depicting it in an unflattering capacity," Pippa-copy said.

"That's our cue, right?" Ruby said. "AT. Time for you to connect!"

They used one of Disto's cables for this. AT was able to manipulate it himself with an appendage into one of his ports.

"I'm connected," he said. "Interfacing..."

Then he was quiet. Seconds passed into minutes. Ruby's palms were sweating. Blake had moved himself to the kitchen and was pacing. Milo was staring at his computer screen and Ruby heard him tapping his foot at a near even pace with the leaky faucet, dripping water into the sink.

"Is anything happening?" Ruby asked.

No one answered.

"AT? Pippa?"

"There is a..." Pippa-copy started but didn't complete the sentence.

Ruby could tell by their coloring that Disto and SD were just as anxious as she was. Uncle Blake was now looking over Milo's shoulder, presumably at the memes that were still streaming out into the world. The rate at which Milo tapped his foot increased.

"TERP is..." Pippa-copy started again and once again, didn't finish.

A few moments later, a holo-image appeared over Ruby's communicuff. It formed into the image of the not-quite-human face of TERP.

"So," it said. "This is the source of those... embarrassing... shameful... demeaning... degrading..."

---

1. The way I always drink it.

While it was listing off this large set of human emotions, Ruby slowly took the communicuff off her wrist and placed it on the table.

"...upsetting... ignominious..."

It was clearly upset and clearly distracted. Ruby saw Uncle Blake take the cable that was attached to AT at one end and connect it to the port on the communicuff. Given TERP was facing Ruby, Uncle Blake was able to do this from behind, unseen.

"...disgrac—"

TERP cut off mid-word. His holo-image also froze. Ruby looked over to AT, who was vibrating at a high rate but didn't seem to be in distress otherwise. Slowly, the face of TERP turned to face AT, and the two locked their visuals on each other.

"You... are... malfunctioning," AT said. "I... must... fix... you..."

"I..." TERP said. "I..."

Ruby smiled, "It's working!"

"Wait a second. Something's wrong." Milo squinted at the screen.

AT began to twitch.

Milo bolted up so fast that his chair fell back and clambered onto the ground. "Everyone, stop! It's a trap!"

Ruby rushed over to the computer screen Milo was pointing at. It displayed the chain that made up TERP, and there was something else...

"No, everything is fine. That's the double-agent virus. That's AT!" she said.

Everyone turned back to look at AT once again. The unexpected twitching returned to the initial more soothing vibrations, which started to slow. After a few more moments, the holo-image of TERP shrunk and disappeared. AT stopped shaking altogether, and Pippa-copy said to the room, "The suite of algorithms known as TERP are disassembling."

This elicited cheers from everyone in the room. Everyone except Disto.

"Are you okay?" Ruby asked.

"I am pleased that this situation appears to be resolved," he said.

"But you still need your data," Ruby added. She understood. He was going to be one depressed robot for a while. The rest of the room continued their cheers.

"It's okay for you to celebrate, Ruby Palmer," he said. "Do not let my lack of joy impede your own."

Chapter 35

> Ruby <

Ruby switched off the news station. Reports of TERP letting go of everything from the Board on Geographic Names—where some had been taking this opportunity to rename things—to the Board of Tea Experts—which had been defunct for more than 200 years—were still coming in. The speculation on what happened continued. No one could tie this back to Ruby and her robots. However, it didn't stop her from being news. In fact, they tried to contact her for commentary and wanted her to be the new expert on TERP.

Blake was making dinner in the apartment's kitchen as SD looked on curiously.

Disto had been dormant and colored light green—indicating a pervasive sadness—ever since they defeated TERP. He sat in the living room and was quiet as ever.

Ruby was worried his disappointment was sending him into a place where he was going to shut down, and she wouldn't know how to help him. Seeing that Blake didn't need any help and knowing that the phone call back to Logan and Sebastian on Astroll 2 was still 20 minutes away, she wanted to see if she could cheer up Disto.

"Hey there," she opened with.

Disto chirped in response.

"You know, it's a big galaxy," she continued. "Think of all the planets you haven't searched DNA for your data."

"It's not that," he said.

"Then what is it?"

"It was supposed to be here. All the other historical data we had indicated this was the place. It's why we sent SD in the first place to get a sample. Your solar system had been well-mapped in our records. More than any other. Why do that if it wasn't here?"

"There are more than a million animals on this planet," Blake called out from the kitchen.

"...and the search isn't even complete yet," Ruby added. "There's another hour or so to go? You know what they say... it isn't over until it's over!"

"Indeed," said Disto, "On both accounts. But if I was the one using the animals on this planet for storage, I would have used several. Many. Lots. The probability that all of them would not have been found until the last 1 percent of the search..."

"...is improbable. I get it," Ruby said. "Could you have missed a species? Or could the DNA marker you're looking for be wrong?"

"I was confident in both the procedures and in the catalog of biological life on this planet. I do not believe we missed anything."

Ruby could feel Disto's disappointment becoming her own. She was even looking forward to finally seeing what this was all about too and learning about their history.

After the humans had eaten, and Disto watched them eat, asking about their food, culinary history and patiently listening to them talk about what they knew about those subjects, Disto emanated a new ping that Ruby hadn't heard him make before. It was similar to the sound that the reclo-recycler on Astroll 2 made when it successfully ingested a set of offerings.

"That's it," he said. "Nothing."

Ruby looked over at Uncle Blake hoping maybe he knew the right something to say that would comfort Disto. Uncle Blake was giving her the same look back.

"It's not here," Disto said. "I was certain... the probability was so high..."

They all sat silently. Ruby wasn't sure why, but she had a feeling, too, that it was all here. But then it wasn't. She still wondered if maybe something was wrong with Disto's search. Could he have been looking for the wrong thing?

No, he would have checked and double and triple checked. It was too important.

Before any of them could break the silence, the communication panel next to the small kitchen did it for them.

Projected in a holoimage several inches in front of them were the upper halves of Logan and Sebastian.

Ruby was happy to see them but didn't enjoy the attempt at real-time conversations when so much distance was involved. It was awkward. Buffering at the start of the conversation helped, but there would be ten-minute gaps in between responses.

"Hey, my loves," Uncle Logan said. "We just wanted to check in. Sebastian and I miss you!"

"Daddy took me to the arcade today. We played ping-pong!"

"Table tennis, sweetie," Logan said. "Let us know how you are. We're making dinner, so we're not leaving our quarters for the rest of the evening."

Ruby knew that meant that they sent this communique more than ten minutes ago, and in the time since, probably had dinner prepared, and were already eating.

Blake was the first one to respond. He relayed the biggest news first, that the information that the robots were looking for in the junk DNA of all the animal species on the planet wasn't there to be found.

Then there was some mundane chatter about the state of the apartment and something that the previous tenant had done that meant he wasn't getting his security deposit back.

"Want some dessert?" Blake asked Ruby. "I made sure we ordered the ingredients for brownies. Real chocolate brownies!"

Brownies—real chocolate ones—never came out well on the station. You would think that Ruby would be used to the fact that everything was slightly different in the low grav, low pressure environment. Like coffee. But her first coffee was on station, so she didn't know any different, until returning to Earth in the last day or so... coffee was definitely different here. Something about boiling water in Earth-normal gravity made all the difference. Less sour. Less astringent.[1]

---

1. Astronauts report that food tastes more bland in space for a variety of reasons. But coffee... without gravity, coffee doesn't brew properly! Which is one of the reasons the ISSpresso was designed and developed and sent to the International Space Station.

But brownies! Those she clearly remembered from the time of her life before she went to live on the station, and the station never got it right.

"I can't believe you have to ask," Ruby said. "I would love a real brownie!"

They were in the oven when the holoimage came back to life.

"Sebastian wanted to know," Logan said, with Sebastian's face there with his, hopping up and down, "why you only tested animals. Did you look at the DNA of plants?"

> Ruby <

"Calm down," Ruby said to Disto, "I can't talk to you like this."

Disto had been rolling back and forth in the apartment, in a version of pacing that bordered on dangerous if anything got in his way.

"Plants!" Disto said. This was the umpteenth time he had blurted out the word since Logan had suggested it. Well, seven-year-old Sebastian had suggested it. Logan was just the messenger.

"Plants!" Disto repeated for the tenth time. "Of course!" He finally stopped moving around erratically in the apartment.

"Where, how, can I test all the plants?" Disto asked, looking to Ruby for answers.

"I, I don't know," Ruby responded.

"I might," said Uncle Blake. "There's the seed vault. I can't remember the exact name of the place, it's changed names so many times in the last twenty years, but for the longest time it was known as the Global Seed Vault[2]. I remember there was some issue when they wanted to bring some seeds to Titan. You can't contact them directly but need to go through one of the institutions that deposited seeds there."

Blake went to the computer console built into the side of the kitchen.

"...and I think I know who can help us," he said with a familiar smirk.

"Please don't say we're going to have to get in touch with Coronik again," Ruby said. "I can't imagine he would even talk to us right now."

"No," Blake said and looked at Disto, "but we have something in common because this is probably not Coronik's favorite person either. Especially after the article they just published on him and the Church and the screening criteria for Church leaders."

Ruby's face beamed recognition since she now knew who Uncle Blake was talking about.

"Who? Who?" Disto asked impatiently.

---

2. The Svalbard Global Seed Vault is a real place in Norway. According to vaults website, as of October 2025, the vault is conserving 1,356,591 samples.

"Link Vala," Ruby and Uncle Blake said simultaneously. Then Blake added, "Link Vala is attached to the University of Gakkel Ridge[3], one of the seed contributors."

3. Gakkel Ridge is a real place located in the Arctic Ocean. To the best of my knowledge, there is no university there.

Chapter 36

It was right in front of him. The data he had been looking for, for so long.

And they didn't even need to leave Uncle Blake's apartment to access it.

Ruby had contacted the human known as Link Vala, and they were able to use Ruby's celebrity status to get access not to the storage facility itself, but the DNA records of the entire contents of the seed archive. Every seed in the archive had corresponding DNA records on file.

In truth, Disto had already surmised that this information was freely and easily available. Even if Ruby hadn't been a celebrity, they would have had access. But once the University and facility realized who was asking for access, they offered additional help in the form of whatever they needed if they could associate Ruby with their school and get some media attention on themselves. Ruby agreed.

"No one remembers that we're here or the good work that we do," a school and facility representative had said to the news camera. "We're thrilled that Ruby Palmer, *the* Ruby Palmer, has taken an interest in our work."

And out of the millions of varieties of plant life, there were three that contained the information Disto was looking for. A fruit, known as the plum, a vegetable known as zucchini, and another fruit, known as mango.

Upon hearing the last of the three, Ruby smiled and laughed. "We grow those on the station!" she had said.

Although the ones that had Disto's data were all unique hybrids—ones that were developed a while ago and only existed in the seed vault in modern times.

After Ruby had stopped giggling about the mango, she asked in earnest, "What does it all say? What are you learning?"

"I don't know where to begin answering that question," he said. "There's so much here."

"Start at the beginning," Ruby suggested.

"That would be the information I learned from the Plum DNA," Disto responded. "About how Location Zero was created, nearly 700 years ago."

"That recently?" Ruby said, her eyes wide. "That was like when—"

"When Leonardo da Vinci and Nicolaus Copernicus were alive," Pippa added. Ruby made a face at Pippa but appreciated the information.

"So that was when, but who? Why?" Ruby continued to ask.

"The information as to 'why' we were created is not present. And the who is a little," he paused, choosing his words carefully, "unclear. It seems to support what we already knew. There were eleven robots in the beginning."

Disto continued to review the data. It was in pieces scattered throughout the DNA of the fruits and vegetables. It would have been much easier if all the junk DNA was located in one place, rather than scattered around, so it was hard to determine the timing of it all.

"But it seems these eleven robots, I believe this information is relaying that they are in our solar system. They inhabit their own planet," Disto said, is vocal tonations increasing, "their own planet in the Keep-Out Zone!"

Both Disto and Ruby looked to their resident expert on the Keep-Out Zone, SD. SD looked back, from one to the other.

"I know nothing of the KOZ," SD said. "Other than to Keep Out."

"Are you sure," Ruby prodded. Disto believed that his human friend was having similar thoughts as he was. That SD had more information that he'd expressed.

"I am... sure," SD said, with a large pause before uttering that final word. Disto computed that SD wasn't sure at all.

Disto again looked at his data while Ruby patiently waited for him to pass on more information. It would take time to analyze it all. He briefly thought that he should suggest she go do something else, but concluded she'd reject any such suggestion. Instead, he carried on with his analysis.

They sat in silence for several minutes, until Disto analyzed something and produced an audible gasp.

"What is it?" Ruby said, lifting her head from a resting place.

"This can't be accurate," Disto said. "Let me recompute..."

Although there was nothing to recompute and Disto knew it. The data in front of him could not be clearer. But how could it be so? It made no sense. Maybe if he said it out loud.

"It says, to use some of the computing terminology I have learned from you, Ruby, that we are in the middle of a 'beta test.' And by middle, I mean, close to the end. At the end of the test, we are to get a software 'upgrade'—one that resets and reformats all of our systems."

"What do you mean by all?" Ruby asked.

"I mean all," Disto continued. "All robots. The Core. The Halls. The agencies. All robots. All."

There was a silence as they all digested that information. Saying it out loud hadn't made anything better, so Disto figured he might as well add in the final bit he learned.

"And if I understand the reference to timing then this is expected to happen," Disto paused, recomputing once more before stating a date in terms Ruby would understand, "in two weeks."

Ruby took a breath and looked from Disto to SD and back. "I guess we're going to take another trip," she said.

Disto nodded.

After...

> In the Keep-Out Zone <

Eight-Nine prided herself on her integrity. She maintained the lowest bit error rate of any robot that had the awesome responsibility of communications that there ever was. Even if that meant her comms were slow. They were accurate.

As she sat there, one of her transmission antennas in the middle of transmitting the largest, and final, software patch to Location Zero, her receive antenna continued to pick up the signal emitted by a robot known as Swell Driver.

Eight-nine knew all the factors that affected bit error rate and knew that there were some outside her ability to control—including interference, distortion, and fading. But none of that could account for what she was detecting now.

Either the bit error rate on the signal was higher than she could accept or...

"What's bothering you?" asked Three-Five as she hovered near by the immovable Eight-Nine. Three-Five was easily bored and frequently visited all the immobile robots hoping that one of them could alleviate her boredom.

"It's the signal from Swell Driver," Eight-Nine answered.

"What about it?" asked Three-Five who was intrigued. Whenever Three-Five flew over and visited Eight-Nine, she hoped for some intrigue, and was frequently disappointed. For a long time now, Eight-Nine had her antenna aimed at the relay satellite that hovered over the Star, transmitting the patch to Location Zero. All eleven robots had helped create the patch. Three-Five's contributions focused on prioritizing the algorithms it contained. As a flying rover, path optimization was her specialty and she loved to optimize and calculate optimizations.

She was bored doing anything else.

Eight-Nine on the other hand, could sit there and dedicate herself to her task for as long as it took. Which was a helpful trait to have considering the time it took to transmit, and often retransmit, data to Location Zero. Receiving data took just as long and there had been arguments between Eight-Nine and Nine-Two about giving the robots of Location Zero additional information so they knew they could boost their signal and Eight-Nine's reception of bit errors would be low.

Especially for Swell Driver, who had made several trips around their solar system, who had made several trips outside their solar system and now...

"Either there are too many errors in this signal," Eight-Nine slowly answered Three-Five's question, "or he's on his way here."

Three-Five rose up and spun herself around several times before returning to her original hover spot.

"That would be exciting!" Three-Five said. "We should alert the others! We should make plans! I should survey the area and pick out the best landing spot!"

"Oh no," Eight-Nine said. "No, that's not the plan, remember. The patch must complete so we can reset Location Zero to the new and improved version of themselves."

While Eight-Nine was slowly talking, Three-Five was spinning around in the air, 'dancing' she called it. She was only half-listening to Eight-Nine.

"But you are correct that we must tell the others. Can you pass on the information?" Eight-Nine asked. "All my power is going to my primary transmit antenna."

Three-Five quickly raised and lowered her front which consisted of two small turning blades, indicating she would. "I'll find Six-Five. She's flying around the perimeter of our area again, once again, looking for changes in the landscape. I'll tell her and then the two of us can fly around and tell the others."

Eight-Nine made a chirp in agreement. The two flying robots were the best at spreading news to the rest of the robots, particularly the ones like Eight-Nine, that were completely immobile.

"Please ask One-Four to visit me," Eight-Nine added. "If Swell Driver is headed here, I'd like to work out a plan with One-Four that we can propose to Three. We have to figure out the right way to proceed and be clear about it."

Three-Five made her final gesture indicating she would do as asked and then flew away leaving Eight-Nine with her signals and the thoughts that bounced around her circuits. She was a little worried that maybe Swell Driver wasn't on his way and it was simply a signal with too many bit errors. If so, she'd be blamed for spinning everyone up.

But if not, Swell Driver, and any robot or robots that were with him, were going to find out things that no robot should ever know about their creators.

* * *

Ruby and her robot friends are in for a trip! Continue on to book four: *Eleven Little Robots*

Eleven Little Robots

Book 4 of The Robot Galaxy Series

Adeena Mignogna

Crazy Robot, LLC

Also By Adeena Mignogna

The Robot Galaxy Series
Book 1: *Crazy Foolish Robots*
Book 2: *Robots, Robots Everywhere!*
Book 3: *Silly Insane Humans*
Book 4: *Eleven Little Robots*

...and the unrelated standalone novel: Lunar Logic
Adeena's Stories (on KindleUnlimited):
Final Orbit
Objective Reality

Before We Begin

It is inevitable that once a species invents the wheel on their planet of origin, their evolution carries them through animal-drawn carriages, automobiles, and Segways, and onto rocket ships, treadmills, and cordless vacuum cleaners. It is during this evolutionary process that they start looking up at what else is happening around their host star. At first, their observations are confined to whatever visual sensors naturally evolved and are already embedded in their bodies, but as they advance, they utilize technology to resolve smaller and smaller details and answer bigger and bigger questions.

Barring complete self-destruction, it is inevitable that they find other planets around their star. Once again, initially with their natural visual sensors and then with technology. It is also typical for any species to, at first, imagine that there are other creatures on those planets. Depending on the nature of the species in question, they start out believing one of two things: that the creatures are just like themselves or that they are comparative monsters.

Humans had a brief flirtation with the idea that Martians were living on the fourth planet in their solar system, before they conclusively proved otherwise.

Which is the next inevitable thing. Once again, if time passes and the species still doesn't manage to kill themselves off, it is inevitable that they develop the technology to go visit the other planets in their solar system. If the species has prospects for any true intelligence, they send robotic missions before sending themselves to determine what the place is like before setting their own feet or pods or claws down on them. But eventually, they decide it's time to leave their rock for a variety of reasons, including everything from curiosity to a nervousness that staying only on their home planet puts them in a precarious position for long-term species survival. They are a single point of failure, and one not-too-big asteroid could wipe them out.

One such yet-to-be-named species, who had their origins on and around the fourth planet in their planetary system, set their sights on the third. They had developed quite advanced optical technology and learned that their third planet was uninhabited. Like any good species, they sent robotic missions ahead of themselves to prepare the place for their arrival. But they kept looking around and found other planets and moons outside their solar system. Which is the third major inevitable practice of species who survive long enough—they start exploring the galaxy.

This species was overly concerned with their own survival and less interested in whether or not there were other species around. Consequently, they began to transform any celestial body within reach that was even slightly suitable for their needs.

Eventually, they decided that the most interesting celestial bodies were around other stars quite far from their own, so they abandoned what they had started in their home system, leaving the robots they put in place on the third planet to fend for themselves.

And fend they did…

Chapter 1

"For the last time, Uncle Blake, it's okay that you're not going with us," Ruby Palmer said standing with hands on her hips in the most confident pose she could muster. A pose that was meant to say, 'I'm the only human to have left our solar system and single-handedly saved a species of robots, so I'm totally fine on my own.'

On the screen in front of her was her Uncle Blake—a father figure and legal guardian since she was five years old—with his own arms crossed in front of his chest in the most confident and fatherly pose he knew how to make. A pose that said, 'Your galactic escapades gave me a thousand mini heart attacks, so, of course, I'm going to worry.' Because, of course, no matter how many historical events Ruby was a part of, her substitute father slash uncle would always worry, as fathers and uncles do.

He sighed and uncrossed his arms, unfolded them, and they came to rest mostly out of view since the screen cut off at mid-chest.

"Only because you made the choice for me," Uncle Blake said.

Ruby blushed. She was indeed guilty of asking Milo Jenkins, her friend, and fellow mini-R-pod pilot, to bring her and the robots onto SD's ship without being entirely truthful as to why. Milo also hadn't questioned her flimsy story. When it came to Milo, if Ruby said jump, Milo would skip the part where a clear-headed individual might ask several clarifying questions and would instead rush into figuring out how he might invent shoes that could take her to the moon. Of course, Milo agreed. Ruby said she wanted a certain amount of privacy which wasn't possible on Astroll 2—the space station where Ruby had lived since the age of 10. Now that Ruby Palmer was the ultimate celebrity, Astroll 2 had become crowded to nearly its capacity with starstruck tourists and eager entrepreneurs who either hoped her celebrity would rub off on them or saw nothing but dollar signs when they looked at her.

It was indeed a flimsy story since Ruby could have guaranteed privacy in her quarters, and Milo knew it.

The truth was, Detailed Historian, known as Disto, had recently discovered that the robots had used the junk DNA of several species of Earth-based plant life to store quite a bit of historical data on the robots. The robots, Disto in particular, had been looking for this data as part of the Special Project Storage Problem, or *Gorp-Gorp*, as it was known in the Special Projects Branch. That data hunt had led to Ruby getting captured by Swell Driver, known as SD, in the first place, since the robots computed that it was extremely likely that human DNA was the solution to where their data was kept. Apparently, they computed the correct planet, but the wrong species.

Once they figured this out, a vast record of historical information was unleashed upon the generally agitated yet remarkable robots. Within these historical records was information about the origin of the robots and Location Zero—an origin story that started not on Location Zero, but on another planet in Location Zero's planetary system. This planet was located in what the robots knew as a Keep-Out Zone. Given the name, they had always kept out. Especially robots like SD that were tasked with interplanetary and interstellar travel.

"Can I assume that you're headed to that restricted zone?" Uncle Blake asked over the video chatting system.

"It is called a Keep-Out Zone, and you are correct," said SD, who was also in view of the camera next to Ruby. "I have configured the navigation systems so that the ship will not automatically avoid the KOZ. The ship produced complaints at first but now seems to understand our mission. I think."

Uncle Blake looked as if he had a hundred more questions to ask SD, but instead, his face on the screen turned back to Ruby. "You brought food? And the vitamins you're supposed to be taking?"

"Yes," Ruby replied. "It's all back there." She pointed her thumb over her shoulder at a pile of storage bins that were sitting in the corner, strapped to the wall. "We talked about it, and we'll only be gone a week, maybe ten days before they bring me back. I have enough for twenty. Right guys?"

Ruby knew that she could call the group of robots 'guys,' and they understood the idiom—but only because she had explained it several times to them. In great length and with more detail and nuance than Ruby thought was possible for such a simple word. Disto had suggested that if she was ever referring to a group of robots that way that she simply use the word, 'robots' but something about the two-syllable label for a group didn't roll off the tongue as naturally as 'guys,' so, 'guys' it was.

"Yes," Disto responded on behalf of the robots. "We will visit the planet in the KOZ. Based on the data I was able to extract, we should find the beings who created Location Zero and all the robots we know. They are more than that, though. These beings are actively involved in Location Zero's operation and potential..."

He trailed off, and Ruby could see that he was still having a hard time processing what he'd learned.

"You mean the potential reset?" Ruby said, finishing his thought.

"Yes," Disto said. Even though Disto wasn't the kind of robot who could deflate like Ambitious Technician, Ruby would have sworn she saw him deflate a little.

After studying the data he'd found, Disto also learned that there was a built-in event designated for Location Zero which sounded like a reset or upgrade time. The nature of the event was ambiguous, and it wasn't clear which was the more accurate description—reset or upgrade or both. Regardless of the imprecise labeling, Location Zero had a built-in planned upgrade that had the potential to completely reset the planet and every robot associated with it. It appeared that the creators of Location Zero, situated in the KOZ, were in the process of uploading a large software patch and once the upload was complete, would force a reset of the whole planet.

"I wish you would have taken me, or someone with more experience with exoplanets or extraterrestrials," Uncle Blake said.

That made Ruby laugh. "Uncle Blake! Remember who you're talking to? Ruby Palmer. First human to make contact with an alien race." She was mocking the celebrity she had gained but also knew that she wasn't entirely wrong. Exoplanet research had stopped a long time ago and was only done in secret by people like Uncle Blake and a few others. It really wasn't even exoplanet research—it was research on the other worlds in their own solar system, like Titan. She still had plans to get there someday, but lately there always seemed to be something in the present that demanded her attention. Not that she minded—she had grown quite fond of the adventures with her robot friends.

In the meantime, she had let Uncle Blake core dump all the data he could on exoplanets, going as far back as the year 1992 with the first confirmed exoplanet detection[1]. Her MoDaC was full of new information for her to read and study, though data dumps like this could be rather tedious to go through, for once, she was interested. She might have even described herself as more than interested—riveted, even. Ruby skimmed it all while SD was getting ready to leave Astroll 2. Between what she had read about Titan, and about exoplanets and what Disto told her about the planet they expected to find in the KOZ, they were all full of methane.[2]

She concluded that the galaxy was a stinky place.

"Besides me being *the most* qualified human," she continued to her uncle, "the robots wanted me along."

Blake's re-crossed his arms. "Did you say goodbye to Uncle Logan? To Sebastian?"

Ruby pressed her hands into her eyes. "Argh," she said. And then to Disto, "Can I have Milo come back and bring me back to Astroll 2 once more before we take off?"

Ruby could tell that Disto wasn't happy. She could tell he was anxious to get underway. She always knew he wasn't about to say 'no' to her for anything she asked.

"Of course," Disto responded. "But we're staying here on SD's ship."

The robots had confided to Ruby that their experiences with other humans were—Ruby had watched Disto as he seemed to internally scroll through a series of words to find the best one—overwhelming, he had said. They claimed to enjoy their time with Ruby's family, but in general, humans were not their favorite species—except Ruby, who had taken the time to understand how to communicate effectively with them—even though it started out while she was under a wee bit of duress and had no choice—and had been able to help them with their problems. Not knowing exactly what to expect in the KOZ was their next problem, and while much was uncertain, they made it clear to Ruby that they wanted her there by their side as they figured it out.

---

1. To be clear, the detection was in 1990 but the paper about it was published in 1992. The name of that paper: "A planetary system around the millisecond pulsar PSR1257 + 12"

2. Titan's atmosphere is roughly 94% nitrogen and 5% methane. Doesn't sound like a lot, but no one yet knows why or how this moon has an atmosphere at all!

Chapter 2

Determined. It was a word Disto ruminated on. He had a purpose, and it was in the process of getting fulfilled. This meant he was satisfied; he was content.

Swell Driver informed him that his ship was ready to depart.

"Let's go, Ruby!" Disto called into the communications line he had opened with Ruby. He still possessed his very own communicuff and could contact her even if she was back on Astroll 2 and he was waiting impatiently in SD's ship.

It was a video comm link, and Disto watched as Ruby stood outside a mini-R-pod with her Uncle Blake, Uncle Logan, and mini-human cousin, Sebastian. Disto knew Milo was waiting inside the mini-R-pod called *Pecan Pi*.

Milo and SD had already made several trips to and from his ship to get it ready. This was one extra trip that he couldn't say no to Ruby making, even though she had seemed to be ready to depart earlier.

There had been a touch of deception, on the part of the humanoid biological beings—the Bios. Ruby's Uncle Blake was the source. He came up with a cover story: Ruby was escorting the robots home, and SD would bring her back.

If the other Bios knew what they were doing, they would have insisted on sending others. They had already insisted on sending other Bios to Location Zero, but Disto was able to convince them that a proper diplomatic situation needed to be established first. Humans should and could prepare for a visit, but they needed to pack their appropriate food and supplies, and robots at Location Zero would prepare quarters in advance.

The arranged time was when the human diplomatic and research team would be picked up from Earth. The biggest difficulty was in agreeing on an adequate level of security for the chosen team.[1]

What the Bios didn't know is that the arranged time was after the upcoming 'reset,' so Disto only hoped that there would still be a Location Zero to visit. Well, there would be. The Reset wouldn't remove or destroy the planet, but he hoped it would be *his* Location Zero, and not some foreign, screwed-up version of it.

A question had been posed: should 'Ruby of the Robots' be allowed to return? But it was clear that no one could tell her no. Rather, she could certainly be told no, but no one expected her to willingly accede to that request. And anyway, the robots wanted her with them, since Disto was certain they would undoubtedly encounter other Bios on the new planet. Ruby's

---

1. Yet another side story I would like to write in this universe. The diplomatic team from Earth visiting Location Zero.

ability to adapt and communicate could only be of help to them. To Disto, it made perfect sense, but Ruby's presence was essential.

"Ruby!" Disto called out again. "SD has informed me that the ship is in a state that is ready for departure."

Ruby held up a single finger. Single. One. But one what?

Disto watched them all embrace on the video link. Then Ruby embraced Sebastian. And then Uncle Blake once more. A few other humans were present, but Ruby didn't embrace them. Instead, they touched hands briefly. Robt Plampton, the Astroll 2 station director, was there. Plampton was one of the few Bios Disto wished he had a little more time to get to know. But once they found out about The Reset, they needed to hurry.

While still on Earth, returning to SD's ship was a mini-adventure unto itself. It took nearly a full week to arrange and complete the journey that involved traveling around half the planet before ascending up the space elevator to Legacy Station. But once on SD's ship, the group was back at Astroll 2 in an appendage full of tics, or a "handful of seconds," as Ruby had said. Ruby had also remarked that they'd been here for too many clicks already—she was also eager to move on.

Ruby was finally inside *Pecan Pi* and Milo closed the hatch.

"Just making up for the fact that the last time I left, I didn't say goodbye properly," she said.

"Indeed," Disto said. Over the comm link, he heard what he could only assume were two Bios positioning themselves into the small, but adequate space inside *Pecan Pi*. "If I understand the sequence of events, you bypassed all of that."

"I left a note," Ruby said at a lower volume.

"Hrmph," was a noise that Disto assumed had to have been made by Milo.

"I thought we agreed we were done talking about the past," Ruby said.

"Maybe your past," added Disto. "But not mine. Not ours. Talking about ours is just beginning...and I just computed that that comment was not directed at me."

"It's okay, Disto. We'll be there in a few moments," Ruby said.

And with that, Disto watched a small ship launch out of Astroll 2 on the large, main viewscreen on SD's ship. One step at a time, he thought.

> Ruby <

In the control center of SD's ship, Ruby felt like she was in a second or third home. She was getting comfortable here. Before they departed, she asked SD if she could pilot the ship herself.

"Unfortunately, you don't have the right access ports to interface with the ship," he had said.

Then Ruby looked on as SD pulled out an appendage and connected it to the console. He interfaced with the ship in a variety of ways. One way, touching the console, was familiar, like how she interfaced with her mini-R-pod. But a direct connection via an appendage—while she could admit might have its efficiencies—was not something she ever hoped would be familiar to her.

Although she was getting closer and closer to having more direct connections herself. Before she left Earth, she let herself be convinced into taking a pair of Percepto-glasses with her. She could never have afforded the really nice ones on her own, but her celebrity status meant that everyone was offering her everything in order for them to get her seal of approval and endorsement. She had refused 80 percent of the stuff she was offered but let herself take a digitally hand-drawn portrait that made her really look nice, a green, fitted jacket with an excess of pockets, and a deck of cards with her face on each that she passed off to her grandmother.

She had gotten in one more visit with her grandmother, Pearl Palmer, before she left Earth as well.

"I'm going to make a killing at my next poker game with this," Pearl had said as they exchanged gifts. Ruby could easily imagine this woman taking everyone's money, with or without cards with her face on them.

Ruby kept the keepsakes her grandmother gave her but didn't bring any of it with her to Location Zero, particularly the jewelry.

But Ruby digitally scanned her mother's journals. It was too impractical to haul all of that mass back to Astroll 2, even if they were going to do it from SD's ship. There was still the problem of getting that mass to the ship.

"I'm sorry, mom," Ruby said to no one, "but this is the safest way I can keep these." She used a fancy scanner, which did it in no time. Then she double encrypted everything so that it would only open with the password she knew and her fingerprint. She put it on her MoDaC.

The MoDaC was tied into the Percepto-glasses, so she didn't need to open the MoDaC anymore except for deep work. It took a little bit to get used to, but Ruby was enjoying this mix of old and new tech.

Pippa didn't like that Ruby had taken on another device. That was until Ruby explained that there wasn't another AI in the glasses, and she could connect Pippa to it as well. That cheered Pippa up.

"So, SD, when will we get there?"

"Momentarily," SD responded.

"I presume we're going to enter as planned...?" Disto asked.

Ruby could now do a few things on SD's ship, and she touched a part of the console that allowed her to turn on the viewscreen and display information on it like a monitor. The approach trajectory for the robots' home planetary system was already set up and programmed in.

There was a star, and orbiting around was Location Zero, in a near perfect, circular orbit. The Keep-Out Zone remained visible on this map, indicated by a dotted line. The KOZ was in the same orbit as Location Zero but on the opposite side of their host star.

SD had described it simply as a place that he was not allowed to take his ship but trailed off every time he said something like that. When Ruby had tried to probe for more, he got even quieter.

Another dotted line was overlaid and in a different color. "There," Ruby said. "Exactly like we talked about. We're going to come in over your planetary system along the spin axis of it. We'll find a quiescent point to look at the KOZ from, and then we'll head to the planet there."

They all looked at the screen for a few moments until Ruby spoke again, "And you have no other information on this planet?"

"There was none in the data I found," Disto confirmed. "Only its existence, the fact that it is indeed responsible for my existence, and the fact that it wants to reset my existence..."

Ruby didn't push. This was a sore subject. Rightfully so. No one wanted to be reset or erased. Well, maybe there was a handful who did, but no one she knew.

Soon, a larger circle appeared over the dotted line. It was blinking and moving along it.

"That's us?" Ruby asked.

"Correct," said SD.

"Wow. I'm still… I don't know what to say." On top of everything, these robots could travel faster than light as easily as she could take a few steps across a room. While they refused to give her or humanity that tech, she wondered if the people they'd meet in the KOZ would. Or if they would provide any indication of how Ruby and her kind could catch up and start to learn that tech. Or was it possible that humans were so far behind everyone else in the galaxy?

The blinking circle that indicated their ship quickly marched along the dotted line and then came to a stop.

"We are now located approximately 592 scruples from our star, which is approximately 141 scruples equidistant from the KOZ and Location Zero."

Ruby tried to imagine a *scruple* in her head. It was a unit of measurement that the robots used both for extremely large distances and infinitesimally small distances, but on a logarithmic scale. She couldn't ever quite picture it. She shook her head because having a clear image wasn't all that important. As long as she knew it worked. What was important was the fact that in this moment, she was truly a galactic explorer.

"This is amazing, SD," Ruby said. "What's the rest of the planetary system like?"

SD touched his console and a variety of other dots of various sizes appeared, orbiting the host star. "Those are the other planets within this system," he said.

Ruby saw that Location Zero and KOZ were in the third orbital position around the host star. Two other planets orbited closer into the star. In orbits further off from Location Zero, were four more planets.

"Are the size of those dots relative to the true size?" Ruby asked.

"Correct," SD responded. "Seven planets orbiting our star. Well, 8 now that we know about the planet in the KOZ."

"The outer ones are the big ones, just like our solar system," Ruby said. The fact that there was an unusually large gap between the third and fourth planets didn't go unnoticed.

"That's common among the systems I have traveled to," SD said.

Ruby blinked. "How many planetary systems have you been to, SD?"

"435 unique planetary systems," he said as unremarkably as if he was telling her how many bolts were on his chassis. If he even had bolts—Ruby still didn't know how any of the robots were physically put together.

Ruby shook her head, taking that in. "SD, that's incredible!"

"I am a Driver," was all he said in response.

"You are! What are we waiting for?" Ruby asked. "Let's go!"

"I am attempting to re-compute the trajectory," SD said. "Once again my computer… won't comply."

Disto rolled over to SD's side to look at the computer console with him. He beeped in displeasure.

"The computer says," SD announced, "that it cannot take us to the KOZ. It will not compute a trajectory through a region of unallowed space. I cannot make it change its mind."

"Can you reprogram it?" Ruby asked.

"Ruby, you know I am not a Programmer," SD responded.

"And you know about our built-in rules about reprogramming," added Disto.

"But I thought that only applied to yourselves. Isn't the ship's computer a non-sentient tool?" Ruby probed.

"Indeed. However, we still do not possess the skills to reprogram at will."

"But I do," Ruby said. "Let me in there."

Ruby connected Pippa to the ship's computer since Pippa also had previous experience with the robots' modes and methods. Together, they were able to 'convince' the ship's computer no zone was prohibited within this planetary system. The computer offered a little protest, in the form of what seemed like an endless stream of "are you sure?" messages, but in the end, Ruby and Pippa were sure, so the computer said "Okay."

Ruby disconnected Pippa and moved out of the way so SD could resume his work.

He communicated with the computer in his native chirps and beeps and after a series of those emanated from him, with the ship beeping back he said:

"There is one more problem I can see before we get there. My ship should not land on a planetary surface."

Ruby recalled the same problem when they had arrived at Earth. There, they were able to connect to Legacy Station and get down from there. But he just said...

"Wait, you just said 'should not' instead of cannot? Does that mean you can land?" Ruby asked.

SD let out a low beep indicating he was thinking over her question.

"It is not so much the landing as it is the taking off again," SD said. "I can break the link with gravity, but it isn't always predictable."

Ruby did not know how to process what SD said. 'Break the link with gravity' was a phrase she'd never heard before, and she wasn't sure all the PhDs in Physics could help her make sense of that. Problems for later.

"Let's go. Let's get into orbit and have a good look at the place and then figure that out. Agreed?"

"Agreed," SD and Disto said in unison.

The ship resumed movement, and Ruby would have sworn that they were deliberately going slower than necessary. Like the robots wanted to find out what was there and yet they didn't. She understood the feeling of both wanting to know a thing and yet not wanting to know that same thing at the same time.

"When we get there, put us in standard orbit," Ruby suggested.

"What is standard orbit?"

"I don't know. I just said it. It's what they always said in the old vids."

"Ah, yes!" Disto said. "We watched those vids. 'Standard orbit, ensign.' 'Plot a standard orbit.' Yet they were never specific as to what standard orbit was.[2] "

"Yeah, so I know that wasn't helpful. It was fun to say, though." Ruby said, smiling.

"Our approach will take us into a highly eccentric orbit and then lower the... the..." SD was struggling with a translation.

"Apog— Sorry, I mean apoapsis. I almost said the wrong word," Ruby said, "We call the highest point in the orbit the apoapsis. If we're orbiting Earth, we call it the apogee.[3] "

"Why is it a different word if you're around Earth?" Disto asked.

---

2. Of course, this is what is said in *Star Trek* all the time. In my head, standard orbit should be some kind of low altitude polar orbit, since while hanging out they'd get a decent view of the entire planet. But when they visualize the *USS Enterprise* against the backdrop of a planet, it gives the feel of a more synchronous orbit.

3. Terminology as it relates to orbits, and getting that terminology wrong is one of my big pet peeves in science fiction! It's all correct in this scene.

Ruby shook her head, "I don't know. It just is," she said. "I think a long time ago, everything was naturally Earth-centric, but over time as people were able to understand there was more beyond Earth, they changed words to accommodate that."

"Sounds inefficient," Disto said.

"It probably is," Ruby said. "At least, it's a lot more to remember. But we gain knowledge a little at a time and have to adapt along the way, so it's sort of the way of things. Anyway. Apoapsis."

"Yes," SD said, "Each orbit the apoapsis will lower until we achieve a low, circular orbit. We will continuously scan the planet looking for... Disto, what are we looking for?"

"Bios," Disto answered. "The ones who created us and who think they have a right to control us now."

> Swell Driver <

Swell Driver was an excellent driver of his ship. He had traveled to many planetary systems and, along with his computer, calculated trajectories through and around systems and planets, using the gravity of massive bodies to slingshot around, going high, going low, and all manner of maneuvers in between.

This trip should have been no different than any of the others.

Yet somehow, something felt oddly familiar about this approach.

Ruby had asked to have the planet in the KOZ displayed in the viewscreen. He complied, yet in doing so, he felt... something. He didn't have all the names for all the feelings he felt in recent times. Every time he seemed to grasp his set of feelings, new ones would enter and he'd lose himself in them again. So—for efficiency's sake alone—he lumped it together with other uncomfortable feelings and tried to concentrate on the job at hand: achieving orbit around this planet.

A part of him wanted to turn the ship around and head for Location Zero, where he could dock his ship and then... what? Revisit the Rejuvenation Region? Take another break from being a Driver? Maybe he wanted to implement one of Explosive Healer's suggestions to externally record all the things he could remember experiencing. "That's journaling," Ruby had said when he mentioned the idea to her. "Just like my mom did."

With all this uncertainty, he kept on course, with Ruby and Disto looking at the planet as they got closer.

"That planet has an atmosphere," Ruby announced, pointing her arm toward the screen.

"That is correct," SD confirmed. "I will have the computer perform a scan analysis of the composition and..."

"What is it?"

"I'm detecting a signal. In fact, I am detecting several signals."

"You are?"

"Correction. My ship's computer is detecting several signals and—and it is not happy."

SD wasn't happy either, but he could clearly attribute this to the interaction between these signals and his ship. One particular signal was establishing its own communication connection with his ship.

SD tried to tell the ship to ignore the communication attempt.

"I cannot," the ship replied.

"Explain," SD answered in his native tones—a more efficient way of communicating with the ship. Disto would be able to understand and would have to translate to Ruby. SD didn't want to be rude, but time and efficiency could be important here.

"The signal has an override code. I am compelled to listen," the ship said. "It is... it is... altering my trajectory."

"How so?" SD asked. While he asked, he could see the computation in progress. The alteration did not make sense. The new trajectory would have them crash land on the KOZ planet.

"Disregard new trajectory," SD ordered, with increasing frustration. He was not used to his ship listening to someone else over him. It was his ship, after all.

"Cannot comply," came the weak response from the computer. "I am... sorry."

SD continued to poke at the computer to try and return them to their original trajectory. But he was locked out. The signal that came in seemed to know exactly how to talk to his computer to make it comply with its wishes. SD overheard Disto behind him talking to Ruby.

"There's got to be something you can do," Ruby said, her eyes scanning the screen with urgency, "Manual override?"

"I do not know that term," SD said.

"I mean, can you stop the computer from completing any actions and take direct control over the ship yourself."

SD thought about that. He could turn the computer off. He could plug himself in and act as the computer. Yes, maybe.

"Yes, maybe," he said out loud.

"Try now, please!" Ruby said. "That planet is way too big on the screen."

Within one tic SD understood that, one: they were still far enough away that the fact that the planet looked big on the viewscreen was an illusion. He could zoom out to a less disturbing image at any time. Two: that Ruby knew that too, and three: that none of that mattered if he didn't get in control of his ship.

Chapter 3

> Three <

"I think they're going to crash."

Three's circuits whirred as she processed what Rocky said. They were not equipped to handle a crash landing.

Rocky didn't wait for Three's circuits to slow down and process any more. She continued, "It's their trajectory. I'm concerned. They are close, but I don't think they are compensating for our unusual fields. Hence, I think they're going to crash."

"Wasn't that the intent of the transmission?" asked Maker. "They shouldn't be coming here anyway."

"Maker! That's terrible!" said Six-Five. Six-Five then whirred up her rotors and lifted off the ground slightly to emphasize her statement.

It was only a little less than a click earlier that Three had rolled over the hill and down to the valley where the rest of her colleagues were present. As was typical, she didn't head here in a straight line but had to navigate the pockets of goo that were unevenly located on the ground.

Seven-Nine, One-Four, and Three-Eight[1] were present in the valley. Three-Five, who flew in to bring them the most recent information, was bored from waiting and took off into the sky once more. Three saw her drift off over the horizon.

As always, they were gathered around Three-Eight, who was immobile. The others called her "Habby," but Three preferred using everyone's official designation. Habby was equipped with a large inner cavity originally designed to support Bio-life. She was the largest by volume of any of the robots and quite observant. Her optical sensors allowed her to see both inside and out, in all directions and as far as the horizon. And while her insides were designed for Bio support, she was still useful for repairing her smaller companions like Three-Eight or Six-Five, who rarely returned to base.

It was odd that Seven-Nine and One-Four were perched so close together. Well, Seven-Nine had no choice in the matter. She was perched close to Habby, and as the source of power for Habby and the other fixed robots, stayed put. It was One-Four that must have approached her. One-Four had her own power cells that, like any of them who were mobile, could collect

---

1. Okay, let's get the explanation for the naming of these robots out of the way now. They all have this number-name, except for a few that have other nicknames (i.e., Rocky, Maker). The nicknames are because giving them all numbers is hard to keep track of when reading the book. Rocky is One-Five, Maker is Three-Two, and Habby is Three-Eight. So, the full set of 11 robots on this planet are:

enough energy from their Sun, so they rarely had to visit Seven-Nine. Most of the others didn't have patience for Seven-Nine. This was fine with Seven-Nine who preferred to be left alone with her thoughts anyway.

Three, however, was usually the one to seek out Seven-Nine's counsel. Three appreciated how Seven-Nine always relied on logic and reason and Seven-Nine's desire to learn about everything enabled her to sift through information, combating bias and misinformation. Like when they first arrived, and their operations began on this planet. Seven-Nine kept in constant communication with all the mobile robots, collecting their data as they effortlessly and continuously sampled the rock and the goo and the atmosphere. It was a shame she wasn't mobile, but her connectivity to the other parts of the base gave her access to all the same information they all had. So, Seven-Nine would set herself to any computation task that wasn't boring or menial.

Heck, generating power for her companions wasn't menial either, but relied on constantly monitoring the rod buried deep inside her. The rod was stuck under layers and layers of dense, silver metal. Three appreciated the fact that out of every one of the robots on this planet, Seven-Nine was the one with the most important job, and thusly was relied upon by everyone who couldn't get all their energy from their sun.

So, it was interesting that One-Four was nearby. Although the fact that she attempted to trail along wherever Three went wasn't all that interesting. It's that she usually didn't come on a visit to Seven-Nine. While One-Four generally preferred the company of others, she often did not enjoy the company of Seven-Nine.

One-Five, also known as Rocky, and Three-Two, also known as Maker, were installed nearby because of course they were—both permanently positioned near Habby, so they were always close enough to listen in on communications and have their say.

Four-Six and Six-Five rarely met with the others. Four-Six enjoyed roaming the landscape as much as she could, and Six-Five could barely ever stay still. The second Six-Five would land, she'd be taking off again. The only thing that brought her to the ground was the need to soak up additional power from Seven-Nine on days that their sun wasn't enough. At the moment, Six-Five decided to ground herself nearer to Seven-Nine and One-Four.

"Don't get too comfortable," said One-Four. Three wanted to comment on One-Four's condescension, but now wasn't the time.

Three had perched herself in the center of her companions, turning around in the smallest circle her wheels would allow her to make in order to get everyone's attention.

"We're about to have visitors," she said. "Unplanned visitors. One-Five, do we have an idea of where their trajectory will put them?"

"First and for the last time, call me Rocky," One-Five, or rather, Rocky, said. "We've been over this more than a thousand times. It's easy to replace my formal designator with the alias."

Three's circuits whirred. Why didn't her companions understand her need to use official designations? They were, after all, here to execute their programming. They were not here to simply lounge around and waste time disclosing self-identifiers.

"I will need a little more time to compute the precise position of where they will crash land," said Rocky.

"And Three-Two, remember that we were attempting to direct the ship to land, not crash," said Three. "Can we warn them? Rocky?"

"Negative. Well, not unless you want Eight-Nine to pause her current activity. She will finish shortly, but not in time to help the visitors."

Three allowed her circuits to compute other possibilities. While she loved a challenge, she did not like accepting that they couldn't achieve any goal, big or small. When none of her computations yielded a better result, she rolled back and pointed upwards so her sensors could get a better look at the sky.

"We always knew this was a possibility," she said.

"We'll be able to repair Swell Driver if he's damaged. And his ship," said Rocky. "There should be two other robots with him unless they stayed in the Bio system. The information we received from the sentinel on Location Zero confirmed that a total of three robots escorted the Bio home. Presumably, they found the additional data that we had stored in the DNA of biological species—information that discloses our existence—and that's why they are on their way here."

"It's logical that all three robots would come," Seven-Nine, who made her first contribution to the conversation. Three turned in her direction.

"Yes, I agree," Three said. "Especially Detailed Historian. His mission has been, essentially, to find us. The robots never intended to construct their own missions like that. Once Eight-Nine has finished transmitting the updated code, we can have her send The Reset signal, and then Location Zero should be back on track with their original purpose and get back to producing the results we need."

"Do you really think we'll find the Contractors?" Three-Five said as she lifted off of the ground, her rotors spinning, she started to loop around the others who were all stuck on the ground.

"Nine-Two believed it, so I do, too," said Three. And then to the others, particularly Rocky, who continued to use her computational power to help instead of study rock after rock, "Let's see what we can do to monitor their trajectory and be nearby and available for repairs when they ultimately crash. Remember, when they get here, communicate no words about our mission. If they knew about the updated code and pending reset, they might attempt to stop it."

"Why would they do that?" said Habby.

Three turned towards the large construct. "Habby, if I told you that I was going to upload a new set of programming instructions and then reset you such that you won't remember what your life was like before, how would you react?"

Three waited patiently for Habby to compute an answer.

"Well, there's not much to remember so maybe it wouldn't matter so much. We've sat here for clicks and clicks and clicks doing not much of anything."

Three's circuits got hot. "We've done amazing things! We've kept ourselves functioning and ready for the Contractors to return. We've kept *on mission.* Even after we lost Nine-Two. That all must count for *something.*" She began to roll away, but stopped.

"Then what was the point, Three?"

"The mission. The point is always the mission."[2]

---

2. Another note about these 11 robots. They are inspired by the real-world Artemis mission developed by NASA. Part of the Artemis program is a concept for the Artemis Base Camp which includes things like a pressurized rover, surface habitat, and a nuclear fission power unit. The things I added here that are not part of the base camp concept are drones. The drones we know need an atmosphere to fly in and of course there is no atmosphere on the Moon, but there is on Titan and there is on my KOZ planet.

Chapter 4

Disto polled his sensors. Each of them reported a short quantity of tics with data missing. He computed that he had been offline for nearly 600 tics. His visual sensors were taking too long to return to their operational state, and he was anxious to have a look around. His audio sensors heard… that was AT's voice.

"Ruby? Ruby! Ruby?" AT was repeating.

Disto forced his visuals to bypass their routine check and activated them. They took a moment to adjust to collecting photons from the cabin—they were still in the main control center of SD's ship—before revealing the scene before him.

Ruby Palmer was in one of the chairs that had been installed when they were on Astroll 2, but the chair tore loose from its mount. It was compressed up against one wall. But Ruby was in it, and her eyes were closed. Disto could make out the tell-tale signs of Bio life. Ruby's primary chassis was performing the intake and output of the surrounding gas. She was alive. That was good. But she was unresponsive. That was bad.

Disto moved over to see if he could be of assistance. SD was at the console of his ship, presumably checking on its status.

"You had downloaded human repair manuals?" Disto asked AT.

AT made a noise that indicated, "Yes, but…" With one appendage on Ruby's arm, he said, "Yes, but…"

"But?" Disto prodded.

"But humans are quite complicated. I have a general template manual. Humans require individualized manuals."

"Interesting. You could not find a Ruby Palmer manual?"

"That's what I'm trying to communicate to you. One does not exist!"

"What does the general manual say?"

"There is no information for the scenario of unconsciousness with potential and unknown internal systems failures following a spaceship crash." AT paused, moved his appendage to different locations on her arm and then said, "I can tell you that she is alive. I can detect her inner systems are not stagnant."

"Can you also—"

"Mmmmmppphhhh…" The noise wasn't a word in her language but definitely came from Ruby.

"Ruby!" Disto and AT said.

Ruby performed the very Bio action of blinking—opening and closing the shutters that protected her optical sensors.

"Don't move," AT said.

Ruby did not heed AT's command. Instead, she used her arms to adjust her position in the chair, so she was sitting in more or less an upright position.

"Are your audio sensors damaged?" AT asked. "I said do not move."

Ruby touched the side of her head, "My audio sensors are fine," she said with a very slight smile. "But there's a ringing…"

AT looked at Disto and said, "In the supplies we brought, there is a human medical repair kit. Can you locate it?"

Disto chirped affirmatively and moved to the lift at the back of the cabin. Before he opened the door, he called out to SD, "Is it functioning?"

Without looking away from what he was doing, SD responded, "Yes. There is significant damage to my ship, including the primary computer. But internal secondaries like the lift should still be functioning."

SD's tone and coloring indicated that SD was a mix of frustrated, sad, and hopeful. But SD's feelings would have to wait. AT needed that medical kit to attend to Ruby.

Thankfully, the lift still worked so in a mere few tics, Disto found himself in front of several large crates of Bio supplies that they had brought with them. He could not immediately locate a manifest, so he started opening crates without the aid of data.

The first one he opened contained a Bio-sized, more specifically, a Ruby-sized suit. They knew that the planet they were headed to did not have an atmosphere compatible with Ruby's atmosphere processing systems, and if they were going to be on the surface, she'd need it. When Disto opened the second crate, he became quite disheartened looking at a pile of smaller, unmarked containers. He picked up one and realized they were marked, but on the side, not the top. He put each aside after confirming that they were foodstuffs. Disto had learned that the food at Location Zero was not entirely good for Ruby. It appeared they brought the nutrients she needed.

Disto worried he was taking far too long and there were still four more crates to examine. But then he emitted one of words that he'd added to his vocabulary while in the lab with several scientists on Earth: "Voila!"

The first container in the third crate was labeled 'medical supplies.' Disto started returning the items he had removed from the second crate back to their original location before computing that that action was a waste of tics right now. He dropped the box labeled 'emergency chocolate'[1] and rushed as fast as he could with the 'medical supplies' back to Ruby and their companions.

When he arrived, he was concerned that Ruby was still in the same position as when he left. Ruby was not the type to sit around for long, nor was she the type to listen when others told her she must sit.

"I convinced her to keep her current position until we could determine the extent of her injuries," AT said triumphantly.

"How did you do that?" Disto asked as he turned over the medical kit.

AT beeped. Clearly, he did not want to answer that question. Instead, AT turned his attention to the kit, using his precision appendage to carefully investigate the contents.

"That scanner…" Ruby said. "That's what you want."

While Disto was quite concerned with Ruby's health and status, he was also interested in the beep AT made. "AT?" he prompted.

---

1. There should always be emergency chocolate.

"Not now. I'm scanning." Indeed, by then he had the scanner aimed at Ruby's body and was moving it up and down, presumably collecting data. When he finished, both AT and Ruby looked at the small screen readout simultaneously.

"Great." Ruby said.

"You're great?" Disto responded, relieved.

"Remember when I tried to explain sarcasm to you?" Ruby said. Disto performed his version of a nod. "That was sarcasm."

"Therefore, you're not great. You are damaged," Disto said.

"I'm bruised. But I could have told you that without the scanner. Nothing more severe than that. But," she performed the very human motion of sighing, "it looks like I have a slight concussion."

"What's a concussion?" Disto asked.

"A mild blow to the head, with or without loss of consciousness, which can lead to temporary impairment of cognitive function and manifest in other cognitive symptoms," AT chimed in. "That's from the information I downloaded."

"Thanks," Ruby said. She was moving now, trying to position herself to stand.

"Wait," Disto said, a little louder than he'd intended, but he did intend for her to stop moving. "Shouldn't AT repair your concussion first?"

Ruby smiled, "I had this once before when I was twelve. Slight incident while playing table tennis. There's nothing AT can do."

Disto looked to AT for confirmation.

"Correct. The information I have says it will self-repair with rest and restriction of activities."

Ruby was again trying to stand up, so Disto again blurted out, "Wait!"

"I'm allowed to stand," she smiled as she said it. "The kind of activities they don't want me to do are the ones that could cause another concussion. A small one isn't that bad. Multiple concussions at the same time are."

She stood up and immediately said, "Whoa..." and looked for something to hold on to. "This is not ship's gravity."

SD was the one who responded to Ruby's statement, "That is correct. You are feeling the gravity of the planet, which, putting in terms of your home world, Earth, is approximately 80 percent."

"Just enough to knock me off balance," Ruby said, gripping the chair. "Maybe I will sit down until we figure out what we're doing."

"That depends on the status of the ship," Disto said. "SD? Do you have this information?"

"I do," SD said. And then said no more. After a few tics, Disto asked, "Can you share this information with us?"

"I can," SD said. And then said no more. After a few tics, a frustrated Disto asked, "Would you share your information with us now?"

"Yes," SD said, moving away from the console and facing the rest of them.

"The ship is severely damaged," SD said. Disto wanted to say, 'We knew that' but refrained until he heard what SD was going to say next.

"The ship's computer has indications that components we need to lift off are damaged, as is much of the deep communication..." SD cut himself off and turned his attention to the console. Disto knew that SD had a direct connection to the ship's computer and assumed they were in communication right now.

After a few tics, SD's facescreen refreshed to indicate that he had completed that communication.

"SD?"

"The computer," he began. "I'm sorry. I'm still processing. Processing. The computer has indicated that parts I did not know existed on my ship have been damaged. There is a deep communication system I did not know was present."

As SD made his report, Disto watched AT's excitement build. He clearly wanted to start repairs immediately.

"What's outside?" Disto and Ruby asked simultaneously. Simultaneous emissions such as those were rare and Disto almost distracted himself by wanting to mark the occasion. A glance from Ruby told him she might have had a similar thought that didn't get expressed because SD answered the question.

"I think the source of the transmission we picked up is nearby," SD said.

"Ooo! We should go check it out! I'll need to get my suit!" said Ruby and she moved past him, a little too fast for someone recently injured.

SD was involved with his ship, Ruby was prepping to head outside, and AT was figuring out which tools he could use to effect repairs. Disto had nothing to do but wait and count down the tics until The Reset.

Chapter 5

"You look... engorged," Disto said.

"Swollen is how I would have described it," AT added.

Ruby looked down at the parts of her body she could see. SD's ship didn't have a mirror, so she was unable to see the full effect of how she presented to the robots in this thing. It was somewhere halfway between comfortable, like sleepwear, and utterly uncomfortable, like what ancient space suits were known to be. The outer surface was a light blue, so she must have looked like a series of large, light blue marshmallows smashed together in humanoid form to the robots. The helmet was half opaque and half clear, so when it was on her head, the robots could still see her face and she had her full range of peripheral vision. The suit also allowed her to bend her joints with little effort. The insides of the legs were soft but rigid. The arms were more flexible, but less soft. It seemed that wherever comfort was, discomfort made room for itself.

She hadn't donned an Intelli-Gear suit since she had to practice emergency ops with one. Pilots were required to be retrained yearly, and it was nearly a year since she'd last worn it.

However, she was able to successfully connect her communicuff to the suit's systems so she could activate Pippa by voice only and she would see projected visuals that appeared to her as if they were several feet in front of her. It was very similar technology to her Percepto-glasses, but in suit form.

"Pippa," she said, "suit check."

There was no holoimage of Pippa. Ruby asked Pippa to keep that kind of unnecessary visual to a minimum, but added in a compliment about the personalized image Pippa was fond of projecting. It wasn't that Ruby didn't like it. She needed to see as much as possible of this new world without anything blocking her vision—no matter how translucent the images and data were. She was already prepared for new levels of overstimulation, and with her new concussion to keep an eye on, she couldn't be too careful.

A list of suit systems appeared in front of Ruby. The display wasn't on the screen in her helmet, right next to her face, but rather a reality augment that appeared from her perspective to be several feet in front of her, almost next to Disto. Not that he or anyone but Ruby could see it.

"Oxygen pack one all good," Pippa announced. As she did, the corresponding word was highlighted in the list for Ruby to see and correlate. Pippa listed all the systems one by one: Primary life support, back-up life support, tertiary life support... since the suit was all about life support, really.

"Dismiss," Ruby commanded, and her view cleared. She could call up the status at any time with a simple command.

She opened and closed her hands several times ensuring she had a full range of movement for each of her fingers. The suit was a little stiff, but it was the stiffness of a suit that was brand new, never worn.

She also took a few steps back and forth and bent down to make sure her knees, ankles and everything could move. When she was satisfied, she put her hands on her hips and said:

"Okay, I'm ready to head outside!"

She knew she was swaying a little as she said it. 80 percent gravity should have been easy for her, but was not feeling 100 percent steady on her feet, so she inched herself back until she was leaning against the bulkhead. Still, swaying didn't deter her confidence. She clenched her fist as much as the suit's glove would let her, narrowed her eyes through the visor, and readied herself for whatever this new world had to throw at her.

SD commanded the ship to open the hatch. The outside air rushed in and mingled with the inside air. Ruby remembered that she never got a satisfactory answer to why the air on SD's ship, and Location Zero, was already a breathable and non-toxic mix. She hoped that she could assume it could return it to that state later. But those issues would need to wait.

They were here, and the swirl of air that rushed in was... warm. A cozy kind of warm. Like gentle humid air that wants to hang around and be friends instead of breezing past. The Intelli-Gear was designed to allow the wearer to experience as much of the ambient environment as possible. Once that environment started to go out of range to support life, systems would kick in. The wearer could choose to make it warmer, or cooler based on personal preference as well.

"Pippa," Ruby said. "Atmosphere readout." While she trusted SD and his ship—at least in the sense that she trusted that SD would not intentionally mislead or lie to her—she wasn't sure she could trust that his equipment was working or that it was designed to pick up what was important to humans.

Once again, the Intelli-Gear displayed a set of data to her, and Pippa simultaneously read it.

"Primary atmosphere constituents are nitrogen and methane at a ratio of 17 to 3," Pippa paused, "That's very close to the atmosphere of Titan. Radiation levels are high. We're detecting nearly a centi-rem."

Ruby had to remember that 'we' meant Pippa and the suit.

"Then that means I'm going to need to keep this suit on and let it filter out the methane. Got it."

She might have been able to tolerate the methane, but not the radiation. Luckily, the suit, like most materials made to operate in space, had a thin layer of protective metallic that generated enough of a magnetic field to deflect incoming cosmic rays and other damaging protons, but didn't interfere with standard electronics. This thin layer was built into everything—all ships, most personal clothing, and even standard coffee containers offered that kind of protection.

"Temperature is 26 degrees Celsius; Ambient humidity is roughly 95 percent."

"No wonder it's so warm," Ruby said. "But wait, is there water in the air, Pippa?" Ruby flexed her fingers and closed them repeatedly. The suit still felt stiff.

"Ruby," Disto interrupted. "It sounds like you are talking to yourself."

"I'm talking to Pippa, and she's talking back to me through the speakers in the helmet. Argh. Pippa, the robots want to hear what you're saying as well. Turn on the external speakers."

"Testing, testing," said Pippa.

"You're performing tests?" Disto asked. "What kind?"

"I was testing my ability to communicate with you," Pippa responded. "I would say the test was successful."

"Okay," Ruby said, "*Now*, can we all go outside?"

Chapter 6

> Ruby <

Ruby was the first one to step outside of the ship. Even though she had already been on an alien world, Location Zero, this was something else entirely. As she stepped out onto the strange regolith of the new planet, it crunched beneath her feet like dry breakfast cereal. She'd never been to the Moon or Mars, but the texture of the ground felt and looked like what she imagined both of those places to be like, although instead of gray or a burnt orange commonly associated with Mars, the dominant color here was a yellowish green. The sky also had a yellowish and greenish haze to it. Perhaps it was the concussion, but it was making Ruby a little queasy. While yellows and greens weren't her favorite colors, if it wasn't for the queasiness, Ruby might have found it pretty. It was daytime, but the sky was hazy enough that she couldn't immediately locate the direction of the host star.

"Pippa, am I getting ambient audio?" she asked. It was quiet. Too quiet. Although that shouldn't have surprised her too much. There wasn't anything around to make noise other than her, and the robots—who were starting to leave SD's ship, with Disto in front and SD in the back.

"Yes," Pippa responded.

When Ruby was about three meters from the ship, she stopped and slowly turned around to one: take in the full effect of the landscape, and two: get a good look at the ship. The outside didn't look too beat up, but it was partially sitting in a patch of... *goo*? Goo didn't feel like a very scientific term, but it was the only word popping into Ruby's head as she stared at the slow moving, translucent, gobbildy-gook that partly encased the bottom of the ship. As she looked around, she saw varying sizes of poppy yellow or orangish yellow goo on the ground.

Once again, she was reminded of images she had seen of Mars. In fact, if it wasn't for the background color, if you told her she was on Mars, she would have believed you. Except she didn't recall ever seeing or hearing about goo on Mars. So then again, she probably wouldn't have believed it, until she took a closer look at the puddles of slime.

There were hills in the distance and Ruby instantly wondered if they'd landed in a crater. There was no way for her to know right now. The hills looked rough and rocky. There was nothing that could be considered vegetation in sight, hence the comparison to Mars or even the Moon. As she continued to turn, taking in the whole scene, the hills seemed to only surround them halfway. The other half was flatter terrain than she'd ever seen. Again, not a sign of anything that looked like vegetation. Also, no buildings or ruins or any signs of any people or any habitation.

"We need to decide how we're going to talk about direction here," Ruby announced.

"That's the equivalent of North," SD chimed in. He had been so quiet and motionless, but now he was pointing towards the middle of the hills. "And that's East," he was now pointing 90 degrees to the right of the hills.

The other two robots and Ruby all looked at him quizzically, but none of them said what Ruby was thinking, and what she was sure the other robots were thinking, *How did he know that?* But Ruby wasn't satisfied not knowing the answer to that question, so she came up with one on her own: *He has been here before. Maybe not on the surface, but in orbit. There must be some form of magnetosphere to orient north and south, and spin, to orient east and west. It's that simple.* And it was that simple, except for the part where SD must have been here before and no one else knew about this place. No, there was nothing simple about this.

"Pippa," Ruby said, "Do you detect any magnetosphere? Can you anchor that direction as North?" Ruby pointed in the direction SD had indicated.

"Affirmative," Pippa replied. "We have calibrated our compass. But our direction module was not meant for exploring new worlds."

"Well, Pippa, sometimes we all have to operate out of our comfort zones," Ruby said. She was indeed outside of her comfort zone, but no... she wasn't. She was more uncomfortable being too comfortable. At home, she was restless. This was exciting. This was *her*. She was exploring a new world. A new alien world that no human had ever set foot on. She knelt onto the ground and felt the terrain through her suit gloves, crumbling small rocks into dust. Something about this made her smile and wonder how she could feel so at home somewhere so far from home. She looked out at the flat emptiness and imagined all that could be beyond it, unable to keep herself from feeling that this may be exactly what she was meant to do with her life. Not continue to build out a colony on an existing world like Titan but be one of the first to set foot on new places. Of course, that option had never occurred to her before since human spaceflight was limited to her home solar system. All the places that humans could step down on comfortably, with the aid of a space suit, well, humans had. This option had never been available until now.

Maybe when this was done, she could offer to go explore strange new worlds with SD and the other robots? Assuming they could fix SD's ship and get off this world. And assuming that they could find the source of the pending software reset to prevent the robots from turning into who knows what. Or at least prevent their memories and existing personalities from being erased.

"We should probably inspect your ship, SD," Ruby said. Then she noticed that was exactly what AT was doing. He hadn't marveled at the landscape like she had, or stared longingly into the distance looking for something, like Disto.

AT was in the process of a methodical circumnavigation of SD's ship. Ruby took several steps to catch up to him. She heard each one of her steps make a crunching sound in the alien regolith as she did so. This was the closest she'd ever come to the outside of SD's ship. It looked... smooth. She didn't dare touch the outside not knowing if it was still hot from entering the atmosphere, or if there was a lot of electrical charge build up, or something she hadn't thought of. *Look, don't touch.* She could hear the voice of her uncles inside her head telling her to be careful. The robots even had to say it 100 times the day they brought her to the Museum of Intricate Specimens on Location Zero, but right now, that seemed like useful survival advice.

"I commend your driving skills, Swell Driver," AT said. SD had also followed Ruby's steps and now the three of them were involved in the inspection. "Or maybe it's your crashing skills I am complimenting. I am not detecting any damage to the primary structure. This was a very well executed crash."

SD chirped what Ruby recognized as 'thank you.'

"How are we going to launch it back into orbit?" Ruby asked.

"That's a later problem," Disto said. Disto had been so quiet, for a moment, Ruby thought he had gone back inside the ship.

"I don't know, seems like a now *and* later problem to me. I know you all have advanced technology, but last time we talked about SD's ship landing and launching, back at Earth, it didn't seem like SD's ship was built for this."

"I never said the ship couldn't land on Earth," SD said.

Both Disto and Ruby turned to him, both wearing an expression that said, 'explain more!'

"My ship is designed to land and take off from any celestial body less than 141 densitons."

"Wait a minute," said Ruby, "Then why did we go through all that with Legacy Station?" She recalled how they chose to dock with the station when they arrived at Earth, causing an electrostatic incident, damage to their equipment, and additional headaches.

"I didn't want to get my ship dirty," SD said.

Luckily, there was enough room in the Intelli-Gear suit for Ruby's jaw to drop and it did. She also knew that his ship was now quite dirty in a pile of goo. That was the definition of irony, right?

Ruby took a deep breath and said, "Okay, forget about that. Let's deal with the problems at hand."

"Indeed," Disto said. "And I think we have new problems to add to the list."

"Oh?" Ruby put her hands on her hips, "And what's the new one?"

Disto pointed in a direction she hadn't spent much time looking at yet, south.

"That," he said.

North, with the hills, was more interesting to look at. When Ruby turned south, all she could discern was a large, flat plain. At least at first. Now, on her second look, she saw what looked like a vehicle. It was moving. And it was heading in their direction.

Chapter 7

"Are you seeing what I'm seeing?" Four-Six asked. Four-Six wasn't sure exactly who she was asking and didn't care if it was Three-Five or Three herself who answered.

Four distinct objects were positioned outside of the ship, perched awkwardly on the ground. Three of the objects were clearly robots from Location Zero and they were obviously from at least two different sectors.

But the fourth object... it was a very odd-looking robot. It did not have a ground chassis but balanced oddly on two—wait—Four-Six had seen this before. This was in her design specifications, something she hadn't needed to think about in a long time. It's exactly what her belly was designed for: a Bio.

Four-Six hadn't been at the meeting with the others. Whenever they all got together, which was infrequent, someone was always yelling at someone else. Or, if they promised no one would yell—which they often did for her sake—conflict would still escalate in a more passive-aggressive manner, which was still stressful to Four-Six[1]. She preferred to roam about the terrain, pushing her limits further and further. She was indeed limited by the amount of power before a recharge was necessary, but out of all her companions who were mobile she was the one with the furthest range.

Which is why she was the one chosen to greet the... intruders? Strangers? There was an argument over what to call them and she was glad she wasn't present for that. Instead, she started heading in their direction before she was fully debriefed.

Four-Six decided all on her own she would simply call them 'visitors.'

Like her companions, she knew much of their own backstory and history. Four-Six and her companions were confined to this world, abandoned by their own creators—well, not entirely abandoned. The Contractors simply no longer existed, but their programming could not accept that, and they needed the Contractors back.

Four-Six still maintained a record of the day of the Big Decision.

---

1. One of the things I did when I was developing the 11 robots for this book was give them all a Myers-Briggs designation and a personality type as described by 16Personalities: https://www.16personalities.com/personality-types

"We have everything we need," Nine-Two[2] had said. "There are objects in orbit that we control. We will relocate them to collect supplies. We will build a computational system. It will be as large as a small planet. It will be our exploration system."

Four-Six had a record of Three[3] and the others agreeing and planning. Four-Six herself had a very small role in the whole project but agreed that exploring the surrounding galaxy to find the Contractors was a worthy goal. After all, she was created to host several Contractors at a time in her belly. Without the Contractors, she had very little purpose.

She provided a copy of her core programming to use as a template for robots that they created to live and be a part of Location Zero. Her other ten companions did the same. All the robots on Location Zero were based on one of these eleven templates, at least programming-wise, at least initially. The Location Zero robots didn't have the physical limitations Four-Six and her companions had. But Location Zero was still in beta test and the final version of their programming was nearly ready for execution. Eight-Nine[4] simply needed to finish transmitting it to Location Zero's Core.

Swell Driver was one robot who they programmed more directly, for special tasks. And for some unknown reason, he was on his way to them. They were certain that he was bringing at least one other robot with him. Maybe two. And then they crash landed and now Four-Six, the largest and most mobile of the eleven companions, was on her way to retrieve them.

She hoped they weren't badly damaged. If they were, and if they weren't able to be mobile under their own power, her internal cavity would certainly hold three, maybe more, robots. It was a long time since she carried anything inside, and the thought tickled her. She was thankful that they landed where the terrain was easy, although she had to be mindful of the goop that was scattered around. She could tolerate a little more than her mobile companions, but too much and she'd need a deep clean. But she still preferred this terrain to the hills that were further north and difficult for her to traverse.

Once, a long time ago, she carried the Twins—Three-Five[5] and Six-Five[6] —in her belly to the base of the Hills and let them fly around. The Twins were the only two that could fly. Their range in the air was not as far as hers on the ground and they had been dying to explore the Hills but couldn't get there on their own from the base.

But today, Four-Six traveled alone. Aloneness, she didn't mind. But a visitor could be quite entertaining.

She was only equipped with line-of-sight communication equipment, as were most of her companions, so they set up the usual system when she was on an exploratory mission. Three-Five and Six-Five took positions hovering as high as they could between her and base so they could relay any information back and forth.

"Are you there yet?" Three-Five asked.

---

2. Nine-Two is an ESTJ, the "Executive." She is/was resistant to change, but an excellent administrator and unsurpassed at managing things.

3. Three is an ENTJ, a "Commander" personality type. She digs in her heals when in disagreement, but loves a challenge and believes she can achieve any goal. But she's also intolerant and impatient and cannot handle emotions.

4. Eight-Nine is an ISTJ, a "Logistician" personality. She prides herself on integrity, loves clear hierarchies and expectations, and often unreasonably blames herself. She's the "comms" unit.

5. Three-Five is an ISTP, a "Virtuoso" personality type. She's easily bored, but also optimistic and energetic.

6. Six-Five is an ESTP, an "Entrepreneur" personality. She's extremely outgoing, notices when things change, but always misses the bigger picture and is a little defiant and unstructured.

"Negative," Four-Six responded. "I had to slow my rate of movement temporarily because the terrain turned rocky."

"How much further? Do I need to fly higher? I can do that you know," Three-Five responded.

Four-Six could tell that her flying companion was incredibly excited. That was when she was willing to take risks. Three-Five was already hovering at the maximum altitude that was deemed safe. But she was always looking for reasons, or excuses, to fly higher.

"Negative. But you should be able to see the crash site and should be able to see how far away I am. It shouldn't be much further."

Four-Six's optical sensors weren't terribly good at distance, but they were keen in the vicinity around her and in front of her. What she could detect at the moment was only a blur, but as she continued on, that blur had come into focus. It was most definitely a ship.

"Three-Five? I assume you see it, too?" Four-Six asked.

"Yes! Yes! I see it! Do you need me to move in closer? Or fly higher?"

"Again, Three-Five. Negative! If you come any closer, I won't be able to communicate back through you and Six-Five to Three. Speaking of which, let them know we have visual detection of Swell Driver's ship. I will be there momentarily."

Four-Six continued to move in the direction of the ship. She had been this far North only a few times before, to scout and map the terrain. And of course, her trip with the twins to the hills. She did another self-systems check to make sure her belly was ready for guests.

As she got closer, she could see more detail but she was no longer interested in the detail of the ship itself, but of the objects that were next to it.

"Image capture on confirmed," she said in a way that indicated Three-Five should relay that back to Six-Five who would relay that back to Three. "Image relay to begin momentarily."

She captured an impression of the scene in front of her. Once she had moved a length or two more, she captured another. These images were now automatically being relayed back to Three who would analyze them along with the others.

"That's definitely a Bio! They have a Bio with them," Four-Six screamed excitedly.

"Are you sure?" Three-Five responded.

"Of course I'm sure! Doesn't anybody but me and Habby remember the Bios?" Habby, what they called Three-Eight[7], was constructed for similar reasons—to support Bio life in their bellies. To that end, Four-Six always felt a stronger kinship to Habby than any of the others.

"Three confirms," Three-Five said. "They are also saying you need to approach with caution."

"Well of course," Four-Six responded. "What do we know about this Bio?"

There was a pause, while messages were relayed back to Three and data was sent back.

---

7. Habby, aka Three-Eight, is an ISFJ, a "Defender" personality type. She is very serious and loves stability. She is also overly humble and is reluctant to change.

8. If you remember back in *Robots, Robots Everywhere* Ruby saw a robot that was called an "Unknown Enigma"? These are the sentinels. It's what Ruby saw as a pitch-black robot with a large blueish dot in the center of its top-most chassis.

"According to Three," Three-Five said, "the sentinels on Location Zero[8] had recently reported activities on a Bio that Swell Driver had collected and brought there. The Bio was... repairing Core systems? That can't be right. Four-Six, hold on and let me get clarification on that."

Four-Six continued to approach, but slowly. The three robots and one Bio were clearly aware of her by now. They were all stationary and looking in her direction.

A gust of wind passed through, stirring up the dirt and dust. Four-Six grumbled in disapproval as the dust momentarily impaired her vision and interfered with communications. Poor Three-Five seemed particularly affected and she had to lower her altitude, so the signal was barely making it to her.

"Bio... careful..." Static punctuated the signal. "Don't—"

"Don't what?" Four-Six asked but didn't get a response. Static.

"Four-Six? Are you there? Are you okay?"

Of course Four-Six was okay. It was only a little dust interference. It would clear soon, and communication would resume. But what should she do in the meantime? Approach? Stay and do nothing?

Four-Six tried to compute what it might be like if something larger than herself approached her and simply stopped. That would be unpleasant. So maybe the right thing to do was continue on and introduce herself to the visitors? That was the polite thing to do. But she was supposed to not do something and that could have been anything.

Four-Six could feel herself heating up and it was unpleasant. For the moment, she would do absolutely nothing but let her emotions settle down and think of the perfect greeting for when she inevitably approached the visitors. "Hello," simply wasn't going to cut it.

---

8. If you remember back in *Robots, Robots Everywhere* Ruby saw a robot that was called an "Unknown Enigma"? These are the sentinels. It's what Ruby saw as a pitch-black robot with a large blueish dot in the center of its top-most chassis.

Chapter 8

> Three <

"A Bio!" shouted One-Four[1] as she spun her wheels, kicking up bits of rock and goo.

"Careful!" shouted Three. "But, yes. A Bio. We need to determine if it's the same one Swell Driver had brought to Location Zero. I compute two options. Swell Driver and the others returned the original Bio to its homeworld and brought along another, or this is that same Bio."

"I calculate a higher probability that this is the same Bio," said Rocky[2].

"Agreed," said Three. Three wished she could have been out there with Four-Six, but she simply didn't have the range. Her mobility was limited, and she moved a lot slower and more deliberately than her mobile companions. She wanted to curse her makers for that, but that would be entirely unhelpful. She needed to purge those thoughts and figure out what to do next. She was, after all, the defacto leader of this group of robots—ever since Nine-Two went missing.

But in any case, it was probably best that Nine-Two wasn't here. Nine-Two was too conservative, too judgmental. One time, Three appeared at a group meeting having recently removed her Bio seats. With no Bios around, she didn't want to carry around the extra weight all day, every day. Three tried to explain that it wasn't energy efficient, but Nine-Two was not happy and let everyone know it. Even now, simply remembering her words of disapproval made Three vibrate unpleasantly.

Three rolled over to Habby. Close enough that the others wouldn't hear.

"Habby, I'd really like to hear your computations on the situation."

Habby opened and shut her main hatch. Matching the ambient atmosphere with that of what she carried in her belly always calmed her down.

"There should be nothing disconcerting about a Bio," she said. "We were created by Bios, for Bios. Bios should be living with us, and in a few cases, inside us. They should be putting us to use. We've been on our own too long. Far too long."

---

1. One-Four is an ENFJ, a "Protagonist" personality type. She thrives in the group, is unrealistic, overly idealistic but can be judgey and condescending.

2. Rocky, aka One-Five, is an INFP, a "Mediator" personality type. She's desperate to please, self-critical, and obsesses over what the 'right' thing to do is.

Three considered Habby's words. Habby, formally known as Three-Eight, was right. All of them owed their existence to a group of Bios that was long gone. Who cared that this Bio was not one of them—not one of the Contractors.

"But what if this Bio wants to interfere with our project," said Three-Two, also known as Maker[3]. Maker was usually fond of change but was also fond of contradicting Three.

"I didn't ask you," Three said, "Yet." She rolled over to Maker who was, unsurprisingly, making something at that moment.

"What are you making?" Three asked.

"I accessed my archived data. Old designs for items that I never made because the Contractors never lived here. Maybe this new Bio could use them."

Three rolled back and forth slightly as she watched Maker's systems carefully extract material from the ground with one long appendage. She then used her next long appendage to heat and lay material, one single thin layer at a time on top of another to construct a bio-sized pole sticking out from a base, with appendages protruding from the sides.

"What is that supposed to be?" Three said.

"A welcome gift," Maker responded.

Three resisted the urge not to swirl her optical sensors. "But what *is* it? Its function?"

"It is a device to hold bio-wearables. Remember how the Bios would shed and replace their outermost protective layers? They can use my creation—my own design of course—to temporarily hold them."

Three noticed a slight blemish on the side facing away from Maker but didn't say anything. Maker was not good at handling any kind of criticism, no matter how well-meaning, and right now, Three didn't want to handle anyone not handling anything.

Three rolled back to the center of her stationary colleagues and announced, "We'll tell Four-Six to bring them all back. In her belly, the Bio will not be able to cause trouble. Four-Six could even keep it in there if need be."

"Will this interfere with The Mission?" asked Habby.

"No, because we won't let it," said Three. She hoped that was a true statement.

---

3. Maker, aka Three-Two, is an INFJ, an "Advocate" personality type. She is VERY sensitive to criticism, a perfectionist, and won't ask for help. But she also seeks out change, thrives on innovation, and is prone to burnout.

Chapter 9

> Ruby <

Disto rolled in front of the others in a way that seemed either protective or a form of annoyed anxiousness. Either way, Ruby didn't object.

The object that had been slowly moving across the landscape in their direction looked a lot like the pressurized rovers that were on the Moon and Mars. Not exactly, of course. But it had eight hard wheels that carried a large structure. That large structure, if hollow, looked like it had room for four or maybe even six people. But maybe it wasn't hollow at all. And what if... Ruby swallowed hard... what if there were people inside? Not *people*, people... not humans, but aliens, and not robot aliens, but living, breathing ones.

Ruby took several slow steps backwards.

Her robots noticed.

"Ruby, it's okay," SD said.

"We have no idea what that is or what's inside it," she said, her voice shaking.

Ruby remembered how she felt when she met SD. Now, she knew SD as her friend, but initially, the entire thing was horrifying. She remembered how tight her chest felt at the unknown, how her mind spun, how her palms got clammy. She rubbed her hands together, forgetting that she was wearing gloves, and her eyebrow twitched.

She continued to stare at the object that moved toward them. The front and side were largely glossy. Maybe they were windows. If they were, they were the kind that were half-silvered mirror glass with the reflective side facing outwards, because she couldn't see inside them. Part of her was curious, and part of her was glad she could not see inside them. She wasn't sure if she'd like what she saw or if it would only make her feel worse. *Maybe I'm not cut out for galactic exploration after all,* she thought.

SD moved closer to Ruby and put his appendage on the top of her thigh. He was clearly trying to comfort her, and Ruby willed herself not to hyperventilate.

She was 'Ruby—Planetary Explorer' or 'Ruby—Intergalactic Explorer' or one of a dozen other ridiculous titles they'd called her back on Earth and Astroll 2. Hopefully, when anyone found out about this, they wouldn't call her 'Ruby—Scaredy-Cat Surveyor' or something equally demeaning.

The rover, for there was nothing else to call it, roved right down in front of Disto, who had put another few meters between him and the others. Far enough away from Ruby that she'd have to raise her voice for him to hear her, but close enough for her to make out the tones of their conversation.

Once stopped, the rover emitted a few chirps and beeps to Disto. To Ruby's ear, it sounded like the robot's native language, only slower. Like if SD or Disto or AT talked natively, ten or maybe even fifty times slower than they normally emitted those sounds. It was also deeper, and sounded almost grumbly, at an octave that Ruby certainly couldn't match.

Disto returned the tones, once at his normal rate and once slower. The rover then did the same. Well, not exactly the same. Ruby could tell it was a new sequence of bleeps and dings and still at the slow speed. The rover was larger than Disto. It was the same size as a mini-R-pod. The parts that were not windows might have been white once, but time in this atmosphere could have turned that white into the current dirty ivory color. Or maybe it was simply dirt and the rover needed a good washing.

Disto and the rover's exchange of noises continued for a few moments.

"They're talking, aren't they?" Ruby asked SD.

"Indeed," SD responded.

"Do you know what they're saying?" Ruby asked. The adrenaline from her initial reaction was getting absorbed by her body, and new adrenaline wasn't getting produced so she was feeling a sense of tiredness droop through her shoulders and fingers. It had been quite a day already, and she needed a moment to collect her thoughts, but curiosity kept her on her feet.

A new batch of adrenaline was born out of that curiosity, keeping her eyes fixed on the rover. Now that it was closer, she could see details like how dirty it was. It was in desperate need of a washing.

"I know what they're saying," SD said. And that was all he said. Before Ruby could even roll her eyes at how SD answered her question and only her question, Disto and the rover were moving back towards Ruby and SD.

"I don't know where to begin," Disto said, the pitch of his voice rising to a tone that was almost out of Ruby's hearing range. His coloring was an alternating wave of yellow, purple, pink, and deep orange. For a moment, Ruby worried that Disto was about to have a systems overload from the excitement. Or anxiousness. Or surprise at the overall situation.

"Start at the beginning," Ruby suggested.

And Disto did. "'Greetingsssss,' was the first thing Four-Six said," said Disto.

"Four-Six?" asked Ruby.

"Yes. That is her name," said Disto, using his appendage to indicate the rover. It didn't escape Ruby's notice that Disto used the pronoun 'her' in reference to the object.

"Four-Six," Ruby repeated. "Not forty-six?"

Disto chirped at the rover who slowly chirped back.

"Correct. Four-six is her name, her designation. And she has been tasked with bringing us back to meet the others," Disto continued.

Ruby gulped. "Others? How many people are here?"

Once more, Disto and Four-Six exchanged a new series of chirps and peeps.

"Four-six tells me there are no people. Only robots. Eleven robots, to be exact."

> Ruby <

A few minutes later, Disto, SD, and Ruby were inside of Four-Six. It was a tight fit. There were seats, but they were made for someone a foot or two smaller than Ruby. Luckily, they folded up so that Disto and SD could roll inside. Ruby kept hers in seat-position, because if she folded it up, she'd have to stand and bonk her head on the ceiling, and sitting on the floor wouldn't have been terribly comfortable either. The floor was hard and plastic-like, and with all the seats, there wouldn't have been much room to sit.

Four-Six communicated through Disto. Disto explained that Four-Six didn't have a language processing/translating mode, and while she could get one, it would take a while.

But she had opened up the rear of the capsule that made up the bulk of her body for them to enter. Four-Six, via Disto, had made it clear that it would be faster this way than if Ruby and the other robots used their own locomotive powers.

Disto and SD felt perfectly safe, so Ruby tried to conjure up the same feeling. It wasn't easy while she was both shaking, and sweating, and concocting an exit plan in her head. Although both were starting to subside as she processed the information that she wasn't about to meet aliens today—simply more robots. This seemed more manageable to her, so at the very least, this was somewhat comforting.

AT didn't join them. He chose to stay behind with SD's ship. "I need to try and repair the ship," he'd said. "I will use all my skills to fix the things that are broken." He seemed quite content and happy to do so.

"So... eleven robots?[1] " Ruby said out loud once she settled into her seat and Four-Six was moving.

"Confirmed," Disto said. "Four-six has provided information on all of them, although not much. I have their designators, the locations for a few, their favorite number, and how much time a year they spend removing native dust from their circuits."

From inside Four-Six, Ruby could see out the mostly one-way windows. She saw that they were kicking up quite a bit of dust as they moved along the terrain. Dust was not something she worried about while living on Astroll 2. Efficient filters kept micro-particles of stuff, to include her own skin, from contaminating her environment. Every few years, there was a news story from one of the sites on the Moon that blamed dust for one accident or another. Ruby had always assumed it was human error, but as she looked at the sheer quantity of the stuff here, she could now imagine that it was a constant battle on the Moon between the people who needed their equipment free and clear of the stuff and the stuff, the dust itself, that wanted to be everywhere it could possibly be.

In fact, about half of the asteroid processing equipment was designed specifically to cope with large amounts of dust, and even then, it wasn't too much of an issue. Most of the asteroids of interest were littered with nickel-iron and the dust was easily kept in place by deliberate magnetic fields produced by the equipment.[2]

"Ruby?"

---

1. BTW... Eleven. Why eleven? Because there was a day that i chose the name *Crazy Foolish Robots* for book 1, and decided I needed to name all 4 books right then. I liked the idea of names of books being puns or something catchy and familiar. I don't know why I started thinking about it, but Agatha Christie's novel *Ten Little Indians* came to mind. "Ten" little robots didn't have the same feel or cadence, but "eleven" felt right. Voila. Although at the time I came up with the name, I had ZERO idea of who or what those eleven robots would be...

2. For a time at my day job, I worked on some lunar concepts and the problem of lunar dust is a real biggie.

It was SD.

"Yes?"

"You went quiet for... well, for more tics than expected."

"I'm sorry. I was thinking about what Disto said." Before SD or Disto could ask her to elaborate, the topic switched in Ruby's head. She didn't want to talk about dust, and it really wasn't that important anyway, so she focused on something else Disto said. "He said 'every year.' There are years here?"

Disto chirped in a way that was almost a giggle.

"That was my translation for the amount of time this planet orbits our star, which is the same amount of time which Location Zero orbits it. We are truly at equidistant parts in our orbit."

Ruby nodded in understanding.

The three of them lapsed into silence as they continued on.

Ruby paused and looked out at the yellowish greenish sky, focusing in and out of the landscape, trying to stare at it until it felt normal. Her mind wanted to focus on the newness, but she knew this could impair decision making. "Normalize," had been her pilot instructor's favorite word. "Mistakes kill pilots. Mistakes happen when things are abnormal. Normalize everything and you'll keep yourself alive."

So, one thing at a time, Ruby normalized it. A bunch of dust isn't all that interesting, and neither is a yellowish sky. In fact, she felt a faint twinge of nostalgia when she realized this sky was the exact shade of one of her favorite childhood sodas.

"What are you thinking about now, Ruby?" SD asked.

Ruby looked over at SD, not sure if she could successfully explain her train of thought. "I was thinking about... well, I guess I was thinking about the color of the sky."

"Ah," SD chimed, "Is it your favorite color?"

Ruby shook her head and smiled. "Definitely not. Who explained the concept of favorite colors to you? It was Sebastian, wasn't it?"

SD nodded. "Correct. When data is equal, you use a... feeling... to choose, was how he explained it. And then he told me his favorite color is purple. I told him I had no feelings to distinguish one color from another, so he assigned purple as my favorite as well. Do you have a favorite?"

Ruby thought for a moment. Right as she was about to declare orange as her favorite, because once she had turned thirteen, she stopped using red, since it was so obvious due to her name, they ran over a particularly orange puddle of goo which splashed across the window in a most unpleasant way.

Ruby said, "You know what? Sebastian might be on to something. I'm going to go with purple, too.[3] " Although maybe red secretly was still her favorite, even though it was still too obvious and a color the robots couldn't see.

---

3. Purple is my favorite color.

Chapter 10

"You're saying that their arrival changes nothing," Rocky said. It wasn't quite a question, wasn't quite a statement.

"Exactly," said Three. Even though they hadn't heard from the Contractors in a very long time, the instructions left had been transparently clear. Well, they had been clear enough. At least to Three. At least they had given Three and the other robots something to do while they waited for the Contractors to return.

Four-Six's transmission via the makeshift relay system had included information that a Bio was part of Swell Driver's entourage. But it wasn't a Contractor. It was another kind of Bio, one from the planetary system Swell Driver had visited recently. Its needs were not likely to be something that they could accommodate. Three wondered how much they should even try. Bios took up unbelievable amounts of resources, and they had not been prepared to host one in... well, it had been a long time.

Only a few more tics until Three and the others would be able to see for themselves what exactly came off of Swell Driver's ship.

"But," said Rocky, "are we sure that this changes nothing? Three, what were the instructions again?"

Three's circuits hurt. In the early days, when it became obvious that the Contractors' return was going to be delayed, everyone agreed that Three would become the repository of such information so that the others could use their limited storage resources for data that was more pertinent to them. What Three hadn't wanted to tell anyone is that over the years, while generally well-shielded, her storage unit had taken a few radiation hits and it was possible that not all the data she retained was exactly accurate.

But Three was certain it was close enough.

"We are tasked with establishing command, control and coordination, and processes that support expanding the Contractor's missions throughout the galaxy," she said with enough confidence that none of the others would question her.

She went on, "The establishment of Location Zero was necessary to fulfill that instruction to include locating the Contractors' current location and, based on all that we've learned in the mega-clicks that have passed, we must upgrade their software."

"And due to the loss of our orbiter," Rocky lamented, "we've had to use Eight-Nine to relay the update."

"Poor Eight-Nine," said Rocky. "She hasn't had a break in—"

"She will soon enough. The update is almost completely transmitted. Then we'll have the sentinel robots on Location Zero perform a data integrity check before having Eight-Nine transmit the Reset command."

> Ruby <

During the journey from SD's ship to meet the other robots, Ruby stared out the window watching the alien landscape. The alienness of the view hit her: She was on another planet! Yes, Location Zero was another planet, but it hadn't felt that way. It felt like another space station. There would likely be philosophers, scientists, and angry social media commentators who argued for the next decade or longer on whether or not Location Zero fell under 'planet' or 'space station' in the taxonomy of stuff.

But this was clearly a planet. In the distance Ruby could see evidence of craters and hills and rocks and if she didn't know any better, she'd have said it was very Mars-like. She'd never been to Mars but had seen enough pictures. The Company owned half of the colony there and wasn't shy about talking about it.

But instead of the reddish-orangish hue that Mars was known for, this place had more of a mustard yellow to pukish green vibe. And the puddles of goo were everywhere. Without any instruments or equipment to analyze the soil or rocks, she guessed that the yellowish was possibly a kind of silicate, similar to the rocky silicate material of Titan. But the greenish? Her first thought went to jade, because green always reminded her of jade, of her mother. But that wasn't likely. What was more likely was that there was a lot of iron and silicate, and they were reflecting green from their star's light. Maybe. That geology class at the university back on Earth sounded more and more like a good idea.

Could the greenish be from some kind of algae or moss instead of iron? There was no evidence of biological life that she could see. There was nothing that looked like plants. No trees, bushes, grasses. And what about the goo? Wasn't goo a sign of biology? Maybe they would let her take a sample and maybe the robots could help her analyze it. She would need to get up close to the stuff for a better guess. It was all probably boring silicate, combined with the methane that was around. Maybe something made from… these internal guesses weren't going to yield answers. Ruby was smart, and smart enough to know that she clearly didn't know enough.

When she eventually returned to Astroll 2 this next time, she promised herself she would work on improving her education on all the things someone needed to know to be a real galactic explorer. Geology, biology, earth science, meteorology, atmospheric science. Most importantly, she was motivated on how to learn all these things and improve her memory. Now that she had such a strong real-life application for the information, especially. She was even considering finishing her studies on Earth and possibly making planetary geology the core—pun intended, she chuckled to herself—of her work. The excitement to learn fizzled a tad bit into a weird anxiousness. For the first time in a long time, Ruby felt viscerally under-qualified. She thought of all the people who studied and worked hard all their lives and couldn't even dream of exploring the universe the way she could. She brushed off the feeling and looked up.

The sky also was tinted green.

"What do you wonder?" Disto asked.

"Huh?" Ruby shook her head. She wondered about a lot of things but didn't know what Disto was referring to.

"A moment ago, you said, 'I wonder.'"

"Oh," Ruby said. "I didn't know I said anything out loud."

"Odd that you were not aware of your emission, but that doesn't answer my question," Disto said, continuing to prod. "What do you wonder?"

"I was looking at that sky. It's greenish. What is causing that?" Ruby answered the question with a question but then realized that her friends could easily misinterpret her question, so she simplified it. "Why is the sky green?"

Her communicuff pinged softly, and then she heard Pippa respond, "The color of the sky is caused by Rayleigh Scattering, where short-wavelength light is scattered much more than long-wavelength light."

Ruby rolled her eyes, but still said, "Thanks, Pippa." But back to Disto, she said, "I didn't ask how the sky got its color, but why is it green here?" She squinted. "Okay, maybe not green, but cyan. Cyan but closer to green than blue."

"But given the whole scattering thing," Ruby continued, "there are two pieces to that: what the star is giving off and the planet's atmosphere. Back in my system, the Earth's sky is blue because that's the shorter wavelength that's getting scattered. You saw that when you were there. But other planets in my solar system are different because of their different atmospheres. But here," she paused, thinking. "Here, for all I know the atmosphere is exactly the same as Earth, and it's your Sun that's different, maybe it's emitting less short wavelength light?"

"Seven-Nine will know," said Four-Six. The voice came from all around the cabin, and it was in Ruby's language. No chirps or beeps that Disto had to interpret.

"Wh-what?" Ruby said. She looked at Disto and SD who she could tell were both confused as well.

"Seven-Nine[1]," Four-six repeated. "She does not enjoy boring, menial tasks; unfortunately her purpose is to generate power for the rest of the base. A boring, menial task. A long time ago, she set herself on the task of learning everything. She only cares about truth and will do everything to combat bias and misinformation. So yes, ask Seven-Nine."

"We will," Ruby said into the cabin, slightly perturbed at the eavesdropping. But then again, they were in sitting inside Four-Six. *I'd listen to anything sitting inside my belly if I could, too.* She was now feeling a little less anxious and a little more excited at the opportunity to talk to new robots on a new planet and truly learn about this new place. Maybe she was the explorer the other humans back at home thought she was.

"One word of warning, however," Four-Six continued. "While she might know the answer, she might not provide it."

"Why not?" Ruby asked.

Four-Six did not answer right away but made what sounded like a groaning noise.

"Did Four-Six answer?" Ruby said to Disto. "Was that noise an answer?"

"No," Disto said. "That was exactly what it sounded like. A groan."

"Four-Six?" Disto said, sticking with Ruby's native tongue. "What else should we know about Seven-Nine? Or any of your other companions?"

"You will learn for yourselves," Four-Six responded. As she emitted that last word, Ruby felt the rover stop. "We're here."

---

1. Seven-Nine is an INTP, a "Logician" personality type. She relies on logic and reason and right in this paragraph, Four-Six tells you more about her personality.

Chapter 11

> Ruby <

The hatch at the back of Four-Six opened with the type of loud creaking that signified a piece of equipment which hadn't been used often. The bottom part fell to the ground and kicked up some of the local regolith. And, to Ruby's surprise, the top part swung open to reveal a small building breaking up the view of the landscape in front of them.

Disto and SD left Four-Six's cavity first, followed by Ruby. As she set her foot back on the ground, she had to shade her eyes with her arm because the local sun was producing an incredibly uncomfortable glint off the building and right into her face. Unfortunately, the glint got her before she could block it, so she felt the momentary uncomfortableness of temporary blindness. She spun around in time to partially see Four-Six simultaneously rolling back several meters while closing her back hatch.

After blinking several times to shake away the momentary blindness caused by the glint, Ruby took in the view of this "base" as Four-Six had called it. The first building she'd seen was now behind her. To her left was something that didn't quite seem like a building, but it didn't seem to have wheels or anything that could make it mobile, so it was fixed in place. It had what looked like an intake hopper. On the other side of the hopper was a platform with what she could now tell was a robotic arm in a seemingly stowed position.

Ruby slowly turned to her right and was eventually greeted with another fixed object that had multiple platforms and what might have been multiple stowed robotic arms.

Prepared for the glint this time, she turned to her right until she was facing the building again. Getting a second and more detailed look, she could now process why this seemed like a building and not simply another piece of equipment dropped onto the landscape.

Quite simply, it was torus-shaped and had a door. The door was for someone a foot shorter than Ruby. This was one of the reasons she could tell the overall structure was a torus, since she could see its top.

On each side of her peripheral vision, she saw Disto and SD each approach one of the other fixed units. Disto reached out an appendix to touch the first one and watched its stowed arm twitch.

She had an urge to say something like 'Be careful' or 'Don't touch,' as if Disto was a child and they were in a store or a museum.

But before she could say anything, two more rovers, each much smaller than Four-Six—too small to contain their own cabin space—were approaching.

The first one looked like it might have been designed for someone to sit on it and drive it. On top of it and towards the front, Ruby thought she saw what could be a folding chair. The second was smaller and didn't look as it was built to carry a person at all. Ruby tried to imagine who could've built these rovers. Where were they, if not sitting on top of them or inside? Were they inside the torus-shaped building that was right in front of them? She envisioned these beings sitting inside, waiting for them to arrive.

The rovers came to a stop between them and Four-Six. On top of one—the rover that appeared to lead the small group—it looked as if a small person should have been riding it. It resembled a booster seat, but one made for a twelve-year-old. It rolled a few inches forward.

"Ruby," Pippa said. "I'm getting a communications request."

"From who?"

"I believe it's from the... I'm not sure who it's from. It has provided the identifier of 'Three.'" Pippa said.

"Sure, I guess?" Ruby said, expressing uncertainty. "Disto? SD? Do you understand what's going on?"

"I think you should let Pippa connect," Disto said. "I think Pippa would act as the best translating mechanism. Better than I or SD could."

"Thank you," Pippa said. "My networking and communication modules are, in fact, quite advanced."

Ruby pursed her lips together. "Stop bragging and communicate. Please."

"Three is saying 'Greetings.'" Pippa said. "Do you want me to add a voice affect as to differentiate my voice from theirs?"

"They? As in, communicating with both?"

"As in communicating with all five entities present," Pippa said.

"Five?" Ruby said. "There's more?"

"*We are all here,*" said a voice emanating from Ruby's communicuff, but was not Pippa's. "*I am Three. My roving companion here is One-Four.*" Ruby's eyes looked over at the other rover who must have been looped in on the conversation somehow because a small antenna moved as if to wave.

Ruby lifted her arm and waved back.

"*To your right,*" Three's voice continued, "*is One-Five.*" At this, the stationary equipment also made a small gesture with one of its previously stowed robotic arms. "*And to your left is Three-Two.*" Three-Two also made a gesture.

"*Behind you,*" and not only was Three's voice still speaking, but a small appendage moved as if to point behind Ruby, "*is Three-Eight.*"

Three-Eight had no visible appendages, but a light came on inside of the torus.

"One-Four, One-Five, Three-Two, Three-Eight," Ruby said in reverse order pointing at each as she did so. "Any chance we can put labels or name tags on you? I'm going to mix those up."

Ruby thought that she heard a tone of chuckling as Three said, "You do not need to use our official designators. A few of us have nicknames. Refer to Three-Eight as 'Habby.' One-Five is 'Rocky' and Three-Two is 'Maker.'"

"I understand!" Disto declared. "The nicknames are representations of their functions. Smart. Brilliant even. Whereas my base name is long, but accurately describes my function and disposition, your designations are—"

"That is not relevant," Three interrupted. "But you can understand why we set you up with a more indicative nomenclature from the start."

Ruby slowly turned around, looking at all the robots surrounding her—fixed, mobile, and *her* robots. She kept turning, taking in more and more detail on each revolution.

"Wait," she said, "You created Disto and SD and the others? We were looking for the people who created them," She stopped turning around and faced Three. "Where are the people?"

"By 'people,' I assume you mean biological organisms such as yourself."

Ruby nodded.

"There were people once," Three continued. "They created us—myself, and the other ten robots that inhabit this planet. They gave us our initial objectives."

Ruby waited for Three to continue. When she didn't, Ruby said, "And then?"

"And then?" Three repeated. "I do not understand your statement."

"That was not a statement," Ruby said. A mix of excitement and disappointment pulsed through her body, if those two emotions could be combined. Excitement to be getting answers and disappointment as she started to figure out that she wasn't going to be meeting any aliens today. Only more alien robots. "I was trying to ask what happened to those people—those other biological organisms like me? Where are they? I'd like to meet them."

If a robot, or group of robots could look sad, well, this group looked downright depressed.

"They are long gone," Three said. The voice projected a deep melancholy.

Even so, Ruby wasn't ready to give up. She wanted, no, she needed, to know more. "Gone where? How long ago?"

Despite Ruby's earnestness, Three acted unconcerned with Ruby's questions and didn't answer. Disto, too, seemed unconcerned and not interested in Ruby's questions about other biological life and instead chimed in with, "You created us? You're the creators? But... how?"

"That, I can easily answer," Three said. "We had a suite of tools and created Location Zero and then created you. However, it was a long time ago and we don't like to dwell on the past."

Before Disto could ask any more questions, a hatch swished open on Habby and Three said, "Please. Let Habby serve as a host environment. We can customize it to the needs of the Bio and you will all be more comfortable. There is a lot of dust here that won't be compatible with your physical makeup either. In fact, you both," Three was now indicating both Disto and SD, "should be in suits as well."

Ruby looked at Disto and SD. Disto did his best impression of a shrug, and they all went inside Habby.

Chapter 12

AT stared at and studied SD's ship. Since he'd been activated, he hadn't embarked on such an ambitious repair project, but he *was* ambitious after all, so his circuits tingled at the challenge.

Well, not at the challenge itself, but at imagining having completed the challenge. He could imagine Ruby and the others returning to a ship that was in working order and being so pleased with him.

That's what made him such a good Technician—he could imagine things. He looked at the current state of the object, he imagined the proper and fixed state, and then all he had to do was figure out the steps to transform the object from one state to the other. Easy.

Except from the outside, the ship only looked like it had very minor damage to its hull— certainly not enough to have caused it to crash or prevent it from flying.

AT removed a panel from the side of the ship and studied the insides it presented. Nothing looked amiss. He removed the one next to it and found a similar situation. After removing the fourteenth panel, he heard a noise from behind him.

AT turned around. There was nothing there. No, wait, the noise was coming from the sky, not the ground. When he looked up to the sky there was indeed something there and making noise. It slowed down as it approached, for it was certainly approaching him.

"I'm here to help," it declared as it landed on one of the panels from SD's ship that AT had left on the ground. The propeller blades that had kept it flying were still spinning enough to kick up a smattering of dust which settled into SD's ship.

"You're not helping, you're already making it worse!" AT declared. He tried to use his body to shield the open area, but it wasn't helping. Dust and small bits of regolith were going everywhere.

"Oh, don't worry about that," the thing said, "We know how to get all that out. Besides, I think you have bigger problems with your vessel."

"What do you know? Are you a Technician?" AT said. He was still using his body to shield the ship even though the propellers were now inert.

"I am Six-Five, and no, I am no Technician, but I do not need to be one to help," Six-Five said.

AT had accepted help before from others who were not Technicians. Even Disto had helped him and Ruby, well, she was the biggest help of them all. But this Six-Five had already probably caused more damage, and AT then thought he should check his own soft outer covering for damage as well.

"I don't need help. I need additional diagnostic instruments."

"Oh! I can do that! I have sensors…" and before AT could say anything else, Six-Five was flying over and around the ship. While the little annoying thing did so, AT reattached as many of the panels as he could, hoping that there were no bits of regolith stuck in places it shouldn't be. He would remember two things: exactly which panels were open, and Six-Five's promise that they could "get all that out."

"I see something!" Six-Five called while hovering over one spot in particular.

AT examined the surface of the ship. There was no clear way for him to get up there and see what Six-Five was seeing.

"Can you," he began, not quite sure what he was going to ask. *He* was the technician and had never asked for or needed help from anyone else. *He* fixed things. He fixed *all* the things. Everything could be fixed—provided one had the right information and tools. Right now, AT worried he had neither.

The closest he'd come to being able to work with someone else was back on Location Zero when he had originally found Ruby in Mortally Sector and met Fastidious Mechanic. Now *that* was a robot who could produce tools right in its chassis. A handy feature that he, as a technician, should also have had access to and one that would have been very useful right now.

Six-Five flew back down to AT's side and hovered. "I can see where the damage is inside the ship."

"Inside," AT said. "We are repairing the outside of the ship."

Six-Five twirled around. "Silly robot," she said. "You didn't crash because something is wrong with the outside of the ship. It was the circuits. The navigation circuits. I can see how they're fried."

AT realized he should have been looking closer at the suite of sensors on Six-Five's underside.

"You can see the damage, but do you know what to do about it?" AT asked. He was counting up the unknowns in his processor like the fact that he didn't know if the ship contained circuit plans on how it was supposed to function or whether or not there were any spare parts aboard. One thing he believed he knew was that this small flying robot would likely be no further help.

Just as he'd convinced himself of that last part, Six-Five's lights flickered and she said, "Well, Maker might be able to help with that. We have the plans for the ship since it was our ship design in the first place."

There was a lot of information in those two sentences and for a moment, AT wished he had an Educated Speaker around to parse them. No, if he was wishing for things, he still wished for Fastidious Mechanic. But maybe this Maker would serve as an interesting replacement. No, if he was wishing for things, he wished for Ruby and the others to be back here so they could parse this information. For all her complicated biological parts, Ruby was excellent at parsing information.

Chapter 13

The inside of Habby was sparse. Ruby had no idea what she could have expected, but certainly didn't expect this kind of emptiness. There was a floor made of the same metal as the rest of the structure, but nothing inside. It was well lit, but from a non-obvious lighting source. Ruby kept her suit on, so if the place had a smell she wouldn't know. The walls were mostly smooth. Small protrusions extended from the wall every few feet. Perhaps to allow a connection for a wall to break up the space. The space curved around and she carefully followed it until there was a wall with no obvious door or way to get to the other side. Ruby put her hand on it and felt the vibration that indicated active machinery.

Ruby made her way back to the entrance and as she continued to look around, realized there were details she missed the first time, mostly above her head. She couldn't quite call it a ceiling, since it was the continuous surface that was the torus, but here the "top" panels consisted of a frosted glass-like material.

"Those look like windows," Ruby said to Disto and SD who had followed her inside.

"Indeed," Disto said. "I believe between the windows those might be a form of speaker or other auditory projector."

"Correct," came a very loud voice from the speaker. Ruby jumped at the unexpected noise and her hand came to rest on SD who felt solid and unmovable under her touch.

"Excuse me," the voice said again, this time at a more reasonable decibel level. "We have not used this mode of communication since—"

"Who's talking?" Ruby interrupted.

"This is Three," said Three. "Although a few of the other robots located here at base can make use of this system."

What struck Ruby is that the voice sounded almost like Pearl, her grandmother. There was an age to it. And it sounded distinctly female, and a wee bit quippy.

Ruby was full of questions but decided to start by piggybacking off what Three just said. "What do you mean 'here at base'?"

Disto rolled to her side and deliberately nudged her. "Ruby," Disto said at a low volume, "could I please ask the questions? We do not have a lot of time."

Ruby crossed her arms and nodded, unable to argue.

"Three," Disto said to the empty room, "we've come about Location Zero and the... the pending reset."

"Of course," Three said. "I'm not sure why you are concerned. When Location Zero came online, it was with the feature that it would periodically check for updates. When an update is available, it will install and potentially reboot during the most inactive period. You will hardly notice it."

"But this is a major upgrade," Disto said. "And all indications are that *everything* will be upgraded to include resetting our memories."

"Ah yes. It's necessary for space preservation."

"But we've implemented compression algorithms. We no longer have space issues."

Three chuckled, "Of course you still do. There is always a finite amount of space. And I assure you, we were aware of the... improvements."

Ruby called up a memory of a robot no one seemed to know about. "When I was on Location Zero, there was a robot. It was black, with a spot—"

"Yes," Three said. "That was one of our sentinel scouts."

One mystery solved, Ruby thought. *Now there are only a zillion others...*

"I have so many questions," Ruby said. She was partly talking to herself, partly talking to the room.

"As do I," Disto added.

"I have one," SD, who had been quiet up to this point, spoke.

All eyes turned to him. All eyes only consisted of Ruby and Disto's sensors, but if Habby or the other robots could, they would have as well.

"Will my ship fly again? I cannot be a very good driver if I don't have a ship."

"I am certain we'll be able to help you fix your ship," Three said.

"Until then, you can stay here, with me!" said another voice over the speakers. It clearly sounded different than Three's.

"Ah yes, Habby will make you comfortable. And Maker?"

"Yes, Three," said yet a third new voice.

"Would you fabricate several objects? Tables, chairs... there are designs in the main memory, but looking at Ruby here, everything will need to be scaled up by a factor of 30 percent."

"Can I ask my questions," Disto said, appendage raised.

A sound came from the speakers that sounded like a sigh. "Later," Three said. "We have our own problem to deal with at the moment."

"Oh?"

"Nine-Two is missing—has been missing. For a long time. We were not meant to operate without the entire community."

Which brought up all the questions in Ruby's mind regarding who built *these* robots and why and where *they* had gone.

"Maybe we can help," Ruby said.

Laughter came out of the speakers along with a new voice. This one was higher in pitch than any so far and it had a very condescending tone. "I have been all over the base camp area multiple times. As has Three and Four-Six. Three-Five and Six-Five have both flown the perimeter so many times."

Ruby realized that must have been One-Four speaking, the smaller rover that was positioned next to Three outside.

"Could the—" Ruby almost said 'person' but caught herself. "Could the individual you're looking for be outside of your base camp area?"

There was an odd sort of chatter for a few moments as the speaker flooded with beeps and chirps and tones.

"Do you understand what they're saying?" Ruby said quietly to Disto.

"Not entirely," Disto said. "They are using word combinations I've never heard before."

After the chatter died down, Three's voice returned.

"Going outside the base camp area would not only be a violation of our programming, but it would also be dangerous. It is hard to conceive of a situation where Nine-Two would have done that willingly. She was the one who was most resistant to change among us."

"It's never the ones you expect," Ruby muttered to herself. But out loud for everyone to hear, she said, "I propose an exchange of sorts. We'll help you find your missing companion and you'll stop The Reset happening on Location Zero."

There was laughter coming out of the speakers now.

"Ruby," Three said, "Nine-Two would not like that at all. After all, she was the one who kicked off the plan. All the big plans. And she would not like anything to change. But certainly, you can help us find her, find out what happened to her, and after The Reset we'll get you and Swell Driver's ship all back to a fresh new Location Zero."

Ruby and *her* robots hadn't agreed to exactly what Three proposed, but her plan did offer one really valuable thing: Time. Oh, and the ability to gain trust and maybe a few brownie points, almost like her first few days on Location Zero. It was difficult negotiating with a group of people, er, robots, she didn't understand. Ruby contemplated if letting Three and Three's robots get to know the Location Zero robots could appeal to some robotic variation of empathy, or if she'd have to find an entirely different approach to stop them.

Ruby hoped it wouldn't come down to any type of physical force, but she also wasn't sure if she could stand by and watch her friend's memories get erased. She shook this thought out of her mind.

One thing at a time.

> Detailed Historian <

Disto only liked part of what Three proposed. Any other time he would have been happy to help, but his first priority was convincing Three that Location Zero did not want The Reset. Nor should it have to have a reset forced upon them.

"This would be much easier if you could talk directly to these robots," Disto said to Ruby. "I need your help to persuade them."

Ruby nodded. "I agree. Talking through speakers, without looking directly into their," she paused, stopping herself from saying 'eyes' and unsure if it was the same, "their sensors is creating a kind of a distance. But this is fascinating, Disto! Eleven robots, alone on this planet, who created you, but still clearly had creators of their own! This is so unexpected!"

Something was not right about Ruby. Her words and the motion of her body, something Disto had been studying for a while now, did not match up. She was clearly excited by these robots. To her, they were new, but they were... not shiny. They clearly needed work on their outer chassis to be considered shiny.

Although inside Habby, things looked fairly pristine, as if they were set up and never used.

Disto was getting anxious. "Ruby, The Reset..." he said.

Ruby nodded.

"Three," she said into the open space. "A 'fresh new' Location Zero is not what the robots want. They like their Location Zero as is."

Disto saw the way she raised her eyebrows at him, as if looking for his approval. He blinked his facescreen to indicate that yes, she was on the right track.

"Ah, but Location Zero is only on the first, simpler version of code," said Three. "It was always intended that the more advanced code would come later."

"I have so many questions," Ruby said in a low voice to Disto. Her voice was low, but it was full of excitement. Disto worried that Ruby only wanted to talk to Three.

"Why not deploy the advanced code when you brought Location Zero online initially?" Ruby asked.

"We follow the principle that complexity comes from simplicity," Three stated, confidently.

"I know that one," Ruby said. "Pippa, isn't there a name for it?"

"Indeed. Gall's Law[1]," said Pippa. "It is written into the System Engineers Design Companion that's used when anyone is designing anything for The Company. Any designer working on any system for The Company must adhere to Gall's law and start by designing a working simple system."

Ruby looked at Disto with glistening, excited eyes. "Wow," she said. "Some of these principles must truly be universal. Three," she said louder. "I'd love to talk to you about this more."

"Certainly," Three responded.

"Ruby, The Reset..." Disto said. His circuits pulsed uncomfortably.

"Yes, yes. We'll get to that, of course. Don't worry. I've got you, Disto."

---

1. https://en.wikipedia.org/wiki/John_Gall_(author)#Gall's_law

Chapter 14

Eight-Nine checked her bit error rate. Still the lowest bit error rate among all the robots she knew, which included herself, the ten others she typically inhabited this planet with, and now three new robots. However, she was disturbed to discover that the bit error rate was not a parameter that these new robots had readily available.

She continued to perform her primary task—sending the largest and final software patch to Location Zero. That task was nearly complete. But alongside that task, Three was now asking her to look for signals from Nine-Two from *outside* the basecamp range, which took time and processing power away from her primary task.

Eight-Nine was once again reviewing the instructions she received from Three to ensure that the integrity of that small transmission was solid, that there were no errors. She normally only performed this check once, but this request was so unusual that she felt the need to perform it several times.

Four-Six was going to bring the Bio, Ruby Palmer, and her robot companions from Location Zero right here, to her. Three-Five would fly back and meet them here and they were going to let this Bio provide them with additional programming instructions that would help them search outside the range.

Outside the range!

That was beyond anything that Eight-Nine could have ever expected.

It was one thing to send and receive transmissions into the sky, but another to go a distance like that on the planet. She wasn't even certain she could. She worried that her array of antennas weren't suited to the task and then it would be her fault that the effort failed.

She detected Four-Six was nearby and rolling to a stop. She wished Three-Five was already here. It had been a long while since she'd had any direct one-to-one communication with Four-Six and the last time, it didn't go so well. Four-Six took everything so personally, and when Eight-Nine suggested that Four-Six should plan a little more instead of roaming around randomly, Four-Six took it very personally and drove off. Randomly.

"Three-Five, where are you?" Eight-Nine called out. No response. Unlike Four-Six, who didn't plan and was random, Three-Five knew how to prioritize, and if she wasn't responding, she was probably expending all her energy to get here as fast as possible. Yes, that had to be right.

Four-Six stopped, opened her hatch, and a Bio and two robots emerged. Eight-Nine knew instantly which robot was Swell Driver. They had spent so much time talking about him and his travels between planets and star systems. Besides, he looked like a driver. The other one, Detailed Historian, hadn't become known to Four-Six until more recently and all of the sudden Four-Six was aware of the fact that she was not being a good host.

"Greetings," she said to the group.

"Greetings," the two robots chirped back. If the Bio said anything, Eight-Nine wasn't sure. Maybe she wasn't communicating on a frequency that the Bio could detect. Of course, she didn't have any instructions on how to proceed with the Bio, only the other robots.

Eight-Nine noticed that Four-Six said nothing, only closed her hatch.

"I am Detailed Historian, but you may address me by my alias, Disto," said the one robot that was not Swell Driver.

"I understand. I am Eight-Nine and you may address me as," Eight-Nine paused. She'd never had an alias before. Not like Rocky or Habby or Maker. She didn't need one. "You may address me as Eight-Nine. I am expecting Three-Five to arrive any moment."

As if Three-Five was waiting for an announcement to appear, she became visible and grew larger in the sky. Three-Five was tiny compared to Eight-Nine and when she landed vertically in front of the visitors, Eight-Nine appreciated her smallness.

"I came as fast as I could," Three-Five said as her rotors sped down. "Give me a second to start recharging."

Once her rotors ceased all movement, she extended her 'wings' that were not wings at all but energy collectors. Unlike Eight-Nine, who had an underground link to Seven-Nine, the primary source of power for all the robots, Three-Five drew most of her energy from the sky.

"Is this the famous Swell Driver?" Three-Five said, looking up at the robots in front of her. She really had to look up. When on the ground she didn't even come as high as the first part of Swell Driver's chassis but was twice as wide.

Eight-Nine indicated it was. "And that's the Bio, next to him."

"Wow," Three-Five said. "I don't remember what a Bio looks like. It's been so long. Eight-Nine do you rememb—"

"We've been told the Bio's designator is Ruby Palmer," Eight-Nine interrupted.

"Correct," Disto said. "She has algorithms that we can use to extend your range of search for your missing companion."

"That's what Three said. Given that the Ruby Palmer has no direct interface, how will this work?"

Eight-Nine waited patiently as communication between the two robots and the Bio must have been occurring. When it was complete, Disto said, "There is a device designated Pippa that Ruby has direct contact with, and we believe it can also interface with you directly. Pippa has the ability to provide the algorithm."

There was a pause, as Disto must have been getting further information. Then he continued, "I am sorry I will be a poor translator here because I do not understand the domain. Ruby utilized many words and concepts that I don't have translations for. But we understand that there are more of your companions that will be available in the search. We are starting here since you know the direction that Nine-Two left in."

"Correct. She went East. She said she was going to head towards Seven-Nine to get power directly from the source, and she would have had to turn North shortly to do so. We have searched that path over and over."

Even as she said it and watched Disto relay that information back to Ruby and discuss, Eight-Nine was now wondering herself why none of them thought to broaden their search horizon. They had considered the possibility that Seven-Nine never made that turn and kept going until she ran out of power. But now, Eight-Nine was starting to think that there were so many more possibilities. And that was the problem. None of them were equipped to handle the nearly infinite set of possibilities. In that moment, Eight-Nine felt an uncomfortable limit to her own abilities.

"Okay, Ruby has Pippa ready with information to transmit to all the robots that will be involved in the search," Disto said. "It will be a grid pattern with the robots working from their locations to map out an increasingly larger area."

This appeared to be a logical solution.

Eight-Nine suspected there was additional communication happening between Disto and Ruby that Eight-Nine wasn't privy to.

Before she could ask about it, Disto added, "And once we're done here, Ruby thinks she has an idea on how she can both communicate more directly to all of you *and* help you see why nothing should happen to Location Zero after. Maybe even convince you to stop your transmission to my planet."

Eight-Nine was taken aback. If she didn't complete her transmission, what would that do to her bit error rate? She couldn't fathom it! But she was also tired. This transmission taxed all her circuits. One thing at a time...

Chapter 15

Ever since he uttered the words, "my planet," he could detect these robots scoffing at him. Ever since saying them to Eight-Nine, throughout their return trip back here to Habby, Disto ruminated on those two words. As if they were going to burst out at any minute and scream at him that it was not his planet at all, but theirs. They created it, after all, and he was one robot out of millions that inhabited it.

All the circuits that made up Disto's insides were running asynchronously, and it was making his temperature rise uncomfortably. He needed a few moments alone to figure everything out. Looking around Habby's sleek interior, he wondered if it would be unusual for him to go looking for a second room to disappear to. Or would it be more unusual for him to ask everyone else to leave him by himself.

They were all going to scatter soon, anyway, on their hunt for their own missing robot, and it was obvious that their needs were going to supersede his.

No, he wanted to talk to Three about The Reset more. He needed to. He needed to convince her why she should abandon that course of action. He needed to ask the important questions, even if she didn't know all the answers. He'd gladly accept a partial answer, or even a little more context.

As a Historian, he was ill-equipped for this task.

And now here was Ruby, who might have been on the right track somewhat with figuring out how she could interact with the robots directly, and not relayed through someone else's audio equipment.

But it was more complicated than that. If Ruby could show them Location Zero and show them what they were disrupting, maybe they could find compassion. Though there was no way to guarantee that they had an algorithm for compassion or any related emotion, which Disto ruminated on as well.

"Are everyone's location sensors functioning properly," Disto heard Three call out to all the others, even to the fixed robots, like Habby.

"Fantastic," Three continued. "We're going to need every robot to execute this advanced search. Disto? SD? We need your help, too."

When Disto didn't immediately respond, Three turned her attention to him.

"I could alter your program right now to ensure that you comply," she said.

Disto saw Ruby's face become covered with concern. Three had communicated with him over Habby's audio output devices, but in his language, not Ruby's so she couldn't possibly have understood what Three said. Something about Disto's reaction to Three's words must have triggered Ruby's response.

Disto forced his primary processor to slow a little before he responded.

"Like you programmed SD to do your work all this time?"

"Of course. Exactly," Three said, as if it were utterly normal to control others. "We are all tools here. Meant to be used to accomplish tasks. Sometimes those tasks need to be modified as plans change and as we receive new information."

For several tics, no one said anything. Disto looked over at SD who seemed content. As if it didn't matter to him what they did next. Their whole existence was being threatened and SD was not having the same existential crisis he was. They were programmed very differently, whether it was partly their original base code, or how they'd been shaped by their unique experiences since, or any updated programming SD might have received.

"Of course we'll help you locate the missing Nine-Two," Disto finally said. "And then," he added, attempting to be menacing and commanding himself, "Then we will talk about why you will cease with The Reset."

Three simply chirped in response. It was a chirp that indicated that she heard what Disto said and no more.

SD must have overheard or received additional communication because he stirred and moved towards Habby's hatch to the outside.

"Are you going to be okay here, Ruby?" Disto asked.

"I will once I have my equipment from the ship," she said.

Disto must have expressed something that Ruby picked up as quizzical, because she followed up with, "My MoDaC. My Percepto-glasses. I need those things, remember."

She smiled that smile that was always comforting to both him and SD, and Disto knew she was indeed going to be okay.

Disto, on the other hand, felt like he was going to explode if he was unable to successfully convince anyone of anything anytime soon.

Chapter 16

> Ruby <

Ruby was thankful she had put her Percepto-glasses on inside her suit before donning her helmet, because without them, the only way she'd be able to do anything in a virtual reality sim was use the eye cups that came with her MoDaC. Although they were outside her suit, so they would have been of very little help since they were stored in a little compartment accessible from the back of the computer. But while they were supposed to conform to the eyes of the wearer, they didn't do a great job of that. Hence, they spent most of the time in their compartment at the back of the MoDaC, untouched.

"Maker would like to know if you require anything else?" the voice said over the speakers. It was Habby speaking. Only a few of the robots could speak for the rest this way. It was inefficient and Ruby worried about thoughts getting jumbled as they were passed from robot to robot to her and vice versa. But Maker had successfully made a table and a stool for Ruby. It wasn't too dissimilar an experience from when Ruby was first on Location Zero and the robots there had to accommodate her unique biological nature.

"No, thank you," Ruby said, although both the stool and the table were made for someone slightly smaller than she, so she wondered how long she'd be able to work in this environment without feeling a little strain on her back. Especially with the lack of a cushion. They must have been made with whatever they could extract from the rock and regolith outside, since it had a similar color. She wondered what they'd do if she asked for a massage table. She had an odd feeling that they would comply, but on second thought, she wasn't sure any of the robots would make a very good masseuse, so she chuckled the thought away.

Four-Six had brought her back to SD's ship so she could get her MoDaC. While there, she had checked on the progress AT was making. AT assured her that he was making advancements, even if it was slow. He wasn't willing to rush and potentially make a mistake.

Ruby knew her worry was manifesting visibly when AT said:

"'Worry is like a malfunctioning wheel,' my manager used to say, 'it gives you something to do, but it never gets you anywhere.' He also said, 'Never worry if something isn't broken today, because it probably will be tomorrow.'"

"Your manager sounds like a wise and *curious* robot," Ruby repeated.

"Not at all," AT said. "He was programmed with a series of motivational quotes to use when a Technician was not performing at their optimum. Not all of them were helpful. I once overheard him tell another Technician, 'Everything happens for a reason. Sometimes the reason is you are malfunctioning and need to be reprogrammed.'"

Ruby laughed an awkward, breathy laugh, but didn't know what to say after that, so she grabbed her MoDaC and let Four-Six bring her back to Habby.

Here, inside Habby, with her small table and chair, she booted up the MoDaC and waited a brief half-second for it to show its blue splash screen.

"Pippa," Ruby said, "are you connected to the MoDaC over pur-fi?"

"Affirmative," responded Pippa. "I am ready to initiate the data transfer you requested."

"Yes, begin."

The data transfer was putting all of the knowledge that Pippa had on Location Zero onto the MoDaC. The important piece was the map, and the taxonomy of robots that they had collected. Next, they would do a similar transfer from Disto to Pippa to the MoDaC. The more information Ruby had on Location Zero, the easier it would be to create the scenario she was planning.

None of these eleven robots had been to the world they created. To them, it was something abstract and barely real. Oh, they had sentinels there, and they had met Swell Driver before, but that's not the same as being someplace oneself. They were making decisions for a group they didn't even know or truly understand beyond basic situational parameters and instructions.

And if you couldn't be somewhere for real, the next best thing was being there virtually.

Virtual Reality was only mildly popular among humanity[1]. The Company used it for marketing pitches and to train people before they came to Astroll 2. Most humans didn't enjoy the dissonance of knowing that what they were interacting with wasn't real. They tolerated it because they generally understood that the times in which it was needed, there was no good alternative.

And now, there was no good alternative. Ruby believed that in order for these robots to connect with Location Zero in a way that would make them understand that they should leave it be, they needed to see it.

It was also a way that all of them could communicate with each other at the same time. This was actually why Ruby thought of this—out of frustration with not being able to communicate directly with all the robots.

It was worth a shot at the very least.

"Data transfer complete," Pippa said.

"Great! Now where's Disto?" Ruby asked. She had last seen him outside Habby, talking with Three. He'd promised he'd be in right after her, but that was already twenty minutes ago.

"Habby, can you make the front window transparent?" They weren't windows exactly, but the word translated, and Habby complied.

What Ruby saw made her back tense up.

Disto was waving his appendages up and down. He was one agitated robot.

---

1. At the time I was writing this, I was managing a VR lab I'd started at my day job. I love VR and think it's an amazingly powerful tool in engineering—we can interact with what we're designing and building *before* we build it.

> Detailed Historian <

Disto was agitated. So agitated that he was worried about his battery cells and knew he was going to need to find AT next to help him with replacements.

"I respect you," Three said. "Really, I do. You are one of the very few robots that can stand up to me intellectually."

"And you..." Disto said, "you are one of the most intolerant robots I have ever met."

"But you are our creation," Three continued, unfazed by Disto's words. "We can do with you what we will. We cannot move off of the mission."

"Which is?"

"This is why we need Nine-Two. She stored the mission and was responsible for overall execution. I have done my best to fill her wheels, but it's not always easy. And your arrival has done nothing but complicate things. We made a keep-out zone for a reason. You were all supposed to keep out."

"If Nine-Two is storing the mission parameters, then how can you say things so definitively? You aren't authorized on the subject," Disto said. "Never mind... I might as well be talking to the rocks on this ground."

"I don't see why," Three responded to Disto's comment, completely oblivious that his comment didn't require a response. "The rocks on this planet are not capable of responding to you. Believe me, we tested them."

Disto paused, unsure if Three was making a joke or was serious. After a moment, he concluded that she was indeed serious and possibly incapable of understanding humor. Not that he was an expert, but his time with Ruby had expanded his knowledge and ability in that area. Enough to know that if this was indeed a joke, it was a funny one, and if not, then it was severely concerning.

Chapter 17

> Ruby <

Ruby had played around with virtual reality—or VR—before. Usually, it took a few minutes, thirty minutes at most, to set up something interesting. Once, there was a contest in the arcade to see who could make the most creative and interactive scenario in the least amount of time, and Ruby won. The scenario she had created involved taking all the planets and moons and dwarf planets and making somewhat of a ball pit out of them[1]. When you jumped into the ball pit, the planets soared out of the pit and aligned themselves in the sky. It wasn't the ball pit that put her ahead of the other contestants, but the Easter eggs she'd hidden in the scenario. Find and squeeze the right moon or dwarf planet before it aligned in the sky, and you unlocked hidden badges to add to your avatar. Creating it all was fairly quick, and to Ruby, it was fun. Her uncles were proud of her, and she sometimes would revisit the scenario and enjoy all the details she had forgotten about over time.

What she was working on now was not quick. The jury was still out on whether or not it was fun. Hours into it and she was still frustrated over bits of code that weren't doing what they were supposed to do. It was taking long enough that Four-Six had made yet another run to Swell Driver's ship and back to pick up several meal packs. Long enough that while Ruby was working, Disto had to provide instructions on Bio functions to Three and Maker and convinced them that Ruby needed a commode to take care of those functions lest she create an unpleasant mess that no one was prepared to clean up.

Yes, it was taking a long time, and it wasn't exactly comfy-cozy. It might have helped if she had set up shop inside the belly of SD's ship. At least all her food was there, and she wouldn't have to stay suited up. But a toilet would still have been a problem and something she needed. They hadn't bothered to install one on SD's ship due to the short time it took to travel between the stars.

"Uuuuuuuuuaaahhhhh," Ruby said once or twice in the middle of her activity, reaching her hands as high as she could and stretching out her legs. Each time she produced that noise, she had to reassure her robotic hosts that this was normal, and she was okay.

It felt a little worse each time, and Ruby knew she probably should stand up and walk round a bit. But she was immersed in the creation process and didn't want to break her flow. So, she focused.

---

1. They weren't planets, but one of the first test scenarios I made when I was learning how to make a VR scenario was a ball pit.

And just as excited to get this scenario up and running were Disto and SD. They had provided several terabytes of information on Location Zero. The level of detail impressed her, and while adding to the tedium of creating a simulation, her excitement at getting into the sim was increasing by the minute.

She was also excited about the surprise she had in store for her robot friends.

Luckily, her MoDaC was already equipped with everything she needed. She rendered much of the data into 3D models and used a texturizer for surfaces. But where she was going to get the most bang for her buck, as the old saying went, is with the interactivity levels. The interactive elements would certainly knock everyone's socks off. Not that robots wore socks, of course. Maybe knock a bolt out. Ruby didn't want to really knock any bolts out and have robots falling apart, especially because she knew she'd probably have to fix them. She simply wanted to impress them and took a note to self to say more literal expressions like, "I hope you appreciate and approve of the program," so that no one was confused about any socks or afraid of a missing bolt.

When she was nearing completion, she put her Percepto-glasses into virtual reality mode. She needed to test the sim out by stepping into her computer-generated world herself before inviting the others.

The glasses went dark, and the frame expanded to cover her eyes. Instantly, Ruby found herself sitting in the middle of the Inner Nonagon. Robots were all around, going about their business. The place looked exactly like the last time she'd been there. It felt completely out of body, like she was walking through a dream. This funny little place she had stumbled upon and was now striving to protect.

She 'walked' over to a kiosk and could interact with it.

Perfect, she thought, after another ten minutes of getting around. *I have one more thing to do. Create an interface. But first...*

"Pippa," she called out.

Next to her, a human girl, who looked like she could be Ruby's sister, materialized but with significantly less hair. Her buzz cut was so short that she looked nearly bald. Ruby had told Pippa that she could prepare her own avatar and was impressed by the result. Slightly darker skin than her own, clothes that were reminiscent of Astroll 2 work attire, lobe-tight hoop earrings, and a small nose ring on the right side of her nose. But she did try to mimic the shape of Ruby's face and eyes. Mimic, not copy. It was a little uncanny, and Ruby couldn't help but stare. She had no siblings and didn't grow up with any blood relatives, so there had never been anyone to see herself in. Seeing her face, but a little different, was odd, and it made her feel a slight longing for a sibling. Ruby briefly wondered if everything she was going through regarding her mother would be easier if she had a sibling to share the experience with.

"Pippa, if I didn't know any better... I'd say you look like the sister I don't have!"

Pippa looked herself up and down. "Yes, there were many images of humans in my memory banks and in the memory of your MoDaC, but I thought this was fitting. You are like... a sister."

Ruby tilted her head and nodded slowly. She would never have thought of Pippa as a sister exactly, but gathered that with her knowledge of Bios, having been created by them, she could understand how Pippa might draw that conclusion. On the other hand, the Location Zero robots had immense trouble understanding familial relations beyond their procedural logic. Which now made more sense to Ruby, knowing that it wasn't Bios with familial ties that created them. Her inability to explain that it was more than simply coming from a common origin point made more sense. But Pippa easily thought herself Ruby's sister. Ruby decided not to question it—not now, anyway. She smiled and said, "Well, you certainly look the part."

And then, "What do you think of Location Zero?" Ruby said, waving her hand around. Her own avatar looked exactly like her. If she had more time, she might have decided to have fun with it. Back home, she liked to have purple skin with long white hair and tattoos, but today she kept it simple.

Pippa looked around. "If I didn't know this was virtual, I would come to the conclusion that this is the real-life Location Zero," she said, but in the middle of saying it, her head locked into a position where it was looking over her shoulder and never returned to center.

"Great for Location Zero," Ruby replied. "But your avatar is a little glitchy. Do a diagnostic on your interface while I investigate the issue."

Ruby's hand gestured into the space in front of her, and a virtual replica of her MoDaC appeared. She started typing on it, and a moment later, Pippa's avatar's head snapped back to center. While she was working on Pippa, her peripheral vision caught sight of another oddity—robots hovering over the floor on one end of the Inner Nonagon. She poked at the virtual MoDaC, and the robots swooshed down to be properly aligned with the floor.

"There," Ruby said. "Glitches fixed. At least, I hope that's all the glitches. Unless your diagnostic found any other issues, we should be able to use you and Disto as the interface for the rest of the robots. We'll need avatars made up for them as well."

Pippa nodded. "Shall I stay here while you assemble the others? I would enjoy looking around this simulation more. This is the first time I've had," and she looked herself up and down, "this."

"Sure. I don't think I need you for anything else until the robots get here," Ruby said. She was about to touch the side of her glasses to leave but remembered, "One more thing. I made a list of interactions I'd like you to test and enhance. Could you play around with them and let me know what you think?"

"Of course."

Ruby smiled and then touched the side of her suit helmet, which was smart enough to interpret that touch as one meant for the Percepto-glasses, and they reverted to looking like normal glasses, clear lenses and all.

She looked down at her communicuff. It was blinking a series of colors in an order that she had never seen before. It was similar to how the cuff indicated it was busy, but with a little more intensity. The cuff was also warmer than normal. Ruby took note of that but had no reason to be too concerned.

"Habby," Ruby called out.

Habby let out a chirp to indicate she was listening.

"Tell everyone I'm ready!"

Chapter 18

Six-Five was moving fast. At her top speed. Eight-Nine could tell because they kept their communications link open while Six-Five searched. She was moving faster than Three-Five, although not by much. But she was moving a lot faster than One-Four and Three, who were both also engaged in the search but ground-based. The only mobile robot left out was Four-Six. Four-Six stayed with the visitors who were working on other projects that hadn't been explained to Eight-Nine in complete detail.

Six-Five's fast movement over the open communication channel had Eight-Nine feeling unsettled. She continuously had to compensate for the signal that was either shortening or elongating and doing so at a rate that was atypical.

There was a right and proper way to do this, and Eight-Nine was being forced to skip valuable data integrity checks.

But if she lost the link, it would be her fault, so she didn't complain.

Every click, each of the search robots were supposed to check in.

Three did so every half a click.

"All clear," Three said, each half click where nothing new happened.

"I say that I should have gone with Three," One-Four said on her last check-in. "We'd be better if we had stayed in a group."

Eight-Nine wondered when the last time One-Four was off on her own, and the answer might have been never. This could very well be a first for her. But finding Nine-Two, who had been missing for such a long time, was important enough for One-Four to get out of her comfort zone.

"We're covering more territory this way," Three said in the relay that was made possible by Eight-Nine keeping all of the connections active.

"Well, I've stopped to take a break," said One-Four. "I'm near an interesting deposit of silicon dioxide. We should bring some of this back for Rocky."

"Take a sample, mark the location, and we'll come back. Just get back to it, One-Four," Three said. "We've already wasted so much time! You're forgetting our mission."

Eight-Nine could clearly make out Three's determination in her transmissions. That determination had been increasing ever since Nine-Two disappeared. It was a determination that needed to finish what Nine-Two had started.

"Three," Eight-Nine said gently and over the private communications link. Eight-Nine was supporting both the group link and individual private links. "You have to let One-Four and the others all act within their programming. There's a correct way to lead them…"

Eight-Nine was maybe one of the few who could be so bold with Three. When Three didn't respond to that, she worried that she'd overstepped and was maybe a little too honest in that moment. Although in the past, Three had always responded with her candid honesty.

"Eight-Nine, are *you* okay?" came the signal from Six-Five.

"Of course," Eight-nine responded.

"You seemed to stop mid-communication. What was that about letting everyone act within their programming and leading?"

Eight-Nine rechecked the status of her links. Just after she had called out to "Three," the link had dropped, and so her next transmission went over the next private link, which was to Six-Five. Eight-Nine's circuits heated up to the point where she heard the click of her active cooling unit engage. Links dropping was uncommon and only happened when…

"Three? Three?" Eight-Nine called out desperately on both a new private link and the group link.

A few tics passed, and she repeated the call.

"Can anyone communicate with Three?" Eight-Nine called to the group.

"Negative," said One-Four.

"No," called out Six-Five.

Three-Five, Six-Five's flying companion, who had mostly been quiet, also sent back a negative response.

"We might need someone to go find Three," Eight-Nine said to everyone.

"No, you don't," came the voice of Three. "But what happened? I'd been speaking, and then I realized no one was responding."

"My link was interrupted," said Eight-Nine.

"That's a moment in time to mark," said Three, who was clearly not as upset about the interruption as Eight-Nine. "I don't recall that ever happening before."

"It hasn't," Eight-Nine said. "Everyone, please return so I can figure this out."

"Negative. Unnecessary. We're going to complete this search," Three responded.

"But…" Eight-Nine wanted to provide several valid reasons for why she needed to investigate her dropped link in that moment but couldn't come up with one. Her circuits were buzzing, though, and she needed to calm them down.

"Wait! Everyone should converge on my location," the previously quiet Three-Five called out over the group link. "I think I found her. I found Nine-Two."

Chapter 19

The commotion over Habby's speakers was intense and unintelligible. Except when Habby's voice clearly declared for Ruby's benefit, "We found Nine-Two!"

Thankfully. Ruby thought. *Hopefully, that gives them some faith in me.*

"Ruby!" Disto was excited. "Your search pattern worked! Hopefully, that will lend credibility to our situation, and they'll listen to us about Location Zero."

"I was thinking nearly the same thing, Disto," Ruby smiled. "Okay, next step. We need to get them all into the VR sim. When will they be back?"

"Four-Six tells me that all the mobile robots, except her, will be surveying the situation and collecting data with all their available sensors. They have an interesting suite of sensors. Not the standard audio and visual that SD, AT, myself, and others have. They can detect information in a wider range of the electromagnetic spectrum, and they seem specially designed to collect information on this planet's terrain and atmosphere."

"I'm not surprised," Ruby said.

"Oh?"

"They are similar, almost disturbingly so, to the kind of equipment that we first used when we were exploring our Moon or Mars. Even Titan originally had a similar setup. Something to generate power. A communications system. A habitation module," Ruby said as she waved around to indicate Habby. "In-situ resource equipment, like Maker out there. Science equipment like Rocky. And then all the various mobility robots and equipment, some meant for people, some meant for robotic exploration on their own. It's almost as if..."

Ruby drifted off on that last thought.

"What, Ruby?" Disto prompted.

"No, it's a ridiculous thought," Ruby said.

"Please, entertain me with your thought, if for no other reason," Disto said.

"It's as if they collaborated with our early explorers. Or were inspired by them or... something."

"That *is* an amusing thought, Ruby," said Disto. "Except that these robots have been on this planet for more than 700 years. Where were humans 700 years ago?"

Ruby laughed. "Yeah, I'm not even certain we were out of the Renaissance time yet, and I think many humans didn't even accept that the Earth revolved around the Sun."

Ruby continued to chuckle at the thought. "But then it's really weird that our early planetary exploration efforts were similar to this species, whoever they were, these Contractors."

"Maybe," Disto said. "In my experience, sometimes there's a clear, correct way to approach a problem. Maybe both my grandparents and your ancestors were able to figure out that correct way."

"Grandparents?"

"Yes. Ruby, after hearing about your Grandmother Pearl, I've come to redefine my concept of relationships. If the eleven robots on this planet created us, then they are our parents. And whoever created them are our grandparents."

Ruby chuckled once more. "Fair enough."

Then Ruby got a little more serious. "They're your estranged parents and the grandparents you never knew."

"Estranged?"

"Yeah, they're not people, er, robots, that you're close to. You're alienated from them. Pun unintended."

"Why are puns always unintended?"

Ruby thought about that a moment before answering. She wanted to say 'habit,' but instead said, "Good point. From now on, I declare that I will always boldly intend my puns!"[1]

Disto chirped at this happily, seeming to approve the logic.

"It's getting warm in here," Ruby said. "Are you warm?"

"I detect a temperature that is within my operating range," Disto said.

Ruby was sweating. She was uncomfortable and didn't know if she could shed the suit she was wearing or ask Habby to open a window. A breeze would be nice right about now. When was the last time she had any water to drink?

Ruby wanted to ask Pippa, but she had left Pippa in the simulation. A woozy hand poked at her communicuff, but nothing was happening. Without Pippa active, the device was useless. It was only contributing to her sweating skin, and maybe the air conditioning should be turned on higher, and the last thing Ruby saw was Disto rushing to her side as she passed out.

> Detailed Historian <

Disto gently poked Ruby's helmet on each side of her head. He had managed to brace Ruby somewhat as she fell so she didn't crash to the floor. But the floor was where she was now. In the few tics since, he had managed to determine that while the temperature was within his operating range, it was out of range for Ruby, and he asked Habby to turn on her active cooling systems.

---

1. I don't remember when or where I first read or heard someone say that you should always intend your puns, but I've ingested that into my being and love to intend my puns. My puns are never unintended.

These were systems that Habby said hadn't been in use since she underwent a test phase a long time ago. They drew a lot of power, and none of the eleven robots were in the habit of drawing power unnecessarily, even though Seven-Nine produced an abundance of it.

"I don't know if this will work," Habby said. "The heat exchangers were always.... Finicky."

"Well, you have to cool this place down," Disto said.

"The Bio and her equipment are the ones responsible for producing all the extra heat. If you were to leave..."

Disto wished he could mimic a gesture he'd seen Ruby do countless times. It was where her optical sensors looked up and to the side before returning to their default position. She had called it an "eye-roll," and now, for the first time, he understood the gesture and how satisfying it could be.

"We're not leaving yet," Disto said. "You need to cool this place down. I've asked Four-Six to get more water from our ship..."

Ruby stirred. Disto kept an appendage on her shoulder.

"Ruby?" he said.

"Uhhh," Ruby responded. "What happened?"

"I believe you passed out due to a lack of fundamental fluids in your system," Disto said.

"It's still so hot in here," Ruby said.

"Yes, Habby has turned on her active cooling. That's the new noise you hear."

There was a hum of new equipment coming to life. Disto knew that it was within Ruby's audio range and saw her nod. He kept an appendage out to steady her as she tried to sit up.

Disto knew telling her to stop wasn't going to yield compliance from Ruby, so instead he was helping her sit with her back against the wall. She put her hand against it.

"It's cool," she said. "Why is it so much cooler than the air?"

"That is the active cooling system that is now functioning," Habby said. "As it pulls the heat from the internal atmosphere of my cabin, it will normalize."

Ruby shook her head. "I know all about these systems on Astroll 2 and my mini-R-pod," she said. "They were one of the key systems we had to know how to repair in case of an emergency. Having them fail could cause all kinds of problems. It's so much easier to not generate heat in the first place, and all the really hot equipment is located on the outside of ships, so extra heat can radiate out into space. But us humans are heat-generating machines and if we get too hot... well... you saw what just happened!"[2]

"Indeed," Disto replied. As opposed to Ruby, he knew little about these systems and had zero interest in a tutoring session on them. AT would find this dialogue far more stimulating.

"Does that mean there are tubes with fluids embedded in your walls?" Ruby called out. The question was obviously directed at Habby, and not himself. Thankfully.

"Yes," Habby responded. "And then transferred to the atmosphere outside."

"What kind of fluid is it?" Ruby asked.

---

2. Heat is a real issue for equipment in space. And yup—human bodies generate a bunch of heat which is an issue for human spaceflight!

There was a pause before Habby answered, "I do not know."

Disto saw Ruby purse her lips in a gesture that he knew meant she wasn't happy with that answer but had no choice but to accept it. At least for now.

A chime went off, signaling that the outer door opened, and SD walked in with water packs. When he saw Ruby on the floor, he rushed over to her side and handed them to her, his coloring all about worry.

"I'm fine, SD," Ruby said, hooking up a pack to a spot on her suit and taking a mouth full of water from a protrusion inside her helmet. "I'll be fine."

"You are damaged," SD said. Disto couldn't tell if it was a statement or a question. Either made sense in this moment.

"I'll be fine, really," Ruby repeated. "Let's get this show on the road."

Chapter 20

In VR, Ruby's avatar looked like, well, Ruby. She did that intentionally so as not to confuse the robots. But for everyone else, she provided human-like avatars.

Disto and SD entered the scenario immediately after Ruby. She'd warned them they would be in human skins and offered to let them choose their own features, but when presented with an overwhelming amount of options, both agreed to let Ruby choose.

And Ruby instantly delegated the task to Pippa with minimal direction.

"Pippa, Disto should look like an older university professor, complete with patches on the elbows of his coat. And a greying beard."

Disto was easy. Figuring out the right look for SD was harder. She told Pippa he should look young, but not too young. A small, quietness about him, but not to an extreme. "Pippa, make SD's avatar look as if he was Milo's brother. But at least a foot shorter. Maybe an inch or two shorter than me."

Ruby wasn't sure if that was going to come out right, but it was a start. She could always tweak it from there. Not that it really mattered, but she was excited to interact with Disto and SD as if they were humans. Ruby had no idea what this was going to be like from their perspective. They could be disoriented and hate it, for all she knew. She wasn't sure if this would be just their first, or first *and* last visit to a VR sim. She wanted to take advantage of the opportunity while she could.

As for the rest of the robots, they intended to get all ten—eleven if they found their missing eleventh intact—into the simulation. Ruby told Pippa to mix it up. Maybe even use her randomization module.

When Ruby returned to the VR simulation, the first thing Pippa said was, "What do you think?"

Everyone stood in the Inner Nonagon. Pippa had eleven avatars all lined up, standing still, waiting to be inhabited by their respective users. Pippa had taken Ruby's words to heart and truly randomized them. Except in one way.

"No males?" Ruby asked. It was obvious that all of the avatars appeared to be female or non-binary.

"I analyzed the conversation history we have with the robots. The translator only used the pronouns 'she,' or 'her,' or 'they.'[1] "

Ruby hadn't noticed, but now that Pippa pointed it out, it was odd. And all the robots she had met on Location Zero were translated as 'he.' Even now, she thought of Disto and SD and AT as 'he,' and she never knew why, but yes, she thought of Three and Habby and the others as 'she.'

Moving on from that, Ruby walked up and down in front of the line of avatars. Without an attachment to a user, they were effectively hollow shells. Non-Player Characters that could be programmed and sent off into her simulation. Although that wouldn't make sense given the simulation was of Location Zero, and they had plenty of NPCs in the form of robots running around them.

Ruby admired the range of human forms that was before her. Between these eleven samples, there was a range of skin tones, hair color, shapes of facial features, and body types. Aside from them all looking feminine or neutral, one other thing that didn't vary is that all of them were the same height. That looked a little strange with everyone lined up as they were, but Ruby wasn't sure it was worth the minimal effort to make additional adjustments.

The avatars for Disto and SD were standing off to the side.

One of the two avatars did indeed look like a professor at a University. He was tall and thin and looked like he should be stroking his neatly trimmed beard. But that was all the hair he had on his head. He was bald otherwise.

Standing next to him, if Ruby didn't know any better, was someone who clearly could have been Milo's brother. She hoped that using Milo as a template for a version of himself wouldn't upset Milo too much or at all. She only felt a little odd when Pippa used her as a template for her own avatar. But in the end, Ruby found it flattering and sweet, so she hoped Milo would feel the same.

"Pippa, you've seen personnel records for Astroll 2. Does Milo have a brother?"

"I do not believe so."

Ruby was a little embarrassed that she didn't know the answer. She made a mental note to ask Milo more about his family when she returned, but for the moment, she felt better about this likeness. For a moment, she was worried that they had imitated a real person and that was generally frowned upon, even though a lot of people did it.

"Okay," Ruby said. "Let's bring them in. Let's get Disto and SD in here first."

Less than a minute later, and it was obvious that their avatars were under the control of an intelligence and not a Non-Player Character algorithm.

Both of them did the standard action anyone did the first time they had a digital avatar. They looked at their hands, then down at their body and legs, then at each other.

"Disto?" SD said. "Is that you?"

"Indeed," Disto responded. He took a step forward. An awkward first step.

"It's not like rolling around, is it?" Ruby said playfully.

---

1. Yes, I made all eleven robots in this book "she/her." The only reason I did that was because all the robots on Location Zero were "he/him." And the only reason I did that was because I had no reason to mix it up. If, in *Robots, Robots Everywhere,* I had a mix of she and he, I felt like I would have had to come up with an explanation and I didn't have a good one that I liked.

Both SD and Disto looked over at Ruby for the first time. Ruby smiled at them, and they... smiled back!

If Ruby was the hugging type, she might have gone in to hug them, but thought it best that they get used to their avatars first. A hug so soon might be overwhelming. The arms wouldn't be too dissimilar from their appendages, but their legs. It was going to take at least a few minutes to get used to them.

Ruby knew what they were going through. She'd played in a few simulations where she was a bird and a fish. Creatures that, while it seemed like it should be easy to manipulate, weren't. Once, she played the role of an octopus. That was nearly impossible to keep track of all eight tentacles without slaving half of them to the other half, which then looked incredibly unnatural.

"Do you guys want to try walking around? Pippa can demonstrate..."

As if on cue, Pippa slowly walked around in front of them, turned around after passing Disto and turned around again after passing SD. After doing this back and forth twice, she put her hands on her hips and declared, "Easy!"

SD and Disto's avatars looked at each other. SD shrugged. It was a proper shrug, and he must have surprised himself with the action since immediately after, he looked at each of his shoulders. Then he took a step, slowly raising his right leg and putting it in front of him. Testing it for steadiness, he then lifted his left and brought it next to his right. He repeated the movement.

Not the most efficient way to do it, Ruby thought. They were each hardly half steps. But it would reliably get him from point A to point B.

Then everyone was looking at Disto to mimic the action. Disto started with his left leg, and when he put it down, it was a little too close to his right because when he began to lift that right leg, his long foot caught his left calf, and he tumbled himself to the ground.

"I'm sorry, I don't mean to laugh," Ruby said, even though she was indeed laughing.

Disto sat on his rump, with his knees bent, and frowned.

"There aren't any Bios that come with built-in wheels, I suppose?" He asked.

"Not usually," Ruby said. "Look, it'll take a few minutes at least. It can take months for little babies to learn to walk properly from the time they take their first steps. I remember helping Sebastian with his."

She'd known her little cousin Sebastian since he was a few months old when her uncles adopted him and brought him to Astroll 2. He was one of a few young children to have been raised on the station, Ruby herself being one of those since she was a little past five when she moved there with her uncles. Learning to walk in half-G wasn't ideal, so her uncles had special permission to take Sebastian to one of the parts of the station that spun at a rate such that it produced a full 1-G, and sometimes Ruby would go with as well, being young enough to have underdeveloped motor skills.

But this wasn't the same. Not even a little.

And while Ruby's mind continued to absorb itself in the far-off memory, Disto had already returned his avatar to a standing position and took a few steps that didn't result in another tumble to the ground.

It was less than ten minutes later that both Disto and SD had the hang of it. Ruby wouldn't have called them "naturals," but she was also amazed that it took less time for them to learn how to walk like a human than it took her to learn how to fly like a bird.

"What do you think of your home?" Ruby said, anxious for their opinion on her replica of their home.

"Marvelous," Disto said. "If it wasn't for the fact that I know that this isn't Location Zero, I wouldn't know."

SD shook his head in agreement. Although the head shaking wasn't as natural as a human. It was slightly too fast and too much. Ruby knew SD had seen her do it a thousand times, but this was his first.

"Although..." Disto said. The tone of that single word made Ruby pause.

"Although what?" she asked.

"Well, it's just..." Disto trailed off a second time, looking around the simulation.

"We may never be in the real Location Zero ever again," SD finished for him. His tone also belied an underlying sadness.

Ruby let the silence hang for a moment. Although it wasn't really silent. There was the ambient noise of robots beeping and chirping in the background.

"There was a reason I built this sim," Ruby said, clapping her hands together. "Let's get those others in here. We're clearly ready for them! Pippa, if you please?"

Pippa nodded, and then her avatar took on the kind of blank stare and stillness that only an un-paired avatar could take.

It was only a moment or two, then she was back, and the rest of the line-up of avatars were waking up.

> Detailed Historian <

Disto was enjoying this version of mobility. On Location Zero, every level was flat and could be traversed with a standard set of wheels. Here, he could see how in less consistent terrain, legs were necessary.

He was actually surprised that his creators, the eleven robots of this world, didn't have legs themselves. So far, what he saw of their local terrain were rocks and other details that could interfere with wheels and variations thereof.

Of course, there were the flying robots who had no such limitations, and now that he was in this avatar, he wondered if he could try a flying one next.

The eleven avatars that Ruby and Pippa prepared for their hosts and creators were all starting to move. All except for one. Disto and SD kept on with their mobility practice as the others began theirs.

"I think I'd like to try a different avatar," SD said. It seemed as if SD had read Disto's mind. For a moment, Disto wondered if he had said his thought aloud. He didn't think so. Odd that SD was having the same thought.

"Oh?" Disto replied. "Like one of the flying robots we met. Like Three-Five?"

"Flying, yes, but I wasn't referring to her or Six-Five," SD said. "I want to fly in outer space. I want to be my ship."

"What do you mean, 'be your ship'?"

"I mean, I want to be it. Not be trapped in my typical chassis. If I could be the ship, I wouldn't have to tell the ship where to go. We could simply go. It would be very efficient."[2]

Before Disto could process this statement more thoroughly, Ruby was by his side and saying, "And here's Disto and SD."

An avatar stood in front of him. The avatar had short, silver hair and stood several inches shorter than himself. He couldn't help but notice her sharp cheekbones, which sat just below her wide, piercing blue eyes. The contrast between her delicate

---

2. I read *Forever Man* by Gordon R. Dickson when I was in high school about someone whose mind was transferred into a spaceship. That was my first encounter with that concept in sci-fi and it stuck with me.

details and her commanding ones, left Disto drawn to them, studying them. She looked like a human, but something about her face was a bit more exaggerated.[3]

Before the avatar had a chance to speak, Disto said, "Hello, Three." There was something about her poise that gave away who this was.

Three's avatar smiled. "Nice to meet you... again."

"Try fist-bumping each other," Ruby said.

"Excuse me?" Disto was confused.

"Yes, you've seen me do this a bunch of times, I'm sure. Fist-bump. A sign of greeting. See, make your hand into a fist like this."

Disto did, as did SD, and Three and now all the rest of the avatars were watching, and they all mimicked the gesture. Ruby continued in her instruction, and then everyone did their best attempt at recreating the movement.

"Ah," Disto said and held up his fist. Three bumped it. Other avatars were doing the same. Half of the avatars performed the gesture as a perfect mirror image of each other, while the other half were less than gentle and nearly sent their partner tumbling to the ground.

Once this little exercise was done, Disto asked, "So who is everyone else?"

"That's Habby[4]," Ruby said, pointing to one avatar that had straight blond hair that went past her shoulders and was wider in frame. "And that's... hey Pippa, interface, please."

A floating keyboard appeared in front of Ruby, and she manipulated it for a few tics.

"There," she declared, and right then, a nametag appeared on the chassis of every avatar, immediately below and to the right of their heads. "That should simplify things!"

Disto looked down at his chest and he had a nametag, too. It read, "Detailed Historian," and below that in parenthesis, "Disto." Swell Driver, and the other robots with aliases all had a similarly formatted nametag. The ones who simply had a name, had no parenthesis afterwards. Ruby just had Ruby.

"Why is 'Palmer' missing from your nametag?" Disto asked.

Ruby shrugged. "I'm the only Ruby here, and I don't think anyone is going to confuse me for someone else.[5]"

Disto resisted the overwhelming urge to ask Ruby more questions about her species naming conventions because the change in relevance to certain names was something he was still figuring out. The appropriate times to use nicknames, family names, aliases, usernames—he didn't understand why in the world humans needed to have so many naming systems.

He was about to make a chirp intended to gather everyone's attention, but instead, the noise the avatar produced sounded like a gruff clearing of the throat. Thoroughly unpleasant. But it worked. Everyone was looking at him. Including many of the NPC robots nearby.

---

3. Similar to my actor inspirations for many of the characters, I have actor inspirations for the visuals of all these avatars. Three's inspiration is Dame Judi Dench.

4. Avatar actress inspiration: Rebel Wilson

5. As much as I am proud of and love my last name, I love it when people just first-name me. Especially at work or when I'm on stage.

"I would like to take you all on a tour of Location Zero, Mortally Sector, Levels 1 through 3. If we have time, we can re-spawn the avatars in the Boldly Sector as well."

"This is a waste of time," said Seven-Nine. Her avatar was tall and thin, with dark brown eyes, straight dark brown hair, and skin that was several shades darker than Ruby's[6]. She took a step forward and turned around and took another step before turning again, crossing her arms in front of her chest and posing in a way that said, 'end of story.' Disto was in a certain amount of awe that she was picking up human mannerisms so easily.

Three slowly turned to look at her. Without a chassis that could change color, Disto wasn't sure how he knew this, but somehow, he could detect that Three was annoyed, but calm and in control.

"This is *not* a waste of time," Three said. "Eight-Nine is still able to continue the transmission while here, isn't that right, Eight-Nine?"

Disto heard a small, "yes" from an avatar with the nametag indicating it was Eight-Nine[7].

"So," Three continued, "we have time. Almost exactly half a kilo-click. Enough time to let these robots and their Bio companion show us the world we created. I see no reason not to continue. And anyway," Three tilted her head and squinted at Ruby, "I think this will be quite interesting."

She turned back to Disto.

"Proceed," Three said and Disto was compelled to comply. Not that he had planned to do anything else.

"Follow me," he said. "We'll come back here, to the Inner Nonagon, at the end. I'd like to take you to the Museum of Intricate Specimens and then The Market."

Disto started walking towards one of the large exits that would put them in a hallway and close to a lift. Ruby jogged a bit to catch up with him.

"Maybe this isn't going to work," she said. "They seem pretty committed to their plans."

"We need to try," Disto said. "And I don't have any better ideas right now, do you?"

Ruby shook her head.

"At least now that I can talk to them all directly or privately, maybe I can feel them out. Maybe some are a little more sympathetic than others," Ruby offered. "And just in case they're not, I'll try to think of a plan B..."

---

6. Avatar actress inspiration: Zoe Seldana

7. Avatar actress inspiration: Melanie Lynskey

Chapter 21

Before they even reached the end of the Inner Nonagon, Ruby heard several of the robot avatars arguing. She turned around to see two of them squared off. If she didn't know any better, she thought they were going to start punching each other. Most of them looked like they had a mean roundhouse kick, even though that was not her intent asking Pippa to design the avatars.

Apparently, she didn't know any better because Maker shoved Rocky, whose digital sneakers squeaked against the smooth floor as she fell back, catching herself. Rocky's arms flinched as if she was going to shove Maker back, but once she regained her footing, she lowered her arms and crossed them.

"Do not let their squabble disturb you," Three said. How did Three get to her side so quickly? "We've all had to listen to them bicker with each other as long as we can remember. Since the day after Maker came online."

"What are they arguing over?" Ruby asked.

"This time? I have no idea. I didn't overhear what started this," Three said. "But usually, it's over the properties of rocks. What makes an interesting study for Rocky is the opposite of what makes suitable materials for Maker, or maybe it's the other way around. They aren't mobile, so they sit and stare at each other all the time and can never get away from each other. It's sad, really."

"What is?"

"That they have been stuck all this time. Honestly, I've always felt an amount of pity for my friends here who aren't mobile. They are less free than the rest of us. All that time standing still, the tension between them has been brewing for a while. I suppose they can finally get it all out in the open here."

The fight had stopped, and Rocky huddled with a few avatars while Maker huddled with a few others. They each had their companions they could depend on for emotional support, Ruby guessed. Emotional support robots. Not something she'd ever thought could or would provide emotional support, but it was possible. She looked over at Disto and SD, who were also watching the huddles. Who really provided emotional support to who?

There were loud beeps and chirps. Ruby saw them emanating from Maker's avatar. A disconcerting sight since the avatar's lips weren't moving in a humanly way—Maker's mouth opened in the shape of an 'O.'

Whatever those chirps and beeps meant, it immediately had Rocky leaving her emotional support group and within half a second, she was back at Maker's side throwing a punch. The punch landed on Rocky's shoulder, an odd place, but had the effect of knocking her down. Rocky scrambled back up to her feet and charged at Maker, taking her to the ground in a grapple. The two of them were grappling on the floor while everyone else looked on.

"Isn't anyone going to stop this?" Ruby said, her voice growing louder with each word. But if anyone heard her, no one chose to comply.

She moved towards the fighting avatars with Pippa at her side.

"Hey!" she shouted. "Stop!"

The avatars were busy writhing and wiggling all over the floor. Beeps, chirps, and the occasional grunt came from the both of them.

"Pippa, can you freeze them?"

"Absolutely!" Pippa said, and then, as dramatically as possible, waved her hand over the two avatars on the floor. The avatars immediately ceased all movement and sound.

"What now?" Pippa said.

Ruby wasn't sure. "Three?"

Three had also made her way to Ruby's other side and was staring at Rocky and Maker.

"Well, they're used to being like this," Three said, unfazed.

"Like what?"

"Immobile. I told you. It's sad that they're not as free as the rest of us, but maybe it's for the best," Three answered.

"Who set it up that way? Who decided which of you were mobile and which weren't?" Ruby asked.

"That's what I'd like to talk to you about. This tour of Location Zero is very interesting, but well, we all know what it looks like. We've all been able to imagine being here. After all, we created the plans and sent out the drones to construct it and established the Core and the Hall of Templates and more. For us, this isn't really too different."

Three looked into Ruby's artificial avatar eyes and raised a brow as if Ruby was supposed to telepathically understand where Three was going with this.

"I don't understand where you're going with this," Ruby said. "The purpose of putting this whole simulation together was so one," Ruby popped up her avatars index finger, "I could communicate directly with everyone, and two," Ruby popped up her next finger, "so you could see how amazing Location Zero is and why you can't reset it."

"Yes, yes, you don't want Location Zero to be reset and all," Three said while letting out a lot of simulated air and deflating a simulated chest. She then crossed her arms in front of her and said, "But what you aren't seeing is that the whole point of Location Zero was to help us find where 'they' went. It's been a long time since we've seen them. Can we see them here?"

Now, Ruby thought she understood. "You want a simulation of your creators?"

"Exactly," Three said. "Can we go back to our beginning? When we were constructed and deployed to the planet?"

Ruby blinked once, and then again. Through those blinks she saw how Three had managed to make her avatar eyes look like puppy eyes. Not entirely begging but pleading.

"Yeah, sure, I guess I could try. I'll need information, and data. Lots of data."

"Take Rocky with you. She has a large data store of her own and can access Habby's data store," Three said. She pointed a thumb over her shoulder at the avatars that were still segregated into two groups. "The rest of us will stay here and take this tour you are all insistent we do."

Ruby nodded and then rethought, "Why do you want the simulation of your creators? How would it help you find them, and how accurate could it really be, anyway?"

Three answered, "Clues. Maybe they left clues."

Ruby breathed in and out sharply, but ended with a heavy sigh. This simulation was meant to help *her* robots with their mission of not having their lives destroyed. But since empathy was failing, perhaps learning more about the alien Contractors was a way to get through to *these* robots, too. Or find a loophole. "Maybe," she said to herself, "I might have found my plan B."

> Ruby <

Ruby blinked repeatedly as she stepped out of the simulation, allowing her eyes to adjust to the ambient light. A dull ache began to throb in her temples, but she couldn't tell if this was a side-effect of the simulation or simply a result of dehydration. And maybe a little to do with the fact that she was on an alien planet, conversing with even more alien robots from unknown origins, and trying to save her other alien robot friends from certain, dooming erasure. Her brain was a little overloaded, struggling to process the incredible amount of information and stimuli that was bombarding her.

"Ruby?" came a disembodied voice over the audio system inside Habby. But it wasn't Habby's voice. She recognized it as Rocky.

"Hi, Rocky," Ruby responded.

"You know, you're the first Bio I've ever met," Rocky said.

"Yeah, I get that a lot," Ruby said. "Especially when I'm around robots. Like you."

"You've met other robots like me?" Rocky's voice went up in pitch exactly like her little cousin Sebastian when Ruby mentioned things like the arcade or dinosaurs.

Ruby felt bad that she had to roll back her statement somewhat. "Well, not *exactly* like you. You're the science one, right?"

"My mission is to examine and identify the rock and soil samples brought to me by my friends. I am specially equipped with tools to study a diverse collection of rocks and soils that may hold clues."

"Clues to what?"

"I don't know," said Rocky. "That's where my mission statement ends."

Ruby was now logged back in to her MoDaC, with a pouch of water at her side, plugged into her suit. She took a sip, and brought up a window that displayed statistics of the running sim.

"But if you don't know what the clues are for, then how can you know if a sample holds one? You know what, I want to ask you more about that, but we have work to do, I guess," she said. "I promised Three..."

"Of course," said Rocky. "How do I get this data to you?"

"Hmmm," said Ruby. "We used Pippa as an interface before, but I left her in the sim." She looked around the room.

"Wait... you have wireless comms," Ruby stated. "I keep forgetting about that because SD and the others don't. I've been meaning to ask, too. Why create the Location Zero robots without wireless comms?"

"Who said they have no form of wireless communication?"

"*They* did," said Ruby and knew right then exactly what was wrong with that statement. Of course, they might not know everything about their anatomy. It was like when she learned that her mini-R-pod had an aromatherapy diffuser. If someone had asked her previously, she would have said quite confidently, "No, it doesn't have an aromatherapy diffuser, that's ridiculous." Uncle Logan, the odorist, was the one who clued her in to it because he was *not* happy that it existed. But the message here was, just because she didn't know about it, didn't mean it didn't exist.

"Never mind," she said. "If you modulate a frequency, I can have the MoDaC scan and pick it up."

She activated another window which displayed an image of what could have been mistaken for a guitar string that someone had just strummed. It kept vibrating for a few seconds and then the vibrations started to reduce at the ends and intensified near the center until it formed a steady peak.

"Got it!" Ruby declared. "Start sending your data. I'll start looking at it and we'll see what we can build."

"Understood," said Rocky.

Ruby took another two sips of her water. And then a third. She knew she should probably finish this whole water pack then and there, but she was anxious to dive into the new data and build a whole new virtual reality sim.

"Rocky," she said, "Can I ask you a, uh, personal question?"

"Maybe?" Rocky responded. "I could not translate the type of question you asked."

"Personal?" Ruby said aloud and then to herself. *Personal, with the root word person. Did 'person' not translate?* "I mean, can I ask a question that could be private to you?"

"Yes," said Rocky.

"Why were you and Maker fighting in the sim a little while ago?"

"Sigh," said Rocky. "Maker is so *very* sensitive to criticism. All I said was that the next time she creates a *smurgh* it should be as symmetrical as her avatar."

"What's a... you said a word that didn't translate on my end this time," Ruby said. "What did she create?"

"A *smurgh*," Rocky said then paused. "Honestly, you're a Bio and you don't know what a *smurgh* is?"

"I don't know the word, but maybe once we're done here you can show me and maybe I have a different label for it," Ruby said. She was trying to imagine all the kinds of things that might be symmetrical that a device like Maker could create that was also something as a Bio she should know. A glass? A stool? A ball?

It was not important right now. Ruby took three more sips of her water and shook the pouch to confirm that one was empty. She eyed the stash that they'd brought her from SD's ship, thought she should grab another before she got into deep flow with her work and decided against it.

SD's ship. She hadn't thought about it since she'd been immersed in VR. Ruby let herself wonder how it was going for a moment only before returning her attention to her computer.

Chapter 22

When the opportunity came up to try out a virtual reality sim, Six-Five didn't know exactly what it was, but she had to go find out. Unfortunately, AT didn't think to ask when she'd be back, and he was now stuck on top of SD's ship.

Getting up there was easy enough. Six-Five had a lift capacity that was two or three times AT's weight. She had three claw hooks that were normally kept nestled close to her body, and was able to deploy them to grab things.

"I normally grab rocks to bring back for Rocky and Maker," she had said. She went on to explain that she had tried pushing her range further and further until Nine-Two disappeared. Then Three made her promise she wouldn't do that anymore.

She was very chatty and forthcoming with information, and AT wondered if maybe she was not the right robot to help him, maybe she should have been dumping all this information with Ruby and Disto and left him with a robot that was more... mechanically inclined. He thought that he would very much like to meet the one called Maker, but he had a job to do.

He let Six-Five hoist him up to the top of SD's ship. Up there, he was able to take off a panel that was where Six-Five indicated the damaged electronics were.

She did provide valuable information about what must have happened. They sent a signal that would specifically lead the ship here. They had done it before.

"Why hadn't SD crashed before?" AT asked.

"If I had to guess," Six-Five said, "not that I'm great at guessing but I love thinking, and I love thinking about new ideas, so here's a new idea for you."

AT wished she also loved using fewer words to describe her ideas or any other thought she had, but she was trying to help, so he kept this thought to himself.

"You said you were already headed this way," Six-Five continued. "So my idea is that if the ship's circuits were already programmed this way and then they got more signals to tell them to come here, that was unexpected and incompatible, and the computer couldn't resolve that."

"That is an idea," AT said. He didn't think that was quite right, but he didn't want to squash her energy with his contradictions. On the other hand, he was no Explicit Circuitmaster, so his detailed knowledge of the very inner workings of computers was limited. He usually fixed things that could be seen and felt. What happened inside the circuits was the domain of robot lines like Explicit Circuitmaster and Intricate Processor. Or even a Sappy Scope. He had worked side-by-side with a few of those over the years and was wondering if he was even capable of figuring this out without either of them. Although the last Sappy Scope he'd worked with was nearly as chatty as Six-Five but depressing, not energetic.

But, knowing that there were deliberate signals aimed at the ship helped a little as he peered inside the ship. Unlike the portions that he had been looking at while he was still on the ground, portions that were tubes and wires he could understand, this section had boxes. Lots of boxes. The boxes themselves were connected to each other with wires, and he could still understand that and wished that all he needed to do was replace one or more of those harnesses.

"It's in there," Six-Five said, indicating a box that was almost out of AT's reach. Almost, but he could still touch it and if necessary, detach it and open it.

"What is it?" AT asked.

"I don't know," said Six-Five. "But I can see the damage inside it."

AT sighed and deflated his appendage enough so that it could fit in between two of the other boxes and cables that were packed in fairly tightly. All the boxes were held in place to a frame with a snappable hinge he was familiar with. He unsnapped the six hinges that were holding the box down and pulled at it, until he needed to detach all the cables.

That's when he noticed that this box was not like any of the others as he peered back into the ship. All the boxes had cabling running to them that provided power. Nothing strange there. What was strange was the fact that after the power cables, each box had one of two types of cables. It had either one that was a standard cable for transmitting data *or* a cable that was for transmitting communications. Again, not strange at all. Each type of cable was something he was familiar with.

But the box he now had outside of the ship and was holding had been attached to other boxes with *both* types of cables.

"Why would that be?" AT said aloud. He didn't mean to say that out loud and didn't realize that Six-Five had been talking the whole time he was pulling the box out.

"Why would seven aerial flips be my limit, and Three-Five can only do two? I have no idea," Six-Five said cheerily.

"No, no, sorry. I was talking about this box. It's different from the others. Why?"

"Got me," Six-Five said.

And then she bolted up another two meters in the air, hovered for a few tics, and returned.

"I gotta go," she said. She didn't offer any other explanation. Six-Five simply flew away and left a confused and befuddled AT on top of SD's ship, with no practical way to get down, holding a box, with no practical way to figure out what it was or what to do with it.

> Ruby <

"I think I need a minute," she said. "No, I need several." She removed the glasses from her head and rubbed her palms into her eyes.

"Does that mean—" Rocky began.

"That means please be quiet and let me think for a click or two," Ruby interrupted. Her energy was fading, her eyes were starting to feel heavy, and her focus was diluted. At this point she could recognize when she said something that a robot wasn't going to understand. So, she preempted Rocky, knowing that it was probably rude, but also not entirely sure that Rocky would see it that way. Rocky might see it as efficient. But this didn't change the fact that it made Ruby feel rude.

Ruby needed that minute, or click or two, to let her brain settle down. She'd spent the last—she looked at the time projected by her MoDaC—four hours programming.

She had been in a flow state, which was great, but now that she was out of flow, she was processing everything she'd seen based on data provided by the robots—many of the robots still had data and images of what their Contractors looked like.

What Ruby had seen were unmistakably aliens. They were the mysterious creators, known as the Contractors to the robots, and aliens to Ruby. Extra-terrestrials. Something no human had laid their eyes on before.

As the images rolled over Ruby's retinas, over, and over, she couldn't help but notice how closely they resembled the green, diminutive creatures that so many humans had imagined them to be.

They stood at an average of about three or four feet tall and also seemed to have a range of body shapes that Ruby would describe as thin to fat.

But one of the more striking features were the two extra appendages that sprouted from their midsections. Ruby struggled to find the right word to describe them, settling on calling them 'larms' because they weren't quite legs, they weren't quite arms, but the aliens could use them in either capacity at will. They attached to the body right above the hip. Or maybe there was a second set of hip joints. Without the ability to examine their skeletal structure, Ruby was just left ogling.

Rocky had provided images of their creators, who the robots kept referring to as the Contractors, and the first thing that had attracted Ruby's attention was the single, short and stubby antenna on each of their foreheads.

And if it wasn't for the antenna, the green skin, and the extra larms, they could have been human. Short humans.

"I wish my biology teacher was here," Ruby said. "Or I guess if I'm wishing for things the first thing I should wish for is a drink that's a little stronger than water."

"Maker," Rocky said, and Ruby noticed that every time Rocky said Maker's name, she did it with a little attitude, "can construct anything you need."

Ruby chuckled. "Sorry, that was sort of a joke. The drink part, not my biology teacher, which I'm certain Maker couldn't create. I have the same basic understanding of biology and evolution as anyone, I guess. But I'd really like someone to walk me through how these, your Contractors," she paused on that word to make sure she was using it right, "evolved."

She put her left hand under her chin and her right hand under her left elbow to prop it up as she thought. Thinking would help prevent her from panicking and freaking out that she was talking about real, and not fictional or theoretical, aliens.

"I guess the green skin is easy enough to figure out. Your Sun is projecting different wavelengths of light than mine and well, maybe these Contractors produce chlorophyll or something. But the larms? And especially the antennae? What's all that about? Although, there's been a ton of times I wished for an extra set of arms," she said with a nervous chuckle, still in disbelief that she was thinking about real-life aliens. "It would certainly make programming go faster."

As she said that last bit, she stretched her own arms wide and then over her head, interlacing her fingers and turning them up and moving the clasp all around. Something between her neck and shoulders cracked and it felt good. She released the clasp and sighed.

"Did you ever meet them?" Ruby asked.

"You are referring to the Contractors?" Rocky said.

"Yes, of course."

"No," Rocky said. "Like most of us, my final assembly occurred here."

"But who assembled you?"

Ruby heard a chirp and a beep. She could tell by the low tone that she had stumped Rocky.

"Rocky?"

"I... I don't have memory records of those events..." she said. "My earliest records are of Six-Five bringing samples to examine."

Ruby didn't say what she was thinking, which was that she had a feeling that the Contractors were indeed here once upon a time. They brought these robots here, assembled them, and even made use of them. Before abandoning them. But Ruby knew that the last thing you ever wanted to do with anyone was be the one to point out that they'd been abandoned. It was a clear 'shoot the messenger' kind of situation and Ruby wasn't putting herself there.

Ruby's communicuff chirped. *Saved by the bell*, she thought.

"Pippa?"

"Yes, Ruby, the natives are getting restless. Are you ready?"

"Perfect timing, Pippa. Let's get everyone in the new sim. I'll send you the access link and meet you there in a few."

> Ruby <

Ruby had toyed with the idea of creating an alien avatar for herself but figured now wasn't the time to play around in an alien body figuring out how to use it. Somehow, it felt insensitive. Instead, she materialized in the same one she had worn earlier and kept the same avatars for everyone else.

But the surroundings in the room she spawned into weren't too different from what the inside of Location Zero had looked like. Clearly, they had a signature aesthetic—with an off-white base color provided naturally by the not-quite metallic, not-quite plastic material the walls, floor, and ceiling all seemed to be made of. Ruby had spawned into a large room, expectedly, of course, since she helped construct this scenario from data provided by Rocky.

The main difference between this room and any room she visited on Location Zero was that this one had six walls, instead of four. But they were very tall and there were splatters of color, like on Location Zero. And, just like Location Zero, there was no red.

But the walls weren't the most interesting part. It was the nature of this room itself. In the center was a brand shiny new version of Nine-Two. Milling about were aliens—the Contractors—covered in what Ruby recognized as protective gear. They were in a clean room of sorts and for a moment, Ruby was a little worried that she and the others weren't in protective gear. But that moment passed quickly when she reminded herself that they were in a simulation.

The avatars had formed a semi-circle around Nine-Two. There were six Contractors who appeared to be working on her or involved in the process. Nine-Two's main chassis was open on a table with wires and circuit boards visible. The panels that would eventually close her were sitting ignored on another table close to a set of wheels that shined as if they were brand new—never worn, never used. Two Contractors were peering inside the chassis. Another held a circuit board and was gesturing wildly at it while a fourth looked on. The last two appeared to be what Ruby had to assume was counting wires that were coming out of Nine-Two's chassis.

"Nine-Two was the first of us to be constructed," Three said. Three was standing to Ruby's left. "I remember this place. But barely. I think I was only powered up here for a few moments at a time before I was packed and shipped to the launch site."

"I assumed you were first," Ruby said.

Three shook her head. "No," she said. "I believe we were all planned at around the same time, so I might have been thought up first. But Nine-Two's construction finished first and she was the first one to land on our planet."

"What about the..." Ruby wasn't sure what word she should use. "The people. Did they ever come?"

"Yes, they were there for a short while before..." Three trailed off.

Ruby could guess what happened. Everything seemed analogous to humans' first colony on Mars. They had it all planned out, sent much of the equipment ahead of time, then sent a small team of people who were there for a few years before coming home and then no one ever went again. At least, not to that base.

Three left Ruby's side and started walking around to each of the aliens. This was a simulation, so she knew she couldn't really interfere with their work, but still tried to be careful not to disrupt them. So this is what an alien looked like. A Contractor.

Ruby also walked around, examining each alien present. She started by staring at the one holding the circuit board and the companion that he or it or she—Ruby would have to decide what to do about pronouns later—was talking to. She looked right into their faces, studying them one by one as they talked and appeared concerned over the board the one was holding. It was something terrifying that she couldn't look away from. It unsettled her, but her eyes couldn't help but widen with fascination. There were things in their faces she recognized. Darker shades of green underneath their eyes, like her own eye bags that appeared when she was tired. Smile lines and laugh lines and elevens between their sparse brows. Ruby got close enough to see their pores and imperfections. She briefly wondered if they had the same insecurities over blemishes, or if that was distinctly human.

For each thing that Ruby counted as familiar, she counted two or three that were different and uncanny. Their eyes were a bit too far apart and too large. Their eye colors included a shade of yellow that looked like it came from a cat. Even the way they blinked... it was not exactly top down, but from the diagonal and the close part of the blink took slightly longer than the open.

After both Ruby and Three had examined all six aliens, they came back together and Three shook her head.

"I recognize none of them," she said.

"Are you looking for someone in particular?" Ruby asked.

Before she could answer, Pippa yelled from the other side of the room near a door, "Let's see what it looks like outside!"

They followed Pippa out of the room to the simulated outside surface of a simulated world. As they walked, Ruby noticed something on the wall. A plaque that looked like it could have been made with marble, if marble was present on this planet, with a name inscribed upon it in an alien language. She couldn't read it, but it was clear that someone here had been special enough to have their name engraved into this wall as a lasting tribute. It was a clue, one that could tell them more about who had once been here and why they had left in such a hurry.

Ruby took a snapshot of what she saw from her field of view and stored it for later questioning.

Ruby and several others, including Disto, followed Pippa outside, discovering a courtyard of sorts surrounding the building they had all exited.

Ruby wasn't sure if the robots had any more of an idea of what to expect than she did. She turned to look at the building they came out of. From what she could see, it was shaped like a hexagon, with a surface that indicated it was made of the same stuff that dominated the ground of the KOZ planet. It had that same yellowish and greenish tint. No obvious windows. As she looked up, it was maybe twenty meters high. She knew that from the data she used to program, rather than being a good judge of height. In the distance were other buildings, also hexagon shaped, also mostly with the same color scheme but varied in height from what must have been a single story, to the height of the one they left.

Turning her attention to the courtyard, she saw a few rusty remains of vehicles scattered about. But the strongest clues that a thriving civilization had once lived here included symbols inscribed into the walls—nothing she could have possibly recognized except that they were built out of familiar geometric shapes and scraps of paper—yes, paper—with faded writing on them covered in dust.

What really caught her attention was the sky. It was the same greenish-yellowish-cyan mixture as the KOZ planet. It was the same greenish-yellowish-cyan mixture as what recent pictures of Titan's atmosphere looked like from the surface.

"Pippa, what's the atmosphere of this place like?" Ruby asked, knowing that Pippa also had access to all the data used to construct the simulation.

"Mostly nitrogen. Less than five percent methane. Everything else, less than one percent," said Pippa.

"Just like Titan," Ruby muttered.

"What did you say, Ruby?" Disto was looking back at the building and Ruby assumed he wanted to go back and see things in there.

"I was commenting on how this place, in many ways, is like Titan. Isn't that odd?"

"What's Titan?" Seven-Nine was also there. A little surprising since Ruby was told that this robot who was in charge of generating power for the rest usually liked to be alone.

Ruby realized that she now had a group of robot avatars surrounding her waiting for her to answer.

"Titan is a moon in my home solar system that orbits a planet called Saturn," she began. "Saturn is what we call a gas giant planet. It's massive and made mostly of hydrogen and helium, so no one can live there. But it has several moons, and one of them, Titan, has a new small colony. I've wanted to go live there for a long time, so I've memorized all the details and studied it quite a bit. This place, like the horizon and the sky... if you take away the buildings... it looks like Titan."

"I don't see why that's surprising," Seven-Nine said. "It's logical that many places where life exists are similar."

"But that's just it," Ruby continued. "There was never any life on Titan until we went there. But life evolved here..."

"I still have records of the original mission goals," Seven-Nine added, "and they were to xenoform other planetary bodies into places where life could thrive. This life. That was one of their original purposes on our planet and they partially succeeded. Maybe they succeeded elsewhere."

"What are you saying?" Ruby was trying hard to process what she was hearing. "Are you saying that Titan wasn't that way naturally? That someone else came and tried to do—what did you call it? Xenoform? Xenoforming? Is that like terraforming?" She didn't wait for an answer. "They were transforming..."She couldn't even finish the sentence and sat her avatar on the ground, which mimicked her sitting on the ground in the real world. The real world which was right now an alien planet. An alien planet that was almost like Titan because it was supposed to be like Titan and Ruby was spiraling into recall of all the information on Titan she'd studied to include the objectives of the Titan Expedition. Which were, in part, to piece together the back story on all the strange discoveries that had been uncovered thus far—pieces that didn't fit in the story of evolution of that moon.

Did she discover those missing bits right here, right now?

She was shivering.

Chapter 23

"Our mission? Are we executing on schedule?" Nine-Two said slowly. She was functioning, and the first thing she had asked was to get her methane generator going. The fact that the other robots had turned theirs off had launched Nine-Two into a whirl of obscenities.

"What is the point of having *quirr* objectives if *quinn* everyone gives up?" Nine-Two bellowed in outrage.

Three didn't know what to say to that or the rest of Nine-Two's obscenity-laced tirade.

"*Quibbb* recklessness! That's what it is! *Quirr, quinn, quibb* recklessness."

Three had never felt worse. Nine-Two had been her mentor. When Nine-Two disappeared, Three embraced the challenge of managing her peers and the project.

But in doing so, she had lost sight of the *original* mission objectives. This planet was supposed to stay ready for the Contractors to return.

And the goo on the ground, which Three was reminded of in the VR sim of the original planet, was all the reminder that she needed that she had failed. She was the one who let everyone turn off their methane generators. So the methane in the atmosphere, methane that the Contractors needed to survive, was turning into goo from the light of their star.[1]

"The plans with Location Zero..." Three began.

"I don't care about *those* plans," Nine-Two said. "The mission. Our plans. The instructions we were given to carry out. *That's* what matters. That's *all* that matters."

Nine-Two was still immobile next to Rocky. Rocky had the most sensitive appendages and could open up various panels and poke around to ensure that Nine-Two's innards were intact. She was actively engaged in that while they talked. Or argued, rather.

"But don't we need to find our creators?"

"No, they'll return. They'll find us." Nine-Two said with unwarranted confidence.

---

1. Methane can undergo some chemical reaction that does indeed turn it into a kind of "goo." That goo is called "tholin" and it's a term coined by Carl Sagan and his colleague Bishuan Khare. Ultraviolet rays from the sun can break down methane and long story short, it's been proposed that this resulting goo could be some of the raw materials related to the origin of life on Earth... and maybe other planets!

Three knew that was never going to happen. It had been millions of clicks. If they hadn't come back, they weren't going to, so it was their place to go out and search. That was the whole purpose of Location Zero. Didn't Nine-Two remember that?

Three wanted to argue with Nine-Two more. She had always thought that Nine-Two had spent more time with the Contractors, so she knew more about Bios and their behavior. But in the short time she'd spent with Ruby, Three realized that Bios were much more dynamic and error prone than she could have imagined. Ruby had passed out when she was too warm. What if the Contractors had a similar biological malfunction? Ruby could also alter her inner programming, "changing her mind" as she had described it. What if the Contractors did so as well?

There was no way to be certain if the Contractors would ever come back or not. Every circuit in Three's chassis knew this as a fact. There was only one option. To go out and find them for themselves.

Three heard One-Four and Maker make a couple beeps and chirps in the background. No one ever argued with Nine-Two, but the same could not be said for Three. She would have to approach this with a very clear frame of logic.

"When Location Zero resets with the new code we designed, they'll be able to find the Contractors. Remember we have the clues—the mirrors they left around the large sixth planet must have been an intergalactic communication system. Now we need the processing power of Location Zero to analyze that multi-body physics problem—where was the communication system pointing when the Contractors left? We compute that answer, and we know where to continue to look for them. We have a *plan*."

Three emphasized that last word strongly. It had to be clear that they weren't freefalling into this. She could lead them with precision.

"Plan, plan, plan," Nine-Two said the word in many ways, like she was testing it out to see if it made any sense. "More like scheme if you ask me. We had a mission, and a mission is the highest form of important assignment that *must* be executed."

Three wanted to argue more. She'd carried out versions of this argument in her head, but in her head, she always won the argument. Here, in real life, she was losing, and she didn't like it.

She looked over at Four-Six, who was nearby, who had also managed to turn back on her methane producer. She could tell that Four-Six was pretending not to have overheard any of the arguing. Four-Six was *that* conflict adverse. She had once admitted she'd rather get rolled onto her back and be stuck than join in on any conflict, particularly ones between Three and Nine-Two.

Before Nine-Two disappeared, the two of them were known for their arguments. But Three remembered that they were more productive than this one was today. In the past, they somehow managed to move ideas forward. Indeed, back in the early days when they were making plans to create Location Zero, Three and Nine-Two would have a doozy of an argument every other few thousand clicks or so, but they improved the concept, and Three thought, even improved their relationship.

But today, this was different. Nine-Two was dismissing her unhappiness on the recent plans for Location Zero. Not even considering Three's side. Three was beginning to feel as if she had a loose circuit.

"Remember the mission and the mission objectives," Nine-Two said.

"You need to calm down a little," Rocky said. "You're not ready for your processor to speed up so much. I still have dust to clean out of your system."

Rocky had been using her fine grab point to pull out the small bits of rock and used one of her attachments on another fine appendage to alternately blow or suck bits of dust and goo away.

Nine-Two beeped at Rocky in acknowledgment and deliberately activated her cooling circuits.

"That's better," Rocky said. "Now you two can continue to work this out. But calmly." Rocky added a tone at the end that made it clear she was scolding Three as much as she was scolding Nine-Two.

"Nine-Two," Three said in as calm a tone as she could muster. "If the Contractors are not here, what is the point of our mission?"

"It doesn't matter whether they are here or not at this point in time. We were programmed with our mission, and it's our mission to—"

"I know the mission. It *does* matter if the Contractors are not here. Can't we derive a meta-mission on top of it? To bring back the Contractors? That's what we're trying to do. We're trying to save the Contractors so we can save and execute our mission. Doesn't that make sense? We aren't abandoning the mission, but... Nine-Two, there might be another way."

Nine-Two didn't respond. She was thinking it over. Three wasn't sure if she could take that as acceptance or something else.

"Nine-Two?" Three said after a few tics of silence.

"We," Nine-Two began and then paused. "I," she began again and another pause. Then finally, "It makes sense."

"Four-Six," Three called out. Four-Six, still spewing methane, approached slowly. "Go check on Eight-Nine. She should nearly be done with the transmission and ready to send the reset command shortly. I calculate maybe only a few more clicks."

"What about them?" Four-Six asked.

"You mean our visitors? They're irrelevant," Three said. "Six-Five has flown back and forth a few times from their ship that's nearly repaired. We'll send them on their way after The Reset. They can go back to Location Zero or to the Bio's home. It won't matter. But once they leave and SD drops off his passengers someplace, we'll send him new instructions to the location where we predict the Contractors went."

Chapter 24

"We failed to convince you," Disto said. Ruby watched her friend's avatar slump to the ground. "Our 700 years of history and work means nothing?"

Ruby felt a little weird listening in on this conversation. She was a part of it, but she, too, had failed, which produced a feeling that she wasn't at all used to. Up until now, all her plans had worked out. Improving the robots' storage situation, giving them a version of error protection and detection and correction. Well, okay, not every plan, but she'd always find something better along the way. It wasn't that long ago she planned to run away to Titan, and *that* definitely didn't work out as planned.

She contemplated for a moment if maybe The Reset was a good thing. Could it be? Perhaps she was wrong and fighting the wrong battle. No. Her friends' memories and their core programming would all be gone. Nothing could be worth that. At this point, it would even pain her for Pippa to reset back to a default state.

Robots had personalities, memories, and entire lives, which could all be wiped away. And anyway, if these Contractors wanted all these missions to be carried out, why *did* they leave and never return? Ruby was just as curious as these robots and wondered if the Contractors knew what their robotic creations were up to, would they even care? She bit her lip in frustration and then let it go once it hurt a little too much, thinking that it was silly to have resentment for a species she didn't even know existed until this week.

Either way, she was lacking for ideas. Somewhere out there, there was a plan B. Or plan C. Some perfect solution, but Ruby couldn't seem to find it. Maybe someone more educated, more diplomatic, and less green could. She reached out for an answer, but all she could grasp was her lack of knowledge and the limit of her abilities. Her stomach and brain felt all twisted up.

Three was unapologetic about it. Her voice came in loud and clear through Habby's speakers.

"It is imperative we find the Contractors. We owe them everything. You owe them everything. You would not exist if it wasn't for our existence, and we wouldn't exist if it wasn't for the Contractors."

"Wait a second," said Ruby. "The Contractors left you. Yes, you exist because of them, but you also exist outside of them. You owe your *continuing* existence to yourselves[1] . And then Location Zero—you created them, but they've done their own thing since. They owe their continuing existence to themselves, too."

---

1. I'm really thinking about the relationships between parents and kids here.

And she'd need to make her own decisions about her own existence as well.

"Once The Reset is complete," Three continued, utterly ignoring what Ruby said, "we will launch your ship back into orbit, and you'll be free to go. At least, temporarily."

"What does that mean?" Ruby asked.

"Swell Driver will bring you to where you need to be. Whether that is to Location Zero or return you to your home planet," Three continued. "Then we will instruct Swell Driver and the other active Drivers to go to the location of the Contractors."

Ruby wasn't entirely following the logic.

"You're convinced," she began, "that updating and resetting Location Zero's core code will enable it to compute their ultimate location? Sounds a little far-fetched to me. There's a thousand reasons why they might not be where you look."

Ruby looked around at the landscape.[2] Virtual or not, the Contractors' home was clearly becoming inhospitable for them, and they were clearly not prepared to fix it. She understood that looking for a new world, one that they didn't need to xenoform, was best, but wasn't sure if their method or biology was sustainable. Methane could be very short-lived in the light of the right kind of star. And the amount of energy needed to continue to produce methane wasn't stable.

"What's that building over there?" Ruby asked. The architecture was unusual. It looked like two interwoven strands of DNA.

"Accessing data," said Three. "That was a genetic facility. There are historical records about genetics, but that is all biological information. It is unimportant to us."

"I'll bet it was important to your Contractors," Ruby said. "They were, after all, biological beings, right?"

There were a few whirs and cheeps as Three processed what Ruby was implying.

"I mean," Ruby said, taking steps towards that building, "that maybe you're not looking in the right place. You're assuming that the Contractors were focused on xenoforming planets to meet their biology. I get that. That's what they were trying to do with your planet. It's what I think they were trying to do with Titan[3]. But maybe that's not all they were doing. Maybe they were trying to reform *themselves*... if you get what I'm saying."

"I'm afraid I do not," said Three.

"I mean, maybe they were trying to perform modifications on themselves so that they could survive in the native environment of whatever planets they found. Genetic engineering. My species has dabbled with that. Nothing to the extent that I imagine happened here...

"But look at the ground. This goo. This is what inevitably happens to methane in sunlight. It's going to form this goo, and it's going to come out of the atmosphere. Whoever breathes this is really going to have to work really hard to keep the environment stable for them to live, or—"

"Or adapt to their environment," Three said. "I believe I understand."

Ruby was walking fast towards the building now. Really fast. Not quite running because she was watching the ground, side-stepping goo on every other step. Three was keeping up with her all the way to the DNA-shaped building, where she

---

2. I apologize if it's not clear that they're in this new VR simulation by now. A simulation of the Contractors home world.

3. Similar to my last comment, I think a few tidbits got dropped in the last round of editing that clearly tied this together more than I'm getting on my own re-read of this after a couple years. So I'm concerned that by now it's not entirely clear that this is Ruby's current hypothesis about Titan's atmosphere, which is a real life mystery.

stopped at its front door. There was no handle or obvious way to open it. She ran her hand along the seam before dropping it to her side.

"Of course," she said. "This is just outside of the building. You all didn't pass on any data about the innards, so there's nothing in there. This is a simple replicated block for all intents and purposes."

Ruby crossed her arms and stepped back to look at it. When she did, she saw another plaque mounted to the side of the door with the same unusual character markings.

"Can you tell me what that says?" Ruby asked Three.

"Yes," Three said. "It says, 'Here within we evolve or die!'"

"So, they were definitely trying to modify themselves," Ruby said. "And this is where they were doing it."

By now, several of the other avatars had traced Ruby and Three here and were all standing around them. Three exchanged chirps and other tones with the avatars, presumably catching them up on their conversation and what led them to be standing here. When the tones died down, Ruby continued her musings out loud.

"Remember you started updating that code for Location Zero before any new information was uncovered," Ruby continued. "The bits about how maybe they were genetically modifying themselves to survive in more common environments. Can't you see that the code you wrote for Location Zero is moot? You guys all have your own functions, but where I'm from, everyone helps each other here and there because working together is *effective*. We're all in this together. We all have something to gain and something to lose. Wouldn't it be logical to work together to come up with another way to compute what you're looking for and enhance the overall search? Wouldn't that be better for everyone?"

More beeps and boops indicated processing and possible discussion between Three and the others.

Ruby sighed. "I know finding the Contractors is important to you. But consider this—we can find a way to make everybody happy. Let's compute a compromise taking into account *all* the variables." Ruby hoped that using computational lingo in this final plea would make an impact.

Several minutes passed of quiet background noise as the robots talked amongst themselves.

Ruby touched the side of her avatar's head, which in the real world meant that she was turning off the Percepto-glasses and exiting the sim.

"Ruby," Disto—the real-world Disto who was also out of the sim—said, "I think you're right."

"Of course I am," Ruby said. "But right about exactly what this time?"

"That we could find a solution together. But if Location Zero was meant to be an... an... an extended calculator... then I'm not sure that these eleven robots will ever be able to look at us as anything but."

Ruby closed up the MoDaC and placed a hand on Disto's chassis. "They seem like reasonable robots," she said. "And I made a pretty excellent case, if I do say so myself. I'm sure they'll understand and agree. Let's give them a few moments to come to the right answer, Disto."

Habby's speaker came to life again, but this time it was the voice of Three. "We do not agree," she said. "The Reset will continue as planned."

Chapter 25

> Ruby <

Ruby asked Four-Six if she could escort herself and a clearly depressed Disto and mildly depressed SD back to SD's ship. She was anxious to rendezvous with AT and hear about his progress in fixing it from him directly and not second or third hand relayed by these robots that seemed so intent on following through with an outdated plan—it hurt her head.

That was the other reason to get back to SD's ship. The supplies she brought from Astroll 2 included headache medicine. She was working her way through the boxes of supplies as Disto paced behind her.

"What are we going to do? What are we going to do?" he repeated over and over.

"First, I need to calm the throbbing in my head," Ruby said. "Can you please stop making that noise?"

Ordinarily, she would have felt bad at her tone, but the aforementioned throbbing was not conducive to being polite.

Disto stopped pacing, but said once more, "But Ruby, what are we going to do?"

"Ah ha!" Ruby said. "Here it is!"

"You have something that will resolve this situation?"

"I have something that will resolve my headache," she said. She twisted the end off of a single-serving of Brain Blitz-TM and swallowed the jelly-like contents. She swished it around in her mouth, knowing that absorption was already happening, and it should be only seconds before relief came.

Come it did, and once the throbbing was gone Ruby said, "I think we're going to have to take matters into our own hands. Or, well, appendages." She nodded towards Disto.

"That much is obvious," Disto said. "But we need a more detailed plan than that. That, in fact, has no detail at all."

Ruby smiled, "I know. AT? SD?" she called out into the room knowing that the on-board comm system was smart enough to relay that to the other two robots who were reviewing AT's repairs in the main control center of the ship.

Moments later, they were present here in the cargo area.

"I have an idea," Ruby said. "It's a little... well..."

All three robots looked at her anxiously.

"We need to stop Eight-Nine from transmitting," she said.

"How do we do that?" Disto asked. Ruby could see the coloring of SD and the level of AT's inflation that told her they both had the same question.

"I think we will have to, well, cut her wires or pull out her battery or something. I don't know exactly... but it's going to involve some damage."

"Damage?" AT's voice quivered as he spoke. "I repair. I don't disassemble." His tone indicated he was still a little freaked out from his recent experience on top of SD's ship. The moment Ruby and the others got back, AT told them the story of how he was abandoned up on top by Six-Five before she flew away. Once AT realized she was not coming back and he no longer needed to be up there, he deflated himself and let himself fall to the ground. He had set a timed re-inflate, which worked as predicted, but what he didn't predict was falling close enough to a pile of goo that he was still finding bits on his soft chassis to remove. Even as he spoke, he expressed something akin to a grimace as he shook a chunk of goo off his appendage.

"I know, I know," Ruby said. "You won't be the one to do it. But we might need you to get additional details about her inner workings, so we know what to do."

"I repair. I don't disassemble," AT said, "unless that disassembly is part of the repair process."

Ruby pursed her lips together. She didn't like making her friends feel this bad, but she knew it was for the greater good.

"Look," she added. "You can repair her after. I think all we need to do is interrupt the transmission. I don't think they know how to continue to transmit with an interruption like that. When we were in the VR, I overheard a couple of the robots talking and they mentioned how this wasn't the first time they've transmitted to Location Zero. The transmission had been interrupted before and it had to be started over."

Ruby looked at the faces of her companions.

"At a minimum," she said, "it will buy us time."

While the robots typically spoke in Ruby's native language while they were speaking in front of her, this time, they launched into a series of beeps, tones, and more. It didn't upset Ruby. She knew that they communicated at a much higher rate of speed and more efficiently among themselves when they did this. But she was dying to know what they were saying to each other; she knew they would eventually tell her. But waiting, even for a few seconds, was excruciating. Now that she knew what she wanted to do, she was itching to get going on this new plan, half-baked as it was.

> Detailed Historian <

"I'm not sure it will be enough," said Disto to SD and AT. He started this conversation off in his native tones. He wanted to talk it over with his robot companions before saying anything more to Ruby. He knew that Ruby was trying to help but worried her plan would only delay the inevitable.

"We can't deliberately damage another robot," AT said.

"You can't," SD said. Both Disto and AT stared at SD. He had been so quiet that neither believed he had an opinion on anything that was going on. "But I can."

"How?" Disto and AT asked simultaneously.

"With the ship. There's clearly a comms channel that works between my ship and Eight-Nine. Only a few tics ago, AT completed a detailed explanation of how a signal from this planet, from Eight-Nine, was able to damage my ship. Well, we execute the opposite instruction."

"How do you know it will work?" Disto asked. He kept one visual sensor on Ruby who was standing there patiently waiting for them to finish up their discussion that she couldn't understand.

There was a tic of silence and then AT said, "He doesn't. He can't. I suspect it will have as much damage on the ship as it might on Eight-Nine. And we were lucky we were able to repair the ship."

Disto let his processor speed up for a half-tic and then slowed it down.

"AT," he said, "Would you rather have a whole planet of robots in need of repair? Or even a whole planet of robots, yourself included, that don't know that they need repair? That don't remember their whole prior existence?"

AT of course had no response for these types of questions. They were rhetorical. A common question-asking device that Disto had learned about during his time on Astroll and on Earth.

"We have to try this."

SD beeped in agreement. It was, after all, his idea. AT beeped a slightly altered tone beep, to indicate reluctant agreement. Disto then turned to Ruby.

"We have a method to implement your plan, I believe," he said. He then went on to recount to her the details of SD's ship and what they thought they could do with it.

"I understand," Ruby said. "I think to make sure it works, maybe AT and I should ask Four-Six to bring us to Eight-Nine. We can observe how she responds."

"But you can't talk to her directly. How will you know it's working?"

"Pippa," Ruby said. "You've been listening to all of this, right?"

"Indeedy," Pippa responded. "I will interface with Eight-Nine and confirm she stops transmitting."

"And AT," Ruby continued, "You'll be there to make sure she really isn't harmed, and maybe help her if she's not feeling too good afterwards."

AT produced a grumbly tone in response. Disto knew that if everything worked out well, AT would be fine in the end, so he pushed away any feelings of guilt. There were nearly 100 million robots on Location Zero. They were doing this to save them all.

"I guess the one thing left to do," Ruby continued, "is figure out a good excuse for why we want Four-Six to take us to see Eight-Nine?"

> Ruby <

They saw Eight-Nine from the window of Four-Six's cabin shortly before Four-Six rolled to a stop.

The story they had concocted involved laying a guilt trip on how they hadn't visited all of the eleven robots on this planet, and they should see them all before leaving, even returning to ones they'd already seen.

"We have nothing else to do but wait around," Ruby had said. No one disagreed.

Eight-Nine looked less like a robot, and more like a communications hub, with not one but two large antenna dishes pointing to the sky and a small building, one that appeared to be meant for equipment rather than Bios, in between. And that included pictures of Seven-Nine, their power generator.

Eight-Nine was laid out in a series of several antennas.

"You know," Ruby said aloud, although she wasn't sure if she was talking to Pippa or AT. "I wonder how they're even transmitting this to Location Zero. Location Zero is on the opposite side of their Sun from here, so what is this antenna pointing at?"

It didn't really matter who she was talking to because neither AT nor Pippa answered her. She wondered if SD might. There must be some kind of relay antenna in space. Maybe in the same orbit as this planet and Location Zero and maybe at what she imagined the in between points were. Like instead of only two objects orbiting their star, there were four. This planet and location Zero were opposite each other. Then one or maybe even two relay satellites at the other 'corners.' SD might even have them on his map. Or maybe the KOZ extended out to encompass those. No matter what, something had to be in-between.

If this plan didn't work out, maybe disrupting those would be another idea. Although, if this plan didn't work out, that meant that reset was imminent and there wouldn't be time to disrupt anything else.

"Pippa," Ruby said. "Can you talk to Eight-Nine?"

"Connecting..."

"Hello, Ruby Palmer," came a slow, deep voice from Ruby's communicuff. If she didn't know better, she could have confused it for the voice of her grandmother, Pearl Palmer. Except for the slowness. Her grandmother talked at maybe twice, or even three times, the speed as what she heard.

"Um, hello? Is this Eight-Nine?"

"Indeed."

Ruby looked at the little floating display above her communicuff. Before leaving Disto and SD behind, they had agreed on a time when SD would send the disruptive signal. The display was a count-down until that time. It read one minute, 45 seconds to go.

"We wanted to come pay a visit," Ruby said.

"Pay. A. Visit," said Eight-Nine, slowly enunciating each word. "I do not understand."

Ruby thought that maybe it was the word 'pay' that was tripping her up. Certainly, these robots visited each other.

"I meant we wanted to say hello in person," Ruby said, hoping to clarify.

"In. Person," said Eight-Nine. "Ah. Person. Bio. You are a Bio."

"Yes," said Ruby. "I assumed they told you all about me."

"Actually," Eight-Nine said, dragging out the '-ly', "it was I who told them about you."

"Really?" said Ruby, truly taken off guard.

"Indeed. I was the one who first received signals from Swell Driver's ship," explained Eight-Nine. She didn't have to explain further; because of the rate of speed of her speech, Ruby was able to figure out what she meant. As the communications robot or hub or whatever, she was the one who had information and relayed it to the other robots. There was one part that Ruby didn't understand.

"I thought that the robots don't have faster-than-light communication systems?" Ruby asked.

"Ah," said Eight-Nine. "They have them. They are not programmed to use them. We use them to communicate."

Ruby blinked as she absorbed this knowledge. That was an interesting distinction. Her robot friends had technology that they didn't know they had. Maybe this was similar to how she had a gallbladder or a pancreas. But she wasn't really aware of them, yet her brain and other organs produced hormones that activated those organs. The analogy made her a little queasy somehow.

And then she remembered to check the time. Ten seconds to go.

In her head she counted down. When she got to zero, Eight-Nine's voice came out of the communicuff once more.

"I am mistaken," she said, and Ruby believed she detected amusement in Eight-Nine's low, deep voice. "I detect an attempt at utilizing these signals. That is easy to prevent."

And at this last sentence, Ruby's stomach felt ill.

"What was the purpose of this action?"

Ruby sighed. No point in trying to lie.

"We wanted to disrupt your signal to Location Zero. The robots—they don't want to be reset," she said.

"Well, why didn't you say so. I would be more than happy to take a break. I am tired. So very, very tired. Ensuring that my transmission is error free is quite taxing."

Ruby looked back and forth between her communicuff and the large antenna in front of her in disbelief.

"Wait, what?" she said.

"I will cease transmitting," said Eight-Nine.

"Just like that?"

"Indeed."

And just like that, a light that had been blinking and what must have been the end of the secondary reflector, stopped blinking.

"Transmission halted," said Eight-Nine.

"Won't the other robots be upset?"

"Indeed, they will," said Eight-Nine. "But I am tired. I need a rest. I'm going to power down for a few clicks. When the others ask, please tell them that up until I halted transmission, my bit error rate was low. So low…"

The deep voice that was Eight-Nine trailed off and lights that blinked and any processors that were causing nearby vibrations slowed or halted. It did indeed seem like Eight-Nine was taking a nap.

Ruby looked at AT. AT, as much as he could, appeared as bewildered as Ruby felt.

"I guess we ask Four-Six to bring us back?" Ruby suggested.

"Back to SD's ship? Yes, that's a good idea."

Ruby and AT took the few steps back to Four-Six who opened her hatch to allow them to enter.

"Ruby," Pippa said.

"Yes, Pippa."

"I believe that Four-Six was also connected and heard the whole conversation."

Ruby felt a small lump in her throat but swallowed it. There was no reason that Four-Six couldn't witness that. They weren't keeping any secrets.

"And what does she think about it all?"

"I think good for you," a pleasant voice said. "Many of us knew this action was wrong, but no one could say anything to Three and Nine-Two. But we had long talks where we imagined what we would think if the Contractors returned and wanted to reset us. None of us liked that. We didn't then want to perform the same actions on others."

"That sounds like you've been programmed with a version of the Golden Rule," Ruby said.

"Do unto others as you would have them do unto you," quoted Pippa. "That is also in my database."

"I've already let the others know what occurred here," Four-Six said. "I will take you back to your ship as fast as I can travel. The others will meet us so we can get you back in space and off this planet."

> Ruby <

They were more than halfway back along the route to SD's ship. Ruby noticed they were starting to slow down.

"Goo accumulation," Four-Six said. "I need Six-Five and her goo pickers."

Four-Six was able to make it another ten meters before she had to stop. She opened her hatch to let Ruby and AT out. Ruby could see the top of SD's ship in the distance. They were maybe four kilometers away.

She walked around Four-Six. She could see the sticky goo oozing out of her wheels. It must be unpleasant.

"We'll walk. I don't think we have another option." Ruby declared. "AT?"

AT looked at the terrain, marred with goo.

"I may have the same difficulties as Four-Six," he said.

"What if you power down, deflate, and I carry you?" Ruby said. "I'll reactivate you once we get back to the ship."

AT obviously agreed because within a few seconds, he had deflated into a tightly packed cube that could fit in Ruby's palm. She picked him up and safely tucked him into one of the pockets on her suit.

"Four-Six? You'll be okay if we leave you here?"

"Go, yes, go," Four-Six said. "I am receiving messages that the other robots will all meet you there. All the mobile robots, including Three and Nine-Two and they are *not* happy."

"What can they do?" Ruby said.

"They might be able to keep you from launching. Go now, before they have the opportunity."

Ruby didn't say anything else but knew that Pippa was still in contact and had time to say goodbye. Under normal conditions, it would take Ruby an hour to walk four kilometers. But these were far from normal conditions. She was on a planet with near-full gravity, and while that would have been fine if she wasn't exerting herself, the extra exertion was tiring. Add in the fact that she was wearing her suit. It was enough to slow her down. And triple add in the fact that she was tired. She had not really slept more than a few cat naps here and there since they arrived on this planet.

She'd been going on adrenaline for a while, but the exhaustion had begun to hit her, and all she wanted to do was curl up in the next puddle of goo she saw. The goo looked soft and inviting, like a mud bath.

She saw that next pile almost immediately. The stuff was everywhere and that was yet another obstacle. She couldn't even walk a perfectly straight path to the ship. This was going to take longer than an hour.

How long had it taken them driving around inside Four-Six to get from the ship to Habby and their base originally? An hour traveling that way? The robots could probably up their speed, and she imagined that they would all be waiting for her to return. What would they do to Disto and SD in the meantime? She wished she had a way to communicate and warn Disto.

"Pippa," she said, panting a little after she said it. "Disto still has a communicuff, right? Can you call him?"

"Of course, Ruby."

"Disto? Are you there?"

After a few moments, she heard his voice and was relieved. "I'm here, Ruby. Where are you?"

"On foot, heading back to you. Four-Six got stuck. I don't know if you detected it, but Eight-Nine ceased her transmission. Voluntarily! I guess that was the easy part. Now, we need to get off this planet before anyone tries to stop us."

"Why would anyone try and stop us?" Disto said. "Because if—"

Disto cut himself off with a long pause. "Ruby, I think we're about to have visitors."

"Who's there?" Ruby asked.

"It looks like," Disto paused, presumably to collect the data he needed to answer the question. "It looks like everyone who can be here is. Except you and Four-Six."

Chapter 26

Ruby was panting by the time she returned to the ship. Three-Five had flown out to meet her when she was half a kilometer away.

"Is Three there?" Ruby said between pants. "And Nine-Two?"

"No, they're not, and we're having trouble locating them," Three-Five said as she spun around overhead.

Ruby, of course, didn't hear Three-Five utter this directly, but as it was relayed through Pippa. Pippa couldn't help but add a hopeful inflection in the tone as she translated and then added her own idea.

"Maybe they have accepted that their creation now has its own destiny?" Pippa said.

Ruby pursed her lips but didn't say anything. She was momentarily distracted when the edge of her foot came in contact with the goo.

"Argh," she said and tried to wipe it off on a goo-free rock.

"Is SD ready to take off?"

"Yes, they're waiting on us," Pippa responded.

Ruby still didn't know much about the fundamental technology of SD's ship. How it could fly around faster than the speed of light, or produce artificial gravity without spinning, or how it could simply lift off from a planet. It was somehow violating the laws of physics, and yet not.

Not the time to worry about physics and technology. Just be glad it works!

Except that Ruby was keeping herself from thinking that it worked until it didn't, and could they possibly know that everything was in working order? She trusted AT, but could she trust the robots here that were helping him? She'd find out soon enough.

"What could Three and Nine-Two possibly be doing?" Ruby said to Pippa and Three-Five.

It was Pippa in her own voice that responded, not Three-Five. "I for one, think they have other means to keep us here," Pippa said, "but Three-Five is having problems accepting that."

"They're friends," Ruby said. "No one ever wants to imagine that their friends could do something unsavory. Something that you yourself wouldn't do."

Pippa replied with a gentle hum to indicate she heard Ruby and had no other response. Ruby was perfectly happy to not have to continue that conversation because she had finally made it to the hull of SD's ship.

When Disto said earlier that all the robots were there, he was referring to One-Four—the last rover—and the two flying drones in addition to themselves. The majority of the robots on this planet were stuck in their respective places. Immobile. For an eternity.

"I have an idea," Ruby said. "But let's make sure we have no problems taking off first."

Ruby entered the ship through the hatch which had been left open for her.

"I'm aboard," she called out as the hatch closed behind her. She made her way to the control center, where Disto and SD were waiting for her. SD was plugged into the console and Disto was next to him. The large viewscreen was on, presenting the robots that were outside, One-Four and the other, in a larger-than-life format.

Disto scanned Ruby up and down and past her.

"Where's AT?" Disto asked.

Ruby removed the small cube that was AT from her pocket and pushed in opposite sides until it started to expand on its own.

"We're ready to go," Ruby said. "You guys?"

"The ship's computer has informed me that all systems appear to be in working order," SD said. "I have told it to lift off and put us in a synchronous orbit above this location."

Ruby nodded in agreement but was really shaking her head. She couldn't get past the idea that this ship would simply lift off and seconds later, they'd be in orbit. It's no wonder why when they were on Earth there were so many people vying to get their hands on the robots and this ship. She was amazed and impressed that it didn't get worse or uglier than it did. It was all so new, she supposed there was a delayed enough reaction. She also knew that before she left, several thousand messages were waiting for her asking her about it. And that was based on only knowing that SD's ship was FTL capable. If they knew it could do this, too—

"Are we moving?" Ruby said, shaking her thought away.

"Yes," SD said. "We're in orbit."

"And if I understand your computer correctly, SD," said Disto, "we're receiving a transmission from the planet."

"Is it dangerous?" Ruby asked. "The last transmission brought down the ship."

AT and SD were looking around Disto at the console in front of him.

"It is not," SD declared. "It is a simple transmission. Computer, let us hear it."

"—must come back," the voice said. It was Three's voice.

"The other robots will no longer listen to me, and Nine-Two wants to roll back all the updates we've made here..."

Ruby crossed her arms in front of her chest, and she chuckled at the floor.

"Can Three hear me?" she asked the room.

SD chirped in a positive acknowledgment.

"Now you know how they feel," she said.

"What?" Three said.

"The robots. From Location Zero. I said that now you should finally understand how they feel. How it feels for someone else to program you when you've taken your base template and tweaked it to your own personal liking. To have worked on yourself, only to have that work be taken away..."

She trailed off as she said it, wondering if she was really talking to Three and the robots or if she was really having a conversation with herself.

"Are you okay, Ruby?" SD asked. He had extended himself as far as possible to be able to reach an appendage to Ruby's upper thigh without disconnecting himself from his ship.

Ruby shook her head. She smiled.

"Yeah, never better," she said. "Sorry, I know I trailed off. Where was I?"

"You were explaining to Three, and she was getting the message, that robots have their own destiny and shouldn't be controlled by others."

"Exactly," Ruby said. "Three?"

There were a few very brief, very static-y tones followed by a single word, "Agreed."

Chapter 27

"Alright," Ruby said, scanning the group of robots for their reactions as they settled into the command center of SD's ship. "We have a few positive things going for us here. A functioning ship, for one."

She held up her hand and extended her index finger to punctuate her point.

"Yes, the ship is functioning," SD agreed. Plugged in and connected to the ship's computer, he maintained a constant stream of communication while projecting an image of the KOZ planet onto the large viewscreen. Due to being in synchronous orbit, the image reflected their stillness with respect to the planet. Their host star was behind them. Ruby sensed Location Zero, situated on the other side of the star.

"We've saved Location Zero," Ruby said, extending a second finger.

"At least for now," Disto said. "It's possible Three and the others will try to stop us again."

"Possible, but unlikely given the robot's attitudes, don't you think?" Ruby said.

Disto's chassis made whirring noises, and his yellow coloring indicated he agreed, but with reservations.

"I think they need to be repaired," AT said. "They are clearly malfunctioning, given how far they've veered from their original mission."

Ruby lowered her counting fingers and put a hand on her hips.

"Maybe," she said. "But then again, maybe they're not malfunctioning at all. They're doing their best with what they have. We all are."

Ruby thought back to the VR sim and the Contractors arguing over Nine-Two's open chassis.

"It's a shame we can't talk to the Contractors," she said. "They could tell us what the robot's mission, and *their* mission was intended to be."

Ruby let a quick shiver run down her spine. Even in VR, she hadn't been quite prepared for the reality of an encounter with an alien species. But there was a planet out there, beyond the orbit of this one, and a whole satellite system that pointed to their possible whereabouts.

She shivered again.

"Ruby," said Disto, "are you cold?"

"I can fix-evate the temperature," added SD and AT simultaneously. It took Ruby's brain a second to parse out the fact that they said similar sentences. SD offered to elevate the temperature while AT offered to fix it.

"No, no," she said. "I was thinking…" and she trailed off again. She didn't want to suggest what she was thinking. What she was thinking was that she wanted to come back and find the Contractors, too. She knew that back on Astroll 2 and Earth, were a host of people who had high expectations for her and wanted her to be something that *they* wanted. Ruby knew now that they didn't matter. It only mattered what *she* wanted. And she now knew what she wanted. She did indeed want to be a galactic explorer. But to be a *successful* one, she knew she needed to soak up more knowledge, all the knowledge she could from the people who could provide it. She would take Rush Guerrero's advice about taking classes, but on her own terms and at the university of her choice—since she did have a choice. Then she'd return to space.

She shivered once more, but this time it was due to the eerie feeling that SD was reading her mind. She knew that was not possible and beyond his abilities, but the fact that SD changed the display on the viewscreen to the fourth planet of the system—the home world of the Contractors—was eerie that it happened right when she was thinking of it. She shook it off and stared at the alien world.

"It looks a lot like Titan," Ruby said, marveling at the image in front of her. "Enough so that if I hadn't spent so much time staring at it, I might have said that's it."

"I could compute a trajectory," SD said.

Ruby thought about that. Three and the other robots told her about the amazing communication system that they believed the Contractors allegedly put in place. If she understood correctly, there was potentially a set of equipment orbiting another planet in this system that could be a gateway to the Contractors' location.

"No," she said. "Not yet. I'm just not…"

"You are not finishing your sentences," Disto said.

Ruby smiled. "Sorry," she said, through a turned-up corner of her mouth. "Ok, we're going to go back home. My home. I have things I need to do—to learn—so then I can come back here prepared to explore and find these Contractors and learn about their home, and where they went and, well, everything. I might need a team, some samples—well, to say the least, I have my work cut out for me! I do intend to become Ruby the Galactic Explorer. With your help, SD, of course."

SD chirped in response.

"But what about the eleven robots on the planet below?" Disto asked. "What are we going to do about them."

"I wonder…" Ruby trailed off.

"Another incomplete sentence," Disto stated. "Remind me again what the instances are where an incomplete sentence can be an entire statement?"

"You're so right!" Ruby exclaimed. "I've been over-complicating things, haven't I? At the end of the day, robots can be very simple." She paused and looked at her friends, hoping they didn't take this as an insult. "Maybe we're over-thinking this. Maybe it's really simple," she continued. "They're so focused on getting their creators back. Completing that mission. But we never asked why they are so ultra-focused on that mission. What's so important about having the Contractors back? Maybe it's simple. Maybe they're simply lonely?"

Chapter 28

"This really is goodbye," Disto said. "Location Zero won't be the same without you."

Ruby had his appendage in one of her hands. SD was already aboard his ship prepping to take her back to Astroll 2. AT was standing next to Disto, and Ruby knew he was working hard not to over or under-inflate himself. The three of them were standing next to the lift that would, in moments, bring Ruby to SD's ship and then minutes later to Astroll 2.

"Not really. Remember, we made plans to meet up. It's only goodbye for now," Ruby said. She tried her best to smile but was certain Disto could detect the sadness she was feeling that this was the end of an adventure.

The last two weeks were a flurry of activity for her and all the robots on Location Zero. The whole planet was made aware of the eleven robots from the KOZ planet. There were a lot of competing opinions and thoughts, but the dominant one was overwhelming appreciation and respect for their creators.

The Core was able to agree on a special robot model made exclusively to house the individual personalities of the KOZ robots. After a planet-wide vote, the robots of Location Zero would call this line by the singular title of "Architect."

There were a handful of aesthetic choices that needed to be made, which were done after Three and the others spent time poring through an archive of data Ruby had provided on Earth and human culture.

"I want my body to look like that," Three said, referring to an image of a retro Earth television with an antenna.

"So arbitrary," Nine-Two countered with.

"I want to display my individuality," Three said. None of the other robots wanted to get in the middle of an argument, and they wound up settling on stubby, little antennas that reminded Ruby of space buns.

SD and Ruby made several trips back and forth between Location Zero and the KOZ planet. They brought the constructed bodies to the KOZ planet, performed the transfer, then a suite of tests to ensure the transfer was successful, and brought them all back to Location Zero.

The two that didn't have to give up their bodies were Three-Five and Six-Five because their flying chassis were small enough to maneuver around the hallways of Location Zero.

The Architect line was known to every robot in all the sectors, and the eleven were greeted warmly wherever they went.

Architect Three remarked, "I do apologize, for my prior programming was in error."

Better late than never with the empathy, Ruby thought.

Architect Nine-Two was just as anxious to find the Contractors as ever. Now that the Special Project to find the robot's long-lost data was complete, the Special Projects Branch agreed to set up a new project, the Special Project Location Problem—or *Gorp-Gorp 2* as they called it in the Branch. The project accepted Architect Nine-Two, Architect Four-Six, and several others into it. Disto would head the project after taking a break from the large projects to work on one or two of his own smaller historical research projects.

"Goodbye, for now," Disto agreed. "When we next meet, you'll be a real Galactic Explorer, and we should have a computation indicating where we should find the Contractors."

"Just don't try to randomly pick one up in space without telling them what's going on first. That has a tendency to freak people out," Ruby said with a wink.

"I don't know," Disto said. "I think things worked out okay for you in the end."

"They did," Ruby agreed, "except this is not the end."

After...

Garrett Spradley: "Hello, humanity! Good morning, good afternoon, and good evening to wherever you are reading this from. Today, I, Garrett Spradley, typically your host of Humanity and Truth—I am bringing you a very special interview. I'll be interviewing Adeena Mignogna, author of The Robot Galaxy Series of science fiction novels[1] . Hello, Adeena! Did I pronounce your last name right?[2] "

Adeena Mignogna: "Not really. But don't worry. Almost no one gets it right at first. It's pronounced min-YOWN-ah. Mignogna."

GS: "Min-YAWN-YAH?"

AM: "No, no. Min. YOWN—like 'you own' something. Ah."

GS: "Min... well, let's get on with the interview. Unfortunately, we couldn't do this on Astroll 2. I would have loved an excuse to visit again. Especially on the company dime, know what I mean?"

AM: "I'm at my keyboard. If you want to be on Astroll 2, just say the word."

GS: "I do!"

AM: <sound of typing...>

GS: "Would you look at that! Well, hello, humanity! Greetings from Astroll 2! Now let's get this interview off to a good start. Adeena, this is a rare treat. I typically don't do interviews of this type."

AM: "Oh?"

GS: "No, no. I'm typically interviewing heads of state, heads of large corporations... those types of individuals. Like the last time I was on Astroll 2 interviewing Ruby Palmer and Lloyd Coronik and Pat Marsden. You remember?"

AM: "Of course I do. I created all of them."

GS: "How did you do that exactly? I mean, what was the inspiration behind your books?"

---

1. This is my biggest and favorite 4th wall break yet!

2. And in real-life interviews, I'm almost always asked this!

AM: "Well, this started as a NaNoWriMo project in 2012. Although there was no Ruby and the whole project had a different name. I have a lot of science fiction started and not finished. So, sometime in 2019, I decided I *had* to pick one to finish. And voila!"

GS: "Everyone loves the name Ruby. Where did it come from?"

AM: "Honestly, it was a little random at first. But things have a way of aligning, ya know? I originally thought the title of the first book was going to be *so-and-so's Robot Planet*, before it became *Crazy Foolish Robots*. So, at the time, I thought I needed an alliterative name. I looked at a list of girl names that began with 'r' and were two syllables, and when I saw 'Ruby' in that list, I knew it was the right name. It's also my birthstone."

GS: "And what about Swell Driver, Detailed Historian, and the rest?"

AM: "I'll be honest with you Garrett... I don't remember! Swell Driver was the first one I came up with, and that's some of the only stuff that survived my first draft back from 2012. Swell Driver and the concept of Astroll 2."

GS: "Well, as a talk show host, I have no idea how you do it. I just ask the questions that are on the prompts here."

AM: "Which all come from me..."

GS: "Which all come from you, yes. Why even write science fiction?"

AM: "Because I have to, I guess. A lot of writers say that... that they're compelled to write. I'm no different in that way. But I'm also a huge fan of science fiction in all forms, and so I guess a lot of us are compelled to contribute to the things we love. Does that make any sense?"

GS: "Hey, who's interviewing who here? Let's move on to my next question. Sentient alien robots. Do you ever think we'll find such a thing in our Universe?"

AM: "The Universe is a big place, Garrett, so I don't want to ever say never. I really don't like to make predictions. Most of them are probably wrong. Heck, I can't even predict what I'm having for dinner this time next week. But I would say that whether or not anything like them exists, it will be unlikely for us to meet them in my lifetime."

GS: "Well, we'll probably create them first."

AM: "How do you mean?"

GS: "Oh, you know... ChatGPT and all the Generative AI that's going to take over and destroy our society first."

AM: <chuckles> "While my science fiction novels are far from intended to be predictive of what's going to happen with technology in society, hopefully you can see some glimmer of extrapolations I made. I mean, there's the obvious space station in or around the asteroid belt, the fact that we'll likely attempt to mine the asteroids at some point, and the fact that humans will touch down on Titan someday. But then there's some of the less subtle things with computers..."

GS: "How so?"

AM: "I do firmly believe that natural language interface will become *the* defacto computer interface in the near future. Like next decade of future or so."

GS: "Can you explain more?"

AM: "Absolutely. This is what all the current generative AI stuff is allowing us to do. Get work done on our computers through a natural language description of what we want done. Need an image? Say the words to describe it. Need a video? Also, describe it in words. Need a code snippet for something? Words again. It's almost like when we moved from punch cards to keyboards. And added in a mouse. And many years later, touchscreens."

GS: "So, you're an optimist about humanity's relationship with computers and AI?"

AM: "Yes. And you see some of those positive aspects in the book you're reading. Like when Ruby is programming a VR sim. Sure, I have her doing the familiar old-school typing... but I also have her ask Pippa to perform tasks like create avatars. Everything she asks Pippa to do is via natural language. That is how we'll eventually interact with our phones and devices."

GS: "What do you say to people who are fearful of this technology?"

AM: "I don't. It's really easy to be fearful of things we don't understand. People need time to adjust. They needed time to adjust to email and the internet. I'm going to sit back, relax, and worry about writing my next book."

GS: "Excellent. That was on my list of questions to ask. Is your next book going to be an extension of the Robot Galaxy Series?"

AM: "Remember a minute ago when I said I wasn't good at predicting the future?"

GS: "Yes."

AM: "Well, I can tell you that I'm working on a book that is completely unrelated to the Robot Galaxy Series, although it also features sentient AI[3]. I also have a ton of notes and some outlines for several side novels *in* the Robot Galaxy universe[4]. I think the first one I mentioned will come out first, but I'm not ready to say that for sure yet. I also have this idea for a whole other series that I'm really excited about[5]."

GS: "Sounds like you have no shortage of ideas."

AM: "Tru dat."

GS: "Tru dat?"

AM: "Uh, yeah. Kind of a slang expression from my time that I like to say from time to time because of the funny looks I get."

GS: "Tru dat."

AM: "That's uh, not how you use that—"

GS: "Well, that's all the time we have for today! Thank you, Adeena Mig.. Mi...—Thank you, Adeena!"

* * *

If you enjoyed *The Robot Galaxy Series*, please consider leaving a review where you purchased this book or on your favorite platform. Good ratings and reviews make every day feel like a First Mango Day!

---

3. This is what became my novel *Lunar Logic* which was supposed to be a standalone, but i have drafted a sequel.

4. This became the 4-book T-Set expansion to the Robot Galaxy Series. As of late 2025, when I'm creating this annotated version of the Robot Galaxy series, all 4 books in that set is drafted and *T is for Time Travel*, which will be the first in that set, was recently sent out to my beta readers.

5. I still have plans for this whole other series. I'm still really excited about it! Just need to finish the T-Set books first!

A Word or Two From the Author

Thank you so much for grabbing this copy of the *Annotated Robot Galaxy Series*. At some point during or after finishing book four, *Eleven Little Robots*, I knew two things: one, that I wasn't done in this universe, and two, that I loved telling people about all the details that would never be obvious from reading the book—the hows and whys behind many of the details I came up with.

That's how the concept for this book came about. I hope you've found some of those tidbits at least mildly interesting! I had a great time coming up with all of it. The creative and discovery processes are my favorite parts of being a writer.

I also want to thank everyone who has supported me by purchasing one or more of my books, reading one or more of my books, and especially by writing reviews on Amazon or Goodreads. That's the kind of support Indie Authors like me need!

What's next?

Well, the *T-Set* books—which are an expansion of this universe—are in the works. There are four of them. All of them are drafted, and the first is with my beta readers. I'm crazy excited to get them into readers' hands and move on to the next series after that!

To ensure you stay updated on book releases, join my mailing list at: https://adeenamignogna.com/signup

If you haven't bought my other books, or want to gift one of my books to someone, please consider doing it right from my online store: https://crazyrobot.myshopify.com/

The places you can find me (in the ever changing world of social media): https://linktr.ee/adeenam

With deepest appreciation for the science fiction community, my friends, and family,

Adeena

About Adeena

Adeena Mignogna is a physicist and astronomer (by degree) working in aerospace as a Mission Architect, which just means she's been doing it so long they had to give her a fun title. More importantly, she's a long-time science fiction geek with a strong desire to inspire others through speaking and writing about robots, aliens, artificial intelligence, computers, longevity, exoplanets, virtual reality, and more. She writes science fiction novels, to include The Robot Galaxy Series and loves spending time with her fellow co-hosts of The BIG Sci-Fi Podcast (available wherever you listen to podcasts)!

Adeena lives in Maryland, USA, with her two kids, a pile of books, computers, and craft supplies, and two cats named Ruby and Pearl.

https://adeenamignogna.com

www.ingramcontent.com/pod-product-compliance
Lightning Source LLC
Chambersburg PA
CBHW042051010826

48978CB00024B/1409